TEARS from IRON

Memories of the Cataclysm, Book I

JONATHAN OLDENBURG

To the t'Okaedrin in my life

ACKNOWLEDGEMENTS

To Alex and Newton who were with me when we first walked the fields and forests of Isfalinis, though we did not yet know her name. And again to Alex, who emerged once more to offer his hand in its conclusion. Without that, I don't know that it ever would have seen the light of day. To Greg and Geoff for their willingness to tell me truths I didn't want to hear. Without their advice, this book would be but a shadow of what it's become. To my parents and my brother for their relentless encouragement. And always and foremost, to my wife.

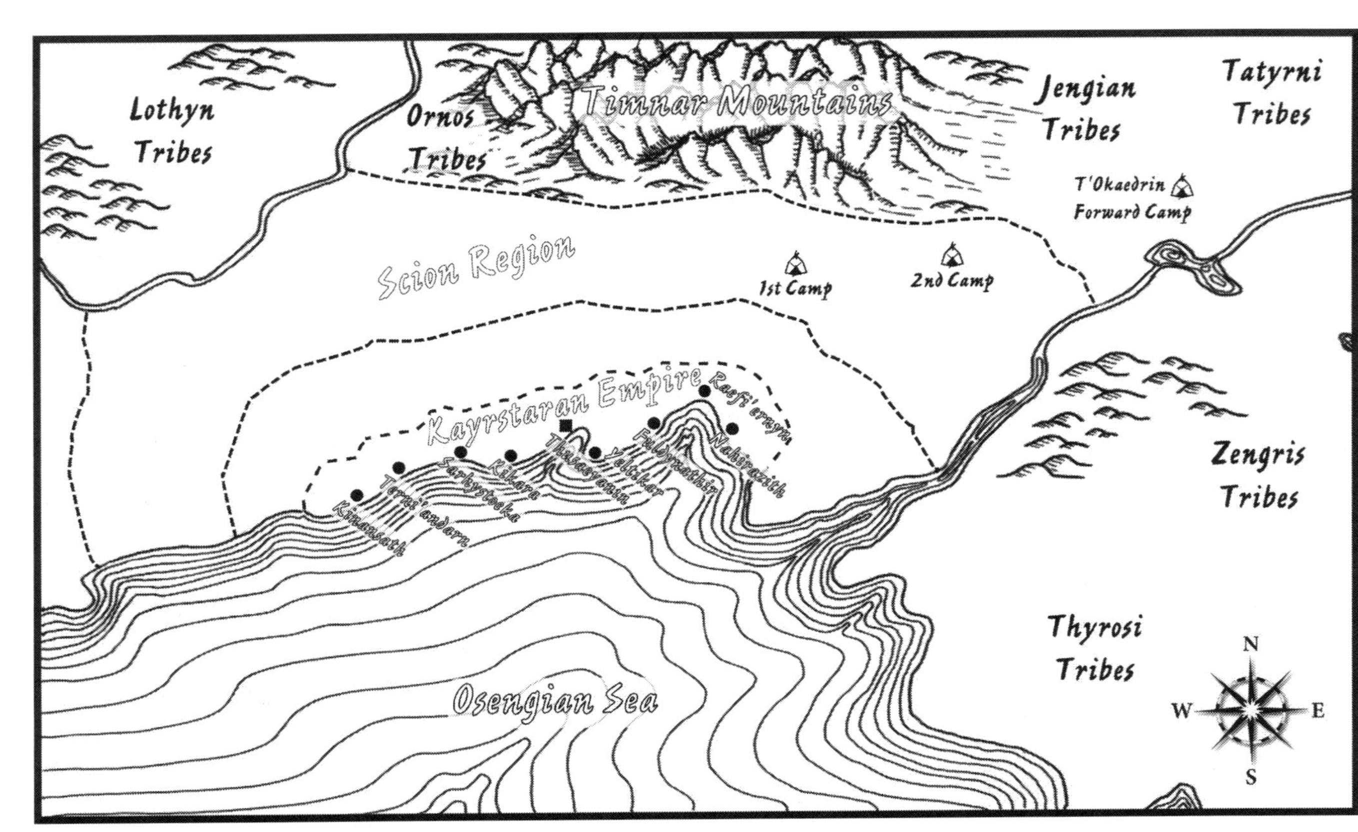
Lothyn Tribes
Ornos Tribes
Timnar Mountains
Jengian Tribes
Tatyrni Tribes
T'Okaedrin Forward Camp
Scion Region
1st Camp
2nd Camp
Kayrstaran Empire
Raefi'ernyn
Kinansath
Terni'andarn
Sarhystocka
Kikara
Thusaeyanin
Yeltikar
Fuldyrathir
Nahirazith
Zengris Tribes
Thyrosi Tribes
Osengian Sea
N
W
E
S

A BRIEF NOTE ON PRONUNCIATION

The Syraestari language makes heavy use of the apostrophe. It serves two basic purposes.

First, an apostrophe denotes when two adjoining vowels are pronounced separately. For example, with "Pi'aernoth" (Sister), the 'i' and 'ae' sounds are independent: (PEE-ayr-noth).

Second, an apostrophe marks where a vowel has been removed when two words are joined together. For example "t'Okaedrin" (The Brothers) is the combination of "te" (The) and "Okaedrin" (Brothers). Rather than the more cumbersome "te'Okaedrin", the "e" is removed in favor of "t'Okaedrin" (TOE-kay-drin)

For a full pronunciation guide, please see the Glossary at the end of the book.

DRAMATIS PERSONAE

T'Okaedrin

Vistus / Belarrin	
Dalric	His Father
Nalsuntha	His Eldest Brother
Bridionis	His Brother
Arcomin	His Brother
Hirnid	His Brother
Liuticar	

Pi'aernoth

Auphni	Vistus' mother
Elestis	a Pi'aernotha Osnoeda
Talikae	a Pi'aernotha Kaupet
Draatha	a Pi'aernotha Kaupet

Scions of the Fallen Tree

Vitarria	
Parvik	
Inban	a Chieftain
Mirnadd	
Sravika	
Henirgar	
Tayrja	
Kitiger	a Chieftain
Fedigni	
Laerdina	
Jarkon	a Chieftain
Grannif	a Chieftain
Dirbructi	

Kalilaer & Wildmen

Wiersa
Yrpel
Regund
Idysha
Zoltha
Chostir
Fritten
Obaudes
Argluf

Syraestari

Kayrstana	Empress and High Lady of Thusaeyanin
Ninanna	Kayrstana's Edrethyn, a Sword-Whisperer
Tazil	High Lord of Raefi'ernyn
Ushtyl	High Lord of Nahirazith
Sizras	High Lord of Sarhystoeka
Zaerina	High Lady of Terni'andarn
Arkesh	High Lord of Yeltikar
Ovirkar	High Lord of Fuldynathir
Jesaelyn	High Lady of Kikara
Tyrnis	High Lord of Kinansath
Aerharyndra	Tazil's wife
Sarroth	Captain of Empress Kayrstana's housecarls
Nethzir	Captain of Lord Tazil's housecarls
Eltirkar	Captain of Lord Ushtyl's housecarls
Onath	a courier
Medreuneth	a sorceress
Imeskir	a Sword-Whisperer
The Shadow-Servant	

PROLOGUE

Isi huddled alone, empty, in darkness deeper than the Abyss.

In the dawning of the world long ago, she had created Song, but she could sing no more. Song was a thing of joy and sometimes sorrow. It could give voice to pain and transform rage. But here in her forsaken prison, none of that could survive. It was a tomb devoid of life, of emotion, of thought.

She strained to summon to her mind the faintest glimmer of the world beyond, the world her kindred had fashioned, sensing that then she could remember the other Etyni and recall hope. But instead of white-peaked mountains, she had a tomb three paces by three. Instead of the warm sun upon her face, there was only the creeping cold that seeped through her flesh to lurk in her bones. There was no blustery wind to dance in her hair and whisper in her ears, just the slow lonely tapping of some distant bead of water.

Though the greatest war the world had ever known was being waged above, she was not a part of it. She was a part of nothing. Isolated, empty. Even time had lost its meaning and she could feel the last vestiges of thought, memory, and life pulling away. There was only the oppressive gloom, bearing down on her soul, and its weight grew relentlessly. Its pressure was still distant, but she could sense Him drawing closer. He gained strength while she wilted and, when He arrived, her doom would be complete.

A sharp click rang in her ears. She sat upright, staring into the darkness, wondering if an age had passed since she'd last heard anything but the singular drip of water.

"Aupeust My'az," a man commanded and faint golden light filled her cell.

Isi almost laughed, feeling the soft warmth of that dim light washing over her skin. She looked up and saw a tall Aestarin standing before her in long robes of black. His skin was pale and smooth. The high cheekbones of his race were particularly strong and his long angled ears pressed against his dark brown hair. Ainii had demonstrated her mastery when she gave the Aestari their shape and this man was one of the handsomest Isi had seen. But the blue eyes staring down at her were shadowed, betraying deep pain and a smoldering rage.

"Are you here to kill me or save me?" Isi asked.

"Of all the Etyni, I think that I loved you most," the Aestarin replied. He extended a hand. "Rise, please, Lady. I cannot speak to you in this way."

'Loved' not 'Love,' Isi noted the words as she took his hand and stood up. "Then you are Syraestari and not Hiraestari."

The anger in his eyes softened and a faint smile touched his lips. "I had expected to hear the name given by our enemies, not our true one."

Resignation filled her. He was one of her captors then. "Why are you here?"

The Syraestari ignored her question and let out a deep sigh. "We just wanted to be free. To know what the other races know. To find ourselves. But we were held captive by that accursed Oath. What else were we to do?"

"It wasn't our intent to curse you," Isi replied. "It was supposed to be a blessing."

"A blessing?" the Syraestari cried, anguish cracking his voice. "I know all the old arguments, the old lies. The Oath bound us in chains and its breaking has doomed everyone!"

"Each soul has a choice."

"A choice between oblivion and damnation." He laughed bitterly. "I once dreamed that there was more, but Cydion deceived us and now I know the truth."

"What do you want of me?" Isi asked softly.

Her gentle tone doused the fires burning in the man's eyes. "Everything I have done, everything I will ever do is for the good of my people." He drew in a deep breath. "You know why you're being held here?"

Isi swallowed. "I fear the answer."

"Cydion intends to devour your soul. The Lord of Death is our master now and we cannot deny him. Not yet."

Isi nodded. She had already been certain of her fate but it was a surprise that hearing it spoken aloud failed to crush what little of her hope remained.

The Syraestari continued, "He nearly consumed Niella but she was rescued by her handmaidens. Diotra sacrificed herself instead, life and soul."

"No," Isi whispered, tears springing to her eyes.

"He tried to devour Henji, too, but she claimed death instead."

"Not Henji!"

"On the Great Bridge of Vasyr, she bled her last. Then her brother died in a futile quest for vengeance."

Isi stumbled back and buried her head in her hands. So many of her kindred gone. It should never have come to this. Vaenna had been right. Highest Above! Vaenna had been right and they should have listened.

The Syraestari spoke, "You may not believe me, but I wish they were still alive."

Isi looked up at him and saw that his eyes brimmed with unshed tears. Anger remained in that gaze, but the pain had grown to overwhelm it. "I believe you."

"Though I wish otherwise, I cannot help you escape." He turned away and his voice lowered as if he were arguing with himself. "I do not dare. It is too soon." He turned back to her, eyes gleaming. "But we will act, I promise you. We shall shed our chains and claim what we were meant to be. We shall leave this sickly land for a home of our own, untormented by Cydion, by humans, by anyone. Not yet, though, I cannot. I am sorry."

"I understand." Bleakness opened up in her. She was certain now of why he'd come.

He blinked and the tears held in his eyes fell to stain his cheeks, though he didn't seem to notice. "I will not see Cydion consume you. That much, I swear I can and will do. There is only one way, though it condemn me forever to the Abyss."

Isi drew herself up. "First, tell me your name, child of Ainii."

"I am Reigliff, my Lady."

Isi nodded. "Reigliff, you must forgive yourself."

"Never."

Holding her gaze with his, Reigliff drew a dagger from his robes and plunged it into her breast.

CHAPTER 1
Belarrin

"And on that final day, Cydion, the Lord of Life and Death stood upon the Hill of Kensethir, triumphant over the broken bodies of the last of the Etyni. Yet even as the peoples of the world trembled before his might, broken Itesa took up the Sword of Zaris and plunged it through his heart. Cydion died, Itesa died, and the world shattered beneath them."

—"The Last Days of the Age that Was" as recorded by Sedryk Imraphel, Chieftain of the Tuenosian Tribes

Vistus didn't like being alone.

He was accustomed to the long hallways of his home resounding with life and laughter but instead the silence was only broken by the quiet whisking of his broom. That singular sound only reinforced his loneliness as he worked his way between the twenty beds of his barracks room.

He was a t'Okaedrin and t'Okaedrin weren't made for solitude. The word meant brother in the language of the blessed Syraestari and a brother without a family was as broken as Vistus' arm. After months of mending, his arm was nearly healed and, any day now, his brothers would return. Then he could be whole once more.

Vistus didn't spend hours each morning cleaning the barracks because he enjoyed it. The task had to be done so he did it. Yet he could drown himself a little in the steady rhythm of the work and there was comfort in the order it imparted. The world beyond was a morass of chaos and evil but here, at least, all was as it should be. Yet he missed his family.

His eyes drifted to the scaled hauberk laid out over his storage chest and the sword and iron-banded shield resting upon it. "I should be out with them," he muttered. His family was braving the virulent wilderness. "If only..."

He flexed his left arm and felt the muscles pull taught over the healing bone. Soon.

Shaking his head, Vistus resumed his sweeping. He moved out into the hallway and worked his way down the long length of the barracks. He paused at each set of doors to clean the adjoining rooms, skipping only those belonging to the few families still present. He didn't see those t'Okaedrin often. Half were out on their daily patrols protecting the nearby Kalilaer settlements and the remainder rested for the same duty at night. Regardless, they were capable of cleaning their own quarters.

It was a slow labor, but he didn't mind. Every task, no matter how simple, had to be done right. His father had taught him that. Yet by the time he was half done his left arm ached and the golden sunlight shining through the outer door called to him. He turned his back on the temptation and raised his hand to wipe the sweat beading on his brow.

The world reeled around him, roaring with a voice more deafening than thunder.

Vistus staggered and then dropped to the floor as the ground rippled beneath him. He splayed his hands wide in a futile attempt at stability as the roof and floor creaked in agony. He clenched his eyes shut, waiting to be buried again. Waiting to die.

But as quickly as it had come, the quake ended.

Vistus drew in a shuddering breath. It wasn't bad this time, but even so he wanted to get out of the barracks. He returned to his quarters to stow his broom first, feeling like that bit of discipline returned a measure of control. But he didn't begin to relax until he stepped outside.

The warm sun and cool wind greeted him as if nothing had happened and he tilted his head back drinking it in. Why did it have to be earthquakes? Every one of them was a reminder of his first family. The family he'd lost.

He looked back at the barracks and saw no sign of damage. This quake had been nothing like the one that caused the old barracks to collapse on him as a young boy, killing everyone he'd known. His survival had been pure luck. Buried beneath a heap of rubble and pinned so close he could barely move, his groping hands had chanced upon a rivet once used to hold the ceiling in place. He'd struck it against the sword buried beside him again and again until someone heard.

"Not today," he said, turning away.

His eyes lifted to the rocky promontory that rose just beyond the barracks and up the high and shining walls of Raefi'ernyn. Just looking at the city of his masters made his heart flutter. The ramparts were a gleaming alabaster unmarred by the earthquake. Behind them, the city's spires stretched even higher to scratch the clouds. Raefi'ernyn was a symbol of nobility and hope. That the unaging Syraestari would claim a broken human child like himself was an honor and a gift he could never repay.

Raefi'ernyn never appeared to suffer from the quakes, but not so their Kalilaer charges. Vistus turned the opposite direction and headed west toward the labor settlements at a run. The camps lay on the far side of the muster field which also served from time to time as a place of punishment for rebels and murderers. The nearest Kalilaer buildings housed potters and weavers. Vistus was happy to see that both of these groups were undisturbed and that the Kalilaer had already returned to their tasks. But beyond them, the corner of a building had collapsed. Ironically, it was in the carpenter's camp. Already, the laborers were scurrying around its ruins and several pairs of t'Okaedrin warriors were present as well. They had no need of him.

Vistus turned to run a slow loop around the settlements, passing by the smelters with their furnaces billowing smoke upward into the blue sky. On the far side lay the farms where workers furrowed the soil in preparation for the planting of the spring wheat or tended the olive groves. Yet Vistus saw no other signs of trouble, not even of an addled Kalilaer trying to flee the settlements. All was at calm.

The run served to steady Vistus' nerves. He enjoyed the sun upon his back and the brisk sea breeze. Perhaps later in the day, provided he finished his other chores, he'd take a longer run along the shore. But the broom and the barracks still waited.

As he neared the barracks again and slowed to a walk, Vistus heard the steady tattoo of booted feet. A smile burst to his lips as he turned toward the forest. It was a vast wilderness that began less than a mile from the barracks and stretched to the distant wall of ice at the farthest bounds of Isfalinis. From its midst, the gray line of the Timnar Mountains jutted skyward where the nearest peak belched a plume of black ash. It was a sign, just like the earthquake, that Isfalinis' long torments weren't over.

But emerging from the fringe of the forest marched rank upon rank of t'Okaedrin warriors. Their helms and hauberks gleamed and their crimson cloaks fluttered as they strode in matched step, rank upon rank. Several hundred paces to the front and either side of the column, Pi'aernotha Osnoeda walked with bows drawn and eyes wary. The Sisters of Iron were skilled scouts and archers holding the same discipline as his brothers. They would not relax until the host reached the encampment and they were satisfied that all was well. The Pi'aernoth were easier to single out than individuals within the greater mass of t'Okaedrin and Vistus scanned the women's faces for Elestis, but didn't see her. She could just as easily be following the rear guard or scouting the far side of the column.

As the army reached the muster field, Vistus was surprised to see that Captain Nethzir wasn't with them. The leader of the Syraestari housecarls always led the forays into the wilderness. Finding his family among the ranks, Vistus was equally alarmed to realize that his father and eldest brother were absent. His heart fluttered with worry. They were dear to him, just like his first family had been all those years ago.

As soon as the t'Okaedrin were released, his family ran toward him with Bridionis in the lead. His best friend was a little taller than Vistus with dark brown hair that fell in heavy locks. They engulfed in embrace and the others gathered round, all fifteen of them. Even Arcomin.

"Amazing!" Bridionis laughed. "You survived without us."

"And you without me!" Vistus realized he was grinning and couldn't stop. They were all here. All except their eldest. "Where's Nalsuntha?"

"He and father rode on ahead last night. They've been summoned to a meeting in the city."

Vistus turned to look up toward gleaming Raefi'ernyn. "An honor."

"Yes," Bridionis said, but then clapped him firmly on the shoulders. "But what of you?"

Arcomin laughed. "Doubtless he's enjoyed lounging on a nice straw bed while we've been mucking in the dirt."

Vistus scowled, trying to think of a retort but Hirnid, ever the peacemaker, spoke, "How's your arm?"

"Almost fully mended," Vistus replied raising it. "The healer predicts I'll be ready for full duties within a week."

"Good, good," Bridionis said as they turned together and began walking back toward the barracks.

"Welcome home," Vistus said, "I've missed you all."

"If you don't act the fool, you'll be with us next time," Arcomin said.

Vistus smiled at him. "Yes, I even missed you, Arcomin."

His brother snorted. "Maybe in the future you'll remember not to charge ahead of the rest of us. If you'd done as you were trained, your arm never would've broken. We fight in a line and stay that way, no matter what."

"I prefer to think that it was we who fell behind," Bridionis said.

Arcomin glowered. "Break ranks again and you might just get yourself killed. Or even worse, one of your brothers."

Vistus didn't reply. He didn't need to. What Arcomin didn't know, what none of them knew was why he'd charged ahead. He'd only told his father and their eldest brother the truth. As he and his brothers had clashed with a band of wildmen last winter, he'd seen several slingers near the enemy flank. Slings were the simplest of weapons, but the stones they flung were deadly in skilled hands. They'd lost a brother to a stone through the eye only last year and Vistus wasn't about to let that happen again. It was a worthy enough price for a broken arm.

"Don't mind Arcomin," Bridionis said as they reached the barracks. The brothers dropped their gear, unslung their shields and swords, and pulled off their scaled hauberks. "He's just missing the dirt he complains so much about. If he could, he'd go back to drudge in the wilderness right now."

"If it meant the death of all the Scions, I would," Arcomin retorted as he retrieved his whetstone from his gear. Sitting on the ground, he set his sword on his lap and unsheathed it carefully. The other brothers did the same, each looking over their weapons.

"No luck, then?" Vistus asked. Sitting beside Bridionis, he picked up his brother's hauberk and looked for any damaged or missing scales.

Bridionis shook his head. "Not even a trace. Once again, the rebels managed to seize our Kalilaer and vanish into the wilderness."

"Weeks and weeks of walking back and forth," Hirnid added. "A couple times we thought we'd found a trail. Once we even came across an old camp."

"Hovels in the mud," Arcomin grumbled. "Twigs and branches for a roof. Savages!"

"It looked like they'd just abandoned it," Hirnid continued, "but like Arcomin said, the crudeness of it made it hard to tell."

Vistus nodded. He'd seen a couple such camps himself. Always empty with the air of being recent, they were enough to tantalize and mock at the same time. As best he knew, no occupied camp had ever been found. The wilderness was just too vast and the Scions of the Fallen Tree knew their wood craft too well. "And the earthquake?" he asked.

Bridionis shrugged. "Just another day in the life. We were near enough the edge of the wilds that the danger was small. Some scrapes and bruises in other families, but that's all."

"Accursed Scions," Arcomin muttered.

This time Vistus nodded his agreement. Long ago, humans much like the Scions of Fallen Tree had marched under the banners of Cydion, the Lord of Life and Death. They'd slain the Etyni, His Highest Above's greatest servants, and unleashed a Cataclysm that nearly destroyed the world. The recent quake was a testament to the continuing trauma of that devastation.

"Vistus, did you notice?" Hirnid asked with a nod toward Bridionis and a gleam in his eye.

Vistus looked over at his friend and, for the first time, realized that Bridionis had a special broach clasping his cloak. It was iron, like they all had, but a wolf's head had been etched on it. "Bridionis?" he asked. But his brother just ducked his head down, focusing on his work.

"He's been wearing that since the day we left," Hirnid said. "But won't tell us where it came from."

"He caught some Pi'aernoth's eye," Arcomin said. "Though with a face like that I can't see how. Just wait until father notices it."

That brought Bridionis' head up. "Father's already seen it. We're allowed to wear small tokens."

"But a wolf?" Arcomin laughed.

Vistus leaned over and elbowed his friend. "So who's the girl?"

"I don't know what you're talking about." Bridionis ducked his head down again to focus on his sword as laughter rang out around the circle.

Conversation quieted as the brothers focused on their work. It was the rule their parents had taught them from infancy. The sword had to be taken care of first and then the armor. Only when that was done would they see to themselves. Even though Vistus' gear required no tending, he assisted his brothers with theirs. As he worked, he could feel the smile etched on his face. This was life as it should be. Together.

"Here comes our eldest now," Hirnid said, breaking the silence.

Vistus looked up to see Nalsuntha walking towards them. Eldest Nalsuntha wasn't the oldest of their family. That distinction most likely lay with Bridionis, but true age didn't matter. They had all become t'Okaedrin as infants, rescued from birth mothers who'd been wildmen or Kalilaer laborers. One or two might even have been freed from the accursed Scions, but Vistus didn't know. Who had born them wasn't important. Those people weren't family and never had been. What mattered was that these t'Okaedrin were his true brothers. And the only age that meant anything was the one their family shared together. Six years ago, they had ceased to be children in training and had spoken their final oaths in service to the Empress Kayrstana. They had become warriors. Since that day, three of their number had proven that trust with the highest of honors by dying in her name.

Vistus set down Bridionis' armor and rose to greet Nalsuntha with an embrace, then his eldest stepped back. "You're looking hale as ever brother."

"And itching for something besides the drudgery of solitude," Vistus replied.

"We'll see what we can do." Nalsuntha grinned.

"Eldest," Hirnid said, "does that mean we aren't condemned to months of guarding the Kalilaer for our failures?"

"That's hardly punishment, Hirnid," Bridionis said, "I, for one, am looking forward to a bit of rest – even if it means sentry duty."

Arcomin growled irritably. "I hate playing mother to a band of traitors when the more dangerous enemy is still out there in the wilderness."

"The Kalilaer aren't traitors," Vistus snapped. "They're doing just what they're supposed to. Only those that run are evil."

"And they all would, given a chance," Arcomin retorted.

"Regardless of what they are, the Kalilaer are necessary," Nalsuntha said firmly. "You should know better by now than to question the wisdom of our Syraestari masters, Arcomin. The empress and her high lords see far more clearly than we do and it is our duty to obey. It is our honor to defend this realm against our own fallen race. That includes protecting the Kalilaer from their baser inclinations."

"Yes, Eldest," Arcomin replied in a rare moment of docility.

Nalsuntha put his hands on his hips as he surveyed his family. "Father is pleased with how you carried yourself in the wilderness. Though we didn't succeed, you were always disciplined, alert, and a true representation of our brotherhood. But our duties for the day aren't done. You have the rest of the morning to finish cleaning your armor and weapons and then yourselves. After the noon meal, resume walking the Kalilaer camp in the same pairs as usual. Except for you, Bridionis, you'll join Arcomin and Hirnid."

"I'm near enough full health, Eldest," Vistus said. "I can go with Bridionis as usual."

Nalsuntha clapped him firmly on the shoulder. "I know that, Vistus, but you and I have a meeting with our high lord."

"High Lord Tazil?" Vistus gasped. He felt all eyes turn toward him in wonder. Tazil ruled Raefi'ernyn and was but one step below the empress herself. Vistus looked up to the fair city and swallowed a lump in his throat.

"Lord Tazil's son will be there, too. As will our father."

"What did Vistus do?" Arcomin asked, the corner of his lips turning up in a malicious grin.

"More likely, what honor is he to receive?" Bridionis asked.

"T'Okaedrin aren't summoned before High Lord Tazil to receive honors." Arcomin laughed.

"They don't administer punishment either."

Nalsuntha shrugged. "I don't know. Father said we'll learn when we arrive." He looked Vistus over. "Your tunic appears clean and in good repair. We will leave immediately."

Arcomin chuckled darkly at that, but Vistus ignored him. "I am ready, Eldest."

"Come then."

As they walked across the t'Okaedrin compound, Vistus felt the eyes of all his brothers at his back. He was as stunned as they were. What had he done to deserve either praise or punishment? He was just a warrior, doing his duty. They had all fought every battle with courage and discipline, even Arcomin, no matter their rivalry. And there had been no pranks or disobedience since his youth. Each one of them had acted out in one way or another, except perhaps Hirnid, and had earned added chores or a turn at the lashing post. But that was all years past. Had he committed some crime without knowing it? But what crime would warrant the judgment of a Syraestari? And not just any Syraestari, but their high lord?

He and Nalsuntha climbed the road up the bluff at a brisk pace, Vistus following his eldest a half pace to the left. The rush of the ocean waves grew louder and louder as they climbed up the long rise toward the gates of the city. The waters below sparkled a perfect crystalline blue, but Vistus attention was pulled to the city that rose before him.

Two Syraestari housecarls stood at the outer gates. The personal warriors of the high lord each possessed centuries of training and experience that earned them the admiration of every t'Okaedrin. Their armor was splendid, leaving Vistus glad he wasn't wearing his own simple scale mail hauberk, however well polished. The Syraestari armor was scale, too, but with banded plates at the collar, shoulders, elbows, and knees. It wasn't just armor, though, but a work of art forged from steel instead of iron. Hauberk and helm were both embossed with gold filigreed impressions of wind, waves, and fire. A full head taller than either of the humans, the two Syraestari looked down on Vistus and his eldest with expressionless faces. Their eyelids, top and bottom, were painted in the Syraestari custom with a thick circlet of black ink.

Nalsuntha and Vistus bowed low, then passed through the gates. Inside, Vistus kept his eyes pointed straight ahead. He knew it would be dishonorable for a t'Okaedrin to gawk, no matter how much he wished to. Yet he risked glances from the corners of his eyes. In the camps below, Syraestari were uncommon sights, but scores strolled the wide streets of the city. Vistus and Nalsuntha bowed low each time they passed one by. They were all tall and slender and walked with elegant gaits. Most wore long robes sewn in flowing patterns that merged one into another without clear shape or end. Their fingers were adorned with rings while gleaming necklaces hung about their necks. Their eyes were all painted, too, though some with greater flourishes than the housecarls. The women were as tall as the men and wore golden rings that dangled from their angular ears. The magnificence of so many august people left Vistus feeling slightly breathless. He knew his awe was but a little less than if he were to stand before one of the ancient Etyni.

The only humans in the city were the women of the Pi'aernotha Kaupet. These Sisters of Stone were dutiful peers to the t'Okaedrin who weren't agile enough to be selected for the scouts and archers of the Sisters of Iron. Vistus had always held Stone Sisters in lower regard than those of Iron. But now, as he walked through Raefi'ernyn, he was filled with a new sense of respect. These sisters were entrusted to live in this great city and see to the daily needs of their masters. It was an unfathomable honor.

A handful of them hurried past, traveling both directions down the main thoroughfare. Many carried clothing to be washed along the nearby river or food from the fields and storehouses. Others weeded the gardens while a few perched on one of the rooftops replacing cedar planks.

Vistus and Nalsuntha followed the main street of Raefi'ernyn directly toward the soaring palace at its center. Despite his desire not to stare, Vistus couldn't stop his head from tilting upward to gaze at the high spires. From his earliest memory, he had stared at the central tower, rising a hundred feet or more above the bluff, but to see the palace in all its magnificence took his breath away.

His childhood imaginings were as nothing before this. When all he'd known were the sturdy but plain wooden barracks of the t'Okaedrin and the simpler camps of the Kalilaer, there was no way he could have conjured anything so wondrous to mind. With white stone walls, arched colonnades, and gabled rooftops, the palace appeared more shaped and sculpted by an artist's hand than simply erected. A wide frieze beneath the roof's cornice portrayed scenes that were no less spectacular. The first depicted dozens of small ships daring a sea crossing amid a raging storm with waves so lifelike Vistus could almost taste the salt water. That imagery blended into a battleground where Syraestari in scaled armor fought with swords and shields against a teeming host of stunted monsters with long arms and fanged teeth. The final scene was a familiar one of Raefi'ernyn standing strong beside the sea beneath a star-filled sky.

Nalsuntha slowed as they approached the central steps and Vistus' attention was so focused on the palace that he nearly stumbled over him. But rather than enter through the main doors, Nalsuntha guided Vistus toward a side entrance next to a stable. The door here was much smaller and watched over by a Stone Sister who smiled as she opened it for them. "Welcome t'Okaedrin. The empress' blessing upon you both."

"And upon you," Nalsuntha replied, formally.

Vistus spared the woman a distracted smile before following Nalsuntha into a long lamp-lit corridor. Dozens of doors lined either side and it was intersected a handful of crossing hallways. Feeling the weight of the meeting fall upon his shoulders, Vistus made no effort to look around. He knew he was coming upon a moment of truth and his heart fluttered in apprehension. They walked most of the way down the hall to a door that looked little different from any other except for a second Pi'aernoth standing in front of it.

At her expectant glance, Nalsuntha said, "We've come at the bidding of High Lord Tazil. I am Eldest Nalsuntha and this is Vistus."

"One moment, Eldest," the woman replied. She paused to run her hands in a smoothing gesture down the pleats of her brown dress, then slipped the door open and stepped inside.

As she closed the door behind her, Nalsuntha spoke, "Whatever this summons might mean, Vistus, you are a good brother."

"I… thank you." Vistus stammered. He might have said more, but the door opened and the woman emerged.

"His Highness will see you."

Vistus swallowed a lump that rose in his throat as he followed Nalsuntha inside. The room was of modest size, perhaps twenty paces across with two thick pillars jutting from wooden walls to the left and the right. The wood was lacquered and carved with forest scenes of trees, wildflowers, and a brook so lifelike he could almost imagine its gurgling voice. On the far side, High Lord Tazil sat with his son, Captain Nethzir, standing at his right and Vistus' father, Dalric, standing to his left.

But as he followed his eldest across the chamber, it was Tazil who claimed his full attention. The high lord was a lanky man who sat with a stiff dignity that transformed his unadorned wooden chair into a throne. His golden hair was tied back by a strip of green linen that exposed his sharp angular ears. Around his eyes, Tazil had applied the customary black makeup but extended it with a flourish like two talons running down either side of his nose. His brown eyes held Vistus' gaze as if they were shackles.

As they reached the three waiting men, Vistus tore his eyes away as he and Nalsuntha bowed to one knee, right fist to floor and forehead to knee.

"Please rise, my children."

The words poured over Vistus, setting his heart to racing even faster than it had been. Children? Spoken so softly, so gently that it couldn't be punishment but something far more wonderful. But he couldn't fathom anything more glorious than to be named child by any Syraestari, let alone his lord. It had to be a dream.

Vistus rose obediently and faced his master. Tazil's right hand, adorned with a half-dozen rings, lifted to rest regally on his chest as he glanced at Dalric, then back to Vistus. "I am given to understand that you are among the bravest of all my t'Okaedrin and also the cleverest."

"I live only to serve, Highness," Vistus said, ducking his head again in a small bow. He felt breathless and was glad that his voice remained steady.

"And you serve well," Tazil replied. "It is for this reason that my son has need of you in the greatest task you will ever face." He nodded to his son.

Vistus knew Nethzir, if only from a distance. As captain of the housecarls, Nethzir also led his father's army, which meant he usually accompanied the t'Okaedrin raids. He showed great personal courage, sometimes even entering the battle. He was a little taller than his father with the same blond hair, though the paint around his dark eyes was embellished only by a slight flaring toward his temples like tongues of black flame. If they had been human, Vistus would have guessed High Lord Tazil and Captain Nethzir to be of an age. But his Syraestari masters were as above him as he and his brothers were above animals. In the dawn of time, they had spurned the poisoned temptations of fell Cydion. Because of their wisdom, the Syraestari remained free of the curse of aging death.

"I am prepared for whatever you would have of me," Vistus said.

Tazil turned to Dalric. "You have trained him to speak as fairly as he doubtless fights."

Vistus' father stood with shoulders back and head straight, the epitome of t'Okaedrin discipline. Dalric had been a grizzled warrior even before Vistus joined the family. Though his sword was buckled at his side, his days of fighting were over. Years ago, his right arm had been shattered at the wrist as he stepped between a wildman attack and a Syraestari. "He is a good son, Highness."

Vistus' heart swelled as Tazil said to his own son, "Captain Nethzir, please explain his task."

"You have been chosen to root out one of the hidden rebel camps that afflict our people," Nethzir said. "When the Scions attack us again and seize any disloyal Kalilaer from the settlements they can reach, you will go with them. You will join with the rebels as if you were a fleeing Kalilaer yourself. You will have to behave like one of them for several days, long enough for them to withdraw to their camp. I will lead several t'Okaedrin families in pursuit. When we reach you, we'll destroy the Scion camp and recover you. Do you have any questions?"

He had nothing but questions. Were it not for the hard expectant eyes of his masters buoying him up, Vistus was afraid he might tremble. But he would not dishonor them, his father, or his brothers. The thought of being the warrior who discovered the Scions of the Fallen Tree filled him with excitement and apprehension. A small part of him quailed at the thought of going alone among the enemy after being so recently reunited with his family, but he crushed that feeling down. "My Lord, how will I signal you?"

High Lord Tazil nodded approvingly as Captain Nethzir reached into a pouch at his side and withdrew a leather cord. It was looped through a small hole in a black stone perhaps a quarter the size of Vistus' palm. "This is a Sapaupan Kaupet, a stone enchanted by the Sorceress Medreuneth. As long as you carry it with you, we will find you."

Captain Nethzir extended his hand and Vistus reverently reached out to take the stone. It rested cool in his palm and the edges shimmered faintly. Here was honor stacked upon honor. That he, a human, should be entrusted with the sorcery of the Syraestari was beyond anything he could imagine.

"It is a challenging task we've given you, but the plan is simple," Nethzir said. "That is why it will succeed. To blend in among the Kalilaer and the Scions, you will have to grow a beard."

Vistus nodded, concealing a grimace. A mark of pride among the t'Okaedrin was the smoothly shaved jaw. With it, they could honor the smooth-skinned Syraestari while setting themselves apart from the Kalilaer as well as the stone-wielding Scions and the wildmen of the northern forests.

Nethzir's voice took on a firm edge. "We have need of you as never before. As you know, the Scions have become more ferocious in recent months. Their raids steal away many of the Kalilaer and ravage our harvests. You're about to enter a battlefield more dangerous than any you've seen. It will be a battle of the mind and of the soul. To triumph, your heart must appear to change, just as your face will beneath its beard. You must become as them if you are to survive. This may require you to speak words that will turn your stomach. You may have to pronounce disloyalties to us and to your brothers."

Vistus swallowed. "I understand, my Lord."

"Good. You were chosen because, of all your brothers, you are the most resilient and adaptable. When we looked for a t'Okaedrin to undertake this task, we were impressed by the initiative and daring you demonstrated when you broke ranks to dispatch the slingers that threatened your brothers. From your father's recounting, I understand this is but the latest example of your adaptability. We have faith that you will triumph. An opportunity lies before us, before you, to bring peace and security to the realm. What is your greatest duty? What is your greatest honor?"

"There is no greater duty than to kill in the name of the Empress," Vistus recited, clinging proudly to the words. He would see these Scions dead for her. For her and High Lord Tazil. "There is no greater honor than to die in the name of the Empress. I live for my Empress, my masters, and my brothers. By them, and for them, I live and I die."

High Lord Tazil spoke. "Go then, Vistus. Serve with honor. We will speak again when you have returned to us."

Vistus dropped down to one knee, bowing until his forehead nearly touched the smooth stone floor. "I obey, my Lord."

"Wake up, they've come!"

Vistus clawed to wakefulness to blink into the lamplight over his bed. Shadows played off the high-beamed rafters of the barracks room. "What? Who?"

Eldest Nalsuntha's hand caught him firmly on the cheek, tearing the vestiges of sleep away. "Scion raid, Vistus. Move!"

"Scions!" Vistus blurted, leaping to his feet. Nalsuntha pushed the Kalilaer tunic and breeches into Vistus' arms and he hurriedly donned them. They were made of a coarser linen than the t'Okaedrin wore, with shorter sleeves and a simple waist tie instead of a belt. "Where? How many?" he asked as he pulled on his breeches.

"About three dozen. They've broken into the pottery camp and two of the farming barracks."

Vistus stamped into his work shoes as he pulled the tunic over his head. As his eyes emerged from the cloth, he saw the black stone necklace dangling from his eldest's hand. "Thank you," he said, taking it and slipping it around his neck.

Nalsuntha clapped him on the back. "We'll see you soon. Hurry!"

Vistus nodded, sparing a glance for his bed. The covers lay back, all askew, and his t'Okaedrin clothes had scattered onto the floor in his haste to dress. Disorder always meant distraction. Growling, he pushed the thought from his mind and ran for the door. His brothers were all up, too, donning their armor and grabbing weapons for the inevitable pursuit.

They paused in their tasks to shout out cries of encouragement. Vistus even heard Arcomin's voice among them. His best friend, Bridionis, and his father stood waiting by the door.

"Go brother!" Bridionis said, grinning widely, and his father added, "Fenr's strength with you, my son."

Vistus met their grins as he ran out the door. "I will see you on the other side."

Moonlit darkness met him beyond. The night was cool and chill, with the full lingering heat of summer still several weeks distant. Stars speckled the heavens, peeking through wisps of cloud.

He turned toward the nearest Kalilaer settlement first. It would not do for him to appear to come from the direction of the t'Okaedrin barracks or proud Raefi'ernyn towering on the bluff above.

Behind him, a t'Okaedrin began ringing the alarm. The harsh call of iron rod striking iron triangle cut through the night air. It was a sound that lifted him up, swelling his heart with pride and courage. He had fought under that harsh chime a dozen times and once, a fainter ring of metal on metal had saved his life.

He passed the potters' camp on his left, its short thick wooden walled buildings rising up as dark shadows in the night. Heart in his throat, Vistus turned northward towards the looming wilderness. He had longed for this moment, dreamed of it, imagining both the victory and glory it would bring. But now that the task was upon him, he was more afraid than excited as a host of doubts rose up before him.

He had to be strong enough. He had to be brave enough. The Syraestari needed him. And he was alone again.

Sprinting for the forest, he could see dark shapes of Kalilaer and Scions racing ahead of him. His feet pounding against the hard-packed earth, tall grasses beating a rapping tattoo against his shins. Running was slower in his crude work shoes than it would have been in his solid leather t'Okaedrin boots, far slower than he'd expected. He was breathing hard as he finally burst through the outer line of trees.

Beneath the forest eaves, darkness was almost absolute, with the moonlight casting only intermittent flecks across Vistus' face. But he did not slow his pace. Trees loomed then passed like black shadows. Branches whipped by, snagging against his tunic, scoring his bared forearms and leaving him wishing for his armor. He breathed hard, drawing in the cool night air.

But as much as he focused on running and not careening into a tree or stumbling over a hidden root, he concentrated on the change that had to come over him from within. He could feel the transformation in his skin and in his bones as he forced his own mind to shift. It was a task that had consumed the long weeks of waiting. More than the growing of his beard, he had readied to become less and less himself even to the donning of a new name. With each step he became increasingly the enemy. A rebel, a Scion.

He caught rare glimpses of others racing ahead of him. They flashed briefly in the moonlight before disappearing once more into the shadows of the trees. The Scion raiders and escaped Kalilaer were fast, faster than he would have guessed. Wildness and fear lent them wings, but he hastened after. If he lost them, all his waiting and preparation would be for nothing.

The beat of hooves echoed behind him and Vistus cursed, "Blood on the Bridge!"

His brothers shouldn't have followed so soon. Panic seized him and he leaned forward, sparing no energy for what might be a long run ahead. Never mind if he broke an ankle on an unseen root or a hidden stone. The t'Okaedrin had to pursue, of course, if they didn't it would have been suspicious. But they should have given him more time. He had to get deep enough into the forest that they would be forced to stop, fearing for their horses. But the hooves pounded closer until they thundered like drums in his ears.

A shadow leapt from the darkness to his right catching Vistus full in the chest and throwing him to the ground. Landing hard, a cloud of dirt spattered across his face. He rolled onto his back, grappling with his assailant. His hands gripped leather clothing with no jingling of metal. His mind seized on that. It had to be a Kalilaer or one of the rebels. A t'Okaedrin would have worn iron scale.

The figure hissed in his ear, "Lie still!" It was a woman.

Vistus stopped struggling, but whispered back. "Kalilaer or Scion?" If she was just another escapee, all would be ruined. He would kill her and follow still, but the delay would be costly.

"Scion," the woman whispered, "now be silent."

Uttering a silent prayer of thanks to His Highest Above, Vistus did as he was told. Moments later, horsemen galloped past on either side. The ground trembled beneath the thunder of their hooves. Only after they were gone did he dare scrub at the dirt in his eyes. Blinking, he stared at the woman. Her blond hair shone where the moonlight caught it. She held a finger up to her lips. Silence.

Not long after, Vistus heard what he knew she'd been waiting for. It was the heavier thudding sound of booted feet. He lay back down on the ground and the woman flung herself beside him as they waited for the dark forms of a dozen warriors to run past. In the dim light he caught the pale gleam of iron helms and scaled hauberks, but the deep darkness of the forest hid himself and the woman from them. After the t'Okaedrin disappeared into the night he sat upright. She sat up too, and smiled at him. "Welcome to freedom."

Vistus breathed deeply, trying to slow his racing heart. He opened his mouth to speak, then stopped himself, thinking. He had to talk like them, think like them. What would a Kalilaer, newly escaped from the camps, say? He scratched at his chin, uncomfortable with the coarse beard. "I was afraid I'd lost you all in the darkness. You really are a Scion of the Fallen Tree?"

"Yes," she nodded. "And you're one now too. My name is Vitarria."

"Belarrin," he replied, giving his false name. He nodded to himself, reinforcing that thought. He was Belarrin now. Rising to his knees, he peered into the darkness. When he was preparing for this task, he'd asked his mother for a name that wildmen might use. In her youth among the Pi'aernotha Osnoeda, she had slain a warrior by the name of Belarrin. There was something poetic about turning the name of a slain enemy into a weapon.

"It's too dangerous to move far yet," Vitarria said, then pointed to the darker shadow of a nearby tree. "We can hide there. If we flee now, the Iron-Men will find us when they give up their pursuit and return. We wait for them to pass before moving on."

"But you know where we're going?" Belarrin asked as they crept over to the tree.

"Yes."

"Thank His Highest Above." His mission would succeed, though he knew she would misunderstand his thankfulness.

"Be at peace, Belarrin. You are free of Finaestari chains now."

Finaestari. It was just as Captain Nethzir had warned him. The Scions spoke lies with every breath. He had learned, while still a young child, that rebels and apostates used fell names to justify their crimes. The Scions twisted history to deny the nobility and grandeur of his masters, naming them Finaestari, 'Dark Aestari,' in an attempt to blacken that which was good. Syraestari meant 'True Aestari', those of their kindred who had chained themselves in service to Cydion. As Vistus, he knew the truth, but the traitor Belarrin wouldn't use his master's proper name. "Free," he said, trying to be as honest as he could. "I'm not sure I quite understand it."

She smiled at him and he grinned back. Vitarria was not what he'd expected. Her face was fair, her eyes bright, bespeaking innocence. He had fought enough Scions to know that they weren't unsoiled ash-born monsters like the troglyds of legend. But he had always faced them across a field of ringing blades and spilled blood. This was different. Perhaps he should've expected as much. That she would be pleasant, friendly, and gently spoken. Even when she spewed her lies, there was the root of belief. She thought what she said was right. It was a pity she didn't know, that none of her kind understood. If they had, perhaps humanity would have swallowed its pride and spared the world the Cataclysm.

But as he assessed her, he realized her demeanor was not that of a warrior. "Where are your weapons?" he wondered.

"I have a knife," she said, patting a short weapon at her belt. Beneath the leather scabbard, Belarrin saw that the blade was stone.

"A knife to fight men with iron? You are very brave."

She laughed. "I did not enter the camps. A priestess only fights when she has no other choice. I came to help you and all the other Kalilaer that made it to the woodland."

"Then I owe you everything. Thank you," Belarrin said. There was irony in that, but he kept it from his voice.

"Of course," she replied. "Now we should be quiet in case any Finnies are about with their accursed Iron-Men."

Belarrin didn't like that name either. Finnie was even worse than Finaestari. A mockery of a mockery. But he held his tongue and the pair peered silently into the dark forest. Beneath the black eaves, his eyes grew more accustomed, but the forest was so shadowed he could see little. No sounds penetrated the night except the rustle of branches in the cool wind, his own breath and Vitarria's softer beside him.

Then he heard the sound of hooves and footfalls in the distance ahead. Belarrin sank deeper into the shadows and Vitarria did likewise. His hand crept instinctively to the black stone that hung around his neck on its string of leather. It was his single link to home, a cool beacon that told him he wasn't alone. It would bring his brothers to him when the time was right. But not yet.

When the t'Okaedrin had passed, their footfalls fading into the distance, he let out a deep breath. Vitarria rose to her feet. "Come, it's time to move."

Belarrin followed her deeper into the forest. They ran at an easy pace, much more relaxed than his frenzied flight from before. The trees and brush grew denser the further they traveled. They became more similar too, especially in the darkness, until each tree that flickered past looked the same as the one before. Belarrin began to wonder if the woman knew where she was going or if they were running in circles.

"Careful," Vitarria said, stopping short.

Belarrin ran up beside her and peered into the darkness. Ahead of them, the ground broke away in a sheer cliff. He could barely see the forest floor below. It was at least twenty feet high, perhaps thirty, and ended sharply at the base. Belarrin suppressed a shiver. The precipice was just one more symbol of the Cataclysm. The cliff had formed recently, perhaps from one of the quakes that had struck in the past few months. Otherwise, the sheer edge would have already begun to wear away.

Vitarria peered to the left and right.

"What are you looking for?" Belarrin asked.

"The path down. I'm sure it's near here."

Belarrin laughed. "How can you tell where anything is in this wilderness?"

He sensed more than saw Vitarria's gentle smile. "It is my home."

She turned to the left and trotted along the edge of the cliff, but not so close a careless step might pitch her over. Belarrin followed, shaking his head in disbelief. His skepticism grew as more time passed. This priestess was no warrior. She didn't know her way. If she got both of them lost, what good would that do him? But there was no other choice except to continue.

Finally after a half mile or more, she stopped. A rope had been tied around a tree and dangled over the precipice. Vitarria grasped it in both hands and quickly slid down. Belarrin swallowed. He didn't like cliffs. He didn't like anything that reminded him of the Cataclysm, especially its earthquakes.

He gingerly took the rope and lowered himself over the edge. Pebbles rattled loose around him as he scrambled with his feet to find purchase against the cliff edge. The dirt, already softened by other climbers, shifted, then gave way. Belarrin clutched at the rope and shut his eyes as dirt cascaded around him. He swung forward, his shoulder striking the cliff wall. "Accursed Scions!" he muttered under his breath as stars flashed in front of his eyes.

But he clung tightly to the rope, allowing his head to stop spinning. Finally, he opened his eyes again. Then, drawing a deep breath, he slowly lowered himself hand over hand. He was not going to trust his feet against the cliff edge again. As his feet finally touched the forest floor, he stifled a gasp of relief.

"What was it you said?" Vitarria asked.

"Accursed Cydion," Belarrin lied. "I hate climbing."

Vitarria looked up the cliff face. "Generations dead and he curses us still. But as long as we live, we have hope." She turned to him. "We'll leave the rope in case any others remain behind us."

Belarrin followed her as she broke into a run again. It was curious the delusions these people held, so close to the truth but not quite. As a priestess, she of all people should've understood. That was what set the Scions apart from the wildmen tribes of the deeper north. The wildmen lived as savages. In crude villages, they eked out a living with tools of stone and bone, growing a little, hunting and gathering more. But the Scions had come from Kalilaer rebels. They'd been taught the truth only to run from it. It was the difference between ignorance and apostasy. For the wildmen, there was hope, but the Scions were beyond salvation.

The pair ran on until the first grays of dawn crept through the forest canopy. Then, Vitarria slowed to a walk.

"Hold!" A voice snapped from the brush ahead.

CHAPTER 2
Stones

"The Cataclysm isn't about you. It was never about anyone. The deaths that flow so readily from it are but an echo of that deeper hidden pain, that rupturing of Isfalinis herself, flesh, breath, blood, and heart."

—Lady Medreuneth

Belarrin froze, but Vitarria barely slowed, replying, "Peace Parvik, it's only me."

"Henji's Blood on the Bridge," Parvik cried as he stepped out from his hiding place, a stone headed spear in his hand. "I was afraid we'd lost you." He nodded over at Belarrin. "Who's this?"

"Another Kalilaer," Vitarria replied. "His name is Belarrin."

Parvik lowered his spear and nodded to Belarrin. "Welcome." Then he looked back at Vitarria and grinned. "Only one stray this time? Some of the Scions might think you're getting lazy."

Vitarria laughed. "Just the one, running alone through the night." But as the words passed her lips, she fell suddenly silent, face paling. Belarrin glanced at her sharply and, seeing Parvik tense, he turned behind him to scan the underbrush.

"What is it?" Parvik hissed softly, "did you see something?"

"No, no, I..." Vitarria shook her head. "It's nothing. Just a sudden thought."

"You're sure?"

"Yes, it's nothing. I'm sorry, Parvik. It is good to be back again."

Parvik relaxed, but Belarrin watched Vitarria closely as a creeping sensation rose in his spine. What did it mean? Did she suspect something? But he'd done nothing peculiar he could think of. When Vitarria met his gaze, he saw no suspicion in her eyes. If anything, there was a drawn sadness to her countenance that hadn't been there before. He shook away the tendrils of fear. In this strange place he was seeing threats that didn't exist.

"Come, Belarrin," she said, a smile returning to her face. But the sorrow remained, too. "Let me introduce you to the others."

Parvik gestured behind him with his head. "They're all waiting back in the clearing. I expect we'll be leaving soon."

Belarrin followed Vitarria into the glade. Close to a hundred people were scattered around it without any semblance of organization. The fleeing Kalilaer wore linen blouses and breeches of simple cut like Belarrin's garb, while the Scions could be marked by their leather clothing, as much of it tanned as not. But even if they had all dressed alike, Belarrin was confident he could have told the Kalilaer from the Scions. The former stood or sat, blinking in the new dawn light, both nervous and excited as if not sure if this were real or a dream. The Scions were more confident, standing alert and ready, though not with the sure discipline Belarrin was familiar with in the t'Okaedrin.

One of the Scions, a man whose brown hair and long beard were streaked with gray, roared with laughter at the sight of them. "Vitarria! I knew it would take more than a few Iron-Men to keep you from returning to us." He strode forward and engulfed her in an embrace. "The tree has fallen," he said softly. The words had the weight of a ritual.

She returned his hug with vigor, replying, "But a new shoot rises." Pulling away, she said, "This is Belarrin. Belarrin, meet Inban, our chieftain."

"I am honored," Belarrin said, then stepped back, startled, as Inban flung his arms around him in a furious embrace. The pungent scents of sweat, dirt, and leather filled his nose. Belarrin could only stumble back awkwardly once he was released, but Inban didn't seem to notice.

"How successful were we?" Vitarria asked.

"A great triumph! Thirty slaves freed and we lost no one."

"Isi be praised," Vitarria replied. "Every time I'm afraid of who I won't see again."

"The Shadow of Zaris guided us as truly as he has before."

Vitarria nodded. "It would seem I was wrong, yet I can't let go of my doubts."

"Then do not," Inban said, giving her a one-armed embrace before departing.

"Shadow of Zaris?" Belarrin asked.

"Yes," Vitarria replied. "A strange figure cloaked in shadows. He approaches one of us only, usually near dawn or dusk, and tells us which Finnie city to strike and when. Every time we've followed his direction, we've rescued a large number of slaves while suffering only a few losses."

"But Zaris was slain in the Great War along with all the other Etyni."

Vitarria lips twisted into a grimace. "I don't understand either. Perhaps he can still touch our world. All I know is that five times he's come and five times we've triumphed. Nevertheless, I doubt. Not very priestlike of me, I know."

"No. A priest above all others must be sure lies do not pull others from the truth," Belarrin answered. Though they had only met a few hours before, he could already feel a companionship with the woman no matter how foolish he knew that might be. It was unfortunate that she was so enshrouded in lies that she could not see clearly.

"Thank you. It does give me hope to think that His Highest Above has turned his face upon our plight. Besides, how can I say different when so many lives have been reclaimed?"

Looking out at the escaped Kalilaer, Belarrin knew he shouldn't have been surprised at their numbers, yet he was. The madness that afflicted his race baffled him. The Kalilaer lived good and honorable lives, just as His Highest Above had intended. They lived in sturdy houses, securely protected by warriors and well fed by the harvests. The hard work they carried out in the settlements was as much for their own good as their masters and certainly was better than a meager life in the wilderness. How could they wish for anything more than that? How could they prefer this grim struggle for survival? Perhaps his time among them would help him understand. If his knowledge helped other Kalilaer avoid this twisted fate that could only be for the good.

As the sky turned from gray to blue with the rising of the sun, Parvik and several other Scions of the Fallen Tree entered the clearing. Inban nodded to them. "It is time to move."

Belarrin joined in with the huddled mass of escaped Kalilaer as they followed the Scions deeper into the forest. Though he walked with them, he also kept himself apart. He could not afford to be drawn to closely among them for fear that one or another might wonder who he was and from which of the Kalilaer settlements he'd escaped. If anyone pressed those questions, he would probably die.

Most of the Kalilaer were quiet, too, looking around at the wilderness with awe-filled eyes. Some whispered softly to each other as if afraid to speak louder and break the spell. Belarrin marveled himself, curious. He had spent many months on campaign in the wilderness, but there was something different about walking through it this time. Perhaps it was because he saw the forest through the eyes of a refugee rather than a warrior. It was curious how such a simple change could be so mesmerizing. There were secrets within its bounds that called to him.

He quickly perceived another difference between the Scions and the t'Okaedrin. When the t'Okaedrin marched through the wilderness, they followed rivers and valleys where the foliage wasn't too dense. That made it easier to move in formed columns and clear paths for supply wagons. The Scions followed no such principles. They walked wherever they willed, undeterred by heavy underbrush, areas of scattered stones mottled by lichen, or downed trees. Yet they seemed to know their way unerringly, bypassing the thickest parts of the forest and moving at a pace that nearly matched the t'Okaedrin in the open.

More curious, though, were the people themselves. The Scions spoke with an ease and friendliness he had only experienced within the bounds of his own family. Even the men and women joked together readily. They spoke whenever they felt like and never seemed to mind who overheard.

Certainly, he had chatted as casually with Elestis, but even that felt different than this. Elestis was a Pi'aernotha Osnoeda, one of the warrior scouts. Over the past few years, they'd become close friends and, if all went as he intended, would become more. When next they met, he would be flush with new triumphs on his shoulder. He was almost certain to win approval from Dalric and her mother to arrange a marriage. Realizing a broad grin had formed on his face, Belarrin smoothed his features. It would not do to draw any questions, not even ones as to why he was smiling.

The chaos in Scion society extended everywhere, as far as he could see. While they walked, he tried to guess their hierarchy but couldn't. Had Vitarria not introduced him to Inban, he might not even have been able to identify their chieftain, let alone sub-leaders.

The rest of the day passed quickly, as did those that followed after it. Despite the sameness of the forest, the Scions had no problem finding their way. Near each midday, they paused briefly and the Scions handed out dried meat. Some of them ran ahead to hunt and trap so roasted deer or perhaps rabbit was ready for eating each night. With the juices of animal flesh dripping down his fingers, Belarrin found those feasts to be the best part of this freedom. It was far better than the bread and mushy stews that were a large part of his diet in the life he'd left.

Each time they stopped, Vitarria always joined him. Belarrin wondered if her peculiar behavior when they'd met Parvik that first morning had stung her so that she took a special interest in him. Belarrin certainly didn't mind. Though she was no Elestis, she was pretty in a wild sort of way, wearing her pale hair loose while the Pi'aernoth always tied theirs back to keep it from interfering with their archery. Vitarria's eyes were a deep green that reminded Belarrin of the untamed forest itself.

"How long were you a slave?" she asked, taking a seat beside him as he ate the evening meal.

"I was Kalilaer most of my life," Belarrin replied. He swallowed. It was hard to force himself to use the words these Scions did. Kalilaer were not slaves. Slavery was ignoble, but what the Kalilaer did was good. They lived and thrived as was intended from the beginning. But he had to speak as the Scions did. "I was enslaved as a child."

"I thought all children were forced to be Iron-Men."

"I must have been a little too old," Belarrin said. Only those under six years of age made good t'Okaedrin. Older children already had ties that were too strong to their birth parents, making them unruly, undisciplined, and sometimes even rebellious.

"Then we must seem very strange to you."

He smiled. "A little, yes."

She grinned back. The sadness he'd noticed in her eyes had faded, but every once in a while, he thought he saw it appear again. "Give yourself time. It isn't always an easy change, but if you listen and watch us you'll see that we are here because we choose to be. No one made us what we are but ourselves and we believe that no one should be held in chains."

He nodded. It was peculiar that the Scions spoke of chains when it was they who had been ensnared by their short memories. If they knew their legends were corrupted and that they clung to the lies of Cydion, there would be no need for this war. But Belarrin knew simple words couldn't sway her no matter how much he might wish it. "I will watch and listen, then."

She nodded, saying nothing, but she didn't leave either.

Somehow, Belarrin found that comforting. With Vitarria around, he felt more secure from those questions he wanted to avoid. There was also something friendly and welcoming in her kind words, different from anything he'd ever heard from his mother, father, Elestis, or any of his brothers. It intrigued him and made him uncomfortable at the same time.

Their camps were haphazard, with each Scion finding a place that suited him best, and Belarrin didn't like it. The chaos was unsettling. He'd been raised to discipline and order and found comfort in the structure of his life. He wanted aligned rows of tents, carefully stacked weapons, and meticulously placed outer pickets.

Only a few days, he told himself each night as he lay back and looked through the canopy of leaves and tree limbs to the winking stars beyond. Clutching the black stone hanging from his neck, he turned his thoughts to happy things. His brothers, Elestis, and the glorious victory that was coming. Sleep came easier with thoughts of home.

The march emphasized the vastness of the wilderness. Every day felt the same, every step identical with the thick looming evergreens, the shorter leafy trees forming a lower canopy, and dense bushes growing wherever the sun broke through. The ground was speckled by downed trees, the trunks rotting with the rich scents of loam and host to a myriad of smaller plants. The ground itself was gently rolling, broken only by the occasional ravine. None, thankfully, were as steep as the cliff of the first night. On the third day, though, they passed along the edge of a clearing that had been burned into the wilderness. The earth itself had ruptured, doubtless from one of innumerable Cataclysm earthquakes that ravaged the land. Liquid fire, the blood of Isfalinis herself, had poured upward before cooling in a mile-long scab of blackened rock.

He followed the others across it, gingerly placing his feet with care. The rocks had crumbled as they cooled, breaking into countless coarse boulders that could easily tear flesh. Only in a few places had greenery pushed through the black wound and he wondered at the severity of it. Perhaps the great rent had been formed by the quake that had nearly claimed his life all those years ago. When they left it behind, disappearing once more into the close-grip of the forest, Belarrin realized that he was breathing heavily, more from the dread recollections than physical exertion.

Belarrin focused on the trees around him, pushing away those dark thoughts. He considered all he'd been told about this forest. It stretched northward for a month of marches and more before reaching a wall of unending ice that stretched higher than the treetops, higher even than Raefi'ernyn's highest tower on its mighty bluff. Of course, none of the t'Okaedrin had seen it, but their masters had. The ice had been a barrier for the Syraestari in their long migration. In those days, the Cataclysm had been even more severe, making permanent settlement impossible. The Syraestari had been assailed by wild humans on every side in desperate search of food in a dying world.

The world was healing now, but still humanity resisted. And as he walked through the great wilderness, Belarrin understood more than ever how the Scions could disappear so fully within it. Finding them was like searching for a grain of sand dropped into the sea. Yet despite the vast sameness, the

Scions seemed to know where they were going. Late in the fifth day since joining them, they arrived at the Scion camp. To his surprise, it was exactly like the handful of camps he and the t'Okaedrin had stumbled upon in their futile searches for the rebels. Post holes around the periphery marked where a fence had once been erected while larger depressions in the center remained as echoes of where huts had stood. A single shelter remained near a fire pit in the middle of the camp. Built for a large blaze, it only held a small one now, and a single man sat huddled before it. A spear lay on the ground at the man's side and a stone knife hung from his belt.

"What happened?" Belarrin asked. "Where is everyone?"

Vitarria smiled. "Peace, Belarrin, all is well."

Noticing them, the man rose to his feet and ran forward. He stretched out his arms. "Chief Inban, welcome!"

Inban strode to greet him in a big embrace. "How far, my friend?"

"Another three days," the man replied, squinting up at the blue sky.

"Press on then," Inban replied. "We are all eager for a good feast and home."

Belarrin turned to Vitarria. "You've changed camps."

Vitarria nodded. "After every raid, those who stay behind find a new place."

"But why?" Belarrin asked, though he already suspected the answer. The Kalilaer he pretended to be probably wouldn't, though.

"Just in case one of us is captured. Even the strongest of us can be broken in time and forced to reveal our hiding place. No one who goes on the raid knows the new location." She nodded toward the man talking with Inban. "That knife you see at his side. That is for himself, should the enemy find him instead of us."

Belarrin's lips thinned. "Grim choices."

"But necessary if we're to survive."

Belarrin nodded. This was just one more reason the t'Okaedrin had never found a Scion camp. The vastness of the wilderness was bad enough. But with this, any search without his guiding stone would be worthless.

They didn't linger in the old camp, but followed the Scion back into the forest. It was a return to the sameness of before, with every step looking like the one that had preceded it. Another three days without change, just like the man had promised. Yet, as predicted, they reached the new camp late on the third day.

It looked nothing like the wildmen villages that lay further north. Those peoples, despite their savagery, had managed at least to build settlements with several dozen permanent buildings with wooden walls and thatched roofs. Vegetable gardens speckled the open places and earthen ramparts surrounding the outer edge. But the Scion camp wasn't carved from the forest. Instead, it filled a large natural glade. It was as chaotic as their makeshift camps on the march, with no real buildings, only crude shelters of bent branches and mud-packed walls, scattered across the field like toys dropped by some giant child. The camp had no gardens or crops, nor any earthen wall to protect it. Instead, a simpler barrier of stacked logs ringed the camp with a single gap about three paces wide. It was only chest-high in the tallest places and would barely slow the charge of a determined warrior, let alone a horseman. Perhaps its only purpose was to provide a short delay and make noise as an attacker breeched it.

As Belarrin and the others cleared the wood line, the Scions in the camp ran forward to greet them. They numbered perhaps two dozen adults and as many children and gave glad cries as they embraced the returned warriors and escaped Kalilaer alike. By the fifth hug, Belarrin found himself shrugging away from the overly friendly greetings, the last one from a burly man, half a head taller than him who reeked of sweat and leather. The Scions greeted each other repeatedly with "The tree has fallen" and "But a new shoot rises."

When Inban, Vitarria, and a few others disappeared into one of the larger shelters, Belarrin wanted to follow. Not so much because he needed to, but because he was curious about these strange misguided people. His mission was not just about destroying this band of rebels. Though High Lord Tazil and Captain Nethzir had never said it specifically, he sensed his purpose was also to understand them and for that, he had little time. He wanted to discover why they had been led so far astray. What was so compelling about the lies they told that pulled them from the good lives the Syraestari offered? But just as importantly, he needed to understand how the Scions functioned. So little was known about them. There were many bands, that much was certain, but no one knew how many. They seemed both uncoordinated and alike, which meant they acted on their own but still communicated. If he could figure out how they did that, perhaps they could find even more bands and destroy them, too. If the Scions were vanquished, then their corruption of the Kalilaer would be ended. Humanity could be saved.

But he stifled his curiosity. Even the savage wildmen had leaders and followers and the Scions would be no different, though they were harder to identify. Belarrin was too new, too much a stranger, to get in close confidence with Inban and the other Scion commanders. He turned away from the large shelter and joined the other escaped Kalilaer around a fire pit in the center of the glade. An enormous bear had been slain and was now roasting over the brilliant coals. Belarrin took a seat on a downed tree and looked beyond the flames to the towering Timnar Mountains rising above the tree line to the north. They were the only familiar sight in this strange place.

"Do you have any experience with the bow, Belarrin?"

Belarrin looked up to see Parvik standing before him. His eyes shifted to the bow in the man's hand. It was shaped from simple wood and bent back with twine. Parvik also held several arrows, fletched with bird feathers. The arrowheads were stone. "No," Belarrin lied.

Parvik smiled. "We'll have you trained then, but don't worry about it for now. I'll get a spear for you, at least. All you have to do with that is point it in the right direction and thrust."

Belarrin nodded, suppressing his scorn. A spear wasn't as complex as a sword, but there was still a lot more to it than Parvik suggested. Instead of commenting, he asked, "You're arming us so soon?"

"We can't begin too early. The Finnies have a hard time tracking us, but if they do, everyone fights or everyone dies. You will be joining the Fallen Tree, right?"

"Of course. Why wouldn't I?"

The man shrugged. "A few refuse. Too afraid I guess, but that makes no sense. Better armed and fighting than living in fear your whole life, right?" Not waiting for an answer, he continued, "We give those that won't join us clothing and spears, then send them northward where they can fend for themselves in some safety. Assuming they still remember how to hunt and track."

"Don't they have troubles with the wildmen?"

"Maybe. But we can't worry about that. The northern tribes aren't trying to enslave us like the Finnies. Those who remain with us here have nothing to fear from the wildmen."

"I see."

"I'll be right back," Parvik said, then walked away.

Looking around the campfire, Belarrin saw Scions talking individually or in pairs with the other escaped Kalilaer. Some held bows that they gave test pulls, while others inspected spears. He rose to his feet as Parvik returned carrying a spear.

Belarrin accepted the weapon and inspected it closely. The shaft had been carefully shaped until it was nearly straight but, once again, the spearhead was made of stone.

Touching it, Belarrin suspected flint. Yet as he held the shaft a short way back from the point, he was surprised by how well balanced it was. It would throw well, yet was long enough to be held and thrust.

"You know your spears at least," Parvik said, watching him, and Belarrin cursed silently. He had to be more cautious.

"A little," he replied carefully.

"Excellent," Parvik replied then tossed him a sheathed knife. "You'll want this too, for hunting – and if the spear fails."

Belarrin unsheathed the weapon and saw that the blade was of flint as well. He slid it back into its leather case and tied it to his belt. "Thank you."

"One day when you've proven yourself, you may even get one of our iron knives. We have a few that we've taken from the bodies of the Iron-Men, but not nearly enough. But don't worry about anything this evening. Just relax and enjoy the end of your long flight from slavery. Tonight is about freedom. Only tomorrow does the work begin again. If you'll excuse me, I need to see to some of the other newcomers."

After he left, Belarrin sat down and stared at the flickering flames of the fire. The more he learned, the more the Scions made sense in their own twisted way They weren't skilled fighters like his brothers, though they were just as determined. Their greatest skills instead lay with remaining invisible. That was how they survived.

The pleasant scents of roasting meat filled his nose and the familiar crack and snap of burning wood his ears. He ignored the chatter of the others gathering near the warmth.

Most of the adults were there, though children laughed and played in the growing dusk beyond. When the meal was ready, their parents corralled them and brought them reluctantly to the fire.

As Belarrin ate, Vitarria and Parvik joined him. She said, "I understand you'll be staying with us."

"Yes."

She smiled. "I'm glad."

"Is anyone leaving?" Belarrin asked.

"A few have refused, but most will stay."

Belarrin nodded, but didn't reply as he sank his teeth into the bear steak. It was as delicious as it smelled. Neither Vitarria nor Parvik spoke as they enjoyed the meal. They were finishing when Inban walked up to stand next to the central fire. Beneath the closing darkness of night, he was a silhouette against the flames. Inban looked out at all the surrounding Scions and Kalilaer.

No, Belarrin corrected himself. These were Kalilaer no longer. They had turned their backs on their salvation and embraced the darkness. They were Scions, too, or near enough as made no difference.

Inban flung his arms wide and bellowed, "Welcome to all of you. We are blessed by each and every soul freed from the bondage of the Finaestari. Your life of slavery is over, but also, I regret, the world you knew before that. The old tribes that once were yours have been destroyed by the Finnies and their murderous Iron-Men. We cannot give you that life back, but we can give you ourselves. Let us be your new tribe. Whether you seek vengeance against your tormentors or to liberate others still suffering under the burdens you so recently bore, we welcome you!"

The surrounding Scions cheered and Belarrin joined his voice to theirs. As Inban sat down, conversations broke out again between each small group of Scions. Vitarria said to him, "I hope this new world you're entering has begun to feel a little less strange."

"A little, maybe," Belarrin admitted honestly. "But I can still barely understand it."

"I know what you mean," she replied. "I probably wasn't much older than you when I lost my tribe, too. Not from the Finnies but from other humans. After wandering a few years, we were found by these Scions and taken in." She shook her head. "I was full of doubt, but in the end I had to accept that there are evil humans just as there are evil Finnies. Perhaps not all of the Finnies are evil, either. I don't know, but I cannot bring myself to believe that all members of a single race are so condemned."

She paused as if waiting for Belarrin to reply, but not knowing what to say, he remained silent. At last, she continued, "I was training to be a priestess even before my tribe was destroyed and my mother gave me a gemstone that symbolized that duty." She raised a necklace that had been tucked beneath her tunic, revealing the stone that hung from it. It was clear white with hints of the palest blue gleaming in a hundred facets, the color untainted by the reds and yellows of the fire.

"It's beautiful," Belarrin said.

Vitarria smiled. "My mother is dead and I was trained in only the meagerest portion of what she knew. I take great comfort from this stone. It reminds me of hope and brighter days. I look at it and think that the world might find peace again. I don't mean just the Cataclysm, but humanity itself. That we might once again return to what we were. Not savages slaughtering each other over the meanest morsel of food or slaves broken beneath the Finaestari heel. I hope that we might wash away all those painful choices we've faced. All those times we've done what we thought was best and yet doubted." She hesitated, then added, "Perhaps I'm just clinging to foolish imaginings. It is just a stone after all. But still..." She did not complete the thought as she put the gemstone away.

Belarrin nodded. "I think you may be very wise, Vitarria." This was not a lie.

"I hope so, but doubt I'll ever know for certain."

Belarrin glanced at her, but she didn't explain what she meant. Instead, she said, "Excuse me, I need to talk to Inban before the evening draws too late."

"Of course."

"Good night, Belarrin."

As she walked away, he stifled a yawn. Beside him, Parvik chuckled. "You must be exhausted after the past few days traveling."

"I'm doing well enough," Belarrin replied.

Parvik grinned. "No need to be brave for me. I remember what it was like when I was freed. Unmarried men bunk together, so if you'd like, you can use the shelter that was built for me. It has a second pallet."

"Thank you," Belarrin replied. Looking around the camp, he realized that there was little he could learn this evening and, if he had a chance to remain silent, he'd take it. "Perhaps I am a little tired," he admitted.

"Then follow me." Parvik stood and Belarrin rose after him.

The Scion guided him to one of the shelters not far from the gate and pointed to a small mound of animal furs. "I'm going back to the fire," he said as Belarrin crawled inside. "I'll try not to wake you when I return."

"Don't worry if you do," Belarrin replied and the other man departed.

Belarrin crawled underneath the fur blankets and stared at the dark ceiling, listening to the laughter of the Scions outside as they rejoiced in their recent victory. He clasped the necklace stone in his hand, feeling its cool weight. "Soon," he whispered to the darkness.

Over the celebration, he could barely hear the wind or the trees. The wind had always been a particularly soothing sound, more so even than the waves rushing along the shore near his home. But this night, the wind wasn't the noise he strained his ears to hear. This wilderness that surrounded him was almost as symbolic as the people who hid in its confines. Worshipping chaos and denying order. Reveling in fear and hating prosperity. Vitarria's words over dinner suggested the beginnings of wisdom, but it was too late for her. It had been too late from the moment she attached herself to their rebellion.

The low hoot of an owl pierced the celebratory laughter of the revelers and Belarrin nearly leapt upright. A flush of anticipation flowed through him, he released his hold on the necklace and shifted his grip to the hilt of the stone knife instead. Waiting was easier now. He was going home.

The Scions outside quieted only slowly as more and more of them found their beds. When Parvik entered the shelter, Belarrin closed his eyes, feigning sleep until the other man lay still. Then he opened them again. There would be no sleep for him this night. He knew he wouldn't find it, even if he tried.

The hours passed slowly and, in the deep darkness of the shelter, Belarrin couldn't gauge the passage of time. Only Parvik's soft breathing broke the stillness.

An owl hooted again and Belarrin smiled. Not much longer now.

On the other side of the tent, Parvik sat up and whispered, "That's like no owl I've ever known. Did you hear it?"

"What?" Belarrin asked, feigning grogginess.

"The owl," Parvik repeated.

The Scion cast aside his blankets and crept to the opening at the foot of the shelter. Pushing away his own blankets, Belarrin crawled up beside Parvik and they both peered out. The moon had long since set and the first grays heralding the dawn were just beginning to creep through the shadowed trees. The two Scions guarding the gate were only dark silhouettes in the night. Both figures lurched, then stumbled, falling to the ground. Parvik gasped, his eyes widening.

Before he could shout the alarm, Belarrin slipped behind him. In a single motion, he closed his left hand over Parvik's mouth and slid his knife across the man's throat. Parvik's teeth clamped down as he convulsed, narrowly missing Belarrin's fingers. But Belarrin held him in tight embrace, feeling the warm blood on his hand as Parvik's body shuddered against his own. Belarrin forced aside surging memories of Parvik's smiling face and his friendly words as he let the body slide silently to the earth. He took a ragged breath.

There was no greater duty than to kill in the name of the Empress.

CHAPTER 3

Vistus

"There is no greater duty than to kill in the name of the Empress. There is no greater honor than to die in the name of the Empress. I live for my Empress, my masters, and my brothers. By them, and for them, I live and I die."

—The Oaths of the t'Okaedrin

Belarrin knelt down on the floor of the shelter and lowered his head to touch the ground. Closing his eyes, he breathed in deeply, then forced the air out in a long sigh. Muscles held taut for days loosened. His fingers clenched and unclenched. Only now, at the end, did he realize the tension that had filled him and how difficult the past few days had been. But life with the Scions had not been as bleak as he'd feared. If Vitarria had chosen the wiser path he might have called her friend. If Parvik had not been the enemy, he might have been a brother. But those possibilities couldn't exist. It did not matter now.

He felt his guise slide away and the t'Okaedrin he'd always been emerged again. Belarrin the escaped Kalilaer vanished and there was only Vistus, the loyal servant of the Syraestari. Vistus was his name, his only name. Just as he had always been. Vistus the t'Okaedrin. Or, in the words of his enemies, Vistus the Iron-Man. The lies could cease.

Vistus raised his head and looked out of the shelter as screams shattered the night. A hundred figures in scaled armor with swords drawn poured out of the woods. The pitiful wooden wall had hardly slowed them. Frightened Scions ran from the shelters to fight with their crude spears and daggers, but the surprise had been complete.

One rebel ran past Vistus with spear raised to throw. Vistus lunged forward. He grasped the stunned Scion by the shoulder, spinning him around. Before the man could ready his weapon, Vistus drove his knife through the rebel's heart. Taking the Scion's spear, he rose to his feet and hesitated. His own family would know him, but the other t'Okaedrin might not. If one of them found him first, he might die like the Scions he hated.

But at the front lines he saw his brethren, just as he knew he would. Eldest Nalsuntha's braided hair whipped through the air like a many-chained flail as he thrust and slashed with his sword. Tall Bridionis and pale Hirnid flanked him, their crimson cloaks rippling as they carved through the wavering line of Scions.

Vistus ran toward his brothers, charging the Scions from behind. He speared one through the back and slashed another's neck with his knife as he shouted, "Brothers!"

Bridionis spotted him through the press. "Vistus!"

The eyes of his other brothers turned his way and they shifted their attack, hacking at the Scions who still stood between them. Attacked by iron from the front and surprised from behind, the rebels had no chance and, in moments, his family surrounded him.

Bridionis flung his left arm around him in tight embrace. "Welcome home, Vistus."

Before Vistus could reply, Eldest Nalsuntha bellowed, "Laughter later, brothers!"

Bridionis turned away, grinning and followed the rest of his family against the withdrawing line of Scions. Watching the enemy, Vistus was reluctantly impressed. Despite their surprise, their pathetic stone weapons, and their hopeless plight, they fought courageously. They stood together, side-by-side if not in disciplined ranks, fighting and dying as valiantly as any brother.

A hand touched his shoulder and Vistus turned to see his father grinning at him. Over his right arm, he carried a red t'Okaedrin cloak which he offered to Vistus. "It is good to see you, my son."

Vistus tied the cloak around his neck, feeling more alive than any time since he'd entered the woods. "I should join them, father," he said, looking back to the battle.

"You've already done your part, allow them the honor of doing theirs," Dalric replied. "Besides, it is almost over."

"I don't understand," Vistus began to say, but fell silent as a second line of t'Okaedrin emerged from the tree line behind the battling Scions of the Fallen Tree. Cut off from their only line of retreat, the rebels had no choice but to stand and die. The end came quickly, leaving only a handful of Scions alive to be taken prisoner. Not one escaped.

A hush fell as the first golden rays of the dawn touched the blood-stained glade, broken only by the crying of Scion children, now taken in hand by t'Okaedrin guardians. Vistus and Dalric turned at the sound of footsteps. Two Syraestari approached. Their steel armor was edged in silver and embossed with flowing patterns like wind and rain. The first was Captain Nethzir, High Lord Tazil's son, but Vistus didn't recognize the second. They walked side by side as peers. The stranger was even taller than Nethzir and lanky with an unruly shock of brown hair and deep green eyes beneath the customary black paint, these stylized with sharp points extending back toward his ears. His lips were set in a grimace.

As they neared, Vistus and his father bowed down to one knee with heads bent forward, exposing the backs of their necks.

"Rise," Captain Nethzir commanded. As they obeyed, he spoke again. "How many losses?"

"Two t'Okaedrin are dead, Lord Nethzir," Dalric replied, "and six have serious wounds but will recover."

"Well done," Nethzir said.

"Thank you, my Lord."

The second Syraestari's gaze was fixed on Vistus. "This is the Okaidir infiltrator?"

"This is him, Eltirkar," Nethzir replied. Vistus knew that name. Eltirkar was the housecarl captain for Ushtyl, high lord of the city called Nahirazith. Vistus wondered why a neighboring captain had joined the raid. "You did well, Vistus. My father will be very pleased."

"Yes, I'm impressed as well," Eltirkar said, though his frown did not fade. Vistus suspected it was near permanent.

Vistus dropped his head in a half bow. "Thank you, my Lords."

"Okaidir Vistus," Captain Nethzir said, "did you learn anything in your time among the rebels that may be useful for us?"

"Yes, my Lord. They change camps after every raid. Only those who are left behind know the new location so no prisoner may be compelled to confess it."

Nethzir nodded. "Yes, we've heard that from the lips of captives."

"Also, my Lord, they are being aided by the Shadow of Zaris."

Nethzir's eyebrows rose. "What does that mean?"

"I don't know and they don't seem to be sure either. I was told that the Shadow tells them where to attack and when. He has done so five times and each raid was successful."

Nethzir glanced at Eltirkar, then said, "We shall have to consider this. After you have had more time to recover, your father will question you further to see what else you've learned."

"Yes, my Lord." Vistus bowed again.

Nethzir turned to Dalric. "Gather the t'Okaedrin and Pi'aernoth."

"Yes, my Lord." Dalric dipped his head in a bow, then took two steps back before turning away. While they waited,

Vistus dropped his gaze and took a respectful step back from the two Syraestari as well.

The t'Okaedrin quickly formed a half circle around the captains and Vistus saw that there were six full families present. With them stood another family of Pi'aernotha Osnoeda. These Sisters of Iron carried bows and had long daggers belted at their sides. Vistus had no doubt it was these who had so silently killed the guards at the gate and around the camp perimeter. He searched them for Elestis' face, but didn't see her. Perhaps she was scouting still.

In the center of the encircling Brethren and Sisters of Iron, a dozen Scions knelt with hands bound behind their backs. Among them was Chief Inban who clutched at a deep wound in his side, his face pale with blood loss. Vitarria knelt, too, at the far end of the line. Ten children huddled nearby, none over six years of age. The youngest were held carefully in the arms of a few of the Pi'aernoth. A few cried, but most were too terrified even for that.

Nethzir glanced at Vistus. "Are any of the prisoners leaders?"

"Yes, my Lord." Vistus replied, pointing. "Inban is their chieftain."

"Dalric, I want the chieftain's wounds tended. He must live to face questioning."

"Yes, my Lord." Dalric signaled Nalsuntha who, with the help of Hirnid, dragged the protesting chieftain away. Inban's eyes met Vistus across the field. "His Highest Above curse you to the Abyss, traitor!"

"Now, remove the children to the supply carts," Nethzir commanded.

Five Pi'aernoth stepped forward to take charge of the children. As they were led through the gate of the camp, a few of the Scion adults whimpered. Once the children disappeared into the forest, Nethzir turned to the prisoners and drew a scroll of parchment from beneath his breastplate. As he unrolled it, Vistus saw the familiar scratched lines of the Syraestari language. Like all of his brothers, he could not read them. In his idle hours, he'd wondered if there ever had been human writing too. But it didn't matter. Reading was not needed to serve.

When Nethzir spoke next, he lifted his voice to echo loudly across the glade. "These prisoners have been found guilty of sedition against the Empire. By proclamation of the High Lord Tazil, all who conspire against their Syraestari masters are condemned to death." He rolled up the scroll and turned to Dalric. "See it done and then come find me."

"Yes, my Lord." Dalric bowed, then turned to Vistus. "We are victorious today because of your courage, my son. I give you the honor of executing the prisoners."

"Thank you, father," Vistus said. As he strode toward the line of prisoners, his brother Bridionis met him and handed him his sheathed sword. Vistus drew it and gave back the sheath. Then he turned to the first prisoner.

The man spat at Belarrin's feet. There was no fear in his eyes, only seething hate. "Coward, I curse you. Let the betrayer know betrayal!"

Vistus ignored him and plunged the blade into the prisoner's chest then stepped to the next one. His lips wanted to twist in distaste, but years of discipline held his expression firm. These Scions deserved their condemnation, but it would've been better had they perished in combat like their companions. That would have been an honorable death, even for the likes of these.

The second prisoner cursed him too. It was a pity that they couldn't understand. They accused him of treason when they were the fools blindly clinging to a lie. He struck this one down and moved to the next. One by one, they died. His stomach turned at the deed, but it had to be done. The price of justice was seldom an easy one.

Stepping up to the last prisoner, he paused. Unlike the others, Vitarria looked up at him with calm eyes. Her face was not contorted by fury or fear as the others had been. Her lips were turned down in the same sad expression that had puzzled him over the days past. Vistus raised his sword.

"I forgive you, Belarrin," she said. Vistus stopped, stunned. His blade hovered uncertainly as he stared into her bright compassion-filled eyes. Then Vitarria whispered in an even softer voice, "His hand in crimson fury shine, taketh my life but saveth thine."

Behind him, his brother Arcomin laughed. "Vistus has a soft heart for this one. Maybe it's time he be given a real woman for a wife to keep him strong." Some of the other brothers chuckled. Vistus felt his cheeks flame with anger and embarrassment. With a snarl, he stabbed Vitarria through the heart. The mocking laughter faded as Vistus lowered his sword and Vitarria crumpled to the ground. Staring into the pooling blood mingling with Vitarria's loose gold hair, Vistus' stomach turned as shame rose up within him. He cursed himself silently. It was supposed to be an execution of justice and duty, not of anger. Not even a Scion deserved that, especially not her.

Cydion blight Arcomin, he thought bitterly. And himself for succumbing to the fool words.

Dalric clapped his hands together once, pulling attention to him, and shouted, "Stack all of the rebel bodies in the fire pit and burn them. Burn anything that is of no use. This battlefield tells a story of what we've done here and I don't want anyone to read it."

The t'Okaedrin and Pi'aernoth scattered to obey, but Vistus remained where he was, eyes fixed on Vitarria. His lips twisted into a grimace. What did it matter that she had forgiven him? She was the rebel, a criminal. She had no authority to forgive. There was nothing to forgive. But he still should not have killed her from anger.

Bridionis stepped up beside him and rested his hand on Vistus' shoulder. "Is something wrong?"

Vistus shook himself and pulled his eyes away from the body. "No." Stooping down, he cleaned Bridionis' blade on the hem of Vitarria's tunic, then handed the weapon back to his brother. "Thank you."

"Of course." Bridionis smiled and turned away.

Looking over to the center of the camp, Vistus saw that his brothers had already begun to pile many of the bodies there along with the wooden hafts of the stone-headed spears. Vistus knelt down beside Vitarria. He was about to lift her body when sparkling light caught his eye. Her pale stone necklace had fallen free to rest in the pool of blood. Its many facets glimmered as they soaked in the morning sun.

Seized by a sudden impulse, Vistus carefully lifted Vitarria's head. He pulled the necklace loose and stuffed it into the pocket of his tunic. Vistus looked around, but none of his brothers had noticed him. It wasn't forbidden to take small trophies from the bodies of the fallen, but he was supposed to ask Dalric's permission. Yet he wouldn't. He couldn't without being asked questions he didn't know the answers to.

He put his arms under Vitarria and rose. Her body was surprisingly light. He walked over to the fire pit.

CHAPTER 4
Brothers

"In its early years, the Cataclysm stole the lives of the great and the weak in equal portion. But as the world calmed, the natural order reasserted itself, freed even from the overzealous fetters of the fallen Etyni."

— Ushtyl, High Lord of Nahirazith

The heavy trudge from scores of booted feet, the creaking groan of wagon wheels, and the weight of the scaled iron shirt about Vistus' shoulders were all heralds of a more familiar life. The depths of the surrounding forest with its sharp greens and deep browns, didn't feel so strange now. It was chaotic, true, but Vistus marched in a column of order through it. He was no longer alone. They paralleled the course of a small river that gurgled over rocks and tumbled branches to their left as it raced to the sea ahead of them.

Vistus' family marched in the central position of honor, third in line and just in front of the wagons. The other families of brethren followed after while the Pi'aernoth scouted ahead, behind, and on either side. Aside from iron shirts, the sisters wore lighter leather armor so they could move quickly and blend into the surrounding wilderness. They would not stand toe to with the enemy, but their archery could disrupt any charge. At their warning shouts, the more heavily armored t'Okaedrin would stand ready. The armies of the t'Okaedrin always traveled in this manner, even in the safest part of the world. By assuming danger was always nearby, they were always prepared.

Each of the families had charge of one of the carts that carried food, tents, barricade posts, and other provisions along with the bodies of the two who had fallen in the battle. They would be buried back home, not in these wildlands. An additional wagon carried the prisoner, Inban, and the children rescued from the camp. Their screams and wails had died down as exhaustion set in. The cries were whimpers now, and so soft they could only be heard when the carts stopped. It was painful for them, Vistus knew, but for the best, too. He had once been one of them, an infant too young to remember it. He couldn't even recall the faces or voices of his birth-parents. But true family was not forged from that kind of blood. He had stronger bonds now, bonds made complete in the blood spilled on the battlefield. Bonds of companionship and endurance, founded upon discipline and tempered by war.

In time the children would come to understand what he knew. That true honor, justice, even life itself came in service to the Syraestari, the only hope against the madness of the Cataclysm and the repeated failings of humankind. These children would be blessed with real mothers and fathers. Their discipline would be harsh – Vistus bore a few scars from the lash – but it would be fair and would lead to wisdom. When they were older, the best of them would be named eldest, like Nalsuntha, and would lead on the battlefield. Vistus looked forward to the day when he would be rewarded for his faithfulness and be named a father with a family of t'Okaedrin of his own.

Vistus smiled widely, remembering the pride in Dalric's voice. He looked forward to seeing his mother, Auphni, again. Though her hair had grayed, she still was the tough Pi'aernotha Osnoeda warrior she'd always been. She was the one who had taught him the stealth by which he had slain Parvik.

"Heavy thoughts, Vistus?" Bridionis asked, walking beside him.

"No, just thoughts of home."

His friend laughed. "To hear you talk, one would think you'd been gone for years instead of a few days."

"In a way, it feels far longer. They were a strange people."

"And ignorant fools."

"Not so much as you might think," Vistus replied.

"Don't tell me you grew fond of them."

"Of course not. But they were clever in their own way. They knew how to travel quickly through the deeper parts of the wilderness without getting lost. Of course they were crude, with their stone weapons and their mud huts. It was strange, though," he paused and they walked a few moments in silence as he gathered his thoughts. "They are as evil as we've always known, but it is a naïve sort of evil, I think. They evoke His Highest Above. They talk of the blessed Etyni, just as we do. But everything they say is twisted around. I wonder if they once knew the truth, but over time have told themselves lies to hide their shame and failures. Now those lies only drive them to do more evil."

"Not anymore," Bridionis replied, grinning. "At least not that group of rebels."

"Yes," Vistus replied, forcing himself to match the smile.

The column angled away from the stream and up along the edge of a ridge overlooking the river basin. The talk of the Scions turned Vistus' thoughts toward Vitarria. He reached into his tunic and clutched her gemstone in his hand. Tracing its surface with his nail, he considered her final words again. Why had she forgiven him? She was the one who had done wrong. And the rest of it had sounded almost like a prayer. Something about her death saving someone.

He didn't know why he had taken the stone. It was an impetuous act like nothing he'd done before. Perhaps from the shame at killing in anger. But that deed had been done and the cause of it made no difference to her, only him. Perhaps it had been what she'd said not long after they had met. How the stone reminded her of hope. Even as she uttered the lies of the Scions she had seemed innocent, as one well-meaning but deceived. A life that, in other circumstances, might have been better lived. Somehow, he didn't want to forget that.

"Are you sure you're alright?" Bridionis asked. "That is as grim a face as I've ever seen on you."

"I'm fine," Vistus said, shaking himself from his reverie. "Killing an enemy you have shared meals with is a very different thing than slaying them on the battlefield."

"Yes, I suppose that's true. Just remember why you did it and how evil they were."

"I know that!" Vistus snapped. Then he shook his head. "No, I'm sorry. It just makes me think of possibilities. What might they have become if we'd captured them as children instead? They could've been saved, instead of doomed to this fate."

Bridionis clapped him on the shoulder. "Ever the far seeing one, brother. We cannot save them all, but remember, we saved the children."

Vistus nodded. His brother was right, of course. He had to cling to the good and let go of the bad.

The world lurched.

Whatever Vistus had been about to say fled his mind as the ground reeled around him. He stumbled back, nearly losing his balance. A thunderous crack ruptured the air. Ears ringing, he tried to steady himself as a shadow passed over his eyes. Vistus looked up to see a great tree lurching towards them. He stumbled forward and grabbed Bridionis by the shoulders, flinging him away then diving after. The tree crashed behind them in a great gust of wind and sound. A thin branch struck Vistus' arm like a whip, drawing a ribbon of blood and pitching him to the ground. The earth heaved madly and Vistus could only grip his head in his hands and pray.

His mind wailed silently. Highest Above, not again. Not again!

He clenched his eyes closed so tightly he saw only red. Behind those lids rose memories of darkness and dust, of penetrating cold and paralyzing fear. Long ago screams filled his mind, blending with the cries of his brothers and the bellowing of the oxen. He held his eyes shut, unwilling to open them and see if he'd been buried alive a second time.

A hand clutched his shoulder, pulling him from his stupor. Vistus looked up into Bridionis' wide eyes. "The wagons!" he cried. "Quickly!"

Vistus staggered to his feet, still reeling like a drunken man, though the world had calmed. He looked beyond the fallen tree and saw that the bluff behind them had given way. One of the wagons had toppled down the steep slope, dragging oxen and driver with it. A second wagon leaned precariously over the brink. Behind the terrified driver, sawing on the reins, children gripped the wooden bars of their cage, wailing.

"No," he whispered. The fear of losing those precious children purged the cloud of old nightmares from his mind. He scrambled over the tree after Bridionis. They ran downslope of the cart and threw their shoulders against the side.

"Quickly, now!" Eldest Nalsuntha shouted as he arrived behind them with a dozen more brothers. "Half behind pushing, half on the side lifting."

They strained and heaved while the oxen struggled against the loose soil, the driver cursing, the children screaming. Sweat broke out on Vistus' brow as he strained, his shoulder driving into the coarse wood of the wagon, his feet sinking deep into the earthquake-churned soil. He could not lose them, he would not! They were just like him, rescued from despair and ruin. Bridionis struggled on his right and Nalsuntha to his left, they strained, pushing with all their might. The cart lurched forward a hand's breadth, its wheel groaning like an injured bull.

"A few more paces, brothers!" Nalsuntha shouted.

Crack!

Vistus' feet gave way and the wagon lurched into him. Darkness closed over his eyes as he heaved, scrambling for purchase, his legs kicking futilely into the loose soil. A scream tore at his ears. His vision cleared and he saw that the front wagon wheel had snapped off. The cart leaned almost to the tipping point and Bridionis had fallen beneath it. His arm was pinned almost to the shoulder between the wagon and the ground. The cart tilted slowly, gouging deeper into his arm and pushing his head away.

Vistus' eyes widened. "Push or it will snap his neck! Push!"

The brothers heaved with him and more t'Okaedrin rushed forward to help until there was no more room, but still Vistus could feel the cart slipping. The ground was too soft, the wagon too heavy, their strength not enough.

Highest Above, he prayed. Not Bridionis, not like this!

He poured all of his energy into the effort until his muscles shrieked and his bones groaned. It wasn't enough. It wouldn't be enough. Around him, his brothers cried out, shouting their exertion and Bridionis screamed as the pressure grew.

Vistus clenched his eyes shut, straining until blood pulsed through the veins of his head like thunder, turning his vision crimson. He couldn't give up. Not for his best friend. Never! Searing lines of gold flashed across his eyes and sounds rose up in his throat. "Volti'etkas yskaesot idritha lestraimes!" he screamed.

His muscles burned with rejuvenating vigor, flexing like he'd been reborn. He sensed more than saw his brothers redoubling their effort. The cart shifted slightly, easing the pressure on Bridionis. Then it moved a little more. A gasp of relief escaped Vistus' lips as Bridionis slid free and tumbled down the slope, but the brothers didn't slow. First one pace, then two, they drove the cart forward. It gained speed, lurching onto the path until, with a shudder it stopped again. Wedged up against a heavy oak out of danger.

Vistus hardly paused to make sure the cart was safe before running down the hill to his brother. Bridionis lay near the bottom, clutching his arm. His face was white, his eyes opened wide, but a low chuckle escaped his panting lips.

"It's..." He drew in a ragged breath and tried again. "It's broken I think."

Vistus knelt beside him, carefully examining the arm. Bridionis clenched his eyes shut, hissing as Vistus' fingers probed the swelling flesh. His skin where the wagon had pressed against him was an ugly purple-blue. Their brother Hirnid ran down to them. "How is he?"

"It's broken, but not all the way through," Vistus said. He felt his lips split into a grin as he looked down at Bridionis. "A bit of rest, a bit of mending, and you'll be as good as new."

"Thank His Highest Above," Bridionis whispered.

Hirnid let out a long breath. "Blood on the Bridge, I'm glad you're still with us, brother."

Bridionis' smile was twisted by pain. "I owe all of you my life."

"We all owe each other," Vistus replied. Then, with a grin, he added, "but that doesn't mean you had to imitate me by breaking your arm."

Bridionis chuckled. "I can think of no better brother to mimic."

"Hold his arm straight, Hirnid, while I make a splint," Vistus said.

Hirnid nodded and took Vistus' place beside Bridionis. Once Hirnid had the arm cradled safely, Vistus scrambled to his feet and ran up the slope. As he climbed, panting toward the top, his mind spun. He didn't understand what had happened. Was it a gift from His Highest Above? The weight of the cart had overwhelmed them. Bridionis, and very likely the children, had been doomed - then everything suddenly changed. And what had he shouted? Meaningless nonsense. He shook his head. It wasn't important. Bridionis and the children were saved. That was all that mattered.

Nalsuntha stood at the top of the rise, shouting at the other brothers. "Get those children out of there. I want everything packed on the other carts. And what won't fit, we carry on our backs. Then burn the broken ones so no rebel can use them!" He turned to Vistus. "How is Bridionis?"

"Broken arm, Eldest. I'm making a splint."

"Good, good."

"Any other injuries?" Vistus asked.

"The driver of the lost wagon died. His family is taking care of him, now. No one else is seriously hurt. See to Bridionis, we've got the rest handled." Turning back toward the cart, Nalsuntha bellowed, "And make a spot for Bridionis! He's riding from here."

Vistus hurried to his family's supply cart. Climbing into the back, he rooted through several crates until he found a rope and a length of linen. On his way back down the hill, he broke two branches off a tree, each twice as thick as his thumb.

"We'll have you fixed up in no time," Hirnid was saying when he arrived. "No Cataclysm will be the end of us. And we can't have Vistus taking all the glory now, can we?" Bridionis' chuckle was half wheeze, half laughter.

Kneeling beside them, Vistus took his brother's knife from its sheath. With a few deep cuts he whittled the two branches down to blunt sticks. Then, with Hirnid's help, he wrapped the arm in the linen. Bridionis' face turned white as the ramparts of Raefi'ernyn, but he gritted his teeth and kept his eyes opened as they worked. As soon as the arm was covered, Vistus braced it with the two sticks and tightened the splint into place with the rope. Then, using the last of the linen, he fashioned a sling to fit around Bridionis' neck. "Good as new in no time," he echoed Hirnid's words.

Between him and Hirnid, they got Bridionis to his feet and then slowly ascended the rise. By the time they reached the top, the carts had been switched out with the children and Chieftain Inban safely loaded on a new one. Two of the t'Okaedrin were stacking kindling by the broken ones. Vistus and Hirnid hoisted Bridionis up on their cart. He lay down without protest and closed his eyes. His breathing was smoother as the panic subsided. Vistus nodded, content. He would heal just fine.

"Ready?" Nalsuntha asked.

"Yes, Eldest," Vistus and Hirnid replied.

"These are for you." Nalsuntha pointed to two leather packs at his feet then turned to face toward the head of the column. "March!"

The cart drivers snapped their reins and the oxen leaned into their harnesses. Groaning, the carts rolled forward behind the column of t'Okaedrin. Vistus picked up their packs and handed one to Hirnid. They slung them over their shoulders and followed Bridionis' cart. Behind them, their brothers lit the kindling and set the old carts aflame.

Despite the terror of the earthquake, the forest appeared little changed. A few more trees had fallen, perhaps, but the damage appeared minimal. Vistus had seen far worse, not least the one that had collapsed their barracks, burying him alive and killing the other t'Okaedrin children of his first family.

Late that afternoon, Nalsuntha halted the march. The sky had long since taken on a reddish cast. Doubtless the mountains, troubled by the quake, were belching fire and ash. At least earthquakes happened less frequently than they once had. His father had told him that they struck at least weekly when he was younger. Now it could be a month or even more between each tremor.

Beneath the crimson skies, the t'Okaedrin unpacked the supply carts. Wooden posts were pounded into the soft forest soil, forming the skeleton of a makeshift barrier around a central camp. The brothers used hatches to cut down and trim smaller trees to expand it into a fence. Within a few hours, they'd erected a wall at least as sturdy as the crude one that had encircled the Scion camp. While they worked, some of the Pi'aernoth returned with a deer they'd killed and a large collection of mushrooms to supplement the food packed on the wagons. Others took the children out of their cage and let them run around a little to stretch their legs under watchful eyes. Chieftain Inban was also taken down and lashed with his back to a sturdy tree trunk. By the time the camp defenses were finished, dusk was settling over the woods and the food stewed in an iron pot over a fire.

Grabbing a bowl for himself and another for Bridionis, Vistus joined him where he sat alongside Hirnid, Arcomin, and a few other brothers from his family. The deer meat was soft and succulent, practically falling apart between his teeth. He wolfed the meal down, feeling the warmth of it spread through his chest then out to his hands and feet.

"How are you feeling?" Vistus asked.

"Better," Bridionis replied. He had to cradle his bowl in his lap, but once that was done ate without difficulty. "With a night's rest, I should be fine to march tomorrow."

"You fell under that wagon on purpose, just to escape guard duty tonight, didn't you?" Hirnid asked. Vistus and the other brothers laughed.

"Not one of my better plans." Bridionis grinned. Then, he glanced over to where Chief Inban watched them. "I suppose the prisoner should eat, too."

"The apostate can starve," Arcomin said with a growl.

"Maybe, but not until he's been questioned." Bridionis glanced down at his arm, then looked over to Hirnid. "Seeing as my hands are full for the moment, can you take care of it, Hirnid?"

"Yes." Hirnid hopped to his feet and headed over to the cooking pot.

As he returned with the bowl of food, Arcomin called, "Hirnid, come here a moment."

Arcomin stood as Hirnid arrived and, extending his hand, poured a handful of dirt into the soup. "Rebels live in filth. We wouldn't want to make him feel like he's away from home, right Bridionis?"

Bridionis met his challenging glare. "Apostates must face justice, not your petty games, Arcomin. This is beneath us."

"Since when did you start loving the enemy so much, brother?" Arcomin asked, sitting down again. "I bet you wished you'd joined them instead of Vistus. That way you'd have been the one to get all friendly with that rebel-woman."

Vistus blanched at that. He didn't like this conversation. Not Arcomin's torments and certainly not what he said about Vitarria, but he didn't trust himself to speak. Bridionis replied, "As I recall he executed her. It has been my experience that Vistus doesn't kill his friends."

"Lucky for you, huh?"

As he spoke, Hirnid walked over to Inban and handed him the bowl. The chieftain took it in his two bound hands. Tied together as they were, the only way he could eat the food was by drinking it. But instead, Inban took one look at it and dumped it out on the ground beside him.

"Cydion-accursed fool!" Arcomin cried, leaping back to his feet. He crossed the short distance to the prisoner and struck him full across the face with the back of his hand. "Rebel dog, you spit upon the kindness of your betters!"

Vistus stood, but Bridionis was faster. "Arcomin!" Bridionis ran to place himself between Inban and Arcomin.

"What? You think you can order me around with one arm tied back?" Arcomin snarled. "Hey Vistus, come pull off your lapdog."

But Vistus could only stand and watch, his heart warring within him as Inban looked his direction. The chieftain's eyes were full of hate and accusation. Vistus felt his blood curdle at that stare. How could an apostate judge him? Yet, Bridionis was right, too. This was a place for justice, not rage. Just like the execution of Vitarria.

Before he could cast aside his doubts, though, Hirnid stepped up next to Bridionis. "Peace Arcomin, you're both right. But it's our place to follow, not command. Our task is to present him to our masters."

"A few bruises would only loosen his tongue," Arcomin growled, but he let Hirnid pull him away. He spared one final hate-filled glance at Inban before withdrawing to the other side of the campfire.

Bridionis and Hirnid returned to Vistus and they sat down again, Bridionis shaking his head. "If he's not careful, he'll lose himself. We're weapons, not judges. This Cataclysm we brought is proof enough that humans should leave such decisions in the hands of our wise masters."

"Wise words yourself, though," Hirnid said.

"What about you?" Bridionis asked, turning to Vistus. "I'm surprised you weren't there beside me."

Vistus could hear the disappointment in his voice. "I know. It's just that… well, Arcomin's words struck close to home. When I killed that Scion woman, I did it because he made me angry. That wasn't justice either."

"It was justice because Captain Nethzir ordered it."

"I suppose."

"But come on." Bridionis laughed. "Let's talk of brighter things, like how long you intend to keep that bear fur on your face."

Vistus reached up to touch his grizzled jaw. "Can I use your knife again?"

"For this task more than any other." Bridionis handed him the blade.

Vistus wet his cheeks and then carefully ran the edge of the blade against his skin. As the coarse stubble grown for his time with the rebels fell away, he couldn't help but smile wider. It felt like the final step to returning to his family

"Just be careful you don't slice that beautiful face of yours." Bridionis chuckled.

"Sage advice from the one-armed man," Vistus retorted. He dried the blade on his sleeve and tossed away the extra water. Then sheathing the knife, he returned it to Bridionis.

"Now there's the Vistus I remember," a woman's voice called behind him.

Vistus spun around. "Elestis!" The Pi'aernoth flung her arms around him and Vistus returned the embrace happily. Releasing her, he stepped back. "It's good to see you again."

"And you." Elestis grinned. "I was afraid of what the rebels might do to you."

"They did nothing."

Her head tilted as her eyes weighed him appraisingly. Elestis was the most beautiful woman in all of Raefi'ernyn. Her hair was a light brown that she usually kept back in a braid. But when it hung loose to her waist, it took Vistus' breath away. "Yes. Yes, I see that. I'm glad. I wanted to come by earlier, but my eldest kept us all out in the forest to be sure no other Scions were lurking about." She grimaced. "This whole wilderness is a nasty place, if you ask me. I'll be glad when we're back in Raefi'ernyn."

"As will I," Vistus said.

Elestis stepped close to Vistus again and kissed him lightly on the cheek. "I have to grab a quick dinner then return to scouting. We'll talk more when we get home. I'm glad you made it through safe and I'm proud. Very proud."

Vistus watched her walk away. There was grace to her movements, like the whisking of a cloud or a running deer. T'Okaedrin and Pi'aernoth only had a part in choosing their mates. The final decision was made by their parents. When the time came, he hoped Dalric and Auphni would arrange his marriage with Elestis. After the recent victory, he felt a renewed confidence it would come true.

Vistus frowned as he watched Elestis get her meal from the cook fire and then walk over to join Arcomin. "What is she doing talking to him?"

"Elestis has many friends," Bridionis replied.

"But him?" Vistus scowled.

"I thought you knew about that."

"Arcomin's a brute and a fool."

Bridionis shook his head, his smile betraying his sarcasm. "Now you condemn him?"

"I'm serious, Bridionis. We have to fight alongside Arcomin, we have to die for him. But that doesn't mean I have to like him. So why are you suddenly defending him?"

Bridionis rose to his feet again, carefully holding his hurt arm. "Hardly. Arcomin is a braggart and a fool, but I think you should be more careful with Elestis."

"What does that mean?" Vistus asked, looking up at him.

"I'm not sure that she's as interested in you as you are in her. She likes you, certainly, but she likes Arcomin, too, and who knows who else."

"She admires bravery and audacity," Vistus replied. "Arcomin hasn't done anything worth talking about. I'm the one who infiltrated the Scions. What can he say to that?"

"Just be careful. I don't want to see you hurt."

"Fine, I'll be careful," Vistus said. But Bridionis was wrong.

A few minutes later, Eldest Nalsuntha came by and gave Vistus his guard shift. He spent the first half of the night staring through the darkness, watching the northward trail they'd marched down. It was hard to completely focus on this task, though, as his mind churned. The past few days had been full of turmoil, not just from the Scions but also from within. He was grateful that Bridionis lived. He got along with his other brothers well enough, except Arcomin at times, but none of them were so close a friend. Bridionis was wrong about Elestis, though. She loved him as much as he loved her and they would be married one day. But thinking of her brought to mind another woman. Vistus reached up to feel the gemstone hidden beneath his tunic. "I forgive you," Vitarria had said and then in anger he'd killed her. Why did this one dead Scion repeatedly invade his thoughts? His mood was dark when his replacement finally arrived near midnight. Vistus returned to his bedroll and fell into a restless sleep.

He was awakened by a loud cry. Instantly, Vistus leapt from his blankets, grasping for his sword. Then he realized the shout came from Hirnid. He was stooping beside the prisoner. "He killed himself!"

Vistus hurried over, cold dread seizing his heart. Just as his brother had said, Inban was dead. The Scion had somehow managed to twist around in his bonds to strangle himself on the ropes. His tongue hung limply from his mouth and eyes bulged wide.

Even in that grotesque position, Vistus could still see condemnation in Inban's gaze.

CHAPTER 5
Belief

"Despite having a unity that once surpassed all of the other races, the Aestari have become a fractured people. Their differences cannot be discerned from appearance. Rather the Schism of their race was founded on philosophy, be they Hiraestari against Finaestari, or if you prefer, Tirnaestari against Syraestari. Indeed, it would not surprise me to learn of additional factions emerging with each successively unresolved dispute."

—"A Study of the Four Races" written by Lord Oegis, servant to the Etyni Oltos

Ushtyl, High Lord of Nahirazith, leaned against the parapet and looked out over the walls of his city. It was a good city, though not yet great. A thousand years couldn't diminish his memory of ancient Syrdranaethin with its hundred spires, each one different and perfect. How their glistening crowns caught the rising sun and shone radiant in red, yellow, green, and blue. With a population of only some thirteen hundred Syraestari, Nahirazith was but a shadow of that lost splendor. But that would change. The new empire forged here could not be allowed to fail, whether it be from dangers without or weakness within.

He stared northward to the wilderness that began a mile beyond the ramparts. That vast forest teemed with humans, far more backward and uncouth even than the crude kingdoms of the Lost Age, before the Great War and the Cataclysm each wrought their ruin in turn. The modern savages had lost all the knowledge of their forbearers, from the forging of metals, to the written word, to sorcery.

Ushtyl drummed his fingers on the hard stone of the wall. Human intelligence had never been the danger, even when they'd made childish play at empire in the long ago age. Now even those inane attempts were gone, replaced by a far more appropriate animalistic barbarity. But starvation had done no more to stave off the threat they posed than their perpetual ignorance. No, the greatest danger from humanity remained their relentless propagation.

The subjugation of the wildmen tribes into Kalilaer workers and the training of their children as compliant t'Okaedrin warriors was a promising solution to that problem. At least it had been before the accursed Scions emerged, making life beyond the city walls impossible for any of his people. But if the t'Okaedrin infiltrator sent to destroy one of the Scion camps had been as successful as High Lord Tazil's messages claimed, perhaps that threat could be removed at last, after over a century of effort. That would mean the only remaining dangers to his people's dominion were those that had arisen from within.

"My Lord," a voice spoke from behind him.

Ushtyl glanced over his shoulder to see one of his housecarls. "Yes?"

"My Lord, High Lord Tazil has arrived and Captain Eltirkar is with him. I had a room prepared for Lord Tazil in the guest quarters and they are both refreshing from their journey. Shall I tell them when to expect you?"

Ushtyl closed his eyes a moment, listening and feeling the sea breeze as it gusted from the south, heavy with scents of salt. "Do you believe in Empire?"

"Yes, my Lord," the housecarl replied, his voice eager. "The human plague has been pushed back and all the world shall bow before our might."

Ushtyl smiled to himself. Like so many of his people, the housecarl was young, not even a century old. He'd been born when Nahirazith was a new city and that meant he had no memory of the dark years of wandering before it. The housecarl was of an age where most Syraestari first began to feel their victory over the sands of time. It was a period of restlessness and energy where the world was filled with possibility. But it was a time when agelessness was confused with immortality. There were times when Ushtyl lamented missing that era of his own life. He had been barely fifty years old when the Great War began. He had just broken his first century when his people fled their ancient homeland after it had been shorn from the mainland by the Cataclysm. Between the war and that harrowing sea crossing, he'd witnessed his people dying in the tens of thousands. No man could experience that and have any delusions of immortality. "Do not celebrate the victory before the battle is won. What we have created here remains fragile, a treasure to be protected. But don't let the hard road ahead dampen your vision either."

"Of course, my Lord." Out of the corner of his eye, Ushtyl saw the younger man duck his head as a sign of respect. "With your leadership, I have only confidence and I am filled with joy that High Lord Tazil sees the world as you do."

"Yes," Ushtyl said, turning to him. That wasn't strictly true, but close enough. Like all his housecarls, he wore the hauberk and green cloak of his station, immaculately cleaned and polished. He was a good man, a skilled warrior, loyal and courageous. The golden vision afforded by his youth was an innocence Ushtyl would use. He would exploit every tool to see this empire complete and whole. Never again would a Syraestari wallow in the dark wilderness, scratching out a living like a beast. Like a human.

"You may tell High Lord Tazil and Captain Eltirkar that I will meet with them directly in the Room of Arching Cedars."

"Yes, my Lord. By your leave?"

At Ushtyl's shallow nod, the housecarl turned to run back the way he'd come along the parapet. Watching him, Ushtyl chuckled to himself. A thousand years and more of life to him, yet the young still ran like humans, as if the promise of age and infirmity lurked on the far horizon.

Ushtyl walked more slowly after him, along the parapet and then down the steps to the streets below. The thoroughfares of Nahirazith were intentionally wide. Narrow streets brought shadow, chill, and dreariness. This was a city of light. The cobbles were cut from white stone and plenty of space was left on either side for trees and gardens to offer shade during the heat of the summer and rich scents year round. Every house was unique unto itself, some fashioned of stone and others wood. Most rose to a second or, more rarely, even a third level with wide balconies and red tiled roofs. The buildings had all been erected by Syraestari, often blending sorcery into the construction to yield beauty unattainable with simpler tools. Common motifs celebrated the elements, from wind to rain, sea, forested glade, or the rising sun. Still, the buildings were not yet what they should be. What they would become again. It took the best soil to nurture trees, the best stones, and the best of ores to erect truly majestic towers. None of which had been found yet. But they would be.

The Pi'aernotha Kaupet who served the households of the city didn't build anything. With their fleeting lives, no human could aspire to such skill. But the Sisters of Stone were charged with simpler repairs, cooking, laundering, and carting away all waste far from the walls. The Pi'aernoth knew him by sight and every one dropped to one knee with head bowed as he passed. The Syraestari showed their respect as well, though with a far more muted dipping of the head.

As he turned down the main avenue, a parchment held by a nail driven into the mortar of a wall caught Ushtyl's attention. In a large scrawl, someone had written, "A refuge has been found! The time has come for us to live as we intended, free of humans and their corruption!"

"Cydion's Abyss!" Ushtyl cursed, tearing the parchment down and crumpling it in his fist. As he continued on, he saw two more. One proclaimed the refuge as a place of safety between the arms of a mountain range. The other said there were no humans anywhere near. He tore these down, too, his mood darkening. The words bordered on treason given the number of lives that had been lost to establish this realm and to ensure its security. If the empress would only agree and assert a ban on such dissention, the cowards would be silenced. But she wasn't certain in her own mind and so the realm wallowed. But Ushtyl had no doubts of the need for this dominion and his people knew it. He would find the fools behind the messages and they would know his wrath. It had been a long time since a Syraestarin had been flogged. Perhaps too long.

His stroll quickened to match his mood as he entered the central plaza of the city. At its middle rose a tall spire, surrounded by fountains of water magically pulled from deep in the heart of the bluff. The stone itself had been carried from the battlefield of Dahiraetin where the empress had raised him and Tazil up to the title of high lord. Dahiraetin and its carnage had taught them all a lesson. They had realized once and for all that the human threat could not be evaded by running. It could only be quelled by domination. The seeds of empire had been born in that moment and the monument was his promise that it would never be cast aside.

Beyond the fountain stood his palace, flanked on either side by two smaller towers. The first was the Sorcerer's Tower, a rounded building edged with columns too narrow for any but a sorcerous hand to sculpt. As yet, it housed but one master sorceress and a handful of acolytes. With time, their number would grow. The tower on the opposite side was square in shape with buttresses almost like ramparts. Statues of the last four Etyni slain by Cydion during the Great War stood guard over each of the corners. Fenr stood tall with his great hammer resting on his broad shoulders. Niella, with back arched and staff raised in her left hand, pointed outward with her right in warning. Next to her was Zaris, leader of the Etyni, with sword clenched between his hands, point downward as a sign of judgment. And last stood Itesa, sister of Fenr, flail spinning in her hand.

Ushtyl turned away to climb the steps of his palace, his mind sobered by the memory of that day. He passed quickly through the atrium and descended to the Room of Arching Cedars. It was his favorite room in the palace, even though it was on the lowest floor. The chamber had been given its name for the dark and elegant wooden planking that formed the walls and ceiling of the interior. The four corners were rounded like the trunks of cedar trees with splayed branches that rippled across the ceiling. It had taken over ten years for his greatest Syraestari woodmasters to carve beautiful motifs of ages past. Each wall recalled elegant memories of the Lost Age, while the ceiling portrayed the triumphs and tragedies of the Great War that had brought its end. It was a dark room, lit only by four lanterns and a hearth on the far side that gave it a sense of solitude and contemplation. He liked to come here alone to consider heavy matters or to talk with people he trusted. As he entered, High Lord Tazil and Captain Eltirkar were seated beside the fire. They both rose to their feet, Eltirkar offering a short bow and the Lord of Raefi'ernyn a friendly smile.

Ushtyl turned to Eltirkar first and an edge entered his voice, "Captain, I want housecarls sent out immediately. Those refuge fools are defacing my city and I want their banners down. Now! Send the housecarls out every morning to tear apart anything new. And I want them caught!"

Eltirkar blanched beneath the tirade. "It will be done, my Lord." He bowed again and quickly withdrew.

As he left, Ushtyl brought a smile back to his face as he faced Tazil. "Forgive my unpleasant words on your arrival. Be welcome, my friend."

"I'm having similar difficulties in Raefi'ernyn," Tazil replied. "My son is diligent in his fight against it, but we're no closer to catching the culprits there either." He rubbed his jaw. "If only we could be certain how pervasive the malcontents are."

"They will make a mistake eventually," Ushtyl said.

"Still, it is strange. I've never known any of our people to act this way. This subterfuge..." He shook his head. "I do not like what it portends. The empress must make up her mind before this indecision tears us apart."

Ushtyl nodded. "All the more reason to be firm in our tasks." He walked over to a small table along the wall and poured two goblets of wine. Returning to the fire, he handed one to Tazil. "I trust your journey was a pleasant one."

"It was. I find the ocean breeze encourages my thoughts."

The door opened behind them and Captain Eltirkar re-entered the room

"And I trust your wife is well?" Ushtyl asked after receiving a nod from Eltirkar that he'd sent the orders to the housecarls. Tazil, unfortunately, made no decision without consulting his wife. She was intelligent and clever, but their collaboration meant Tazil never moved quickly on anything.

"Lady Aerharyndra is well and she sends her greetings. Thank you."

Ushtyl gestured both Tazil and Eltirkar back to their seats, then sat down across from them. "The raid was a success?"

"Perfectly, as your captain witnessed," Tazil replied. "I am likewise thankful for the efforts of Sorceress Medreuneth."

Ushtyl nodded. "She is always eager to ply her arts." Unfortunately, that seemed to be all she cared about. Of the problems of the Scions and the establishment of the empire, she always was indifferent.

"The Okaidir Vistus was able to fully infiltrate the Scions and lead my army to their camp. Not a soul escaped. We also captured the Scion chieftain. He will be put to question as soon as he reaches Raefi'ernyn."

"Excellent. How did the Okaidir fare?" Ushtyl asked. His concern wasn't for the human, but for any corruption an infiltrator might bring back to the larger circle of t'Okaedrin.

"Vistus will be fully questioned after the army returns to Raefi'ernyn in about two days. His father and eldest have sensed no change in him. He was ordered to execute the surviving Scions after the battle and did so. There was the slightest hesitation with the last, a woman, but his father believes it stems from the typical t'Okaedrin distaste for executions. They prefer to kill on the battlefield where honor is earned."

Ushtyl shrugged. Humans were tools to be used or cast aside. He couldn't understand Tazil's fascination with them. "So he will be ready for his second task, then?"

"Yes. He also reported one thing of interest. Apparently, the Scions are being aided by a creature they call the Shadow of Zaris."

Ushtyl snorted. "Zaris and all the Etyni died in the Great War."

"Perhaps Zaris can touch the world still. Or perhaps, it is one of his Cyrleni. The fates of the Etyni's servants are not all known. Regardless, the Scions attributed this creature's influence to their recent successes."

"Then among our other tasks, we must identify this Shadow and how he knows so much about us."

Tazil glanced over his shoulder at the table set against the wall opposite the wine table. "Shall we discuss the next stage of the plan, then?"

Ushtyl looked to Eltirkar. "Are you prepared, Captain?"

"Yes, my Lords," Eltirkar replied.

They stood and walked over to the table. A map laid out upon it showed the empire along the coast and the wild regions to the north. Eltirkar traced his fingers over the wilderness above Nahirazith and Raefi'ernyn. "The scouts have located a dozen wildmen villages, my Lords. One is Tatyrni, a couple are Zengris, and the remainder are of the Iachian tribe."

Ushtyl waved his hand impatiently, the jewels on his fingers flickering brightly in the torchlight. Captain Eltirkar was competent, but had the unfortunate tendency to fixate on unimportant details. "I don't care what tribes they are. Once they're Kalilaer, it won't matter to them either. What is your plan?"

"The t'Okaedrin of both cities will join forces here." Eltirkar pointed to a location midway between the Nahirazith and Raefi'ernyn near the edge of the forest. "The march north to the site of the forward camp will take about ten days. Once it is established, we will carry out the raids in two separate attacks, six villages on one day and the rest two days later. In this way, we will avoid having too many prisoners at our forward camp at once. We'll need to commit five families of t'Okaedrin and a complement of Pi'aernoth archers at each of the villages to be certain of success. Another force of at least five families will remain at our forward camp to defend it."

"Will this completely remove the wildmen tribes from that region?" Tazil asked, his eyes and nose pinching in contemplation.

"As best we can tell, we found them all, my Lord. But the wilderness is quite dense so we cannot be completely certain. And of course, humans have the unfortunate tendency to fill any unoccupied space. It is quite possible that new clans could move in when these are destroyed."

Ushtyl frowned as he looked down at the map. That was the eternal problem. For every village they destroyed another seemed to rise in its place.

"I appreciate your assistance with the next infiltration," Tazil said, turning to Ushtyl.

"You had but to ask, my friend." Ushtyl was more than happy to help the other high lord. It allowed him to take the plan for his own and step into full command. He'd done it before. The decision to establish a dominion here on the backs of enslaved humans instead of continuing the futile search for a refuge had been Tazil's idea, too. But Ushtyl had become its champion and everyone thought of it as his now. The curious thing was that Tazil never seemed to mind. Ushtyl wondered if he even noticed. He glanced over to Eltirkar and saw a bemused half-smile on the captain's lips. It was the closest Eltirkar ever came to a grin and suggested he had made the same observation as Ushtyl. And that he approved. "Our involvement will leave Nahirazith vulnerable and that concerns me."

"I regret that the greater risk must be yours. I and Raefi'ernyn pledge that we will come to whatever aid you require."

"I'm also concerned about the perception with the city," Ushtyl said. "My people are feeling the bite of the Scion raids as never before. Last month, several dozen farmers escaped and we lost part of the spring harvest before we could bring it in."

Tazil nodded. "They're getting more audacious. But if all goes well, that problem won't last."

"Until we are successful, better to say nothing about our plans. Ignorance is preferable to anticipation and failure."

Tazil smiled, his eyes glittering in the lantern light. "Come, my friend. All will be well. The Empress will see the fruits of our labor and there shall be no more talk of abandoning this home we've forged."

"Yes," Ushtyl replied. "That will be the end of it."

CHAPTER 6
Postures

"The child depends instinctively on the parent. But the child learns. To walk, to talk, to think, to disagree. It is the nature of things for that child to one day no longer be a child. But who decides when that day has arrived? The child, or the parent?"

—Erpitha of Algathnarhil

If there was one word to describe what a warrior experienced on campaign, Vistus would've picked marching, not fighting. Or perhaps boredom instead of excitement or fear. The days of the return march drifted one into the next without change. The only difference compared with his journey out was the company, and for that Vistus was glad. Here among his brothers, he didn't have to dwell among the apostates and the doomed. He wasn't forced to continually face his own doubts. No, this was his family. These were dutiful warriors like himself living exactly as they were meant to. Unfortunately, that did mean boredom.

So when evening fell, his brothers did what all warriors not on sentry duty did. They slept. But Vistus did not. Perhaps his claim to have left doubts behind was a lie, at least in the dark hours. It was then that he saw Vitarria's eyes wherever he looked and heard her voice whispering in his ears.

"I forgive you," she had said.

He sat with his back against a tree near the edge of camp, the nail of his forefinger running over the gemstone he'd taken from her body. Musing without purpose, only knowing he was troubled.

The scuffing of boots nearby surprised him and he looked up to see Nalsuntha approaching. Before Vistus could leap to his feet, his eldest gestured for him to remain where he was, then dropped to a crouch beside him. "I think it's time we talk."

Vistus clutched the gemstone tightly. Had Nalsuntha noticed his theft? He kept his voice even. "About what, Eldest?"

Nalsuntha scooped up several pebbles and one by one tossed them away, skittering across the ground. After a time, he spoke. "It's been several days since your ordeal and tomorrow we will reach Raefi'ernyn. I wanted to give you time to work through what you've experienced before we talked. But I think we should speak while we're still out here."

"I don't understand."

Nalsuntha tilted his head, looking at him. "You're the first ever to be sent among the enemy."

"Yes, Eldest, I know."

"We care, all of us — your father and mother, your brothers — about what it might do to you. Our masters care too. You remember Captain Nethzir's warning?" When Vistus nodded, Nalsuntha continued, "Their needs come first, always above our own, but they aren't family like we are. I expect the Syraestari will want to talk to you, perhaps even High Lord Tazil himself. We must be careful, after all. The danger we put you in is far greater than merely facing an enemy with a spear. Do you understand?"

"I think so."

"I am sure the rebels said things you hadn't heard before. Lies to make you doubt."

Vistus met Nalsuntha's eyes. "There is no doubt."

"Good."

"They hate us of course," Vistus said after a moment. He chuckled darkly. "Some called us traitors. Others even pitied us, thinking we've been blinded without seeing the veil that has fallen over their own eyes."

Nalsuntha sighed. "It is a weakness of our race that we would rather devour a hand offered in guidance than admit our own flaws. That is why the Syraestari are our masters. They have the wisdom we lack. By trusting them and obeying their commands, we overcome our greatest failing."

"I am grateful to have been raised t'Okaedrin and I've thanked His Highest Above every day since the battle for the children we rescued for the same future."

Nalsuntha smiled and, slapping him affectionately on the knee, rose to his feet. "I'm glad to see you came through your ordeal so well."

"You have no need to fear for me," Vistus replied. "The more I think on them, the more I hate them. It is good to be surrounded by my family again."

"Welcome home, Vistus," Nalsuntha said, then walked away.

Vistus loosened his grip on the gemstone. Closing his eyes, he leaned his head back against the tree, feeling his heart pulse as it always did when he contemplated the rebels. He did hate them. He knew that. But still he couldn't escape Vitarria's haunting words. Vitarria! Why did he focus on that name, but none other? He had to stop. She was just an apostate priestess. He had to forget her name forever.

Vistus pulled out the clear gemstone and raised his hand to throw it away. But no. Images flooded through his mind, memories of the rebel priestess talking about hope, of her forgiving him, of her dead in a pool of blood, slain by his furious hand. He couldn't do it. Perhaps when he was home, he could hide the stone away for a little while and try to forget. Perhaps that, but he couldn't bring himself to leave the stone behind forever. With a deep sigh, he withdrew to his tent in search of rest. It came only fitfully.

With the next day's march, the trees begin to diminish in number. The sun broke more and more radiantly through the thinning canopy overhead. Then the forest ended entirely and they stepped out onto the coastal plain.

A wide smile spread across Vistus' face as he felt the sunlight shining full upon him. As far as he could see to the south and east and west, the sky gleamed a brilliant deep blue. Beneath it the grasses ran, swaying in great ripples beneath the unfettered wind. Overhead, he heard the distant cry of a bird of prey on the hunt. Salty scents of the sea drifted upon the breeze, welcoming, embracing him with memories of home. In the far distance, he could see the water. The plains dropped away to a wide shore dotted with groves of olive and apple trees. Then, beyond a golden beach, lay the pale rippling blue of the sea to the edge of sight.

"Lelpfios' Blessing," Bridionis murmured beside him. "It is good to be back."

Vistus nodded.

Freed from the close woodlands and with their journey's end in sight, the column of t'Okaedrin picked up their pace across the plain. They reached the Kalilaer settlement first. It was a sprawling area that could never be mistaken for a village or town. From the bluff above the sea, and extending at least a half mile toward the forest, the plain was speckled with fields planted with wheat and lintels. Scattered across the Kalilaer plain were collections of buildings, each grouping marked an artisan camp with as many as a dozen structures apiece. In some, the Kalilaer wove linen, in others they shaped pottery, or smelted iron for the Syraestari blacksmiths. Mineshafts dotted the area, marked only by the large wooden crossbeams that the miners used to send up their ore in exchange for food.

Looking across the field, Vistus counted five groups of t'Okaedrin horsemen maintaining their constant vigil. More pairings walked through the artisan camps. They watched both the Kalilaer for the few dissidents that might cause trouble and also the forest edge for the raid that could happen without warning. A few Syraestari were visible, too, though most spent little time outside of their cities. He had heard rumors that they wanted to change that, but not while the Scion threat remained. Most of those in sight wore long linen robes dyed in sharp hues of red, green, grey, or black and trimmed in silver and gold.

Raefi'ernyn itself loomed up to the left on a small hill overlooking the plains. Vistus wondered if he would ever enter the city again. He defied any fool rebel to pass beneath the towering gatehouse and claim that humanity was equal to the Syraestari.

And below its splendid ramparts, at the base of the bluff, lay the buildings he called home.

After the families had been dismissed from the muster field, Vistus and his brothers gathered around their cart and began unloading supplies. Vistus was handing down a barrel of salted meat when a group of women rounded the building. At their head walked Auphni. His mother was always easy to distinguish by the wide braid of gray hair that dangled to her waist. It swung to the left and the right with each determined stride. Seeing them, she raised her hands and cried out, "My sons, welcome home!"

Vistus jumped off the cart and along with the rest of his family, gathered around her. "Where is Vistus?" she asked from the middle. His brothers stepped back and allowed him to step to the center where Auphni engulfed him in a great hug. "It is good to see you again, my son. Dalric said you did wonderfully." Letting him go, she took a step back and her gaze passed over all their faces. "You all did well, my sons.

And I am glad to see you've returned safely. You honor me, your father, and our masters."

"Thank you, mother," Vistus said and his brothers echoed him.

Auphni put her hands on her hips. "Now where are these children you rescued?" Vistus pointed to the cart and her eyes lit up. "Highest Above, you did well indeed." She turned to look back at the group of young women trailing her. They were all Stone Sisters. "Come on, girls, don't dawdle. It's time to bring these brothers and sisters to their new families."

Vistus watched the women take the children away. He wished he could remember that part of his infancy. They were frightened now, but soon they would learn all that he had learned. They would come to see the world through the eyes of t'Okaedrin and Pi'aernoth, most blessed of all humanity.

"Ushtyl is preparing Nahirazith for the campaign as well," High Lord Tazil told his wife. "He sends his greetings."

They sat in their usual places, relaxing on their wide couch in main room of their quarters, a warm fire on the hearth before them. Aerharyndra sat back, reclining slightly with one leg crossed over the other. Her right hand reached over the arch of the couch to hold his while her left cradled a wine glass on her lap. The firelight flickered gently across her sharp features and glowed in the auburn hair that cascaded over her shoulders.

"I understand the need for collaboration, but why Ushtyl?" she asked. "Why not Sizras instead?"

"Sizras wants nothing to do with any action that might tie us more strongly to this land." Tazil frowned. "Lately, it feels like every serious conversation we have turns into an argument over dominion or refuge. I don't want to strain our friendship any more than I have to."

"I don't like Ushtyl," Aerharyndra said, her nose flaring slightly as it always did when she was annoyed yet knew he was right. "His thirst for glory can't be sated and he happily takes credit for other's work. Your work."

"I care nothing for that, so long as we are safe and happy."

She squeezed his hand gently. "Husband, you are too good. Ushtyl sees everyone else as a plaything. He can't abide anyone that stands in his path."

"That's why I'm not in his path. We need each other, so there's nothing to fear."

"I hope so, husband."

Tazil squeezed her hand. "This is all for the good. It will make us stronger. Our people finally will be secure enough that they can begin to live safely beyond the city walls. Then the empress, Sizras, and everyone else who doubts will see that is the best path for us"

"That will be good. We weren't intended to live in cages, no matter how beautiful."

The Empress Kayrstana loved to walk in the garden during the cool of the morning, before the heat of the day came to its full strength. Her garden was encircled on all four sides by covered patios that led into the palace proper. One day, when all was in order, when the tumultuous high lords had been shown their place, when the pernicious Scions threat was crushed, she would build a greater garden. She already had begun consulting with one of the master craftsmen in her idle moments. But that was an ambition for lighter days. For now, she loved this smaller space. As spring slipped into summer, it was a riot of colors and fragrances. Fruit trees stretched their limbs across the smoothed stone path, green buds intermixed among the leaves. She had slipped off her shoes to better feel the caress of the grasses beneath her feet. It might not have been an imperial thing to do, but only those she trusted were near. The Pi'aernotha Kaupet gardeners had withdrawn, as had all the royal courtiers. Only two people remained. High Lord Tyrnis stood on the far side of the garden, waiting patiently as she had requested, while a pace to her right and one behind, her ever-present shadow followed.

Kayrstana turned to her. "Lady Ninanna, please walk with me."

"As Your Majesty wishes," Ninanna said, quickening her step to fall alongside.

Her words were said with a calm and respectful dignity, just as they had been since Kayrstana's first memories. Ninanna was her Edrethyn – her guardian and protector. She had watched over Kayrstana since before she was able to walk. Ancient even then, Ninanna had a patience Kayrstana could only dream of emulating.

Kayrstana glanced at her out of the corner of her eye. The Lady Ninanna stood half a head higher than Kayrstana, with long golden blond hair that fell to the small of her back. The locks were tied back by a red cord, but a wayward strand had escaped to hang loosely down the side of her face. Upon her back was slung a greatsword forged, it was said, by her long dead husband in the days before the War. Before even the Schism of the Aestarin. Ninanna wore the black robes of a Sword-Whisperer and that, as in all things, was a mirror of who she was. Part, but apart. For all that Kayrstana loved her as somewhere between an older sister and a mother, Ninanna was not like her. She was not like anyone else among her people. Ninanna's path from Tirnaestari to Syraestari had not been forged through the foreswearing of their ancient Oath to the Etyni. No, Ninanna still looked upon humans as equals. It was a regrettable insistence that continually lowered her in the eyes of all but Kayrstana. Ninanna's path to the Syraestari had been bloodied by betrayal, leaving behind the bodies of her beloved husband and son. Kayrstana knew little more than that. Only that Kayrstana's father, the Emperor Taerdranin, had seen unmarred possibility in Ninanna and had asked her to guard the life of his only child. Why she had agreed, Ninanna had never said.

"Lady Ninanna, how much time have you spent with the other Sword-Whisperers this past year?"

"A few days, Your Majesty."

"I expect you must miss their company."

"At times, but both they and I understand our duties. I am content."

Kayrstana stopped and knelt to smell a lily, its yellow petals radiant as they reached out toward the sun. It was ironic that Ninanna had formed the Sword-Whisperers almost a thousand years before, yet did not lead them. She wasn't trusted enough by the lords and ladies to be placed in such a position. Peculiarly, there had been no similar protest over her guardianship of Kayrstana.

"I have a task I need of you. I fear you won't like it, but it does have the benefit of placing you in the company of your Sword-Whisperers."

She sensed Ninanna stiffen. "You wish me to leave your side, Your Majesty?"

Kayrstana rose to her feet. "Only for a time, my friend. The empire is increasingly troubled and I have need for one on whom I can depend. There are so few."

"If there is a task you'd have of me, you only need to ask," Ninanna replied.

"I know and I thank you." Kayrstana smiled, meeting the woman's deep brown eyes. "And I know you will worry for my safety in your absence. I promise to keep a ring of t'Okaedrin around me and will not leave Thusaeyanin until your return."

"What is your need, my Empress?"

"As you know, the high lords are becoming increasingly turbulent. Their incessant bickering over the future of our people, refuge or dominion, is bad enough. But even worse, they resist the demands I make of them."

"It was the long migration before Dahiraetin, Your Majesty," Ninanna replied. "The high lords grew accustomed to the greater authority afforded them when our people had to disburse to forage and survive. Now that we've established a new realm, they resist a return to the old ways."

"I wouldn't have expected you to agree with them."

"I don't, Your Majesty. And so long as you move slowly and hold to your courage, I believe you will prevail. But I also understand their stubbornness, especially with the newer high lords like Ushtyl and Tazil who could little remember the old empire."

Kayrstana nodded. "I am particularly watchful of those two. It has come to my attention that Ushtyl and Tazil are planning a raid deep into wildman territory. I want you to take two ranks of Sword-Whisperers to Nahirazith. You are to inform them that I've placed you in command of the raid."

Kayrstana scanned Ninanna's face for a flinch. She knew her guardian well enough to catch the slight twitching of Ninanna's lips. "They will resent my presence."

"I expect so. But they need to know that I am the empress and what they do, I do. You are to become my Hand, representing me in this matter."

"You know my opinion of these raids. This enslavement of humans is neither honorable nor beneficial."

"I know your thoughts and respect them," Kayrstana replied, though they both knew she didn't agree. "I wouldn't have asked you were there a better choice."

"With each raid, we fix ourselves more deeply to these lands," Ninanna said. "When we settled here, it was only to be for a short time while the earthquakes and fires of the Cataclysm raged. We were supposed to abandon this place and find a final refuge, a home where we could live apart and free as we dreamed from the days Cydion bound us in servitude. Isfalinis is healing, the snows are in retreat. The time has come for us to find a new home."

"I've heard as much and often from High Lord Tyrnis," Kayrstana replied. "But there are many things still to consider. As long as we remain here we must solidify our position and I won't restrain Ushtyl and Tazil's raids. But I need my presence among them and authority over them reinforced. Will you do as I ask?"

"As always, Your Majesty," Ninanna replied, bowing. This time Kayrstana could not detect any dissatisfaction, though she knew it existed still. Because of that obedience, she hated sending Ninanna. It was a strain in the trust they'd developed over so many years. But she wouldn't shirk from what was necessary.

Kayrstana smiled. "Thank you, my friend. I'd like you to depart tomorrow morning. For now, I give you leave to prepare for the journey. I'll also have word sent to the Sword-Whisperers and will have a letter for the high lords ready by the time you leave."

"Your Majesty." Ninanna bowed again, then departed.

As Ninanna crossed the patio and entered the palace, Tyrnis approached Kayrstana. Of the eight high lords and ladies, he was one of the few she could depend on – and even then, not fully. As with all nobles, he was ambitious. But he had always been loyal and his face bore the scars of his service to her people. The same battle at Dahiraetin that saw hundreds dead, including two high lords and the leader of the Sword-Whisperers, had taken one of his eyes. His pale blond hair wisped gently in the cool breeze as he bowed before her.

"You realize, Your Majesty, that you are sending her into the Abyss."

"I know, High Lord," Kayrstana replied. "But whom else is there that I can trust?"

"None so fully," Tyrnis answered. "But it is a grave risk. Ushtyl and Tazil are clever and their dislike of Lady Ninanna is well known, Ushtyl's particularly."

"Yes, but it's also her chance for glory. When Lady Ninanna succeeds in this, even her greatest detractors will be unable to deny her prowess. I haven't told her, but I intend to give her command of the Sword-Whisperers as a reward for her triumph."

Tyrnis nodded. "It has been a long time since Dahiraetin."

"Yes," Kayrstana replied, "the Sword-Whisperers have been leaderless for too long. Ninanna was always worthy of it, regardless of what else people see."

"Speaking of Dahiraetin," Tyrnis said, "I have news."

"Oh?" There were times when it felt like everything was related to Dahiraetin. On that day of grief and pride, so much had changed.

"I have found a place of safety, Your Majesty." It had been in the wake of that dreadful battle that the first seeds of empire had been born. They'd realized that running was futile.

There were always too many humans and not enough food, no matter where they went.

It had been the very same high lords she mistrusted now who had reached that conclusion. Newly appointed in the wake of Dahiraetin, Ushtyl and Tazil had brought forward the recommendation of carving a new land built upon the labor and arms of captured humans.

"Where?" she asked.

"To the northwest," Tyrnis replied. "It took my scouts over a month to reach on horseback. They report that the ice wall is in retreat, revealing new lands. They confirmed finding a valley between two arms of the mountains. The land is defensible on its open side by a large river. But more than that, the land is lush and it is ripe with newly exposed ores, enough to reforge cities like Syrdranaethin and all those we lost. We can rise again, and not just with the crude stone and wood we use here."

"Confirmed?" Kayrstana asked. "I wasn't aware you were searching."

A rueful smile touched Tyrnis' lips. "I must confess, Your Majesty that I was not. It had been my intention to, but I thought it too soon. No, a letter was left on my nightstand. I dismissed that outright, of course, until it was followed by maps of impressive detail. I couldn't ignore such evidence, but on the chance it was a fool's errand, I wanted to be sure before bringing it to you."

Kayrstana frowned. She knew who the messenger had to be and was not pleased. He took far too many liberties.

"If it took your scouts a month, how long would it take our people to march?"

"Nine months, I'd guess, perhaps more."

"The memories of our wandering are too strong upon us. I doubt the people would put up with that."

"They would if you guided them, Empress. That great distance will put the humans far away. For the first time since we broke from the Tirnaestari, we will truly have a chance to be our own people."

Kayrstana hesitated, then shook her head. "No, High Lord Tyrnis. I will not. I can't even begin to think about such an undertaking until the high lords are firmly under my guidance. You've always stayed true, but most of the others have grown too comfortable with no rule but their own. Another journey would only embolden their resistance."

"But, Your Majesty—"

"No, High Lord." Kayrstana rested her hand on his wrist to take away the sting of her words. "I will not. Not yet."

Tyrnis sighed. "Yes, Empress."

"If there is nothing more, High Lord, I'd like some time in contemplation alone."

"Of course, Your Majesty." Tyrnis bowed, then withdrew.

After he'd gone, Kayrstana took a seat on one of the garden's stone benches. It was strange, but already she felt Ninanna's absence. The Sword-Whisperer had been such a shadow, such a friend. Yet the tasks were too important. There were risks as with all great endeavors. In this, she had to dare all and, if necessary, Ninanna herself would be sacrificed for the good of the people. Kayrstana shied from that possibility but couldn't deny it. Ironically, it was Ninanna herself who had taught her that leadership required painful choices.

CHAPTER 7
Whisperer

"Just as the Schism sundered the Aestari, so the Second Schism split the Sword-Singers. From that crucible arose the Sword-Whisperers, children born from the mind and heart of Ninanna the Outcast. To this day, I do not know whether to hate and fear them or to respect and honor them."

—Eloezyntir, a Captain in the Sword-Singers

The wind gusting through Ninanna's hair had grown decidedly more chill with the setting of the sun. One strand of her thin blond locks had broken free from her braid. Irritated, she brushed it past the long point of her ear, even though she knew it would slip free a moment later. Letting out a sigh, she snapped the reins, urging her horse into a trot. The other nineteen riders instinctively matched her gait. As in all other things, the first lesson of the Sword-Whisperers was that they were but one piece of something much larger. Power came through acting in concert.

Out of the corner of her eye, she saw her lieutenant spur alongside. "Why the hurry tonight, Lady Ninanna?" Imeskir asked. When she glared at him, he laughed. The motion twisted the long red scar that ran from hairline to jaw along the right side of his face. Two fingers' widths to the left and the blade cut would have taken his eye. "What would the people say if they knew that the glorious Lady Ninanna hated sleeping on the ground where rocks dig into her back?"

Imeskir defied the traditional Sword-Whisperer manner of dour reticence. Perhaps for that reason, Ninanna liked him most. It was important for a warrior to uphold a grim reputation on the battlefield, but too much of it stole all joy from life. It was a feat Ninanna struggled with in herself. "I endure the hard ground when I must, but I do not long for it," she told him. "Besides, I saw you squirming over some roots yourself last night."

Imeskir rubbed surreptitiously at his back. "Then I'll hold my tongue and our honor shall be preserved. Still, when we depart these lands again, I expect it will be roots and rocks that await us with each setting sun."

"Yes," Ninanna replied grimly. If they ever left. Kayrstana was a good empress, but she was still young and finding herself. In the meantime, she was susceptible to all those voices that urged comfort and power over stability and independence. The constant bickering of the high lords made finding the clear path even more difficult

But Imeskir must have mistaken her somber tone. "The price of civilization, I fear, is that we've forgotten the value of hard living." His head tilted back and he laughed. The moonlight gleamed off his wind-rippled hair until it looked like the pale plumage of some exotic bird.

Pushing away her grim thoughts, Ninanna laughed with him. The empress had spoken true. It was good to be in the company of the Sword-Whisperers again.

The last few miles of their journey to Nahirazith passed in silence and Ninanna steeled herself for the confrontation that was to come. It would be better with the morning, but Ushtyl might be awaiting her. As the walls of the city rose up before them, the warriors straightened in their saddles, the grim mantle of the Sword-Whisperer falling over them. Even at this late hour, they had a stern reputation to uphold for the people of the city.

A housecarl standing beside the gate recognized their robes and two-handed blades and waved them through. Ninanna guided her company down the wide thoroughfare. She'd been to the city more than a hundred times since its founding over a century ago, but always accompanying her mistress. This time, leading the Sword-Whisperer ranks, it was a different form of somberness that fell over her. She looked at the dark buildings rising two stories high on either side. Over a thousand Syraestari lived here, huddled in their fine houses, their verdant gardens, their cobbled streets. Behind high stone walls they looked northward to the wide forests and looming mountains with increasing apprehension. Their homes had become palatial cages as fear of the humans grew even while the threat of the Cataclysm lessened. But they could cope with the danger posed by the scattered human peoples, hungry and regressed to tribalism by the ruin of the world, if only they found their courage. Instead, the Syraestari had chosen the path of slavery. She didn't know the exact numbers, but hazarded that closing on five thousand humans now dwelt in chains beneath the walls of each of the nine imperial cities, some with swords but most with threshing flails, potter's wheels, or carpenter's hammers.

A few torches gave the stables of Ushtyl's palace some illumination, but above their small spheres of golden light, the towers rose black against the night sky. Their form was only visible by the blotting of the stars. As Ninanna's company arrived, several Pi'aernoth rushed out to greet them, rubbing the sleep from their eyes when they didn't think the Whisperers were looking.

Ninanna handed her reins to a dark-haired human woman who barely stood as tall as her chin, then turned to Imeskir. "Take care of the ranks. I'm going to see if High Lord Ushtyl is still awake."

"By your command, Lady."

Stepping into the entry hallway, she saw a Syraestarin approaching and recognized Eltirkar, captain of Ushtyl's housecarls. Still in the full arms and armor of a housecarl, he strode toward her with a stiff and determined gait, his eyes locked on hers.

"Good evening, Lady Ninanna," he said, bowing his head slightly as he arrived.

"Good evening, Captain Eltirkar." She gave him an equal bow. At different times, she would be superior to him, or him to her. Here, in this place, she suspected it would be

Eltirkar who held the authority. At least until she asserted hers in the empress' name.

"On behalf of my lord, welcome."

Though the words were proper, she detected a hint of anger in his tone. It wasn't unfamiliar to her. There were few enough Syraestari, now, that she was known to all and liked by few. Most who knew her reputation responded in the same way as Eltirkar. Some doubtless concluded that only a person of feeble prestige could found an order as respected as the Sword-Whisperers but be denied authority over them. The majority, however, despised her for her past as a Tirnaestari outcast. Some wounds even two millennia could not heal. But for her it was an old and familiar pain. Enduring it, she kept her voice level. "Thank you. Will I be attending him tonight?"

"Both he and High Lord Tazil have already retired, Lady, but I can show you to your quarters."

"Thank you." Ninanna wasn't sure what she felt about Tazil being present in the city. She had deliberated approaching him first, but Tazil tended to follow Ushtyl's lead. That being said, when he stood alongside another high lord, Tazil could be a redoubtable antagonist. But at least she would have a full night's sleep in a real bed before facing the two high lords. Their opinion of her was as bleak as the captain's. When Ushtyl had still been a young man, she'd opposed his entrance into the Sword-Whisperers. He'd been too ambitious and unwilling to surrender himself to the greater whole, a necessity in the mutual warfare that was their greatest strength. But she'd been overruled and that, coupled with his very different outlook on the world, only perpetuated his grudge. They'd been unfriendly peers until he left the Whisperers upon his elevation to high lord.

Eltirkar guided her down the hallway. Here away from the center of the palace, there was little decoration. Nevertheless, here she saw tribute to the masonry skills of master craftsmen. The stones of the walls, floor, and ceiling had been fitted together nearly seamlessly, the arched supports every dozen paces were perfect curves that contrasted elegantly with the hard edges of the regular joins. Lanterns had been set with precision to provide good light down the length without requiring more than was necessary. They passed by a score of adjoining rooms and a handful of connecting corridors before Eltirkar stopped near the end and opened a door. Gesturing within, he said, "Good night, Lady Ninanna."

"Thank you, Captain" she said, stepping inside and allowing Eltirkar to close the door behind her. Within lay a small anteroom containing a straw pallet where a Pi'aernoth could sleep close at hand. Through the next doorway lay her own room. The walls were plastered and well made, but the furnishings were simple. Along the far wall, a tall closet had been set alongside a narrow table with a chair. The woodwork was well done, but inelegant. Filling most of the room was the bed itself, covered in linens and furs. An oil lamp sat on a second, smaller table beside the bed.

She was still standing on the threshold when the outer door opened. Ninanna turned to see the same Stone Sister who'd taken her reins enter the anteroom carrying her saddlebags. She bowed deeply, perfectly balancing the heavy burden as she moved. "I am Talikae, my lady, your Pi'aernotha Kaupet. Can I bring you food or wine?"

"No, thank you," Ninanna replied.

Talikae crossed the room to set the saddlebags on the table and began undoing the ties but Ninanna interrupted her. She hated the idea of this slave woman doing work she could do herself. Unfortunately, Ninanna had learned that the Pi'aernoth's training was as pervasive as the t'Okaedrin's. If she simply ordered Talikae to stop, the human would only be hurt. Better to give another useful task. "I will unpack it myself. Please bring me a basin of water, hot if it's available."

"It is, Lady," Talikae said, bowing again before withdrawing. She returned a few minutes later with a steaming bowl and a cloth. When Ninanna dismissed her, she said, "I will be in the anteroom, Lady, should you require anything else."

"Thank you," Ninanna replied. "I don't expect I will. The rest of the evening is yours."

As soon as the door was closed, Ninanna washed her hands and face in the water. After the cold night, the warm water against her skin felt wonderful. She carefully removed the ring of black paint around her eyes. At times she'd contemplated adding more elegant flourishes as was popular within the nobility. The empress certainly had encouraged her to, but the Sword-Whisperers stood outside such things. Still, she longed to give in to this one note of elegance.

Looking over at the still-packed saddlebags, she let out a sigh. Unpacking could wait until morning. She removed only her linen sleeping robe and changed into it before crawling into bed. Then she blew out her lamp, slid her knife under her pillow, and closed her eyes. The sleep of the road-weary came quickly.

A sound brushed the edge of Ninanna's hearing. Her eyes shot open. She stared into the dark chamber, straining her ears, but there was only silence. She could not recall the sound that had wakened her, only that it was. She carefully slipped her hand under her pillow, reaching for her knife. It wasn't there. Cydion's Abyss!

Still there was no noise and in the darkness she could see nothing. Ninanna drew in a slow, deep breath, remaining still. Then in a single motion she sat upright, commanding, "Eusy'arjev vled loesyns!"

The lamp beside her bed flared to life, basking the room in its brilliant rays. The unnatural shadows lingered around the walls as if the flame's light was muted by a layer of smoke. On the far side of the chamber, a black-robed figure sat in the room's single chair. It lifted its gaze to stare at her, revealing a white mask beneath its heavy cowl.

A shudder passed down her spine. She drew a deep breath to steady her voice. "Just kill me and be done with it."

"I am not here to kill you," the figure said. "If I were, you already would be dead."

Ninanna hid a grimace at the truth of those words. What had happened to her that she'd allowed her guard to slip so much?

A hand withdrew from the deep folds of the creature's robes to toss her sheathed knife onto the bed beside her. "I took that only to be sure you wouldn't do anything rash."

"And to prove you could." The robed figure did not move. There was no need to acknowledge what was obvious to both of them. She left the dagger where it lay. She wouldn't show fear. "If you've done anything to the Pi'aernoth in the room beyond..."

"I kill only when the need arises. She sleeps still, unknowing."

Ninanna stared, trying to pierce the mask to the face that lay beneath. Cold blue eyes met hers. "Who are you and why do you disturb my sleep?"

"I am the Shadow-Servant."

"The Shadow-Servants are all dead and the world is better for it."

"Are they? And how did they die?"

"If you've claimed the name, then you should know," Ninanna retorted. "They died in fire and blood breaking our peoples' shackles to Cydion in the last hours of the Great War. It was the only good thing any of them had ever done. They were assassins, spies, and murderers who warrant no admiration from me. You're a fool to take on their name."

"Perhaps. And perhaps you're right about the fate they deserved." His hand emerged from the folds of his robes a second time. This time he held what had once been a bladed weapon, but only the hilt remained. He tossed it onto the bed at Ninanna's side.

She picked it up carefully. The hilt was sized for a knife blade. She recognized the masterful craftsmanship and style from the last years of the Lost Age. It had a round grip and a small spherical pommel. The guard was straight behind the blade, but split in front to curve slightly up and slightly down toward the fingers. Weapons of this style that she'd seen before were usually gilded and had a gemstone set in the pommel, but this hilt was seared black and the leather of the grip was burned away. Its only color was the faintest gleam of steel where the blade had once met the guard. But the blade was not broken. Running her finger across the join, she couldn't detect even the faintest ridge. It was almost as if the blade had been burned away.

Ninanna hissed, dropping the black hilt to the covers, eyes locking on the creature across from her.

"You know that weapon," he said.

It was the knife that had been driven into the back of Cydion, the Lord of Death. When she spoke again, it was an effort to keep her voice steady. "Why are you here, Shadow-Servant?"

"Only to talk."

She picked up the knife hilt and tossed it back to him. His hand emerged from the robes to catch it, then disappeared again. "I meant what I said, Shadow-Servant. It would be better had you died."

"Perhaps you're right, but it would seem I survived."

"Why me? Why now? And who else knows you live?"

"The empress knows and her father before." At Ninanna's sharp look, he continued, "For what it is worth, your guardianship has presented a nearly insurmountable challenge. I rarely speak with her."

Ninanna felt her cheeks burn. She did not need veiled complements from this creature. She gestured at the shadows lining the room. "Why all this?"

"There are many who wouldn't want us to speak."

"Myself among them."

The Shadow-Servant's laugh rang too natural in her ears. "I've approached you because in this age I find that there are few people I can trust. You are rare because the word you give is the word you keep. You are rarer still for your tempered ambitions."

"I think you may be insulting me."

He leaned forward. "My point is that, though you seek advancement, you do not do so over the bodies of your rivals."

"I am curious at an assassin speaking to me of trust and ambition. Not the least because he broke into my room." She was goading this killer, but even knowing that, she wouldn't stop. She wouldn't allow herself to be afraid of him.

"A fair point. I embody neither trust nor mercy." His tone hardened as he continued. "I have always held one single ambition. All I do, all I have ever done is for the good of our people."

"I've heard much the same from the lips of tyrants."

"This I promise you. Should the good of our people demand it, never doubt that I would plunge a dagger through my own heart."

Hearing the coldness in his voice, Ninanna believed him despite herself. "You still haven't told me what you want."

"A crisis approaches. I know you have never been fond of this dominion we've built upon the enslavement of humans. You long for a return to our old ways of isolation. But the recent raids of Tazil and Ushtyl only strengthen the claims of those who would remain. Further, they incite the Scions and wild humans against us, making any withdrawal more difficult. The empress remains undecided, but the day is fast approaching when she will make a choice or one will be forced upon her. I fear that choice." The Shadow-Servant eyes grew even more intense. "I have found a place of refuge."

"A place for our people?" Ninanna could only ask in surprise.

"North and west of here," the Shadow-Servant replied, "It would require a march of many months to reach. The wall of ice is in retreat, revealing new carved plains and verdant woodlands. There is a lush land between the arms of two great mountain ranges that could protect and hold our people – if only we would seize it. It is rich with the life, the rocks, the ores of the old world. Tyrnis sent scouts who have confirmed it."

"High Lord Tyrnis knows of you?"

"No. He doesn't know the messages came from me."

"So you manipulate just as your kind did before the Cataclysm." It was hard to imagine any of the Shadow-Servants surviving the fiery counterattack that followed their assault on Cydion. From what Ninanna had heard, the entire hillock had been seared bare for a hundred paces. But as startling as that revelation was, she was even more surprised at his claim to prefer a retreat to solitude over building an empire of human slaves.

"Tyrnis is an honorable man. He would be as unhappy that I live as you are. He would never have investigated had he known the truth. And time grows short. But that is only half the crisis." The Shadow-Servant sat back. "There is a struggle growing between the empress and the high lords. I am sure you've seen it. The high lords do not wish to surrender the autonomy they gained during our years of wandering. The fools want an empire without an empress."

"It is common knowledge that both High Lord Sizras and High Lady Zaerina resent the empress' latest dictates," Ninanna replied, "but they are both advocates for refuge and not dominion."

"Yes, the battle lines are still unclear. We cannot yet see who will be a friend and who will be an enemy, but the lines will be drawn and blood will flow. Of this I am certain. There is too much pride, too much certainty in each of us. Whether the cost will be another Schism of our people, I don't know. Nor do I know whether the cost will be a few lives or thousands, but there will be a price and it will be paid. I want that cost to be small."

Ninanna narrowed her eyes, wondering how much of her mission he'd guessed. "You seek to manipulate the empress through me."

"No. I know my reputation breeds mistrust."

"Then why are you here?"

"For the moment, I ask for little more than your vigilance of Ushtyl, Tazil, Sizras, and all the high lords. In the end, more will be required of you whether you believe me or not. The decision whether to remain here and carve an empire of humans or retreat to a place of our own will be made. If you truly believe in withdrawing then you must know that the longer we remain here, the harder that choice will be. The empress and the high lords must gather soon. And they must believe that there is no future in this place. If you won't do this for me, do it for the good of the empress, for the good of our people. But if you will not, you are useless to me."

"And I become a threat to be removed."

"No." The Shadow-Servant hesitated a moment, then said, "But I know such words won't convince you. Unlike you, I am not to be trusted." He leaned forward. "A thousand years I have confided in no one and few even before that. But I must trust now as I never have. There is an itching beneath my skin. I feel a dark dread in my dreams and I know we may be facing our doom. A Schism, or worse. I am certain we are again living in days of prophecy."

"I give no credence to prophecies," Ninanna said. "Their meaning becomes obvious only after the event is past. Vaenna's warnings did nothing to avert the Schism, the Great War, or the Cataclysm."

"Our failing, not hers," the Shadow-Servant replied. "Are you familiar with her Third Prophecy?"

Ninanna shrugged. "I've read it, though that was long ago."

Reaching into his robe, he withdrew a scroll and set it on the bed by her feet. "The opening stanzas have been on my mind in recent days." He began to recite:

"Tears from iron, blood from stone,
The heavens tremble, the earth doth groan.
His hand in crimson fury shine,
Taketh my life, but saveth thine.
A voice to rise beside the sea,
In wind and wrath from calumny.
By night he comes alone to slay
Forgive them then upon that day.

A land in pain, a people bound
The ice doth melt, a refuge found.
While towers rise with fetters fine,
Forged iron chains itself to bind.
A choice appears to flee or stay,
The war complete or cast away.
Harbinger raise thy final hand
Stayed at last by crimson brand.

In the tempest where all is set,
The storm, the wind, the cry beget."

Ninanna shrugged. "I remember the style, but don't see its use."

"Listen to the words, really hear them."

Ninanna sighed and rolled her shoulders. Once she had believed that prophecy held value, but that was before her world had been torn apart. That was before she had been riven from her husband and son. Before they had died. She closed her eyes a moment, then opened them again and, picking up the scroll read the words.

"Tears from iron, blood from stone, the heavens tremble, the earth doth groan," the Shadow-Servant said, his voice soft. "Can there be a truer picture of the Cataclysm? The rivers and seas have long been called the 'Blood of Isfalinis' while stone and iron are her flesh."

"Why, then, would Vaenna name the Blood twice and the Flesh twice when she could just as easily have spoken of the Heart and the Breath of Isfalinis? The Cataclysm has wracked the world with erupting mountains and ferocious storms as much as earthquakes and floods."

"I don't know, perhaps these two are more important," the Shadow-Servant replied. "But see, she also tells of a land in pain and ice melting. That's happening today. The walls of ice to the north are in retreat."

"Maybe," Ninanna admitted, "But that speaks nothing to this specific moment. The Cataclysm has been ending since it began, just like a mortal human child starts dying from the womb."

"So you're a philosopher as well as a warrior." Ninanna nodded her head slightly at the compliment as he continued, "I believe the later lines give the answer. 'While towers rise with fetters fine, forged iron chains itself to bind.' That is the very picture of our realm. We have built it on the labor of humans. Did you know the wildmen call the t'Okaedrin Iron-Men?" At Ninanna's nod, he continued, "And that's the crux of it. The prophecy says we bind ourselves." His laugh was a sharp rasp. "Can that be anything but a warning against the dominion we've begun to forge? If I am correct, then we're binding ourselves as surely as we bind humanity. How can it be any other way? If we rely on others for our livelihood, we give them sovereignty over us. We become weak and they become strong."

"Now you're the philosopher," Ninanna replied.

"And then there is the choice," he continued. "To flee or stay, to complete the war against humanity or cast it away. That is what matters."

"But what about the other lines," Ninanna asked. "Vaenna was slain in the final battle against Cydion. Why then would she say, 'Taketh my life, but saveth thine'? She's dead and Cydion certainly never saved a life."

"I think it's metaphorical. It is another description of the Cataclysm where some are killed by the chaos of chance while others are saved."

"But why 'my life', then?" Ninanna pressed. "It has been a long time, but I don't recall any other prophecy of hers using words like that. For that matter, whose voice rises above the sea? Who is the slayer and who deserves forgiveness? Who is the harbinger?"

Although only a little of the Shadow-Servant's mouth was visible beneath his mask, she could see it twisting into a frown. "I don't know."

"And that is why prophecies are useless. You have forced a few lines without understanding the rest."

"No!" The Shadow-Servant sat back in his chair. "We don't understand everything, but what we can see is clear enough. The Cataclysm is coming to an end and with it, a crisis looms."

"You think a prophecy can end the Cataclysm?" Ninanna interrupted, fighting down a laugh.

"Will the Cataclysm end because of the prophecy or does the prophecy merely predict its conclusion? I doubt even the Etyni could answer that question." He glared at her as if challenging a reply. When she didn't respond, he continued, "More importantly, this enslavement of humans is destroying us and pulling us into ceaseless wars. It must end. This empire must be cast aside with a return to solitude regardless of what the other lines mean."

Ninanna opened her mouth to retort but closed it again immediately, seeing the trap. The easy conversation of bantering philosophy had lulled her and now he struck. This Shadow-Servant knew her past. He knew her compassion for humanity and wanted her to agree that slavery was a crime. A crime against all that His Highest Above had intended. But he wouldn't bait her into speaking it and so doom herself. In a cold voice, she asked, "You want me to do more than just watch Ushtyl and Tazil. What is it you really seek?"

"I want to end the enslaving of humans."

Ninanna laughed. "Do you think me a fool?"

"I know that you are not, Lady Ninanna, and that is why I am here."

"You, the Shadow-Servant, want to help humanity? You're an assassin, a murderer, a butcher."

"Yes, yes, yes I am!" he cried, rising to his feet. "But always with reason. Always for the good of our people."

"So you have already said," Ninanna snapped. "And exposing sympathies within me for the humans will achieve that end? Just stick a blade through my heart and be done with it."

The Shadow-Servant sat down, his eyes blazing. "You condemn me? I know you won't confess it, but your love of humanity is known. Yet what have you done? You pine and fret and worry and watch. I have acted where you will not. Why do you think their raids have been so successful lately? I have walked among their ragged bands and given them direction. They call me the 'Shadow of Zaris' and they listen and succeed. But you, you sit and do nothing." He leaned forward. "And what of our own people? You plead in the empress' ear, but she doesn't listen. She must come to see! I am making all our people see. Who do you think is leaving parchments across the nine cities proclaiming a withdrawal from here? The high lords believe it a conspiracy. No, it is only me. Just me. And that's why I need you."

Ninanna could only sit in silence at the Shadow-Servant's tirade. If what he said were true, then perhaps he really did mean what he said. Perhaps he did want human slavery ended and this empire abandoned. But she well remembered the machinations of his kind, the trickery and deceit luring one choice only to betray in the end.

"You are a Shadow-Servant," she said. "I cannot trust you."

He let out a long slow sigh and she almost believed the despair in his voice was real. Almost. "You do not believe me. Of course you don't believe."

"How can I?"

The Shadow-Servant clasped his gloved hands on his lap and closed his eyes. Ninanna watched him carefully, measuring the distance to her dagger which still lay where he'd tossed it, and recalling to her mind its balance. If she had need for it, there would only be a moment. But perhaps, just perhaps, he spoke the truth. She shook her head. It would take a lot more than a show of passion from a master manipulator to convince her.

Finally, the Shadow-Servant opened his eyes. "You think you know me and so you doom me." He let out a slow sigh. "I shall ask nothing of you then. I urge only vigilance for its own sake. Read the prophecy for yourself and consider it. When I can prove I mean what I say, I shall return. Will you do that, at least?"

Ninanna tilted her head, staring into his deep blue eyes. His request appeared reasonable enough, but no. All it took was a simple innocent step for a Shadow-Servant to get its knife in you. The real one, not the one you thought you saw. She couldn't agree so easily. "On one condition."

"Yes?"

"Which Servant were you? I want your name."

"No." He shook his head. "I cannot do that."

"Then I won't help you."

"For something as petty and trite as a name?"

"If it were petty and trite, you'd tell me," Ninanna replied.

"You don't understand."

"But I do." Ninanna leaned forward and wrapped her arms around her knees, staring at him. "You are a creature of shadow and darkness, one of veils and illusions. Your name leaves you vulnerable. It symbolizes that small corner of yourself that you've kept apart from all that you do. I knew most of your kind in the Age past and demand to know which of them you are. If you are Traevlyn or Izdyrgarith or Nemithtar, this I swear. One of us will not leave this room alive. It is said that there is always a cost when dealing with a Shadow-Servant. But know this. There is a cost a Shadow-Servant must pay to deal with me."

He recoiled at that and, for the first time, she could sense him losing the fierce control he held on himself. Not even his mask and robes could hide it. "You would cast everything away on a name?" he hissed. "You would refuse to help your people? The humans you love? You know I'm right, even though you won't admit it. But you'd throw it all away? Just for a name?"

"No," Ninanna replied. She kept her voice cold and wondered if she were about to die. "It is you who would cast everything away on a name. Speak it or we are done."

The Shadow-Servant's eyes burned beneath his mask as though he sought the words to say.

"You want me to trust you," Ninanna told him. "Then you must trust me. Price for price."

A bitter chuckle broke through his lips and he slumped back in his seat. He shook his head, then after a long moment spoke. "Reigliff. My name is Reigliff."

A chill flickered across Ninanna's skin and the fine hairs on her arms stood on end. Perhaps it might be true. A thousand years had passed since she last had heard Reigliff's voice. "The son of Traevlyn? Traevlyn who founded the Servants?"

"Yes."

"Then you truly are a murderer."

"Yes." His eyes flickered. "Do we kill each other, now?"

"No."

"Then consider what I have said and watch as you've promised." Reigliff rose to his feet. He moved slowly as if weary, soul and body. "Trust for trust. Price for price. Kargats zathoes."

Shadows flooded over the room at his command, even blotting out the burning lamp's glow. Then the darkness faded and this time the light pierced to the walls. The chair across from Ninanna stood vacant. She let out a long sigh, then picked up her dagger. Sinking back into the bed, her fingers played across its hilt as her mind raced.

CHAPTER 8
Oath

"The journey from our old shattered realm to the shores of the Osenjian Sea was a long one, plagued by troglyd monsters and human barbarians. Amid that toil, how could we remain whole? As I look back now, it is not surprising to me that our people splintered from the unified empire we had known to lesser domains, each relying upon their own lord."

—High Lord Sizras of Sarhystoeka

Ninanna slept poorly, her mind filled with the words of Reigliff and apprehension over her meeting with High Lord Ushtyl. The Shadow-Servant had been right about one thing. She did care about humans and abhorred their enslavement. Killing them, as she had done countless times during the Syraestari migration, was one thing. Humans had died at her hands even when all Aestari followed the Oath, before the Schism severed her people. It was the nature of kingdoms and empires that they fought regardless of race, but enslavement was evil.

As a child, she had stood along the shore of Lake Henjis and had sworn that she would look to the good of the other races as much as her own. Though the Tirnaestari had loosed her binding to the Oath when they cast her out, she'd refused to give it up herself. That choice was her own to make. But there was little she could do actively about humanity's current predicament. No other Syraestari believed as she did. The closest ones to allies were those who wanted nothing to do with humans. If the empress could be convinced to seek out the refuge, then Ninanna would fulfill both her oath to humanity and her oath to her people. She had too many enemies, though, and if she stood too strongly against slavery she'd quickly find herself marching to the executioner's block.

Ninanna awoke near dawn and, rubbing her eyes, tried also to rub away the clouds over her thoughts. After lighting her lamp, she washed her face again in the now-cold water. She was unpacking her saddlebags when Talikae entered with her breakfast. It was a mash of eggs, ham, and a thick slice of warm bread. The food was simpler than she was accustomed to in the empress' court, but still quite good. Talikae then brought her another steaming bowl of water and a linen towel. Ninanna used it to wash her face again and her hair, then carefully painted the rings of black makeup around her eyes.

Feeling a little more refreshed, she left her room and found Imeskir with the other Sword-Whisperers in the courtyard behind the palace. They were inspecting their armor and weapons. Imeskir sat on a long stone bench in the shade of a pair of oak trees. His greatsword was stretched across his lap where he checked it over with a whetstone. However, he wasn't giving his blade much attention. A cluster of a dozen women, artisans and lesser nobles alike, surrounded him. His lips were twisted into a half grin, as close to a laugh as he would allow outside the ranks of the Whisperers. Compared with the grim demeanor of the other warriors, he might as well have been roaring in merriment. But seeing Ninanna, his mirth faded. "Excuse me a moment, ladies. I have duties to attend to."

They laughed softly and, as Imeskir rose and walked toward her, they parted to let him pass. Not a few looked sharply at Ninanna, jealousy poorly masked in their gazes.

"You always find quick friends in Nahirazith," Ninanna commented.

"You'd think the scar would scare them away." Imeskir traced the red line along his cheek.

"I think that's what draws them."

"Perhaps, my Lady," he replied, glancing back at them. Facing Ninanna again, he said, "We were well lodged last night and treated courteously, though the housecarls were gruff as might be expected."

"Good."

"When will High Lord Ushtyl meet with you?"

Ninanna looked past Imeskir's shoulder to see Captain Eltirkar striding towards her. "Now, I suspect."

Perhaps sensing her unease, he said, "I'm sure you will do well. You always do."

"Thank you, Imeskir." She smiled. "And be kind to your ladies."

"I always am." He flashed her a quick grin before turning back to the waiting women.

Ninanna held her place, waiting on the captain. Arriving, he clasped his hands behind his back. "If you are ready, the high lords will meet with you now."

"I am. Thank you, Captain."

She followed him around to the front of the palace and up the wide white steps. They passed through the great outer doors, crafted from thick banded oak and etched with emblems of wave and wind. Eltirkar led the way across the wide pillared atrium and up another winding flight of stairs to the upper level and the far end of the palace. Four housecarls stood before a pair of double-doors which they opened wide at the pair's approach. As Eltirkar passed, they gave him deferential bows followed by quick glares at Ninanna. The large chamber beyond was built entirely from white stone. The only decorations were simple etchings near where the walls met the ceiling at twice the height of a normal room. The beauty of the chamber came from its wide windows that opened to the east, allowing the rising sun to flood the room with its majestic light. The only furniture in the room were two chairs with a small table between them near the windows. Tazil sat to her right and Ushtyl to the left and both nursed goblets of wine.

Eltirkar and Ninanna dropped to one knee before them and the captain said, "Lady Ninanna, my lords."

"Thank you, Captain Eltirkar. Welcome, Lady Ninanna," High Lord Ushtyl said. Eltirkar rose to his feet and moved to stand beside his high lord while Ninanna straightened and held her place. Ushtyl continued, "Your arrival last evening was unexpected. What brings you to Nahirazith?"

Ninanna suspected that was a lie. It was unlikely Tazil would've made the journey himself but for knowledge of her. Spies ran thick in the empire. "I apologize for the surprise, my Lords, I only just received my orders from the empress four days past."

Ushtyl leaned forward, steepling his fingers. "And what orders were those?"

Ninanna had long considered her response to this question and decided to draw on the full language of the court. "Her Imperial Majesty, the Empress Kayrstana wanted to impart to you both the importance to which she ascribes your upcoming mission against the wildmen tribes. She praises your efforts and wants to lend you the full support of the imperial throne."

Behind the high lords, Captain Eltirkar bristled at her words. Ninanna quirked her eyebrow, surprised at his impudence. But Ushtyl lifted his hand and Eltirkar stilled. "Why did the empress send her Edrethyn, sworn to guard her body and soul, with an escort of two full ranks of Sword-Whisperers? A simple envoy would have sufficed." He swirled the wine in his goblet contemplatively. "To my knowledge you have remained close by her side for a thousand years."

Ninanna paused. She'd anticipated this question and knew her response had to be delicate. "Only Her Imperial Majesty can speak to why I was sent. She commanded and I obeyed."

"She does not trust us," Tazil said. Ninanna turned to the second high lord as he set his wine goblet down on the table and sat back, glancing over at Ushtyl. "The empress does not trust us."

Ninanna said nothing. There was nothing she could say. Tazil's statement was true and everyone in the realm knew it. The high lords had, of necessity, enjoyed great autonomy during the migration when the Syraestari had to scatter to gather what little food there was. But now that cities had been built and farms planted the disbursement was no longer necessary and they resented Kayrstana's reassertion of her authority.

Ushtyl's eyes narrowed to slits. "Why is it that you're really here? It is more than just for praise and congratulations."

"It is, my Lords." Ninanna nodded. "Her Majesty wants it made clear that she blesses your raid and, in the interests of encouraging greater unity within the realm, she has sent me as her Hand to lead it."

"She is mad!" Captain Eltirkar burst out. "I knew she would try something like this, my Lords. Not only is the empress trying to steal your glory, she's trying to steal your entire army!"

Ninanna flinched, but not at the anger. That was to be expected. It was his impudence toward their monarch. She hadn't anticipated that. Certainly the high lords were ambitious but for one of their lieutenants to speak such open defiance was indefensible.

Ushtyl's face had tightened to a dark mask. When he spoke, his voice was soft and cold. "The empress has overstepped her authority, Lady Ninanna. Everyone involved in the raid is a citizen of Nahirazith or Raefi'ernyn. They are housecarls holding oaths to myself and High Lord Tazil. The empress is not even providing reinforcements to protect our cities while our armies march. Only the High Lord Arkesh has graciously offered to do so by drawing from his own household warriors."

"The t'Okaedrin and Pi'aernoth serve the empress," Ninanna replied, keeping her voice measured and calm. As she continued, Captain Eltirkar's face darkened even further until it nearly reached a shade of purple. The two high lords were far more restrained, but anger flared in their eyes. "They kill and are killed in her name. My Lords, it is not my desire to sound impertinent. I was given no latitude in this and bear a sealed letter from Her Majesty to show how seriously she holds this expectation." Reaching into the satchel at her side, Ninanna drew out the document. Neither of the lords appeared inclined to take it, so she stepped forward and set it on the table between them.

"My Lords," Eltirkar stepped forward. "This was to be my command. Captain Nethzir and I haven't spent all our labors only to have this false-Syraestari, this human-lover, steal away our glory and yours."

Ushtyl kept his eyes on Ninanna and when he spoke, his words were cold. “You do not flinch from these accusations, Lady.”

“I am quite familiar with what others say about me,” Ninanna replied. “But they are always just words, intended to draw me to anger. I will not become angry. I know who and what I am regardless of what others might claim. I know where my oaths have been given and to whom they have been held for twice the years that either of you have lived. My blood and my honor remain untarnished.”

“Perhaps,” Ushtyl said, his tone skeptical. “But that doesn’t change the fact that the empress has no authority to give that order. This isn’t her army, but mine. Yes, the humans are sworn to her, but they are entrusted to me. We don’t need you. Nor do we need her help in building bonds between high lords.”

Ninanna sighed. “I regret, Lord Ushtyl, that I cannot accept that answer. These commands come from my liege and from yours. Both of us have the duty to obey. I regret that I will not be silenced on this, not even if you cast me into prison.”

“Perhaps she should be imprisoned!” Eltirkar cried.

“Will you jail my Sword-Whisperers along with me?” Ninanna asked, gaze flickering to Eltirkar. “They, too, hold obedience to the empress. I know the fondness the people of Nahirazith hold for the Sword-Whisperers. Such an act will raise an outcry. Remember, those who accompany me were the very ones who held the battle lines at Dahiraetin, protecting your people against the onrushing horde.”

"You're blade was not drawn at Dahiraetin," Ushtyl said, eyes narrowing.

"The same can't be said for my second, Imeskir. It was his rank that stood at the apex of the storm and did not break. Your people remember him still and the price that was paid." She paused, then added, "I apologize for the firmness of my reply, but it is necessary. It is a duty that I am oath-bound to perform."

"Throw her in prison, my Lords," Eltirkar snapped, "Those consequences will be nothing compared with giving her control."

"No." Tazil's firm, yet quiet tone stilled the angry captain. Tazil turned to look at Ushtyl. "Still, I'm troubled. Perhaps it would be better to stop the raid rather than succumb to this."

Ushtyl shook his head, but said nothing.

"I have an assurance to give that might make your decision easier," Ninanna said. "As commander, I have no intention of altering your plans. I know both Captain Eltirkar and Captain Nethzir's reputations on these matters. I won't be a pawn though. If there is a part that needs changing, I will give that order, but I agree to consult with the captains on it first. Furthermore, I will take no credit for the outcome. All glory will go to you and your warriors."

Ushtyl looked up at her, his eyes measuring. "Is this from the empress?"

"No, she gave no instructions on how I run my command. This is from me, on my honor."

"Excuse us, a moment, Lady Ninanna," Ushtyl said.

She nodded and withdrew to the back of the room. As she did, her eyes met Eltirkar's. His gaze still held the full venom of his fury. That he was so unrestrained was troubling. Ushtyl and Tazil had rejected his advice, but they hadn't silenced words bordering on open rebellion. As for the high lords, it was evident that they had shifted from anger to calculation. They were older, more mature and measured than the captain. She saw doubt in Tazil's eyes. That high lord disliked acting quickly on anything. Clearly he wanted more time to consider, but from Ushtyl's firm posture, it was obvious he'd already decided. As she had anticipated before arriving, if Ushtyl decided, Tazil would follow.

She returned at Ushtyl's summoning wave. "If you will swear as you have promised, we will allow you command of the army," Ushtyl said.

Ninanna nodded. "I swear I do not intend to alter anything of what has been planned and will do so only after conferring with Captain Eltirkar or Nethzir. I swear that all glory and honor for this raid belongs to the High Lords Ushtyl and Tazil and to the people of Nahirazith and Raefi'ernyn."

"Then it is done," Ushtyl said. "You may leave us."

Ninanna bowed again and withdrew, glad that this time she was not accompanied by Eltirkar. She might have to watch her back with that one. No lord or lady had been assassinated since the onset of the Cataclysm, but that didn't make it impossible.

She found Imeskir, seated on the bench where she'd left him. The group of Syraestari women around him had nearly doubled in size and they hung on every word he spoke.

"They were all around us now," Imeskir was saying. "Our lines to the left and to the right had broken, but we fought on, back to back, just five of us still alive and all alone. There was nothing else that we could do. To flee was to be run down and besides, we didn't know if our people were safe. As long as we stood, the enemy had to face us. And so we fought by blade and by voice. The human flood that had precipitated the battle was gone now, revealing what had given them their maddened ferocity. Troglyds in the tens of thousands flooded out of the mountains, driving all peoples before them in a panic. The troglyds were not affected by the fear we can pour out in waves of sorcery. Their minds are too feeble and filled with a lust for killing that cannot be sated. But we could still strengthen ourselves and speed our blades. The swords whisked and cut, a wall of hardened steel that drove the monsters back. Their corpses piled around us, the ground thick with the black sludge that is their blood. We had fought so long that the flesh of some of their dead had already begun to slough away, returning to the mountain ash from which Cydion had formed them in ancient days. Dust clouds whirled around me and I could see no more than a few dozen paces, but everywhere I looked the battlefield teemed with the fell creatures.

"I confess," he paused, "that the thought entered my mind that this must have been what the battles of the Great War had been like. Bleak and without hope. My brothers to the left and to my right had already fallen. I could see that one still moved feebly from grievous wounds. I wished

I could at least have ended his misery, if not healed him, but there was no respite.

"Even with our chants we were weakening. Stumbling over a troglyd body, I was too slow and took the long slash you see upon my face. Blood poured into my eyes half-blinding me. I took a cut in my upper leg and another across my left wrist. Only able to wield my blade one-handed and weakened from loss of blood, I knew my end had come. Three of us remained and my two companions were in a worse way than I. So I prayed to His Highest Above for a quick death."

A murmured gasp ran through the crowd. They had heard the story many times before, but hung on every word. The woman sitting next to him, perhaps five hundred years in age, leaned forward to rest her hand gently on his wrist. She was attractive, with red-brown hair, and clothed in a fine green linen robe, but if Imeskir noticed the touch, he gave no sign. His eyes had a faraway look as he continued, "But then, the troglyds reeled back. Three figures emerged from the haze. They were Sword-Whisperers, too, but fresh and at the height of their power while we and even the troglyds were exhausted. They carved a path to us and one of them shouted that our people were safe.

"None of us could run and we could barely walk. So we stumbled back under the protection of our kindred. It was a sight to behold, the likes of which I cannot tell you. Their helms were drawn closed and my mind addled, so I didn't know them at the time. I only learned the names of Dyrnin and Aetinar afterwards. I honor their memory, for they fell that we might live. Who would ever pay the price of one life for one? I have often wondered that such blood could be exchanged so easily. For why did I deserve to live while both of them had died?"

"What of the third warrior?" the woman seated beside him asked.

A sad smile formed on Imeskir's lips as he turned to face her. "That is why I tell this tale, for I long to know the ending. He was a storm of fury and darkness. Sometimes I wonder if that warrior alone could have held back the entire horde. But as for who he was, I cannot say. As soon as we reached the main Syraestari lines, I collapsed. After I healed, I asked among my companions who it had been, but none knew. Sometimes I wonder if the rescue had been a dream. Yet what then of Dyrnin and Aetinar? Their sacrifice was no illusion and I will not dishonor them by even imagining it as such."

He let out a deep sigh and bowed his head a moment. But when he raised it again, his characteristic grin, so unlike the other Sword-Whisperers, had returned. "Do not mourn for me, my friends, for I lived. Mourn those who did not." Looking up, he saw Ninanna waiting and said, "Please excuse me, I must be about my duties. But thank you for listening to my tale."

They murmured softly as he stepped between them. He bowed slightly to Ninanna and then the pair turned together to walk across the courtyard. "Why do you persist on telling that story?" Ninanna asked. "I know it gives you nightmares."

"With each telling I feel I get closer to knowing those eyes that stared at me through that helm."

"But you still don't know?"

His laugh was tinged with sadness. "If I did, Lady Ninanna, there would no longer be a need for me to recount it. No, I do not know. Sometimes I even imagine it was you." He glanced at her out of the corner of his eye, but when she said nothing, he continued, "I know that would be impossible. You were with the empress. It has happened to me before. I spend too much time around one person or another and start seeing their face behind that helm. So I will continue telling my tale and one day I will discover the truth."

"I wish you'd allow yourself some peace. Is it really worth the nightmares?"

"It is. I have to know." He sighed, then looked at her. "But please, enough about me. What about the meeting? Did it go well?"

"I succeeded, but I'm not sure if it went well."

High Lord Ushtyl stared out the broad windows into the small garden below. The sun had risen to half its height to fill the room and courtyard with its warm rays.

"I should have anticipated this," High Lord Tazil said beside him, "but I did not. Every time I think I've come to understand the empress, she surprises me again."

"Yes, she is clever," Ushtyl said, contemplatively. He had known of Ninanna's coming weeks ago. It had been his recommendation on his last secret visit to the empress. Ninanna was just the first step of breaking the high lords to

Kayrstana's will. Once that was done, he would become the prince consort. A single step from the imperial throne itself.

"Will Ninanna's word be enough?" Tazil asked, half to himself.

"She always keeps her oaths," Ushtyl replied. "That, at least, I cannot say against her."

"It's all about perceptions. We must make it clear that Ninanna is a figurehead. If the people know the campaign came from us, then the triumph might yet remain ours."

"For now."

Tazil looked at him sharply. "You think this move is but the beginning, then?"

Ushtyl shook his head. "Not the beginning, and definitely not the end. The empress seeks to consolidate imperial power at the price of our noble rights. She will attack and attack until every high lord is brought fully to heel."

"Hammer of Fenr," Tazil cursed. "You're right, of course. We must act together to preserve what we have earned through blood and tears before she devours us one by one."

"High Lord Tyrnis and High Lady Jesaelyn have always been devoted to her."

"But not the others. Together we are strong enough." Tazil shook his head. "Of course that means we need to have faith in each other and not look each to our own cities."

Ushtyl turned to the other high lord, weighing him with his eyes. Tazil was intelligent and could see distant ends, but he sometimes missed what lay just in front of him. "Do you think Sizras and Zaerina would join us? They both want to cast aside our dominion and flee for a pittance of a refuge."

"In this I think they would," Tazil said. "I'm on friendly enough terms with High Lord Sizras, and High Lady Zaerina usually follows his lead."

Just like Tazil followed Ushtyl's lead, though he did not see it. Ushtyl smiled. "Reach out to them, then, and I will contact Arkesh and Ovirkar. We should meet after the raid marches north."

"A just plan," Tazil replied, excitement tinging his voice. The high lord was a passionate man, once he found a path to follow. "If the two of us work together, we can show the others that they can, too. I will ask Aerharyndra to assist with the messages. My wife is better at delicate words than I am."

"Then we are agreed."

"Yes." Tazil looked toward the door, a twinge of annoyance touching his face. "Now that the issue with Lady Ninanna is resolved and we've decided on this course, I must return to Raefi'ernyn. My son has already begun the preparations for the raid, but there is still much to do."

"Carry my greetings to your wife and Captain Nethzir," Ushtyl replied.

"I will, thank you."

As Tazil left, Eltirkar stepped into the room and closed the door behind him.

"You did well, Captain Eltirkar."

"Thank you for saying so, my Lord, even though I failed."

"You did not fail. You proved what I already suspected to be true. Lady Ninanna cannot be goaded by slander against the empress or by attacks on her own character."

"It will make her difficult to control."

"She is uncontrollable, but not invulnerable," Ushtyl replied, turning to look out the window again.

"Was there anything else, my Lord?"

"No, Captain, thank you."

Ushtyl's gaze dropped to the garden below as Eltirkar withdrew again. The flowers had lifted fully and opened their faces to the sunlight. So it would be for the Syraestari. A smile found its way to his lips. There were so many possibilities. So many opportunities and he would seize each one. First the Scions destroyed, then the high lords mustered. He had to act quickly to hold their unity long enough before those dissenting against the empire broke away. There were two battles to resolve, dominion and power, and the t'Okaedrin lay at the heart of it. As did Ninanna, for now. With her on the campaign, the high lords would be easier to control in their anger. Even better, with her gone, she could no longer poison the ears of the empress with words against the empire. He had hated her since she tried to stop his acceptance into the Sword-Whisperers. Now, if he balanced everything right, he would destroy her.

CHAPTER 9
Duty

"There is no race more peculiar than humanity. The short years of their lives leave them brash and relentless. I have seen honor in a human youth, greater even than the most venerable of my Aestarin people. But I have seen evil within them, too, the depths of which would make even the soul of Siona, tyrant of the Ie'dhae, appear radiant."

—Tayrjeth of Dydinsenon

Vistus ducked as the wooden sword whistled past his ear. He rose from his crouch, striking out with his own blade. Hirnid broke the attack on his shield, but the blow staggered him and he stumbled back. Vistus struck again, a little lower. Hirnid ducked his shield to block and withdrew another step. Vistus followed, swinging high, but as his blade fell, Hirnid lunged forward and broke the attack mid-swing. Surprised, Vistus stumbled back as his brother charged, punching outward with his shield. Vistus barely deflected the blow and brought his blade up to counter. A hardened point pressed against the scaled armor of his chest. Vistus looked down to see Hirnid's sword there. Had it been an iron blade, it would have punched through, opening his stomach, no matter the armor.

Vistus lowered his sword and shield. "A triumph to you, brother."

Hirnid smiled. "I win again. Did those rebels soften you in the few days you were with them?"

"If Hirnid is too much for you, I can always step in!" Bridionis called from nearby. His arm still in a sling, Bridionis could do little during the morning drill but watch.

Vistus laughed. "I don't think I'm that far gone."

Around them, the rest of their brothers sparred. The practice field echoed with the dull thuds of wooden blade striking blade. Further away, another t'Okaedrin family lifted heavy stones over their heads while a third practiced archery and throwing spears. A low-hanging cloud of dust marked a fourth family running circles around the muster field in full armor.

Though the sun was but newly above the horizon, Vistus was already bathed in sweat. He wiped a gloved hand across his brow, enjoying the cool breeze as it brushed against his face. The sky was clear, promising another bright summer day, though the nearest of the Timnar Mountains still had a brooding look where a thin line of smoke trickled from its peak. Vistus pulled his gaze away from it, not liking to think about the earthquakes. His nightmares had redoubled in the days since their return from the raid. It was a mark of shame that the torments of childhood had come to him again. He could only pray that his brothers didn't notice his nighttime thrashing.

"Brothers!" Nalsuntha's shout rang out across the yard. Vistus turned to see their eldest striding toward them. "Gather to me."

The sparring t'Okaedrin stopped immediately and ran over. Those in front knelt on one knee while the rest, Vistus, Hirnid, and Bridionis included, stood in a half circle behind. Their steamy breath curled up through the still cool morning air as heat rose from their shoulders.

Nalsuntha's green eyes gleamed in the light and a wide smile stretched across his face as he looked at each of them in turn. "I have great news, brothers. High Lord Tazil was pleased by the success of our last raid."

"Honor to the Empress!" the brothers shouted. Bridionis slapped Vistus on the back and he grinned back.

When they had fallen silent, Nalsuntha continued, "High Lord Tazil is proud of the discipline and prowess of his t'Okaedrin and word our family has reached his ears. Even now he prepares a campaign larger than any we've seen. We will not face the Scion rebels, this time, but the wildmen in the foothills east of the Timnar Mountains. In a few days' time, a host of thirty-five t'Okaedrin and seven Pi'aernoth families will march northward."

A gasp passed through the listening brothers. Normally, a dozen families at most marched and Nahirazith only had twenty-five families of adult t'Okaedrin. "Where are all the families coming from?" Arcomin asked.

"High Lord Ushtyl from Nahirazith is committing many of his families as well," Nalsuntha answered. He crossed his arms. "Our first task will be to establish an outpost in the woodlands. From there, we will attack as many villages as we can before the wildmen become aware of us. Our goal is to take prisoners. The adults will join the Kalilaer and the young will be trained as t'Okaedrin and Pi'aernoth."

Vistus' smile broadened. It was good to be part of the family again, a warrior instead of a spy. This was simpler. Better.

"Your morning training is over," Nalsuntha said. "You will spend the remainder of the day checking your weapons and armor. See the smiths if need be. I want everything in perfect order by the setting of the sun. Honor to the Empress!"

"Honor to the Empress!" the brothers echoed.

"Vistus, follow me."

"Yes, Eldest," Vistus answered, falling in beside Nalsuntha as he strode back across the practice field. Vistus looked at his eldest, wondering why he was being singled out. He eyed the wooden poles where the lashings took place and suppressed a shudder. Why did his mind always move towards toward guilt? Nalsuntha could just as easily called him for something good. Vistus suddenly felt very aware of the Scion gemstone around his neck.

But Nalsuntha marched past the lashing posts without a glance and out of the t'Okaedrin encampment. To Vistus' surprise, they followed the path up toward Raefi'ernyn itself. The great stone walls rose above them.

Passing down the streets this time was just as mesmerizing as the first. It took all of Vistus' resolve not to stare at the wonders of the city. At the tall columned buildings, the wide tree-lined thoroughfares, or the elegant Syraestari striding along them.

As before, they skirted the main entrance of the palace and headed toward the stables. In a nearby courtyard, twenty Syraestari warriors drilled. Though he had never seen one before, their greatswords and black robes marked them as Sword-Whisperers. The t'Okaedrins' pace slowed as they became mesmerized by the practice. Each of warriors moved with a swiftness unfettered by the size of their blades that Vistus could only envy. Their weapons connected and clashed in a rhythm that could almost be called a song. Watching them made him feel like his own drills with the t'Okaedrin were more akin to little boys clumsily trying to beat each other with sticks.

Nalsuntha shook himself as one breaking free of a dream and Vistus forced himself to do likewise. He followed his eldest brother into the palace. They returned to the same room as before.

When the Pi'aernoth opened the door for them, Vistus swallowed a lump rising in his throat. On the far side of the chamber, his father stood before High Lord Tazil, Captain Nethzir, and a Syraestari woman. The high lord was dressed in a deep green robe embroidered with black lines. His gold necklace was nearly a hand's width wide, embossed with at least five red stones each the size of Vistus' thumb. Captain Nethzir wore armor so polished that it gleamed in the light of the room. The woman he did not know. She was taller than the two men, yet willow thin. Her raven black hair hung loose, with long locks curving across each side of her face, nearly hiding her sharp blue eyes. Her eye paint looked like talons and mimicked her hair, sweeping along the ear then arcing across the cheeks toward her nose. Yet she wore the simplest gray robes Vistus had ever seen on a Syraestari. A single silver ring encircled the middle finger of her left hand.

"Rise, t'Okaedrin," High Lord Tazil said. His voice was soft, like a whisper of wind, but heavy with self-assurance and power.

Vistus stood beside Nalsuntha and kept his eyes respectfully averted away from the high lord's face. Just like the last time, his heart thundered in his chest. Not once, but twice he had been called before his master, last time with a task and this time in triumph.

He felt the high lord's gaze upon him. "You are named Vistus, yes?"

"I am, my Lord."

"You may raise your head, Okaidir," Lord Tazil said, his tone gentle but overpowering. Vistus lifted his eyes to meet his master's. They were of a rich brown hue that soaked in the flickering torchlight. In that gaze he saw the knowledge of centuries. "I have been told of the success of your task."

"Thank you, my Lord," Vistus replied, pleased that his voice didn't tremble.

"We have done what has never been done before. A camp of the rebels was found and destroyed. This wouldn't have been possible without you. You are an honor to your family." Tazil raised his hand, palm open and up. "Captain Nethzir." The armored Syraestari at his side nodded and, extending his hand, set a thin golden ring in Tazil's hand. "Because you have brought honor in a way that no t'Okaedrin has since the beginning of their service, you shall be rewarded as uniquely. Give me your hand."

Swallowing to fight his racing heart, Vistus lifted his right hand and the high lord slipped the band onto his middle finger. "Thank you, my Lord."

"I've also spoken with your father. We are all impressed with your work and you're well on your way to being placed over a family of your own."

Vistus' heart thundered in his chest. "Thank you, my Lord," he said, realizing his voice was breathless.

"Now, to the task at hand," Tazil's tone became more abrupt. "You have already been told of our next raid against the wildmen?"

"I have, my Lord," Vistus replied.

"The attack is only the first step of our plan. We will have need to call upon your unique skills again." Tazil paused a moment, before continuing, "You might say that your previous task was a test to see what you're capable of. And you have proven to be very capable indeed."

Vistus kept silent, unsure if he could speak, as joy merged with sudden apprehension.

"You won't be joining your brothers in the raid," Tazil said. "Your battle will be in the greater war that follows. When the captives are brought in from the wildmen villages, you will join them in the guise of a new prisoner yourself. You will be brought back to work alongside them in the Kalilaer camp. Not here, but the camp at High Lord Ushtyl's city of Nahirazith. There is too much risk that a Kalilaer in the Raefi'ernyn settlement might recognize you."

"My Lord..." the whisper escaped Vistus' lips before he could stop it.

"Yes?" High Lord Tazil's brows narrowed.

Vistus shrank beneath those piercing brown eyes and regretted his weaknesses. He had allowed himself to speak when he should have held his tongue. Because he wanted to stay with Elestis, because he wanted to fight alongside his brothers, because he was afraid of all the torments of last time, of Vitarria and Parvik. "Forgive me, Lord, I spoke out of surprise and it is to my shame. I live to serve the empress. I die to honor her."

A sharp gleam entered Tazil's eyes, but when he spoke his voice was surprisingly gentle. "Anyone, man or Syraestari, may be taught to swing a sword. But the truly great learn to wield other weapons, as you have. And worry not." His lips slipped upward into a smile that didn't quite reach his eyes. "Your brothers will be sent to Nahirazith to watch over you. Unfortunately, you must serve as a Kalilaer for an unknown period of time. It is necessary to establish you as one of them. Slipping you into a group of fleeing Kalilaer as we did before worked for that short task, but your role now is far more dangerous. When the Scions of the Fallen Tree attack next, you will flee with the other Kalilaer and then your true mission will begin. Do you understand me so far?"

"Yes, my Lord."

"You are to live among the rebels and become fully one of them." A frown crossed his face as Tazil continued, "Unfortunately, with the Scion chieftain's death, we know nothing more than you have told us. Not your fault, of course, but unfortunate nevertheless. We don't know how many camps there are, nor how they communicate with each other. You are to learn how they do this and locate as many camps as possible. Identify who their leaders are. Once that task is complete, you will signal your brothers. Then the t'Okaedrin will descend on your camp to destroy them and bring you home. Do you understand?"

"Yes, my Lord," Vistus replied. Despite his apprehension, he couldn't deny the thrill of excitement that stirred within him at the challenge he was to face. "How will I signal my brothers?"

"A good question," Tazil said and turned to the Syraestari woman standing beside him. "Lady Medreuneth, will you explain please."

"Very well," she replied. Her voice was sharp and clipped. Vistus wondered at her authority that she didn't name High Lord Tazil by his title. She looked over at the Syraestari warrior. "Nethzir, please assist me."

"Yes, Lady." He strode to the table at the side of the room. When he returned, he carried a shallow bowl half filled with water.

"You have the necklace you were given last time?" Lady Medreuneth said, turning to Vistus. He had to fight not to shrink from her piercing gaze. Yet as she spoke, he sensed her focus was far away, as if contemplating knowledge he would have to study ten lifetimes to even begin to comprehend.

"Yes, my Lady," Vistus replied, pulling the black stone from around his neck. He was glad he'd decided against stringing it on the same leather loop as the pale gem he had taken from Vitarria's body.

"Good." She inspected the stone, but didn't take it. "You were not instructed on the nature of the Sapaupan Kaupet before. It isn't wise for the ignorant to dabble even on the edges of sorcery. But this time, unfortunately, you must be told. Attend." She reached into the folds of her robe and pulled out a second black stone, identical to Vistus' save that it had no hole for a necklace. "These two stones have been attuned with the raw power of the Flesh of Isfalinis. With the earth, as shaped by Fenr and Itesa. The stones were once one, but have become two while remaining one." Lady Medreuneth didn't appear to perceive his confused look as she reached back into her robe. She pulled out a wide leaf, rounded on one end and pointed on the other. She carefully lowered it into the bowl that Nethzir held so that it floated gently upon the surface of the water. Once the leaf steadied, she set the second stone to rest gently upon it. As soon as her hand moved away, the leaf turned to point at Vistus. "Move your stone back and forth," she instructed.

Vistus did as he was told and watched, mesmerized, as the leaf turned wherever he held it.

"As long as you keep that stone, we will be able to find you, just as we did before," High Lord Tazil said. "Scouts will follow you, but at a distance to be certain they aren't discovered. Once they're sure of the location of the Scion camp, they will withdraw. This time we will only attack when you call. After you've gathered all of the information you can, but not before, you are to destroy the stone."

"How, my Lord?" Vistus asked, staring at the black object. It was cool in his hand and its edges seemed to draw in the torchlight causing it to shimmer faintly.

Lady Medreuneth answered him. "Breaking one of the Sapaupan Kaupet severs the bond with its other half. The t'Okaedrin will attack the place it was destroyed. If it is cast into the fire, the stone will burn like wood. But be careful. It will burn quickly, but also brighter than normal flame and hotter too. It may be safer to crush it. The stone is hard, but not so hard as normal rock. It can be shattered between two rocks."

"Once you destroy the Sapaupan Kaupet, the attack will happen within two days," Lord Tazil said. "Do you understand everything we've told you?"

"Yes, my Lord."

"You have already honored the t'Okaedrin. Serve well in this and you will be more honored than any brethren who have come before. I and High Lord Ushtyl have placed a great deal of trust in you. Find everything you can about these Scions of the Fallen Tree, their camps, their leaders, and their plans." High Lord Tazil's eyes hardened. "Do not panic and call for rescue too soon. You must learn all you can or I will be greatly displeased. What is the greatest honor?"

"There is no greater honor than to die in the name of the Empress," Vistus recited.

"Indeed." Lord Tazil looked at Dalric first, then Nalsuntha. "Have you anything to add?"

"No, my Lord," they both replied.

"Good. Okaidir Vistus, you are dismissed. You will do well."

"Thank you, my Lord." Vistus bowed low then backed away. At the door, he turned, opened it, and stepped into the outer hall.

He walked down the corridor in a daze, thumbing the golden band encircling his finger. The weight of it felt odd on his hand. He was supposed to be done with the rebels, except where he met them at the edge of a sword. He was supposed to be home with his brothers, with Elestis. But at the same time, eagerness welled within him. No t'Okaedrin had ever faced such a challenge. When he triumphed in this, he would be the greatest brother who had ever lived. He would win the hand of Elestis for certain and they would become parents of their own t'Okaedrin family. No one could deny him!

His thoughts sobered as he reached up to touch the gemstone hidden beneath his shirt next to the Sapaupan Kaupet. When he destroyed these Scions, he would prove to himself that he really was a man, that he really was t'Okaedrin. He would banish the ghosts of Vitarria and Parvik forever.

Stepping through the outer door of the palace, he was so focused on his thoughts that he almost forgot to bow before the Syraestari guard. He did so in a clumsy stumble. Walking through the streets of Raefi'ernyn and then past the outer gates toward the t'Okaedrin camp, he focused on maintaining his decorum despite the excitement surging within him. He reached up to touch his chin. He'd have to begin growing a new beard. That was unfortunate. It itched horribly and made him feel filthy and crude, just like the Scions were.

Outside the city, he followed the path down the bluff. A strong ocean breeze rushed northward from the radiant blue waters to his left, full of life and promise. Nearing the camp, he saw a family of Pi'aernoth practicing their archery against the hillside. Elestis was among them. Casting aside decorum, he ran to her and, flinging his arms about her, lifted her in full embrace.

"Vistus!" She cried, breathless as he set her down. Her lips firmed and she pushed away, eyeing her family.

He could feel their gaze upon him, but didn't care. They were not Syraestari, it didn't matter so much what they thought. "I'm going in again, Elestis!"

"In? I don't understand."

"Back to the Scions. This time I'm going to destroy them all!"

Her eyes did not light up like he'd expected. "You were supposed to remain here with us."

"Just one more time, then we will be together."

"But I thought you were done with infiltrating."

"They need me..."

"How long will you be gone this time?"

"I don't know. It will be longer, for certain."

Elestis eyed him uncertainly. "Longer, how much longer?"

"I'm not sure, maybe months?"

"Months!"

"I know it's a long time, but this is better. They all-but promised me a family when I returned. We can be wed."

Rather than join his excitement, she sighed and his heart lurched. "What is it, Elestis?"

"I don't know, Vistus. It will be so long. Who knows what could happen between now and then. Being among Scions that long is far more dangerous than last time."

"I'll be careful. I know what to expect this time."

"But if they discover you, you'll die."

"They won't and you and my brothers will always be nearby."

"I..." she began to say, but her mother's shout interrupted her. "Elestis! Enough talking with that Okaidir. There will be time for that another day."

Elestis' eyes fell. "I have to go, Vistus, we'll talk later." She turned and walked back to the waiting Pi'aernoth.

Vistus watched her go, his excitement broken. In his mind he ran all the words he'd said through his mind. He could have explained himself so much better. If only he'd thought it through, first. But all he could see was Elestis' crestfallen face. With a sigh, he turned away.

Night lay across the land. Raefi'ernyn rose a looming shadow to blot out half the starlit sky. All was still but the softest rustling of the breeze rippling faintly through the grasses and the more distant rush of water driving against the shore. Reigliff moved silently through the darkest shadows along the side of the t'Okaedrin barracks.

Ahead, he heard the faint chink of mail as one of the two human guards shifted his position. The t'Okaedrin were alert and well trained, but not skilled enough for a Shadow-Servant. They stood near the outer fence rather than the door, doubtless under the false belief that no one could enter the compound without passing through the gate. But over the millennia, he had slipped into many places more heavily guarded than this. He tried the door and found it unlocked. A little bit of oil at each of the hinges ensured it opened smoothly and silently. Sorcery might have served just as well, but he believed in many tools.

The hallway beyond lay in deep darkness. The torches had been doused and the only illumination came from starlight filtering through a few tiny windows. It was too easy. Reigliff smiled faintly. Most of the times he'd come closest to death had felt easy, too. Creeping down the corridor, he passed by a long row of open doorways, both to the right and to the left. Beyond each, deep breaths and soft snores betrayed the presence of sleepers within.

Near the end of the hall, he paused and peered into one of the rooms. It was like any of the others, with a score of beds, half on either side of a central walkway. He listened carefully for several long minutes, his sensitive ears picking out each individual sound and straining to hear any noise that did not fit. To hear anything that suggested an Okaidir was awake. Satisfied, he stepped inside. He edged down the middle of the room, careful that no footfall caused a floorboard to creak. He scanned each resting face in turn until he found the one he sought midway down on the left side.

By appearances, there was nothing to set this human apart from any of the others. He appeared no different than any of the thousand or more t'Okaedrin who led similar lives. The man's hair was unkempt, his face thin but not gaunt, the arms lying above the blankets strong and muscled.

After a long moment staring down on him, Reigliff leapt upward with gloved hands extended. He easily caught hold of one of the ceiling's crossbeams and silently pulled himself up to perch upon it. If he was going to spend any time in a room, he preferred to be up near the ceiling. He was less likely to be observed where shadows lay heaviest and, if he was, the superior height gave him the advantage when he attacked or when he fled.

He stared down at the Okaidir named Vistus and pondered.

His meeting with Ninanna had been as successful as he'd expected, if not all he had hoped. But he had come to learn that hope was a myth. All chances were sculpted. After her meeting with the high lords, he had followed Tazil back to Raefi'ernyn. In the broader picture, Tazil was not normally a man he would be overly concerned with. Ambitious but not relentless, he was a family man. His wife was a good influence upon him, tempering both his impulses and his hesitations. His son was young still, but a warrior showing promise both in courage and in circumspection. But after Dahiraetin, Tazil had proposed abandoning the search for a land of their own in favor of founding an empire. Because

Ushtyl had taken charge of the idea, most thought he was the source, but Reigliff remembered clearly. Tazil had also been the founder of the t'Okaedrin. And now he was at the center of the resistance to Empress Kayrstana's consolidation of power. Yes, answers lay with Tazil. But Reigliff did not even know the question.

Not long after his arrival home, Tazil had met with the human sleeping below. An infiltrator on a second mission to destroy the Scions. He should have anticipated such a bold scheme from the High Lord of Raefi'ernyn. Reigliff's own interference as the "Shadow of Zaris" had transformed the Scions into a greater danger, spurring a response. Now Ushtyl and Tazil needed the Scions destroyed to secure their empire, just as much as Reigliff needed the Scions to remain a relentless threat.

Using humans to fight the humans. That had been the mad inspiration of the t'Okaedrin, as short-sighted as it was brilliant. With human warriors, there was no reason to risk Syraestari lives. With human slaves, there was no reason to waste Syraestari talents on the mundane. But with no purpose to give his people focus, decay could be the only result, until the mass of human slaves bred beyond all ability to control them. They would be full of knowledge and resentment until their anger inevitably burst into a sudden flame that consumed his people.

And this human lay at the center of the high lords' plan. Reigliff had long believed in singular moments that changed fate. Such as that moment when Ainii, the Aestari Shaper, was found murdered. That singular event had shattered the

Aestarin race beyond all hope of reconciliation, bathing both sides in the blood of the Schism. Or the moment at the close of the Great War when all the Shadow-Servants, working in concert with their greatest Sorcerers, had shattered the Syra-estari bondage to Cydion. In his heart, Reigliff sensed that another moment had arrived.

But why this man? Though Vistus appeared unremarkable, there was a sense about him Reigliff couldn't quite name. It was something in his manner, in his voice, that suggested doubt and hidden torment. Not just the simple questions that all thinking creatures faced, but a haunting. He couldn't identify it any more closely than that, but had long since learned to trust his instincts.

Beneath him, Vistus stirred uneasily in his sleep. His arms flailed gently, as if struggling dully against some dark nightmare. He mumbled wordlessly as his head shook back and forth. Then Vistus lay still, his body tense, and a single clear word slipped between his lips. "Ae'irpiva..."

Reigliff lurched back, almost losing his grip on the cross-beam. He clung to it with clenched hands as his heart raced. It was impossible. No human could know that word, least of all a t'Okaedrin!

A Word of Power.

As ancient as the shaping of the world, a word which harnessed the raw energy of creation, giving command to Isfalinis' breath. Spoken in a dream, without understanding, it had had no effect, yet Reigliff trembled still. How was it possible for Vistus to know such a word? There had been no human sorcerer in centuries!

Could this human be a Siharrin – one of those few souls gifted by His Highest Above with an instinctive grasp of sorcery? If such power lay within Vistus' grasp, then death and destruction truly would follow in his wake.

Reigliff's hand slipped down to one of the knives at his belt. This threat was greater than the war between empire and refuge, greater than the squabbling of the empress with her high lords. Vistus could unleash a slaughter greater than Dahiraetin and summon forth grim echoes of the Cataclysm itself.

But as his blade slipped free of its sheath, Reigliff hesitated. Vaenna's Prophecy. Wonder filled him as he silently mouthed the prophetic words, "A voice to rise beside the sea, in wind and wrath from calumny."

Was this him? A sorcerer capable of harnessing the wind itself? A t'Okaedrin whose entire life was built upon lies taught by his masters. Just as importantly, were Vaenna's words an encouragement or a warning?

Reigliff looked down upon Vistus and frowned. In sleep, the human looked as harmless and weak as all of his kind. Hardly a threat even with a sword in his hand. An illusion, perhaps of Reigliff's own making.

He pushed the knife back into its sheath, praying he had made the right decision.

A fine layer of dust swirled around Vistus' boots as he approached a Kalilaer Camp. It was one of dozens below

Raefi'ernyn, each of which performed a single task. Large open spaces separated the camps of the settlement so it was almost impossible for malcontents to escape without being noticed.

This particular camp was devoted to making fabric. It had several buildings in addition to the barracks where the Kalilaer were secured each night to keep them safe from the predations of the Scions. Normally when it was his task to watch over the camps, Vistus had passed through them little mindful of what the Kalilaer were doing. It was their work, not his, and never before had it held meaning for him. But now, he lingered, curious and apprehensive.

In one of the buildings, walled on three sides and open on one, he watched a handful of men and women working with flax. They ran hands and combs through the rough fibers, tearing at them. At the next, Kalilaer fed the prepared flax through a series of rapidly spinning wheels. In the last building, he could hardly understand what was being done. Linen thread was passed back and forth through a wooden contraption using a device that looked almost like a double-headed wood spear point. It made no sense except, on the end closest to the toiling Kalilaer, a square of fabric gradually took shape. He shook his head. If he had to infiltrate here, he didn't know what he would do.

He turned to his Hirnid, standing beside him, and saw a wide grin on his face. No doubt his brother anticipated his thoughts. Growling under his breath, Vistus stormed through the camp. One of the Kalilaer, walking between two of the buildings, dropped down to her knees as he passed, but he paid her no notice.

They didn't speak until they were outside of the camp, then Hirnid put his arm companionably around Vistus' shoulder. He chuckled. "I think I will enjoy watching you work a loom."

A loom? Is that what that strange device was called? "Toil first, but honor later. I think it is you who will be jealous of me, brother."

Hirnid grinned. "Not I. Others maybe."

Vistus believed him. Hirnid was a good brother. Not so close a friend as Bridionis, but a good man nevertheless. He was faithful and stalwart, but would never be an eldest or a father. He was too much of a follower and not enough of a leader. "Come on. Let's finish our patrol of the other camps. I may have to join them soon, but that doesn't mean I want to linger here now."

But as he passed through the potters, the woodworkers, the smelters, and the farmers, he felt a measure of dread. None of it was work for a t'Okaedrin. It was honorable toil, he told himself. Kalilaer were good people living as they ought. Not all were content, but that was the poison of their old wildmen ways and the Scions that tempted them. Once all humans were firmly under the guidance of the Syraestari, such corruptions would end.

None of that really helped. He didn't want to be Kalilaer. He didn't want to be away from his family. But he was an obedient t'Okaedrin so he would and he would do it well. Better get it over with, though. He found himself looking forward to their departure.

CHAPTER 10
Chained

"Highest Above, we have lost our way. Our fathers have been consumed by fire, our wives drowned in the deeps, our children swallowed up in the earth. The Lothyn assail us from the right and the Iengian from the left. Give back to us the knowledge of iron. Remind us of what it was to be a people with a homeland. Return to us the words that pull down fire from the sky and drive back the storm. Forget us not in this time of woe."

—Lament of Tentifar, High-Priest to the Isyren Tribes

High Lord Ushtyl paused and, closing his eyes, listened. The wind brushed faintly at his ears and, more distantly, more magnificently, it rustled in the boughs of the great forest like the relentless tide that was his army, his empire. But here, around him, there was silence. Not a sound to be heard from the host of nearly a thousand t'Okaedrin and Pi'aernoth.

Nodding, he opened his eyes. Behind a single rank of Syraestari housecarls stood row upon row of human warriors grouped by family. There were forty-two families total, thirty-five t'Okaedrin and seven Pi'aernotha Osnoeda. The men wore scaled cuirasses, iron helms, and leather greaves. On their backs were slung banded wooden shields while iron swords hung at their sides. Their crimson cloaks swirled in the noonday sun. The women wore shorter iron-scaled shirts and iron helms, but otherwise their armor was leather. Their cloaks were brown, the better to blend into the wilderness. Bows were slung on their backs and short swords hung at their belts.

Allowing a smile to form on his lips, Ushtyl turned to Tazil. "I doubt as large an army has gathered on a single field since the last days of the Great War."

Tazil nodded. "The heralds shall remember this day as the birth of the new Syraestari dominion."

Before them, at the head of the army, stood Lady Ninanna and the Captains Eltirkar and Nethzir. Ninanna turned to the high lords. "They are yours to command, my Lords."

Ushtyl nodded to Tazil who stepped forward and in a booming voice cried, "Draw!"

Instantly the waiting ranks of t'Okaedrin drew their swords and unslung their shields while the Pi'aernoth unshouldered their bows and each strung an arrow. The front ranks knelt while the back ranks remaining standing. Silence fell again upon the field. Then Tazil bellowed, "Sheath!" The t'Okaedrin and Pi'aernoth returned their weapons and then stood waiting once more. Then Tazil shouted, "T'Okaedrin! Pi'aernoth! What are your oaths?"

The humans replied as one voice that rolled like a wave of power across the plains. "There is no greater duty than to kill in the name of the Empress! There is no greater honor than to die in the name of the Empress!"

As they fell silent, Tazil turned to Ushtyl. "I am pleased."

"As am I." Ushtyl turned to Ninanna. "Commander, you may begin your march."

"Yes, my Lord."

As Ninanna faced the army to give her commands, Ushtyl and Tazil turned away and walked to their waiting escort of housecarls for their journeys home.

Ushtyl knew he shouldn't have felt surprise at how tightly Ninanna had kept her word, but he did. Despite her feelings against him and the mission, she had changed nothing of Eltirkar's plans. When told that her Sword-Whisperers were not needed in the raids, she had agreed that they would only defend the forward camp. But that didn't mean all was calm.

Reaching their horses, Tazil turned to him. "Having seen to our security abroad, now we can see to our rights at home."

Ushtyl nodded. "I will be meeting with Arkesh and Ovirkar in a few days."

"Success on both fronts, my friend."

"Success," Ushtyl replied, lifting his foot to his horse's stirrup.

"We will always be nearby," Dalric said.

Vistus nodded, his mind already far away. He sat between his father and Bridionis on a bench inside the forward camp's only building. They were in a small alcove next to its side door separated from the main room by hanging curtain. Waiting. Two weeks ago, they had begun their march through the forest. Up until a few days past, this place had been just an empty clearing surrounded by endless wilderness. But with so many families to share the labor, the tall wooden walls had gone up quickly. The chances of anyone discovering the camp, let alone attacking it, were small. But if that happened, they would be prepared. It was the kind of order that set the t'Okaedrin above the wildmen.

Vistus scratched at his bearded chin. He'd begun growing it again as soon as Tazil had ordered him to infiltrate. It had drawn more than a few stares from the other families as he helped build the fortifications. But only Arcomin had mocked him for it, claiming Vistus was becoming a wildman himself. Vistus wished he had his golden ring to shove in his brother's face, but it was safely stowed away in his chest back home. He wouldn't be able to blend in with the Kalilaer if he wore it. He'd also placed Vitarria's gemstone in the chest, but at the last moment had taken it out again. Try as he might, the ghosts of that raid still haunted him and, strangely, the nightmares were always worse when he took it off. He kept it hidden on one of two leather strings around his neck. The second held the Sapaupan Kaupet.

Dalric spoke, "The prisoners that came in today are from three different tribes: the Zengris, the Iengian, and the Tatyrni. Scouts say that all Zengris mark their faces with blue tattoos. The Iengian men are known to use ritual scarring on their forearms. Only the Tatyrni have no obvious markings, so pretend to be one of them."

Vistus let out a sigh, thinking on how much the raid earlier that day had cost. Word had arrived with the prisoner column that Eldest Nalsuntha was dead. He'd take a wildman arrow through the eye. If Vistus hadn't been assigned the task of infiltrating, he might've been named to replace Nalsuntha. Instead, his rival Arcomin received the honor. Vistus forced away his grief and anger. He had to concentrate. "Will there be only Iengian and Zengris near me, father?"

"We will make sure of it."

Vistus nodded. He could hear the prisoners beyond the door. Most were silent, but some wept and a few moaned. Before today, it was unlikely that these tribes had ever heard of the t'Okaedrin or the Syraestari, other than vague rumors of Iron-Men. By now it would be clear to them just how crude and backward their own lives had been. The defiant had already died, the rest would kneel. Unlike the Scions who'd chosen a path of apostasy, the ignorance of the wildmen gave them the chance at salvation still.

"I know this will be hard for you, Vistus," Dalric said. "But we will always be nearby. Your brothers will check on you frequently when you are in the camps. They will treat you as a stranger and a Kalilaer, of course. You must not let your deceit falter or the other Kalilaer may kill you, and all this effort will be wasted."

"I understand, father."

"I've arranged for Elestis' family to be sent to Nahirazith, too." Vistus' heart leapt as his father continued, "But the Pi'aernoth only guard the perimeter of the camps so you will not see her except, perhaps, from afar."

"Thank you, father."

Dalric smiled. "Do not thank me, thank our masters."

Vistus glanced to his right. Through a small gap in the curtain, he could see into the main chamber of the building. Captain Nethzir, Captain Eltirkar, and a Syraestari woman in the garb of a Sword-Whisperer stood around a table in the center of the chamber, talking quietly. The woman terrified and mesmerized him at the same time. Her name was only ever spoken in hushed voices. Rumors said Lady Ninanna had founded the Sword-Whisperers thousands of years before. Trying to contemplate the great ages of the Syraestari dazed Vistus' mind. To span centuries, or even millennia, with faces as unblemished as a human in early adulthood was incomprehensible. Eternal youth - except for the eyes. He had seen her eyes, once, and they were ancient. Regardless of what the rumors claimed, all Vistus knew for certain was that Lady Ninanna was the most beautiful Syraestari he'd ever seen. Elestis was like a tiny wildflower next to Ninanna's lily, a tiny star before the sun. But in that lovely face, in those brilliant brown eyes, he sensed a deep sadness, the likes of which he'd never seen in another. Beyond that, she had the same relentless aura that all Sword-Whisperers carried, suggesting a might and prowess not to be reckoned with. In its own way, this sense of power was even more potent and focused than that of a high lord. He was glad he never had to speak with her.

"How soon, father?" Vistus asked.

"A few minutes more and full darkness will be upon us. Just in case one of the prisoners' hoods have slipped, we don't want to risk anyone seeing you. The commander will tell us when."

Vistus leaned back and closed his eyes, feeling the moment of change approaching. He had thought once would be all, but now it was upon him again. He forced in deep breaths of air, feeling the crude leather clothing against his skin and the dirt he'd rubbed on his arms and face a few hours before. The harsh stubble of his beard itched ferociously and he had to fight not scratch at it. The two necklace stones hung cold against his chest.

The muscles of his face twitched into a frown, then smooth again, as he cast off his Okaidir self. He had practiced this over the past several weeks, sloughing off his old life much like a snake might cast off its skin, except he was becoming something else. It had been difficult, forcing himself to see his brothers through foreign eyes. How does one cast away the only life one had ever known? He realized he wouldn't be able to hide himself completely. He would still be himself but he had to live a different past. He could no longer be Vistus the warrior, the brother, the son, the servant of the Syraestari. No, he had to become a crude wildman, with no knowledge of iron or swords, discipline or civilization.

A hand touched his shoulder. Vistus opened his eyes to see Dalric standing over him. "It is time."

Vistus nodded and stood. Holding his wrists together, he extended his hands so Dalric could bind them. Then Bridionis gave him a quick embrace with his good arm. "You will do well."

"Thank you, brother," Vistus replied. He drew in another deep breath, feeling muscles loosen as he became Belarrin once again. That name had served him well before and it would carry him home. He sighed, feeling Vistus slip away until only Belarrin remained.

Dalric opened the door and Belarrin stepped out into the night.

Torches flickered from various points along the edge of the prisoners' wooden enclosure. It was just enough to cast the hundreds of cowering shapes within as a sea of shadows. Dalric walked beside him to the enclosure gate and handed him his black hood. Then his father gave him a final smile and lifted his hand high to signal. A loud clash resounded through the fort in reply as one of the brothers beat a metal gong.

In that moment of deafening noise, the guards opened the enclosure gate and Belarrin stepped among the prisoners. They stirred in fright at the unknown sound, most looking around blindly but unable to see for the hoods pulled over their heads. Before the noise faded, Belarrin found a seat among them and then pulled on his own hood.

Blinded in the darkness, there was nothing more for him to do until morning. He was just like any other prisoner. He realized his heart raced and his hands were sweaty. Trying to calm his nerves, he lay back against the ground. His head jostled the foot of another prisoner who pulled back, muttering an anxious apology. Closing his eyes, Belarrin tried to sleep, but among the whimpers and moans it was a long time in coming.

The crash of a gong wrenched Vistus from clouded dreams of darkness and cold, pulling him to wakefulness. He stared around blindly, seeing nothing as the sharp scent of rough twine filled his nose. Drawing in a deep breath, he chided himself. He was Belarrin, not Vistus now. Forgetting that could get him killed.

The other prisoners stirred restlessly around him. Some began whimpering again, but even from the silent ones he could sense a tension in the stilted sounds of their movements. The enclosure gate creaked open and boots scraped in the dirt.

"You!" a voice broke the uneasy quiet. It was Arcomin, yet to Belarrin's adapting ears, the tone was harsh and brutal instead of a reminder of home. "Up!" His brother shouted and feet scuffled. "Over there!"

The Kalilaer around Belarrin fell quiet and the air thickened with unease. Belarrin felt it inside, too. He didn't like it. This wasn't like before. That time, he had cast off his Scion guise the moment his brothers arrived, but now he was the enemy among his own family.

More t'Okaedrin shouted, grabbing prisoners and sending them out of the enclosure. Their voices drew closer until rough hands took Belarrin by the shoulders and wrenched him upward. He stood unsteadily as his hood was pulled from his head. Blinking in the raw light of the dawn, his eyes focusing on the face in front of him. It was Arcomin.

No recognition appeared in Arcomin's eyes as he roared, "Don't look at me, you swine! Do you think you're better than me?" He struck Belarrin open-palmed on the side of the head sending him sprawling into the dust. "Get over there!"

Ears ringing, Belarrin scrambled back to his feet. His urgency was only half-feigned as he hurried to the line of prisoners forming outside the enclosure. His face flushed with shame as he did, still feeling burning imprint where Arcomin had hit him. He did not understand. The t'Okaedrin didn't strike the prisoners unless they disobeyed. Wildmen were ignorant, not evil. It was just Arcomin taking advantage, the fool!

Two t'Okaedrin took his hands roughly, but not so violently as Arcomin, and tied his wrists to a rope linked to the prisoner in front of him. Then they extended the rope to bind the prisoner that followed after. All of the wildmen stood wide-eyed in a long line that ran down the center of the camp, binding one to another.

The prisoner in front of him was a huge man, a full head taller than Belarrin and broad at the shoulder. His forearms were marred by a crossing pattern of scars. The man behind him was far less remarkable except for three blue tattooed lines across the right cheek of his face. Iengian and Zengris, just as Dalric had promised. Scanning the ramparts, Belarrin did not see his father or Bridionis. It was for the best. A clean break until it was time to return home. If only Arcomin had been absent, too.

Prisoners continued to file out from their enclosure as directed by the t'Okaedrin. Once half the men and women joined Belarrin's line, a second one was started. Belarrin knew his line was headed for Nahirazith and the other for his old home of Raefi'ernyn. On the other side of the fort, a smaller group of young children, none above six years old, were guided to several large wagons. Unlike the adults, they would not be forced to march. Unlike the adults, they were destined to be t'Okaedrin and Pi'aernoth. Belarrin suppressed a smile. Looking at those frightened faces, he knew they were headed to better lives. The best of all lives.

When all the prisoners were bound into their lines, Arcomin shouted loudly to be heard by all. "From this day forward, you are Kalilaer. 'Laborer' in the tongue of our masters. Each Kalilaer is allotted five swallows of water. Each loaf is to be shared between four Kalilaer. If you take more than your portion, you will be killed."

Faces paled and a few moaned. The Zengris behind him whimpered softly and Belarrin tried to mimic the man with an expression of dejection. When an Okaidir arrived with Belarrin's portion of food and drink, he tore off a hunk of bread and took his five swallows. The water was warm and bitter, the bread dry and tasteless, but he had eaten worse before. He forced it down, knowing he'd need his strength for the ordeal ahead.

After the meal was completed, the gong rang again and the line of prisoners began to move with his brothers falling alongside. Standing near the gate itself were four Sword-Whisperers in long black cloaks and dark armor with enormous swords slung upon their backs. They watched without expression and the Kalilaer shied away. Belarrin didn't blame them. Although the Whisperers had not been involved in any of the village raids, no Kalilaer needed to be told to fear them.

Beyond the gate, the line of prisoners walked through the glade surrounding the fort and then into the forest itself. Trailing the column were three ox carts, two loaded with food and water, the third with the children. They marched at an agonizingly slow pace. Belarrin had been on such expeditions plenty of times, but always as a captor. The t'Okaedrin could walk at their own stride with legs stretched out comfortably. But Belarrin's gait was shortened to an awkward shuffle as he tried to avoid stepping on the heels of the man in front of him and hoped to be spared the same by the prisoner that followed after.

Near midday, the t'Okaedrin halted the prisoners in a small clearing. While most of the brothers stood along the edge of the column, watching, Arcomin and Hirnid walked up to the first captive. Inwardly, Belarrin groaned. This was not a task for Arcomin. He took too much pleasure in tormenting prisoners. Had Nalsuntha still lived, he would never have allowed it. But Arcomin was eldest now and could do what he wanted. Drawing in a deep breath, Belarrin tried to force an inward calm as he watched. All the other prisoners stared too, more than one shifting restlessly from one foot to the other. They already knew what to expect from their marches from their ruined villages to the forward camp.

Hirnid stood behind the first prisoner, hand on the hilt of his sword while Arcomin grasped the Kalilaer's head between his hands. The prisoner whimpered softly as Arcomin raised the eyelids with his thumbs. Satisfied, he stepped back and looked the man up and down. Then he glanced at Hirnid.

"No blood," Hirnid replied.

Arcomin nodded and the pair stepped to the next prisoner. Each inspection was quick, but thorough. The Kalilaer were too terrified to do anything but stand petrified, though a few wept as they waited. The other t'Okaedrin remained at a distance, half watching the prisoners and half looking out into the woods.

Arcomin and Hirnid stepped up to the tall Iengian in front of Belarrin. As Arcomin reached for the man's head, the prisoner snarled and pulled away. Arcomin reacted instantly, driving a mailed fist into the man's stomach. The Iengian doubled over and collapsed to the ground. Belarrin was jerked forward as the rope tying him to the Iengian drew taught. He stumbled to his knees before catching himself.

Instantly they were surrounded by t'Okaedrin. As Arcomin pulled the Iengian upright, Hirnid grabbed Belarrin so strongly he thought his arms might wrench from their sockets. Only when the prisoner line steadied did Hirnid release him and step back. Drawing in deep breaths of air, Belarrin tried to stretch his arms to work out the pain, but it was difficult with his wrists bound together. The Iengian did not resist again as Arcomin inspected his eyes. Stepping back, he looked at Hirnid.

"Blood on his left side."

Arcomin nodded and, narrowing his brows, stared the Iengian in the eyes. "If you so much as flinch, I'll open your stomach. Flinch, then. I'd like nothing better."

The Iengian's face flushed crimson in fury, but he made no move as Arcomin lifted his tunic. "Minor cut. It'll heal." He released the shirt.

Arcomin stepped over and grasped Belarrin's head between his palms. The leather of his gloves was coarse, the scaled mail cold. Belarrin glanced only a moment into Arcomin's eyes before forcing them down meekly. He saw a dark light in his brother's gaze and the edge of a smirk on the lips. Arcomin's thumbs pressed down onto his eyes far harder than they needed to. For a quick moment, Belarrin feared Arcomin was going to gouge them out. It was all he could do not to flail helplessly. But then Arcomin released him, stepped back and finished the inspection.

When Arcomin and Hirnid stepped over to the Zengris behind him, Belarrin let out a gasp of air as a cold sweat poured over his forehead. His mind reeled as he grappled with the feelings rising up within him. Only slowly did he realize that it was true fear. Even though his feigned enemies were his brothers, his life was wholly under their control. He was utterly powerless. There was no reason for him to be afraid of his brothers, yet he was and he didn't like it. He did not want to be Kalilaer. He let out a deep breath as it dawned on him, perhaps for the first time, that he truly was. And he was utterly alone.

As the inspection continued down the line, Belarrin regained control of himself, steeling his heart and mind for the road ahead. About halfway done, Arcomin said of one prisoner, "Dazed eyes, blood on the chest."

"No," the prisoner whispered softly as Hirnid dutifully untied him from the line. The prisoner's voice grew louder, "No, no, no! I am well. I can walk!"

The man struggled against his bonds, trying to pull away as the large Iengian had, but he was not so strong. Arcomin's blow across the face dropped him to his knees. "Is this all you have, mewling wildman?"

Arcomin took a step back and drew his sword, sending a palpable shudder echoing down the line. The Iengian next to Belarrin took a step forward, bellowing, "Mirnar! No, Mirnar!" He charged forward in a fury, but Belarrin had anticipated it this time. He leaned back and dug his heals into the dirt to keep from being flung after the enraged Iengian. The Kalilaer on the other side did the same and between the two of them, managed to slow the madman. Hirnid dashed forward and brought the pommel of his sword down on the Iengian's head, dropping the man into a dazed heap on the ground.

"Anyone else want to be a hero?" Arcomin roared, waving his sword. "How about you, Mirnar? You hate me don't you? Fight me and die. Or just die."

Belarrin's gaze shifted from Arcomin to his other brothers. He saw Bridionis take a step forward and even Hirnid blanched. But as eldest, now, they would not countermand Arcomin. Why had father picked him, of all of them? Arcomin was the strongest, to be sure, but was that enough?

The bowing prisoner looked up from his crouch and wiped a hand across his mouth where Arcomin had struck him. It came away bloody. But Mirnar's dazed expression had vanished, replaced by a snarl of rage. With a bestial cry, he lunged forward, hands outstretched for Arcomin's throat.

Futility. Arcomin's blade swung down, striking him at the collarbone, rending flesh. Belarrin turned away, his heart a mix of disgust.

"Any other fools?" Arcomin asked, stepping over Mirnar's body, his blade crimson with blood. "No?" He sounded disappointed. Arcomin turned to glare at the stunned Iengian beside Belarrin. "If that one can walk by the time we march, he lives. Otherwise, kill him."

Belarrin looked down at the Iengian, hoping the man stayed down. It would be much better for the Iengian to die and leave the rest of them in peace. Yet, looking over to the body of Mirnar, Belarrin could not deny a small flutter of nerves in his own chest. He knew he should not have felt it, but that didn't help. He should not be afraid of his brothers. There was no need to be. They were his link to escaping this false mantle he bore. But at the same time, being Kalilaer and seeing another's fate meted out so easily jarred him. Anger rose up against that fear. None of the prisoners should be afraid because of Mirnar's death. His execution made sense despite Arcomin's shameful brutality. The man was too weak to survive and would've died anyway. This was quicker and necessary.

They didn't understand and blame for that lay at Arcomin's feet. It was one of the tasks of the t'Okaedrin to teach the Kalilaer the truth of what they were to become. To teach them that it was right. But the Kalilaer all had pale faces, some with gazes locked upon the corpse and others with eyes fixed away while Arcomin and Hirnid finished their inspection. After it was done, food and drink were handed out as it had been that morning. By the time Belarrin finished eating, the Iengian was sitting upright. When it came time to move, he stood and marched. Belarrin frowned at his back and wished his brothers had just killed the man.

CHAPTER 11

Welcomes

"This is the day to make our weakness our strength. If humanity in all of its numbers preys upon us, then let us sculpt humanity into a shield. Syraestari no longer need die to defend all we love. If humans prey upon us, then let humans also die to defend us."

—High Lord Tazil on the Field of Dahiraetin

The afternoon passed slowly as they walked through the depths of the forest. The sense that it was all exactly the same and yet chaotically different clashed in Belarrin's mind. Each step felt identical, yet every tree and bush was unique. The tree trunks varied in shades of brown and gray with bark coarse or smooth. They were crowned with dark green needles or lighter toned leaves, some of which had fallen to carpet the floor in browns and yellows. Rocks lay scattered here and there, interposed by rotting trunks of downed trees speckled with lichen and stinking faintly of decay. Compared with the noise of the passing column, the wilderness lay silent. Belarrin could hear nothing above the heavy tromp of feet, the moans of despairing prisoners, the metallic chinking of the t'Okaedrin arms and armor, and the dull creaking of the ox carts.

Late in the day, but well before sundown, the t'Okaedrin halted the column and held another inspection. Fortunately, the Iengian didn't struggle this time and no prisoners were killed. Another meal was passed out. This time, along with the bread and water, they were given thin strips of dried meat.

When all of the prisoners had their food, Arcomin bellowed, "Sit down! You sleep where you lie. If you're lucky." Several of the t'Okaedrin chuckled.

Belarrin was glad be off of his legs. He was in excellent shape, able to run half a morning in full armor, but the stunted pace of the prison line exhausted him. Gnawing on his strip of meat, he watched his brothers build a fire and cook their own meal. The smell of roasting meat made his mouth water.

"What are you?" A hard voice demanded

Belarrin turned to see the Iengian staring at him. The man's eyes narrowed and the corner of his lip turned up in scorn. "I'm a prisoner, just like you," Belarrin replied.

The Iengian eyed Belarrin's unscarred forearms and snorted. "You are nothing like me."

Belarrin fought down a wave of anger and, keeping his voice as even as he could, replied, "What does that matter?

We're bound together and marching off to work in their camps. Does anything else really make a difference?"

A wolfish growl rose up in from the man's throat. Belarrin stared back at him. Blood on the Bridge, the wildmen really were animals. But before he could think of any reply, the Zengris behind him leaned over and said, "Don't mind that Iengian. He knows, just as we do, that all the real warriors are dead. Only we fools remain."

The Iengian's growl deepened and his mouth twisted into a snarl.

Belarrin realized he had to end this before his brothers came over. "It isn't important now, who or what we were. Our homes our gone, our people dead. We're all prisoners now and not enemies." He looked over to the fire in the center of the camp. Bridionis was leaning forward to take another piece of roasted meat. Belarrin swallowed, forcing his new self to speak as he stared at his family. "They are the enemy."

The Iengian scowled, then snorted and turned away, but the Zengris laughed bitterly as he looked at the fire. "An enemy is someone you can fight. All we can hope to do is live another day."

Belarrin nodded.

The Zengris turned to Belarrin. "I am Wiersa."

"Belarrin."

"I'd like to say it's an honor to meet you, Belarrin, but I wish I was far away. I'm going to sleep and I hope can dream of a better place than this."

"Good luck." Belarrin let out a groan as he lay down and closed his eyes. He longed for pleasant dreams, too, but knew those would be far different from what Wiersa might imagine.

Hirnid leaned his back against a tree trunk. The nearby cook fire had faded to a dull red glow, still alive enough to give off faint waves of heat against the growing night chill. Most of his brothers were on watch or had withdrawn to their bedrolls to rest before their turn came. But Arcomin sat beside him, leaning toward the fire's warmth.

Among the line of sleeping prisoners lay Vistus, his brother. This mission was so different from what he was accustomed to and he didn't like it. Brothers were supposed to fight side by side. Last time they'd been marching to Vistus' rescue, at least. But this time he was here among them, yet not here. And even worse, Nalsuntha was gone. Hirnid had been charging beside him when his eldest went down with the arrow in the eye. As blood sprayed over him, Hirnid had stopped, stunned, forgetting all else but his brother. All of his training, all of his discipline had vanished as he knelt down beside Nalsuntha and witnessed the vacant stare in his other eye, the slack jaw, the body limp with death. At least the others had been intent on the enemy. No one had witnessed his weakness when he'd allowed brotherhood to overshadow duty.

But to his greater shame, Hirnid didn't know if that was wrong.

He looked up as Bridionis approached the fire. Bridionis gave him a distracted glance and nod before walking over to Arcomin and crouching beside him.

Arcomin looked over. "What is it?"

"I wanted to speak with you, now that we're alone."

"There is no call for concern."

"You might disagree once I speak."

A look of suspicion entered Arcomin's eyes. "What then?"

"I'm uneasy what happened today with the execution of that prisoner."

Arcomin laughed. "What? Don't tell me you're getting soft, brother."

"Of course he had to die, he was going to anyway," Bridionis replied. "But I'm troubled by the pleasure you took in it. Especially when you challenged any other to face you."

"Certainly I took pleasure in it. The death of any apostate is a blessing."

"But these aren't apostates. They aren't Scions."

"They would be, given a choice."

"It is our duty to deny them that choice."

Arcomin's face twisted into a snarl. "You accuse me of not knowing my duty."

Bridionis held both hands up, palms out. "No, certainly not. I'm worried that in your anger you stepped very close to disobeying the orders from our masters. Nalsuntha's death has taken a toll on all of us."

"Nalsuntha has nothing to do with it." Arcomin gestured toward the line of prisoners. "You saw them, their defiance. This is the only time to break them before they get among the rest of the filthy Kalilaer and spread their poison. Belligerence must be culled until only docility remains. You saw that oaf in front of Vistus. People like that must be broken or slain, I don't care which."

"The Kalilaer are not our enemy. They rely upon us to protect them even if they don't understand it. Every one of them is needed to work the land. Our masters will be furious if we kill any that should've lived."

Arcomin grabbed the front of Bridionis shirt and pulled him close. "Are you challenging me?"

Hirnid considered intervening, but Bridionis appeared undisturbed. "No," he said calmly. "You are my brother and you are my eldest. I can worry for you."

Arcomin snorted and released Bridionis' shirt. "Don't worry for me, brother. Worry for Vistus. He's the one leaping into the maw of the beast." He glanced over at Hirnid. "And what are you still doing here? Go get some sleep or I'll throw you on watch right now."

Hirnid scrambled to his feet. "Yes, Eldest."

The pleasant dreams Belarrin sought did not find him. He tossed and turned through the night, tormented by nightmares of buckling earth, of collapsing barracks and falling timbers. Wooden beams pinned him down so he could hardly move. The earth so cold, his throat so dry, his lungs burning from his cries for help. Praying to be rescued, afraid to die. He struggled beneath the weight but his hands would not respond.

Belarrin lurched to wakefulness, sitting upright and tearing at his bonds, a cry of terror dying unspoken on his lips. Chest heaving, he looked down at the ropes tying his wrists together. It was all he could do not to tug at them again. But he sighed and tried to relax his mind. Gray twilight had begun to pierce the forest. Overhead, tree limbs groped outward like black shadows across the dim sky. The t'Okaedrin had begun to stir. They donned their armor first while weapons lay ready nearby. Then the swords were belted at their waists and shields were slung over their shoulders. The morning meal was simple and they ate quickly before moving away from the dead fire.

"Up!" Arcomin's voice rang out through the camp. Prisoners groaned as they pushed themselves up from the hard forest floor. These turned to moans of despair as the children awoke in their ox cart cage and began wailing. Those who moved too slowly were kicked to wakefulness by t'Okaedrin walking the line. Wiersa was one of those stubborn ones until a sharp kick from Hirnid drove him upright. After the Okaidir was out of earshot, he grunted. "As if I didn't have enough bruises already."

The t'Okaedrin gave another inspection and checked the rope bonds, then passed out a small breakfast of bread and water. Arcomin was restrained this time, at least. Perhaps Bridionis and the others had talked some sense into him. There was no place for cruelty in the t'Okaedrin. Discipline was hard, cold, and immediate, but without rage. Viciousness only lent credence to the lies of the rebels.

When the meal was finished, the column set out once more. The day felt no different from the last. Each tree might have been the one before. They might have been walking in circles. He'd undertaken many such long marches before, as a t'Okaedrin, and he didn't enjoy them then. As a prisoner, it was far worse. He sensed they were traveling slower than the journey out from Raefi'ernyn, which meant he had perhaps as much as two weeks of dreary nothingness to look forward to. And beyond that, mundane toil in the Kalilaer camps.

The only events to break the timelessness were the pauses for the midday meal or the evening stop. But there was no pleasure in either. The food was miserable and rest was impossible to find. The Iengian in front of him, at least, seemed calmer. He grumbled often and glared at prisoner and t'Okaedrin alike, but made no violent movements. In the evenings, Wiersa usually talked to Belarrin briefly. Neither had enough energy to speak long. Wiersa had a dry and bitter wit, but he held no secrets either. "When I heard the warning shouts, I hid in my hut," he confessed one evening. Chuckling bitterly, he continued, "I might have escaped if flames hadn't forced me out. I wonder now if I'd have been happier burning alive."

Belarrin forced himself to laugh at the other man's words as he fought down a wave of scorn. His many battles against the wildmen had taught him that some were worthy of respect for their courage if not their wisdom. On the field of battle, he might even have respected the brutish Iengian next to him. Vistus' hand shifted up to touch the gemstones hidden beneath his shirt before he could pull it away. Vitarria had not died a warrior's death, but she had faced it unflinching and that was courage, too. It wasn't found only on the field of battle. But was it courage that she died clinging to what she believed? Did it matter that that belief was apostasy? That it was a poison that threatened to drag the world back into darkness? He shook his head, forcing the thought away. It was a path he didn't want his mind to take.

One night they were camped on the edge of a clearing. A full moon beamed down through the canopy of leaves to cast the line of prisoners in silvers and gray. Belarrin's stomach rumbled from too little food as he lay on the ground. His ankles ached and the backs of his knees throbbed. He knew he was strong, but this kind of walking could exhaust any man. He closed his eyes and tried to dream of the wide-open plains, the cool brush of the salty wind on a warm day, and the perpetual rumble of the ocean surf pounding upon the sandy shore.

"You're a priest."

Belarrin opened his eyes and looked up at the huge Iengian looming over him. For once, the beast-man's eyes were thoughtful. "What?"

"You're a priest," the Iengian repeated.

Confused, Belarrin sat up and felt his necklace fall against his chest. Looking down, he saw the black stone and the clear gemstone dangling free. The moonlight had fallen upon the pale gemstone and it sparkled in the white light. He grabbed them in his bound hands and shoved them back under his shirt. "No, I am not."

"Then how did you get the stones?" Wiersa asked.

Belarrin turned to see the Zengris watching him, too. His mind raced. "My father was a priest." He hesitated, hoping they thought him choked up as he picked his words. "My sister was training to be one, too."

Wiersa's voice softened. "Did the Iron-Men kill them?"

"Yes," Belarrin replied. Recalling raids he'd carried out before, it wasn't hard to come up with a lie. "My father died first, in the doorway of our house. I tried to protect my sister, but there were too many of them. I was knocked senseless and, when I awoke, I was staring into Vitarria's empty eyes." He remembered the real Vitarria's lifeless gaze as she lay at his feet, the blood mingling with her hair. To his annoyance, the strangled sound in his voice was not feigned as he continued, "The necklace dangled free and I grabbed it before the Iron-Men noticed."

Wiersa nodded, admiration filling his eyes. Yet his tone was disappointed. "So you don't know the rituals?"

"No."

"A pity." He sighed. "Not that it would've done much good, I suppose. His Highest Above has abandoned us."

The Iengian spoke. "I misjudged you, Tatyrni. That boldness is worthy tribute to the fallen. It is a deed worthy of an Iengian." Then he laughed. "I am named Yrpel."

"Belarrin." He replied after a moment's hesitation.

Yrpel turned his gaze over to where the t'Okaedrin were eating their meal and a growl rose up in his throat. "Your words give me half a mind to tear their heads from their bodies right now."

"Not with hands bound and us all tied together," Belarrin replied.

"I do not want them to think they've broken me."

Instead of observing that they already had, Belarrin said, "There are better ways than getting yourself killed, and me with you."

"Perhaps there are." Yrpel roared with laughter so loudly that several of the t'Okaedrin turned to look their direction. Belarrin quickly laid down and Yrpel and Wiersa did the same.

One of the t'Okaedrin walked over, though Belarrin didn't open his eyes to see who. After a long moment, the man muttered, "Fool Kalilaer" and walked away.

The next morning, they finally marched out of the woods.

A cool wind greeted Belarrin, brushing across his face, welcoming him home. But he was not home. This was Nahirazith instead of Raefi'ernyn and he was arriving in bondage. Yet the settlement that lay ahead could have passed as a twin of his home with its sweeping fields and orchards, its scattered Kalilaer camps and the t'Okaedrin barracks under the shadows of a mighty Syraestari city. Seeing Nahirazith for the first time, he realized that the home of High Lord Ushtyl was at least as magnificent as High Lord Tazil's. Its highest tower soared far higher than Raefi'ernyn's and gleamed golden in the rising sun.

"Spear Cydion through the heart and call me a fool," Wiersa whispered behind him. A ripple of gasps spread through the ranks of prisoners as they first beheld the stronghold of their masters. If iron and sorcery weren't enough to prove Syraestari might, then Nahirazith surely would.

As the column marched through fields of waving green grains, the toiling Kalilaer paused to stare at them, their expressions indiscernible at the distance. Bitterness, perhaps, at another defeat of the savages who preferred their "freedom" to a better life. Or happiness at more workers to share in the burden. It mattered little.

Four t'Okaedrin on horseback keeping an eye on the field workers slowed their mounts to watch the prisoners march past. Bows were slung upon their backs and iron-headed spears rested easily upon their pommels.

Beyond the fields, the path wound through several of the working settlements, a potter's camp, a bakery, a tailoring camp. Each of them just a few buildings with wide open space in between. The other prisoners murmured apprehensively as they took it all in, numb shock written upon their faces.

Belarrin's brothers guided the prison line toward the side of the settlement closest to Nahirazith and onto a long barren field large enough to hold several thousand men in ordered ranks. Along the northern side, a dozen small angled wooden platforms had been erected.

"What are those?" Wiersa muttered darkly.

Boards, Belarrin knew they were called. The last two at the far end of the field each held Kalilaer, a man and a woman. They were bound by ropes at their wrists and ankles that were stretched taut. Under the strain, their limbs were splayed at sharp angles out from their bodies, forming the shape of crossed swords. The Boards were raised slightly to increase discomfort and also allow the prisoners to be able to see and be seen as they suffered. The skin of each of the captives was red from too much sun. The man lay in a stupor with his tongue lolling and eyes closed, but the woman gasped for breath as she lifted her head to watch the lines of new laborers arrive. It took great effort, though, and she dropped back with a groan.

The t'Okaedrin halted the column in front of the two captives. It was a not so subtle way to show new Kalilaer the price of resistance. The t'Okaedrin ignored the man and the woman as they performed one final inspection on the new Kalilaer. Satisfied with what they found, they gave out a meal of bread and water.

Biting into his portion of the dry bread, Belarrin found himself longing for the meat of a deer or a boar, dripping in its own juices. It would be a long time before he enjoyed a feast like that again.

Once everyone was fed, the t'Okaedrin walked down to the far end of the field where they spoke with several Syraestari in long flowing robes.

"What are they going to do to us?" one of the prisoners asked in a hushed voice.

"Work us in the fields until we die," Wiersa replied dryly.

"What have they done with my wife?" another man asked.

"And where are my children?" a woman said, crying.

Belarrin listened silently, the answers were all obvious. Wiersa had come the closest though even he didn't understand. They would all work, but unlike in the wilderness it would be orderly here. They would all be guided by their masters. No one who worked hard would starve or suffer any want. There would be no famine here, no freezing through the cold winter, no death upon the tusks of a wild boar or at the hands of a rival tribe.

"There are fewer guards now," Yrpel said, glancing both directions down the line.

A sharp laugh burst from Belarrin's lips, drawing a glare from the big Iengian. "We wouldn't make it far with these ropes. Do you think we can run faster than the ones on horseback? The forest is a long ways a way."

"Better to die than serve," Yrpel growled.

"Better to live and find another way."

Yrpel's brows lowered and he glared past Belarrin to the t'Okaedrin. "Fine. But later, we will act."

The woman on the Boards raised her head again. In a rasping voice, she said, "So they're enslaving Zengris now too."

"What do you mean?" Wiersa asked.

A hoarse laugh escaped the prisoner's lips. Or perhaps it was a wheeze. "The Finnies hunt farther and farther out." Belarrin flinched at the disrespectful name and forced his face to relax.

"Finnies?" Wiersa asked.

The woman's brow furrowed. Her brown hair, caked in sweat and dirt, clung to her forehead. "Did you think those slave-warriors ruled here? Your masters are the Finaestari, only don't call them that to their faces. Not Finnie, either.

They don't like it. Call them Syraestari. 'Master' works fine too."

"I don't see the difference," Wiersa said.

The woman opened her mouth to respond, then fell back, coughing. It was a deep scratching rasp that made her whole body heave. But for the ropes binding her limbs, Belarrin was sure she'd have doubled in on herself in pain. He wondered what she had done to draw such punishment. The Syraestari weren't harsh in their demands for the Kalilaer, expecting only obedience. After a long moment, the woman relaxed and laid her head back, drawing in deep breaths. Then she raised her head again and said, "They see the difference and that's all that matters."

"Please rest," one of the prisoners said.

"No, anything is better than lying here alone." The woman let out another short cough.

"What have they done to you?"

"I fell asleep when I shouldn't have. They caught me dozing behind a furnace. But don't worry, it takes more than a night and a day on the Boards to finish Chostir." The woman coughed again. Then clearing her throat, she continued, "They'll cut me loose at sundown and back to the smelters I'll go." She glanced over at the man tied next to her. "But this fool spit in a Finaestari's face. He's unlucky that the Finnie didn't kill him then. He's here until he dies. "

"How long have you been a slave?" Yrpel asked. The Iengian's voice was almost a rasp itself, but from anger instead of pain.

"Fifteen years, maybe? I don't know and it doesn't matter anymore. All of my people are slaves now, or dead. I work in the smelters and, if you're lucky, you will too. The least fortunate go to the mines."

"What about our children?" one of the women asked.

Chostir shook her head. "You don't want to know."

"Tell us, please!" the woman's voice was joined by dozens of others.

"They'll be trained as slave-warriors, just like those that captured you."

"Impossible!" Yrpel bellowed as the line of prisoners broke into wails.

Chostir lay back and coughed sharply once more. After it passed, she raised her head again. "The Finnies take children young and bind their souls to absolute devotion. They'll make monsters of any child you bear here, too. So don't." Absolute silence met that pronouncement and Belarrin's heart churned within him. Everywhere he turned he heard lies. It was enough to send him into a white rage. That isn't what happened at all. If only they weren't so blinded by ignorance.

"A bit of advice," Chostir said. "If a Finnie is anywhere near you, drop to the ground. If it's one of those Sword-Whisperers with the huge swords, kiss the earth like you're a worm. They're sorcerers and will turn you into a torch as soon as look at you. Better them, though, than the Shadow-Servant."

"What is a Shadow-Servant?" Wiersa asked and Belarrin shook his head in disbelief. Chostir had gone from spewing lies to telling myths.

A new voice spoke from behind Belarrin, sharp and filled with authority. "I think you would have learned to hold your tongue, Kalilaer."

Belarrin turned to see Captain Eltirkar striding toward them with another Syraestari warrior at his side.

"I'm sorry, Master, forgive me," Chostir said, her face paling. "I meant no harm. I only told them to be dutiful."

"No doubt." The Syraestari's lips thinned. He turned toward the lines of new Kalilaer and in a booming voice, said, "I am Captain Eltirkar, governor of this camp and servant to the High Lord Ushtyl who reigns over Nahirazith." He paused and his brows lowered. "If it has not already become abundantly clear, you are here to work as Kalilaer. You shall always be Kalilaer. You shall live out your short lives here. You shall die here. I know your intellect is akin to that of cattle, but you will understand this. If you work hard and are obedient in all things, you will be housed and fed and shall live in reasonable comfort. But if you are lazy, discontent, or harbor rebellion in your hearts, you shall be punished. The deaths of those that dare to defy their masters will be a painful example to those that outlive them. That is all."

Eltirkar turned to the Syraestari beside him. With a grimace, Belarrin mentally corrected himself: Eltirkar turned to the Finaestari beside him and they spoke quietly. After a moment, the second Finaestari bowed his head slightly. Then Eltirkar left the field and his companion walked down the line of prisoners. Reaching the far end, he turned and retraced his steps until he stood facing Belarrin. Belarrin could not tell if he was recognized or not. He didn't know the Finaestari. What if there was some confusion and he were taken to the mines? The thought of the darkness of those tunnels made him shiver. The warrior pointed at Belarrin, Wiersa, and Yrpel. "These three."

T'Okaedrin rushed forward and cut the ropes connecting Belarrin and his two companions to the rest of the line. Some of the other prisoners whimpered as the three followed the warrior from the field. Other Finaestari approached the line to claim more Kalilaer for different duties.

Belarrin eyed Yrpel, afraid the larger man would try something desperate now that their hands were free, and shook his head fiercely. Yrpel glanced over at him and frowned, but finally nodded.

They walked in silence through the camp and Belarrin saw with some relief that they were not headed toward any of the mines. No one had told him where he was to be assigned, but it would have to be close to the edge of the encampment if the Scions were to have the best chance at freeing him. They passed by several groups of buildings, each with a Kalilaer barracks side by side with several shops. Some of the clusters had carpenters, others cooks or tailors or weavers. In between lay large gaps where no one could walk unmarked. The Finaestari's pace was steady and unhurried, but Belarrin's heart raced inside him. Just like a real Kalilaer. The thought stunned him and he glanced from Yrpel to Wiersa. Yrpel's brows were drawn and his teeth set while Wiersa's cheeks were pale and a sheen of sweat gleamed on his forehead. Belarrin was surprised he wasn't sweating too.

But then he saw that they approached three buildings. The barracks was wide and block shaped while the other two opened on the side facing them. In front of the buildings loomed two conical clay mounds about twice the height of a man. A plume of smoke billowed from one of the cones and another from the farthest building. Several smaller clay lined pits lay in the center of the complex. Belarrin let out a sigh of relief. It was a smelting camp. When he had walked guard duty in the past, he'd seen Kalilaer working at these odd structures. He didn't understand the process, but knew it would be work he could handle. More importantly, it was one of the sets of buildings near the outer edge of the encampment.

As they drew near, a Kalilaer ran out from the left building. Though he didn't appear to be past his middle years, the man's hair was so gray that only his bushy eyebrows hinted that his braided hair had once been black. The man dropped down to one knee before the Finaestari and bowed low. "I am here to serve, Master."

"Three more to work," the Finaestari said, then turned on his heel and walked away, not even pausing to make sure that the new Kalilaer remained. Glancing after him, Belarrin knew why. Even more than as a t'Okaedrin, he could feel the authority and awe towards their masters. Dissent was unfathomable.

CHAPTER 12
Furnace

"When I close my eyes, I still see the towering golden spires of lost Ilera and the radiant blue of Lake Esverin speckled with the white masts of a hundred ships. But then I waken to a sky choked with ash and fire, to water gray, muddy, and brackish. I crouch in my crude hut of rotting deerskin and clutch my knife of stone. Before a sputtering fire, my family shivers, hungry and too tired to weep. I pray for the day His Highest Above will end my life."

—Author Unknown

The Kalilaer rose to his feet and passed his dark brown eyes over the newcomers. He was a short man, barely reaching Belarrin's chin, but his shoulders were broad and his forearms were more massive than on anyone Belarrin had ever met. "Welcome friends."

Dumbfounded at the pleasant greeting, Belarrin didn't respond. His companions were silent, too. After a moment, the older man's lips curved upward into a smile. "I am Regund and I will explain things. But first, what are your names?"

"I am Belarrin," he said, and gestured at the still stunned Zengris. "This is Wiersa."

Before he could say more, the tall Iengian spoke, "I am named Yrpel."

"Excellent," Regund replied, then he shrugged. "As excellent as it can be for any of us, at least. You have been assigned to smelters and we can make good use of you."

"I have no interest in serving the Finnies," Yrpel growled.

Regund frowned. "Then kill yourself and leave the rest of us alone. If you want to live, you serve just as we do."

Yrpel looked around. "I see no guards making you work."

"If we don't work, we aren't fed. They don't have to guard us closely, just kill us when we run. There is no escape, so we work." Regund turned back toward the smelting camp and bellowed, "Zoltha, Idysha!" Two Kalilaer came running from the camp as Regund faced Belarrin and the others again. "We work for food. If we don't work, we starve. If we work well, we eat well and the t'Okaedrin leave us alone. If you work very well, you may be rewarded. The best of us become blacksmiths and live good lives." His lips twisted slightly. "As good, at least, as any of us could hope for."

"What are t'Okaedrin?" Wiersa asked.

"Our human guards, the slave-warriors," Regund said as the two Kalilaer he called arrived, a man and a woman. The man was lanky and, though he was nearly as tall as Belarrin, gave the impression of being smaller. Yet his eyes were bright and knowing. The woman was almost as tall with striking green eyes and fiery red hair that hung almost to her waist. She would have been pale in complexion, but for the heavy layer of soot covering her arms and face. They both stared appraisingly at the newcomers.

The man spoke, his voice naturally soft. "The huge one will go with you, Regund?"

"Yes, Zoltha." Regund nodded. "Yrpel will accompany me to the forges. We shall see how each of you do and can move you if needed. Belarrin, you will learn smelting from Zoltha and Idysha can teach Wiersa charcoaling."

Wiersa's face split into a grin as he looked at Idysha. He winked at Belarrin. "Looks like I'm the lucky one."

The woman snorted. "We'll see if you say the same at the end of the day."

Zoltha walked up to Belarrin and extended his hand. Belarrin took it uncertainly as his trainer said, "I hope you are a man of good judgment. Smelting requires wisdom, patience, and a steady mind."

"You will find that I am."

"Good," Zoltha replied, then turned on his heels and led the way back to the center of the smelting camp where the four smaller clay pits lay. Belarrin saw that Idysha and Wiersa walked to the taller conical mounds while Regund and Yrpel headed toward the farthest building. Half of the central clay pits were unused, but a pair of Kalilaer stooped over one while a young laborer barely out of childhood worked a pair of bellows at a second. The youth looked up as Zoltha arrived. "Fritten, meet Belarrin."

"Welcome," Fritten said.

Unsure quite how to respond, Belarrin said, "Thank you."

"Fritten, Belarrin will partner with me the rest of the day," Zoltha said. "Start the first burn on the next batch of ore."

Fritten nodded and, releasing the bellows, rose to his feet. Belarrin glanced into the youth's blue eyes, but saw no annoyance there. Was it better to work the bellows or prepare ore? Fritten seemed indifferent to either.

As the youth departed, Zoltha sat down and took Fritten's place. Belarrin saw that the two bellows were connected to a single tube that ran through the wall of the clay pit. The pit itself was filled with charcoal and gave off an intense heat, though there was no smoke. "It is important that the bellows be worked constantly," Zoltha said, "pressing down on one while raising the other. Our most important task is to keep the fire at the same heat."

"Is there something else in the pit?" Belarrin asked.

"Yes, iron ore is layered between charcoal, both in equal measure. It looks like there's enough room to add more." Zoltha gestured with his head at two wood crates set to one side, his hands still moving in a steady rhythm on the bellows. "Go ahead, add ore first and then charcoal."

Belarrin did as he was instructed. In one of the crates he found a mound of reddish stones. "This is iron?" he asked, skeptical. "It doesn't look like it."

"That's ore. It won't look like iron until after Regund is done hammering it. Drop several shovelfuls into the pit." Belarrin nodded and scooped the ore in. When he was done, Zoltha said, "Now the same amount of charcoal."

Belarrin dropped the charcoal into the pit then asked, "Now what?"

"Now we wait until the fire has burned down enough to put in more."

"How long does it take?"

"You in a hurry to go somewhere?" Zoltha's laugh was friendly. "We work until dusk. Here, take a turn at the bellows."

Zoltha gave Belarrin his place by the pit. It took Belarrin a moment to get used to the feel of the bellows, but once he did, he focused on trying to maintain the same pace as the other man.

"Good." Zoltha nodded.

"How do you know if the fire is hot enough?" Belarrin asked.

"A good question," Zoltha said. "I didn't think to ask it until my third day. If the charcoal is smoking, it is too cold."

"I see," Belarrin said, wondering how that had been discovered. Zoltha probably had no idea. After a few minutes of working, he asked, "I don't understand what this does."

"Iron gathers at the bottom of the pit where the air blows and the fire is hottest. Sometimes if you look into the pit, you can see it glowing. The other parts of the rock melt away and leave only the iron bloom. Well, mostly iron," he added. "When we're done here, the hammerers like Regund pound out as many of the impurities as they can before it goes to the smiths."

Belarrin lost himself to the rhythm of the bellows. The strong whooshing noise blended with the ring of hammers from the far shop. Waves of heat emanated from the pit, but smoke only came from the charcoalers if the wind gusted from the wrong direction. When his arms got tired, Zoltha took his place and Belarrin added more ore and charcoal to the smelter. For the first time since his infiltration of the Kalilaer had begun, he felt tension begin to ease from his shoulders.

He was happy that his companion was not talkative. Zoltha only spoke when it was time to switch or add more ore. Occasionally he heard Wiersa chattering distantly at Idysha and was glad for the peace here. The less he had to speak to these Kalilaer the better. He didn't really want to know them any more than he had to, and they certainly couldn't get to know him. T'Okaedrin walked past the camp from time to time, though none entered it. Belarrin didn't recognize any, for which he was glad.

As the sun approached the horizon, sending red streamers across the blue sky, the charcoal had burned low again. Belarrin stood to gather more, but Zoltha stopped him with a raised hand. "That's enough for today. We'll let the furnace cool overnight and take the iron bloom out in the morning."

Belarrin nodded as Zoltha rose to his feet. Looking eastward, he said. "Come, I think dinner is arriving."

Following Zoltha's gaze, Belarrin saw four Kalilaer approaching. Fritten was one, but he didn't know the others. They carried several large pottery bowls. Two were tall and narrow. He recognized them as common containers for water or wine. For the Kalilaer it would be water, of course. The other bowls were wider, shallow, and steamed in the cooling air.

All of the laborers from the smelting camp gathered around. Belarrin counted about twenty in number. As he came closer, he saw that the shallow bowls held a thick stew of mashed grain, turnips, and onions along with the less desirable cuts of cattle or pigs. Regund and another Kalilaer emerged from the nearest building with pottery cups that they handed around. Then each of the laborers took their turns getting stew and water. Once that was done, they gathered near the smelters, which still gave off waves of warmth in the cooling evening.

Belarrin followed Zoltha and took a seat on the ground. The food was dull, but still better tasting than the bread they'd eaten on the march. He looked up as Wiersa took a seat on his other side. The man's face and hands were damp from washing but his fingertips were still black.

Wiersa grimaced. "I don't think I'd be able to get all the soot from my hands if I jumped into the sea."

Idysha laughed from the other side of the circle. "Who are you trying to be pretty for, new blood?"

Wiersa tilted his head to the side and grinned at her. "Well…"

Idysha met his look evenly. "In that case you'd better go back to scrubbing and not return till next snows have fallen."

The other Kalilaer laughed at that, but Belarrin could only grimace. As the laughter quieted, Regund looked at the newcomers, "What is life like in the wilderness, now? Are the tribes still battling each other, or are they making peace to fight the Finnies?"

"I hadn't even heard of the Finnies until I was captured," Wiersa said, his smile replaced by a glower. "We'd heard vague rumors of Iron-Men, but nothing more."

"The Iengian still fight anyone who will face us," Yrpel said loudly from the other side of Zoltha. "How else will we prove who is strong?"

Regund shook his head. "And so the Finnies enslave us all."

"Would you have us scurry around like mewling lambs?" Yrpel's brows lowered. "I will not be called weak."

"Of course not." Regund sighed.

"What do you hope for, Regund?" Idysha said, leaning forward to look at the older man. "I haven't been a slave so long that I forget the life before. There was never enough food. Only those strong enough to fight could protect their families."

"So human fights human and the Finnies triumph."

Belarrin glanced between the locked stares of Regund and Idysha, then noticed that most of the other Kalilaer were grimacing with heads bowed to eat their meal. It was an old argument, he sensed, and a meaningless one. Why did they care what the wildmen did now? They were Kalilaer and that was better. They never again had to worry about starvation or being slaughtered by a rival clan.

Zoltha turned to Belarrin, perhaps as much for a distraction as wishing to know the true answer. "What about you?" he asked.

Belarrin hesitated as all eyes turned on him. He realized he could use his reluctance to end all such questions at once. "We fought when we had to," he admitted, then dropped his gaze and more quietly added, "But I don't want to talk about it. What good is it talking about what was? It's all gone now."

"The wounds are still raw for many of us. I understand and am sorry," Zoltha said. The other Kalilaer in the circle shifted awkwardly or turned to gaze up to the crimson-stained sky, deep in their own thoughts.

"Belarrin's family were priests, though," Wiersa blurted. "Show them your necklace!"

Belarrin wanted to strangle the Zengris, but with all eyes on him he reluctantly pulled the clear gemstone out from under his shirt, wondering again why he'd worn it in the first place. Several of the laborers gasped aloud. Zoltha leaned forward, his eyes wide. "Highest Above bless us. Is that one of Isi's Tears?"

Belarrin looked down at the pale gemstone. It glimmered faintly as it drank in the starlight. "I'm not sure," he admitted.

"I don't understand why the Iron-Men didn't take it," Wiersa said.

Anger flashing, Belarrin opened his mouth to speak, but Zoltha answered first. "They only loot the dead, not the living."

"What does it matter to them if we live or die?" Yrpel snapped, but shame lay heavy in his voice. "We were all too weak to withstand them."

"The Finnies want slaves, not corpses," Zoltha answered, "and the Iron-Men obey their masters without question." Belarrin nodded in agreement. At least one of these Kalilaer understood. Zoltha continued, "I've heard the Iron-Men even worship His Highest Above and all the Etyni, but their rituals are twisted from the lies their masters have told them."

Belarrin stared at the other man as heat rose to his face. Zoltha looked back at him, but if he sensed any anger, he didn't show it. "Could I see the stone?"

Belarrin wanted to protest, but he couldn't think of an excuse. As he pulled the necklace over his head, the black stone fell free from his shirt and dangled against his chest. Belarrin wanted to shove it back, but decided the safer course was to ignore it. He handed the pale stone to Zoltha. The other man raised it to his eyes and stared at it. "I am almost certain that this is a Tear of Isi," he said, his voice dropping almost to a whisper. "How did you come by it?"

"I think my family has always had it," Belarrin said. Then, unable to contain his curiosity, he asked, "What is a Tear of Isi?" He knew who Isi was, of course. One of the ten Etyni, she had brought music into the world. During the Great War against Cydion, she'd been murdered by the very humans she had sought to protect.

"I'm not completely sure," Zoltha replied. "The priest in my tribe had one before I was born, but during a quake, the earth opened up beneath him and the stone was lost. Yet this is how my mother described it to me."

"But what is a Tear of Isi?" Wiersa echoed Belarrin's question.

Zoltha laughed bitterly. "I know little more than you, I'm sure. I always loved the old stories before my people were enslaved. But what my mother told me was a legend at best. It was said that when Cydion first blackened the world with his armies that Isi wept crystal tears. These were given to all the races and kingdoms of Isfalinis so that they might know that the Etyni grieved with them." He shrugged. "I don't know how much of it is true, but I pray it all is. There is power in the tears of an Etyni. It almost gives me hope."

Despite himself, Belarrin felt enthralled by the other man's words. Zoltha might be wrong about many things, but it was clear that he was a thinker.

"What is the black stone?" Zoltha asked, pointing at the other necklace.

Belarrin blinked. Sometimes the simplest lie was the best. "I found it several years ago and liked it so I made it into a necklace."

"I've never seen anything like it," Zoltha said.

Yrpel leaned forward and stared at it. "It looks like charcoal. I could crush it with a hammer and find out."

"No!" Belarrin cried, stuffing it back under his shirt. He took the other necklace from Zoltha's hand and slid it back over his head as well. "It is a reminder to me of home."

"I meant no offense, Belarrin." Yrpel raised his hands, palms out.

"Just the same, I'll keep it from your hands."

The Kalilaer chuckled at that. Then Idysha gasped loudly and jumped to her feet, her eyes staring behind Belarrin. He turned to look over his shoulder as three figures approached.

Two were t'Okaedrin and the third was a Kalilaer woman in ragged clothing. Her walk was more of a stumbling shuffle as they approached. She looked vaguely familiar. Then he realized it was the woman from the Boards. She was shorter than he 'd realized, the brown locks of her hair plastered to her face by sweat and dirt.

"Chostir!" Idysha cried, running toward her. Zoltha leapt to his feet and followed after. Together they helped the woman walk the final distance.

The t'Okaedrin followed more slowly, then stopped a dozen paces away from the group of Kalilaer. "Inside!" one of them commanded.

The Kalilaer rose to their feet and obediently filed into the barracks. Regund handed Belarrin two cups of water. "For Chostir," he said, then grabbed a bowl of the stew. Belarrin followed him into the building. Once everyone was inside, the t'Okaedrin shut the door behind them and an iron bar rattled into place, locking them inside.

The Kalilaer barracks barely resembled a t'Okaedrin one. Instead of beds, each person was allotted a straw pallet. Nor was there any storage chest or any sort of privacy except for a wooden partition that stretched down the middle, dividing the women's half from the men's. There were no windows, leaving the interior stuffy and full of the stink of sweating humans.

The Kalilaer huddled around the sitting form of Chostir, a cluster of shadows in the near darkness. Regund knelt down beside her and handed her a bowl. "We kept some food for you in case you survived the Boards." At a gesture from him, Belarrin stooped down and handed over the water.

"Thank you," Chostir said, her voice rasping. She hurriedly drank both cups of water then tore into the stew.

Zoltha glared down at her, "You are a fool, Chostir. One of these days they'll leave you on the Boards forever."

Chostir paused from shoveling the food into her mouth and looked up. Her grin was barely visible in the darkness. "Can't be much worse than what they've already done to me."

"You're not listening to me. You could have died!"

She shrugged. "What is the alternative, Zoltha? If I don't defy them, then I become what they want me to be. I'd rather be dead than break forever."

"There are better ways, safer ways."

"I'm tired of being safe!" she cried. "That's what they want from us, but it's a lie. If I have to suffer on the Boards to remember who I am, then that's what I must do." Her voice choked with tears. "I can't lose that. It's all I have left."

No one responded and, one by one, each of the Kalilaer drifted off to their pallets. Belarrin found an empty one and, curling up on it, tried to find sleep.

CHAPTER 13
Courage

"The Cataclysm destroyed our memory but left us our identity. It was the Finaestari who stole that away, leaving humanity shorn of tribe and clan."

—Thane Henirgar of Merania

"How do I know Sizras isn't behind whatever rabble is posting treason all over our cities?" High Lord Arkesh asked. He stood taller than Ushtyl, with a shock of curly brown hair and dark brown eyes, edged with paint that flared back toward his ears.

High Lord Sizras glared at Arkesh, his muscular arms crossed in front of his chest. "As if I would ever stoop to subterfuge." He turned to Ushtyl. "Why did you ask that we meet with you? I have nothing in common with this man."

"Nor I him." Arkesh snorted.

Ushtyl leaned forward, resting both palms on the table between them. "I know, my Lords, that you have your differences. That you, Sizras, want to abandon this dominion for a refuge while Arkesh believes in securing our home here. But despite this disagreement, we are all more alike than different. I've heard both of you express dissatisfaction at the empress' efforts to curb our noble rights."

"That does not make us alike," Sizras replied. "And I know your proclivities are the same as his, Ushtyl. It was only at the behest of Tazil that I came at all. Him, I respect, even though we stand apart."

"My belief in dominion is well known," Ushtyl answered. "The high lords are evenly split on the matter, four in each camp with the empress remaining undecided. Until she summons us all to convene, I believe there cannot be an answer." Ushtyl spread his hands wide in a placating gesture. "But that is not the only question facing us. If we can agree to set the debate of empire and refuge aside, I believe we can work together for the good of us all."

Sizras' brow furrowed. "I'm displeased with Kayrstana's impositions, but I am not a traitor to the throne or our people."

"Traitor?" Arkesh sputtered.

But Ushtyl pushed to his feet, hands out in a placating gesture. "Neither are we, Sizras, and treason is not what I suggest."

"Speak plainly, then," Sizras replied, "for my patience is thin."

Impossible man, too full of his own honor and pride. But Ushtyl knew such thoughts were unhelpful and pushed them down. Instead, he kept his voice soft and calm. "I have no stomach for rebellion either, Sizras. But that doesn't mean I'll stand idly by why the empress devours our privileges. The empress is our ruler, but we are her lords. Just as we offer her fealty and service, so she entrusts each of our cities to us to rule as we see best. We have lead each of our peoples through the darkest part of the Cataclysm with courage and great sacrifice. We have shown ourselves to be lords of competence and valor, never shirking from the threats of humanity or the ruin of the world. Despite this, she encroaches on her obligations to us. We are fully in our rights as high lords to prevent her from seizing that which is not hers to take. Our housecarls, our cities, our people."

Sizras rubbed his chin. "What did you have in mind?"

"An alliance of high lords. I believe that all but Tyrnis and Jesaelyn will join us. When the empress pressures any one of us beyond her authority, we stand together to resist her."

"I will stoop to nothing dishonorable. No artifice. Anything I agree to will be plain to all. My people and yours, everyone knows how I stand on such matters and I will state it plainly."

"Not subterfuge, then," Ushtyl replied. Though if all went well, he thought he might bend Sizras on that matter. "But we, as concerned peers, can surely align against the predations of our liege. Where one might crumble, united we can prevent her continued seizure of our rights."

"Such as your desire to command your own raid."

"Yes," Ushtyl replied. "For centuries, each high lord has had the authority to order his armies for the good of his people. To fend off incursions and counter against threats to the realm. But now the empress wants to centralize our warriors under her direct control despite the skill with which each of us has seen to our obligations."

Sizras frowned, considering. "With the constraint that I will have no part in trickery, I am willing to meet the others."

"And you, Arkesh?" Ushtyl asked. "When I spoke with you and Ovirkar before, you sounded agreeable."

"I will work with Sizras and Zaerina if they agree to root out whoever is causing dissention in our cities," Arkesh said. "Every few days I see new rubbish trying to rally support for their so-called refuge."

"That I will not do," Sizras said. "These actions cannot be considered crimes when even the high lords are undecided." He turned to Ushtyl. "It would seem you will have to decide between us."

Ushtyl suppressed a growl of frustration. "You would cast away your rule for this, Arkesh? If you walk away, Ovirkar will follow and we will be too few. The empress will triumph and we will all cower under her thumb."

Arkesh's lips twisted in distaste and he flashed a glare at Sizras. "Fine, I agree. Kayrstana has taken to meddling in the training of my t'Okaedrin, now. She seems to think the increased Scion raids a justifiable reason. As if I cannot protect my own people!"

"Good, thank you Arkesh. And thank you, Sizras. I know you both hold the good of our people in your hearts."

"Just to be clear," Sizras said with a glance to Arkesh, "I will tolerate no discussion of dominion. If I see that motive in this collaboration, I will leave and I'm sure Lady Zaerina join me. I would choose to be a broken lord fully beneath the empress' thumb before I relent on this."

"Yes, yes," Arkesh replied. "I already consented."

"Then we have agreement." Ushtyl said. He poured out three goblets of wine and passed them out. "To our success, then, my Lords."

"To our success," they echoed.

He took a long slow drink.

Night passed slowly. Belarrin lay on his pallet and, despite his weariness, stared into the darkness and listened to the surrounding snores. He'd expected life among the Kalilaer to be easier than among the newly captured wildmen or among the Scions of the Fallen Tree. It was and yet it wasn't. The Scions were apostates, beyond salvation, while the wildmen wallowed in barbaric ignorance. But the Kalilaer were living a good and noble life. They weren't slaves as they claimed, but lived as humans should live in worthy service to the Syraestari. He wasn't a fool and knew that many were unhappy with their lot. Else the Scions would have no power. Yet knowing and seeing were two different things. They were as willful and defiant as Parvik and Vitarria, only bowing from fear and want. From people with such beliefs, he would've expected sullen barbarity as among the wildmen, but that wasn't the case either. After only a few hours working at Zoltha's side, it was already obvious that the man contemplated deeply despite having an outlook just as blinded as the others. Even Chostir, misguided though she was, had enough self-possession to think about who she was and who she wanted to be. But how could people who had lived in the wilderness, without civilization and only tainted legends to carry them, be like that?

It would make blending in among them more difficult. He had to be careful that they didn't see through his deception. Yrpel had been too blinded by his rage and Wiersa his bitterness to see anything clearly. But these Kalilaer might. Especially one as clever as Zoltha. He would have to embrace this false self he'd created even more fully if he was to succeed.

He did not know when he finally fell asleep, only that when he opened his eyes again, dull gray light slipped through tiny cracks in the walls. After the doors were unbarred by the t'Okaedrin, Zoltha showed Belarrin where the well was outside. They carried water into the barracks while several of the Kalilaer ran off to pick up the camp's breakfast ration. Belarrin washed his face then joined the other Kalilaer outside where they shared their bland meal of mashed grain and vegetables. They ate quickly and no one seemed inclined to talk. Belarrin was glad of the quiet.

As they finished, Zoltha turned to him. "I'll partner with you again today. First, we'll see how yesterday's bloom fared."

Belarrin nodded and, after they rinsed out their bowls and left them in the barracks, they went to the smelter. Clearing the cold charcoal and ash away was a filthy but quick task. Reaching down inside, Zoltha pulled out the iron bloom.

"That's it?" Belarrin asked, surprised. The bloom was the size of two clenched fists. The central lump of metal still looked vaguely rock-like, with coarse ridges of discolored ore crisscrossing its outer surface.

"That's it," Zoltha replied. "When our camp is at full strength, we have enough workers to make four of these a day. There are a handful of other smelting camps around here too, and that adds up to a lot of iron. More importantly, it gets us our food."

"I don't understand."

Zoltha gestured with his head to Belarrin's right. "Look."

Turning, Belarrin saw two Finaestari approaching. Both wore robes, one of deep green and the other black. "They inspect the iron we've made each morning. If they're satisfied, we eat well. If they are unhappy, we get less food. If we create steel, they reward us even more than normal."

"Why don't we just make steel, then?"

Zoltha laughed. "If only it were that simple. Steel is made the same way as iron, but the heat has to be kept perfect throughout the process. We do our best, but there's no way to know until the bloom is done." He shrugged. "Frankly, I can't really tell steel from iron, but the Finnies can."

Though he knew the answer, Belarrin asked his next question because he knew a normal Kalilaer would wonder. "What makes steel better?"

"Under heated iron can be soft, causing weapons to lose their edge quickly while overheated iron is too brittle. Steel is neither. More than that, I can't say for sure. Maybe the blacksmiths know." In a hushed voice, he added, "Silent now, while the Finnies are here."

As the two Finaestari walked up to the smelters, Belarrin dropped to his knees like all the other Kalilaer. The pair strode up to Zoltha. "Give," the one in black said.

"Yes, Master," Zoltha replied, holding up the bloom.

The Finaestari took it and said, "Tethyntoes chatimtriv dipesar."

Out of the corner of his eye, he saw the Finaestari hold the bloom up close to his ear. After a moment, the Finaestari grunted and dropped the iron to the ground at his feet. "Good iron, no steel."

Belarrin remained on his knees as the pair walked over to the next smelter. Once they had seen all the blooms, they headed to the furnaces where Regund and Yrpel worked. Only then did Zoltha rise to his feet. Belarrin and the other Kalilaer stood, too.

"Those two come by every morning. Sometimes they inspect the blooms, but they usually just look at the hammered ore. It's always the same pair." Zoltha grinned as he continued, "I call them Cydion and Veduk."

Belarrin's jaw dropped. "But those are..."

"The Lord of Death and Siona's chief lieutenant." Zoltha laughed. "I know I must obey the Finnies or pay with my life, but behind their backs it helps to resist at least a little."

Belarrin found himself smiling. The small act of rebellion was amusing. It was like Chostir, but perhaps safer. Unless, of course, the Finnies overheard him. "Cydion and Veduk."

"Cydion's the one in black. Veduk rarely talks." Zoltha stooped to pick up the bloom. "We'll prepare the smelter for today's burn and then give this to the hammerers. By then, the Finnies should be gone."

Preparing the smelter was much like the work from the day before. First, Zoltha checked to make sure that the clay walls were undamaged and that the tube for the bellows was in place. Then they loaded up the pit with charcoal. No ore was to be added until it reached full temperature. Once everything was ready, Belarrin followed Zoltha up to the hammerer's building.

Smoke was already billowing out of its chimney and the air rang with the sound of the hammers. Inside, Regund worked a set of bellows at a furnace of stone rather than clay. Yrpel and several other laborers gripped glowing blooms with iron tongs and hammered at them, their muscles bulging and sweat streaming down their faces.

"They remove the last of the impurities this way," Zoltha shouted to be heard over the ringing.

Belarrin nodded. These blooms looked more like what he expected. The iron Yrpel worked was smoother. Golden sparks flared out with each strike of his hammer. Yrpel looked over at them briefly, nodding, before returning to work. Zoltha showed Belarrin a bucket where they stored the unhammered blooms before leading the way back to the smelter.

The work was much the same as the day before and, by midday, Belarrin began to find it tiresome. He recognized the challenge of keeping the fire at the right temperature.

Also, he realized, the labor at the bellows would keep his muscles strong since he couldn't drill with a sword. But that didn't help the long unchanging hours. T'Okaedrin walked by from time to time, eyeing the Kalilaer at work. Only once did they enter the camp. Whenever they approached, the Kalilaer not at the bellows bowed low, but the one pumping kept working, though he bowed his head, too. Not even the presence of the brothers was an excuse to risk letting the smelting temperature drop. More rarely, Finnies walked by the camp. Except for Cydion and Veduk that morning, none entered it, and most gave the working Kalilaer no attention at all.

As the sun began its descent, Zoltha suddenly straightened from where he'd been standing over the smelter and looked to the east. "Cydion's Abyss," he cursed. "More of them?"

Without pausing in his pumping of the bellows, Belarrin looked over his shoulder. A long line of prisoners marched onto the field where he'd arrived yesterday. There were at least another hundred there. It had to be the second group of Kalilaer from the other villages. Again, he asked a question to which he knew the answer. "It isn't normal for them to bring in this many at once?"

Zoltha shook his head, his face pale. "We rarely see more than one group a month, but now two in two days? Highest Above, what is to become of us?"

Belarrin had no answer he was willing to give. As they worked the bellows, they watched the prisoners arrive and be separated out. Belarrin was grateful that none were assigned to the smelting camp. If any real Tatyrni tribesmen arrived, he might have been exposed as a fraud.

When all the prisoners were gone, they turned their full focus back to their work and the rest of the afternoon passed only slowly to the rhythm of the bellows. By the time they stopped for their evening meal, Belarrin was glad for the break in routine. But they had barely begun eating when Regund said, "Iron-Men approaching."

Belarrin followed the other Kalilaers' lead as they set down their bowls and knelt down with heads lowered to the earth. Although he knew this was an appropriate sign of respect, he chaffed to be on the other side once more.

The t'Okaedrin stepped into the middle of the circle of Kalilaer and one said, "I remember you." Belarrin grimaced as he recognized the voice. Glancing out of the corner of his eye, he saw Arcomin with Hirnid beside him. They stood in front of Yrpel. "Get up, Kalilaer," Arcomin ordered, "and look me in the eyes."

Yrpel rose slowly to his feet and straightened. The tall Iengian towered over the two t'Okaedrin.

"No ropes on your hands this time, Kalilaer," Arcomin said. "Think you can kill me now?" When Yrpel did not reply, Arcomin turned to Hirnid and laughed. "I told you he was a coward."

Belarrin sensed more than saw Yrpel tense. "Don't do it, Yrpel!"

The t'Okaedrin spun towards him and Belarrin quickly dropped his head again. A moment later, Arcomin's boots stepped into Belarrin's vision. "So, there are two fools in this camp." Arcomin drove his knee into Belarrin's shoulder, dropping him flat to the ground. "Get up!"

Forcing his clenched jaw to relax, Belarrin stood.

"Look at me."

Reluctantly, Belarrin raised his eyes to meet Arcomin's. They'd been brothers for over fifteen years, neither knowing whom had been rescued from the wildmen first. They had endured the strict discipline of childhood and had fought, side by side in dozens of battles. Though they were rivals, they were brothers stronger than any bond of blood. But now, as he met his brother's gaze, Belarrin couldn't see even the smallest hint of recognition. Within Arcomin's eyes lay only contempt and loathing. As had happened on the march to Nahirazith, Belarrin realized he feared his brother as he knew all Kalilaer must fear him.

"Do you give the orders here, Kalilaer?" Arcomin asked. When Belarrin hesitated, he roared, "Answer the question!"

"I'm sorry, Master, I meant no wrong."

"And what about you? Are you a coward, too?"

"No, Master."

Arcomin spat in his face. Belarrin was so startled by the attack that he took a step back, clenching his fists. His lips twisted into a snarl, but the dark gleam in his Arcomin's gaze stopped him. He drew in a deep breath and forced his hands to relax as the spittle dripped down his cheek.

"Apparently you are," Arcomin said, then drove his fist into Belarrin's stomach.

Belarrin braced for the blow at the last moment, but the pain of it doubled him over, driving him to his knees. Arcomin's mocking laughter echoed in his ears and Belarrin's face flushed red with anger and shame.

Hirnid stepped up beside Arcomin and bellowed, "Everyone in the barracks!"

All around him, the other Kalilaer scrambled to their feet. Gathering up their food, they headed into the building. Belarrin rose last and dared a glance at his brother. Arcomin's eyes were locked on his, lips twisted in scorn. Belarrin was tempted to hold that gaze, but he didn't know what Arcomin might do. Instead, he ducked his head and hurried to the barracks. Silently he made a promise. When he returned to the t'Okaedrin, they would exchange more than simple words.

As the iron bar slid into place, locking them inside, Yrpel turned on him. "Why did you speak for me? I fight my own battles!"

"Fine then," Belarrin retorted. "Fight them next time and die, you fool! That's what you want isn't it?"

Before Yrpel could reply, Regund stepped between them. "Peace, Yrpel, Belarrin is right. The Iron-Man was just looking for an excuse to open your stomach. If you resist, you die. The Finnies only care about having good workers, but some of the Iron-Men are pettier. They enjoy fighting when they cannot lose."

Belarrin turned on Regund, glad the darkness hid his clenched teeth. That wasn't true. Or at least it shouldn't have been.

"I'm sorry, Belarrin," Yrpel said, then let out a long sigh. "But I vow on my life and yours that all Iron-Men will die in the end."

Belarrin only grunted and pushed away from the group. He felt their eyes on him, appreciating what he'd done, as he sat down on his pallet and finished his dinner. Then he curled up and closed his eyes to be free of their stares.

He couldn't deny Regund's words no matter how much he wanted to. How could any of them believe anything else with Arcomin providing the truth of it? T'Okaedrin shouldn't behave like that. They guarded the Kalilaer and protected them, as much from themselves as the Scions. But they didn't scoff or torment. Certainly, the Kalilaer were beneath them in honor and courage, but they were good people doing what was right. Arcomin always had the tendency to push the edge of what was honorable, but he was stepping beyond it now. Was it because Belarrin was here and vulnerable? Or was it his way of grieving the death of Eldest Nalsuntha?

Belarrin squeezed his eyes tight. In this place, he'd had no time to mourn the death of his brother and he still couldn't. Not until he was home again. Nalsuntha had been such a good eldest. He deserved so much more.

Belarrin rolled onto his side, trying to change the course of his thoughts. But thinking of how he'd intervened in Arcomin's torments only darkened Belarrin's mood. He couldn't say why he'd spoken. It didn't matter if Yrpel died or not. For that matter, only a few days ago, he'd wanted Yrpel dead himself. What scared him most was that he could not be sure of the answer to his own question. He might have just been angry at Arcomin's intrusion, but he couldn't drive away the thought that he was no longer indifferent to Yrpel's fate.

Only slowly did sleep come to him, leading to a new day much like the one before it. Cydion and Veduk came by early to inspect the ore and then he and Zoltha started up the smelter. Zoltha was an easy man to work with and the pair fell into a steady routine. Several hours after midday, Zoltha was adding ore to the smelter when he looked up and said, "Those Iron-Man are back."

Since Belarrin was working the bellows, he only bowed his head and continued to work. But a lump rose in his throat when he saw Hirnid stop near the edge of the camp. Arcomin entered alone.

Zoltha knelt to the earth as Arcomin walked up. "You, Kalilaer! Stand up!"

Belarrin obediently scrambled to his feet. As soon as he did, Zoltha rose and took his place at the bellows.

"You thought you were safe at the bellows, didn't you?" Arcomin asked.

"No, Master," Belarrin replied, forcing his eyes down. If he met Arcomin's gaze he feared he might lose control.

"That's right you aren't. I know a troublemaker when I see one. What is your name, Kalilaer?"

"Belarrin, Master."

"Your name is Dog now, got it? And I've got my eye on you. I see a slow death on the Boards in your future."

"Yes, Master."

"Look at me, Dog."

Reluctantly, Belarrin raised his eyes just as Arcomin struck him with his fist. He hadn't seen it coming and the blow caught him square in the jaw. Belarrin stumbled back. He tripped over the edge of the smelter and sprawled on the ground beside it, stars flashing before his eyes.

"Remember that!" Arcomin laughed, then turned to stride away.

Belarrin pushed to his knees and fingered his jaw, amazed that it wasn't broken. What madness had taken Arcomin? They'd always been rivals, but this was crazy.

"You are a very brave man," Zoltha said.

"Hardly," Belarrin replied, spitting blood and shifting to a sitting position. Would Hirnid restrain him? Could he? Hirnid was a good brother, but he was a follower. If only he told Dalric. His father would put a stop to this. Wouldn't he?

"Nothing broken?"

"No."

"Take as long as you need, I'm good on the bellows for a while yet."

"Thank you." Belarrin sighed as Regund, Chostir and a few others ran up. They gathered around him and Idysha followed after them with a bowl of water in her soot-stained hands.

"Thank you," Belarrin said again, taking it.

"I've never seen such rage before," Regund said. "The Iron-Men like to torment us when they get bored, but not with this much attention. Especially with so little cause."

"I guess I'm a lucky one." Belarrin grunted.

"Maybe it's all the raids they're doing," Zoltha said. "There seem to be more Iron-Men about than normal. They might have lost one of their own in a battle and are taking it personally. Did any of them die when your village was attacked, Belarrin?"

"I don't know, maybe," Belarrin could only stammer as his mind turned again to Nalsuntha, dead of an arrow in the eye.

They all nodded and Chostir said, "If we're lucky, that one will go on a raid and get killed."

"One can only dream," Regund replied.

Idysha stepped forward and rested her hand on Belarrin's shoulder. "If he returns, we won't be able to intervene, but we all are with you."

Surprised at the gentleness in the woman's tone, Belarrin looked up to see genuine concern in her eyes. He had never heard that much care from anyone, not even Elestis or Auphni. "I…" He didn't know how to respond. "I don't know what to say. Thank you."

Once they were sure he wasn't seriously hurt, the others returned to their work. Unwilling to be cowed, Belarrin took his turn on the bellows as soon as he could and the rest of the day passed in undisturbed toil.

That evening as they ate, Yrpel said, "If these Iron-Men keep coming back, we must do something. We must escape!"

"Foolish talk," Regund replied. "You'll never make it. There are few guards here, but they are numerous closer to the forest. They have horses and bows while you have nothing."

"But this is madness!" Yrpel said.

"Regund is right, Yrpel," Idysha said. "I want to be free of this as much as you, but we cannot be rash. Slaves don't escape without help."

"Help?" Wiersa asked.

"The Scions of the Fallen Tree," Idysha replied.

At the mention of that name, Belarrin's ears perked up, but Regund snorted. "The Iron-Men are too strong, even for the Scions. I've seen their raids before. Most who run end up dead or recaptured. Only this time they're sent down into the mines and never see daylight again."

Fritten nodded. "Who would want to live in the woods anyway? Don't you remember what that life was like? We ran from place to place, always afraid of being attacked by other tribes, always afraid of starving. Here, all I have to do is work hard and do as I'm told. That's a better life than anything those Scions could offer."

Belarrin nodded as he looked at the younger man, weighing him again in his mind. He had taken his youth for naivety before, but he alone seemed to understand.

Idysha, however, did not. "I'd rather starve than give up hope for a life beyond these chains," she snapped. "This life is empty. We breathe in the charcoal dust all day until we can hardly stand it and eat gruel for every meal. We can't walk more than a few hundred paces without punishment or death. The only time I'm happy is in my sleep. You can keep your chains, Fritten, I will put my faith in better days."

Zoltha spoke, his voice softer than the others, but with a confidence that turned all ears to him. "Faith is what matters most.

"Faith in what?" Chostir asked bitterly. "The Etyni? His Highest Above?"

"Yes."

Chostir laughed. "And what can they do? The Etyni are dead. Cydion murdered each of them before he, too, fell. They are on the far side of the grave and cannot help us."

"The Etyni aren't like us. Death cannot destroy them," Zoltha replied.

"If they could help, they wouldn't have let us end up here."

"His Highest Above is greater than all of that."

"What kind of god would let the Cataclysm destroy the world?" Chostir snapped. "Not a living one! The Etyni are dead and gone. So is His Highest Above, if he ever was. If he ever cared. We are alone. We will die alone and this is the end of everything." Her last words were choked and tears sprang from her eyes as she rose to her feet and stormed off into the barracks.

They watched her go in silence, then Idysha stood. She turned to Zoltha. "I don't know if His Highest Above hears us or not, but your faith gives me comfort."

Zoltha smiled sadly. "Sometimes I doubt too, but it is all I have. I must believe or there is nothing left."

Idysha nodded, then turned to follow Chostir into the barracks.

As she left, Belarrin looked from one Kalilaer's face to another, marveling at the passions in each of their voices. Not one agreed with another, but they all believed strongly. Even the foolish arguments were made with a certainty he had to admire. Even more startling, he understood them all. After only a couple days, he could feel Idysha's desperation, Regund's despair, Chostir's bitterness, and Zoltha's faith. They were all wrong, all except Fritten. But he understood.

CHAPTER 14
Dreams

"It is not difficult to understand how someone living in abject misery might cast all aside in one desperate grasp for hope. But those who live in relative ease and make the same drastic choices with the same dire consequences I cannot comprehend. Is it courage or is it folly?"

-Erpitha of Algathnarhil

Ninanna awoke to the sensation of motion. She opened her eyes, listening, but the room was silent. Darkness was complete. The air smelled faintly of her leather armor and the lilac soap she'd washed with the night before. All seemed as it should be, yet she knew it was not. She slipped her hand beneath her pillow and was glad to find her knife still there. She inched it out silently from its sheath, listening.

Most likely it was Reigliff again, but she had lived too many centuries as a bodyguard to trust assumptions. Sitting up, she hissed, "Eusy'arjev vled loesyns."

Light flooded over the room as her bedside candle burst into flame, revealing the robed figure of the Shadow-Servant sitting in the chair. "Kind of you to leave me my knife this time."

"I trusted you to be more circumspect." Reigliff shrugged, then added in a biting tone, "I suppose I should offer you congratulations on the enslavement of a few hundred more humans."

"Get out!" Ninanna spat as anger and shame flooded over her.

"So that does bother you? I was beginning to wonder."

Tightening the grip on her knife, Ninanna fought against the waves of emotion roiling within her. She kept her voice cold. "A wise man does not goad the person he's begging for help."

Reigliff bowed his head. "I take your point."

"Why are you bothering me?"

"I wish to continue our conversation from before."

"Then come at a normal hour and leave me my sleep."

"At the hours you prefer, you're generally in the company of those I have little care for." At Ninanna's shrug, he continued, "I gave you my name in return for vigilance. What have you seen?"

"Nothing unexpected," Ninanna said, leaning back against the headboard. "Just the usual bickering and posturing."

"Have we all grown so complacent?" The Shadow-Servant growled. "I've heard housecarls and lords cursing the empress openly. They only do so because their high lords accept it."

"I've cursed you many times, but that doesn't mean I'm plotting you harm."

"I shall take that as a comfort," he said, dryly.

Ninanna crossed her arms over her knees. "I know your name, now, yet you insist on wearing your mask. Have you come to believe your own theatrics?"

"Interesting that you think I wear a mask to hide who I am. I do not need to conceal what is never seen."

She shrugged. Maybe it was a mark of madness. "You said you wouldn't return until you could prove your point. I hope there is more to this meeting than your own type of posturing."

"It would seem that I lied, though I doubt that surprises you. I've come because I learned something new that might cause you concern." When Ninanna didn't reply, he continued, "Are you aware that your raid's greater purpose was to infiltrate a t'Okaedrin among the new slaves?"

Ninanna sat up straighter. "What? Why?"

"Ushtyl and Tazil hope that when the Scions next attack, the infiltrator will escape with them. They want to track down the Scion camps and destroy the whole rebellion. If they succeed, it could mean the end of all human resistance. It would only be a matter of time before all tribes within several hundred miles of our border were subjugated."

Ninanna kept her face smooth, even as anger roiled within her. The high lords knew her Oath, but they'd used it against her. No, she amended, she had allowed them to by deceiving herself. When she'd taken command, Ninanna had told herself she did so because her people were in danger. A truth that was also a lie. Her people were living close to the edge of losing all they had. This war had always been one of annihilation, or at least one of subjugation. But this newest raid had pushed the war closer to its conclusion. Her raid. She wondered if the empress had known the high lords' true purpose.

Reigliff tilted his head. "Though you try and hide it, I can tell the fate of the humans troubles you."

"What I believe is no concern of yours." Reigliff did not reply, his eyes locked on hers. Ninanna felt her anger rise. "You play with me, Shadow-Servant, and I won't allow it. You claim you want my help, but your every act is to manipulate. First you goad, then you cajole, then you bait. If you were anyone else, I'd ask if you knew about the infiltrator before our march north. But I cannot trust any answer you give. You don't want an ally, you seek a pawn. It's all your kind has ever sought. I am not yours to be pushed wherever it suits you. I am who I am and will act as I choose regardless of your schemes. If you knew anything about me, you would know that for truth. Not even your name gives trust. I want nothing to do with you."

Reigliff did not stir. Not even his eyes flickered to suggest anger, remorse, or frustration. When he spoke, his voice was soft but without emotion. "Go your own way, then, Sword-Whisperer and be who you will be. But as you do, consider turning your path toward the infiltrator. As a Kalilaer, he calls himself Belarrin and you will find him at the smelter nearest the city."

"Why would I do that?

"You may find the words he whispers in his dreams curious. Words like 'Ae'irpiva.'"

Ninanna could not stop her eyebrows from rising. "Does he know what it means?"

"I don't know."

"This is another lie, another trap of yours."

"No."

"Then explain to me how a t'Okaedrin could know a Word of Power."

"Are you so certain it's impossible? When we live in days of prophecy, even the possible is bent by fate."

Ninanna snorted. "By that reasoning, you have nothing to be afraid of. Fate will provide."

"You misunderstand me. Fate provides the tools, but it is up to us how to use them. Prophecy only predicts the conflict and the dangers, but the description of what follows is always painfully vague."

"And yet you're surprised that I don't believe you."

"As you wish. Don't be surprised if I call upon you again."

"I have no doubt you'll know how to find me," Ninanna replied, dropping back to her pillow.

Reigliff bowed his head. "Kargats zathoes."

Shadows closed over the room for the length of a breath, then faded to reveal she was alone again. It was peculiar that he insisted upon such theatrics even though she was unimpressed. Though he strived to set himself apart, he couldn't conceal that he was driven by normal and understandable desires. It was nice to know that he had more weakness than just those of character.

She rolled onto her shoulder to blow out her candle, then lay back down on her pillow. In a few days' time, she would be done with her final tasks from the campaign. She'd relinquish command back to Ushtyl and Tazil and return to Thusaeyanin. When she arrived, she would ask the empress about the infiltrator. It was unlikely the conversation would be pleasant.

When the next morning dawned, Ninanna rose feeling unrested and troubled in spirit. As much as she hated to admit it, Reigliff was right. She hadn't done enough to safeguard humanity. Unlike the rest of the Syraestari, she'd never foresworn their ancient Oath. She was still devoted to the well-being of the other races as much as her own. Yet she had become a slaver herself and an aid to those who sought to destroy the human resistance.

How had it happened? How had she slipped so far away from who she once was? Thinking back, Ninanna couldn't even see the path. It was so slow, step by step, convincing herself she was but one person doing all that she could.

She tried sitting at her table and focusing on her final report to Ushtyl and Tazil, but it seemed that every word she wrote spoke the lie of who she had become. When her Pi'aernoth servant walked through the door carrying a breakfast of warm bread and a goblet of wine, Ninanna looked up and asked, "Are you happy, Talikae?"

The human set the bowl down and, bowing, said, "My Lady, I do not understand."

"Are you happy?"

"I am honored to serve one so revered as you. I hope my service has been to your liking."

"It has."

"Then I am happy, my Lady."

Ninanna ground her teeth. She was certain the woman was not stupid. Nor did she detect any guile. Had the Pi'aernoth training beaten all sense of self-will from her? Ninanna rose from her chair and sat on the bed. Gesturing to the chair, she said, "Please sit."

"My Lady?" Talikae gasped. "I couldn't, please forgive me, it wouldn't be proper."

"It is proper because I have asked it of you, correct?"

Talikae flushed and bowed. "Yes, my Lady." Hesitantly, she walked forward and sat down on the very edge of the chair.

Ninanna suppressed a sigh. It was something, she supposed. "Do you dream, Talikae?"

"I… I think so."

"What do you dream about? No." Ninanna paused. "No, I mean, if you don't mind my asking, please tell me what you dream about."

"My Lady has only to ask and I will tell."

"That's not what I mean. Dreams are a personal thing and if you feel awkward at all, then I don't want you to tell me."

"I..." Talikae flushed, lifting her eyes for a moment to meet Ninanna's before dropping them again. "I do not mind, my Lady. You have been very kind to me. I don't remember my dreams very well. I think I have dreamt of the sky and the forest and the ocean, but I don't remember much more. Please forgive me, my Lady, it is silly."

"No it isn't. I dream often of those things too," Ninanna said. "Have you ever been into the forest?"

"No, my Lady, that is a task for the t'Okaedrin and the Pi'aernotha Osnoeda, not one such as myself." She hesitated, then added, "Truth be told, my Lady, the forest frightens me."

"Why is that?"

"It is an evil place full of feral beasts, monsters, and wild humans who would destroy our cities if they had a chance."

"How do you know this?"

Talikae looked up at her again, confusion written on her brow. "Because my mother and father have told me it is true, my Lady. That is why the t'Okaedrin and Pi'aernotha Osnoeda go there to bring peace to the wilderness."

"How do your parents know?"

"I suppose their parents taught them, too," she said after a moment's thought. "If they taught us wrong, I'm sure our Syraestari masters would have corrected them and us."

"I have lived close to half my life in the wilderness," Ninanna replied. "It has its dangers, certainly, but it is not so evil a place as you believe. It has a unique beauty. All around there is jubilant life, filled with sounds and smells."

"Yes, my Lady."

Ninanna smiled softly. "There is nothing wrong with dreaming of the forest. Nor do you need to be afraid of it."

"I will remember that, my Lady," Talikae said, her face flushing again.

Ninanna rose to her feet and instantly the human bounded up as well. "I have made you uncomfortable, Talikae. We need not speak further on it."

"I am sorry if I said the wrong thing, my Lady."

"You did not. Thank you for speaking with me. You may go now."

"Yes, my Lady." Talikae bowed low and departed.

Ninanna watched her leave, a frown forming on her lips. The slave masters had done too good of a job, locking the human minds into hidden prisons. How young had Talikae been when she was taken? A year, perhaps two or three? She knew only what she'd been told and had facing punishment for any errant thought her whole life.

"Blood on the Bridge!" Ninanna cried. Picking up her goblet, she flung it against the far wall. The wine splashed in a stain of crimson as the glass shattered. Ninanna collapsed back onto her bed, tears filling her eyes as she realized Talikae would be the one to come and clean up the mess. The human woman wouldn't understand why the glass had been broken. Probably, she would even worry that she'd failed somehow. "Blood on the Bridge," Ninanna said again in a hushed voice. "What monsters have we become to fashion such prisons?"

Walking to the other side of the room, she picked up the pieces of the shattered goblet. Once that was done, she would find a cloth and scrub the wall.

Late that afternoon, Ninanna was sitting alone in the palace garden, enjoying the sun and the flowers when a Syraestari approached. He offered a slight bow, "Lady Ninanna, I carry a letter from Empress Kayrstana."

"Thank you, Onath," she replied, accepting the offered message. "How is Her Majesty?"

"She is well. A guard of a dozen t'Okaedrin watch over her in your absence."

"Will she be expecting a response?"

"She gave me no instructions on that, my Lady. I am departing in the morning should you wish to send a reply."

"Thank you, Onath."

"Good evening, my Lady."

Ninanna smiled as he bowed and departed. Though young and seemingly only a carrier of letters, Onath was one of the most reliable members of the imperial court. He was the only one Kayrstana trusted to carry personal correspondence and had long since mastered the social graces that came with his task. He would go far.

She rose from her seat and entered the palace. If Onath was the messenger, then it was likely the empress sought discretion. That meant reading the message in her room rather than a public place. She sat down at her desk and carefully unsealed letter.

Lady Ninanna,

I congratulate you on your triumph against the wildmen tribes. I have received your initial report on the success of the raid and have also heard word from the High Lords Ushtyl and Tazil.

That being said, I was sorely disappointed in the agreement you made with the high lords. This was to be a triumph for the empire, a bonding that would bring our people closer together. Instead, you claimed no glory, but passed it all onto those two men. This will only serve their goal to rebuff my authority. When I gave you this task, I had thought you understood my mind better than that.

Because of this, you must make further steps to assert imperial authority over the high lords. The time of wandering and independent action are over. They must understand that they are not peers, but servants to the imperial throne. Therefore, before you return to Thusaeyanin, I have another task for you to complete.

Your report on the raid has made it clear to me that I do not have a firm grasp on the size and strength of my armies. If we truly are to unify as a people and protect ourselves from the incursions of the Scions of the Fallen Tree, I must know what arms we can bring to bear.

Therefore I direct you to make a full count of the housecarls, t'Okaedrin, and Pi'aernotha Osnoeda in all the cities of the realm. I want you to account for each warrior by weapons and armor. Also count each sorcerer and sorceress trained sufficiently to fight on a battlefield. Additionally, tally all of the weapons and armor that each high lord keeps in his armory. Finally, I require an estimate on how quickly each city is forging new weapons and armor.

You must make it clear to the high lords that this is the order of the empress and as servants it is their duty to obey. Do not reach a secondary accord with them. You understand my intent on this and I will not have you subvert my authority a second time.

I have already sent letters to each of the high lords of your mission so they will be ready to assist you. Thank you, my old friend. I know it was not your intention to disappoint me and regret the hard words I have had to include here. You will do well.

By my own hand,
Her Imperial Majesty
The Empress Kayrstana

Ninanna stared down at the letter, her cheeks burning at the rebuff. But what had the empress expected? That the high lords would just bow knee to her because she demanded it. They'd been independent for far too many centuries to be brought quickly under heel. Such a task required time and gentle care, not this running roughshod over sensibilities. And if taking command of their raid was a rebuff, a close census of each city's strength would be a slap in the face. This was the very opposite of what she'd always recommended. It seemed the empress wanted her to be a weapon to crush her vassals.

Ninanna was so focused on the letter that she barely noticed when Talikae entered with her evening meal. "Thank you," she said absently as the human bowed and turned toward the door.

Then realization hit her. Ninanna straightened and looked at Talikae. The woman was walking more slowly than normal and limped slightly. "Is something wrong, Talikae?"

"No, my Lady," the woman turned and bowed again. But as she did, she couldn't hide a wince.

Ninanna was on her feet in a moment. "What happened, Talikae?"

"It is nothing, my Lady. I made a mistake and was corrected for it. Please forgive me, my Lady."

"There is nothing to forgive."

"Yes, my Lady."

Ninanna sat back down, troubled. After a moment, she said, "Please send your mother to me."

"Yes, my Lady." Talikae bowed again and withdrew.

A few minutes later, a soft but firm knock sounded on her door.

"Come in," Ninanna said.

The door opened and an older human woman stepped through. Her dark hair was streaked with gray and wrinkles lined her face and hands. The woman bowed low and said, "You have summoned me, my Lady. How may I be of service?"

"Rise, please," Ninanna said. When the woman straightened, she continued, "I understand that Talikae was lashed. What was the reason for it?"

"I'm sorry if her punishment has disturbed you, my Lady. We did not mean to inconvenience her services."

"You haven't. What were the lashes for?"

"It was a petty thing, my Lady. Just idle words a woman her age should know better than to say or think. Please think nothing of it, my Lady. The slight has been corrected."

"What did she say?" Ninanna pressed.

The woman flushed slightly as she answered. "Forgive me, my Lady, but the girl said she would like to see the forest someday. It was a fool thing to say, a fool thing to think with all of the dangers out there. I have explained to her again how treacherous the forest is and how good you are to protect us, my Lady. I am sure it will not happen again, my Lady."

Ninanna opened her mouth to scold the woman, but closed it again. What would be the point? She wouldn't understand any more than Talikae. It was a nice trap. Ninanna realized that if she pressed further, she would only cause more beatings for the poor human slaves. But mere silence couldn't be the answer either. She sighed and said, "Be confident that Talikae is serving me well and I have no complaints."

"I am glad, my Lady."

"You may go, thank you."

"Yes, my Lady. Thank you, my Lady."

Ninanna turned back to her desk and leaned forward, kneading the small of her back with her fist. Though it seemed smaller on the surface, Talikae's problem was far bigger than the squabbling of high lords. But Ninanna had no idea how to even begin unraveling that nightmare of lies.

Sometimes it felt like there were too many problems in the world to solve them all. She reluctantly turned her attention back to the letter. The census would not do. A trip to Thusaeyanin might bring the empress to understand the dangerous road she traveled down. But Ninanna knew such a conversation wouldn't be pleasant.

She folded the letter and then carefully fed it into the flame of the oil lamp, watching the fire slowly consume it. When it was a pile of ash, she rose and began to pack her bags, her meal growing cold on the table.

Watching Arcomin and Hirnid leaving the smelting camp, rage simmered in Belarrin's heart. His brothers' fifth visit to the camp in as many days had ended like all the others. The only difference this time was that they'd been waiting when the barracks door was unlocked with the dawn. Belarrin turned back to Yrpel. The Iengian had stooped to his knees, one hand rubbing his chest where a new bruise was doubtless forming. He clenched his other hand into a fist. "I'll kill them all, I swear it!"

"You did well," Regund told him.

"Cydion's Abyss, I curse them! I curse the Finnies, the Etyni, and His Highest Above! No man should have to live like this. I'll tear them limb from limb!"

"Easy, Yrpel," Zoltha said, kneeling beside him. "Curse them if you like, and the Finnies, too. But do not curse the Etyni or His Highest Above."

"And why not?" Yrpel cried. "When I needed them most, they weren't there. What have they ever done for us?"

"I don't know," Zoltha said quietly. "No man can know what might have been or what will be."

"Words do me no good."

"Perhaps not." Zoltha turned to look after the t'Okaedrin and repeated himself more softly. "Perhaps not."

Yrpel grimaced, then eyed Zoltha. "Since these chains have fallen on me, I find I have ceased to care about the Etyni. But because my words trouble you and I respect you, I won't speak them again."

Belarrin and Zoltha helped Yrpel to his feet and they returned to the other Kalilaer gathering for their morning meal. As Yrpel sat down again, he said, "But curses or not, I don't know how long I'll be able to endure this torment. I will kill them, I swear it."

"You would only throw your life away," Idysha said. "I've seen too many good man do so."

"There are times when it is worth throwing life away. And what else would you have me do? Pray for rescue? Wait on these Scions of yours?"

"Keep your hope," Idysha said, her voice gentle. "Don't let them break you. We will all have our revenge in the end."

"What about the Hiraestari?" Wiersa asked. "Where are they?"

"What are Hiraestari?" Fritten asked, his youthful face peering around the circle.

Not surprisingly, it was Chostir who answered, "They were like the Syraestari, except they were friends of humans."

"Legends only, now," Idysha said.

"Lies, more like." Regund growled.

"I don't understand your anger," Wiersa said.

"There's a reason they only exist in legends, Wiersa," Zoltha replied. "If they still exist…"

"Or ever existed," Regund interrupted with a scowl.

"If they were what the stories say about them," Zoltha continued, "They would have done something long before now. Half the slaves I've talked to have myths like your own, so ancient that we cannot know what the truth is. The other half have never heard of them. Whatever they were, the Hiraestari must be dead and gone, lost to the Cataclysm."

"Or they're lies spread by the Finnies to make us believe some of their kind are capable of good," Regund said.

They weren't mere legends, Belarrin knew. Unlike his companions, he had more than myths to draw upon. He had the memories of his masters, untarnished by a thousand years of retelling. The Hiraestari were corrupted, their souls filthy and tainted by dark Cydion. More than one of the Etyni had fallen during the Great War, felled by their blighted hands. It startled him how many of the wildman and Kalilaer stories touched near to the truth only to get what was most important backwards.

As if mirroring his thoughts, Wiersa sighed. “We have forgotten so much.”

“Enough of this!” Chostir said. “Our lives are bleak enough without dwelling on it. If I wanted to brood more, I’d go back to the Boards. Tell brighter stories than that. Have I ever told you of the city built on a waterfall?”

The others groaned. “Enough, enough.” Regund laughed. “Everyone back to work if you want to eat this evening.” They dispersed with lighter hearts.

Unfortunately, Zoltha decided that Belarrin was trained enough to work with other Kalilaer and paired him with Chostir. Fritten couldn’t disguise his relief as he joined Zoltha instead. But Belarrin was told, not only about the city of waterfalls, but also a whole host of other tales. Each was more fantastic than the last, from cities of gold so large that a person could walk all day to a kingdom ruled by a queen that was human and a king who was Hiraestari. She nattered on almost without ceasing and, to make matters worse, the stories distracted her. Belarrin spent a large part of the day reminding her to hold the rhythm of the bellows. But every time he wanted to snap at her, one glance at her face stopped him. He remembered the haunting pain on Chostir’s face from the night she’d fled, despondent, into the barracks. But when she told her stories, a soft smile touched her lips and her eyes held a faraway cast as if she lived for the moment in a brighter place. Despite the folly of it, he couldn’t bring himself to break her spell.

From time to time, he glanced over at Zoltha who was working Fritten and caught a bemused smile. Belarrin grinned himself and turned back to his work, no longer listening to Chostir but dreaming his own dreams. Of his return to his brothers, of the glory he would win, of marrying Elestis and becoming a father to his own family. Unlike Chostir's tales, his were possible and lay just beyond the horizon, beyond the smelting fire.

The day passed to the tempo of Chostir's speaking and the steady whoosh of the smelting bellows. The evening meal was, thankfully, quieter than the morning and they all shuffled obediently into their barracks when their t'Okaedrin guardians arrived.

As Belarrin fell asleep that night, he contemplated the morning conversation and his time working with Chostir. More and more it was becoming apparent how much this group of once-strangers had come to depend upon each other to survive. They bickered frequently, but there was an underlying sense of need and even respect. They were a family.

Belarrin's eyes shot open. No! Not a family. Not his family. He was t'Okaedrin, not Kalilaer. Even worse, most of these would choose the Scion path if they could. The calm of the camp, the camaraderie of hard work had all combined to make it feel normal. But he couldn't allow himself to feel normal. He did not want this. He couldn't come to love them as brothers and sisters. One day, the Scions would come and they would flee. Those who fled with him would cease to be dutiful Kalilaer and become apostate Scions. There was no family here. Whatever he thought of them, however much he might like them, he couldn't allow himself to forget that they were the enemy. And he would have to kill them, just as he had Vitarria and Parvik.

That night, he slept poorly, tormented by dark dreams where the Scion attack never came. His beard grew long and gray as days passed into months, into seasons and years. His family forgot about him, and he them, until only the Kalilaer part of him remained. Until there was only the endless toil at the smelter.

CHAPTER 15
Patience

""For fifty years I have devoted myself to knowledge. I lovingly found a place for every precious tome in our glorious library. There, we recorded our wisdom, our history, our laughter, our fear. And then, in a moment of ash and fire, it was gone. What use is knowledge, then, if it falls so easily through the fingers?"

—Thavayyan of Estrya

The onerous work that came with the next morning did little to dispel the bleakness of Belarrin's dreams. He traded pairs often, now, sometimes working with Zoltha, sometimes Fritten, and sometimes Chostir. Fritten was easier to work alongside than Chostir. He was dutiful about his work and content to a degree that Belarrin found startling. Fritten had no ambitions beyond making iron. He didn't care about the rumbling surf that was always at the edge of hearing. He didn't notice the beauty of the distant mountains when the setting sun gleamed upon them. Nor did he seem to care if it were cloudy or bright. He was the perfect Kalilaer and, to his own amazement, Belarrin increasingly found him distasteful. He actually longed for the eternally chatty Chostir no matter her inevitable distractions at the bellows. At least with her, he knew a mind worked behind the eyes.

But most of all, Belarrin enjoyed Zoltha's company. There was something calming about the man's steady faith that made him more stable than anyone else in the camp. He was patient, quiet of voice, and best of all, rarely talked

Days slipped into weeks, without change. Each morning Cydion and Veduk gave their inspection. Each day they fired a new bloom. Each evening they sat in their dinner circle for a few moments before being banished to the barracks, talking as much to distract themselves from the emptiness of their lives as anything else.

On a day, much like any other, Belarrin worked beside Zoltha. Both were silent as fit their personalities and the babbling of Chostir across the camp was only a soft murmur almost completely drowned by the steady wheeze of the bellows. It was Zoltha's turn to pump and Belarrin stocked the charcoal and ore.

Fritten's angry bellow shattered that quiet. "Enough Chostir! I don't care about your stupid stories. Your fool lies. There never was a city of water or anything else. Only a child would think otherwise. Concentrate on the bellows or you'll ruin the bloom!"

Belarrin and Zoltha turned as Fritten leapt to his feet and stormed toward them. Behind him, Chostir stooped forward, abandoning all effort on the bellows, and burst into tears.

"I can't work with her anymore," Fritten said, his voice ringing louder than the hammers of the smithy. "You or Belarrin, sure, but not her."

Zoltha glanced to Belarrin as if to hand him the bellows so he could calm the situation, but Belarrin shook his head and rose to his feet. "Easy, Fritten, I'll talk to her."

"Talk? That's all she does," Fritten snapped. "Talking will get us a half-portion of meatless gruel and a day lashed to the Boards."

Rather than reply, Belarrin walked past the angry youth and approached Chostir. He saw Regund appear at the entrance of the smithy, but waved him back, too. More than once, a thought had come to his mind as he'd worked with Chostir and Belarrin regretted not speaking sooner.

"What?" Chostir's voice was choked as he knelt down beside her. "Maybe it would be better if I was sent to the Boards again. Then at least you'd have peace from me."

"No one should seek to get punished, Chostir," he said as gently as he could. He'd seldom found it easy to talk to women. He got along well enough with Elestis, of course, but even then he often stumbled over his words. Vitarria had been surprisingly easy, but that might have been because he knew she would die. Here, though? He hesitated. It was like going into a different kind of battle and he wished he had a sword. "You have a good memory for stories," he said.

"They aren't lies, no matter what Fritten said." Chostir shrugged, then bowed her head. "But it doesn't matter, does it? That world is gone and we'll never see anything like it again. Just work and death."

"Maybe not," Belarrin replied, immediately regretting the words. Why would he want to encourage her for anything but the life she had. It was the best life. A good life. But he knew she wouldn't see it that way. "You know many stories. Do you know songs, too?"

"Yes, my mother sang to me all the time. My tribe liked singing, too. But I have no voice for it. They always teased me when I joined in."

"That doesn't matter. You know the songs? You like them?"

"Yes." She looked up and met his eyes. Her tears had formed runnels in the dirt on her face. "They remind me of home, but how can that be better? That's just as far away as any of my stories."

Belarrin formed his lips into a soothing smile. "Because songs have a rhythm, just like you need with the bellows."

"I don't understand," she replied, but by the light growing in her blue eyes, he saw that she was beginning to.

"Sing your songs to yourself and pump the bellows with the rhythm. It will keep your pace steady."

The ghost of a smile appeared on her face. "And I won't give up on my stories. I will dream of a better life."

"A better life," Belarrin lied his agreement.

"Thank you."

"Of course," Belarrin said, rising to his feet. "I'd better rejoin Zoltha now."

Chostir nodded and turned her attention back to the bellows. This time as she pumped, she worked with a focus Belarrin hadn't seen before. He saw that Regund had disappeared back into his smithy to work, but as he walked over to Zoltha, Idysha approached him.

She rested her hand on his shoulder and smiled. "You are a good man, Belarrin."

He didn't know how to reply to that and could only offer a half smile in return. She wasn't looking for more and withdrew to her charcoaling.

As Belarrin knelt down beside Zoltha, the other man said, "That was well done, my friend. And very clever, too. Whatever made you think of it?"

"The t'Okaedrin," Belarrin replied with a half-truth. "When we were captured, I saw that they marched in step by using songs. On our journey here, I tried the same for myself, if only to keep from stumbling over Yrpel's feet the whole way. It occurred to me that the same could be used on the bellows."

Zoltha chuckled. "Very well done. I wonder that none of us ever thought of it before."

From that point forward, Chostir ceased to be a problem. She sometimes hummed to herself, but she was so focused on her songs, that she only regaled her stories during breakfast or dinner. Fritten even agreed to continue working with her. But Belarrin's act also garnered new respect from the others. Those who hadn't heard, learned from those who had until he seemed to be accounted nearly as wise as Zoltha.

Much like the tempo of Chostir's songs, there was a rhythm to this life that Belarrin found himself growing more and more accustomed to. But that only increased his alarm. No matter how hard he fought it, he could feel the normalcy of the smelting camp seeping into him. Days passed quickly, but his nights were filled with tormented dreams. He felt the bonds on his hands from his first march as a Kalilaer, chaffing his wrists. He felt the shattered crossbeams of his collapsed childhood barracks crushing down against his chest. And each day he awoke to his new prison. He was inescapably bound in the body of a Kalilaer and could only pray, like the others, for rescue by the Scions. The morning meal chased the worst of those nightmare images from his mind, allowing him once more to feel the almost comfort of the routine toil at the smelting bellows and so the cycle continued.

The only events to break the continuity of his labors were the visits by various t'Okaedrin. Each day, they passed through at different times, always in pairs. Aside from Cydion and Veduk, Finaestari walked by only rarely. One day, however, Belarrin saw the tall grim Sword-Whisperer who had commanded the raid pass by. He was so surprised to see a Finaestari of her stature that he gapped openly for a moment before he caught himself. But as he lowered his eyes, he saw her looking right at him. Two more times after that she walked by, and each time he sensed she stared his direction. It made the skin on the back of his neck itch. He knew what such warriors were capable of. If she took offense, he'd be lucky to die slowly on the Boards, no matter his mission.

But far more distressing were the almost regular visits from Arcomin. Belarrin received the worst of his attention, followed by Yrpel. But Arcomin tormented each of the men in turn. All except humble Zoltha whom he didn't seem to notice. Belarrin soon had a series of bruises lining his chest and back. Hirnid usually stepped in when Arcomin got increasingly violent, but did little more. Perhaps Hirnid was uncertain since Arcomin was now the eldest. But Belarrin saw no one else from his family, though he longed most of all to see Bridionis and Dalric. He didn't see Elestis either, though his mind often turned to her as he toiled silently at the bellows. But it was unlikely he would ever see her out on the camp perimeter. That left Arcomin as his only constant tormented reminder of home. His violence became so pernicious that the other Kalilaer even remarked upon it. Regund, who'd been in the camp for ten years or more, had never seen such behavior. The only solace Belarrin could take from their alarm was that no suspicion fell upon him. Instead, there was admiration at his courage and restraint.

When he waited for sleep each night, Belarrin prayed that the Scions would come and free him to begin his task. He prayed that Arcomin would leave him in peace. But the Scions did not attack and Arcomin kept returning with ruthless frequency.

One afternoon as summer was drawing to a close, Belarrin worked alongside Chostir. He pumped at the bellows and Chostir, not having to maintain a rhythm for the moment, was regaling him with another ludicrous story. This time she told him about a tower, hundreds of feet high, that had supposedly been built by humans before the Cataclysm. She fell silent when Arcomin and Hirnid again walked into the camp. Belarrin bowed his head, but continued working.

The two t'Okaedrin walked past him and advanced on Zoltha. It was the first time Arcomin had accosted the quiet man. Zoltha rose obediently to his feet at Arcomin's command.

"What about you?" Arcomin asked his favorite question, absurd though it always was. "Are you a coward?"

His head bowed, Zoltha replied, "I submit to your authority, Master."

"That isn't what I asked."

"I do not know the answer, Master. Is the rabbit a coward for fleeing the hawk?"

"You taunt me!" Arcomin snarled and struck Zoltha in the face. The bowing man took the full brunt of the blow and collapsed to the ground. Blood poured from his nose. Seeing the crimson stain on the ground, a kernel of rage flared to life in Belarrin's stomach.

"What do you have to say to that?" Arcomin demanded.

"I have nothing to say, Master," Zoltha replied. "I am here to serve."

"How about now?" Arcomin shouted, driving his foot into Zoltha's stomach. "Are you a coward?"

The Kalilaer doubled over, wheezing, "Yes, Master."

Tears stung Belarrin's eyes as Arcomin kicked Zoltha again. Why did Arcomin care about Zoltha? Zoltha wasn't t'Okaedrin, he was Kalilaer. He served obediently, doing all that was demanded of him.

"Kiss my feet, swine!" Arcomin commanded. Zoltha struggled to obey, but before he could, Arcomin kicked him again, catching him in the jaw.

The seed of anger in Belarrin sharpened. Kalilaer were a part of the order of things. They labored as was expected of them, but they were not mindless beasts. If he had ever thought that before, he didn't now. This wasn't justice, this wasn't honor.

"Kiss them!" Arcomin yelled, shrugging off Hirnid when the other Okaidir put his hand on Arcomin's shoulder. That only seemed to infuriate him more. "Don't you see it, brother? Can't you see behind their eyes? They all hate us. They all want to kill us. It is written across their hearts. They have no loyalty, no wisdom, no courage. But I'll show them courage!" He drew his knife.

"No!" Belarrin leapt to his feet. Only when Arcomin turned on him did he realize what he'd done. His face flushed red and Belarrin met his brother eye for eye. A nagging part of his mind questioned what he was doing, but that quiet voice drowned beneath his rage.

Arcomin's voice softened, but grew far uglier. "No?" he hissed.

Behind Belarrin, the bellows fell silent as Chostir watched in shock.

"If you want to kill someone, then kill me," Belarrin said. He walked slowly over to stand in front of Zoltha.

"Perhaps I will, Dog."

Looking into his brothers eyes, Belarrin realized that Arcomin just might. But Hirnid grasped Arcomin's knife arm firmly in his own hand. "No," he said, "you will not."

Arcomin turned to glare at the other man, but he let Hirnid take the knife away. "Fine." Arcomin spat, then turned back to Belarrin. "But no Kalilaer defies one of the t'Okaedrin. No Kalilaer looks me in the eye. You will be punished."

Belarrin didn't resist as Arcomin flung him to the ground and bound his hands behind his back. "You're going to the Boards, Dog. Let's see if you're brave enough for that!"

Ninanna stepped into the empress' private wing of the palace at Thusaeyanin. Despite being absent only a few weeks, it was strange to see that nothing had changed. The walls still held the gleam of finely polished cedar, the high plastered ceilings painted with images of trees, and flowers. The only difference was the presence of four t'Okaedrin guards outside Kayrstana's receiving room. They wore cloaks of purple instead of the usual crimson, but otherwise could've been the same as any others of the brotherhood.

The leader of the guards bowed as Ninanna arrived. "Lady Ninanna, Her Imperial Majesty was not expecting you."

"I know. If she is free, I need to speak with her."

"Of course, my Lady."

He bowed a second time then opened one of a pair of double doors and slipped inside. A moment later, he returned. "She will see you."

"Thank you."

This time both doors were opened wide for Ninanna to pass through. The receiving room beyond was one of the smaller chambers of the palace, intended for the empress to meet with groups numbering no more than a handful. Despite that, it still had a throne near the center. The throne was a grand thing, carved from the heart of an oak tree with swirling lines that seemed to blend the ceaseless waves of the ocean with the rippling grasses and flowers of an open field. A finely woven carpet stretched out from the throne with three benches set on either side for guests. The left wall had high windows sufficient to bask the room in sunlight while maintaining privacy.

The empress sat upon her throne. She wore a fine green linen dress trimmed in gold thread that matched the crown set in her towering curls of hair. Four additional t'Okaedrin stood near the doorway and they pulled it shut behind Ninanna as she walked down the carpet. At the feet of Kayrstana, she bowed low.

"It is good to see you, my friend," Kayrstana said, extending her right hand. Ninanna kissed it, then rose to her feet. The empress looked past her to the four guards. "You may leave us. For centuries, my entire guardianship was entrusted to this woman. I will be safe in her care."

Ninanna didn't turn, but she heard the doors open and the quiet shuffle of boots as the t'Okaedrin exited.

"Please sit, my friend," Kayrstana said. As Ninanna withdrew to the nearest bench, she continued, "I have done as I said in your absence. I've remained in the palace and chose the best twenty t'Okaedrin from all of Thusaeyanin to watch over me. They were taken from their old families to form a new one without father or mother, though there is an eldest who spoke to you. They are doing well."

"I am glad, Your Majesty."

Kayrstana straightened her back and folded her hands in her lap. Ninanna recognized the manner as the empress donning her mantle of rule. "Now, why are you here, Lady Ninanna? I hadn't expected to see you. Did Onath fail to reach you with my message?"

"He delivered, Your Majesty. That is why I've come."

"Were my instructions unclear?"

"No, Your Majesty, but I'm concerned by them. I am your Edrethyn, but these are the tasks of a Hand."

"I wish you to be more."

"Your Majesty, the oath I swore to you and your father was your protection, heart and mind. I cannot do that if I am not at your side."

Kayrstana smiled. "My friend, that is exactly what you're doing. I am safe here. You've seen to that by your diligence in how both the palace and city were built. The t'Okaedrin are brave and obedient men and, though they lack your singular skill, they are many and as courageous and dutiful. They will see to my physical safety. But that isn't the safety that concerns me. As long as the high lords continue to pull against the threads of my rule, my place is weakened. They must be brought into obedience as befits the vassals they are."

Ninanna couldn't argue against the empress' words. Her duty was more than just physical protection. It always had been. "Your Majesty, what you've asked me to do is more than bringing them to heel. It will embarrass and enrage them, perhaps even to the point of open rebellion."

"If they rebel, then I will see them broken," the empress said harshly. Her tone softened as she continued, "But they will not. They are too aware of the limits of their own authority for that. They will not be happy, but they will comply. They will also come to see you as my Hand. That honor hasn't been bestowed upon anyone since the days of my grandfather." Her tone grew sharper again. "This would have been easier, indeed it might not have been necessary at all if you'd done as I intended with Ushtyl and Tazil."

"If I failed you, Your Majesty, then I apologize," Ninanna replied.

Kayrstana sighed. "Perhaps I expected too much. I had thought after so many years you understood my intentions even if they weren't spoken."

Ninanna fought down a stab of guilt. Perhaps she had known what the empress wanted deep down, but she'd ignored it because she did not like it. For centuries, Ninanna had been a mentor and guide to a young empress who grappled with what it meant to rule. But Kayrstana was older now and coming into her own. The relationship was changing and only time would tell what it would become. But that didn't mean Ninanna had to become a blind follower. "Your

Majesty, for this census there are many better choices than myself. The high lords don't like me and they do not trust me."

"That is why you are the perfect choice. That and the fact that your loyalty to me is known to be unwavering. You must make them comply without stretching beyond the bounds of decorum. I know you're capable of this task, otherwise I wouldn't have asked it of you. You were the only one from among all the Aestari who was able to transcend the Schism to be both Tirnaestari and Syraestari. You have stood by my side through the final throes of the Great War, the mad crossing of the waters in the Cataclysm, and all that has followed since. I know you will do well."

Ninanna bowed her head. "I will do as you command, Your Majesty." But whatever the empress thought, Ninanna would be watchful for any sign of rebellion. Of course, that might have been exactly what Kayrstana had intended.

The empress smiled. "You will do well, my friend."

"Your Majesty, I have heard rumors that a refuge for our people has been found."

The empress glanced at her sharply. "Do not pay too close heed to those miscreants that plaster our cities with rumors and ill-chosen words. There is turmoil enough on the matter without idle lips stirring up tempers."

"Then there is no refuge?" Ninanna asked. If Kayrstana lied to her, she didn't know what she would do. Kayrstana had come to hold more and more of her own secrets, but Ninanna had never to known an actual lie to pass between them.

"No." Kayrstana shook her head. "I did not mean that. Such a place has been found."

"Then have you given further thought to our departure?"

Kayrstana stiffened. "I have not and nor do I intend to. High Lord Tyrnis has filled my ears with the same words until I am weary of it. I will tell you what I told him. No decision will be made until the high lords are fully obedient again."

"Yes, Your Majesty." When Kayrstana was like this, Ninanna had long since learned it was futile to push. It might even be harmful.

"Now, was there anything else, my friend?"

Ninanna hesitated as she considered asking the empress about the infiltrator Reigliff had told her about. But whatever the answer, Kayrstana would couch her reply with the justification that it preserved the realm. Ninanna had already pushed today and further questions would only yield anger. If only she knew how to better fulfill her oaths to both peoples. "No, Your Majesty, that was all."

The empress shoulders relaxed just slightly as if she again set aside her mantle of rule. "Then let me say it is good to see you again, Lady Ninanna. I look forward to the completion of your task. Though the t'Okaedrin see to my safety, you will always have a place by my side."

"Thank you, Your Majesty." Ninanna stood and bowed, then withdrew.

As she walked back down the corridors of the palace, heading toward the stable, her mind raced. All she had sought to do had been turned around. The empress was growing in her self-confidence. If only Ninanna could be as certain of her growth in balance and circumspection. But she knew wisdom could only come with experience. Kayrstana had to be able to stumble before she could truly stand.

The fire gave off a warm light as it crackled in the hearth. The room was quiet and the rich scent of mulled wine filled her nose. At the end of a long day of meetings, discussions, and deliberations, the Empress Kayrstana treasured her time alone. She sat in the antechamber outside her bedroom, curled up on a couch, reading. "The Philosophies and Histories" by Councilor Maelohn of Aveonfaili was an ancient book from long before the Cataclysm, before even the Schism.

He had been one of the main opponents of the Aestarin Oath, the Oath that Ninanna held still, which bound their people in servitude to the other races. But unlike many of his peers, Maelohn had opposed violence. Ironically, his murder by the Tirnaestari had done much to cause the Schism. Though the pages of the book were cracked and carried the dusky smells of great age, Kayrstana had long ago realized how much she enjoyed reading it. He had a natural prose that made her feel as though he sat across from her, speaking. At times, she wondered if the Schism would have occurred, had he lived. But even more, in these present days, she found wisdom in his words regarding the other races. Regarding humans. They weighed heavily upon her mind, nearly as much as the tumultuous high lords. When their threat was taken too lightly, devastation had followed, but the path ahead was unclear.

The pressure had grown ever since the mysterious Shadow-Servant brought his message of refuge. By his description, it sounded a wondrous place, reminiscent of their lush homeland in the Lost Age. But it was far away and her people were not prepared for such a journey. When she had delayed making a decision, the Shadow-Servant had gone to Tyrnis instead. That made Kayrstana grind her teeth. Her father had told her the Shadow-Servant could be relied upon to watch over herself and her people, but the creature's interpretation of what was best for the Syraestari didn't always match her own. She had been certain her father knew the Shadow-Servant's name though he'd never shared it. All she knew was that her father had saved his life at the end of the Great War.

It felt like the greater part of her day was spent allowing others to speak, urging and pleading their visions of a brighter future. High Lord Tyrnis, Lady Ninanna, and the Shadow-Servant stood on one side while many of the High Lords stood on the other. Was that what an empress was? A listener? It didn't feel right. Her subjects should listen to her as much or more than she did to them. But how could she proclaim anything when their loyalty was doubtful, when she was uncertain in her own heart?

She looked up as the door to the anteroom creaked open. Her t'Okaedrin guards and Pi'aernoth servants would never enter without knocking. The only one to sneak past them, unwelcomed, was the Shadow-Servant himself. But it was not him.

In the doorway stood High Lord Ushtyl.

A warm smile flooded across her face and Kayrstana could feel her heart flutter within her. He was so handsome, his shoulders rolled back, his posture perfectly straight. Rich brown hair flowed from his shoulders and his blue eyes, sharp and cold for so many others, held a secret warmth. And Ushtyl was certain where she doubted. He knew what he wanted and took strides to claim it without hesitation. Kayrstana was glad that their ambitions matched so well. She was likewise glad that, even as her heart raced, she was able to hold his certainty restrained. For all of his pressure toward remaining in these lands, she would make the final decision in her own mind.

As she set down her book and rose, he crossed the room to her. He bowed low at her feet and kissed her ring before standing again. When he did, she slipped her arms around his waist, drawing him into an embrace.

"I didn't expected to see you," she said. "A second unasked for visit today, but this one more welcome."

Ushtyl drew back to look down on her. "Second?"

"Lady Ninanna. She is unhappy with the census I ordered."

"Unfortunately, but not surprising. The census is important."

"I know," Kayrstana replied, "and you must not make it easy on her. The other high lords cannot suspect you've allied with me against them."

He rested his hand gently on her shoulder. "They will not. Already, they are certain I am at the heart of resistance to you."

Kayrstana let out a slow breath and nodded. "I know it is necessary, but I dislike this subterfuge."

"The only way to bring them to heel is if they resist too strongly. The people will see the need and will support you."

"But you must not push them so far into rebellion that they cannot come back."

"I won't. The aristocracy is a necessary evil to any rule."

She smiled. "Except for you."

"You have my heart, my empress. Your will is mine."

Kayrstana's heart fluttered again, but she stepped back and took her seat on the couch. Ushtyl walked over to a table on the far side of the room and poured himself a goblet of wine. Then he returned and sat on the far side of the couch.

"As glad as I am that you're here," she said. "Why is it you've come? It is a great risk, should anyone see you."

"I was able to slip away unmarked," Ushtyl replied. "I came because this will probably be the last time we can meet until this adventure is over. From here forward it will be too dangerous."

"Then the high lords are well in hand?"

"Yes. Though Ninanna gave too many concessions with the raid, she still has stirred up anger. It was enough to push Tazil, and he, in turn, pushed Sizras and Zaerina. Ovirkar and Arkesh were much easier to convince."

Kayrstana shook her head, her mood darkening. "So many. To think that only two aside from you have stayed loyal. What does that say about the heart of our people that so many of our high lords look only to themselves?"

She thought for a moment that Ushtyl might argue. He was, after all, a high lord himself. And he was ambitious, too. She would be blindly in love not to see that. But at least he had pinned his hopes on her. Once this ordeal was over, their relationship could at last be made public. She could finally take him as her Prince-Consort.

"The census should have the right affect," Ushtyl said. "But even with it, the high lords will move slowly. They resist the reach of your hand, but are reluctant to step toward outright rebellion. Tazil and especially Sizras will be my tools of restraint. They are both careful men and have joined reluctantly. With my subtle assistance, they will keep Arkesh and Ovirkar from overreaching. Once the lords are brought again to heel, I think you will be able to expect obedience from them all."

"Good. I trust your wisdom on this matter. You must be careful how much you push."

"I am always careful, especially where your position is at stake," he replied gently. "But matters are more difficult because of that secretive group of Syraestari flooding our cities with inane talk of running away to a hidden refuge." Kayrstana frowned. She suspected the Shadow-Servant was behind that, somehow. But of course, he wouldn't admit it. Ushtyl must have read something on her face because he asked, "Do you have any suspicions on who they might be?"

"Only possibilities," she answered. "And I won't act on them. I know you're position on the matter and I respect it, but I am not yet willing to reach a decision. Until then, these people are irksome to say the least, but they've done nothing wrong."

"They are a dangerous nuisance," Ushtyl said firmly. He took a sip of his wine, then continued, "they threaten everything I've crafted between the high lords. As you know, among those that resist your rule, many advocate dominion while nearly as many want us to abandon these lands. It's hard enough to keep them allied without these meddlers stirring up the people."

"I realize that. Nevertheless, I will not stop them," Kayrstana replied. "I trust your skill on the matter. If you need me to push the high lords further, send another message through Onath."

"Of course, Kayrstana," he replied, his voice softening. She could hear his passion in everything he said, but if they were to wed, he had to learn that her word on matters of empire would always be final. Nevertheless, she relied heavily upon his advice. Not only was he a fine warrior and loyal to the core, but he understood intrigue as few others she'd known.

"How long?" she asked.

"I must move slowly, as I said. The t'Okaedrin infiltrator will be the key. His triumph on breaking the back of the Scions will be a moment of triumph for you and all the people. It is upon his return and the completion of that task that we should be ready."

Kayrstana smiled. "Then I will school myself to patience."

Ushtyl matched her grin. "Yes, my love. I wish that we could see each other before then, but I'm afraid it wouldn't be wise."

"We still have Onath. He is to be trusted."

"Yes he is and no one suspects his knowledge. To all, he is but a messenger."

Kayrstana let out a sigh. She could feel the conversation coming to a close, though she didn't want it to. That seemed the eternal plight of the ruler, but she would do as her role demanded. She rose to her feet. "Then if there is nothing more, I regret that you should be on your way."

"Of course." Setting down his wine goblet, he rose to his feet.

They held each other in a long embrace. "Until the other side," Kayrstana said softly in his ear.

"Until the other side."

CHAPTER 16
Boards

"He who knows no pain and feels no fear, him I do not know. But you who wail in the darkness, you who stand above the gaping maw of the Abyss though your heart trembles within you… you, I might call brother."

—Excerpt from Parys First-Born's last words to the Sword-Singers before the Gates of Vesgaerdryl

As Arcomin and Hirnid dragged him away between them, Belarrin fostered the burgeoning hope that his brother's attack had all been part of a scheme to get him away from the camp for a moment to meet with the t'Okaedrin again. But that flaring desire was dashed as they marched him to the field where he'd first arrived in Nahirazith as a prisoner.

As they pushed him down onto the Boards and began binding his arms and legs with ropes, Hirnid muttered under his breath, "You shouldn't have done that, Vistus."

"Me?" Belarrin hissed back. After so long, it was strange hearing his true name. "What are you doing? I should gut you both for trying to ruin my mission!"

Arcomin growled, but it was Hirnid who replied, "You'll do no such thing. We have orders to give you trouble. It inspires loyalty to you from the other Kalilaer, but now you've gone and made a mess of things."

"You made this mess, you fools! I had everything..." He cut off in a cry of pain as Arcomin pulled his rope taut, stretching Belarrin's left arm so tightly it felt like it might tear from his shoulder. A moment later, Hirnid did the same with the right, drawing another shriek from his throat. Belarrin clenched his eyes shut as he gasped for breath and fought down a wave of panic. This wasn't like when the barracks collapsed. He wasn't trapped. He would be freed. Opening his eyes, he saw Arcomin smiling down at him.

"You've got to face the Boards," Hirnid said, "just like any other defiant Kalilaer. If we did anything different, they would be suspicious. I'm sorry, Vistus, but it must be done."

He and Arcomin took the ropes around his legs and pulled them tight, too. The pain of each of his arms and legs being pulled in different directions left Belarrin breathless, but he managed to retort through gasps of pain, "I might believe you if Arcomin wasn't enjoying himself so much."

Arcomin laughed, though it was half a snarl. "Leave us, Hirnid, I will talk to our brother alone." Hirnid hesitated a moment, then nodded and withdrew. Arcomin was eldest now, after all. When Hirnid was gone, Arcomin turned back to Belarrin. "You know how much I've worried about you, brother."

Belarrin stared at him, hating, but said nothing.

"Surrounded by Kalilaer, I worry for your soul, my brother. I must keep it safe."

"My soul?" Belarrin spat. "What about yours? Does it make you feel strong to beat helpless Kalilaer?"

"They aren't helpless. They're apostates in the making."

"Ever think that you're making them that way?" Belarrin asked. "They're doing what is right. Leave them alone!"

Arcomin shook his head. "Champion of wildmen and Scions. How far you've fallen."

"Kalilaer."

Arcomin leaned forward until his face was inches from Belarrin's face. "Is that the lie you tell yourself? The others may not have noticed, but I did. I saw your expression when you had to execute that Scion woman." He smirked. "Did a fair face and pretty smile twist your soul, brother?"

A shiver of fear crept up Belarrin's spine, but his anger was stronger. "Fool. I see jealousy in your eyes."

"An eldest jealous of a Kalilaer and a lover of Scions?"

"If you're so certain," Belarrin retorted, "why don't you tell father? Why don't you tell Captain Nethzir?"

Arcomin's complexion darkened. "You are the blessed child who can do no wrong. They wouldn't believe me."

"Because it isn't true."

His brother crossed his arms. "I will let them see for themselves."

"Let them see," Belarrin said. He wanted to strain against the ropes pulling his limbs taut, but that would only make the pain worse. "Let them see me drive the Scions to their knees!"

"I await your pleasure." Arcomin laughed.

"How did you end up as eldest anyway?" Belarrin retorted. "I can think of a whole family of brothers more capable."

Arcomin sobered. "It likely would've been you, had you been around. But since you prefer the company of savages, you can hardly lead. I am here, though. I am here with our brothers. I am here with Elestis."

"Stay away from her!"

"Perhaps you should tell her to stay away from me." Arcomin's grin was feral. "You never really bothered to understand her, did you? Elestis doesn't want a man she'll never see. She wants someone here, not lurking with barbarians. She wants someone like me. Someone whose heart is truly t'Okaedrin. Someone strong. And there's nothing you can do about it."

Belarrin's face burned red with anger. "Perhaps not now, brother. But I promise you this. We will have more than just words when this is done. And if you ever hit me again, I'll kill you no matter the cost to me or my mission."

"Then kill me," Arcomin retorted and struck him in the chest. With his limbs drawn back as they were, Belarrin could do nothing to deflect the blow. He heaved on the Boards, his eyes watering as Arcomin said, "Captain Eltirkar will pronounce the judgment on you. Enjoy yourself, Vistus, and pray the pain of the Boards will flay your apostasy away."

When Arcomin walked away, Belarrin leaned back and drew in ragged breaths of air, trying to calm himself. Not just from Arcomin's taunts but from his own rising terror. Unable to move his arms or legs, it was too much like the earthquake that had buried him.

"Highest Above, help me," he hissed through clenched teeth. He didn't know how he was going to survive it without going mad. "Curse Arcomin!"

Slowly the initial panic began to subside and he breathed a little easier. But the tension in his limbs was relentless and he knew it would only get worse. The afternoon sun gleamed down on him and he turned his eyes away. He lifted his head and looked out toward the smelting camp. The Kalilaer working there were small in the distance. They could see him too, if any looked his direction. But why would they? They had their work to do if they were to eat. Besides, he wasn't one of them, no matter what Arcomin claimed. He'd only been surprised by Vitarria's forgiveness. Nothing more. He still was confused by it, but that didn't matter. He was t'Okaedrin to the depths of his soul.

Looking the other way, Belarrin could see the t'Okaedrin barracks beneath the towering walls of Nahirazith. He had never been in those particular halls, but that was far more of a home to him than life among the Kalilaer. If he could ever get back there.

Laying back his head, he gasped, "Why me?"

Why had he been chosen to infiltrate the first Scions? Why was he infiltrating the Kalilaer now? There were thousands of t'Okaedrin, but he'd been picked. He closed his eyes and tried to clear his thoughts. Perhaps this punishment was for the best. He was beginning to sympathize with the Kalilaer, but they needed no sympathy. Their lives were good lives. It just wasn't his life. He could only pray that the Scions would attack soon. But not until he was free of the Boards and able to join the escape. That thought filled him with new panic. What if the Scions attacked while he was still tied up, condemning him to months, if not, years more as a Kalilaer?

"I am t'Okaedrin," he whispered. "There is no greater duty than to kill in the name of the Empress. There is no greater honor than to die in the name of the Empress. I live for my Empress, my masters, and my brothers. By them, and for them, I live and I die."

Yes, this was good. He had to harden himself for what lay ahead. In the Kalilaer lay weakness and they weakened him, too, if he allowed it. He shouldn't have risen to Arcomin's torments. If he had still thought as a t'Okaedrin, he wouldn't have. He had to be hard.

The sun was touching the far horizon, sending long streamers of crimson light across the plains, when horse hooves sounded in the distance. Belarrin opened his eyes and lifted his head. A Syraestarin rode toward him at a slow walk, an Okaidir on foot ran at his side. As they drew closer, he recognized Captain Eltirkar and Hirnid.

Captain Eltirkar reined his horse in front of the Boards. Looking down on Belarrin, he shook his head. "I expected better from you, Okaidir."

"Forgive me, Master," Belarrin said. "I have failed."

"Not yet. I will not allow you to fail."

"Yes, Master."

"How is your resolve?" Eltirkar's eyes narrowed.

"It is strong, Master."

"Then explain this folly?"

"A weakness, Master. I had not hardened myself sufficiently for living with the Kalilaer. I am aware of that now and it won't happen again."

Captain Eltirkar stared down at him, eyes piercing like spear points. Belarrin fought not to squirm beneath that gaze, knowing to look away was to fail. Deep in those green eyes lay the passage of centuries, a power and a wisdom he knew he couldn't even aspire to. Shame rose up within him as he sensed all of his failings, his weakness of spirit. After the shame came anger. He should have been stronger, he was stronger. He would persevere and show Eltirkar, Arcomin, and all the others his courage.

After what felt an eternity, Eltirkar nodded slightly. "You must be punished, of course."

"I understand, Master."

"Two nights and two days. You will be cut loose at sundown. I expect you to survive."

"Yes, Master." It took all of Belarrin's will not to flinch at the judgment. Two days? Could he endure that without going mad? A nagging corner of his mind mocked him. Chostir had. And she wasn't even t'Okaedrin.

Captain Eltirkar turned to Hirnid. "Water him."

Hirnid bowed his head. "Yes, Master." He took a leather flask from his waist and, stepping up to the Boards, held it up to Belarrin's lips. Belarrin drank eagerly. The water was tepid and leathery, but he'd tasted worse. He drank it eagerly until it was gone.

"Honor to the Empress," Hirnid said to him.

"Honor to the Empress," Belarrin replied then watched his brother walk away. Captain Eltirkar had already departed.

Belarrin lay back, trying to ignore his rumbling stomach. It had been many hours since he had last eaten and he would get no food until he was freed. Since he wasn't condemned to die, water would be brought each sunset, but that was all. His muscles already ached and he tried to relax them as much as he could. There would be more pain toward the end and the wearier he was, the worse it would be. But knowing and achieving were two very different things.

The evening brought coolness with it. A chill wind gusted off the sea, filled with scents of salt and seaweed. He shivered, feeling his limbs tighten. Sleep eluded him. The dreams were as bad as waking, every one of them pulling him beneath the collapsed barracks of his childhood, pinned and blinded in the darkness, a heavy weight on his chest, barely able to cry out. When he jerked awake for the twentieth time, he laughed bitterly and stared upward at the stars cycling through the heavens, his mind and body in a fog of agony.

Daylight meant relief from the cold, but it carried its own price. The sun brought blazing heat and blinding light. He squinted against it, twisting his head to the left and the right, but was unable to quell the brilliance behind his closed eyelids. Sweat burst out on his forehead and trickled down his armpits. An itch formed there that he couldn't scratch. The more he tried not to think of it, the more it grew, spreading until his whole body was aflame.

He roared in his torments. Unable to relent any longer, he writhed in his bonds, flailing helplessly knowing even as he did that the agony it brought was greater than the pain he sought to relieve. But it was different pain and that was worth the price.

"Worth the price," he mumbled. Was it really?

Did Dalric know the depths of what he endured to obey? Did High Lord Tazil and High Lord Ushtyl? Did His Highest Above, looking down from on high see his devotion? Was it even worth it? It had to be, because he had nothing else. Nothing to free him of these Cydion accursed Boards. No other way to get free of those weak Kalilaer. It was the only path to home and it couldn't come soon enough.

At dusk, Hirnid came again with a flask of water. The heat and sun had put Belarrin into a stupor and he was barely aware of his brother. Yet Hirnid held the flask up to his lips and poured slowly so he could drink every drop. One clear thought rose to Belarrin's mind. He owed Hirnid.

"Thank you," he managed to rasp.

Hirnid nodded. "You are strong, brother." Then he departed, leaving Belarrin alone again in the encroaching darkness.

It was colder than the night before, or at least it seemed that way. Belarrin could hardly think through the agony. He dozed fitfully, his mind filled with fever dreams until he could no longer tell when he was asleep or awake. Vitaria's face appeared with blood on her cheeks and matting her hair. Parvik, too, with his throat opened and gushing crimson. The two stones, black and clear, lay cold against his chest, colder than the night, so cold they burned. A cowled figure rose up before him with a white mask and piercing eyes. It whispered, "Ae'irpiva" before disappearing again. The word remained emblazoned across Belarrin's mind long after the dream faded beneath other nightmares. Then Belarrin was buried in the collapsed barracks once more until he awoke, screaming his torments.

Sunrise brought no joy, not even to the weak but alert part of his mind that knew he was nearly free of his torments. But that thought made the day pass even more slowly. The sun crept across the sky, searing against his lids. For the Empress. For the t'Okaedrin. For the world His Highest Above intended. He tried to force the mantras through his mind, pushing beyond the agony of his tattered muscles, his parched throat, his gnawing hunger.

And then daylight faded. Hirnid stood before him and another of his brothers. Praise His Highest Above that Arcomin wasn't there. Belarrin shrieked as they loosened the bonds that held his arms and legs. It hurt to draw in his stretched out limbs, but he did it anyway as he fought to regain control of himself. He balled up, rolling onto his side and blinking eyes too dry to weep. He crushed the moan that tried to force its way up from his throat. No, he had survived. He was t'Okaedrin and he would endure.

Belarrin forced his limbs to uncoil. He couldn't contain the groan that escaped his lips as he sat up and faced Hirnid. His brothers watched him, trying to remain stiff and aloof, but their eyes betrayed their concern. For that, Belarrin was grateful. Then Hirnid stepped forward and held the flask to his lips one more time. Belarrin was glad his brother kept hold of it. If he'd been made to lift the flask himself, he would've trembled so much that drinking would have been impossible. When he was done, Hirnid stepped back.

"It is time for you to return to the smelting camp," he said.

Belarrin nodded and scooted to the edge of the boards. When he put his feet on the ground and tried to stand, they almost gave way beneath him. His brothers didn't help, of course. They would not help a Kalilaer. Belarrin caught the edge of the Boards with his hands and steadied himself. He drew in deep breaths of air, grateful that his lungs didn't burn as much as before. When he felt the trembling diminish, he straightened. "I am ready."

Each step he took was unsteady, but Belarrin was proud that he didn't trip or stumble. His brothers stood on either side, silent sentinels, but they were much more than that. They were reminders of the home to which he belonged.

As he approached the smelting camp, he saw the other Kalilaer sitting and eating in their customary circle. They all stood as soon as they saw him. "Belarrin!" Zoltha cried, running towards him. The man's nose was bruised dark red and black from Arcomin's blow. Ignoring the t'Okaedrin, Zoltha slipped his arm around Belarrin's shoulder steadying him. Idysha ran up on the other side and did the same.

"Into the barracks!" Hirnid snapped.

The Kalilaer gathered their meals and hurried into the building. Inside, they gathered around him while the t'Okaedrin closed the door. The metallic ring of the lock bar sliding into place echoed hollowly in Belarrin's soul. The great gulf between himself and his family had formed again. While on the Boards, he had been tormented, but at least he'd been able to look upon Hirnid and see a brother. But now the bond was severed once more, not to be reforged until his task was done.

Chostir handed him a bowl of gruel and Belarrin tore into it eagerly. It was the best food he'd ever eaten. The other Kalilaer were silent as he devoured his meal. Only when he was done did he look up and realize that all eyes were on him. Even in the darkness of the room, he could sense their attention. It was Zoltha who spoke, "I owe you my life."

Belarrin opened his mouth to argue, but Zoltha silenced him. "Don't protest, it won't do any good. You did what the rest of us were too afraid to do. You are the best of all of us and we all see that." The others nodded, even Fritten.

"He's shivering," Idysha said.

Someone grabbed a fur blankets from Belarrin's pallet and Idysha draped it around his shoulders. Then she stooped to kiss his forehead. Belarrin looked up at her in surprise and she grinned impishly.

Regund spoke, "Zoltha has said what we all feel. We cannot let the Iron-Men do this to you again. We will protest to the Finaestari if we must, even if they send us all to the Boards."

"No," Belarrin rasped, his voice still weak. Zoltha handed him a cup of water and he drank from it eagerly. Belarrin tried again. "No, you must not. We will endure."

After a long moment, Regund sighed. "Very well, since you wish it."

"Thank you," Belarrin said looking around at the circle of huddling Kalilaer. There was a strange warmth here that he didn't understand. He'd never experienced anything quite like it. There was an innocence to these Kalilaer, where nothing was demanded or expected. It wasn't like his own family. He cringed. Only moments among them again, and already his resolve was weakened by their kindness. He would prove Arcomin wrong. His soul was t'Okaedrin. "Thank you," he repeated, trying to control the edge that had entered his voice. "But I am very tired."

"Of course," Idysha said and the others murmured their assent. They helped him back to his feet and over to his pallet. Then they left him and those who remained awake withdrew to the opposite side of the building where they carefully spoke in quiet whispers. For once, sleep came quickly and without dreams.

But it felt like only moments later that Zoltha was gently pushing him awake. "I wish I could let you sleep longer, but the t'Okaedrin have just unlocked the barracks and I know they won't allow it."

"I understand," Belarrin said, sitting up with a suppressed groan. His muscles still ached, but the sharper pain was already fading. A few days, he knew, and he would be back to normal.

After the punishment, it was actually refreshing to work the smelter again. Compared with the troubled thoughts coursing through his mind, compared with the many duties usually demanded of him as Okaidir, it was such a simple task. It was a task he could lose himself in, if only for a time.

Zoltha partnered with him again. The man probably would have tried to work the bellows all day if Belarrin had not insisted. But Belarrin did, even if he couldn't pump long before his arms began to ache. The strength was still there, it was his endurance that had been battered.

That night, after they were sealed in the barracks, he lay on his bed surrounded by the breathing of the other Kalilaer. There was a strange comfort in that soft murmur. There was a bond here, much like that which existed between him and his brothers. But these Kalilaer had never fought side by side. Nor had they known each other their whole lives. Some, like himself, Yrpel, and Wiersa, had only been there a short time, but still the bond existed.

Chostir had approached him earlier in the day while they were both gathering charcoal and ore for their smelters. "I know I tell stories a lot," she said. "I tell them as much to distract me as anything else. I know no one believes me, but I believe this. I understand what you went through on the Boards and I know what it means that you came back to us. The foolish things that got me there were nothing, but what you did gives me more hope than I've ever felt."

Belarrin could think of no way to respond, but she spared him his hesitation by resting her hand gently on his wrist a moment before turning back to her work.

He still didn't know what to think of those words. Nothing had forced obligations between these Kalilaer, but they chose them anyway. Was that a choice that apostate savages would make? And how did that compare to Arcomin's behavior? His brother, his eldest? The Kalilaer behaved differently. They behaved better.

Belarrin's eyes shot open. No.

That was the trap that had snared him before. A trap even Arcomin saw. They weren't better. This was just a temptation, luring him from the path of right. But their unfettered affection was powerful. It tore at him, heart and mind.

He needed to be away from this place and back with his family before it completely destroyed him. And not just for that. What was Arcomin doing to Elestis? Was he turning her against him as he'd promised? She had to be rescued from his lies. His family had to be rescued from him, too. Arcomin was growing into the worst kind of fool who would tear apart all Belarrin held dear merely for spite.

Belarrin reached up and touched his forehead. No, he had to regain control of himself. He dropped his hand again to touch the grizzled chin and beard that marked him as

Kalilaer, not t'Okaedrin. He could not and would not return to his brothers a shameful failure to face punishment and scorn. If he bowed to his fears, the punishment he faced would be deserved. There would be no honor. There would be no Elestis. He shifted his hand to rest upon the two gemstones about his neck. He had to remain, whatever the cost to himself. The cool black stone was a tie to his masters, the Syraestari to whom he owed all devotion. The bright clear stone a tie to Vitarria and Parvik. Deaths he had to cleanse from his conscience by destroying the Scions and proving himself right. That is what he had to do. Patience.

He closed his eyes and sought sleep, but the telltale snick of wood sliding against metal pulled him to wakefulness. Belarrin sat up from his pallet and was surprised to see the door swing open to reveal a star-studded sky beyond. The silhouette of a man darkened the threshold. In a loud hiss, the intruder said, "Follow me to freedom."

CHAPTER 17
Scion

"I have long believed that history teeters upon the edge of a blade, where the slightest shifting decides the fate of thousands. Some pray to the Etyni, perhaps because they were physical beings who once walked this world, shaping it with Words of Power. Others bow before the world itself, the raw power of its fire and wind and water or beseeching the spirits they attribute to the trees and rivers. But I worship His Highest Above, for at all moments it is he whose breath falls upon the blade."

—Words recorded by an unknown author
in the last days of the Lost Age

Belarrin scrambled to his feet as, around him, the other Kalilaer awoke.

"Hurry!" Their rescuer hissed, stepping into the room. "There's little time before the Iron-Men come. Follow me unless you love your chains."

Those words roused the others. Belarrin quickly kicked on his boots then hastened to the door, the other Kalilaer moving with him. But then one shadowed figure stepped in front of the rest. It was Fritten. "No! You can't go," he cried.

"Get out of our way, Fritten," Yrpel snapped.

"You'll all die," Fritten said. "I can't let you. You must stay here where it's safe."

"Safety means nothing to me," Yrpel said. "I don't want to kill another slave, but I will if you won't get out of the way."

"I'll scream!" Fritten replied. "I'll warn the t'Okaedrin so they'll stop you."

A growl rose up in Belarrin's throat, but before he could act, Regund stepped up behind Fritten. He wrapped his broad arms around the smaller man, clamping his hand tight over the youth's mouth. "Go," he hissed.

"But what about you?" Idysha asked as others scrambled for the door.

"Leave me. I can't go anyway. I've been here too long to scratch out survival in the wilderness."

"But..."

"It's not so bad a life and it is all I know now."

"Then be well, Regund," Idysha said before stepping through the door. Belarrin followed after her, pausing only to clap Regund on the shoulder. Fritten struggled in the large man's grasp and his eyes blazed, but no sound slipped through the fingers tight around his lips.

Outside, the night was dark and moonless. In the distance, dark shapes scrambled between the shadowed buildings, running toward the forest. The smelting Kalilaer all huddled outside the barracks, uncertainty and fear mixing with elation on their faces. Around them stood eight rebels, six men and two women, armed with spears and bows.

"No more time to waste," the man who'd spoken earlier said. "Quickly now, run to the woods and stay together."

As soon as he was done speaking, he turned and began to run. The Kalilaer followed in a mass with Belarrin near the middle. He could see tall Yrpel near the front and Idysha beside him, her long hair streaming in the wind. Their liberators kept to the outside, with three following behind. As the group broke past the last of the buildings, fires lit the night behind them and the harsh clamor of the t'Okaedrin alarm broke the air. Belarrin trembled despite himself. It was a warning he knew well, but never from this side of it. Before it had always been a siren song of home, a remembrance of the day he'd been pulled from beneath the collapsed barracks. But that memory was tainted now, leaving a chill of fear rising up in his throat.

The other Kalilaer panted for breath as they ran as fast as they could. Belarrin was surprised how much of an exertion it was for him, too. Work at the bellows had kept him strong, but it had been weeks since he'd last run. The cold night wind rushed into his face, burning his lungs, tearing away the last vestiges of sleep.

Wiersa ran beside him, chanting softly with each exhaled breath. "I knew it, I knew it. The Scions came, they..."

Blood spattered across Belarrin's cheek as Wiersa collapsed in a gurgle, an arrow piercing his throat. Others shrieked at the sight of six horsemen emerging from the darkness to their right. Iron blades gleamed dully in the light of the fires as the t'Okaedrin charged.

Belarrin cursed under his breath as the distance between his brothers and his companions closed. They shouldn't have been here. Not for his group!

The nearest t'Okaedrin slashed with his sword and a Scion fell. Chostir stumbled at Belarrin's feet, the point of an iron-headed arrow punching through her shoulder. Acting without thought, he grabbed her good arm and pulled her upright again. Her face was pale, her tunic bloodstained, but he pushed her onward toward the forest, cursing aloud, "Black Spawn of the Abyss!"

A t'Okaedrin reared before him and Belarrin threw himself to the ground, rolling beneath the warrior's swinging blade, past the thundering hooves. He scrambled to the dead Scion and, grabbing his spear, whirled to face the horseman. Fools! He didn't want to kill brothers.

As the horse galloped toward him, Belarrin took a quick sidestep to the rider's left side, away from his slashing sword, and thrust upward with his spear. The point took the horse in the chest. It shrieked and tumbled, casting off the rider. Belarrin leapt, even as the t'Okaedrin fell, and drove the spear through the vulnerable gap between helm and scaled shirt.

Firelight played across the man's features and Belarrin offered a silent prayer of thanks. It wasn't his family.

He looked up and, glancing to his right, saw that the fleeing mass of Kalilaer had begun to pull away from the pursuing t'Okaedrin. Turning to his left, he saw why. Five Scions formed a thin line a dozen paces behind him. Facing them were an equal number of t'Okaedrin. Without iron weapons and facing skilled warriors on horseback, the rebels were as good as dead. One fell, even as Belarrin rose to his feet.

Catching movement to his right, Belarrin turned and saw Yrpel and Idysha fall back from the running Kalilaer. Running up beside him, Yrpel stooped to pick up the sword of the t'Okaedrin Belarrin had slain. Then he grabbed the knife from the dead man's belt and tossed it to Idysha. "Come on!" he cried.

Without waiting for him, they ran to join the fighting Scions. Belarrin hesitated, his eyes drawn to the other Kalilaer, now disappearing into the darkness. Rejoining them would ensure he reached the forest while Yrpel and the others died buying them time. Infiltrating the Scions was all that mattered, not these fool Kalilaer. But with a wordless cry, he turned to follow Yrpel and Idysha. Fool! They should've meant nothing to him.

Still cursing, Belarrin charged the nearest t'Okaedrin. As he closed the distance, he threw his spear, catching the warrior in the chest. The armor deflected the point, but the force of it staggered the man and he tumbled from his saddle. Idysha pounced upon him even as Belarrin closed and she rammed her knife through his eye.

Belarrin grabbed his spear as a second horseman charged. He thrust upward with his crude weapon, forcing the horse to rear, prancing out of range.

"Back," Belarrin cried to Idysha. The woman obeyed instantly, scrambling toward the rest of the Scions. Belarrin withdrew more slowly, thrusting again and again to keep the horseman at a distance.

He spared a glance behind him to see that another Scion had fallen. The remaining three were pushed back to back with spears extended. There was blood on the ground. At least one was wounded. The three Kalilaer joined the circle, Yrpel with his sword and Idysha with a spear she'd retrieved. Feeling his own spear in his hands, Belarrin was overwhelmed by a sense of futility. Six undrilled warriors with stone weapons and no armor against four disciplined iron-wielding t'Okaedrin on horseback. There could be only one outcome.

The t'Okaedrin circled. There were no archers among them and, for a moment, Belarrin wondered if they were waiting for Pi'aernoth. But no, they'd lost two of their number when it should have been a bloodless battle. They were methodical now. When they charged, it would be as one, bearing down from all sides. Dismounted, there might have been a chance, but not like this.

Light from the distant fires gleamed off their helms, but their eyes lay in shadow. They should have been his brothers, not his death. The Cydion blinded fools! Bitterness gave way to fear and fear to rage. The futility, to end like this. Not like this! Not in the garb of an enemy, killed by a friend. His eyes were fixed upon the points of the iron swords. The blades that would pierce his flesh and steal his life.

His chest was on fire, his head was ice, like looking through a dream. Terror and rage curdled within him, setting his heart to racing. It thundered behind his eyes until it seemed he looked through a veil of crimson. He thought his head might burst from the pressure of it.

"Not like this!" he screamed as the t'Okaedrin charged. Lines of piercing gold flashed across his vision, the light of the fires, the gleam of the sword points. "Ae'irpiva saepadai aitivys!" The sounds tore from Belarrin's throat. Nothing he knew, nothing he understood, but the pressure on his mind vanished.

A whispered hush filled the air in the moment of time before the t'Okaedrin horsemen struck. A moment of calm, a moment of nothing before swords fell and the final breath.

The night shrieked to life. Belarrin staggered as a gale wind ripped through the darkness behind him. It tore past into the closing rank of t'Okaedrin like a thing alive. The horses reared, screaming in terror as the wind buffeted them, driving them stumbling back. Their riders sawed at the reins, but to no avail. The gale was a thing of nightmare, relentless in its fury. One by one, the horses tumbled to the ground, dragging their hapless t'Okaedrin with them.

Belarrin stumbled forward through the harsh wind, squinting against the sudden flurry of raised dust and shredded leaves filling the air. The t'Okaedrin nearest to him struggled, his leg pinned beneath his writhing horse. Belarrin's spear pierced him through the gap in the armor beneath the arm.

Raising his arm to shield his face, Belarrin turned to see the Scions killing the other t'Okaedrin. He knelt down, shielding his head against the gale fury and whispered a silent prayer. "Thank you."

The wind was already gone. It truly was a gift from His Highest Above. A miracle proving Belarrin's task was blessed, even from above.

"Hurry. Run!" One of the Scions yelled. It was a woman. Her blond hair shone pale in the darkness as she turned toward the forest.

Belarrin looked up. In the distance, the Kalilaer camp was still churning like an overturned beehive. They weren't free yet. He jumped to his feet and turned to the forest. Nearby, Idysha grabbed Yrpel by the shoulder. The large man stood over one of the dead t'Okaedrin, a snarl on his face. But at Idysha's urging he tore away and the three of them raced after the Scions into the woods.

As the forest closed around them, the others' features faded to black silhouettes. They sprinted on, barely heeding the bushes and trunks that rose up on either side. Half the time it felt that Belarrin was stumbling as much as running, in a forever fall. One of the Scions tripped and crashed into a bush. Branches snapped as he cursed, but the man lurched to his feet in a moment to continue his run.

Belarrin's legs began to burn and his breath came ragged from his throat. But still he followed, past all strength. He, a t'Okaedrin, was not about to be outdone by Scions and Kalilaer. Yet even his resolve was waning when the woman in the lead finally slowed and stopped.

They gathered around her, lungs heaving. "Any wounded? How bad?" she managed to ask between breaths.

"I…" one of the Scions began to say, then he stumbled forward and collapsed to the ground.

"Darr!" The woman cried, falling to her knees beside him. The other Scion joined her at Darr's side as Belarrin, Idysha, and Yrpel watched, dumbfounded. "Mirnadd, he's bleeding in the side," the woman said.

"Here, help me turn him," Mirnadd said. Belarrin and the others hurried forward and, as a group, they managed to gently lay Darr on his back.

The wounded man stared upward, his eyes fixed on the woman, his breath coming in short pained gasps. "I… I'm sorry… Sravika…"

"Don't speak, Darr," the woman said, the faint starlight sparkling in the tears falling down her cheeks. "Just rest. We'll get you healed in no time."

They tore back Darr's shirt to reveal a sword gash in his side. Belarrin winced at the depth of it. But undeterred, Mirnadd washed the wound. Then Sravika, using a bone needle, tried to stitch it closed. It was hard work. Blood flowed over her fingers making the needle slick. It was futile work, too. By Sravika's tears, Belarrin sensed she already knew. But that didn't stop her efforts. Nor did she relent as Darr's breathing slowed or when his eyes dulled. Then he breathed no more and still Sravika worked.

Letting out a sigh, Mirnadd touched her hand. "He's gone, Sravika."

"No, we cannot…"

"It's too late."

Her whole body shuddered as she dropped her hands. "We should've stopped sooner. If we had, we might have..."

"We all would have died," Mirnadd replied, gently. "Darr knew we had to press on.

He didn't protest. He understood."

"But..."

"You did what had to be done, Sravika. We had to get enough distance. Darr knew that. We all knew that."

Sravika bowed her head a long moment, then reaching out with her hand, closed Darr's vacant eyes. "Highest Above, welcome your champion home."

She let out a long deep breath. Then she and Mirnadd rose to their feet and turned to face Belarrin and the others. It looked a struggle for her to bring a smile to her face, but when it came it was warm and friendly. "My name is Sravika and this is Mirnadd. What are your names?"

"Belarrin," he replied, then the other two introduced themselves.

"Welcome to the Scions of the Fallen Tree, my friends." She glanced at Mirnadd, then added, "Hopefully Henirgar was able to guide your companions to safety. In the morning we will rejoin the others, but for now we need to find shelter."

"What about the Iron-Men?" Idysha asked.

"They don't usually pursue too far into the forest," Mirnadd replied. "But if they do, we'll be hiding."

They continued at a slower pace deeper into the woods with Mirnadd and Yrpel carrying Darr's body between them. After a short search, Sravika found a cluster of bushes, almost dense enough to be called a thicket. She knelt down, then crawled on her chest beneath the stretching brambles. "This will do," her voice called softly from within.

Idysha crawled through next, then Mirnadd and Yrpel with Darr. Belarrin kept watch as they did, then entered last. The interior was tight with countless intertwining branches, but once he pressed enough down, Belarrin was comfortable enough. The brush broke the chill night wind. It was a good hiding place, he admitted to himself. He doubted his brothers would search in a place so dense. Not when the forest was filled with thick underbrush.

The others settled into the branches, sitting back more than lying down, and remained silent. In moments, he heard the heavier breathing of Idysha's light snoring, but the others faded more slowly. For Belarrin, there was little desire to sleep. He felt more focused than he had in a long time. His mind and heart raced from the battle he shouldn't have survived. Finally being free was exhilarating. It was unfortunate that brothers had to die to see the task done, but they should have known better and he had no regret in his choice. Not when he'd seen His Highest Above intervene so directly. Such a wind! It had been a miracle.

Small patches of moonlight filtered through the canopy of tree limbs, needles, and brush. In that faint light, he saw tears stained Sravika's cheeks. Her eyes were open, too. There was something familiar in them, wild and feral. Yet there was more than that. A sorrow lingered there, too. It reminded him of Vitarria's gaze, just before he struck her down. Sravika's eyes were a deep blue, though, instead of green, and sparkled faintly in the dim starlight. Unkempt locks of golden hair fell across her face, but, lost in her fury and grief, she didn't seem aware of them. Nor did she notice Belarrin's gaze. Discomforted, he looked away and closed his eyes. After a long time, sleep came.

High Lord Ushtyl looked out from his balcony high up in his tower. Below him, he could see dozens of his people lining the parapets to look down on the Kalilaer settlement below. The cacophony of battle had faded now, returning to the silence of night. Near the far side of the settlement, a handful of buildings still burned out of control. One of the woodworking camps was ablaze, he thought, but until daylight he couldn't be sure. Shadows moved around it, doubtless t'Okaedrin making sure the blaze was contained and didn't spread to the nearby crops.

A sharp knock sounded on the door of his quarters. "Enter," Ushtyl called over his shoulder.

Behind him, the door opened and he heard footsteps cross his room. Captain Eltirkar stepped beside him on the balcony and offered a quick bow. "My Lord, the report has come in."

"Did we succeed?"

"Yes, my Lord. The infiltration is complete."

"Excellent." Allowing a Scion triumph galled, even if it led to ultimate triumph. "Is that a woodworking camp burning?"

"Yes, my Lord. The rebels struck a smelting camp, a woodworking camp, a farming camp, and a pottery camp. We recaptured most of the woodworkers and all the potters. Curiously, two smelters remained behind. Because they failed to sound the alarm, I was thinking of sending them to the Boards for a day and then down into the mines."

"Not necessary," Ushtyl replied with the wave of his hand. "Humans are cattle and you expect too much of them. We need smelters more than miners. Just have them reassigned to another camp."

"It shall be done, my Lord."

"What else?"

"About twenty Scions were slain though I'll have firmer numbers by morning."

"Tally any supplies lost and notify High Lord Tazil. He's agreed to support any needs we may have." At Eltirkar's nod, Ushtyl asked, "Any losses of our own?"

The captain hesitated, then said, "Yes, my Lord, more than I'd have liked."

That tore Ushtyl's gaze away from the burning buildings. Meeting Eltirkar's eyes, he asked, "How many?"

"Six t'Okaedrin, all horse warriors."

"Six? That's unheard of."

"I know, my Lord. Even more troubling than their deaths is their disobedience. All six died pursuing the smelting Kalilaer."

Ushtyl's brows lowered. "I gave strict orders!"

"I know, my Lord. I don't know what happened."

"But the infiltrator escaped?"

"Yes, my Lord. His body was not found among the dead and the Sapaupan Kaupet points northward into the forest."

Ushtyl crossed his arms and turned back to the night. "Then be glad nothing worse came of it, Eltirkar. Those fool t'Okaedrin deserved their deaths. If they'd stopped the smelters, I'd have ordered them flayed alive."

"Yes, my Lord. But even so, the brothers are very angry. They thirst for revenge. Rumors are passing through the city among our own people as well."

"I will address them and allay their fears in the morning, Captain. Was there anything else?"

"No, my Lord."

"Then you're dismissed. I want those brothers to know that their fallen are their own fault. When we give orders, they will be followed exactly as given."

"It will be done as you command."

As Eltirkar retreated, Ushtyl pulled his gaze from the burning buildings to look north toward the deep darkness of the wilderness. Now he could only wait.

CHAPTER 18
Rising

"I remember the day the Great War began. The lilies were in bloom and my children played in the garden beneath the sun. They are dead now."

—Elvarie of Oneilla

Belarrin and his companions awoke with the dawn. Mirnadd passed around some dried meat from a satchel and a leather flask of water. When they were done, he said, "Time to go."

Sravika nodded. "We'll leave Darr's body here. I wish we had time for a better burial than this."

Mirnadd crawled through the thicket first and Belarrin followed last. Pushing through the final wall of branches, he stepped into the midst of the open forest, brilliant and golden-green in the new morning sun. He saw that Yrpel still carried the t'Okaedrin sword from the night before. Idysha had slipped her iron knife into her belt. Like the two Scions,

Belarrin had only the spear he'd taken in the fight. As much as he wanted Yrpel's sword, he realized the spear was better. He was too familiar with the use of a sword. Even touching it might betray him.

"This way," Sravika said and headed deeper into the forest.

By gauging the position of the sun, Belarrin knew they were walking north, but more he couldn't say. Sravika's certainty about their path made him marvel. It was much like the time he'd followed Vitarria. The wildness of the forest struck him, just as it had then, and recalled his amazement at the ability of these rebels to travel unerringly through it. How could such a savage and ignorant people, unable even to forge iron, know this one thing so well?

Among the deep shades of the evergreens, leaves had begun to yellow and orange with the onset of the fall. That caused Belarrin's heart to skip a beat. This task had taken him away from Elestis and his brothers for far too long already. But, so long as he was back home by winter, he would be content. The thought of scratching out a meager survival in a snow-bound wilderness made him cringe.

As they walked, Sravika turned to him. "What was it you said last night during the battle?"

"What?" Belarrin asked.

"When we were standing back to back, facing the final charge of the Iron-Men. You shouted words I didn't understand. It sounded like a battle cry in a strange language."

He had said something, Belarrin realized, now that she mentioned it. Strange that he'd forgotten. But the whole battle was a haze. He remembered heat and cold, anger and fear. He remembered the miracle of His Highest Above. "I don't know. Most battles I have been in become little more than a shadow on my memory. It might have been a shout of rage. I remember being certain we were going to die."

Sravika nodded. "As was I."

The brush ahead quivered and Belarrin instinctively tightened his grip on his spear. But a moment later, a woman in rough leather clothing burst from the foliage. She might have spared a glance for him and the others, but her attention was fixed on Mirnadd. She leapt forward to fling her arms around the startled man, sending the long locks of her dark hair cascading around him.

Mirnadd stumbled back, laughing. "Easy woman."

After planting a long kiss on his lips, the woman stepped back to look him over. "What did they do to you?" she asked, tracing a thin cut on Mirnadd's cheek with her finger. Any closer and it would have been a fatal strike rather than a thin scratch. "Accursed Finnies, they'll have to answer to me for this!"

"Then answer they shall," Mirnadd replied, embracing her again.

Sravika's lips twitched in amusement as she turned to Belarrin, Yrpel, and Idysha. "Tayrja is Mirnadd's wife. They're but a few seasons wed, if you couldn't tell. We'll leave them to their greeting. The others should be just ahead."

They pressed through a thin layer of brush and stepped out into a clearing. Nearly a hundred people filled the glade. Half were in the rough work clothes of the Kalilaer, while the

Scions wore mostly leathers and furs. Belarrin's eyes shifted to a group seated off to their right. They saw him at the same moment.

"Belarrin! Yrpel and Idysha!" Zoltha cried, leaping to his feet and rushing forward to embrace them. He was closely followed by a few others from the smelting camp. "We feared you were all dead. Highest Above be praised!"

Yrpel laughed. "It takes more than a few Iron-Men to keep this Iengian down. I finally began my revenge.

"Were any lost?" Idysha asked.

"A few," Zoltha replied, his smile fading.

Belarrin nodded. "I saw Wiersa fall. What about Chostir?"

"She should live," Zoltha said, turning to look behind him. Belarrin saw the brown-haired woman sitting down with her back against a tree. Her face was pale and her eyes were closed. "Henirgar was able to clean and stitch her wound. Provided there's no infection, she will recover."

"Good," Idysha said.

Sravika stood off to one side, smiling as she watched the exchange. Then she turned to embrace a Scion man who walked up. "Henirgar, my friend! The tree has fallen."

"But a new shoot rises," the man answered. There was more than a simple greeting in his voice, though. It sounded like both a prayer and a battle cry. His brow furrowed. "I'm glad to see you, too, Sravika. After those Iron-Men attacked, I feared the worst. But Blood on the Bridge, no one else survived?"

"Mirnadd lives," Sravika replied. "He's with Tayrja. We lost the others."

"Cydion's Abyss! I saw Tallonin fall, and then Gotirnas took an arrow, but all the others?"

Sravika's eyes dropped and her voice shrank to barely above a whisper. "Darr escaped the battle with us, but his wounds were too severe. Mirnadd and I are lucky to be alive. If Belarrin, Idysha, and Yrpel hadn't remained with us, we would be dead, too."

Idysha shook her head. "It wasn't our doing. I felt the breath of Lelpfios himself upon us last night. The Lord of Wind and Rain was watching."

Henirgar's eyes widened as he looked questioningly to Sravika. She nodded. "A gale wind cast the Iron-Men from their steeds."

A smile formed on Henirgar's face. It was almost wolfish. "If the Etyni themselves are watching over us, then the Finnies will fall indeed."

"Highest Above let it be so," Sravika replied.

Henirgar turned to Belarrin and the others. "But thank you also, my friends, and welcome to our family."

"Please excuse me," Sravika said. "I had better speak with Chief Kitiger."

As she left, Belarrin walked with Zoltha, Idysha, and Yrpel to rejoin the other Kalilaer rescued from the smelting camp, but his attention remained on Sravika. She headed over to a small group of Scions centered around an older man of middling height with dark hair and broad shoulders. His stance was straight-backed, exuding confidence and authority. Even had he stood alone, Belarrin knew he would've picked the man as leader of this group.

Chostir's eyes flickered open a moment as they joined her and the others. She closed them again and let out a slow sigh. "Good. I am glad you made it. I could lose no more."

"Rest," Zoltha said, kneeling down beside her. "We'll be moving soon and you must keep your strength."

She didn't protest. Her breathing was regular. That was promising. Belarrin turned back to watch Sravika's meeting. He wished he could join them. If he was to learn about the Scions, he needed to be where the decisions were made. How did one camp communicate with another? It was impossible that they all acted alone.

"Bless you for saving us," Idysha said to Henirgar who had followed them. "Do you rescue as many as this in each attack?"

"No," Henirgar said, his eyes playing over the crowded glade. "Every raid costs us lives we can ill-afford. We were bolder this time, striking four camps instead of just one. The gain was great, but the price was nearly as high."

Idysha's voice softened. "How many were lost?"

"Twenty-two." Henirgar's lips thinned to a slit and his eyes flashed with anger. "Those liberating the farming camp escaped unharmed and the raid on the woodworking camp didn't lose many, though nearly half the slaves were recaptured before they reached the forest." He shook his head. "Those sent to the potting camp were all slaughtered and you saw what your own escape cost. Eight Scions went in and only three came out."

Idysha's head bowed. "I am sorry."

"No!" Henirgar cried. At her flinch, he continued more gently. "Don't let regret fill you, but anger. Every life paid shall be repaid. Twenty-two were lost, but fifty-one Scions survived. Twenty-two were lost, but forty slaves were freed. We came with seventy-three and return with ninety-one. Each raid demands a terrible price, but none us can flinch from it when our time comes." He glanced from Idysha, to Belarrin, to Yrpel and a smile broke out on his face. "But come, my friends. Now is not a time for sorrow, but rejoicing. A day ago you wore chains, but now you are free."

Yrpel roared his laughter, slamming his fist into his open palm. "Yes!"

Henirgar nodded. "The Cydion-accursed Iron-Men grow more and more dogged, but no matter how they try, they cannot overcome us as long as we hold our resolve."

Belarrin grinned with the others, but his eyes were fixed on Henirgar's face. There was more here than was spoken. Behind the brave words, he sensed that perhaps Henirgar was hiding that not all Scions were so certain.

While they stood together, the meeting of the raid leaders ended and Sravika walked back to them. Her face was drawn and eyes shadowed, but her smile was genuine. "Get ready to move. It looks like we're the last of the survivors. It is time to bring you home."

All around the glade, Scions and freed Kalilaer gathered what belongings they had. Unlike the t'Okaedrin, there were no pack animals, no carts filled with supplies. Only packs and satchels that were carried on the back or slung over the shoulder. Belarrin took one such sack which he realized held dried strips of meat and joined the line marching northward. Chostir was too weak to walk on her own so Zoltha and Idysha supported her on either side.

The Scions traveled without the disciplined ranks of the t'Okaedrin, but despite that, the pace was quicker than Belarrin would have expected. He couldn't see who set its direction yet there was apparent order within the chaos. He caught fleeting glimpses of scouts on the flanks and guessed there had to be more ahead and masking the trail behind.

Late that afternoon they stopped in another glade. Several of the scouts must have run far ahead, for they had managed to find the time to hunt a deer which already roasted over a fire pit.

Kitiger walked to the center of the glade and stood next to the fire. "It is a good day, my family," he said in a loud voice. Belarrin sensed Sravika grimace beside him, but she quickly smoothed her face as he continued, "We have all fought bravely and broken forty slaves from their chains!"

A cheer rose up, both Scion and freed Kalilaer lending their voices.

When they quieted, he continued. "To you, my new friends, let me offer welcome. I am Kitiger, the chieftain of this band. Ours is the dream to see no human in bondage. To see the Finnies and their Iron-Man servants driven into the sea and destroyed. I know many of you have fought bravely already, both while cruelly enslaved and in yesterday's battle for freedom. You have lost friends and family. Alas we all have.

"In a few days we will rejoin the remainder of our band. There, it is my hope that all of you will become a part of our family and avenge the evils that you've already suffered so that no one else will have to endure the same. If you will not, we understand and will send you northward with spears and food. But I believe that you all will remain and see this tyranny ended. The tree has fallen, but a new shoot rises!"

Scions shouted the greeting back at him and the former Kalilaer joined in. When they fell silent, Kitiger said, "Now may you find sorrow and joy in this feast. Sorrow for those lost and joy for those found. And pray that His Highest Above continues to protect and guard us."

After a smaller cheer, Kitiger stepped away from the fire and everyone gathered around the pit to gather their meal. Belarrin took his portion and sat down on a log next to Zoltha. The deer was delicious, gamey yet tender. He was surprised when Sravika took a seat on his other side.

"I told Kitiger of your bravery last night," she said.

"There was little choice. If we didn't fight, we would have died."

"It requires courage to stand with meager weapons against the Iron-Men. It is always our hope that freed slaves will choose to join us. With time, they become honored warriors welcomed with open arms around our fires. Yet few have a chance to prove themselves until after their escape."

"You have no need to thank me," Belarrin replied, trying to keep the curtness from his voice. He didn't want to think of the blood of his brothers on his hands. "Yrpel and Idysha were glad to met out some revenge."

Sravika smiled. "I thank you all, nevertheless."

"I noticed you were troubled during the chieftain's speech," Zoltha said to her. "What's wrong?"

She shook herself and blinked her eyes hard. When they opened, they had cleared again. "I don't want to trouble you. You are newly freed and that is good."

"Please tell us."

Sravika sighed. "I'm worried and sad. We lost too many during the raid. The Iron-Men are growing increasingly clever. Rumor has it another of our camps was completely destroyed a few months ago. We don't know how."

"But this raid saved many people too," Belarrin replied.

"I do not know them!" she cried, her eyes flashing. Then she drew in a deep breath. "No, I'm glad for everyone saved. Yet the cost is in friends, some of whom I've known for many years."

"I see."

She glared at him. "I'm not just being sentimental."

Belarrin raised his hands. "I wasn't suggesting that. Earlier, Henirgar said much the same thing. But he also said that so long as more are freed than are lost, triumph is inevitable."

Sravika sighed. "If we all shared Henirgar's passion, I might agree. But many doubt, and I confess I sometimes wonder, too. We rescued twice what we lost, yes, but those Scions who died were each battle-tested warriors. Many Kalilaer will make good warriors too, with time. How many years have some of your kindred toiled in slavery? They must be trained again, they must rediscover their martial fervor."

She laughed bitterly. "Truth is, this raid is better than many. Sometimes we lose more than we save."

"You're saying this war is futile."

She looked over at him, eyes probing. "I hear the question behind your words, Belarrin. You wonder that here, on the morrow of your rescue, we unburden our fears to you. And you not even a Scion yet." She smiled. "With some, I might hesitate, but not you. Nor Yrpel or Idysha either. You three fought and bled with us. There is a binding in such a thing that unclouds words." She turned away, her gaze fixing on the fire pit, eyes unfocused in contemplation. "The war may be futile, I don't know. But that doesn't mean it isn't a war worth fighting. But if nothing changes we will lose in the end. Each year they are stronger and I fear we may be weaker."

"If the cost of each raid is so great, might it not be better to attack in larger numbers? A larger host might defend itself better from the Iron-Men and rescue more Kalilaer." What he didn't add was that, by nature of its size, such an army would be harder to hide from his brothers.

But Sravika's eyes brightened. "Exactly! I've said as much in the council."

"Not all agree, though," Zoltha said.

She shook her head. "Fear holds them back. Fear that in such numbers we will be easily found. But it's a gamble worth taking. Otherwise, it will be decades or centuries before the back of the Finnie empire is broken. How many more must die in slavery?"

"Tens of thousands," Belarrin answered. Despite himself, he found he liked Sravika, much as he liked Yrpel, Idysha, and the others of the smelting camp. But he would use her because he had to. She was his tool to draw the Scions together so they could be eradicated.

"And even if we fail, there will always be more Scions," Sravika said. "They will never be able to destroy us all."

Sravika matched the grin that formed on Belarrin's face. He was glad she didn't understand the reason he smiled.

They turned as Idysha joined them, kneeling beside Sravika. "Chostir is exhausted from the march," she said. "Even with our help, walking is too hard for her."

"Could we build some sort of stretcher?" Zoltha asked.

"None that drags on the ground," Sravika replied. "Our trackers already have to work hard to hide our path. But one that is carried, yes." She smiled softly. "I can help."

"How far are we from your village?" Idysha asked.

Sravika grimaced. "It is more of a camp than a village. But we're about four days away from our old site, depending on the pace we keep."

"Old site?" Zoltha asked. "I don't understand."

"We have to move after every raid, just in case one of us is captured and tortured to give away our location." Sravika looked around at all the Scions in the glade. "No one here knows where we're going. That's why we have to return to our old camp first. Someone will meet us there."

As darkness fell, Belarrin helped the others make a stretcher for Chostir. They found two sturdy pieces of wood, each nearly a thumb's width wide and relatively straight. Between them, they bound leather to form the harness. With all the help, it was quick work. Afterward, Belarrin found a place to bed down beneath a tree near the edge of the glade among the others from the smelting camp. Wrapped up in his cloak, sleep came quickly.

When the march resumed the next morning, each group of freed Kalilaer continued to stick together. The former woodworkers walked toward the front of the line and the farmers further behind, while Belarrin's group stayed near the middle. They traded turns carrying Chostir. Relieved of walking, the color came back to her face and her strength began to return. Unfortunately, this meant she was able, once again, to regale those who carried her with stories. But now they were told with a smile on her lips. Sravika, Henirgar, Mirnadd, and Tayrja walked with them, too. Belarrin suspected that the same was true for the other groups of Kalilaer and the Scions who had rescued them. It was a well-thought plan to forge strong bonds between the old and the new.

When they next stopped to make camp and eat, Belarrin's group formed a circle that was so similar to what they'd done back at the smelting camp that he almost laughed. Sravika sat opposite him and, after eating, picked up a stick and idly traced lines in the dirt at her feet as they talked. They connected in a crisscross pattern that Belarrin found vaguely familiar.

"What are you doing?" Zoltha asked beside him.

Sravika looked up and smiled sheepishly. "I don't really know." She set down the stick and reached into the satchel hanging from her shoulder to pull out a rolled up piece of parchment. It crackled dryly as she laid it flat on her knee. "I took this from the body of a Finnie about a year ago. I know it has to be writing, but I don't know how to read." Belarrin's stomach heaved at her words. A dead Syraestari? Highest Above! It hadn't happened in Raefi'ernyn or he would've heard of it. Such a loss was a tragedy, a shame on all t'Okaedrin. He blinked to wash the sting from his eyes as he stared at Sravika. Had she committed the heinous crime or was it another? To rob such a one who sought only to restore civilization to a world awash in the Cataclysm. He had to shake himself free of the spiraling dark thoughts. High Lord Tazil had warned him he would have to set aside sacred things. He'd warned that Belarrin might have to partake in evil for the greater good.

"The Finnies are smarter than us only because they remember," Sravika was saying. "They still write down their knowledge for others to read. Sometimes I think that if I could figure out those words, we could write things too. We could become as wise as them."

Zoltha crossed the circle to sit beside her. Looking down at the parchment, he frowned. "Why does it matter what it says?" He picked up Sravika's stick and scratched a line. "That is now an 'S'." He marked two crossing lines. "We'll call this an 'R' sound and here is 'Ah'." He continued, making up a symbol for a 'V', an 'Ee', a 'K', and then added a second 'Ah.' Sitting back, he announced, "There, S-R-A-V-I-K-A."

She laughed and Belarrin found himself longing to smile with her. The pure delight in her voice was captivating. He turned away frowning. Only moments ago, she'd spoken of murder as if it were nothing. He couldn't allow the Scions to enchant him as the Kalilaer had. These people weren't friends or family. They were the enemy. Among the Kalilaer, he at least could tell himself they were living as was intended, but not so the Scions. And now, even the Kalilaer had shown their own apostasy. But how could they not? How could he stop them? He liked them all, even Sravika!

She was still laughing. "But how am I to remember the letters?"

"Easy." Zoltha walked over to the fire and picked out a piece of charcoal that had cooled near the edge. Returning to his seat, he took Sravika's leather pouch and drew the same markings on it in ash. "Now you'll never forget."

Despite himself, Belarrin moved closer so he could see the scratches better and, more importantly, so he could see the original Finnie parchment. It definitely was familiar but why, he couldn't say. He had seen Finnie writings before, but it was more than that. There was something about the way the lines crossed that tugged at the edge of his memory.

As they set out the next morning, Sravika again joined Belarrin and his companions. "I spoke with Kitiger and the other leaders last evening," she said. "Because there are so many new Scions, we think it would be best if each of the three new groups appointed one of their own to join our council. That way we can be sure every need is met."

"We choose Belarrin," Yrpel said.

"What? No!" Belarrin blurted, but even as he did, his mind seized on the opportunity. As a leader, he would have a greater opportunity to come to understand the Scions.

"Who else would it be?" Zoltha said and Idysha nodded.

"I don't know what you see in me," Belarrin said, keeping his protests feeble so they would be brushed aside.

"Tell Sravika about how he stood up to that Iron-Man," Yrpel said.

Idysha laughed. "I've never seen such a thing before. He actually stepped between a furious Iron-Man and Zoltha." As Belarrin heard her recount the tale, he was sure Idysha embellished it. He hadn't felt as courageous as she described, just frustrated and angry.

When Idysha finished her story, Sravika looked at Belarrin. "You continue to surprise me. I am certain you'll do well. The task of a councilor isn't onerous. If one of your people has a problem, they come to you first. We all work together to provide help wherever it is needed. The council occasionally meets separately from the others, but not very often."

"What can I say but that I will do my best," Belarrin replied.

"Ha!" Yrpel slapped him hard on the back. "Like you could do anything less."

The next day, they reached the old Scion camp. It was much like the abandoned camp Belarrin had seen during his first infiltration. Only fleeting signs remained that anyone had ever lived there. An ashen scar where the fire pit had lain. Post holes marking the outer fence. Wider, but shallow holes, marking where individual shelters had been carved out. As before, a single man sat near the center of the glade. He was of middling height, stocky and broad shouldered. He'd lost most of his hair, except above the ears. What remained was dark brown with flecks of gray. He rose to his feet and walked towards them.

"Oh." A soft sigh escaped Sravika's lips. "Poor Fedigni."

"What? Why?" Yrpel asked, but Sravika didn't answer. Nor did she enter the glade and Belarrin realized everyone else had stopped, as well. All except Chief Kitiger.

Fedigni looked up at the long line of standing Scions and hesitation entered his steps. He turned to the approaching chieftain and his face crumpled. Beside Belarrin, Sravika shook her head sadly. They were too far to hear the words spoken, but Belarrin saw Fedigni ask a question. Kitiger answered and Fedigni sank to his knees, a great wail tearing from his throat that echoed over the forest.

Sravika bowed her head. "His wife is one of those who died during the raid."

"Then it isn't time for tears." Yrpel growled. "It's time for rage. For revenge!"

"Quiet you fool," Idysha told him, but her tone was soft to take away the sting of her words and she rested her hand gently on his arm. More quietly, such that Belarrin could barely hear, she said with a note of pride, "They cannot all be Iengian."

Sravika tore her gaze from the weeping man and the chieftain who held him in calm embrace and turned to Belarrin. Her own face was drawn with a grief of her own, but she kept her voice clipped and strong. "You have the food in your pack. Come, let's eat and give Fedigni a little peace. We will move on before long."

They ate in silence. As he chewed on a morsel of dried venison, Belarrin looked around at all the faces he'd come to know. Each was drawn, sad or angry, and full of remembrance. Everyone among them had suffered loss. One did not become a Scion, he realized, without weathering death. Slain husbands and wives, parents, friends, siblings, and children. Much the same could be said of the t'Okaedrin. His brothers fought with iron, but that didn't make them invincible. He'd been very young when his first brother died in battle. His mind turned to Nalsuntha. How long had it been since he had contemplated the death of the brother who had been his eldest? There was an emptiness there, he knew, but it blended with the greater void caused by his separation from his family. Only when he was home would he truly be able to feel that loss.

"Did I ever tell you," Chostir broke the long silence. "About the great graveyard of the lost age?"

Yrpel groaned loudly. "Only a half a hundred times. And three times yesterday."

"That's not true!"

He grimaced. "Well it feels like it. I almost think I could tell all your stories myself."

"Well why don't you then?" Chostir asked. "You have a nice voice. I'd like to hear your stories." Belarrin joined the laughter of the others. The bleak moment broken, they were ready when word came that it was time to continue their march.

CHAPTER 19
Branches

"There are those who denounce all lies, but I am convinced that they live in a fog of ignorance. The general, the captain, the king must live in perpetual deceit. He must smile in adversity, and joke in misery. He must laugh as he charges the enemy ramparts, knowing that the act may very well cost him his life. For only in such falsehood will those he commands see that what must be done, will be done."

--Prince Yujin of Sarnoth

As the Scions set out again, Belarrin caught occasional glimpses of Fedigni through the trees. The grieving man walked near the head of the Scion band. Kitiger traveled beside him, but throughout the day, many of the other Scions joined them for a time, including Sravika, Mirnadd, and Henirgar. Each, no doubt, paused to offer their sorrow, but from the hunch of Fedigni's back, Belarrin wondered if the man welcomed it. Would he, had he just learned his wife was dead?

By evening, the greater bleakness had lifted from the Scions who gathered for the evening meal. Fedigni was with them, yet withdrawn into himself. There would be others, Belarrin realized, when they arrived at the new camp. Fedigni was not the only one of them to have lost someone close. As Sravika had suggested earlier, every one of them was dear. In their own way, the Scions were a family just as the t'Okaedrin were. No. Belarrin shook his head, angry at the comparison. They were completely different. Yet there was a resilience he had to admire. They faced death. They grieved, they raged, but then they pressed on with life through the sorrow.

Before the meal was shared, Kitiger rose to speak. "My friends, my family," the chieftain said. "We are nearly home. Another couple days march, Fedigni tells me. We grieve his loss as our loss. Remember that we have had days, already, to feel our sorrow but our family at our home has not. We will feel it, remembering it again with them. With them, we will remember who we are and why we're here. We will remember why death and life is worth the price. We will celebrate our newfound brothers and sisters."

"Kitiger!" Henirgar called from his seat not far from Belarrin. "Two days more, you say?"

"Yes?"

"It seems to me, that will put us in crabapple country."

"What?" Mirnadd blurted.

"I believe that's true, Henirgar," Kitiger said, a grin growing on his face.

"No!" Mirnadd cried as gales of laughter broke out around the fire and, beside Mirnadd, Tayrja rocked backward in laughter so far she nearly lost her seat. Even a glimmer of a smile edged Fedigni's face.

Belarrin and the other smelters looked around, bewildered, but Sravika was laughing too hard to be any help.

"Something must be done," Henirgar called.

"I expect it will be, my friend," Kitiger said. "I expect our homecoming feast will be a fine one indeed."

Yrpel said, "I take it Mirnadd doesn't care for crabapples?"

His question was met only by more gales of laughter.

As they set out the next day, Belarrin took a turn with Mirnadd carrying Chostir. She continued to grow stronger, but both Sravika and Idysha insisted she not walk on her own yet. Belarrin didn't mind too much. Chostir's tales had become like the rushing of a river, a sound he could listen to and enjoy if he chose, or ignore. Besides, he didn't want his arms to grow weak without the usual t'Okaedrin drills.

Yet when Yrpel took his place, Belarrin was happy for the relief. He fell a little behind the others, watching them as he walked. They traveled in what might only loosely be called a column. Sravika chatted happily with Idysha, while Zoltha was a little further ahead, his head bowed in silent contemplation. Yet, though Zoltha was apart, it was only a little. There were invisible ties that bound the survivors from the smelter together. Those ties were branching out, to incorporate Sravika, Mirnadd, Henirgar, and Tayrja as well. Peculiar how easily that happened. The binding of t'Okaedrin into a brotherhood was begun from a young age, but he wondered if the loyalty here wasn't just as strong.

He turned as Kitiger joined him. "Chieftain."

"You are the one named Belarrin?" Kitiger had a deep voice with a natural firmness to it. Yet there was gentleness in his tone, too. Surprising for the leader of a warband.

"Yes."

"Sravika told me of your fight during the raid. She and Mirnadd owe you their lives."

"I owe them mine, too," Belarrin replied. "I hope she told you Yrpel and Idysha were as much a part of it as myself."

"She did." Kitiger nodded. "I applaud your humility. We are one family, unlike the wildmen. Those who seek glory for their own sake can be as much a danger to us as an asset. I hope she didn't break your trust by telling me?

"No, but I'm surprised to be talked about so much."

"I want to get to know all the new members of our family."

"So you know how best to use us."

Kitiger glanced over at him, a wry smile forming on his lips. "You're a sharp one, my friend. Yes, that is part of it, I don't deny. If we're to win this struggle, we need every advantage we can find. But we also want to be sure that all needs are met. As you've seen, we mourn every loss."

"And celebrate every triumph."

"Of course! We aren't made of stone." Kitiger laughed, then said, "I understand those from your smelting camp chose you as their councilor?"

"So it would seem," Belarrin replied.

"You will meet the other new councilors soon, then. Those rescued from the woodcutting camp picked Argluf and those from the farming camp picked Obaudes."

"I look forward to meeting them and the other councilors."

"For the moment, do you have any questions for me?"

Belarrin thought about it. He knew he would. But the deeper questions of how the Scions survived and evade his brothers took a greater level of trust than he suspected he'd earned. "None at the moment."

"If you do, please ask." Kitiger clapped him firmly on the shoulder. "I am pleased to have met you, Belarrin. I sense a good heart in you and a strong arm. I'm glad you're with us."

Belarrin nodded deferentially. The response was instinctive and the degree to which he meant it surprised him. As Kitiger walked away, Belarrin stared after him. Here was a man who had learned how to lead. He was strong, that much was obvious, but felt no need to proclaim it. Instead, his voice was calm and assured. The kind of voice that gave the listener confidence in himself.

His curiosity tantalized, Belarrin watched Kitiger throughout the remainder of the day. The forest was thick enough and the column long enough that he wasn't always in sight. When he was, however, Kitiger always walked beside individual Scions, whether they were from the raiding party or a rescued Kalilaer. Each conversation ended with a firm smile from Kitiger that left the listener with an invigorated step. Yet thinking back to his own words with Kitiger, Belarrin couldn't sense any duplicity. What kind of man was it to inspire so well and yet remain fully honest, too. A great general in the making, or the worst kind of fiend.

"What's Kitiger's story?" Belarrin asked Sravika as the afternoon lengthened.

"Perhaps you should ask him."

"You told him mine," Belarrin observed.

Sravika's face flushed. "Forgive me if I said more than I should have. I thought it worth passing on."

"You didn't say too much," Belarrin replied. "But why are you reluctant now?"

"I'm not. I only meant that he would tell you. But I'll tell you what I can."

"Who was he? He was once a slave, I assume."

"Yes."

"But what about prior that? Was he a chieftain of wildmen, too?"

"He doesn't talk much about his life before slavery," Sravika answered. "I think he wants to set it aside as he encourages all of us to do. We are Scions now. But no, no he couldn't have been a chieftain. He was only a youth when he was taken. He worked the mines."

"The mines!" Belarrin's eyes widened. As t'Okaedrin, he was all too aware of the Kalilaer doomed to the mines. They lived in the same pits in which they worked, passing up ore in exchange for baskets of food. A Syraestari with several t'Okaedrin guards descended into the mines once a week to check on the work and make sure there were no escape tunnels being dug. But the miners never left the pit once they entered. "I cannot imagine living without the sun."

"Nor I."

"But how did he escape? I can't imagine it was easy."

"That story you'll have to ask him," Sravika replied. "But yes, it was in a Scion raid long before I knew him."

"Perhaps I will, when there is time."

The next time Kitiger came into view, Belarrin had more reason than ever to watch him. Anyone who had escaped the mines was a man worth keeping an eye on.

The great fire burned in its pit at the center of the new Scion camp, casting waves of warmth against the cooling day. Its light joined with the red hues of the deepening sunset. Upon the open plain, such a fire would have drawn eyes for miles around, but deep in the forested wilderness there was no such concern. Over a week north of Nahirazith, there was no chance a roving band of t'Okaedrin might stumble across it. No chance except for the stone that hung around Belarrin's neck.

The celebration had begun as soon as they'd reached the new camp earlier that afternoon. The thirty or so adult Scions who had remained behind had flooded new and old alike in warm embraces and cries of joy. The cacophony was nearly overwhelming. In the course of just a few minutes, Belarrin had been embraced by dozens of people he'd never met before. Children ran through the jubilant throng, their own laughter rising above the greater noise. Some of these flung their arms around Belarrin with eyes sparkling. Most were too young to understand the cause of the celebration, but as children they needed little goading for merriment.

He sat with the other survivors of the smelting camp as but one part of a larger circle of Scions, old and new. Watching and smelling a pair of deer roast over the blaze, he enjoyed the companionship of surrounding life. The Scions had, seemingly by instinct, gathered into those groups they knew best. Belarrin counted seven in all. Belarrin and the former smelters comprised one while those rescued from the farming and woodcutting camps two others. Sravika and her friends, along with a few others whose names Belarrin couldn't recall formed a fourth and Fedigni led a fifth. Belarrin knew no one from the final two groups.

As he watched the rejoicing throng amid the company of his own friends, Belarrin sensed pools of sorrow as one Scion or another learned who hadn't come back. The more he observed, the more he realized that his initial observation was flawed. It wasn't a semblance of sadness. No, the grieving permeated them all. The joy and laughter of survival and success were but a thin layer over the deeper mourning and loss that had been its price. Laced with that grief, he sensed a ragged fear in the too-loud voices, the drawn eyes above wide smiles. Hidden, but raw. Surprisingly, however, the sorrow and fear seemed in no way to diminish the celebration.

The truth of that staggered Belarrin far more than the idea that triumph and loss could mingle. It sobered him, pulling him away from the celebration in truth, pulling him to introspection.

He'd faced repeated losses throughout his life, of brothers and near-kin in the unceasing wars against the Scions and the wildmen. But the pervasiveness here was far more than he'd ever felt. For the first time it struck him. Over twenty had died of the seventy who'd ventured out on the raid. When he including those left behind, that meant nearly one in four had perished.

Battle had become second nature to him. But with the intensive training he received as a t'Okaedrin and the iron armor and weapons he used, losses had always been small. True, he'd lost his entire childhood family in the earthquake disaster. But since then, he might expect one or two dead in his family over the course of a year and most years none at all. Not ten times that on a single day.

Sitting between Zoltha and Yrpel, feeling the heat of the fire and the warmth of the gathered band, he could only shake his head and marvel. They were mad. Every last one of them. Each of them awaited their turn to die. Even if he didn't have his black stone pulling the t'Okaedrin here, these people were doomed. Maybe not this year, perhaps not next, but with those losses, how could they even dream of survival?

Yet as he stared into the many sets of eyes, each glowing in the fire light, he saw that they knew. They all knew. And they remained. They roared with laughter to drown out the terror lurking beneath. They wept silently when no one looked. But they remained. He could only shake his head.

"My family!" Kitiger bellowed, rising from the seat he'd taken near the fire. He turned in a wide circle to look upon all of them. "My family, we have returned and our numbers have grown!" A roar rose up to meet that pronouncement, loud enough that Belarrin wondered if his brothers could hear it miles away as they surely were. Yrpel, not surprisingly, was loudest of all and Belarrin couldn't resist laughing as he clamped hands over ears. "Forty new brothers and sisters, once in chains but now saved are among us and we welcome them. They are as we are. Free. Their old lives have fallen away, but that isn't the end. As long as one of us lives to draw breath, that is not the end." He paused and his voice dropped. "But we cannot forget the price that was paid. The price we all one day might pay. Family and friends lost, but never forgotten."

Kitiger stepped back a moment, his body silhouetted by the fire. Then he took a seat and silence filled the glade. The burning wood popped and the roasting deer sizzled, the evening breeze touched cool against the skin in sharp contrast to the fire's warmth. The sun dipped below the trees and gray shadows crept across the camp.

Fedigni rose to his feet and took a hesitant step forward. He clutched a twisted tree branch the length of a sword in his hand. "My wife." His voice rasped, barely audible above the crackling fire. Fedigni swallowed and began again. "My Kiiatra. Even had she known, she would have gone. It was her way. That is what I will remember." His head bowed to the branch in his hand and he grasped it all the tighter. But then, in a sudden move, his head lifted and he tossed the wood onto the fire.

A soft murmur passed through the crowd, visceral.

Sravika stood, then, and Belarrin saw she also held a branch. "Darr hid his pain," she announced. "He was sorely wounded, but he didn't speak. Had he, we would've stopped and he might have lived. Had he, we would've stopped and might have been caught and slain. He died that we might live."

She tossed her branch onto the fire and the Scions murmured again. This time, a little louder, such that Belarrin thought there might have been words in it.

One by one, dozens of Scions rose. Each spoke a couple words and added to the flames. Each time, those gathered spoke their reply. Louder and louder it grew into soft words, then to loud ones. "A tree has fallen. A tree has fallen. A tree had fallen." The words grew more firm with each repetition, stronger, as if both fear and sorrow burned with the wood cast into the fire.

Movement behind him turned Belarrin's head. Looking up, he saw Chostir standing, a branch in her hand. "Wiersa died in front of me," she said. "I saw the arrow pierce his throat. But he died with joy for he was free." She tossed her branch into the fire. Then, almost as an afterthought. "I will miss his laughter."

"A tree has fallen," the Scions chanted and Belarrin joined with them. When he closed his eyes, he could still feel Wiersa's blood upon his face. He missed that laughter, too.

Idysha stood next and walked forward with a branch. "I don't know if this is right, but I feel I must speak for Regund who did not die. He stayed behind in chains to stop Fritten from sounding the alarm. This is for Fritten, too. He was little more than a boy and couldn't hope to understand. I hope they fare well where we left them."

"A tree has fallen." The chant was as unrelenting as any other.

A few more came forward and then Kitiger rose to his feet and stood beside the fire. He held a young sapling cradled in his hands. "We will miss them all, those we knew and those we did not. Those who died in the first days of the Finaestari and those who died yesterday. Those who died as slaves, those who died free. We will miss them all and we will not forget. Highest Above, let these fires consume us if we forget."

He bowed his head and silence spread across the glade, but this time only for a moment. When he lifted his head again, his eyes were bright and his voice loud. "But we live. We have survived another day. We have not forgotten or turned from our task. Those who were lost have found a home. Those who departed have returned to us. Let not those who died for your freedom stir guilt in your hearts. That isn't what they would want. No, let that sacrifice solidify our purpose. Let it strengthen our resolve. Let it lift up our souls. Celebrate their lives. Celebrate our lives!

Like the batting of an eye, the sorrow that permeated the glade vanished beneath cries of gladness. Kitiger turned to a woman sitting not far from him. "Laerdina, I understand you have something special planned for this celebration."

Laerdina stood. She was a slight woman with shoulder length brown hair and weather creased cheeks. She was probably in her forties, though hard life in the wilderness might only have made her appear that way. Her eyes twinkled as she said, "Yes, the children have been very busy." Her voice raised to a call. "Come children, show us what you've found!"

From behind the circle of Scions, a dozen children emerged from the deepening evening, each carrying a large basket in their hands.

"In celebration of this night, the children have worked hard to gather gifts for each of you." At her signal, the boys and girls began making their way through the crowd, handing a small object to each of the Scions they passed. The giving of each gift elicited a chuckle that gradually grew into a roar of merriment. Belarrin and the others near him peered around, trying to see what they were. Finally a child passed their way. Taking a gift in his hand, he blinked. Crabapples?

"And for our greatest hero," Laerdina had to shout to be heard above the laughter. "To our brave Mirnadd, a ten-fold treasure!"

The youngest child of the group, a girl of no more than six years, approached Mirnadd and handed him a basket almost as large as she was. Looking down at her, the grimace vanished from Mirnadd's face. He plucked one crabapple gingerly from the basket and rose to his feet. He offered the little girl a deep bow, then scooped her up in his left arm. "From such a generous spirit, how can I do anything but accept?"

"Eat it, eat it..." the Scions chanted.

Mirnadd lifted his right hand holding one of the apples and the chanting shrank to a dull murmur. "But can I consume such a gift? No, it must be treasured always!"

"Eat it, eat it..." the chanting continued.

Mirnadd gently lowered the child to the ground who ran laughing across the open space to a waiting woman's embrace. Doubtless, that was her mother. Then Mirnadd turned in a slow circle, listening to the chant. Finally, he cried out. "As you wish then! Let the feast begin." Then he chomped down onto the apple to the cries of merriment from the surrounding crowd.

With more order than Belarrin might have expected, the Scions filed in groups up to the campfire to take their cut of the deer. There also were stewed turnips and more crabapples. His stomach rumbled at the richness of the scents as he returned to his seat.

His companions chattered around him as they ate, laughing together as Yrpel said, "So I still don't understand. Mirnadd doesn't like crabapples?"

"What do you think?" Idysha chuckled.

"I don't think that he does. But why? They're delicious."

But Belarrin found he couldn't join them. Not fully. A part of him wanted to, to feel that warmth. To feel that life that flowed through this glade. It was a life born of joy and sorrow, fear and loss, each more intense than he'd ever experienced. That they could contain their grief and worry after so many deaths was almost more than he could fathom. It was there. He could see it. But they had controlled it. Because it was shared, he realized. Amazing.

He looked down at his plate, surprised to see that the meal was gone. It had been delicious. But he could hardly remember the eating.

As the laughter and loud conversation gradually faded to contented fullness, Kitiger stood again beside the central fire. "Thank you all," he announced. "Thank you Laerdina for this fine feast. Thank you Mirnadd for your gracious relenting to the gift. Thank you all, my family."

Cheers met his words, quieter than before, doubtless on account of the full stomachs.

"But before this evening comes to an end, I know we must look to the future," Kitiger said. "Winter is drawing closer. Do we raid again before its full strength or prepare ourselves for the season of want?"

"Attack!" Someone shouted.

"Unbind more chains before the snow!"

Kitiger smiled at their cries. "Yes. We will raid once more. There is time yet before the winter comes." He waited for the jubilant cries to quiet before continuing, "But there is much that must be done. I trust your councilors will see to it. Please do as they ask and all will fall into place. The first task is the building of the remaining shelters here. Then, Laerdina, please see to the gathering of provisions. We will raid, but we must gather for the winter at the same time. Fedigni, please do as you do best, and find us a secure place for our next winter camp. Chirdar and Sravika, I trust you to see to the arming and preparing of our new brothers and sisters. They must be ready to join us to free those left behind. Some have already tested their metal."

Yrpel rose to his feet and, drawing his sword, waved it over his head. "And some have brought the metal with them!"

That brought a wave of laughter, but Belarrin flinched back from the large man. If he wasn't careful with that blade, he'd hurt someone.

"Yes, I see that you did," Kitiger said, chuckling. "For those who have not, there is no shame. I know what it was to spend years as a slave, to forget how to fight with my hands, if not in my heart. We are here to help you. Those here who have been among us know your tasks. You have done them countless times before. And of course, to our new councilors, Obaudes, Argluf, and Belarrin, please help us find the strengths of each of your people and where you need the most help." More cheers, then Kitiger said, "Let the merriment continue as long as it will this evening. But tomorrow, the work begins again. Thank you and may his Highest Above bless us."

Belarrin watched as Kitiger quietly withdrew from the gathering. Those who he passed by, reached up to clasp his hands, but few if any words were said. Then the chieftain disappeared into the darkness beyond the light of the fire. Belarrin shook his head. The man knew how to speak. But for the stirrings of his own heart and his own purpose, Belarrin would've easily followed.

He returned his gaze to the Scion gathering where many had withdrawn to find their rest, but many remained including others from the smelting camp. In watching them, he felt he was beginning to understand why they believed as they did for all of its folly, yet he remained baffled just the same. All of the courage, the joy, the grief and the fear, but it still wasn't enough.

When he saw Sravika rise to her feet, Belarrin followed her, compelled to seek an answer. In the darkness beyond the fire, she was but a dark silhouette in the night. Sensing his footsteps behind her, she turned to him. "What is it, Belarrin?"

"I don't understand," he replied. "I've counted the numbers and I cannot see it."

"What can't you see?"

"One in four of your people just died."

"But the rest of us did not."

"It can't continue like this. Not with these losses. You're all dead, one way or another. How can you see any other end?"

Her reply was gentle. "What other choice do we have?"

"I don't know. I just..." Belarrin ran his hand through his hair, thinking, trying to give voice to the confusion warring within him. But he couldn't. Why was he asking anyway? He was with them to bring their destruction. Seeing them this close to the edge of existence should have been cause for joy. But he felt no joy.

Sravika's voice grew quieter still. "You plan to leave us."

"No," Belarrin stammered. "I just can't understand."

Her smile was a soft shadow in the starlight. "Neither can we. That is how we carry on." She lifted her hand to gently touch his forearm. "Sleep well, my friend. You are free."

She turned away and retreated into the night, leaving Belarrin to stare unseeing after her. Her answer was a riddle, yet somehow he knew the truth lay within it. If only he could understand.

CHAPTER 20
Unity

"Your greatest enemies lie in the contented or in the desperate. Were I able to choose the state of my subjects, they would always be unhappy."

—King Attyrsian of Himnon

Crouched on a tree limb, Reigliff watched the end of the revelries through the canopy of leaves. The great Scion fire gradually faded from flames to deep red embers that throbbed like a living heart in the center of the glade.

Vistus had long sense disappeared into the darkness but still Reigliff remained, his mind wrapped in thought. He'd watched all through the festivities, intrigued and amused by their rituals. These Scions were the great menace that terrorized his people – that created specters of doom in Syraestarin minds? Scattered bands of humans just like this one, each huddled in the wilderness as they struggled between hope and desperation.

Yet, as he listened to their chants Reigliff realized that the Scions had discovered a secret that had always eluded his own people. One that was a source of unrelenting power. They had learned how to die.

It was ironic that these creatures, with lives little longer than a breath, had discerned a secret beyond the ken of the ageless Syraestari. They hadn't merely learned how to let themselves die, but how to let those closest to them perish. It was a truth that just might shatter an empire.

But Reigliff's greatest focus remained on Vistus. All evening, he'd watched the thoughts racing across the t'Okaedrin's face. Human expressions had always been close to inscrutable for him, but some things couldn't be hidden. Vistus had doubts. And that gave Reigliff cause to hope.

He'd nursed his own share of misgivings over the past few days. On the night of the escape, he'd lain hidden nearby when the t'Okaedrin attacked Vistus and the fleeing smelters. Almost, he'd acted himself to kill the fool t'Okaedrin who might have ruined everything. But he couldn't. Not without exposing himself and risking Vistus. So he remained silent, waiting to watch his Siharrin die. Perhaps he'd misunderstood the prophecy after all. But then Vistus spoke and wind was given life.

Vistus was just who Reigliff hoped him to be. There was no cause for doubt now. Yet there was so much Reigliff still didn't understand. The prophecy remained unclear. Also, he itched to find out what Ushtyl was plotting, but that would have to wait. He couldn't leave Vistus yet. If only he could trust Ninanna. His own reputation hurt him there, as much as her stubbornness, but he had to believe she would come around. It was hard for him to admit how much he needed her trust him.

"This is madness." The High Lord Arkesh growled. "Even as we speak, Ninanna is crawling through my barracks, counting everything I own like a dog worrying a bone."

Tazil nodded. "I had to endure a week of the same infamy. It was a galling intrusion. A violation."

"We must act," Arkesh said. "No more delays or we will all become little better than human slaves, dancing upon the empress' every word."

Ushtyl looked around the circle of high lords and saw agreement on all their faces. They were gathered in his favorite chamber, the Room of the Arching Cedars, where the lack of windows and glowing golden torchlight lent an air of conspiracy, confidence, and yet warm familiarity. That he'd called this meeting during Arkesh's census wasn't a coincidence. Of all of them, he was the easiest to predict. Arkesh lacked a subtly possessed by the others and every choice he made was in his own best interest. His people tended to love him because their happiness was a means to his ambitions. His opportunism made him less trustworthy than his peers, but it, along with his impatience, made him the easiest to manipulate. So long as Arkesh saw this association as the best path to securing his own power, he would be at the core of it, driving it forward like a farmer driving plow oxen.

"That makes half of us despoiled," Ushtyl said. "Only Ovirkar, Sizras, and Zaerina remain, but we all know their turns are coming."

"Curious that the two who oppose dominion are still untouched," Arkesh grumbled.

Zaerina, the only high lady present, leapt to her feet. "What is this, Ushtyl?" she demanded, her gaze passing from Arkesh to Ushtyl and back. "I was assured there would be no talk of this."

Sizras rose to stand beside her. "Lady Zaerina is right. You made a promise to me, Arkesh, but it seems your word means nothing."

Ushtyl suppressed a growl as he stood and raised his hands soothingly. "You did promise, Arkesh. There will be no talk of refuge or dominion."

"I only spoke what I've observed." Arkesh's eyebrow arched.

Perhaps he was more in control than he appeared. Ushtyl ground his teeth. "And you think this happenstance makes them in collusion? If you're dissatisfied, Arkesh, we will leave you in the cold and to the Abyss with you." Before the man could respond, he turned to Sizras and Zaerina. "I apologize, this was never my intent."

"Fine!" Arkesh snapped, raising his hands. "I misspoke. My only defense is that Ninanna's presence has made me irritable. It will not happen again."

Sizras stared down at him a long moment before sitting again. "See that it doesn't."

Zaerina's glare at Arkesh was longer, but she glanced to Sizras and grudgingly took a seat beside him. Ushtyl drew in a deep breath and allowed his heart to calm. Corralling these high lords was like dancing in a wildfire. "The question is, what do we do about it?" he asked.

Sizras spoke, "With each victory, our rights our diminished and her authority increases. We aren't some petty human kingdom where the empress can do whatever she pleases. We are Syraestari and our realms have always been guided by collaboration and consensus between the high nobility and the throne." Ushtyl nodded, pleased at Sizras' ability to move past his annoyance with Arkesh to the root of the meeting.

"Our best answer would have been refusal of the census," Tazil said. "Unfortunately, this meeting took too long to arrange and those who resist Ninanna's incursions now would be vulnerable. But we must make sure we all agree to refuse whatever new demands the empress places before us. We must stand together or she will divide us."

"You're right, but it may be too little, I think," Ushtyl said. "If we do nothing now but wait, the empress will have two triumphs over us in only a few weeks. First, she forced Ninanna to take command of mine and Tazil's raid and now she sends the same Ninanna to meddle more directly in our affairs." He scanned around the room, hoping they had taken the bait. The idea could not appear to come from him.

"Then Ninanna's the problem," Arkesh said. Ushtyl suppressed a smile. Arkesh's predictability would be as valuable as he'd hoped.

"She's only the Hand of the empress," Tazil said. "I said before that her inspection felt a violation, but she did everything on her part to ease the sting. I believe she is no more pleased with her task than we are."

"Besides," Ovirkar added, "she's only a middling Sword-Whisperer who hasn't seen battle in what, a thousand years?"

"She's been a warrior since before the Schism," Sizras replied. "She was a Sword-Singer first, and that's no small honor. Then when the Tirnaestari cast her out, she founded the Sword-Whisperers. These are not the marks of a weakness."

Ovirkar waved his hand dismissively. "She formed the Sword-Whisperers, but she never commanded them. She lacks the fortitude. Since the Great War, she's been nothing but a glorified bodyguard over a ruler who has never been threatened."

"Regardless, that isn't what I meant," Arkesh said. "This is politics, not warfare. By giving her command over the raid and now the census, the empress has made Ninanna a symbol of her rule. Take away the symbol." He snapped his fingers. "Take away the rule."

"I will not be party to an assassination," Tazil said.

"Nor I," Sizras replied and Ovirkar nodded.

Curiously, Ushtyl noticed no protest from Zaerina. Perhaps she wasn't a complete follower of Sizras. "An assassination would do no good anyway," Ushtyl said. "She'd become a martyr, loved in death where she wasn't in life." He glanced over at Arkesh to see if the man took his hint.

"Not dead, then," Arkesh said, "but dishonored."

Sizras laughed. "Ninanna dishonored? I hardly think so. She has kept every oath she's made for three thousand years. Most people scorn her beliefs, but not one of them would question her honor."

"Contrive it, then," Arkesh replied. "The testimony of two or more of us can't be discounted, even for one of her reputation."

Sizras turned to Ushtyl. "I promised collaboration, but said I would partake in no conspiracy."

"Is there another way?" Ushtyl asked. It was vexing having to continually test and balance the ambitions of his peers. Their inane sensitivities were frustrating, making it clearer and clearer that so many lacked the will to truly see and do what had to be done regardless of how distasteful the task might be. If Sizras wasn't held in such high regard by the other high lords, Ushtyl might have striven to cut him out entirely. But the truth was, he needed him. For now, at least.

Sizras' lips thinned to a line. "There is always a choice." He turned to look upon the other high lords. "I won't protest if this is the path you choose to follow, but I will not be a part of this deed."

"But you would allow it to happen?" Ushtyl asked.

Sizras closed his eyes as if examining his own heart. After a moment, he opened his eyes again and nodded. "With the greatest of reluctance."

Ushtyl looked around the circle. "What do the rest of you say? Do you agree the removal of the empress' symbol is necessary?" He was pleased to see answering nods except, to his surprise, from Tazil.

Tazil shook his head. "Ninanna and I have never seen eye to eye, but I cannot be part of destroying someone simply because I don't care for them. Like Sizras, I won't protest, but neither will I partake in it."

Zaerina spoke. "Since most of us are in agreement, I say we proceed." She turned to Sizras. "I am sorry, my friend, but I believe this sacrifice is necessary."

Sizras nodded, his eyes sad. Standing, he said, "Then I will take my leave of you all. Know that should the empress make further demands of any of us, I will resist her and expect that you do the same for me."

Ushtyl stood, too, eager for the day when his long-suffering could finally end. "Sizras, Tazil, I respect your choice and I will stand with you, even though you aren't a part of this."

The others nodded their agreement as Tazil, too, rose. After he and Sizras were gone, Arkesh leaned forward. "I believe I have a plan, but I cannot act on it alone. Ushtyl, if you will join me, I think we can ensnare Ninanna."

"I will assist."

CHAPTER 21
Hunter

"When the horizon teems with the legions of the enemy, sun gleaming off helm and blade, who should one look to for courage? Is it the braggart or the jester? Is it the grim soul or the trembling one? I have found valor and cowardice among them all. For it is only in the forging fires of war that one man can measure the mettle of another. Indeed it is the only way to learn one's own heart."

—King Trion of Estrya

"Ha!" Sravika grinned at him. "You look like a new man. Hunting always seems to do that."

"It does?" Belarrin asked, doubtful. They passed along the edge of a small clearing. Mirnadd, Henirgar, Yrpel, and Idysha walked ahead of them, barely visible through the trees.

"I've seen it many times before. And besides, it's better than building shelters." Belarrin chuckled at that, then she continued, "I've seen expressions like yours many times before. Slavery does something to a person, even those only in bondage for a short time. Freedom after does something, too. The thirst for vengeance is as strong as the lingering fear that the escape was an illusion. Being surrounded by Scions might lessen the fear, but not the rage. Out here, though…" She lifted her head toward the sunlight and spun in a slow circle. "Out here in the forest, you can let it all fall away. If only for a day."

Belarrin frowned. It was true that there was something pleasant about being away from the Scion camp and the memories of being a Kalilaer. And Sravika's company was nice, too, though she was nothing like Elestis. She was sadder, yet more joyous, focused but not meticulous, and perhaps a little naïve. It was unfortunate she'd taken to the wrong side. If Sravika had had proper training as a child, Belarrin suspected she would've made an excellent Pi'aernotha Osnoeda. It was too late now, though. She was too old and too rooted in a world of lies to be saved.

Glancing over, Belarrin saw her watching him, reading the expressions that flitted across his face. Uncomfortable, he turned away, hoping he hadn't given away too much. "Did you feel that way after you were freed?" he asked.

"I was never a slave."

Belarrin turned to her, startled. "I'd assumed that you, Mirnadd, and Henirgar were rescued as a group. You stay together just like my companions from the smelters."

"That's how many of the sections of a camp begin, but things change. People get married or die. They make new, closer friends. Over time old groups may break apart or become small enough that several join together. She shrugged. "Not all of us had to be freed from the Finnies. Some, like Henirgar, grew up in the Scion camps. Others, like myself, came from broken tribes."

"You mean survivors from Finaestari raids?"

Sravika's voice dropped and the happiness he'd heard in it before disappeared. "Not always." Intrigued, Belarrin wanted to ask more, but stopped himself. She clearly was reluctant. Perhaps another time.

Up ahead, the others had stopped. When Belarrin and Sravika joined them, Mirnadd said, "There are several good deer trails near here. Let's break into pairs and see what we can find."

Yrpel grinned. "Idysha and I can head out together."

Idysha chuckled at that but Mirnadd said, "Best if each of you newbloods pair with one of us until you get to know this region better." At Yrpel's grumble, Mirnadd added, "Don't worry, I'll keep Idysha safe."

Idysha laughed. "Clearly, you don't know me very well."

They went their separate ways, Mirnadd and Idysha, Yrpel and Henirgar, while Belarrin followed Sravika. "We don't want to stay too close to the others," she said. "With luck we'll each have a deer to bring back to the camp."

They walked for what felt like a couple miles, though in the depths of the forest it was hard for Belarrin to be sure. The path wound around thickets and across ravines, between tall evergreens and shorter trees speckled with the dying colors of autumn. The wind was muted by the great trees, often little more than a flutter, a faint murmur through the branches. Unlike his t'Okaedrin brothers, Sravika didn't stay in the valleys, but wound over ridge and across basins with an uncanny knack for picking the clearest path, even when it wasn't evident until they were upon it. He also marveled at how quiet she was. A squirrel or rabbit would've made more noise. For all of his own care, he felt like a lumbering ox.

Sravika stopped and gestured with her spear. "Good deer path ahead. I killed several near here earlier this summer."

Belarrin knew he lacked Sravika's experience, but he'd gone hunting at least a dozen times while on the march as a t'Okaedrin. He pointed to a collection of shrubs nearby. "That brush should give enough concealment."

Sravika nodded. She slipped amid the green leaves and sank down to her heels. "I'll let you have the first throw. See what you're made of."

"As you wish." Belarrin crouched down beside her and matched her grin.

They waited silently, watching the sun flitter across the forest floor. The air was cool but comfortable and thick with scents of pine needles. Belarrin's fingers twitched on the haft of his spear. It was the same one he'd taken the night of his escape. No one had told him the name of the dead Scion who'd owned it before. He never asked. It was his now and he'd killed more than one brother with its stone point. That thought should've bothered him more than it did. But they'd made their choices just as he had. There had been no other option if he was to serve their masters. And he did not want to die.

He listened to his own breathing and Sravika's. Both drew slow and easy breaths, softly, alert. There was little scent to her, perhaps some sweat from the journey, but it was faint beneath the deeper smells of the wood. He looked at her out of the corner of his eyes. Her gaze was on the forest ahead. The bright light piercing the thin canopy of leaves shone as it reflected in her blue eyes. Her golden hair hung loose, with faint strands wisping in the soft breeze. There was something of a deer in her, poised and tense, ever aware. Something of a wolf, too, in the sharp confidence she exuded and the sense of coiled violence.

The hint of a smile touched her lips and her gaze drifted to meet his. "You're a Tatyrni, right?" she asked in a soft voice, barely louder than the wind.

Belarrin frowned, uncertain of what lay behind the question. "Why do you ask?" he replied as quietly.

"I've never met a Tatyrni before."

"Oh?" That was fortunate. His father had chosen a good tribe for him to mimic. He just hoped she didn't press any questions too far. He'd hate to have to kill her. When that time came, hopefully another brother would do the deed so he wouldn't have to. Belarrin twitched instinctively as that thought passed through his mind. He knew he should be angry with himself about coming to care for these people, but even that was becoming harder to cling to. Vitarria had been the first, curse her, and it had grown worse. But whatever his feelings, he wouldn't allow them to turn him from his task.

"Are all Tatyrni as peculiar as you?" Sravika asked.

"I don't understand."

She turned her head to look at him fully. "You're a strong man and a skilled warrior. I've seen that often enough before." She hesitated before adding, "But you're a poor hunter."

Belarrin glared at her. "I know what I'm doing!"

Her smile took away some of the sting. "Of course, but not so well as I'd have thought. Were you in your chieftain's retinue? That would explain it."

"Yes," he lied, praying she'd be content and stop asking questions.

"So you are peculiar, just as I've said." She turned to look at the forest path ahead. Sravika must have been aware of his continuing stare, though, because she said, "I've never known an armsman who risked his life for anyone but his chieftain. But you did that for Mirnadd and myself. I certainly never met one who would take another's punishment like you did for Zoltha on the Boards. Every armsman I've ever known was too proud for his own good."

She'd named his two greatest regrets. For a fellow t'Okaedrin, Belarrin wouldn't have thought twice about risking his life or enduring punishment. But what had possessed him to risk everything for a Kalilaer? And then for a pair of Scions? Was he truly the man he wanted to be? The man he needed to be? Belarrin turned away from Sravika and looked out to the forest ahead, muttering, "Anyone can change."

He caught her grin out of the corner of his eye. "I see that. A good change, too, I think."

Belarrin didn't agree, but mercifully Sravika fell silent.

Morning had slipped past when movement flitted through trees. Belarrin's breath caught in his throat as he peered forward and he sensed Sravika stir slightly too. Three deer stepped out onto the trail. The first was a buck with many-pronged horns while the others were smaller. They paused and the buck craned its head to look around as the others nibbled at leaves.

Belarrin measured the distance with his eyes. They were still too far for a spear throw. He needed them at least a dozen paces closer. Sravika was right. He wasn't the best of hunters. A better one might act even at this range. He flexed his fingers on the spear haft, loosening muscles for the throw.

The deer took a few more hesitant steps forward, then paused to eat again, trading turns looking around. The buck stared at him and Belarrin froze, not even daring to breathe. Then they took a few more steps. They were close enough now, if only the buck would duck its head to eat. Belarrin allowed himself a slow breath through clenched teeth.

Finally, the buck turned toward a shrub. Belarrin leapt from his hiding place with hand back to throw. Twigs snapped with his passage and deer heads shot upright as they spun to flee, but Belarrin was too close for them to escape. He flung his hand forward, launching the spear.

Crack!

A deafening roar shook the woodland as the ground churned like an ocean wave. Belarrin lurched forward, his throw going wide. Sravika's scream behind him was barely audible above the snapping of trees and the rumble of torn earth. The ground rose up and Belarrin met it hard, cracking his jaw on the packed dirt.

Not again! The thought tore through his mind as he struggled to push back visions of the collapsed barracks, the memory of darkness and pain.

A shadow passed over him and he looked up to see a huge cedar toppling toward the hiding place he 'd just left. "Sravika!" the scream tore from his lips as he stumbled to his feet. But the distance was too far, the ground too unsteady. She pushed up to her knees, eyes widening in horror at the tree falling toward her.

There was no time for thought. No time for doubt or questions. Only panic.

The world around him turned crimson, like blood pouring across his eyes. Bright lines of gold flashed before him. He leapt forward, screaming madly. "Ae'irpiva ykstaivus amakae'onin!"

Belarrin struck Sravika at the shoulders and, grappling her with his arms, pulled her close as he tumbled past. A massive shadow plunged across his vision followed by a resounding crash. Belarrin hit the ground and rolled, tucking Sravika's head into his shoulder to protect her from the worst of it. Then they fell still, his body atop hers, and he stayed there, shielding her as the world broke around them. Heavens and earth crumbled and raged like a wounded bear, deafening, thought-numbing, until only fear remained clenching his heart.

An eternity passed before the Cataclysmic fury subsided. Opening eyes he'd clenched shut, Belarrin realized he was panting for breath. He could feel Sravika's racing heartbeat beneath him. Gasping, he pushed himself to his knees and allowed her to rise as well. She sat up and they stared around them, breathless. Chaos reigned across the wilderness. Some trees remained standing but most nearby lay toppled across the broken earth like an overturned rack of spears. The mountains were visible in the distance now that the forest canopy had been torn away. The nearest peaks belched black clouds into the sky as ribbons of crimson fire poured down their flanks. They were too distant, fortunately, to be any threat.

Still, seeing that raw fury bubbling up from the heart of Isfalinis, Belarrin felt suddenly small. Everything was small. These rebels. His brothers. Even his Syraestari masters. What creature could match such incredible power?

"You are mad," Sravika whispered. Then she broke into a laugh, half joyous, half crazed. "I should be dead!"

"Those who should die usually don't." Belarrin grunted and rose to his feet, his heart gradually slowing. He wondered that he'd saved her only to bring her death later. It had been instinct, he told himself, and that was all. If there'd been time to think, he would have let her die. It was a much less bitter end than the doom she was fated to face. Unwanted, the vision of Vitarria returned to his mind. Her eyes were too similar to Sravika's, as were her sharp nose and narrow jaw. He shoved the thought away angrily. Being haunted by one was enough – he didn't need two!

"The deer got away, but I can think of worse things," Sravika said, chuckling. Still brooding, Belarrin didn't reply. Sravika flashed him a look, her brows narrowing with concern. Then she said, "We should go check on the others."

Belarrin retrieved his spear, then followed her silently. This time, their passage through the forest was slower. Many trees had snapped, leaving obstacles in their path, while others leaned, threatening to fall at any moment. Sravika looked to her left and right, muttering sometimes as she tried to keep her bearing. Belarrin said nothing. He wouldn't be able to help anyway. Not that he particularly wanted to, either. She was as dangerous an enemy as any he'd encountered, using weapons like friendship and kindness instead of sword or spear. He cursed how again and again he proved vulnerable to such ploys.

Belarrin looked back over his shoulder from time to time, watching the mountains and their bubbling fire. His legs still trembled faintly. At least the nightmare of the collapsed barracks didn't paralyze him this time. No, he shook his head bitterly. Instead he almost died to save his enemy.

He stopped suddenly, remembering. He'd screamed something when the tree began to fall. Recalling it was hard, like a dream fading after waking, but they were words. He was sure of it. Somehow they were familiar.

A cold sweat broke out on his forehead. It was like when the t'Okaedrin attacked. He'd screamed then, too. His vision had been tinged with red and golden lines that burned before his eyes. The same thing had happened when the cart almost crushed Bridionis. Belarrin wiped his brow. What was happening to him?

"Sravika, do you have that Finaestari letter?"

She stopped and looked back at him. "Yes, why?"

"Can I see it?"

She gave him a quizzical look, but reached into her leather satchel and drew out the parchment. Belarrin stepped up to her and looked over her shoulder. A shiver crept up his spine. The markings looked like the golden lines blazing in his vision.

"What is it?"

It took an effort to pull his gaze from the parchment to look at Sravika. Her eyes were drawn close in worry. "I…" Belarrin realized he was breathless. "I'm not sure I know." He couldn't think, not even to come up with a convincing lie. Was he going mad?

"You can trust me with whatever it is," Sravika said, her voice gentle.

"I know…" Belarrin stammered, searching for words even as he tried to understand himself. "I'm not sure what I'm thinking. Not that I can put into words, anyway." He rubbed his brow again. "I feel a little lightheaded."

"You did just narrowly avoid getting crushed by a tree." Sravika smiled. "When you think you can tell me, I'll listen."

She turned away and began walking again. Belarrin followed her, grateful that for once she didn't press her questions. Yet he was baffled. How could she give trust so easily? And why did he feel so willing to trust her, too?

Dusk approached by the time they returned to the clearing where they'd separated from the others. All four were there already with a fire burning. None were seriously hurt by the earthquake, though Yrpel sported several long scratches on his face and arms from diving through brush to avoid a falling tree.

"We were worried about you," Mirnadd said, looking up from roasting a couple skinned rabbits over the fire. He and Idysha had also killed a deer before the earthquake struck though Yrpel and Henirgar returned empty handed, too.

"We almost killed one," Belarrin said, dropping down into a crouch beside the fire. "I threw just as the earthquake struck. Of all the Cydion Accursed luck."

"Close doesn't put food in the stomach." Mirnadd grinned.

"He did pull me clear of a falling tree," Sravika replied, then smiled. "Belarrin may not be the best hunter but he does know how to keep me alive."

Belarrin joined the others laughter, but when Mirnadd clapped him on the back, a foul taste arose in Belarrin's throat. Was what he planned for these men and women a betrayal? They would see it that way, but did that make it true? He closed his eyes and drew in several deep slow breaths, trying to steady himself. When he opened them, the others were all chatting easily, all except Sravika. She sat across the fire, watching him with lips pursed with concern.

She saw his unease even though she didn't understand, he realized. He had to be better about hiding it. Off all the dooms that awaited her, he didn't want to kill her just to keep his secret.

"Still," Mirnadd said, "You've timed your return well. Dinner is ready."

Belarrin took his portion of the cooked rabbit and his mouth watered before he even began to eat. It was as delicious as it smelled, gamey yet tender. He surreptitiously licked the juices dripping down his fingers while Henirgar expounded on the day. "Yrpel spent most of the day filling my head with the greatness of his tribe. From what he said, I wonder that the Iengians haven't overthrown the Finnies all by themselves." Belarrin laughed despite himself, remembering his first encounter with Yrpel's overblown pride. "How about you, Idysha?" Henirgar continued. "What tribe did you come from?"

"I was Iengian, too," she replied, staring into the fire. She looked over at Yrpel and grinned mischievously. Yet Belarrin sensed a serious undertone to her smile. "Not that you could tell. We women are more subtle than our men. We don't have to scar our arms to prove our courage." Yrpel roared with laughter as she continued, "I don't know what to say. We hunted, we planted a few crops. We had trouble with other Iengian tribes and some of the Zengris but had only heard vague rumors of the Iron-Men before they came. My husband died in that attack along with most of my tribe. I lost many dear to me, just as everyone has. I never understood why I lived, but knew it wasn't because I was fated to be a slave." Her voice dropped to a whisper. "And now I am not."

No one spoke as all eyes stared into the fire. Only the pop of the burning wood broke the stillness as plumes of smoke lifted to the darkening sky. Wiping the tears from her cheek with the back of her hand, Idysha looked up. "What tribe did you come from Henirgar?"

"I have no tribe but the Scions," Henirgar replied. At her confused expression, he continued, "I think my parents were Iachians, but I don't really know. Before I was born, they were taken by the Iron-Men. My mother was pregnant at the time and I think that is how both were captured alive. When she gave birth, the child, a boy, was taken from her to be raised as an Iron-Man."

"Blood on the Bridge," Yrpel cursed.

Henirgar looked at him and nodded. "Scions rescued my parents a year or two later and I was born soon after." He let out a wistful sigh. "I always thought my mother was weak because she never recovered from the taking of my brother. I think that despair may have killed her in the end, but I'm sure that my unkindness didn't help. Yet now that I begin to understand, she is not here for me to tell."

"I don't see how the Iron-Men can do what they do," Yrpel said. "Can't they see they're slaves, too? Don't they know they were stolen from us?"

Rescued from you, Belarrin thought, but he held his tongue.

"How can they know when none of us can tell them?" Henirgar replied. "They only hear what the Finnies want them to hear. They only know what the Finnies teach them."

"Then they're evil," Yrpel grumbled.

"Are they?" Henirgar asked. "I'm sure most Scions agree with you, but I have my doubts. One of them had the same parents as me and I don't think I'm evil. If I'm not, how can this lost brother of mine be?" He shook his head. "No, I think they bear chains heavier than any other slave. Not even their minds are free."

Sravika leaned forward, her chin resting on her hands. "I had never considered them that way. Maybe they are to be pitied."

White-hot rage flared through Belarrin. Not pitied! Not by ones such as these. His tongue clung to the roof of his mouth, wanting to scream his condemnations. But he did not. He could not. Cydion's Abyss! Even the Boards were less torture than this.

"Pitied, yes," Henirgar agreed with Sravika. "But still they must be slain. They are too bound to be freed."

"Yes." Sravika's voice was solemn.

Belarrin nodded. At least he could agree with that, though the roles were reversed. If he hadn't been so troubled, he might have laughed at the irony. Pity, respect, and fear went both ways, but it didn't matter. In the end, t'Okaedrin had to kill Scion and Scion had to kill t'Okaedrin.

"Only they can decide if they want to be saved," Henirgar said. "It's happened once before, that I know of. One of the Scion chieftains used to be an Iron-Man."

"What?" Belarrin's stunned voice joined Yrpel and Idysha's.

Henirgar nodded. "Twenty years or more ago, from what I understand. One day he just left his Iron-Man camp and walked into the forest." He smiled at their gaping expressions. "I could hardly believe it when I heard myself, but Kitiger has met him. I hope I will too, one day. If there is a legend among the Scions, he is it."

"How about you, Belarrin?" Yrpel asked. "You've never said much about yourself."

Belarrin blinked, then spread his hands wide. "I don't know what to say. My story is much like any other tribesman turned slave."

"You were an armsman to your chieftain," Sravika said.

"Really?" Yrpel said, admiration gleaming in his eyes.

Belarrin shrugged. "It hardly seems important now."

"Ha! Always the humble one." Yrpel laughed. "You did admit that your father was a priest."

"He was?" It was Sravika's turn to be curious.

"But I wasn't," Belarrin replied.

"He has his father's priest stone, though," Yrpel said. "Show them the stone."

Belarrin glared at the Iengian, regretting he'd ever kept the gemstone. Fool Vitarria and her eternal torments. But there was nothing he could do but pull it out from around his neck.

"Zoltha said it is a Tear of Isi," Yrpel said as Belarrin held it out.

Sravika's face turned white as a winter's sky. When she extended her hand, it trembled. Grudgingly, Belarrin gave it to her. Sravika lifted the stone to her eyes, inspecting it closely. Her voice came out in a hush, "It is one of Isi's Tears. I'd never thought to see another."

"Another?" Yrpel asked.

"Yes." Her voice was stronger now. "My sister had one."

That caught Belarrin's attention. "You said your tribe wasn't taken by the Finnies."

"No, we humans are skilled enough at destroying ourselves." There was a reluctance in her voice as she spoke,

"My people were the Isyren. Our bards told legends of a great past, but I only knew us as a broken people. We were a handful of clans, too small to cling to anything. Wherever we went, other tribes drove us onward in unending flight. The last and worst were the Lothyn. They attacked us relentlessly, and like wolves against a herd of elk, they preyed upon the weakest of us." Her eyes stared into the fire, seeing far away. "When I was about twelve, my sister became priestess for our clan, though she was only a little older than I. Our numbers were just too small. But then, one night, the Lothyn fell upon us, burning our huts and killing all they could find. I managed to escape out into the forest with a few others, but my sister and I were separated as we fled. When dawn came, only two others remained with me. We searched for her as long as we dared, but with the Lothyn so near, we couldn't linger. We found no one and had no choice but to flee. We wandered, hiding every night in fear, foraging what food we could. After two years without a home or family to call our own, we were fortunate enough to stumble across the Scions who took us in."

"I remember that day," Mirnadd said grinning.

Sravika smiled, too, though her eyes were sad, "We'd been hunted so long that I could barely comprehend a people who didn't want to kill us. Instead, they sheltered us and still do. Of my two companions, only I remain, now that Darr is dead." She looked down at the gemstone in her hand. "But yes, this Tear is identical to the one my sister Vitarria wore."

Belarrin's heart skipped a beat. His head felt suddenly cold, light as numbness poured over him. All he could hear for a moment was the blood rushing through his heart, barely muffling a sudden scream rising up from his soul. His throat constricted, but he managed to speak the word burning within him. "Vitarria?"

"Not just my sister, but my best friend," Sravika replied, her gaze still locked on the stone.

It was all Belarrin could do not to seize the stone from her grasp and fling it away. Panic warred with shame, only to be met by rage at his shame until panic took him again. His mind reeled and he was barely aware of Yrpel asking, "So you never learned what happened to her?"

"No, but I like to think that Vitarria survived, too." A sharp laugh burst from her throat. "Who knows, maybe she met another Scion band."

I killed her.

The thought overwhelmed Belarrin's mind as Vitarria's blood-stained face filled his vision. That had been his task. He had brought in his brothers and killed her sister. And soon he would kill Sravika, too. Sister and sister, dead and dead at his hand. He realized he was shaking and took several deep breaths, struggling to still his mind.

"I'm sorry, Belarrin," Sravika said.

"What?" His head snapped up, wary.

"I'd forgotten that the death of your own sister was so recent. I didn't mean to bring out your own painful memories with my own."

"I will be alright," he said more gruffly than he intended. Sravika smiled gently, seeming to take it as a sign of his sorrow and not his guilt.

"Thank you for letting me hold the stone," she said, setting the gem in Belarrin's open hand. As she withdrew her hand, she gasped. Resting in his palm, Isi's Tear blazed a brilliant crimson. Not the reflected light of the campfire but a radiance all its own, sharper, magnificent, terrifying.

"Highest Above..." Sravika whispered recoiling back as if watching a snake. Belarrin pulled back, too, drawing his body as far as he could from his outstretched arm. The stone burned cold in his hand, like a beacon fire from which he could not retreat. When Sravika spoke again, the words fell from her lips like a mantra. "Tears from iron, blood from stone." Her eyes met Belarrin's and his heart lurched. She knew. Somehow she knew. "I..." she stuttered as tears poured down her face. Lurching to her feet, she ran into the woods.

Belarrin stared after her, stunned. She had to know. He'd seen it in her eyes. But why not denounce him? Why not kill him? "I don't understand." His words came out in a hush.

Idysha stood up and ran after Sravika, disappearing into the night. "What does it mean?" Yrpel asked.

"I don't know," Belarrin said, eyes dropping to the crimson stone in his hand. "I don't know."

No one had an answer and silence fell over the camp. He closed his hand around the stone, cutting off its light, but he could still feel the heat of it in his palm. Slowly, he drew in his hand again, clutching it to his chest as questions raced through his mind. Should he run? Should he strike out and kill them before Sravika told his secret? But he couldn't. Not like this. He knew he had to, but he couldn't. And so he waited. Waiting for death or murder. Whatever might come.

After a few minutes, Idysha emerged from the forest. Belarrin scanned her face carefully, but saw no sign of her knowing. "She just wants to be alone for a little while," Idysha said, sitting down at the fire again.

"But why is it red?" Yrpel asked, looking from Idysha to Belarrin and back again.

"It is the tear of an Etyni," Henirgar replied, his voice hushed and reverent.

"But why red? Why now? What does it mean?"

"How should we know?" Mirnadd snapped.

Belarrin knew. It marked her sister's killer.

"But..." Yrpel began to say again, but Idysha cut him off. "Enough, my friend. Sravika weeps and the stone bleeds. It is from an Etyni long dead. What more can we know but awe and wonder and grief?"

Reluctantly, Yrpel nodded. Mirnadd cleared his throat. "Perhaps it would be best if everyone got some sleep. I will remain awake for Sravika."

No one protested and they all curled up in their cloaks around the fire. With a reluctant stare into the forest where Sravika had disappeared, Belarrin did the same. But he didn't fall asleep. With one hand, he clutched the warm gemstone. He felt that it should burn at the touch, but it didn't. With his other hand, he gripped his stone knife and waited. He would only kill tonight if he had to, but he wouldn't die easily either.

It was much later that he heard Sravika returning to the camp. She walked with a slow and heavy step. With each pace, Belarrin waited to hear her voice cry out, condemning him. He clutched his knife tighter. But she knelt down next to Mirnadd and whispered something softly in his ear. He replied just as softly then they both found places to sleep by the fire.Belarrin remained awake, still not trusting. Waiting to fight. Waiting to die.

CHAPTER 22
Morning

"There was a time when I believed that regret was a weakness of lesser men. But now, as I look back upon my blood-stained footsteps, as I stare down at my blackened hands, I wonder what I have become."

—Marshal Dartrinan of Fhineros

Belarrin jerked awake. He blinked in the faint grays of the emerging dawn and cursed himself for falling asleep. If he'd died, he would have deserved it. His time among the Scions had left him weak. Letting go of the hold he still had on his knife, he sat up. Mirnadd was already awake, crouching beside the ashen remnants of their fire and gnawing on a bit of roasted rabbit left over from the night before. He nodded as Belarrin joined him, handing over a flask of water.

"Heavy words last night," Mirnadd said. "I, for one, could use some levity."

Belarrin grunted noncommittally as he took the flask and sat down.

"Come now." Mirnadd grinned. "It can't be as bad as that. The sun has risen, the mountains still stand, and not a single tree fell on us while we slept."

Belarrin couldn't stop a slight smile from forming on his face.

Perhaps encouraged by it, Mirnadd said, "The night is for yesterday and for tomorrow. Each of those might hold its share of sorrow and hope. But day is for itself. Alive and in this moment, we live and that is cause for celebration."

"So be it," Belarrin said. He didn't want to think on the stone anymore, or Sravika or Vitarria. Something else, anything else, if only for a while. "Do you really hate crabapples so much?"

Mirnadd chuckled, then glanced up at Belarrin. "The truth?"

"The truth."

"They aren't my favorite, to be sure. I find them too tart. But no, I don't hate them."

"Then why? Just for the show of it?"

Mirnadd's grin widened. "Not at all. At least not originally. Tayrja loves them. By hating them, everyone else gives me more and I give them to her."

Belarrin laughed aloud. But a stirring across the cold fire stilled the sound in his throat. He looked over as Sravika pushed aside her cloak and sat up. As she shifted to a position closer to the fire pit, Belarrin eyed her, watchful while trying not to appear watchful. He silently handed her the water flask. As she took a long drink, he braced himself for what she might say.

Sravika looked over at him. "I must apologize for my behavior last night. Even years later, the loss of my sister can strike me so hard I cannot speak." She laughed bitterly. "I can barely think."

Belarrin stared at her. She didn't know. He'd been so certain last night, but if she did she would have flayed him alive or worse.

Mirnadd spoke, his voice gentle. "You may find her again."

Sravika shook her head. "No. I'm certain she is dead. It is a loss I must accept. A loss I must forgive."

"Last night you said something about iron and blood," Mirnadd said. "What did it mean?"

Sravika shrugged uncomfortably. "It is from a poem I once learned. One my sister taught me. Seeing the gemstone turn red brought it back to my mind." She took another deep swallow from the water flask and glanced at Belarrin then looked away again. In that momentary meeting of eyes, Belarrin froze. Anger, fear, and sorrow. He'd seen all three. She looked at him again. "Belarrin," she began, then her gaze dropped to the fire pit between them. When she continued, her voice was soft, tentative. "I'm afraid that the words spoken last night may have opened old wounds for you. We have all lived lives surrounded by death. Death creates doubt and guilt to gnaw at the soul. It wasn't my intent to hurt you and, if I did, please forgive me. If there is anything from your past that weighs upon you, you must forgive that, too. None of us are free of regret. What was done before is done. What we do now is all that matters."

Again it felt like she knew, else why would she speak words like that? Or was that his own guilt condemning him? But if she did, she wouldn't forgive. She would avenge. And he couldn't forgive himself. Either there was nothing to forgive or he was beyond forgiveness. The Tear of Isi felt suddenly hot against his chest, a burning fire. He grabbed it and pulled it free of his neck. Mercifully, the stone had lost its crimson glow, returning to the clear faint blue it always had been. He held it out to Sravika. "I think you should have this."

She drew away. "No, I couldn't. I have no right to it."

But he had to get the stone away from him, now that he knew the truth. "Then it is a gift. Please, for me."

Sravika looked up at him, this time without turning away. Her eyes, radiant in the new morning light, were deep pools of blue across which flitted a host of emotion, each too quick for Belarrin to discern. Finally, she nodded. The hand she held out trembled as he dropped the necklace into it. "I won't refuse your kindness, but when you want it back, it is yours." She clutched the stone to her chest and shook her head. "You are a strange, strange man, Belarrin."

"You have no idea."

Yrpel sat up, yawning loudly as he stretched, driving the moment of quiet away. Belarrin, for one, was grateful for the distraction. Yrpel's noise roused the others and they all ate a quick meal of the cold leavings from the night before. Then they scattered the ashes of the fire and headed back for the Scion camp.

They took turns by pairs carrying the slain deer, its legs slung to a spear. It wasn't much meat for a hunting party, but they were more concerned about what the earthquake might have done to their camp. The others chatted idly while they walked, but Belarrin didn't join in. He kept apart, even as he traveled in their company. Each time he allowed himself to get closer to them, his task became more painful. He couldn't risk it anymore.

As they walked, the degree of devastation in the forest diminished. Fewer trees were knocked down and they encountered no rents torn in the earth. Near midday, they reached the camp to find that only a couple trees had fallen near the edge of the glade. Several of the shelters had collapsed, too, but no one was seriously hurt. Belarrin lent a hand cutting new tree limbs for struts and packing mud with smaller branches to seal the walls.

As he was taking a break, drinking from a flask of water, Sravika approached him. She pulled him aside to the edge of the camp and he reluctantly followed. Her hand crept up to touch the Tear of Isi around her neck as she said, "I wanted to be sure you were well. I sensed a weight upon your shoulders today, Belarrin, as we walked back to camp. Whatever it is, whatever you've done, you must let it go. Forgive yourself. This is a place of new beginnings."

Her eyes were wide, innocent. If she truly knew what he'd done… He crushed the thought. "I will try."

She grinned. It was a beautiful smile. "Good," she said, then turned back to the camp.

Watching her walk away, a fire welled up in Belarrin's heart. It burned behind his eyes. Rage? Remorse? He didn't know. Both sisters, Vitarria and Sravika, had forgiven him. One was already dead by his hand and the other soon would be. One who knew what he was and the other who did not. "Black Abyss of Cydion!" He flung his empty water flask into the forest.

He sank down to the ground and, propping his elbows on his knees, cradled his head in his hands. Nothing he did made anything better. Who were these people that gave such friendship with so little reservation? Who was this woman who treated betrayal as kindness? They were sorcerers, all of them, enchanting his soul despite all he could do. He clutched the black stone necklace, glad it was the only one around his neck now. He'd been a fool to think he could infiltrate these people. Perhaps it would be better if he just destroyed the Sapaupan Kaupet so he could return home.

And admit defeat in front of Arcomin, his rival? In front of Elestis? No. He just needed to keep his mind clear. With a sigh, he rose to his feet and fetched the flask he'd thrown. Then he rejoined the others. Though he worked side by side with Sravika, he didn't look at her. Even the sight of her brought conflict to his thoughts. The repairs complete on one shelter, they began the construction of a brand new one. First, they stripped cut tree limbs, a difficult task with only stone tools. Then these were bowed into arches, each end thrust into the ground before being packed tighter with a splayed branches and mud.

As they worked, Kitiger approached. "Sravika, can I speak with you?"

"Of course." The pair withdrew a short distance but were still close enough that Belarrin could hear them.

"I've been thinking about what you've been saying these past few months," Kitiger said.

"You have?" Sravika asked, then sudden excitement entered her voice. "You have!"

"Yes." Kitiger's tone remained measured. "I'm still uncertain, but I believe the time has come to weigh it fully."

"Yes, I understand. What do you need me to do?"

"You are ever eager, my friend." Kitiger chuckled softly. "I know you told me Belarrin believes as you do. It seems Obaudes is the same. Though I haven't spoken to Argluf yet, I wouldn't be surprised if he makes three. I don't know if it is courage, brashness, or both, that flows through the veins of our newest kindred. We need them, if we are to survive, but are they wise enough yet to understand the battle we fight?"

"Does our experience make us wiser than them?" Sravika asked. "Too often, I fear we are ruled by our pain and by our fear."

Kitiger's answer was gruff. "That's why we're talking. I will neither let rash risks nor fear destroy our people. I haven't decided, but it is time for us to talk. All of us."

"Then you're contacting the other chieftains?" Sravika asked. Belarrin's ears perked up as he strained to hear. The Scion bands did speak to each other, then. But how?

"The nearest two," Kitiger said. "But before they come, before I announce anything, I have a task for you."

"Speak it then."

"Fedigni has always been passionately opposed to this idea. You must speak to him."

"He is grieving," Sravika protested.

"Do you want this or not, Sravika?"

"Of course I do," she replied. "If we continue as we are, we won't endure. We suffer grievous losses with each of our raids without becoming more than an annoying gnat buzzing in the Finnies' ears."

"Then calm him. He is the voice of the dissention. If he accedes, then the others will follow him. I won't have this family broken apart over this. We nearly came to blows, once, and I will not risk that again."

Sravika was quiet for a time, then she said, "You chose this moment because he is vulnerable."

"I chose this moment because I see our frailty, just as you do. We must decide. The wind has shifted and it is time. Now, will you do this for me or shall I recall the messengers to the other bands?"

Sravika sighed. "I will do it."

"Thank you, Sravika," Kitiger answered. "I know the task is not an easy one. But you have great compassion and wisdom. If anyone can bring our family fully together, it's you."

As Sravika returned to the shelter, Belarrin resumed his work, hoping she didn't suspect him of eavesdropping. But if she did, he was spared the conversation by the arrival of Mirnadd.

"Belarrin, care to help me set some traps?"

"Anything I can do to help."

"We'll find some good runs together and next time you'll be the one to set and recover the traps."

He nodded, then followed Mirnadd into the forest. Mirnadd had an expert eye and they worked quickly and efficiently. They set snares with twine and tensed branches along some runs and deadfall traps on others. As they stood up from placing one, Mirnadd said, "Sravika seems quite taken with you."

"Me?"

Mirnadd laughed. "You'd have to be blind not to notice."

"I suppose I have." Belarrin shrugged uncomfortably. This was not what he wanted. He needed to create distance, but the only thing he could think to say was, "I'm not sure I feel the same."

Clapping him on the shoulder, Mirnadd said, "Of all the people I've met, both in my own lost tribe and among the Scions, you can't do any better than Sravika. Well, except for Tayrja, of course, but she's taken."

"Of course."

"Good." Mirnadd's face furrowed with mock gravity. "And be sure that you don't forget!"

Belarrin grinned despite himself, then cursed. Every time he laughed with them would be like a sword cut on his soul when it came time to end their lives.

As if sensing his preoccupation, Mirnadd fell silent and didn't speak again except a few words as required as they set their traps. Belarrin appreciated the silence. Here was a man who understood boundaries and the value of silence.

On their way back to the camp, Mirnadd said, "Tomorrow you check and reset the traps by yourself. We'll see how good your memory is. If all goes well, you can take this task from now on."

CHAPTER 23
Siharrin

"All my life I have endeavored to understand 'the person.' What makes a king a king, a lord a lord, or a peasant a peasant? What makes a man into a paladin, a miser, or a rogue? Yet for all my studies, I have never been able to answer the simplest question of all. What makes me, me?"

—Master Kirhman of Karnott

The next morning Belarrin woke early as he usually did. The camp was barely touched by the grays of the new day as he headed out into the forest to check the traps. He might not be the best hunter, as Sravika had observed, but his memory was sharp and he found the first trap easily. It held a rabbit. He deftly unhitched it from the snare and reset the trap before heading for the next one. It was empty, so he left it in place. The third held a squirrel.

He knelt down and carefully loosened the twine around the squirrel's neck so the trap could be used again. As he prepared to reset the snare, movement flickered at the edge of his vision. Instantly wary, Belarrin leapt to his feet and turned with spear extended.

Less than five paces away, a figure sat cross-legged on the ground. A thick black cloak covered arms, legs, and body while a deep hood shadowed a face hidden behind a white mask. Primal terror clutched for Belarrin's heart. He didn't need to know what this creature was to know it was dangerous.

The figure did not stir. Its eyes watched him silently, piercing from beneath its mask. When he felt his voice would be steady enough, Belarrin said, "I do not intend to die easily."

"I would not expect a t'Okaedrin to do otherwise."

It knew what he was. Belarrin swallowed, hoping he hadn't betrayed recognition of the name. "Who or what are you?"

"I am Syraestari. Is that how you address your masters?"

Syraestari. That was how it knew. Belarrin slowly lowered his spear, but he didn't relax. He'd never heard of a Syraestari like this one. Seated as it was, he couldn't determine its height and all its features were hidden beneath the heavy robes and mask. "Forgive my insolence, my Lord, I did not know you."

"Nor would I expect you to. I am a Shadow-Servant."

Belarrin's heart thundered in sudden fear. Shadow-Servants were a myth. Stories told by parents to frighten errant boys. Shadow-Servants came for t'Okaedrin children who did not obey. He shook his head, forcing down his dread. He was not a child and wouldn't be afraid, even of this. "Shadow-Servants are killers. Is that why you're here?"

"In the years since your birth, I have ended far fewer lives than you." The Shadow-Servant must have noticed Belarrin's flinch because it said, "That troubles you? Perhaps you contemplate the most recent of those deaths?"

"I regret killing brothers, but they left me no choice."

"There is always choice. Yet I am more curious if the Scion dead trouble you."

"I take no pleasure at executing prisoners, even when it is just."

"I see."

When the Shadow-Servant said nothing else, Belarrin's fear grew and his anger with it. "My Lord, if you're here to kill me, then kill me. If not, then say why you've come. I will be missed soon."

"I am not here to kill you."

"Then what is it you wait for?"

"I'm curious at a t'Okaedrin who holds a spear ready to battle a Syraestari."

Flushing, Belarrin shifted the spear to a rest position on his shoulder. "Even more curious, now," the Shadow-Servant observed. "What shall I call you? Vistus? Or do you prefer Belarrin?"

"What does it matter," Belarrin replied, his anger getting the better of him. "You know who I am. What do you want, Master?"

"I know you, perhaps more even than you know yourself. Yet I don't know you and I wish to." The Shadow-Servant's head tilted to the side. "A riddle, yes?"

Belarrin decided to play the Shadow-Servant's own game. If every answer was turned on him, then he wouldn't speak until he had reason. Silence fell between them. Neither moved, Belarrin standing, Shadow-Servant sitting, eyes locked and weighing.

After a time, the Shadow-Servant chuckled. "So you learn. That's good. But do you remember? What is your first oath?"

"There is no greater duty than to kill in the name of the empress."

"And are you ready to kill?"

"Yes," Belarrin replied, deciding on obedience. There could be no other answer to a Syraestari, even one as strange and ominous as this creature.

The Shadow-Servant's eyes narrowed. "Ae'irpiva." A burst of wind brushed past Belarrin, tousling his hair before fading. The hairs on his forearms tingled. He watched the creature, uncertain of even what to begin to think.

"Stand there if you like, or sit, it matters not to me."

Belarrin hesitated. Shadow-Servants were supposed to be legends. And even if it wasn't here to kill him, t'Okaedrin didn't sit in the presence of their masters. He remained standing. "What do you want, Master?" he repeated.

"You've already answered my question. You are prepared to kill in the name of the empress."

"As I have said," Belarrin replied.

"Then if I commanded you, on behalf of the empress, to drive a spear through Zoltha's heart, you would do so?"

"Yes," Belarrin replied, but his heart faltered inside him.

"And would you slit Sravika's throat from ear to ear?"

"Yes!" He prayed that this Servant wouldn't test him. Not on Sravika.

"A pity. I thought you capable of learning." The Shadow-Servant sighed heavily and dropped its gaze to the ground at Belarrin's feet. It was not the response Belarrin had expected. He stared at it, puzzled and, after a long moment, it lifted its head again and met his eyes. "After weeks working as a slave, after all your time here, listening to these people and seeing how they live, still you answer without hesitation?"

"I am t'Okaedrin," Belarrin replied, "not a slave. And neither are the Kalilaer."

"They work where they are told, sleep where they are told, go where they are told without the possibility of question. They pray that they will be allotted enough food to survive. They pray that they will not be beaten. They live and die at the whims of their masters. Many even long for death so they might escape a life without hope. How is that not slavery?"

"They are doing what is right and you shouldn't mock them for it."

"It isn't mockery. Pity, perhaps? I wonder, were any of them happy?"

"Fritten was."

"Could such a child even understand what happiness means? Too old when he was captured to become a t'Okaedrin, he was sent to the smelters while still too young to even care for himself. A decade and more he has toiled there until all his previous life is a vague dream, a forgotten memory." The Shadow-Servant head titled. "And what of the others? They fled the instant a chance was given, though many died in the attempt. Was it worth the risk to Wiersa who fell? Was it worth the cost for the Scions who died as well? If not, why do they try and try again in the face of so much death?"

Belarrin shook his head. What was this creature? Syraestari didn't know Kalilaer by name, yet it knew Fritten and Wiersa, how they had lived and died. It knew Sravika and Zoltha. He realized his anger hadn't relented. Syraestari shouldn't make him furious. They were his masters. But this one did. "They deserve every death. They rebel against all that is right."

"If that's true, why did you save Sravika, Mirnadd, Idysha, and Yrpel from your brethren? You took a great risk intervening when it would have been easy to abandon them to their fates. You nearly sacrificed the task you were given."

"I..." Belarrin could only stutter. How did it know about that?

"And who told you that the Scions rebel against what is right?"

"My father and mother," Belarrin snapped. "Why are you questioning me? Everything I say, you have taught us that we might know the truth."

"So it all leads back to the Syraestari?"

"Yes!"

"So the Syraestari are wiser. We know what is right for humanity better than humans do?"

"Of course!" Belarrin cried. "You live for thousands of years. You are wiser and stronger. We're a broken and corrupted people. We fought alongside Cydion and wrought the Cataclysm. We are to blame for the desolation of the world!"

The Shadow-Servant laughed. The mocking lilt burned Belarrin's ears and brought fire to his cheeks. "The power of a well-placed lie," it said. "Some humans aligned with Cydion, to be sure, but it was we Syraestari who were his staunchest servants... until we betrayed him in the end."

"Lies," Belarrin snapped. "You cannot be Syraestari. My masters don't speak this way."

The Shadow-Servant stirred for the first time. It flowed more than moved, surging upward, black robes and cloak writhing in the faint morning breeze. Standing, it towered over Belarrin's head, fully the height of any Syraestari and taller than most. "Then would you prefer if I named myself the Shadow of Zaris?"

Belarrin stumbled back as if physically struck. "No."

"I am both, but neither is what you expect. A murderer, a monster that frightens children, a Syraestari. Or a manifestation of one of the fallen Etyni come to guide the Scions to secret victory."

"Impossible," Belarrin could only stammer.

"I've told the Scions where and when to strike. Five of their bands I have found and over twenty times have I directed them."

"Including the one that I infiltrated the first time," Belarrin replied. "They told me so. I joined them and brought their destruction."

"Unfortunate. I hadn't anticipated that."

"But you know everything about me."

"Not everything," the Shadow-Servant replied. Shifting its robes, it descended back into a sitting position. "I wasn't aware of you until after that raid. I first saw you when High Lord Tazil gave you your second task."

"If you are Syraestari, then why have you turned against your people?"

The Shadow-Servant's eyes gleamed. "Ah, now we are getting to the root of the question. I do not act against them. They only think I do. You may believe I act for the benefit of the Scions, but it is not the plight of humanity that moves me. I do not care for your race. You humans are as foolish and short-sighted as you've said, but that doesn't mean my people are always wise. No, slavery is a disease that weakens the Syraestari. While your people toil, mine do nothing. They soften and waste away. There are fifty or more, among my people, who could track the Scions back to their camps, just as I have done. The Scions are clever and know how to conceal themselves, but they're hardly perfect. Yet the task would require my kindred to live in the wilderness, skulking and waiting for a Scion raid to follow. Weeks or months, perhaps, they would have to live hidden in the forest, and they won't do it. They've become so enamored of the life they've chosen that my people would rather cower behind their comfortable walls and depend on Kalilaer and t'Okaedrin to save them. Not even a single voice has been raised to suggest doing what I have done."

Belarrin could only shake his head in denial.

"You think us wise, but we are fools. We are also liars. As I said, we were the traitors of the Great War, even though our reasons were sound. In our pride, we were deceived by Cydion and bound to him in servitude. We suffered an enslavement of our own that we only escaped in the last battle of the war. We saw our opportunity and drove a knife into his back, breaking the chains once and for all."

"Lies. By your own mouth you are liars."

"Yes, but I was there," the Shadow-Servant said, its voice fading to a rasp. "I was there in that moment when Cydion turned upon us, his once-loyal servants, and seared away the greatest sorcerers who dared at last to stand against him. I was there when the Etyni fought upon Mount Kensethir, when Itesa struck down Cydion in his moment of triumph."

"Why should I believe you over all the other Syraestari?" Belarrin asked. His mind whirled and he realized his voice was half pleading. If the Shadow-Servant spoke truth, then everything he had done was built on a foundation of lies. "You claim to be a creature of myth, a murderer."

"Then don't believe me." The Shadow-Servant drew back. "Human lives are feebly short, but even human memory perseveres when parents pass what they know to their children. The t'Okaedrin imitate names such as father, mother, brother, and sister, but these are an illusion. You have no such ties to the past. But the wildmen still remember, even when those stories are tarnished with time. You have heard what their legends say. How can it be that all the tribes tell the same story, even as they fight and die at each other's hands? Iengian, Zengris, Iachian, and Isyren each share the same memory. For though they wander blindly in the wilderness, they are peoples untouched by Syraestarin deceit. It is impossible that they could join together to concoct a common lie to give all their children. Not like my people could lie to you. If the wildmen share the same stories, then there must be truth within them."

"I cannot believe them." There was nothing more he could say. He thought of Dalric and Auphni. They were his true parents no matter what this creature claimed, more so than his unknown birth parents had ever been. Dalric and Auphni loved him and would not lie to him. Nor were they fools to accept a lie. All the Syraestari he'd known had treated him with justice, affording him a place he could feel proud to take. They permitted him the honor of fighting for the defense of right. It was impossible for them to lie, not when they had given him so much.

The Shadow-Servant touched his hand to his chest. "In your heart, you know I am right, even as your mind denies it." He lowered his hand. "But enough of this. Time presses on and we have other matters of equal importance to discuss."

"I have nothing to discuss with you," Belarrin replied, knowing the response was petty, but his mind churned with doubts.

Surprisingly, the Shadow-Servant didn't remark on that. "Then listen as I tell you something about yourself that even you don't know," it said. "I do not doubt that you are a proficient warrior. All of the greatest t'Okaedrin are. Certainly you are strong, resilient, and skilled in all manner of weapons. Even so, it would be a miracle for you to kill four mounted and fully armed t'Okaedrin with only a stone-headed spear."

Belarrin shrugged uncomfortably. He didn't like thinking about those deaths. "It wasn't just me."

Instead of arguing, the Shadow-Servant nodded, then said, "How did you manage to outrun a falling tree yesterday to save Sravika?"

"I don't know what you mean."

The Shadow-Servant chuckled. "It has always amused me how Siharrin consistently refuse to see what is obvious to others."

"Siharrin?"

Instead of answering, it said, "Ae'irpiva. Does this word mean nothing to you?"

"I don't know Syraestarin."

"The word isn't Syraestarin. It is far more ancient, older even than the formation of this world. But you have said it yourself at least three times. You spoke it once and a gust of wind staggered your t'Okaedrin pursuers, knocking them from their horses. You spoke it a second time and a tree that would have crushed Sravika instead fell harmlessly aside. Indeed, before you even began your infiltration, you mumbled it while in the throes of a nightmare."

"A nightmare?" Belarrin shook his head. "How do you know any of this?"

"I've been watching you, Belarrin." The Shadow-Servant paused and tilted its head to the side again. "Belarrin, yes, that is how you think of yourself now. I can see it in your eyes. The mantle you've taken has seized your soul. But do not weep for the passing of Vistus. Belarrin is a far better man."

"I don't know if you are Syraestari or not," Belarrin growled. "But whatever you are, say what you have to say and cease your mocking."

"It is only mocking so long as you refuse to see. It is truth, and when you understand it, all will be clear. Yes, I've observed your toil in the camps as you learned smelting from Zoltha. As you grappled with the taunts of your so-called brother. As you were taken to punishment on the Boards. There, in the throes of your delirium, do you not remember me and the single word I spoke?"

Belarrin's alarm grew with each new word. Memory of the pain of the Boards returned to his mind and the hovering pale mask. "Ae'irpiva," he whispered. "But you were only a fever dream... what does it mean?"

"Wind and yet so much more," the Shadow-Servant replied. "It is a Word of Power wrought before there was time, before Isfalinis had shape, before even the Etyni lived and breathed. A word shaped by His Highest Above at the beginning of all things. Ae'irpiva." When he spoke it this time, he lingered over it, filling the sound and silence that followed with reverence. "It speaks to the deep strength at the heart of a storm, the gust which staggers, the surge of power that topples and tears. It is a word of creation and destruction, a word of changing, a word of life, a word of motion. It is the very 'Breath of Isfalinis'."

Belarrin heard special emphasis on those final words. "I still don't understand."

"You are a Siharrin."

Belarrin growled. "Enough of your riddles and half-answers. Just say what you will without clever words. What is a Siharrin?"

"A sorcerer."

"That's absurd!" Belarrin blurted, but even as he uttered the words, he felt a flicker of understanding in his mind. It was like a fire flaring to life deep within him, a shudder rising up from his soul.

"But a Siharrin is no ordinary enchanter," the Shadow-Servant said. "Most sorcerers, like myself, learn Words of Power from a teacher, master to apprentice, or sometimes from the study of ancient lore. To forcefully pull Words directly from the Residue of Creation is terribly dangerous. Most who dare it have their minds seared away, reducing them to gibbering simpletons. It would be more fortunate to die outright, as a few do. But occasionally a Siharrin emerges, perhaps once a millennia. You are the first I have discovered since the Cataclysm began. Perhaps it is a gift directly from His Highest Above, perhaps it is driven by prophecy, or maybe only simple chance. I don't know. But the mind of a Siharrin can navigate the Residue of Creation, drawing out Words of Power as no one else can. The price is that the knowledge flees as soon as it is spoken."

Belarrin shook his head, but then he remembered the cart of children nearly toppling over Bridionis. Somehow they had found the strength to right it again. And then there was the earthquake when he was a child. When the barracks had collapsed, killing everyone inside except him.

"Now you see," the Shadow-Servant whispered, its hooded gaze staring deep into Belarrin's eyes. "Your life begins to make sense as it never has. Because of your fascination with wind, I must conclude that you have an affinity with the 'Breath of Isfalinis.' The wind, the storms, the rain and the sky. All that passes above our world. There are eight alignments in all, some similar and some different. You may be able to touch the 'Heart of Isfalinis' where fires burn and volcanoes tremble or perhaps the 'Spark of the Heavens' from whence life was drawn, Aestari and Human, beast and flower. Others will be impossible for you, such as the 'Flesh of Isfalinis' and all words that carve the stone and soil or enchantments that strengthen the will. Likewise my own greatest strength is beyond you. Within the Veil of the Heavens light is hidden and darkness falls, the mind falters and doubt arises."

"You're explaining all this as if I believe you."

"Don't be a fool," the Shadow-Servant snapped. "Of course you believe." Not allowing Belarrin to respond, he continued lecturing, "When you consider wind, or any of the other alignments, don't think only of that which you feel upon your face. The Breath of Isfalinis is far more than wind. It is movement, persistent, shapeless, and swift. It is the fury of the storm that brings the cleansing rain. It is perceptive, finding any nook or cranny. It has a voice to speak, a harmony of clattering leaves and rustling grasses, or rippling waves and writhing smoke. It is all these things and more. Each of these manifestations has its own Word, but you can find them all."

"Is..." Belarrin hesitated. Speaking would acknowledge the truth of this creature's words. But he had to know. "Is it these Words of Power that I see before my eyes?"

"You see them?" the Shadow-Servant's said, surprised.

"I see golden lines. It looks like Syraestari writing."

"It is possible," the creature replied after a moment's thought. "No one knows much about the Siharrin. I do know this, though. Now that you are aware of what you are, you will be able to conjure magic intentionally. All it requires is focus. Consider what you need and concentrate upon it. The words shall come to you. Start small. Even for Siharrin, conjuring Words of Power can be an exhausting act and stamina only comes with practice."

Belarrin sagged to his knees, overcome by everything. He cradled his spear in his arms. That, at least, was solid and unchanging. Something he understood. "But why are you telling me any of this?"

"I've come to expose the great lie you've heard all your life and to reveal a truth even you didn't know."

"If that's true, and I'm not saying it is, then what do you want from me?"

"Nothing."

"But..."

"Your mind is full and your heart doubts. We have spoken long enough and your companions will begin to wonder." The Shadow-Servant rose to his feet. "I know you are uncertain what to believe, so I will leave you with this final question. Are you certain you are here because His Highest Above blesses the task given you by High Lord Tazil? Or did He bring you here that you may find and follow a better task? Perhaps you live, perhaps you are here, because you can do something no one else can. There has never before been a man who was t'Okaedrin and Kalilaer, Scion and Siharrin."

"You want me truly to become a Scion, then?"

"I want nothing from you but the answer to that question." The Shadow-Servant gestured behind him with his head. "You will find the produce from your other traps. I collected them to give us more time here. "Go now, Siharrin, and find the truth. The fates of two peoples hangs in the balance. Kargatsasir dotenada!"

Darkness billowed out of the Shadow-Servant's cloak like a dark fog, it swirled around him as if driven by its own hidden currents until he was completely enveloped. Then the dark faded like smoke wafting from a fire. Of the Shadow-Servant there was no sign.

CHAPTER 24
Between

"The power of words to move a soul to dare everything, even to dare life itself, has always intrigued me. I speak not only of the great orators, but of lesser words, too. It might be a chant, a greeting, or even a simple title. Men, in the hundreds of thousands, have given their lives for so little as this. "

—Emperor Mardinathis of Etaria

Belarrin let out a long sigh, feeling the tension flow from his tight shoulders. He stared at the spot where the Shadow-Servant had sat. No trace remained of its presence. Belarrin might have called the meeting a dream, a delusion, but for the line of trapped animals it had left behind.

"It cannot be true," he whispered.

But the Shadow-Servant was at least partially right. Belarrin's mind was at war with his heart. Which to trust? He'd sworn an oath to his masters, an oath of duty and honor. He couldn't cast that aside easily. Nor could he cast aside his family. But he didn't want to see Sravika, Zoltha, or any of the others dead, either. It was strange and a little frightening to be honest with thoughts he'd always fled from before.

Belarrin rose to his feet and walked over to the trapped animals. He added the ones he had collected on his own to the row before turning toward the camp. As he walked, his mind contemplated sorcery. Of everything that was said, that was the least daunting, however inexplicable.

He stooped to pick up a leaf from the ground. Raising it before his eyes, he examined it. Was sorcery really as easy as the Servant had said? What if he wanted the leaf to burn? Belarrin focused his attention on it.

Burn.

Nothing happened. Narrowing his eyes, Belarrin concentrated as hard as he could.

Burn!

He stumbled beneath a wave of dizziness as red tinged the edge of his vision. His forehead and cheeks felt hot, but the warmth faded quickly. Shaking his head, he cleared his mind and waited for his body to steady. Then, taking a deep breath, he focused on the leaf one more time. He concentrated as hard as he could, willing, yearning. He wanted to believe. He had to believe in something when faith in all else lay shattered around him. Just this one thing! Burn, leaf!

A veil of crimson light washed over his eyes. The hairs on his arms curled as if he stood too close to a blaze, then lines of gold seared bright before him as a welling pressure rose up in his throat.

"Eusy'arjev tae'oekym rykatriv naeroda'oesys!"

Belarrin cried out in alarm and stumbled back as the leaf burst into a column of flame. It tumbled, burning as it fell. Before it reached the forest floor, the leaf disappeared in a cloud of soot and ash. Belarrin stared at the spot where it had burned away and burst out laughing. He hadn't been sure he believed until this very moment.

It was incredible. It was so simple!

He knelt down and touched the ground beneath where the leaf had incinerated. His joy died. If the Shadow-Servant was right in this, what did that signify regarding its other claims? If the Shadow-Servant's other claim was also true, then everything he had ever done was a lie. What did that make him? A murderer. Belarrin trembled as he resumed his walk.

As he entered the camp, Mirnadd found him. "I was beginning to wonder if you got lost."

Belarrin shook his head and raised up the trapped animals. "No, I was just enjoying the morning. We had a good catch."

"Excellent."

Tayrja and Chostir joined them as they skinned the animals. The fur was too small to be of much use, but they collected the meat and placed it into a clay cooking pot. Tayrja and Mirnadd teased each other as they worked, laughing happily.

His mind was still preoccupied, and Belarrin had no desire to join in. But Chostir leaned over. A wide grin split her face. "I was talking to Sravika. You remember the story I told you about the city built on a waterfall? She's heard of it, too."

"I didn't know that," Belarrin said absently. He did not want to hear any more of her far-fetched tales. But even as the thought entered his mind, he hesitated. This was what the Shadow-Servant had talked about. Two people from two different tribes sharing the same story. The person he really needed to talk to was Zoltha. As soon as they were done preparing the animals, he excused himself and sought out his old friend from the smelters.

Zoltha was sitting near the cold cook fire with a pile of thin branches lying next to him. On his lap lay the beginnings of a basket. He looked up as Belarrin approached. "A good morning to you, my friend." He hesitated and smiled. "Or I should use to the greeting given here. 'The tree has fallen.'"

"But a new shoot rises," Belarrin replied, grinning at the man's easy demeanor.

Zoltha grunted, adjusting his seat. "Care to give me a hand?"

"Of course," Belarrin replied, sitting down beside him. "But I've never woven a basket before."

Zoltha laughed. "Then we're back in our old places. I taught you smelting, I can teach you this." He handed Belarrin two bundles of branches. "The first smaller group you'll notice are thicker. Those will form the frame, all centered at a single point. The other bundle has thinner branches that you'll weave through the stronger. I've already soaked them in water so they'll bend more easily."

Belarrin watched closely as Zoltha talked him through the steps. It was nice to let the deeper worries fall away, if only briefly, and to focus on something so mundane. The simple toil of it was refreshing and mind-clearing. He centered the thick branches and used twine to hold them in place as Zoltha had instructed. About a hand's width from the middle, he carefully bent each of them to form the corner where the base and sides would meet. Then the actual weaving began. Over and under he guided each strand in a continuous circle around the basket. When he wasn't careful, it slipped out of place, but by moving slowly, methodically, it was much easier.

Across the camp, about fifteen Scions had gathered to practice with their weapons. A few sparred, but most just worked with the weapons, practicing thrusts and parries. Belarrin glanced away from his work from time to time to watch. Sravika was with them, along with Yrpel and Henirgar. He also recognized Obaudes from the group of freed farmer Kalilaer. Even though they practiced as a group, they didn't practice together. They were individuals, each one separate and apart, even as they trained side by side. That lack of discipline, almost as much as their lack of iron, is what doomed them in battle against the t'Okaedrin.

Some, Sravika included, practiced with swords they'd taken from fallen t'Okaedrin. The versatility of the sword was different than the brute slashing of the axe or the stabbing of a spear. But they were like children, just beginning to fathom its potential. Their movements were sometimes too rushed, sometimes too slow. When they thrusted, it was as if they expected the enemy to be twice as far away. When they slashed, they anticipated the enemy to remain still like a tree. They understood the sharp edges and tip of the sword, but not its heart.

He shook his head. Was the Shadow-Servant right? Were these people more his family, more his brothers than the t'Okaedrin? What about Bridionis? Or Hirnid? He let out a deep breath. Life had been so easy and certain when he knew what was right and what was wrong. But now… He glanced over at Zoltha. "How do you have such faith?"

The other man laughed softly, gently. "Because most of my life I've had nothing else." There had been no question why. Perhaps that was what Belarrin loved most about Zoltha. No challenge, only candor. Zoltha grimaced at the basket in his lap. "No, that isn't fair. But I've never been particularly good at anything. I was a lousy warrior and a pathetic hunter. Unfortunately, I made a fair slave, but I'm not proud of that. Even here I'm not sure what I can do, so I help where I can. Weaving baskets. Skinning deer. Building shelters. I don't think you can understand. You're good everything you do."

"Not everything," Belarrin replied, trying to keep the defensiveness from his voice.

"Forgive me," Zoltha said, looking up. "I didn't intend that as an attack or as unguarded jealousy. You have always been fair with me. Not everyone has."

"I'm not good with faith," Belarrin said. "I was once, I think, but these past few months have changed everything. How are you so certain and confident? Even as a slave you were."

Zoltha coaxed an uncooperative branch into his basket before replying. "I guess I've found that when life fails your dreams, you have two choices. You can give up or endure. Enduring is the harder choice of the two. It helps to find joy in the little things." He smiled. "A well-smelted bloom, a well-crafted basket, a meal shared with friends, even in suffering. But beyond that, you must find hope. I don't pretend to have the answer on finding it. For years, I had little hope in this life, but now that we are free, perhaps I can find it again. But if there is to be no hope here, I will always find it in the life that lies beyond the grave. Not even a Finaestari sword can take that from me."

"But isn't that just giving up?"

Zoltha shrugged. "It depends on what it does to you, I suppose. Some people with no hope in this life become dark and bitter, letting it consume them from within, but I won't allow that. I will not let my hope of the next life rob me of what joy I find here. Just because my hope may grow or shrink from one day to the next doesn't mean I'll stop trying. I suppose that's the difference."

"But where does your faith come from?" Belarrin asked, turning the conversation to root of his question and the doubts the Shadow-Servant had set in his heart. "I paid little enough attention to the Etyni and such matters when I was a child. But now that I've lost my past, I wonder. And none of my own people remain to tell me."

Zoltha quirked an eyebrow. "Your father and sister were priests and still you don't know?"

Belarrin feigned a chuckle as he considered how to answer that question. But thinking up this lie wasn't difficult. "I was a fool, too focused on fighting to pay attention. But I'm admitting my ignorance now. Tell me about the Great War and the Cataclysm."

Zoltha set his basket down and stretched. "No one really knows for sure what happened. Too much was lost in the ruin. I've asked plenty of other slaves around the cook fire. I've asked a few of these Scions, too, and they're no more certain."

"But do they all agree in what they do remember?"

"In most things, I suppose, though there is more unknown than known."

"Can you tell me what you've heard?"

"You truly don't know any of it?"

"I remember some, but act like I'm a small child who has never heard before." Belarrin grinned.

Zoltha smiled back and shook his head. "You truly are a strange man, Belarrin."

"So I have been told."

"Ha!" Zoltha reached down to pick up a new branch to weave.

Behind Belarrin, the wood and stone weapons thudded as the Scions continued their practice. That sound filled Belarrin with nostalgia of home, yet it haunted him with doubts, too. He tried to dismiss such thoughts from his mind as he leaned forward to listen Zoltha.

"It is thought that the war started with an eruption. One day the mountain peaks exploded, belching darkness and fire into the heavens. A quarter of the world was consumed beneath that inferno alone. When the fires cooled, an army of ash monsters poured out across the land. I've heard as many names for them as tribes I've met. Trowglid and Trouglide, Kawglyd, and Krogild. All similar, yet different. Even our words have been lost. With them marched the Eday, Siona's accursed spawn. Veduk, you'll remember, was the greatest of them." Belarrin matched his grin, remembering Zoltha's names for the two Syraestari in the smelting camp. "Other tribes have named them Iedta, Yeedhay, and Eedtay. I don't know which, if any, are correct. Perhaps the Finnies with their long memories know, but I wouldn't expect the truth from them.

"Those kingdoms of man that dared stand against such a host, died. There was no choice but to flee, leaving the weak and the old behind to their fates. The Etyni entered the world to stand against Cydion, but the Lord of Life and Death had grown too strong feasting upon the souls of the dying. Blessed Henji fell first, spilling her blood upon the bridge. It is a sacrifice not one tribe I know has forgotten. Not one will, I'm certain of it. But one by one the Etyni died fighting beside the humans they sought to protect until, in the end, only four remained to stand at the final battle."

Zoltha paused and looked down at the basket in his hands. Slowly he turned it, but he was not looking at the basket. His eyes were far away. "Of all the legends, this one I've heard from every tribe and people I met among the Kalilaer. For everyone, the story is the same. On a hill above the raging mass of battle, Cydion met and felled each of them.

First Itesa and Fenr, her brother. Then Niella, and in the end, even Zaris died."

Zoltha set the basket down gently as if it was made of the most fragile Syraestarin porcelain. "In the darkest days of my own life, I have pondered that moment. There have been times when I close my eyes and think that I can see it all unfold before me." His voice rasped as he continued, "What despair must have entered the hearts of all the armies of men, to look up and see the death of all hope? To see the beginning of an eternal age of darkness and torment? Could faith ever have faced as great a crisis as that?

"Perhaps it was a final test, a great weighing of souls. I wonder what I would have thought in that moment, had I been there. What would I have felt? Would I have surrendered and died, or would I have clung to hope even then?"

There were torments here, beyond the story. Afflictions in the very depths of Zoltha's soul, yet he spoke them anyway. Without fear or shame. Belarrin watched him, in awe as much of Zoltha as of the story. Would that he could ever trust anyone enough to lay his own heart so bare.

Zoltha slowly shook his head. "It was then that Itesa, though dying, marshalled the last of her failing strength. Even as Cydion bellowed his triumph and terror over the world, she took up her sword and drove it through his heart. Freeing us all. Savior and foe collapsed, dying together in that moment of wonder."

A long sigh escaped Belarrin's lips and he looked down, realizing that the basket had fallen from his hands. The clack of weapons continued behind him, undiminished. Somewhere, across the camp children laughed. Sounds, so normal, felt strange as his mind fixed upon Zoltha's words. He'd heard the end of the story from the lips of his mother and father, but never with such passion. Itesa epitomized nobility and sacrifice, he'd been taught. She symbolized what all t'Okaedrin should aspire to. Even now, despite all his other doubts, he knew he could still be certain in believing that. But for whom had Itesa died? Scion or t'Okaedrin?

"In that triumph lay a new despair," Zoltha continued. "During their battles, Cydion and the Etyni had unleashed sorcery unseen since the creation of the world. But that was nothing compared to the raw unveiling of their deaths. The fall of such divine beings, so quickly and in all their numbers, cannot pass quietly. It tore the world apart. The remnants of the nations that lived through the war were ruined by the Cataclysm that followed. Knowledge was lost, wisdom and skill faded. Even memory became but a dark and impenetrable shadow. The survivors scattered in search of food, fighting over the last scraps. Towns and villages were abandoned to gather dust and collapse beneath spreading vines. Walls of ice descended from mountains that quaked in endless unrest until, beneath them, there remained only our crude tribes with little recollection of what we once had been." He looked up at Belarrin and smiled sadly. "And then there came the Finaestari to enslave us."

Belarrin let out a slow breath. A part of him didn't want to speak and break the spell of the story Zoltha had woven. But there were questions he had to know the answer to. "Did humans fight for Cydion?"

"I imagine many did. It wouldn't have been difficult for the Lord of Life and Death to tempt the ambitious, the greedy, or the terrified with promises of power and life. But at least as many opposed him or there couldn't even have been a final battle."

"What about the Finaestari?"

To Belarrin's surprise, Zoltha hesitated. He'd seen the man pause plenty of times to prepare his thoughts, but this was different. Zoltha was reluctant. "I don't know," he finally confessed. "There are so many fragments of stories and so much that is wholly lost. In my heart, I want to cry out that of course they fought alongside Cydion. They are monsters."

Belarrin leaned forward, trying to keep the challenge from his voice. If he caught the Shadow-Servant in one deceit, than everything else he said was a lie, too. But what if the opposite were true? One way or another, Syraestari had lied to him. Either the Shadow-Servant or everyone else. "You don't think the Finaestari fought for Cydion."

"No, that isn't it either," Zoltha replied. "I think they did both."

"Some fought on each side?"

"No, they changed sides."

"How is that possible?" Belarrin asked.

"I've heard a fragment of story only twice. According to those legends, the Finaestari were among Cydion's greatest servants until the final battle. Before Cydion faced the Etyni, it is said that the Finnies betrayed him, wounding him deeply. Perhaps it was even weakness from that wound that led to his final downfall."

Just as the Shadow-Servant had said. "So they were heroes," Belarrin concluded. And if they were such heroes, then they were masters worthy of following.

"Perhaps." Zoltha shrugged. "Yet if that myth is true, no memory of their motivations remain. And if they were heroes then, they certainly aren't now."

Belarrin grimaced. It was as if Zoltha heard his every conclusion and stated the opposite. He wanted both to be true. His life had always been for his masters and he wanted it to be a good life. He wanted his masters to be good masters and the deaths he had wrought to be just. Vitarria, Parvik, and all the others who had fallen beneath his blade must have died with good reason. But there was honor and wisdom in Zoltha. Sravika, Mirnadd, and Yrpel were as valiant as any t'Okaedrin warrior. And, he realized, he cringed beneath the ancestral guilt for the ruin of the Cataclysm. He wanted it all, but that was impossible.

If only he could hear words as honest and unveiled from his parents as he had from Zoltha. Better yet, one of the Syraestari. He needed truth from someone great like Captain Nethzir, High Lord Tazil, or that Sword-Whisperer.

"That's as troubled an expression as I've ever seen," Zoltha said.

Belarrin glanced over at his friend and frowned. So much for discipline. But if he couldn't tell Zoltha exactly what bothered him, perhaps there was another way. It all came down to faith, after all. Faith in the wildmen legends or faith in the stories of his childhood. He picked up his basket and resumed his weaving before answering. "We started by talking about faith. I suppose I've always just taken the world as I see it and never thought deeper than that. Is it belief in the Etyni or in His Highest Above that gives you hope?"

Zoltha let out a long breath. "No easy questions for me, are there?"

Belarrin shook his head. "Not today."

"I'm no wiser than you, my friend. Any answer I give isn't true just because I believe it. I believe what I believe, but what is true is true, regardless of whether I believe it or not. I search just like you."

"But that's what faith means."

"Exactly." Zoltha nodded. "And my faith is in His Highest Above. That doesn't mean I dismiss the Etyni. The Etyni were great and powerful, but they weren't perfect. Blood on the Bridge, Cydion was one of them! But they're all dead and what good can the dead do now? That leaves only His Highest Above."

"But if He's so perfect, how could He allow the Great War? Or the Cataclysm? You remember Chostir's questions when we were smelting?" Belarrin gestured at the camp around him. "How can He allow us to sink to this?"

"I don't know," Zoltha replied. "But maybe it comes down to choice. Just as what I believe does not determine what is, so all people must be allowed to decide what they believe. If we were denied that choice, we'd be the very beasts that the Finnies try to name us. It is that choice which led the realms of humanity to fight against Cydion. It is that choice which allows the Scions to fight to liberate those bound by the Finnies. But choice bears its own price. It allows us to fight and kill each other. It allowed humans to side with Cydion. It allows humans to fight on behalf of our enslavers. Everything we choose has consequences, but if the consequences didn't exist, then our lives would be without meaning. For us to be able to choose, we must be allowed to create a Cataclysm."

That was it.

Belarrin looked down at the half-finished basket in his hands with the branches weaving in and out. It wasn't pretty, with a strand askew here and one not quite tight enough there. But it held together, the reeds pushing and pulling against each other, binding themselves with their own strength. Yet one misplaced branch could rip it all apart. He could see the difference between the Scions and the t'Okaedrin, now. The world in which the t'Okaedrin lived had no choice. Humans were weak, flawed, only suitable to be servants who obeyed without question. But he knew humans had choices. If they didn't, he couldn't have these doubts now. If they didn't, the Scions wouldn't exist. Zoltha's story, on the other hand, explained the triumphs and failings of both humans and the Finaestari. The t'Okaedrin story justified neither. And that made what Zoltha said real like nothing else could. It was ugly, like the basket, but whole.

Warmth flooded over him, like the sun bursting through a cloudy sky when the world lay damp and cold after a heavy rain. Belarrin closed his eyes, feeling his heart race as his shoulders straightened from a heavy weight falling away. It was a new feeling, fresh, and unknown. The burden he had carried was not new, he realized. No, he had borne it from his earliest memories.

Beneath the weight of such truth, he couldn't lie anymore. The Finaestari had wreathed themselves in lies and he wouldn't be like them. Nor could he be who he had been. He let out a long sigh. He was t'Okaedrin no longer. His eyes opened. "Zoltha, there is something I must tell you."

"Yes?"

"I'm not everything you think I am." He hesitated a moment, but resolved to press on. "Nor am I…"

A scream tore through the camp, slicing through Belarrin's words like a knife. He leapt to his feet and grappled for a weapon as he scanned for danger. The shriek had come from the direction of the sparring area.

"That sounded like Sravika." Zoltha stood up beside him.

CHAPTER 25
Silence

"There is a moment in every life where a choice is made, sometimes knowingly, sometimes not. It may not be recognized for days, years, or ever, but what befalls after can all be traced back to that single source."

—Aivym of Eswaikosir

A cluster of rebels gathered in a circle on the practice field. The warmth in Belarrin's soul vanished beneath chilling fear. He sprinted toward them with Zoltha following.

He heard Yrpel's words first, pleading, "I'm sorry. I don't know what happened. Highest Above, what have I done?"

Heart cold, Belarrin forced his way through the gathered Scions to see Sravika lying on the ground, soaked in her own blood. Her eyes flittered and lips quivered. Her face had faded to a pale white. Idysha and Henirgar knelt beside her. Henirgar's hands covered a wound in her chest, but with each beat of her heart more blood pooled up through his fingers. He looked up at Belarrin, tears staining his eyes. "The wound is too deep to stop. It will only be a few minutes now."

Belarrin's knees gave out as he fell down beside her. The deaths of Parvik and of Wiersa flickered through his mind, the death of Vitarria, too. But none of those were as dreadful as this. Not Sravika. Anyone but her. Not when he had finally come to see the truth. When he had come to understand.

Sravika's head turned and she looked up at him. Her lips parted and she whispered, "Forgive Yrpel. I wish that..."

Belarrin took her hand, feeling the blood slick between their fingers. Not like this, not now when she was supposed to live. There was so much to tell her. So much to confess. That he was the monster who had killed her sister. That by her death, Vitarria had saved him. That he could see it all now, who he was and who he had to be. That she was beautiful, more radiant than anyone he had ever known. Filled with kindness and wisdom and life, like he had never before witnessed. That she had shown him what it was to live. Not now. "Not now!" he cried.

He felt Henirgar's hand rest gently on his shoulder. "I'm sorry, Belarrin, there's nothing we can do."

"No," Belarrin whispered through clenched teeth. He shook his head, sending tears down his cheeks, staining the ground. She had to survive. She had to be healed. She had to be...

Belarrin drew in a ragged breath. The Shadow-Servant claimed he had some skill. He turned to Henirgar. "Let me."

"It is too late, Belarrin."

"Let me!" he roared.

Henirgar flinched back and Belarrin placed his hands over the wound and closed his eyes. He felt Sravika grasp his wrist. The grip was so feeble. No, he had to focus. He had to see the way, he had to know what it was to heal. He had to save Sravika.

He concentrated until the world shrank to his heartbeat, thundering in his ears and her heartbeat fluttering weakly beneath his hands. He had to close the wound and heal all the damage within. There was no other way, no other chance. He could not fail in this, not like he'd failed Vitarria.

A rumble welled up in his ears, deafening. With eyes closed, he could see nothing. There was only the feeling of Sravika's hand clutching his, weakening. The sharp scent of her spilled blood. So red. Like the setting sun. No, not dusk and death. He shook his head. It was like the rising sun, rising to life. Warm and radiant. He felt it pour over him like a gentle breath, glowing crimson as the dawn.

Brilliant lines of gold, gleaming like the newborn sun blazed before his eyes and words poured from his lips. "Sinahastir aifys Sravikasae ondae!"

Power flowed out of him, over him, over Sravika beyond anything he'd ever imagined. It was real, tangible, like being doused in a rushing river. It was wondrous, alive. His soul laughed at the joy of it and, beyond sound, he heard her soul laugh too.

Then the vision vanished leaving him suddenly cold, weak. Normal. Belarrin opened his eyes and the world spun around him. Faces staring, treetops, sky and ground. He was falling. Hands reached out to catch him.

"He's waking up." Zoltha's voice pierced the fog over Belarrin's mind.

He opened his eyes, gasping for breath. He lay on the ground with his friend kneeling over him. The dizziness was gone and, though he felt weak, that was all. "I'm fine," he said. "How is Sravika? Help me up."

Zoltha obeyed immediately and, putting his arm around Belarrin's shoulder, raised him to a sitting position. The Scions still encircled them, perhaps the whole camp, adults and children alike, with eyes staring at him like he'd become some sort of mythical beast. Awe, wonder, joy and fear. But Belarrin barely noticed their gazes as he found Sravika. She was lying beside him with her head propped up on Idysha's lap.

Her eyes met his. They were a radiant blue that gleamed in the sunlight. She smiled and when she spoke her voice was soft but strong. "Three times you've saved my life, Belarrin, and each time I understand you less."

Belarrin grinned back as tears of joy fell down his face. He could think of nothing to say. She seemed to understand and, still smiling back, closed her eyes.

Henirgar cleared his throat. "She's still weak, but the wound is completely healed. There is barely a scar. Blood on the Bridge, Belarrin, who are you?" Chief Kitiger stepped up next to Henirgar, his eyes asking the same question.

"I don't know," Belarrin replied. Back, before Sravika's injury, he had been about to tell Zoltha everything. But now, surrounded by all of these Scions, men and women who hated the t'Okaedrin, he changed his mind. They wouldn't understand. They wouldn't trust him if they knew the truth. "I think I may be some kind of sorcerer." He hesitated and looked over at Sravika. "We need to care for her first."

"He's right," Laerdina said, kneeling down next to Idysha and Sravika. "Her wound has been healed, but she's still weak. She needs food, rest, and a change of clothes. Tayrja, give us a hand!"

Mirnadd's wife stepped forward and, between the three women, they got Sravika standing. Sravika gave him a faint smile before allowing herself to be guided away. Then Kitiger sank down to one knee and said, "Perhaps you should start at the beginning, Belarrin. We've never seen anything like this. We are filled with joy and hope, but understand that in the unknown there is fear as well."

"I don't know where the beginning is," Belarrin replied, thinking fast. "I've only just begun to understand myself. Looking back now, I think I can see strange events in my childhood, but recently it was that gust of wind as we escaped the camps that unhorsed the Iron-Men. I think I may have created that without realizing it."

"I remember the wind but I would never guessed it was you," Mirnadd said and Yrpel nodded. "I wondered if Eicai had risen from his eternal slumber to cast down our enemies."

"I see lines in gold, then I speak and things happen. It happened again during the earthquake. A tree was falling toward Sravika and I think I pushed it so it fell safely away from us. Then I remembered the parchment Sravika had shown me a few days earlier. It looks a little like what I see in front of my eyes."

Kitiger frowned. "Finnie letters?"

"Maybe," Belarrin answered. "But where did the Finnies get their letters from? Where did we get ours from, when we knew how to write? From the Etyni, probably."

"The Etyni would have taught all the races sorcery in the beginning," Zoltha said, "and they would have taught writing too. Probably everyone wrote the same way once."

"So what do the words you say mean?" Kitiger asked.

Belarrin laughed ruefully. "I don't know. I can't even remember them. I have no idea what I said when I healed Sravika or when I moved the tree or unhorsed the Iron-Men."

"That doesn't sound like anything I've ever been told about magic," Kitiger replied.

Chostir spoke up, "I was told a legend once about an old man who had lost his mind. He couldn't even remember his own name but he lived in a hut near a bridge and healed anyone who came to him for help."

"What do we know about magic anyway?" Henirgar asked, eyeing Chostir askance. "Nothing at all. And why are we arguing about it? Sravika should be dead, but she lives. Don't you understand what that means? We have a sorcerer!

Someone who can stand toe to toe with the Finnies. We can really free all the slaves, just as we've always dreamed!"

Kitiger nodded grimly. "We can destroy the Iron-Men, every last one of them"

A great cry of excitement rose up from the surrounding Scions, with shouts of "Free the slaves!" and "Kill all the Iron-Men!"

Looking into each of their eyes, those of the Chieftain Kitiger and Belarrin's friends, Mirnadd, Henirgar, Zoltha, and Chostir he could see the jubilation in their eyes. The thirst both for justice and vengeance. Vengeance upon people like himself. Belarrin realized his decision had been correct. He couldn't tell them who he was. They would kill him for the Scion-murderer he was. He couldn't blame them. He could only join them and keep his secret.

As the excitement quieted, Belarrin shook his head, "I don't know yet. This is too new for me, too. I need to be able to control it and direct it more quickly and easily."

Zoltha rested a hand on his shoulder. "You'll have to be careful, too. If you collapse in a raid like you did just now, a Finnie sorcerer would destroy you."

"But we'll figure it out," Henirgar said eagerly. "You'll figure it out, I mean. This is hope like we've never had!"

Hope. This is just what Zoltha had talked about. Belarrin looked up at his friend as the surrounding Scions broke into eager chatter – all except for Kitiger, who eyed him uncertainly. The chieftain's expression looked a lot like Dalric's when he was weighing a heavy matter, and Belarrin didn't blame him. The matter was weighing heavily on him too. But for all of his past, he knew he could help them. He was a Scion. They had freed his soul and that was cause for rejoicing.

His companions came by, clasping him on the shoulder. Mirnadd, Henirgar, and Zoltha. Chostir embraced him with laughter in her eyes. Argluf, Fedigni, and many others he knew less well came by. But Yrpel approached last of all, his expression one of woe. "Belarrin you have saved me almost as much as you did Sravika. If she had died at my hand..." he choked off. It was strange to see the large man scrubbing at his face with his great hands.

"What happened?" Belarrin asked, though remembering Yrpel's recklessness exuberance at the welcome feast, he could guess.

"I don't know. We were both working with the iron swords, just feeling the weight of them. I was swinging it to the left and right. I thought Sravika was further away, I was sure she was, but then I felt the too familiar tug of a weapon piercing flesh." He paused a moment and drew a ragged breath. "I turned and there she was, lying on the ground behind me as you saw her. I don't know how it happened, I'm so sorry!"

Belarrin smiled gently and clasped the Iengian on the shoulder. "It was an accident, my friend. She will be fine now. We all know you meant no harm."

"You are kinder to me than I deserve."

"No. Just be more careful."

The excitement lasted the rest of the day. At the evening meal, the other Scions chatted happily, surrounding Belarrin with their cheer. Kitiger and some others were more watchful, still, doubtless uncertain of what he and the future held, but they were far outnumbered by the joyous. The enthusiasm was too much, though, and Belarrin ate as quickly as he could, then fled.

Leaving the campfires behind, he walked to the furthest part of the glade, sat down, and leaned back against a downed cedar. The firelight glowed faintly against the spreading boughs of the forest and he could see a few stars glimmer above the tree tops. The sound of revelry was present, but muted with no single voice distinct above the babble. It was cooler, too, with a soft wind that was pleasantly sharp.

He let out a long sigh, pondering the day's events. When he had left that morning to collect the traps, he had been a different person, still certain of the way of t'Okaedrin. There had been doubts, certainly, but he had remain fixed on his task. The Shadow-Servant had pushed him into those doubts, though, and Zoltha had, in his own devout way, gently convinced him.

But was it all just a rush of passion? In his heart, he had doubted long ago. But now that he was calmed, did he truly believe? Belarrin closed his eyes and forced his mind to consider Dalric, Auphni, Bridionis, and Elestis. Whatever the truth, he loved them still. Did that mean something more? But then there was Sravika, Zoltha, Yrpel, and Mirnadd. How could these two groups of people who were so important to him stand so opposed to each other, even to the death?

He looked up at the sound of footsteps on the leaves as Sravika stepped into view. "No, stay seated," she said as he started to move. He did as she asked and she sat down on the log near his head. "You aren't the easiest man to find."

"Too much attention."

She laughed gently. It had a musical ring to it, like the water of a creek tumbling over rocks. "Then dare I thank you again for saving my life?"

"From you, I'll accept it. But remember that you saved me from the slave camps first. I think that makes us even."

"Hardly."

"Then I don't care who owes what."

She shook her head. "I know I've said this before, but you are a remarkable man. All the strongest men I've known have been full of their own power, prideful and demanding. But even in your sorcery, you're humble."

"I don't feel humble." Belarrin scratched the stubble on his chin. "It isn't really that at all. I think we all have a place in this world and I've finally found mine." Belarrin hesitated as the truth of his own words sank in. As a t'Okaedrin he'd been taught about his role in the world. Doubt had shattered that confidence, but now he'd found a new, better place. He glanced over at Sravika, staring into her smiling eyes. He could tell her the truth of his past. Of anyone in the camp, she would hear him out and understand.

A shadow fell over his thoughts. He had killed her sister. He had manipulated her trust and had come here to murder her, too. No, she wouldn't understand, no matter how much he'd changed, and the news might very well break her. He had done so much harm and he loved her smile. He didn't want to destroy that, too. "Can we talk about something else?" he asked. "Anything else. I'm tired of being the center of conversation."

"Just so long as the topic isn't me, either."

"But you feel recovered?"

"Yes. I'm still a little weak, but eating has helped with that." She glared down at him. "But we weren't going to talk about me."

"I don't mind silence," Belarrin replied.

Sravika nodded and slid off the log to sit beside him. They stared into the forest and up at the stars, feeling the cool breeze. Belarrin felt a touch on his arm. He didn't move as Sravika slid her fingers forward to grasp his hand in hers. The warmth of her touch flooded over him, setting his heart to racing. Yet he felt cold too, hot and cold, exhilarated. He glanced over at her and she looked back, a soft smile on her lips and eyes soaking in the night. What about Elestis, though? The thought peeked at him from the corner of his mind. Was she forever lost to him? But perhaps this was better.

He prayed the moment would never end.

CHAPTER 26
Lies

"There will come a time in your life, my son, when a hard choice will be demanded of you. You may have to choose between duty and love or perhaps honor and peace. The decision you make will determine who you are and how you will be remembered. I cannot advise on which path to take, but you must take one. To sit down at the crossroads is to embrace calamity."

—Queen Cathryn of Tuenosia

A knocked sounded on the door and, after a pause, Captain Eltirkar stepped inside. "Your pardons, my Lord Ushtyl and my Lord Arkesh, but Lady Ninanna is here and insists on seeing you."

Ushtyl glanced over at his compatriot, thinking of the last time Ninanna visited. He'd sat in this same room with Tazil, that time, and she had stolen command of their armies. Was it irony that brought her back again to the same place?

He set down his goblet of wine and glanced over to Arkesh who nodded. "Let her enter."

"As you wish, my Lord." Eltirkar's nose wrinkled. "Since it is Ninanna, would you like me to remain in attendance?"

"That may be wise."

Eltirkar gave the half-bow appropriate for a commander of his housecarls, then withdrew from the room. A moment later, Ninanna appeared with Eltirkar behind her. He closed the door and stood beside it as she crossed the room. The Sword-Whisperer had as stern an expression as Ushtyl had seen on her in a long time. She strode forward to stand before the two high lords and gave a bow slightly shallower than Eltirkar had given.

"Lady Ninanna," Ushtyl said. "I didn't expect to see you here. I assumed you were still pillaging Yeltikar and the rest of High Lord Arkesh's domain."

"I'm not here to see you, High Lord Ushtyl, but High Lord Arkesh."

Arkesh swirled the wine in his goblet. "What is it, Lady Ninanna?"

"You know exactly why I'm here, High Lord. I have orders from the empress, as you well know, to inspect all the warriors, arms, and armor in Yeltikar. But when I sought to enter the armory in your palace, fifty of your housecarls stood before me to block my path."

"Perhaps they resent your presence."

"They can resent my presence all they wish, but to defy the direct command of the empress is treason."

Ushtyl's eyebrows rose. The demeanor of Ninanna was completely different from when she'd approached him and Tazil to take command of the raid. Perhaps her meeting with the empress had given her a backbone.

"Treason?" Arkesh asked. "That word sounds overly harsh. I'm sure it is all a misunderstanding."

"It is defiance, my Lord," Ninanna said. "I have seen it often enough to know its mark. Need I remind you that the Empress Kayrstana is your liege just as she is mine? I was there when you swore your oath before the great wandering."

Ushtyl raised his hands in a placating gesture. "Peace, both of you, before anyone says something they'll regret." Ninanna crossed her arms, but gave him her attention though Arkesh continued to glare at Ninanna. "Might I offer you some wine, my Lady."

"Thank you, but no, my Lord. I have ridden all through the night to deal with this problem and mean to depart as soon as it is resolved."

"Of course, but let us sooth tempers, first."

Ninanna sighed. "Very well. I will take some wine."

Ushtyl nodded to Eltirkar who walked to the far end of the room and poured a goblet. He brought it stiffly to Ninanna before withdrawing back to the door. Ushtyl smiled. "There. Then let us drink to the good of the Syraestari people. I think we can all agree on that."

"To the Syraestari," both Ninanna and Arkesh said, each taking small sips from their goblets.

"Now, Lady Ninanna." He leaned forward and put a smile on his face appropriate to casual conversation. "I have often been curious. I heard that the dagger your carry was forged even before the Schism. Is that true?"

Ninanna blinked, surprise at the question evident in her eyes. "It is, my Lord."

"It is wondrous that things of such age have survived the Cataclysm. Might I see it?"

"Yes, my Lord." She unclasped the dagger from her belt and handed it to him, still in its sheath, hilt first. "It is only modestly remarkable. The smith gave it the slightest enchantment to help it keep its edge."

Ushtyl slid it partway out of its sheath and saw that the blade was just as she'd described. "Yet it is remarkable that something that once was so simple for our people can now be forged by only a handful of our best smiths." He glanced over at Arkesh, who looked to Ninanna.

"If you don't mind, Lady Ninanna?" the other high lord said.

"Of course, my Lord."

Ushtyl slid it back into the sheath and handed it to Arkesh. He drew the blade fully and tested its weight in his hand. "Perfectly balanced."

"Yes, my Lord. It was a gift from my husband."

"I see," Arkesh replied. Then, in a sudden movement, Arkesh twisted the blade in his hand and slashed it against his own left forearm, opening a river of blood. He dropped the dagger to the floor, and stumbled back. His chair toppled to the floor with a crash. "Treason!"

Ushtyl was on his feet in an instant, his goblet of wine flying from his hands as he leapt for Ninanna. She had tensed too late as he bore into her, carrying her bodily to the floor.

"What madness is this?" Ninanna cried out as she struggled beneath him. The outer doors flew open and a half-dozen housecarls ran into the room.

"Silence assassin!" Ushtyl snapped, driving her head into the floor. He'd never seen her fight, but she was a Sword-Whisperer, even if she'd spent the past millennia on the easy duty of guarding Kayrstana. He felt her tense, readying for a fight, and grabbed her by the back of the head again. But then she slumped forward, all resistance leaving her body.

"Bind her!" Ushtyl ordered Eltirkar. "Hands behind her back, and see to High Lord Arkesh!"

Eltirkar took Ushtyl's place over Ninanna and, twisting her hands behind her back, tied them roughly with a length of twine another housecarl brought over. Standing, Ushtyl glanced over to Arkesh who held a bandage up to the wound in his arm.

"It wasn't deep," Arkesh said, wincing. "I saw her prepare to lunge the moment before she struck."

Ushtyl shook his head. "Madness! I never would have guessed such brazen hatred from one such as Ninanna. To think she was the empress' right hand." Ninanna grunted in pain as Eltirkar and another housecarl wrenched her to her feet. To Ushtyl's surprise, her face was a blank mask. "What do you have to say for yourself?" he asked.

"Concoct what lies you will, High Lord," she replied evenly. "My protests here among your pawns would fall upon empty ears. I will not dance to your tune."

"You attempted to murder a high lord, in front of witnesses, no less. I'll have you beheaded for this."

"Not on your authority. Only the empress may order the execution of an Edrethyn."

"So be it," Ushtyl snapped. "Eltirkar, I command you to escort Ninanna to stand trial before Empress Kayrstana immediately. Take ten housecarls with you and see to it that none of the Sword-Whisperers know of her going. I'll not risk good warriors being dragged into treason on account of old loyalties."

"I had better go, too," Arkesh said.

"Are you fit enough to travel?"

"Yes, if your healer will see that the wound is properly bound."

"I'll have her summoned immediately." Ushtyl turned to Eltirkar. "Go quickly and securely."

"As you command, my Lord." He and the other housecarls turned Ninanna and dragged her from the room. She did not look back.

After the door closed behind them, Ushtyl turned to Arkesh. The high lord met his gaze with a half-smile. The plot had begun.

Imeskir paced restlessly outside the stable. It had been hours since he and Ninanna had arrived from Yeltikar. Hours since she'd headed off to her old quarters to make herself presentable before going in search of High Lord Arkesh. Imeskir had stolen a little sleep in the barracks to recover from their long ride, but minutes stretched into hours that left him anxious and worried.

He looked up at the darkening sky and ground his teeth. The first of the evening stars twinkled silently in the heavens and a gust of cool night air brushed around him. Enough was enough. Someone had to know something.

Imeskir reentered the palace and this time made his way to Ninanna's quarters. His heart skipped a beat as he saw the outer door of her room open wide. Walking through, he saw that the inner door was open, too. The chamber was empty of her travel gear. A Pi'aernoth worked within, sweeping the floor. "Where is Lady Ninanna?"

The Pi'aernoth looked up, startled, then immediately collapsed down to her knees with head bowed low. "I do not know, my Lord."

"What happened to her belongings?"

"My master's warriors came in and collected them. I was told to clean the room for the next guest."

"Was her sword here, too? Did they take that?"

"Yes, my Lord."

Imeskir cursed under his breath.

"Has something happened, my Lord?"

"I fear so," he said, his mind racing.

"I pray not, my Lord. The Lady Ninanna is a good woman. She was very kind to me."

"Yes, she is a good woman," Imeskir replied, reaching a decision. "What is your name, Pi'aernoth?"

"It is Talikae, my Lord."

"You will say nothing of me coming here, Talikae, not to anyone."

"Yes, my Lord, I obey."

As Imeskir left the room and wound his way through the palace corridors toward the guard kitchen it was an effort to keep his pace normal. One truth of warriors was that they gossiped over their meat. If there was truth to be had, he prayed it would be found there.

As he approached, the sound of laughter greeted him. He slowed his steps, listening.

"Bloodied her face up good, too," a man said. "I envied High Lord Ushtyl today. All human-lovers deserve as much."

"Too kind if you ask me," another said.

"And I thought Sword-Whisperers were supposed to be the best warriors of the realm. All stone-faced and glaring down at us simple housecarls," said the first. "But she did nothing. Just lay there while she was trussed up like some pig headed to the roasting pit."

Laughter met those words and Imeskir's heart turned cold. A third man said, "Still, to think she actually attacked High Lord Arkesh. I never would have believed it."

"Nor I, said the first man. "It's a fine world we live in where the empress has to protect her people from her own guardian. And now she'll have to pass judgment on her old friend."

"What if she tries to escape."

"Escape? She didn't even fight arrest. Captain Eltirkar will see her safe to Thusaeyanin, you can be sure of that."

Imeskir turned and ran for the stables, little heeding who marked him now. And if any obstacle stood in his path, he would carve it open with blood.

A sudden chill pulled Belarrin awake. He opened his eyes, listening for the quiet breathing of Zoltha and Yrpel, but heard only silence. Yrpel was never this still. Belarrin let his eyes wander around the interior of the dark room, but saw nothing. The air was stale and cold. He could only think of one possibility.

He sat up and, in the deepest recesses of the shelter, a pale mask glimmered in the faint light. Hood and cloak blended invisibly into the darkness. "Do you ever simply walk through a door?"

"No," the Shadow-Servant said.

Belarrin looked over at the still forms of Zoltha and Yrpel. "If you did anything to them..."

"Nothing harmful. They lie in a deeper sleep so that they won't disturb us, nor we them. A veil of shadow surrounds us so we might speak unhindered."

"Why are you troubling me?"

"I sense that you have reached an answer to my question."

Belarrin eyed the shadowed figure. It spoke to him like it wanted to be his guide, like a father, but it wasn't. It was a spy, a murderer, a Finnie. The feeling was peculiar. The old part of himself still wanted to bow in awe while the new part felt anger and doubt. Both halves knew fear. "What am I to you?"

"My chance," the Shadow-Servant replied.

"Your chance? Why should I care for your chances? You're a Finnie. If you know my answer, then you know that you're the enemy now. What makes you any different from the rest of them?"

The Shadow-Servant rocked back, and barked a laugh. "It has been a thousand years or more since I have been accused of being normal. Tell me, human, did any of your masters explain sorcery to you? Did any of them work for the liberation of your people?"

"No," Belarrin admitted.

"I am like them, but I am not like them," the Shadow-Servant replied. "An ally whether you see it or not. And if you find my benevolence hard to believe, then I assure you again that it is not for your people that I act, but mine."

Belarrin eyed the creature. "What do you want with me?"

"We both seek the same ends, if for different reasons. My people must leave this wretched land, but they don't want to. They have grown fat and comfortable on the labors of humanity. But if this war your Scions have brought becomes untenable, they may be convinced. I want my people hounded until that happens. Force them to see the folly of this supposed dominion we have carved. Then we will depart and you'll be left in peace."

"Where do you want to go?"

"Does it matter?" the Shadow-Servant asked. "It is away from here. Away from humanity."

"You want my new family to fight my old one. As usual, humans will do all the dying."

"Then do nothing and humans will still die. It is the nature of the world in this age, and all that came before, that humans fight and humans die," the Shadow-Servant replied. "If you are afraid of that, then perhaps you should give up. Run away and hide. But if you want to see the world change, then slavery must end. As long as the t'Okaedrin fight for my people, only humans will die. That is the price of freedom. If that is, in fact, what you desire."

"Perhaps we should leave, then," Belarrin retorted. "We should leave you and your people alone to rot here and find ourselves new homes free of slavery, free of Finnies."

"If you like, then go." The Shadow-Servant's even reply was startling. "But do you think you'll convince your new family to run from the battle they've fought all their lives? A few may agree, but after the great blood price they've paid, your Scions won't give up so easily. Do you believe that Sravika would agree to this? If she doesn't, will you flee without her? If High Lord Ushtyl believes he's lost contact with you, he will descend upon this camp and destroy all who remain."

"You are Finaestari. I do not trust you."

"I came here to bring you the truth. You have found it and you may do with it as you please. My hope has been that once your mind was freed you would see more than the world at your fingertips. That you would recognize the failings of my people, but also see that not all Syraestari are evil just as they are not all good. We fight a common battle, but if you wish to fight it alone, I won't stop you."

"As simple as that?"

"As simple as that."

"Then if I told you to leave, you would do so."

"I would," the Shadow-Servant replied. "Because I know the path that you will take. But before you do, consider the possibilities if we worked together. I've aided Scion bands many times already and will continue to do so. I've seen you with your new people. I know you care too much about them, especially Sravika, to cast any chance aside. You cannot hide how you look at her. I watched you run to her side, risking everything to heal her."

"If you were there, why didn't you help? I was nearly too late."

"You saved her yourself."

"But if I hadn't, if I'd failed. What would you have done then?"

"Nothing. If I stepped into your camp, the Scions would have fallen upon me. How many would I have been forced to kill so that I could save Sravika?"

"I've witnessed enough Syraestari sorcery to know such things can be done from a distance."

"It was too great an opportunity. I dared believe that in her injury, you could no longer ignore what you knew to be truth."

"Even if she had died."

"Without hesitation. I have risked far more, I have lost far greater than this. The future of both our peoples hinged upon you seeing through the lies that have bound your soul."

Belarrin shuddered, feeling Sravika's blood on his hands again, remembering her eyes as life slipped away. Yrpel's anguished cry rang out in his mind, tormented yet confused, too, about how such an injury might have happened. "It was you," he whispered. As soon as he heard his own words, he knew them for truth. All the veiled words hid this one fact. The Shadow-Servant had needed him. "You wounded Sravika."

The Shadow-Servant didn't stir as a single world fell from its lips. "Yes."

"But why?"

"You had to understand."

"I already believed!" Belarrin roared. His face flushed with heat and his palms dampened with sweat. But the Shadow-Servant was unmoved by the confession.

"You had decided with your mind, but you had to believe in your heart. The two are very different things."

"So you tried to murder the person I care most about in the world."

"If I had intended her dead, she would be. But yes, I attacked her. The certainty of that moment drove all doubt away. Even knowledge of what I have done does not sway you. You know that the t'Okaedrin are a lie."

"And you are the master of lies!" Belarrin clenched his fists. It was all he could do not to throw himself at the creature. "You're no better than the rest of your manipulative, deceitful, murderous kind."

"All of that I am, but I am not your enemy.

"You are now," Belarrin told him, his furious anger turning suddenly cold, hard.

"Do you think Sravika is the first person whose life I've weighed in the balance to bring about a greater purpose?"

"Whatever you may claim, whatever your reasons, you don't seek an ally. You want a tool to do your bidding."

"If that's all you see, I won't be able to convince you otherwise."

"No, you won't. I want nothing to do with you. Leave me and mine alone."

"Then so I shall." The Shadow-Servant leaned forward. "Do whatever you will do, Belarrin. Whether you name me enemy or friend, I am not your war. You know what is. Kargatsasir dotenada!"

Inky darkness flooded the narrow confines of the shelter blacking out even the faint starlight. Panicked, Belarrin fumbled for his spear, but even as he did, the deeper darkness faded to reveal that the far corner where the Shadow-Servant had sat was empty.

Nearby, Yrpel snorted in his sleep, then rolled over and began to snore softly.

Belarrin let out a deep sigh and sank backward to his sleeping pallet. He should have grappled for Words of Power, not his spear, when the sorcery filled the shelter. Old instincts came more easily.

He stared upward at the darkness overhead, his mind racing. He couldn't deny that the Shadow-Servants words and deeds had convinced him that the t'Okaedrin lived in chains. But that didn't make its actions right. That didn't make him beholden to the creature. He would fight against his old masters, but not because the Shadow-Servant wished it.

Belarrin sighed. Was he any less a liar? Any less an evil? He had murdered countless Scions including Sravika's own sister. And he had to keep lying. It was the only way he could remain free. It was the only way he could remain alive and help his new family. But how could they break free of the black stone that hung around his neck like an anchor? And what would Sravika think of him if she knew what a monster he was? There could never be redemption to wash the sins of his past away.

CHAPTER 27
Wind

"When I was young, I believed in a plan. The future was all that I would make of it, limited only by my own will to shape it. But no man can know where his path will lead. I have realized that few of us ever bother to look behind. Only when we do can we see the truth. We are, all of us, blundering in the dark."

-Parys First-Born

When the first grays of dawn pierced the opening of the shelter, Belarrin was still awake to see them. He arose quietly and crept past the still sleeping forms of Yrpel and Zoltha to the door. He had to get away from the camp for a while, away from everyone so he could think and consider.

But as he stepped outside his shelter, he froze. A dozen paces away, Sravika sat atop a boulder. "After yesterday's excitement, I had a feeling you would try to slink off alone again."

Belarrin sighed. "I need to figure out who I am."

"What does that mean?"

"I need to learn to use this sorcery," he replied with half the truth, cringing inwardly at the truth he couldn't confess. "It would be best if I were alone. I don't want to hurt anyone."

"What if you hurt yourself? You collapsed after healing me, so I should go with you just to be sure."

Despite his simmering remorse and anger, Sravika's easy tone brought a smile to his lips. "You sound like Zoltha."

"Zoltha is a wise man."

"That's true. But..." he hesitated, then firming his jaw, forced himself to meet her gaze. "I am not the hero you think I am."

If she was surprised by his words, she didn't show it. If anything, her eyes grew more earnest. "I know exactly what you are."

Belarrin shook his head. "No, you don't. Nor do I deserve what you think of me."

"Perhaps not, but you also don't know what I see." She paused, looked away a moment, then met his gaze again. "I know you are haunted by a specter from your past. You don't ever have to share it with me. Nor shall I ask. Whatever it is, you must forgive yourself. Whatever it is, I shall not judge you for it."

"You keep saying that, but you don't understand..." Belarrin cried out, his face flushing.

Sravika raised her hand, cutting him off. "Whatever it is, Belarrin. This I promise by the blood Henji shed on the bridge."

Belarrin let out a deep sigh and turned away, hating himself. If she knew the truth, no matter her promise, she would despise him with the fury of a hundred Cataclysms. It was but one more weight to add to his burdened shoulders. One more sin to bear. One more reason to hate Finnies for shaping him into the creature he had become. One more reason to hate himself for being too weak to face his own judgment. "I suppose I won't be able to convince you not to come with me today."

"No." Sravika laughed, her voice light again. She reached into her satchel and tossed him a strip of dried meat. "And, since I'm looking after you, eat that. You have the bearing of a man too preoccupied to notice his own hunger."

"Thank you." Belarrin took a bite into the tough meat. It didn't taste bad and, though salty and cold, was still reminiscent of venison. "Is there another clearing near here we could go to?"

"Yes, follow me." Sravika jumped off the boulder and led the way out of the camp.

As they set out, Belarrin found that he was more glad of Sravika's company than he'd expected to be. It meant he wouldn't be able to think too much. Perhaps that was better after all. He was exhausted by all the regret coursing through his mind. He should have shunned her company, but couldn't bring himself to say the words that would drive her away. There was something about her that caused him to laugh and smile when there was no cause for either. There was something warm about her presence, even stronger than he'd felt for Elestis. Belarrin shied away from what that thought meant.

As they passed one of the Scions on guard at the edge of the camp, the man greeted them, "The tree has fallen."

"But a new shoot rises," Sravika responded. The man's tone had been cheery but seemingly indifferent to the words. Sravika's reply, however, was almost reverent.

"I still don't know what that means," Belarrin told her.

Sravika chuckled. "There is no secret message. The answer is right on the surface."

"I don't understand."

"Where are your people, Belarrin?"

He shrugged uncomfortably as he lied. "I don't know. Dead, mostly."

"We are all the offspring of fallen trees, of lost and scattered peoples," Sravika said. "But here, with the Scions we have become something new. A new shoot rises from the ruin of the old, stronger and wiser. The answer to my question 'Where are your people' is 'Right here.'"

Belarrin nodded. "Yes, I think I'm beginning to understand."

"Sometimes I feel like I am still outside looking in, too," Sravika said. She hesitated a moment and Belarrin glanced her way. But her face was an unreadable mask. "I still think of my people, of my sister, and I rage and grieve. But this is my new people, my new family. And here we are." She stretched out her hand as they stepped into a small glade. It was no more than twenty paces across, but it would be enough for Belarrin to have some room for whatever happened. Not that he was entirely sure what that would be. "So now what?" Sravika asked.

"I don't know," Belarrin replied as he walked to the center of the clearing. He turned in a slow circle, looking up at the sky brightening with the dawn. It was a deep blue with patches of cloud gleaming orange and red in the new day's light. "Up until I healed you, almost everything I think I did had to do with the wind. That might be a good place to start."

"Maybe something small first."

Belarrin nodded and picked up a small fallen branch. Most of the leaves were still attached, some green, others aging to brown. "A breeze to rustle this branch."

Sravika said nothing, for which he was grateful. He suddenly felt very nervous. It was a personal thing, he realized, touching deep into his soul. Sharing it with another, especially when he had time to think about it, was awkward. Even if it was someone as warm and accepting as Sravika.

He drew in a deep breath and tried to imagine what the branch would look like moving beneath the wind. Nothing happened. He wished it to move. Nothing happened. What had he done back with Sravika? He shuddered at the memory, but forced himself to recall it. There was urgency welling up in his heart and he'd felt more aware, not of the world before his eyes, but the one behind it. Yes, that was what it had felt like when the veil of red had fallen across his vision. Belarrin paused and exhaled. Staring at the branch, he forced all of his thought into that one need. For a breath of wind.

The sorcery arose as a sensation, this time, a faint stirring of the hairs on his arm. A phantom breeze brushing his cheek. He felt a sensation of the branch flickering before it moved, before the words rose up in his throat. "Ae'irpiva to-sykas moerpylys!"

The sprig leapt to life in his hand, rustling fiercely in a breeze he couldn't feel. Blinking the golden lines from his vision, Belarrin stared at the branch. A few moments longer it danced in his hand, then fell still.

He heard Sravika laughing behind him and realized he was laughing too. He turned to her and shook his head. "I suppose I shouldn't be surprised by it, but I am."

"It's wonderful," she replied, breathless. "I think surprise is the perfect word for it. Are you dizzy at all?"

"No. Maybe because it was a small thing." Belarrin looked down at the branch. "Perhaps I should try something larger."

Her brows knit and concern entered her voice. "Nothing too big."

Belarrin nodded and, turning away, dropped the branch. It was easier to concentrate when he couldn't see her. He bowed his head, focusing again, reaching for that need, that sense of life and wonder. The words came easier this time, branding across his eyes in glistening gold. "Ae'irpiva soery-toelevai moerpylysoel!"

He raised his hands and tilted back his head as a gust of wind whipped through his clothing, tousling his hair, and pushing the grasses of the clearing flat against the ground. It was cool, refreshing, and he had the sensation that if he breathed in just a little more, he could catch the scent of creation itself. The wind blew longer this time and he reveled in each moment of it, freeing his mind from thought, enjoying the wonder. When at last it faded away, he lowered his hands slowly. A fleeting sense of dizziness echoed in the back of his mind and was gone. But it had been faint, far more distant a feeling than when he'd healed Sravika.

A scratching sound caused him to look at Sravika. She was sitting on the ground with a tanned deer hide out in front of her and was marking it with a piece of charcoal. "What are you doing?"

She looked up at him. "Writing down what you said."

"But you don't know how to write." He walked over to her and knelt down beside the hide. Sravika had drawn a few lines across the top of it. They were similar to what he saw in front of his eyes when he used sorcery, but different. More rounded.

"I have decided that I do."

"You've decided?"

She grinned. "Zoltha was right. We don't need to know the Finnie alphabet or that of our ancestors. All writing requires is someone with focus and a bit of imagination. So I decided to make up my own letters. Each symbol is a sound." She pointed to two lines that widened from a point. "I decided that this is the 'M' sound since it looks like a mountain." Then she pointed at a circle. "This is the 'B' sound for Belarrin because it looks like the gemstone you gave me."

His stomach lurched, but Belarrin kept his voice even as he asked, "Shouldn't that be 'S' for Sravika since you have it now?" He wanted to suggest that it be 'V' for Vitarria.

Sravika laughed. "It's my alphabet so I can make whatever letters I want."

"So what does the whole thing say?"

"Well the first word is 'Belarrin' since you're the one talking. Then you should know the rest 'Airpeva tosikas morpilis'."

"I don't know those words."

"Of course you do. It's what you said when you made the branch move."

"But I don't know them. The words come to me and I speak them, but afterwards I can't remember what I said."

Her eyebrows rose. "Is that normal?"

Belarrin shrugged. He couldn't tell her what the Shadow-Servant had said. Instead, he just replied, "I don't know, but that's how it works for me."

"Then it's twice as important I write them down. If you don't know what they are, at least I can record them."

"But you don't know what they mean."

"Does that matter?" Sravika hopped to her feet and walked over to the center of the clearing. Picking up the branch, she said. "Airpeva tosikas morpilis!"

Nothing happened.

"It doesn't work like that," Belarrin said, joining her. "I have to concentrate. I feel this sense of urgency, a greater awareness. It's hard to explain."

She nodded and closed her eyes. Drawing in a deep breath, she exhaled slowly then repeated, "Airpeva tosikas morpilis!"

Nothing happened.

Sravika sighed. "I suppose it was too much to hope."

He swallowed. "I don't think sorcery is like that. I think for most people, they'd have to know the words before they do anything."

Sravika smiled at him, but Belarrin could see the disappointment in her eyes. "I may have said them a little wrong, too. That probably matters. I'll just have to keep writing everything down. Eventually I'll figure out what the words mean and how to say them exactly. Then maybe I can try again."

"That's a good idea," Belarrin said, not wanting to crush her spirit.

"What next?" Sravika asked.

Belarrin scratched his chin. "I'd like to try something else with wind. It doesn't just blow. It also goes places nothing else can, finding things, pulling sound with it. It's fast, too, quicker than a Finnie on horseback."

"You sound like a poet." Sravika grinned.

Belarrin barely heard her, his mind racing. "I wonder…"

He concentrated on the Scion camp and the fire pit where they took their meals, remembering what it sounded like, what it felt like, to sit there among the others. He longed to hear, pulling in his breath and forcing the need. A seed of doubt glimmered in his mind. Did he know what he was doing? Was it madness? But he crushed his misgivings, focusing deep down.

He had the sensation of stars flashing across his mind, pin-points of light, ever in motion, some dim, some brilliant across a canopy of darkness. When the words suddenly poured over his eyes, they came like the shock of falling into an icy pool. "Ki'anpahityn soefili'os iv'yheunzemosa'ojoe lyrsenith'yndo amdelisti'a!"

"...are a clever leader," Fedigni said. "I know why you sent Sravika. She's always been kind despite our disagreements."

Belarrin stumbled back, startled at the sound of Fedigni's voice. It seemed to hang in the air, arising from nowhere. Belarrin stared at Sravika and she met his gaze, eyes wide. "You hear that too?"

She nodded as the voice of Chief Kitiger filled the air. "We both care about you."

"That isn't why you did it. Not this way. You need me to keep my mouth shut."

"You may not believe it, but both are true. You're my friend and my heart weeps for your loss. But I won't deny your accusations. What are we, Fedigni?"

"Fools, Kitiger. We are fools."

"That isn't..."

"You can stop your speeches." Fedigni's laugh sounded dry and bitter. "Neither you nor Sravika understand. I am a broken man. When I close my eyes at night, all I can see is revenge."

"Fedigni."

"No, I'm not angry with you, nor with Sravika. I know you care and I thank you for it. My anger is against those who killed my wife. I want them dead, Kitiger. I want them all dead, Finnie and Iron-Man. My caution is gone. If you want to join all the Scion bands together and make the Finnie cities weep with blood, all I want is to be in the front rank. There will..."

His voice faded away until the quiet sounds of leaves stirring in the wind filled the glade. Belarrin realized he was staring with wonder into Sravika's eyes. She smiled at him as she, too, became aware again of her surroundings. "That was amazing, Belarrin."

"I had no idea that was even possible."

Her smile faded as she sat down and crossed her legs. "Still, I'm sorry for Fedigni. I hope he doesn't feel ill-used by me. He is a good man."

"They were talking about the Scions joining together for a larger raid, weren't they?"

Sravika nodded. "Fedigni has always been the strongest opponent. He and his wife. It's unfortunate that things had to turn out this way for him, but it's good to finally have everyone in agreement. We've fought about this for years."

Belarrin hesitated as he considered his words. He'd wanted unity because it would make the Scions easy prey for his brothers. But now? "I must confess that I'm beginning to have my own doubts."

"What do you mean?"

He swallowed. There was no easy way to explain, other than to say it. "I'm worried that unity is too dangerous. It's far more likely to get us all killed than anything else."

"I don't understand. After we rescued you, you said the very opposite. You had the same idea yourself!"

Belarrin shook his head. "I was different then." He decided to use Fedigni's reasons. "I was angry and afraid. I wanted only vengeance. But my head has cleared now."

"And my mind has not?"

"That isn't what I meant. I mean only that I've had time for my heart to calm. Our only advantage is our secrecy. They never know when to expect an attack and, once done, we disappear into the wilderness before they can follow. I doubt the Iron-Men could wish for anything more than for us to be bold. If we join together, we won't be able to hide."

"Our warriors are courageous. We are not weak."

"That isn't what I meant either." Belarrin's mind raced. There had to be a way he could make her see without revealing the source of his knowledge. "The Iron-Men you see during the raids are very different from when they attack a wildman village. With Scion raids, they're always scattered and, by the time they retaliate, you're already disappearing into the forest. But in battles, they're methodical, disciplined, and relentless. They have the advantage of surprise, not the other way around. The only possible outcome is our destruction."

Sravika flinched, her eyes filling with hurt. "Are you saying I can't understand because they didn't slaughter my people?"

"No!" Belarrin cried. This wasn't working at all. "They are skilled beyond what you give them credit for."

"The same is true for you and us."

"But they're disciplined. They fight in ordered ranks. They march like a relentless wall, unassailable. And they have iron! In the end, no matter the will of the warrior, iron will always defeat stone."

Sravika's voice was small, sad but full of hope. "But now we have you."

"Yes, but the Finaestari have dozens of sorcerers with hundreds, maybe thousands, of years of knowledge. All I am doing is flailing here, hoping to stumble upon things they've known even before the Cataclysm."

"The Finaestari don't fight."

"Not yet, maybe," Belarrin replied, "because they haven't needed to."

"Because they are cowards."

"How can we know that if we haven't faced them? Their warriors are terrifying. Sravika, I've seen them. What they can do with a weapon makes even the Iron-Men look like children. And they're sorcerers, too, or at least their Sword-Whisperers are."

"I know you're afraid, Belarrin. We all are. But we must overcome it or else all humanity will end up in chains."

"This isn't fear, Sravika. I've seen what they're capable of and we are insufficient against it."

"Then what are we supposed to do?" Sravika cried. "Give up and die? Curl up and weep?"

"Of course not," Belarrin replied. "But we cannot pretend to be similar to the Iron-Men. We're nothing like them. We can't sacrifice the secrecy that keeps us alive to fight them as true warriors. The Iron-Men are taken from infancy and trained every day of their lives with iron weapons and armor. They drill under the eyes of Finaestari a thousand years old. What do we have by comparison? Freed slaves and wildmen refugees with stone weapons. They live in stone cities on the heights while we claw out an existence in mud hovels little different from a rat hole or a wolf den."

Sravika's face crumpled. "We aren't rats! We're people trying to survive the only way we can."

"That's not what I meant," Belarrin protested, but she didn't listen.

"I can't believe you think that of me, of us!" Sravika cried, jumping to her feet as tears poured down her face. "I thought you saw what I saw, loved what I loved. I thought you would fight with me to save it." She fled into the forest.

Belarrin stood to follow her, but hesitated with arm extended. "Sravika!"

But she didn't stop. He dropped his hand and sighed. "What am I going to do?"

There was no answer.

He sank back to the ground, staring at the grass before him, overwhelmed by helplessness and uncertainty. If only he could tell her who he really was, then she'd understand. She would understand that he knew what he was talking about. That he was right about the Iron-Men. But then she would know he killed her sister. Then she would want him dead, too. They all would kill the Iron-Man spy.

He let out a long slow sigh, then rose to his feet. He'd spent too much time in his own mind. Back home, drilling with the sword had helped clear his thoughts. If only that were possible here. He tried practicing with magic, using life and fire as well as wind, but his heart wasn't in it. The joy he'd experienced with each new incantation was crushed beneath his regrets. Perhaps this severing of his friendship with Sravika was for the best. What future could they have with Vitarria's blood on his hands? But if it was for the best, why did it hurt so much? For the first time, he dared to allow the thought to enter his mind. Did he love Sravika? Is that what made the pain so great? If only there were another way, if they had lived different lives.

He realized he was pacing and his path had taken him to the edge of the glade. A small bush grew nearby and he recognized it as a variety that bloomed with bright blue flowers in the spring. He knelt down beside it and thought of Sravika. The flowers would be beautiful next to her own deep blue eyes. He closed his eyes, drawing to mind her gentle smile and the way the sun shone in her golden hair. Finding the words he sought was easier than he'd expected, they burst from his lips in lines of gold to the racing of his own heart. Life poured into the plant and it grew before him, sprouting out buds that burst into a dozen flowers, each the size of his palm.

In awe, he plucked one of them and stared at it, smiling.

But what was he going to do with such a flower? Give it to Sravika? She might like it, but it was just a flower. His smile vanished. There could be no future between them. It was only a fool's dream. They were who they were. He was still a liar and a murderer and this was only a flower.

"What was I thinking?" he snarled. In a sudden fury, he drew a spell of fire and incinerated the bloom in his hand. It fell to the ground in ashes.

He turned away.

CHAPTER 28
Shorn

"Fear is what we had become because we had allowed it to happen. But at Dahiraetin, we passed through the fires of that fear. Upon that field, we found that the time had come. We stopped running."

—Lady Aerharyndra of Nahirazith

The Empress Kayrstana walked into her throne room, heart in throat. It was never supposed to have ended this way. She'd known the sacrifice of Ninanna was a possibility, but had refused to countenance it. Yet here it was, and she felt helpless to stop it. Leadership meant hard choices. Ninanna herself had taught her that, though neither could have expected such words to lead here.

Kayrstana loved Ushtyl and trusted him. It was that love and trust which drove her forward, casting doubts aside. She knew she had to be hard if she was to maintain what hold she had over the high lords. Even a moment of weakness and the lords would consume her. If Kayrstana faltered, Ninanna would be the weakness they sought.

But for all of Ushtyl's exhortations, Kayrstana knew she could never be as hard as he wanted. She had to save Ninanna. Not from condemnation, that was impossible now, but from death. She owed her old friend and guardian more than that, but could see no way to offer more without losing everything.

Her hopes for a small hearing had gone unmet. Word must have gone out as soon as High Lord Arkesh and Captain Eltirkar entered the city with their charge. Ninanna's unpopularity would have drawn many, while others simply were pulled to the drama. The throne room was packed with the lower nobility swarming both sides of the long lower floor. The balconies above them were even more crowded.

As she came into view, her chamberlain thumped his spear against the stone floor, raising a booming echo that silenced the room. Looking neither to her left nor to her right, Kayrstana strode slowly toward her throne, guarded on each side by four of her chosen t'Okaedrin. After this, they would have to become more than a temporary replacement for Ninanna. Perhaps they deserved a new title to mark their more regal role.

One of the first lessons of her childhood had been maintaining composure even when her heart raced within her. She climbed the dais with royal patience, her eyes lifting to the radiant window above it. It was circular in shape, ten paced across and tinted with yellow and red that gave the impression of the sun itself shining over her reign. She'd chosen robes of crimson and gold to match it. This day, of all days, she needed to remind the world of her authority without actually asserting it. The arrest of Ninanna was a blow to her prestige, but if she handled the hearing with strength, it would be a small one.

At the throne, she turned for the first time to truly survey the surrounding crowd. They watched in silent wonder, perhaps overcome by the magnificence of the afternoon sun streaming through the window to light upon her person in a glowing penumbra. Or perhaps, they merely waited in baited breath for the coming judgment.

Her eyes lowered to the main aisle that ran the length of the room. Standing midway down was Ninanna. Though her hands were bound behind her back, she stood as straight and tall as if she were positioned protectively at her old place beside the imperial throne. But her golden hair was disheveled by a long night bound in the saddle with no refreshment. Dried blood crusted her upper lip. Her black robes were stained with dirt. Kayrstana's lip twisted in quiet anger. Even prisoners were worthy of respect. It was a mark of shame on Arkesh and Eltirkar, but she doubted anyone else would see it that way. They stood behind Ninanna, well-groomed yet somehow less imposing, though accompanied by a score of housecarls, both her own and High Lord Ushtyl's.

She nodded to the brown-haired man standing just beneath the throne. Sarroth was both her captain of the guard and chamberlain. A century younger than herself, he was shorter than average for a Syraestari, but broad shouldered and strong. Seeing her gesture, he turned to face the room and shouted, "Her Imperial Majesty, the Empress Kayrstana, Guardian of the Nine Cities, Keeper of the Staff of Kayrkir, High Lady of all the Syraestari!"

As he fell silent, everyone knelt. Ninanna, her captors, all the gathered audience. All but the t'Okaedrin who dutifully surrounded her throne. In that moment, Kayrstana's gaze swept over the gathered crowd. Her eyes lit upon one man in the balcony to her right. It was Imeskir, the only one present in the black robes of the Sword-Whisperers. That was a small blessing, at least. Better for Ninanna not to be tried in front of her compatriots.

Kayrstana lowered herself onto her throne, allowing the curled tresses of her black hair to cascade around her shoulders. "Rise," she commanded. The faintest murmur passed through the assemblage as they stood. She turned her gaze on Arkesh. "It is our understanding that you have charges to bring, High Lord."

"Yes, Empress. I accuse Lady Ninanna of the attempted assassination of a high lord of the land."

"By which you mean yourself?"

"Yes, Empress." Another rustle of murmurs through the crowd, quickly stilled.

"Have you evidence or witnesses?" It occurred to her that even in this moment of trial, she had claim to a small victory. Though they removed her Hand, Arkesh and all the other rebellious high lords couldn't deny that only she held the authority to condemn a Syraestari to death."

"Both, Your Imperial Majesty. I have brought the dagger Ninanna used in the attack. In addition to myself, Captain Eltirkar and High Lord Ushtyl were witnesses to the crime. Though Ushtyl was unable to make the journey, I have a letter from him. I am sure you will recognize the writing as in his hand."

"I am sure I will," Kayrstana said as Arkesh handed the dagger and the letter to her chamberlain who carried them up to the throne. It only took a moment's glance for her to recognize the blade which she handed back to Sarroth. As she opened the letter, Arkesh continued, "Additionally, all the guards I have brought with me were present moments after the attack began and saw Ninanna detained."

Kayrstana nodded, her eyes dropping to the letter.

Empress Kayrstana,

It is with a sad hand that I must write to you of the events of this day past. I was conversing with High Lord Arkesh when Lady Ninanna demanded an audience. Though it was an unexpected interruption, I permitted it. Ninanna was irate over the delays in her census of High Lord Arkesh's estate. It was only a matter of confused directives, but she was inconsolable no matter how myself or High Lord Arkesh tried.

Then, to both our surprise, she claimed High Lord Arkesh was destroying the future of our people. She drew her dagger and leapt forward. Arkesh responded more quickly than I, rising and stumbling backward against his chair. He raised his hands to ward against the blow and received a deep gash along his forearm. I immediately lunged forward, taking Ninanna from the side and carrying her bodily to the floor.

Hearing our cries, guards emerged and assisted in detaining her. As she was taken away, she showed no remorse for this grievous deed.

I regret that I must share this news with you, for I know you have long counted her a friend. I, too, was hopeful to count her friend after the success of the raid against the wildmen in which she took part, but this is not to be. I had come to admire her as a warrior and thought her a woman of honor. In my heart I must believe that it was a singular lapse as she carried out her duties – a bowing to the great pressures she must have felt yet been ill-equipped to endure. But I must cast my own opinions aside and demand full justice be carried against her. Crimes against a high lord are but one step beneath crimes against the imperial throne itself. No matter the cause, there can be no mercy.

Please consider this my testimony on this matter. There has been some turmoil in Nahirazith as a result of this attack and I must remain behind to see to it.

Dutifully Yours,
Ushtyl
High Lord of Nahirazith

Kayrstana could only shake her head. Between the lines of Ushtyl's letter, she sensed hidden meanings. Doubtless this was part of the rebellious high lords' schemes to weaken her.

She knew that if Ushtyl had any choice, he would've protected Ninanna. Like him, she wanted to deny that the attack was possible. But he would never contrive such a thing. He loved Kayrstana and knew that she loved Ninanna as much as she would a sister. If only. Kayrstana stopped herself. If only Ninanna could've been more restrained.

Kayrstana raised her head. "I have read the words of High Lord Ushtyl. I will now hear the testimony of the witnesses."

"Yes, Empress," Arkesh said. He took a single step forward, then began, "I had traveled to Nahirazith to consult with High Lord Ushtyl on our mutual concern over the recent Scion raids." As he continued his story, Kayrstana only half listened. She knew there could be but one outcome. Between Ninanna's bloody dagger and the host of witnesses against her, she had no choice. The rest of the trial would be but a drama acted out for Arkesh and the many onlookers. They would search her for any sign of hesitation or any leniency for her old friend. Even the tiniest hint would be perceived as weakness that could only encourage their rebellion. Thus, Ninanna had to be condemned to die for her crimes. That was the only possible penalty for such a heinous act. But Kayrstana wouldn't allow that to happen. Though she would condemn Ninanna, Ninanna would not die. Kayrstana would see to it that she escaped her cell before the execution. It was the best she could do and would have to be enough.

When Arkesh finished his testimony, Captain Eltirkar spoke, and then one by one, the guards. Through it all, Ninanna remained silent and unmoving, with eyes fixed upon the empress' face. Kayrstana could see in that gaze that Ninanna knew. Kayrstana could only hope that her old friend understood. Ninanna would not die for this, but the trial had to go on.

After the accusers finished, Kayrstana turned to Ninanna. "Lady Ninanna, do you confess this crime? There are many witnesses who testify against you."

"The claims were given by three men who covet your power. Captain Eltirkar, even more than the others, has denounced your involvement in Nahirazith. Arkesh and Ushtyl both resist your rule. They know I am your guardian and that I have become your Hand in the census you ordered. That motive alone makes their testimony suspect."

"What of the guards?"

"They only know what they saw. They entered a room where High Lord Arkesh was bleeding from a gash to the arm with my weapon lying on the floor between us. They saw Ushtyl kneeling over me, constraining me. Their high lord, the hero."

"How was your dagger used if it wasn't you?"

"We were discussing Lost Age metallurgy, I saw no reason not to give the weapon when asked."

"If you are innocent, why did you not resist or even protest?"

"Because I did not want to kill," Ninanna replied. "It seemed wiser to appeal to you."

Kayrstana could only marvel at the evenness of her answers. Ninanna stood condemned and humiliated before all, but still didn't shrink. It almost made Kayrstana believe. She wanted to. It was inconceivable that Ninanna would lie to her, but it was even more unbelievable that Ushtyl would. She shied away from that impossible dilemma. It didn't matter anyway. Ninanna had no witnesses and the people had already decided against her. There could be but one outcome.

Arkesh stepped forward again. "Your Majesty, see how easily these lies rise to her lips. It is clear that this was more than an act of sudden rage. Ninanna planned this and now has conceived convenient lies, hoping it will create doubt in your heart. She plays upon your old history, abusing your ancient friendship."

Murmurs of agreement echoed throughout the hall. It wasn't a surprise. If Ninanna had been more popular, they might have believed otherwise. But her insistence on continuing her Oath to the humans had caused too much harm. If Ninanna were found innocent, everyone would believe Kayrstana sacrificed justice to keep a friend alive. Sadness and regret welled up in her, but Kayrstana kept her voice steady as she said, "Lady Ninanna, have you anything else to say concerning the weight of evidence brought against you?"

The firm resolution in Ninanna's gaze softened to sorrow. "I see in your eyes, Empress, that you will condemn me on the word of these rivals because you are afraid. Fear steals your courage and pulls you from the path of justice. After I am gone, you will come to learn that descending into tyranny may seem like the safest answer, but it isn't the right one and I fear you will find the final cost too high."

Gone. The word Ninanna spoke hovered over the throne room, drawing silence with it. Though no judgment had been spoken, she knew she would die. The audience knew she would die. The inevitability was written in the air. And even now, Kayrstana's Edrethyn tried to instruct her on the ways of honor. It was surprising to think that Ninanna had lived two thousand years and still believed that honor was the highest calling. That the needs of the people, of the empire, didn't sometimes demand a harder price.

Kayrstana drew in a deep breath. After everything else, the words felt too weak for their meaning, but she had to speak them. "Lady Ninanna, it is the judgment of this throne, that you are guilty of the crime of attempted assassination against a high lord of this realm. You are stripped of all titles and honors, all trust and friendship. You are no longer my Edrethyn. Your name shall be shorn from the annals of the Syraestari. Furthermore, you are sentenced to die before the headsman's axe. This shall be done with the rising of tomorrow's sun."

Ninanna didn't flinch beneath the condemnation. When Kayrstana fell silent, she said, "Am I to be stripped, also, of the right of speech accorded all condemned Syraestari since the foundation of this ancient realm?"

Kayrstana frowned. Enough was enough and it was time to end the farce of a trial. But she could think of no way to deny the request. "Speak then, but be quick for I have little patience."

"No patience for the servant who guarded you for a thousand years? Nothing for the one you once named friend?" For the first time, emotion entered Ninanna's voice. Pain. "Two thousand years, I have been a part of this people. I came alone amid the darkness of the Schism to become Syraestari. I was permitted, but never accepted. Twenty centuries of unrelenting service given gladly and without complaint, but ever have I been doubted and scorned. I have been cursed a human-lover for refusing to foreswear my Oath. Yes, I care about the fate of the other races, but I have never sacrificed my duty to the Syraestari. Yes, I believe enslavement is evil, as harmful to us as to humanity. But regardless of my beliefs and my service, I have always been forced apart by all but a few. It was your father, the Emperor Taerdranin who accepted me for who I was and you afterwards."

Grief tore through Kayrstana as she heard these words, followed by regret. Every word was like a knife stabbing into her heart. Every word was true. Could it be that Ninanna's claim of innocence was true? It didn't matter now. She was already condemned in the eyes of the people. Kayrstana crushed down her doubts and kept her composure steady. There were prices to pay that not even Ninanna could understand.

Be silent my old friend, Kayrstana silently urged Ninanna. I will rescue you, but you must trust me as I've trusted you.

But Ninanna didn't understand. Her head began to bow as she spoke, her voice dropping gradually quieter compelling those in attendance to lean forward to better hear her. "We swore the Oath of the Edrethyn, me to be your guardian, and you to be my shield. It is a two-edged sword of trust and duty. You know my heart, my soul, my devotion as no one else alive in this world. You know that I would not murder anyone, not even if you'd commanded it upon pain of death and eternal condemnation. You know how sacrosanct an oath is to me and you know each of the oaths that I bear. When I swore to be your guardian, you touched my shoulder and swore in the ancient words of our people that you would accept my fealty. You swore to guard me against those who sought me harm just as I swore to give my life to protect your body and soul. But now that is gone."

Ninanna's head lifted and her voice boomed across the crowded hall. "My liege, my Empress, you have cast aside everything you said to me upon that day, and for what? Idle ambition? Cowardice? You bow at the feet of liars, grovel before the masses, and cast away your most loyal servant. You treat me as though I were a stranger, rushing to hasty judgment. Is this truly what you have become?"

Kayrstana's face burned beneath the tirade, as much from anger now as from shame. It was all she could do to keep her voice calm as she replied more curtly than she'd intended, "You have spoken, Ninanna, as is your right. Now the deed is done and to the headsman you must go."

"Thus your oath to me is broken," Ninanna cried, "and thus is my oath to you shattered. Until this moment, you held my loyalty, my obedience, my fealty, but now your words carry no weight. Though my heart breaks, you are nothing to me!"

Kayrstana surged to her feet, as gasps at the impertinence filled the room. Her face purpled in rage. "Guards, take her away!"

"No, Kayrstana," Ninanna retorted as Captain Eltirkar stepped up behind her and laid a hand upon her shoulder. "By your own mouth, you have rescinded your authority over me."

"Guards!"

But then, Ninanna moved.

Her head swung back, smashing Captain Eltirkar in the forehead. He crumpled, unconscious, but as he did, her bound hands slid the dagger from his belt. Ninanna pivoted, turning her back on the empress, her fingers deftly swinging the blade to slice through the bonds at her wrists. A heartbeat of stunned silence, then chaos. The housecarls around Ninanna charged forward with blades drawn.

"Setrinas teferal!" Ninanna shouted. A sphere of shadow formed around her, then burst outward in a flash of crackling energy. It struck the onrushing guards and lifted them from their feet, flinging them back a dozen paces. Shouts of anger turned to fear as the gathered crowd fled for the doors.

"Protect the empress!" Sarroth bellowed to the t'Okaedrin and, drawing his sword, stepped in front of the throne. The t'Okaedrin closed ranks behind him as he said, "Your Majesty, you must go to safety."

"No," she replied, surprised at how calm her voice sounded. All that unfolded now, unfolded because of her. She might be a coward as Ninanna named her, but she would witness.

In the middle of the room, Ninanna knelt down to draw the unconscious Eltirkar's sword from its sheath as the housecarls gathered to attack again. High Lord Arkesh was at their head, his face red with anger. Ninanna advanced to meet his charge, deflecting his killing stroke, then pivoting to strike the housecarl behind him in the head with the flat of her blade. He crumpled as she swung away again, clipping another guard in the shin and knocking him to the floor.

The doors beyond filled with terrified onlookers seeking to escape, but Kayrstana could see there was no danger. Not to them. Only to the housecarls. Ninanna shifted and moved among them, quick as the wind, vague as a shadow. She chanted as she battled, a whisper that pervaded the room, rising above the screams and roars. There was fear on its breath, but Kayrstana did not move. Only one other remained at his place. The Sword-Whisperer Imeskir in the balcony watched the battle as a man transfixed.

Whether the housecarls attacked one by one or all together, it made no difference. Where ever their blades were, Ninanna was not. She slid among them, her sword flashing in the golden sun, striking head and shoulder, wrist and ankle. But always with the flat of the blade.

"Die human-lover!" Arkesh cried, his voice as frustrated as it was furious. He charged in with sword raised high.

Ninanna caught his attack with her guard, then turned at the hips, propelling him into the ranks of circling housecarls. Arkesh regained his footing and lunged again and Ninanna met him again. Blade locked against blade, then she flicked her wrist and spun. Her sword twisted around Arkesh's, tearing it from his grasp to clatter on the floor. Even as it fell, her left hand swung out, catching him full in the face. Arkesh staggered back, stunned, and she struck again with the palm of her hand. He collapsed to the floor.

Silence fell. The room stood empty but for Kayrstana, Sarroth and her t'Okaedrin guards, the wary and bruised housecarls, Ninanna, and above them all, Imeskir looking down.

Ninanna turned to face the empress and Kayrstana blanched beneath that stare of absolute pain. Perhaps she should have fled as Sarroth suggested. Ninanna advanced slowly toward the throne, the grip on her sword white-knuckled. Kayrstana trembled, but could not turn away from that gaze. Below her, Sarroth advanced a step, his own blade raised to a guard position.

But Ninanna stopped five paces from him and extended her left hand, palm up. "My husband's dagger. I will have it back, Kayrstana."

A part of her wanted to resist, but Kayrstana knew it would be a useless gesture. It would be petty, too. As if by clinging to this one defiance she might claim that all that had happened wasn't her fault. As if it weren't deserved. Ninanna's words stung, they burned like a tongue of fire. As they should. At least, Kayrstana reminded herself, Ninanna would live. "Give her the blade, Captain."

Without taking his eyes off Ninanna, Sarroth picked up the dagger and threw it to her. Ninanna caught it in her left hand, then turned away. The release of that gaze felt like the tearing open of a wound. No one stirred as Kayrstana's once-guardian strode down the center of the chamber, the few housecarls still alert blanching.

Ninanna stopped below where Imeskir watched from the balcony. A seed of doubt entered Kayrstana's mind. Why did he do nothing? She was the empress and she was under threat, but he only watched. What did that say of Sword-Whisperer loyalty?

Into the quiet of the throne room, Imeskir spoke in a voice barely above a whisper. "It was you on that day. I did see your eyes beneath that helm. I should've known it wasn't an idle dream."

Ninanna looked up at him and smiled. It was a gentle expression and one of overwhelming sorrow. She must have known what Imeskir meant, though Kayrstana did not. If Ninanna replied at all, she couldn't tell. A moment the gazes of the two Sword-Whisperers locked, then Ninanna picked up Arkesh's sword from the throne room floor and ran through the open doors.

CHAPTER 29
Beneath

"I can no longer be silent. Yes, in our arrogance, we brought ruin upon the peoples and the world that we had shaped from love. But the answer now is not to withdraw in fear of what new harm we might wreak. Can you not hear their wails as they writhe in the throes of their agony? I, for one, shall not leave them to suffer alone, even if by acting I consign my soul to the Abyss."

—Lady Henji at the Council of the Etyni

Ninanna wept.

She huddled in upon herself, crouching beneath a great cedar tree with only a small sputtering fire for comfort. And it was no comfort. Nothing mattered anymore. She cried for rage, for sorrow, for frustration and folly and shattered dreams. She was twice cast out, twice betrayed by those she had dared to love and respect. She had given life and soul to both halves of the Aestarin people in turn, but both had rejected her. She could think of but one moment in her life worse than this one.

Only that dreaded day she had learned both her husband and son were dead. She was alone, so alone.

It had not been easy, carving out a place for herself among the Syraestari. They were forever suspicious of one who would not renounce the Oath, but she'd been confident and certain of who and what she was. Now that, too, had been shorn away. What did anything matter? The past had been a lie and the future was meaningless. Perhaps it would be better if she just laid down and died. There was no one to weep over her grave. No one who would care if she were gone.

Footsteps sounded at the edge of the small glade, but Ninanna didn't bother to look up. She half-hoped it was Eltirkar or Arkesh coming to end her life. But the new arrival walked to the other side of the fire and sat down opposite. Still Ninanna didn't look up. She stared into the crimson flames. Each step she'd taken had felt so right, but somehow it had gone all wrong. She didn't know what she could have done better.

The flames shrank as the night deepened, from sputtering flames to glowing embers, while the moon crept its course across the heavens and Ninanna lay imprisoned behind the bars of her despair. Once she started down the road of doubt, it was impossible not to question every choice she'd made in the past thousand years. Had she been a fool to ever take guardianship over Kayrstana? Had she always lied to herself that she could find a place among the Syraestari? And what of her Oath. The ravages of the Cataclysm, the ruin of the world, had clouded her vision. Was Reigliff right about the compromises she'd made? Had she allowed herself to succumb to indolence? She dreaded the answers to each of the thousand questions rushing through her mind and so pushed onward to each new one afraid to stop. For if she relented, she might have to face the truth. She wasn't strong enough. Perhaps she never had been and that was the greatest, hardest truth.

A ragged breath tore past her lips, breaking her from her reverie to realize the newcomer was still there, sitting across from her. She let out a long sigh and looked up. "No elaborate entrance this time?" She didn't even trying to keep the bitterness from her voice.

"No." Reigliff's voice was surprisingly gentle.

She stared into his sad, solemn eyes and trembled in her grief. "I loved her! She was like a daughter to me and I a mother to her."

"I know."

"It was I who taught her what it was to be an empress. More than any other! I taught her the price that leadership exacts, and that the price must be paid. I taught her loyalty and sacrifice, honor and love for the people. And for what? To be thrown away, a broken vessel trampled underfoot. She cast me aside like some distasteful stranger, without even the smallest show of sorrow. All I was, all I had done, were as nothing to her."

"It was never my wish that you would feel this pain."

She scrubbed her cheeks with the back of her hand. "But you won in the end, didn't you?"

"I have won nothing."

"Yes, you did. You've showed me that my life is a lie. That all my dreams are nothing. That my hopes for our people were built on a crumbling foundation."

"That wasn't my intent."

"Of course it was."

"No, I want only for you to see that our hopes must be fixed upon something more."

"So now you have me, a broken women. What now?" she asked. But Reigliff didn't reply, he only stared at her behind his white mask stained crimson by the dying embers. "What!" Ninanna cried, the rage of it all burning her throat.

"I don't think I like you like this."

"Neither do I! But you should have thought of that before."

"I did not guide the empress' decision."

A growl rose up in Ninanna's throat. She leapt to her feet and stormed into the forest. The light of the fire quickly faded leaving her surrounded by the darkness beneath the trees. She stopped, her fists clenched as blood raced to heat her face. Then with a cry of fury, she returned to the fire. Reigliff sat unmoving.

"You!" she cried, pointing her finger at him. "All your meddling, playing with high lords and Scions, pushing and pulling from the shadows with no regard for whose lives get thrown down by the heaving anger of giants."

"The battle of empress and high lords would have happened whether I prodded or not," Reigliff replied. "I may have hastened this moment, but little more."

"Then what do you want from me? To hear that you were right? That the high lords are self-serving fools and the empress is the ficklest of them all? To hear that I care about humanity as much as I do the Syraestari? That I'm as much Hiraestari as I'm Syraestari? That I have failed my Oath and, in my lethargy left humanity to be plundered? Yes, yes I admit it all! I am a weak, feeble, broken woman who thought she could bring about something better, only to leave everything in ruins."

"I knew all that about you already," Reigliff replied. "The noble part. The savage part is your grief speaking. You're all those things. Syraestari and Hiraestari, lover of humans, follower of the Oath, even if that lay dormant for a while."

"Kind words I don't wish to hear." Ninanna sank down to sit beside the dying fire again. "Just leave me be."

"I knew all those things even before I freed you from your first prison," Reigliff said. "The one your old people threw you in."

Ninanna lifted her head, mind spinning as memories of another dark day flooded over her. Images of a prison cell and another night of hopelessness as she faced another headsman's axe. But a man had come with face hidden in shadow and had set her free. That night, she'd thought it was her husband's doing, but he'd been working on another plan. A plan that would've dragged him into ruin with her. Instead the doom was her own. Because of this man. "That was you?"

"It was," Reigliff replied. "You wouldn't recognize my voice. It has changed since those days. I freed you, not because I agreed with you, but because I was unwilling to see your life cast away. There was possibility in you then and there is possibility now."

"Forgive my lack of gratitude in this moment. The pain of all that's happened since washes over me. It seems even now I haven't changed, from headsman's axe to headsman's axe, traitor to traitor."

"It wasn't for gratitude that I told you. You've lost your purpose and I need you." Reigliff picked up several broken pieces of wood he must have brought with him and tossed them onto the embers. Then he blew, bringing the fire sputtering back to life. First the dead leaves caught, then the smaller branches until healthy flames licked upward again. "I was out watching the Scions and so only just learned what happened. Don't be too hard on yourself, Ninanna. We both have lived too long to avoid a thousand mistakes where, should we dwell too long, the despair of it might consume us. Cling instead to the truth that even your greatest enemy cannot deny that you've always sought to do what you believed was right. And for all your devotion, all your sacrifice, I cannot believe the empress would simply cast you away."

"I don't need your pity."

"I never pity," Reigliff replied. "Such an act, to cast away her closest friend and ally, is not in her character."

Ninanna shook her head. "You're wrong. I was wrong. It doesn't matter now."

"But it does. There is something more that we haven't seen."

"She tried to humble the high lords and overstepped herself by placing her faith in me. Given my unpopularity, I was too easy a target to discredit. The accusation against me left her feeling alone and afraid. She made a stupid choice thinking she could save herself."

"But she's not stupid."

"Enough!" Ninanna raised her hand. "I don't want to talk about it. She threw me to the wolves and the reason doesn't matter. Thinking about it only drives the knife deeper into my heart. I am done."

"Of course, please forgive me."

Ninanna gave a slight nod, then stared gloomily into the fire. "Is that the reason you found me? If so, you can leave now."

"To curl up and die? No, I'm not leaving yet I'll not leave until you find life again."

"Then you may be waiting a very long time."

"I don't think so. You just need a new purpose."

"While the wounds are still raw from the old? I hardly think so."

"This is exactly the time. I know the power of despair on the Aestarin soul. We both witnessed it in the Schism, the Great War, and the Cataclysm. I saw Aestari by the thousands lay down and die because they'd lost hope. You're too necessary for such a fate."

Ninanna snorted. "Necessary? I am unneeded, unwanted, and would pass unmissed."

"What about your Oath?"

"My Oath?" Ninanna looked up at him, suspicion entering her mind.

"You said you regretted not living up to your Oath to humanity. Can you pass so easily from this life without rectifying that?"

"Who are you to talk to me about my Oath?" Ninanna snapped.

"I've offended you," Reigliff said, rising to his feet. "I will leave you to your death."

"Stop!" She cried as he turned to go. "Can you ever do anything without manipulation?"

He paused and looked back at her. "We each go most easily to our strengths."

"I don't like it."

"But it worked."

"To the Abyss with you, Reigliff. Yes. Sit down." As he did as she instructed, Ninanna could see from his eyes that he was smiling behind his mask. "What?"

"I knew you were still in there, beneath all the grief."

"That's not necessarily good for you," she said sourly.

"I'll accept the risk."

"What is this about my Oath?"

"I need your help. As I told you once, I've been assisting the Scions with their raids. They call me 'the Shadow of Zaris,' because they think I bring justice. My intent is to make this land unlivable for our people. We must remember again who we were, abandon this lethargy, and seek out our own refuge."

"Why not keep doing as you have been?"

"I plan to, but it's no longer enough. Not with the t'Okaedrin infiltrating the Scions. It is to the infiltrated Scion band that I've given my greatest focus, but I can do so no longer. Belarrin, or Vistus if you prefer, is Siharrin. I've confirmed it. He has an affinity for the Breath of Isfalinis. I showed him the truth of this and he has begun to come to terms with his potential. But what should have been my greatest success is my greatest failure. He realized that his t'Okaedrin life was a lie." Reigliff hesitated. "But he no longer trusts me."

"Why not?"

"I pushed him too hard and earned his enmity."

As Reigliff explained what happened, Ninanna fought down a wave of disgust. "This is why I've never trusted you," she said. "You're willing to use anything, hurt anything, destroy anything in your path to see your purpose done. You see only tools for your ambitions, to be burned up then cast aside. What you've done to Belarrin is just like what Kayrstana did to me."

Reigliff bristled. "I seek neither glory nor power nor anything else the empress or the high lords call ambitions. Those are ephemeral things that fall to dust the harder one clutches."

"What you clutched became just as much dust. When Belarrin moved too slowly for your liking, you nearly killed someone close to him. Can you blame his hatred? There is no limit to what you would do to reach your goal."

"My every act is for the good of our people."

"Not good enough!" Ninanna cried. "No matter how noble your goal, it means nothing if you sacrifice your honor along the way. The outcome will always be dark and sullied. Keep telling yourself whatever comfortable lies you please. Say them enough and perhaps you'll believe them even as you blindly step ever closer to Cydion's abyssal heart." Ninanna bowed her head, her voice lowering to a whisper. "We are not tools and neither are you. We're all people with lives, with souls, each of which matters as much as the whole."

"Then I have lost you, too."

Ninanna couldn't tell if the sadness in his voice were real or feigned. She met his gaze to be sure her words sank in. "You've never had me. And what do you care, anyway? There are many more pliable tools to be found than in one who is nothing. Not Hiraestari, not Syraestari, neither a Sword-Singer nor a Sword-Whisperer. Twice cast out and twice alone."

"Do you think any of that matters to me? I don't care what titles you're given or what names you bear. Blood on the Bridge, how can I convince you? How can I show you how important this is? What more can I do to show you that you're more than a tool to me?" The anguish grew in his voice. Could it be real? Ninanna didn't dare allow herself to believe. "Do you want oaths?" he asked. "I will swear whatever you demand. Do you want me to draw my own blood and swear upon it? It shall be done! Do you want me to free a hundred slaves? I'll do it. Do you want to see that I still have a soul, that I'm still capable of pain, that I..." He hesitated, then drew in a deep raking breath that rasped and rattled in his throat. "Then that is what I must do. Highest Above blind me in your light, that is what I must do."

"Reigliff, I..." Ninanna began to say then stopped as he flung back his hood. Bowing forward, he pulled the mask free of his face and raised his head to look at her. Ninanna's breath caught in her throat. His entire face, from forehead to chin, from ear to ear, was a red, pink, and white mass of half-healed scar. Ooze seeped from still-open wounds. His too-normal eyes blinked above swollen cheeks and beneath seared brows. Ninanna opened her mouth to speak, but her throat strangled her voice. A shudder passed through her and she drew a deep breath barely managing to whisper, "How do you endure?"

"I endure," he said from lips more scar than flesh, "because I have to."

"The pain of it. How do you not go mad?"

"The pain is far less than I deserve," Reigliff replied, his voice calm and steady now. "I wear it now like any other garment. I've born these wounds from Cydion for nearly two thousand years. I know now that they will never heal. It does not matter. No one has looked upon my face since the world broke beneath us. I have shown no one because if they see my weakness, they won't hear my words. Is it enough that I unveil my own hidden pain? What else must I do for you to trust me?"

"It is enough."

Reigliff nodded and returned the mask to his face. Ninanna felt a stab of shame that she was relieved when his gruesome visage was hidden once more. As if reading her thoughts, his voice sharpened. "Do not pity me! Never pity me. I showed my face because I want your trust, not your sympathy. We all have burdens to bear and this is mine. If I thought it would bring pity I never would've shown you and to the Abyss with our whole world!"

"Then I will not pity you," Ninanna replied.

She could sense his hard smile beneath the mask. She marveled that he could ever smile. "Good."

"What is your plan?"

Reigliff bowed forward to stare into the embers, his barely revealed pain vanishing again. "No matter how much I doubt, I cannot pull away from the conviction that everything revolves around Belarrin. He is a part of the prophecy, the 'voice that rises above the sea, in wind and wrath from calumny.' He must be assisted in whatever it is that he is fated to do."

"I put no stake in prophecy, but I will watch over him for my Oath. Because this slavery must end."

"Thank you. Knowing he is secure eases the burden on my mind. I know Kayrstana's betrayal has cut you to the heart, but I cannot shy from the feeling that there is something behind it beyond fear. I must find out what."

Ninanna could only nod. He was probably right, but it hurt too much to even think about. She sighed. "Before I go, I'll need my sword."

Reigliff's eyes gleamed behind his mask. "For that, I already have a plan."

Arkesh sat up in his bed with a groan. His chamber high up in his palace at Yeltikar was dark with only hints of dawn light bleeding through the window's closed curtains. He had not slept well in days. Not since that accursed Ninanna stole his sword and escaped. He could feel his shame in the presence of the other high lords and half suspected the housecarls snickered whenever he passed. That Captain Eltirkar had been so quickly disarmed was his only redemption, pathetic though it was.

Arkesh had sent most of his housecarls out to hunt her. If his honor hadn't been enough motivation for them, the empress' reward surely was. But of Ninanna there was no sign. She probably had already fled the realm to go wallow with her beloved humans.

Rising, Arkesh donned his morning robe from the bedside chair where his Pi'aernotha Kaupet had left it. He walked to the nearest windows and pulled back the curtains. Dawn light met him, streaming over the distant Timnar Mountains. He looked down onto the streets below, already bustling with his people about their daily business. His people. No defiance from Ninanna or meddling from the empress could take them from him. His shame would pass, fading from memory just like the unwanted Ninanna would, and life would return to normal. Unless chance upon chance, she were actually caught and executed. Then he would know true joy.

For the moment, it was time to face the day. Arkesh turned to his dresser and froze. There, upon its highly polished walnut wood top lay his sword. The one Ninanna had taken. It had been shattered into a dozen pieces from hilt to point, but was laid out to appear almost whole.

"Abyss consume your soul, Ninanna!" He roared.

Sudden dark dread came over him with the rising of a new thought. Blood rushing to his face, he dashed from his room without bothering to change from his robe. He flew down the winding steps of his tower as quickly as he could. Ignoring the startled looks of courtiers, housecarls, and Pi'aernoth, he descended down into the lower cellars.

"Keys!" He roared to the housecarl standing guard outside the armory.

"My liege?"

"Open the Cydion-accursed door!"

"Yes, my Lord."

As the housecarl scrambled to obey, Arkesh asked, "Has there been any disturbance since last evening?"

"No, my Lord," the guard said, opening the door. "All has been quiet."

Arkesh pushed past him and saw what he had dreaded. The sword rack where he'd secured Ninanna's two-handed sword stood empty.

CHAPTER 30
Searching

"But you, oh Ithia, your deeds are not unknown. The voice that was silent shall scream in the scourge fires. Peace is a dream surrounded by pain. Writhe until even memory is forgotten and pray for the cleansing waters that shall quench the inferno."

—The Curse of Lelpfios

Belarrin awoke well before dawn, determined to disappear from the camp before Sravika awoke. Several days had passed since their argument and since then he'd done his best to avoid her. It wasn't always easy. She had become fast friends with Idysha, Chostir, and the others from the smelting camp. If he drew away completely from everyone else, they'd become concerned and that could only make matters worse.

But he had withdrawn in upon himself. When Sravika was around, he could feel her eyes on him, burrowing into his soul. It was for the best, though. Better this small pain for her than the larger agony of the truth. What he wanted and, perhaps what she wanted, too, was impossible. His soul was too tarnished, his crimes too great. He could only make it up to her as best he could. He wasn't sure how, but he was going to save her life. He was going to save as many of the Scions as he could.

The black stone around his neck had become a burden, reminding him of the t'Okaedrin lurking not far away, waiting on his call. It filled his thoughts. His brothers knew where the camp was, where he was, and he could think of nothing to turn them aside. But he had to. He'd thought so long and hard upon it, that his mind ached. If only he could share his secret with someone he trusted. But that was impossible. Not even wise Zoltha would understand.

No, he had to clear his thoughts. He had to go a day without thinking about Sravika or Vitarria. Without thinking of the meddling Shadow-Servant or the t'Okaedrin raiders waiting on his summons to destroy what he'd grown to love.

There would be only sorcery.

He pushed his practice beyond wind. The Shadow-Servant had used strange words to describe sorcery. He had called the wind Breath and said it was more than just the breeze. He'd also said Heart and Spark and used terms like volcanoes and life. Volcanoes spewed living fire that flowed like water. Inspired, Belarrin created a small flame that hovered above his shoulder, lighting his way to the small practice glade. Curiously, it stayed alight as long as he focused on it, but as soon as his thoughts shifted it vanished for lack of fuel. If he could create fire without anything to burn, he wondered if he could create light without fire. To his surprise, shaping a sphere of golden light was easier even than the fire. It felt different, too, as if the two were only vaguely related. When he'd created fire, there had been a sensation of the hairs on his arms curling even as an echo of warmth passed over him. But as he shaped the shining sphere, there was none of that. Instead there was a feeling of brilliance, like the yellow light of the sun falling upon him, but with as little warmth as a cold winter's day.

Each of the sensations as he cast were tantalizing, yet the joy he'd felt on that first day of practice with Sravika was gone. And try as he might, he couldn't keep out the errant thoughts which inevitably darkened his mood and sent him back into regret and fear. How could the Scions be so blind to their weaknesses that they eagerly longed to cast away their single advantage? Surely they could see they weren't the equals of the t'Okaedrin. It wasn't pride. It was folly!

How could he tell them in a way they'd understand? The only way he could see was to confess who he was. But would they even believe him then? The confessed traitor? No. They would kill him.

Realizing he was already brooding by the time he reached the glade, Belarrin forced himself to relax and concentrate. He spent several hours working with the Breath of Isfalinis. He conjured gusts of different sizes and from different directions. He gave himself the swiftness of wind, or at least something more akin to it, sprinting across the glade in half the time he normally could. He pushed tree limbs back to the point of snapping. He even found that wind could improve his hearing, not just channeling words from far away as he'd done before, but giving greater perception of all the woodlands around him. Under that spell, he sensed the rustle of every leaf on every tree around the glade. He heard a pair of rabbits scramble through the woods and a bird take flight. He half expected to hear the footsteps of Sravika approaching, but did not. A part of him longed for her to come find him, just as the rest of him wished she would stay away. But if she did come, they'd have to speak. He would see Vitarria in her eyes. And all of the pain would return to him again. He clutched his head, realizing it already had.

He screamed his frustration. Would that he could be free of this forever guilt and shame. But that was impossible. It was who he was. He had done what he'd done and no amount of regret could remove that stain upon his soul. Fury welled up in him without release, no target to fight, no enemy but himself.

A bitter chuckle escaped his throat. That was an implacable foe. There was no greater enemy than his own soul.

He would have wrestled with it if he could, tearing it out of his chest, no matter the cost. If not that, he would bend it, break it. The Shadow-Servant had said manipulating shadows would be impossible for him. No, he would find them. He would surround himself in shadows and let his soul burn in the darkness.

Belarrin clenched his eyes shut and drew upon his rage, his frustration, his self-loathing. He poured it into his mind, crushing it into a hard stone in his soul. All of his thoughts, all of his self. Awareness grew, as it had a few times already, of tiny points of light blazing out of darkness. They were dimmer, this time, as if further from reach, and they grew fainter the harder he concentrated. But he wasn't about to relent. He roared his fury, reaching out for the words he knew he should find. His heart pounded in his head, but he gave it no mind. His soul would kneel. He would find the shadow! He had turned away from so much already, failed repeatedly in all that really mattered and every triumph was tainted by regret. How was it that, though he'd always striven to do the right thing, the best thing, it always hurt so much?

The pulsing in his head grew louder, drowning out all sound, all thought, but still he didn't relent. All of his self focused on the points of gleaming light. His heart thundered to the point of bursting as the golden lines he sought finally blazed before his eyes. Throat rasping, words tore through his lips.

Belarrin blinked. Something cold rested against his cheek. He coughed and opened his eyes wider. He lay on the ground with the chill forest floor for a pillow. The sun gleamed through the trees to cast him in its warm glow. With a groan, he pushed himself to a sitting position. The pounding in his head had gone, but he still trembled from it.

He chuckled bitterly. He'd been warned.

When he felt steady enough, Belarrin rose to his feet and resumed his practice, once more working only with what he knew was in his grasp. But now he spent much of the time in silent contemplation, thinking on what each of those words meant. He worked more with the swiftness of the wind. He tried a spell that helped him move quicker, not just his legs but his arms. As he lunged around the glade with an imaginary sword in his hand, he laughed at how he'd look to an observer. But his movement definitely was quicker. In battle it would give a powerful edge. It wouldn't be enough, though. Not against all his brothers and their Finaestari masters.

By late in the afternoon, his stomach was rumbling with hunger and he felt weak and unfocused. Even small spells in enough quantity were exhausting, he realized. But he was reluctant to return to the camp. As dusk fell around him, though, his hunger convinced him. It was full dark when he arrived. All of the Scions had left the warm fire for their beds or guard duty. Only glowing red coals remained and, sitting facing them, Sravika.

He cursed silently, then let out a deep sigh and joined her. As he sat down, Sravika handed him a bowl of stew. He ate eagerly even though it had gone cold. When he finished, he set the bowl down and stared into the embers. The scents of ash and, more faintly, cooked venison, hung in the air only disbursed intermittently by cool gusts of the night wind. Clouds had passed over the sky that seemed to hang, looming, just above the treetops. Boots scuffled on pebbles as, in the distance, a guard slowly walked his rounds along the forest edge.

"I shouldn't have said we live like rats," Belarrin said at last. "I only meant we have so little. We don't have much more than the slaves do, and in some ways less."

"But we choose this life while they cannot," Sravika replied, her voice soft.

"I know, but..." Belarrin hesitated. "I don't think I can say any of this without making you angry. I don't want you to be angry with me."

"Nor do I wish to be."

"Or disappointed in me either."

"Belarrin." She turned to look at him for the first time. "I am not disappointed."

"Yes. You are. And you should be."

"No." The hint of anger entered her voice. She drew in a deep breath and it disappeared. "Not in the way you mean. I'm frustrated because I thought we agreed and now we don't. And it is so important."

"Whatever comes, Sravika, I am here with you. I'm frustrated, too. And afraid."

"Then let's not talk about it."

"But we need to."

"Eventually, yes. But I'm so tired."

Belarrin nodded and they fell silent, staring again into the embers. A part of him wanted to hold her hand like they had once before, but he did not. Nor did she. But they sat side by side, saying nothing until the fire faded to nothing. Then they each returned to their shelters. Yrpel was snoring when Belarrin entered. He lay down on his pallet, eyes wide open, wishing he could sleep as easily and soundly.

The next morning, he allowed himself to sleep until dawn. There would be no more hiding from Sravika. At least not directly. Still, he couldn't allow them to become too close. That would only make the pain greater in the end. No matter what he did, an unpleasant clash of truths was inevitable. One way or another she would learn who he was, eventually. No lie could endure without an ending.

He left his shelter and walked over to the cold fire pit. His friends from the smelter, along with Sravika, Mirnadd, and Henirgar, were eating a light breakfast of ground meal and gathered fruit.

"It's good to see you again," Zoltha said as Belarrin took a seat beside him. "You've been so preoccupied lately we've hardly had sight of you."

"Is everything going well?" Idysha asked. "Sravika says you practice sorcery all day."

"Don't let him fool you," Mirnadd said. "We all know he's out there dozing in the sun while we labor about the camp here."

Belarrin laughed. "If only it were so easy."

"Have you discovered anything that will drive the Finnies into the sea?" Henirgar asked.

"Nothing so grand as that. Mostly I'm just trying to understand what I'm doing." He frowned, struggling for a good analogy. "It's like fighting with a spear. If you spend too much time thinking about it, your enemy will kill you. I need to know how to do what I need to do until it becomes instinct. And I need to know what is impossible for me."

The others nodded and Zoltha leaned forward. "What can you tell us? Not to press and I'm sure it's hard to explain. But is there anything we could understand?"

Belarrin considered before he answered. He had to be careful about everything, given that the source of most of his knowledge was the Shadow-Servant. "It feels like sorcery is of different types. All the times I think I may have used it accidently in the past related to wind, like when we fought of the Iron-Men. Then, of course, I was able to heal Sravika. I imagine that may give me some skills related to living things, but I don't know. I was also able to make a leaf burst into flame, but that was harder. Creating fire may be at the edge of my abilities. There are some things I don't think I can do. Things related to darkness, certainly." He grinned sheepishly. "I tried to surround myself in shadows. It didn't work so well." He explained all his thoughts on wind and its different uses, how he could make himself move more quickly or hear better. "I'm trying to think of other things as well, not just from wind."

"Can you pull iron up from the ground so we don't have to fight with weapons of stone?" Yrpel asked.

Belarrin shook his head. "The earth is like the shadows, it's beyond my reach."

Yrpel sighed wistfully. "Could you imagine it, though? All of us armed and armored like the Iron-Men. That would give them a surprise!"

"We'd still have to learn to fight like they do," Belarrin replied, carefully avoiding eye contact with Sravika. That touched far too close on their argument.

"What about spears?" Chostir asked.

"Iron heads for spears or blades for swords, it's all the same thing."

"Not the heads, the shafts. You said you could affect living things." She grinned. "The trees spears came from were once alive."

Belarrin's brow furrowed. "I don't know."

"What good is changing the shaft, though?" Yrpel asked. "It's the spearhead that has to be strong enough to pierce the enemy's armor."

"Then don't use stone spearheads. Sharpen the shaft to a point," Chostir replied.

"Make one for me and I'll try this evening," Belarrin told her.

"Of course." She grinned.

As he rose to his feet, Mirnadd said, "Have a good nap out there today."

Belarrin laughed. "I'll do my best."

Chief Kitiger approached him as he left. "A few words, if I may."

"Certainly, what is it?"

"Nothing serious," the older man said with a soft smile. "Or at least nothing too serious. Your people seem to be settling in well."

"I'm glad. They are good friends."

"Each is finding their place. Yrpel and Idysha are strong warriors already. Zoltha is as wise a man as I have ever known. Chostir, I'm not so certain of. She works very hard, but I think she struggles to find her place."

Belarrin looked back at the small brown-haired woman and remembered the first time he'd seen her tied on the Boards. "Look deeper. I think you may just find she's the strongest of all of us, in her own way."

"What do you mean?"

"She has learned how to endure as no one else I've known, living beyond hope and faith, voicing the questions we've all felt. But despite that, she has never lost her dreams."

"Dreams?" Kitiger chuckled. "I cannot remember the last time I had time for dreams."

Belarrin nodded. He couldn't either. "Maybe we should start. Dreams are where ideas begin. What kind of a people can we be without dreams?"

Kitiger's smile faded. "Perhaps you are right. I will consider. Thank you, my friend."

As the chieftain turned away, Belarrin wanted to yell after him that they were all doomed. That a band of t'Okaedrin waited nearby and the only way to survive was to change camps. But he could remember the hunger for vengeance in Kitiger's eyes after Sravika had been healed. He'd been no different than the others, longing for the destruction of the Iron-Men. And of Belarrin, though he didn't know it. Instead, Belarrin asked, "You have no questions on sorcery?"

Kitiger faced him again. "No questions, but I will listen if you have something to say." The chieftain shook his head and laughed. "Truth be told, I don't know what to think of it. I'm not very good with the impossible, Belarrin. I trust that you have this gift for a reason and that it will, in some way, help us defeat the Iron-Men and free our people. But as to how you can use that gift, you'll have to tell me."

"I'm still searching."

Kitiger clasped him firmly on the arm. "Let me know when you have found the answer."

Belarrin watched the chieftain depart, impressed again at his wisdom and his perception. Kitiger truly was a leader to admire. As Belarrin turned to continue on his way, he saw Sravika ahead of him, standing near the edge of the camp with a tanned deerskin and a piece of charcoal in her hands.

"More writing sorcery?" he asked, walking up to her.

"If you'll let me," she replied.

"I don't think I could say no," Belarrin replied, though he wished he had the strength.

CHAPTER 31
Rain

*"Twice-burned charcoal blazes hotter than wood.
So, too, does the twice-tested man."*

—Unknown Scion of the Fallen Tree

When Belarrin and Sravika returned again that evening after a day of hard work, Chostir was waiting for them with a spear in her hands. Belarrin's other friends quickly gathered around as he took the weapon.

"I used an Iron-Man knife to make the point as sharp as possible," Chostir said.

Feeling the weight of the spear, Belarrin sensed that something was possible, though he wasn't quite sure what. Just a feeling in the back of his mind, almost instinctual. But as he considered, he became aware of all their eyes on him. After working alone, or nearly alone, the past few days in the glade it was strange.

"Can everyone step back a little please," he said. They quietly did as he asked, all their attention rapt on him and the spear.

"Perhaps if you turn around, Belarrin," Sravika suggested quietly, then withdrew herself.

Belarrin nodded and did as she said. With his back to them, facing out to the forest, he could still feel their gazes, but it was more distant. He lowered himself to a kneeling position with the spear still cradled in his hands. The grain of the shaft was mostly smooth, but he could still feel it between his fingers. There had been life here, once. Was that enough?

What he needed was for the spear to harden, but how to do that? Blacksmiths hammered iron, but iron wasn't alive. How did a man become hard? By becoming cold, closing in on himself, tightening. Like iron, in its own way. Perhaps there was truth in both. He needed the spear shaft to tighten in on itself.

Belarrin closed his eyes and tried to concentrate. Behind him, he heard the nervous shifting of his watching friends, the evening fire crackling in its pit, more distant Scions talking, children laughing. He pushed them all away until there was only darkness and silence. This time was different. He didn't know what he sought, not really. Only the outcome. He relaxed his mind and, instead of pushing for the words, let himself be pulled. He felt he could see pinpoints of light flecking his vision, most distant, a few close. As he focused, some drew closer and others farther, letting need drive him but without direction.

It was almost a surprise when golden light flashed across his eyes and words burst from his throat. "Nynoeka strati-nethlevai yndajah!"

He opened his eyes and looked down at the spear. At first glance, nothing had changed. But then he realized it seemed slightly smaller, both in diameter and in length. The grains beneath his fingers felt finer. Its color might have been a shade darker, too, though he couldn't be sure.

He rose to his feet and turned to the others, their eyes flashing between him and the weapon expectantly. "Chostir, please test its strength."

She took it gingerly, as one might take one of the glass goblets that Finaestari master craftsmen shaped.

"You won't break it treating it like that." Belarrin laughed.

Chostir looked up at him and her face broke into a wide grin. She walked over to a large boulder on the edge of the clearing. Holding the spear near the point with one hand and the butt with the other, she brought the shaft down against the edge of the stone. It bounced off, unblemished. She laughed as she shifted her grip to the center of the spear then lunged with all of her might, stabbing the stone like she might an Iron-Man. She nearly fell forward as the spear point deflected off the rock. Raising it again, she tested the point with her thumb and quickly jerked away. She stuck her bleeding thumb in her mouth. "Hard as iron, I cannot believe it!"

"Harder, maybe," Belarrin said, walking over to her. He doubted an iron blade would hold its point after such a thrust. Taking the spear from her, he inspected it. "I will do this with every weapon we have."

"Will that exhaust you?" Sravika asked as she and the others rejoined them.

"I don't know. I'll be careful," Belarrin replied. He turned back to Chostir. "Thank you for this. This is something I never would've thought of, and it makes all of us stronger, not just me. You've given our warriors an edge we've never had before."

Chostir beamed as Sravika stepped forward to give her a warm embrace. She was still grinning when they joined the other Scions for the evening meal. The dinner was a stew of venison, tubers, and crabapples. Mirnadd made a show of his distaste for the fruit again before digging into his food with relish.

As they were finishing, Kitiger rose to stand in front of the fire. He lifted his hands to draw the attention of those still fully in their own conversations. The gathered Scions quickly fell silent, shushing their more energetic children.

"My family. My friends. A new day is upon us. The Scion way has always been one of change with every act bringing joy and sorrow, greeting new family and bidding old farewell. But more than ever, change has come." He glanced over to where Belarrin sat among his friends. "I know that many here believe that the events of the past few days herald possibilities beyond our wildest dreams, the allure of triumphs heretofore unthinkable. But we must not let our enthusiasm overreach our wisdom. I've spoken with Belarrin and we must find the best way to use his abilities. Haste could bring death for him and catastrophe for our family. But tempered boldness could break the chains holding so many of our kindred in slavery."

As Kitiger paused, murmurs passed among the attentive crowd. Belarrin could hear few of them, for his focus was solely upon the chieftain in front of him. The t'Okaedrin within him was fascinated by Kitiger and how he lead the Scions, sometimes firmly, other times with gentle nudgings, and occasionally it seemed, merely adjusting to the currents flowing around him.

"This, I suspect, you all know and have begun to ponder," Kitiger continued. "But there is more, too, that is changing. Those of you who have been with us through the seasons, know the debates that have wracked our family over the future of the Scions. Every death brings not only its grief, but worry for the uncertain tomorrows where more deaths might await. We grieve for those lost and fret over how close we've always lived between triumph and destruction. As we persist, will our children be stronger or will we leave them weaker?"

This time when he fell silent no one spoke. It seemed to Belarrin that every Scion was leaning forward to hear the conclusion that had to be coming. Kitiger took another small step forward. "After careful consideration with your council leaders, I have decided the time has come for us to change what we are. I've reached out to the neighboring camps and their chieftains have agreed to hear our words. A few days from now, two will arrive and we will discuss whether or not our bands should join together as one."

Loud cheers nearly drowned Kitiger's last words with Yrpel's voice loudest among them. Belarrin looked over to see Sravika grinning widely. She saw him and her smile faltered. It reappeared a moment later with an edge of defiance to it. Belarrin felt no compunction to join the celebration, however. Not when he knew that unity could only bring destruction.

He looked out over the camp to see if anyone else appeared concerned, but saw no sign, not even from Fedigni. If some still worried as he did, they were unwilling to show it. Belarrin felt as though he sat in his own small circle of silence, surrounded by happy friends.

Only one chance remained open to him. He had to convince the other two chieftains that unity was a dangerous idea. If their camps were as divisive as his own had been once, it just might work. Only a few days ago, he would have done all he could to learn how the other chieftains were contacted. But now, he knew it was better that he didn't have the answer. There was safety in secrecy. Yet even if he convinced the other chieftains, that only solved part of the problem. He had to figure out how to get the Scions here out of reach of the t'Okaedrin who waited nearby.

He left the warmth of the campfire and found his bedroll. But rest was once again a struggle. Every time he fell asleep he dreamed of Vitarria. Her pale face hovered before him with blood-stained hair and cheeks. Only her eyes seemed alive and they were full of recrimination. Though she said nothing, he could hear words deep in his mind.

You killed me and I forgave you. Don't kill my sister, too.

Long before dawn, he gave up his futile efforts at sleep and rose. Fleeing the camp, he sought solitude in his sorcery glade. He hoped Sravika wouldn't follow him. Even if she didn't want to discuss what Kitiger had said, her presence would be a torment. In her face he'd see Vitarria, and when she spoke, he'd hear Vitarria's voice.

Belarrin looked up and realized the sun had risen to cast its warm rays over the tree tops. How long had he been standing, brooding, in the middle of the glade? "I would flee, if I thought it might do any good," he whispered, half to himself and half to the specter of Vitarria that filled his mind. "But they know where the camp is now. It wouldn't do any good. I cannot return to them, I cannot stay here. I cannot keep the stone or throw it away. The Scions wouldn't leave if I told them. More likely, they'd execute me and I'd deserve it. Highest Above, what can I do?"

Footsteps stirred behind him and he knew who it was before she spoke. He let out a deep sigh.

"You didn't think you could lose me so easily, did you?" Sravika's voice had laughter in it.

"No," Belarrin replied, turning to face her. As he did, her smile faltered. Her expression reminded him more of the sadness he'd seen during their hunting trip than the guilt he'd seen last night. But a moment later, her grin returned in full.

She had a bundle of about twenty spears slung on her back. Lowering them from her shoulders, she said, "Chostir and the others stayed up late last night removing stone heads from spears and sharpening the points."

Belarrin nodded. It was better to act as if there was no argument between them. They were just here as they always had been. The death of her sister, the unity of the Scions, the fear of his family. None of those existed in this glade. Here, there was only sorcery.

He did everything he could to drown his focus into the crafting of each spear. With each casting, he found the words he needed more easily, but he also felt strength flowing out of him. It wasn't nearly as easy as working with the wind.

When the twenty spears had been hardened, Sravika took them back to the camp while he rested. By the time she returned with a new bundle, he was ready to begin again. He was glad he didn't have to create the spears at the camp. It was easier to work here. To forget all the hard truths that he still had to face.

With the second set of spears, the task took longer and the third and fourth sets were even more difficult. He had to pause several minutes between each one before continuing on.

"You need to rest," Sravika told him when she arrived with the fifth set. "There will be time tomorrow."

"No," Belarrin replied, fighting off a wave of exhaustion. He could feel time running out. The chieftains were coming soon to lead the Scions to their final choice. Meanwhile, his brothers waited, doubtless with growing impatience. Each day the unavoidable moment when everything collapsed drew nearer. There was no time. No time for anything and he was out of ideas.

After Sravika left with that set, he sat down with his back to a tree on the far side of the glade and closed his eyes. For once, Vitarria's face didn't hover in front of him. He let out a deep breath as sleep overcame him.

When he opened his eyes again, the sun was over the tree line, stooping toward evening. Sravika sat a few paces away, legs crossed, watching with an expression of sorrow etched on her features. But as soon as their eyes met, the grief vanished to be replaced by a warm smile.

"These can wait," she said, patting the pile of spears beside her.

Belarrin grunted as he pushed himself to his feet. "No. I want them all done tonight." She didn't protest and handed him the first. The sleep had helped, but he could still feel the exhaustion clinging to his mind as he worked. Each time he sought the words that would harden the spears, he felt those curious stars drift through his mind, waiting for the slashes of golden light. There was something else to that surrounding darkness beyond the drifting stars, like distant clouds of crimson faint and barely discernable. He hadn't noticed them before and, in the fleeting moments he concentrated on them, he felt dread in the pit of his stomach. Yet he also couldn't deny a glimmer of longing, too.

At last, as twilight began to fill the glade, he finished his work. On their return walk to the camp, he was glad for Sravika's supportive arm around his waist.

The mood at the dinner feast was one of jubilant excitement, both for the new weapons and for the coming chieftains, but Belarrin didn't have the energy for it. He withdrew early to his shelter and fell asleep. The next day, he didn't return to the glade. Instead, he spent his day helping Zoltha, Idysha, and Chostir fletch arrows. After the exhaustion of sorcery, it was good to do something mundane with his hands – and to laugh again. The hauntings of his past and the helplessness that lay before him disappeared, if only for a few moments.

The morning after, though, he knew he had to continue his practice with sorcery. Whatever path lay before him, he had to be prepared. But when he and Sravika arrived at the practice glade, he stood in the middle of it at a loss for what to do.

As if reading his mind, Sravika said, "Why don't you try something you're sure you couldn't have done when you first started and see if you can now?"

Belarrin nodded. Rubbing his jaw, his mind turned to all he had done and learned. He looked up at the cloudy sky, thinking. "Yes."

Running to the edge of the glade he leapt up to catch the lowest branch of a tree and pulled himself up. Reaching down, he offered his hand to pull Sravika up, but she scrambled into the tree even more easily than he. She grinned at him. "What now?"

"I need to get higher." He reached for the next large limb above him, scaling higher and higher. He paused from time to time to look over his shoulder, then shook his head and climbed higher. Only when they were most of the way up the tree did he stop.

Climbing up next to him, Sravika perched easily on the limb. "You aren't going to try to fly like a bird are you?"

"Not likely." He pointed beyond the treetops on the far side of the glade toward the distant peaks. "Watch."

He kept his eyes open, sensing that he needed to see this time to find what he sought. Then he reached down inside himself, pulling upon the need as he had always done. The pinpoints of light flashed readily before his eyes and he pushed through them, seeking, his mind balanced between urgency and readiness. The slight tingling on his skin as the hairs on his arms stood on end told him he'd found what he sought. He lifted his eyes to the gray heavens as the words poured easily from his lips, "Itsoe'azhestva ryhota sypansypa!"

Beyond the familiar golden lines, a single brilliant streak of white flashed from the distant clouds to touch the mountainside. A few moments later, their tree trembled with the deep rumble of thunder.

"You..." Sravika swallowed. "You called lightning down from the sky. That's incredible!"

Belarrin realized he was smiling. The thrill of life flowed through him, like bonds connecting him to the world. It was intoxicating, drawing him forward, reaching for more. In a rush, he realized he was focusing again as even greater ideas entered his mind. The words came to him with startling quickness. In that moment as they blazed across his eyes and he opened his mouth to speak, the air shifted. It was like the heavens themselves had drawn breath. "Aezhita taeyhanyth olaes!"

He felt power welling within him, welling beyond him, filling his mind, filling the sky. He lifted his head to see the gray clouds overhead darken. Droplets fell upon his brow and he laughed at the wonder of it. Sravika was laughing, too, though her voice felt far away as the pressure filling his mind redoubled. A wave of dizziness washed over him and he slipped into darkness.

"Belarrin?" He heard Sravika's voice. Urgent. "Belarrin!"

Shaking his head, he opened his eyes and realized that Sravika's arms were wrapped tightly around him. His hair and clothes were damp. As far as he could see in any direction the heavens had opened with rain. "Was I out long?"

"Long enough to frighten me. How do you feel?"

"A little better now." He looked down and, seeing the ground far below, felt suddenly dizzy. "I think that may have been too much."

"If you're strong enough, we should climb down before the tree becomes too slick for handholds."

Belarrin nodded and reached for a nearby limb. He descended as quickly as he could, with Sravika following after. She had just dropped to the ground beside him when a boom of thunder rattled the forest.

"Was that you?" she asked.

"No."

"But you caused the rain, right?"

"Yes." He looked up at the clouds. "I think I should be careful about spells like that. It has unintended consequences."

"Like causing you to faint dead away?" Sravika asked dryly.

Belarrin laughed. “Yes.”

A second crash of thunder caused Sravika to shiver. “Is that what the Cataclysm was like when it first began, I wonder?” Sravika murmured, “Powers that, once unleashed by the Etyni, could no longer be controlled, until it tore the world apart.”

“Maybe.” Belarrin shuddered, vowing silently to be careful.

Returning to the camp, they found several of the Scions complaining about the rain. Belarrin decided not to tell them he’d caused it. Sravika must have read his mind because she glanced over at him with laughter in her eyes.

It drove everyone from the evening camp fire to their shelters where they huddled through the night. The thunder and lightning roared to the tempo of Belarrin’s nightmares until a final crash wrenched him to wakefulness. Belarrin looked up at the roof of his shelter, panting softly. He realized that the rain had ceased falling, leaving the wilderness to rest quietly. If only he could do the same.

CHAPTER 32
Tomorrow

"Humanity is a divisive race. They argue for the pleasure of it and fight over any petty provocation. It is this truth, more even than their fleeting lives, that dooms them."

—Spoken by Maelohn of Aveonfaili at the Council on the Oath, Lost Age

From the edge of camp, Belarrin watched the arriving chieftains in silence. Crimson sunset gleamed over the trees, basking the glade in its rich glow. Most of the band had gathered near the center around the roaring fire. Sravika stood next to him, but as the new arrivals came into view he felt a wall rising between them. The argument they'd avoided was coming to a head and more than that. He could feel his brothers lurking nearby, like an itch between his shoulder blades, and he still didn't know what to do.

The two chieftains, followed by several members from their bands and the envoys that had been sent to meet them, walked up to Kitiger. One chieftain was a tall giant of a man, as big as Yrpel and as broad at the shoulder. His right eye was missing and a long scar stretched down that whole side of his face, even up to split his dark hairline. The other man was nearly as tall but lanky, with sharp green eyes and bright blond hair tied back in a braid.

Chief Kitiger strode out from the fire to meet them. They embraced and, in the surrounding hush, their greetings were heard by all.

"The tree has fallen."

"But a new shoot rises."

They talked a moment quietly, then Kitiger turned to the watching Scions. "I'm pleased to introduce Chief Jarkon and Chief Grannif. Please welcome them."

As the Scion's cheered, Henirgar turned to Belarrin, smiling wide. "That's him!"

"Him? Who?"

"Jarkon! The chieftain who used to be an Iron-Man."

Belarrin turned to look again the chieftains. Jarkon was the larger, scarred man. Another t'Okaedrin here! Belarrin could only shake his head in amazement. But if this chieftain had come from the same place, then perhaps Belarrin could confess who he was, too. Perhaps that was the answer he'd been looking for. Belarrin swallowed, steeling his resolve. He had to talk to Jarkon alone. If anyone could understand, Jarkon would. And Jarkon would know how to tell the others.

Kitiger spoke to the two chieftains, "I know you're tired from your journey. Shall we feast and celebrate tonight and begin our discussion in the morning?"

Chief Grannif clapped his hands, grinning. "Good food and good friends. I can think of nothing better."

Jarkon nodded his agreement. "But for our meeting, I suggest we start with a smaller group and only broaden the discussion later. I imagine you have officers of some sort?"

"Council members, yes."

"Might we start there, then?" A half-smile formed on his face, lopsided from the scar tugging at his lip. "If the words they've said on the matter are half as strong as my own peoples', I imagine they know all the concerns well enough. And if not, we can always bring it to your people in the evening."

"It will make a good beginning," Kitiger replied. "My shelter will be large enough for all of us." He turned to face everyone gathered around the fire. "For now, my family, let us enjoy our meal together with those of the same spirit. May His Highest Above grant us wisdom in the days ahead."

As the meal began, Belarrin found he couldn't keep his eyes off Jarkon. He wanted to talk to him, to understand. It was more than just the desire to confess who he was and free these people from the hidden crisis. He wanted to know why Jarkon had left the t'Okaedrin. What had made him see the truth? And how did he join the Scions? How could Belarrin, likewise, reveal who he was to his friends without breaking them or himself?

But others wanted to speak to Jarkon and Grannif just as much. An ever-growing cluster of Scions gathered around the chieftains until it became clear there would be no chance for a private word this evening, at least. Hopefully on the morrow. But until then, Belarrin found he couldn't focus on the festivities. Sravika, Henirgar, and his smelting friends had been talking continuously through the meal and Belarrin couldn't recall one thing they'd said or any of his own replies. He needed answers from Jarkon and a resolution to the meeting. All hung upon that. He was weary of the weight of it.

Until he could have those answers, solitude seemed preferable. Departing his friends, he found Mirnadd, who was setting up the watches for the evening. "I'll take a turn at guard so someone else can enjoy the feast."

"You certain? You've been working hard and if anyone deserves to rest it's you."

"Too much on my mind," he replied honestly. "Maybe the night air will clear my thoughts."

"As you wish," Mirnadd replied. "You can take Yrpel's place. I'll assign him to later in the night."

Yrpel was more than happy to trade and, as laughter rose from around the campfire, Belarrin stepped out into the forest. With his spear clutched in his hands, he found a good place to watch over the darkening wood. The forest was too dim at night to see much of anything, so rather than pacing in some sort of round, he found a place halfway between the guards on either side of him. Sitting down and keeping still, he closed his eyes and listened. In the darkness, he would hear any threat long before he saw it.

The night was half spent when Yrpel came out to replace him. His grin was so wide that Belarrin could see it easily in the darkness. "You missed some great fun, Belarrin. The stories Grannif tells, ha! And Jarkon." Yrpel hit his chest with his fist. "There is a man after my own heart and never mind that he used to be an Iron-Man. Anyone can see now he's twice the Scion I could even hope to be."

"I'm glad you were able to join in."

"Sleep well, Belarrin."

"Good night."

He returned to his shelter and crawled inside. Zoltha was already asleep. Belarrin found his own pallet and curled up beneath his blanket but, as it had so often, sleep eluded him. It finally arrived in the form of nightmare. He stood in the center of the Scion camp, now a smoldering ruin of collapsed huts and scattered bodies. Before him lay Vitarria, Parvik, and a host of others he'd slain, some with faces he recognized and others he did not. He looked down at the blade in his hand and saw it stained with crimson. "No..." he whispered.

Belarrin turned as Zoltha approached. "You were supposed to be my friend."

"I... I am your friend," Belarrin replied.

Zoltha's brows lowered in confusion. "Then help us." He rested his hand upon Belarrin's shoulder. But as soon the contact was made, Zoltha staggered back shrieking as blood poured down his face.

"Zoltha!" Belarrin rushed forward, but Zoltha fell to the ground, his body pale and lifeless.

"Help us."

Belarrin turned to see Mirnadd reaching out to him with his hand. Belarrin pulled back, but was too late. As soon as Mirnadd touched him, he screamed. Blood streamed from eyes and nose as he stumbled forward, dead.

"Help us." It was Henirgar, with Chostir behind him.

"No, stay back!" Belarrin cried. He turned and ran, stumbling over the mounds of corpses in his haste. But no matter how far he ran, there was no end to the camp, no end to the burned out shelters, the sea of bodies. Every time he looked over his shoulder, he saw his friends chasing after.

"Help us!" They wailed in voices already full of agony.

But he was never fast enough. One by one they reached him and died. Henirgar then Chostir, Yrpel, Tayrja, and Idysha. Even the t'Okaedrin he loved chased him, pleading in desperation. But Bridionis, Hirnid, and Elestis died just like the others until there was only Sravika.

Frantic, Belarrin turned, trying to ward her off. "Don't touch me!"

Her eyes fixed on his. "I forgive you." Then she reached out and died with a scream that tore Belarrin's heart open. He collapsed beside her, staring into her face, white and bloodless. Empty eyes stared into his.

Belarrin lurched to wakefulness to see Zoltha kneeling beside him. As his friend reached out, Belarrin recoiled back from his touch. "No, don't!"

But as Zoltha grasped him by the shoulder, nothing happened. "Are you well?"

Belarrin drew in a ragged breath. "Nightmare."

"A deep one," Zoltha replied. "I had a hard time waking you. The chieftains are about to meet."

"Good." Belarrin sat up and ran a hand through his hair, trying to chase off the lingering fetters of the dream. "Good. Thank you for waking me."

When he crawled out of the shelter, he was surprised to see daylight. He couldn't remember the last time he'd overslept. Walking over to Kitiger's shelter, the threads of nightmare clung to his mind. Was he condemned to destroy all he loved?

The others were all present, standing in a loose cluster near the entrance. Belarrin joined Argluf and Obaudes, the other two who became councilors after being rescued in the last raid. Kitiger began by introducing everyone. When he named Belarrin, Grannif greeted him with an exuberant embrace that left him a little breathless. "Ha! A sorcerer. It's so amazing that I can hardly believe it."

Obaudes turned to Chief Jarkon. "The others tell me you were once an Iron-Man. Is that true?"

"It is," the large man replied. "Though it has been many years. Before you were born, I'm sure."

"I hadn't thought such a thing possible," Obaudes said.

Jarkon's grin was kindly, though the long scar diminished the effect. "All things are possible, I've found, where the heart of man is concerned."

"So I see." But Obaudes still looked uncertain. For Belarrin, though, he had no doubt. There was a difference in how Jarkon carried himself compared with the other Scions. It wasn't anything he could lay a finger on, just a measure of certainty, of self-discipline and control that reminded him of his t'Okaedrin brothers. Yes, Jarkon would have answers for him.

Kitiger ushered the group to the center of the structure where they took seats on the ground in a circle with the three chieftains at the furthest end. "As you both know," Kitiger said, nodding to the Jarkon and Grannif, "I've asked you here to consider the question of whether our bands should unify or not. The debate between my people has been fierce at times, but I believe we've all come to a consensus that it is a matter worth undertaking."

Belarrin cleared his throat. At Kitiger's glance, he said, "I must confess, chieftain, that I've begun to entertain misgivings."

A frown grew on Kitiger's face, deepening to displeasure before he could conceal it behind a gentle smile. He glanced warily at Fedigni, before saying, "Apparently, I misspoke. Nearly all of us have come to a consensus." But Fedigni made no sign of asserting his opinion. He carried the same grief-wracked face as the day he learned of his wife's death. "I recommend we proceed with what my people had all agreed to, prior to today," Kitiger suggested. "As I'm sure is the case with your people, the debate has been a long and hard one with all voices heard on all sides and I'd avoid revisiting it if I can."

Chief Jarkon leaned forward, his eyes fixed on Belarrin. "Still, I would hear his reasons. When one stands apart, the causes are seldom arrived at easily."

The once-Iron-Man's eyes were sharp and piercing. Belarrin turned to look at Sravika before speaking, even though he knew she could be of no support on this matter. But he was surprised when she smiled encouragingly at him. "It's like this," he said, turning back to Jarkon and the other chieftains. "I think we underestimate the Iron-Men and if we bind together, we will destroy that which makes us strongest. Our secrecy. I remember the Iron-Men when they attacked our village. I watched them on my march to the slave camps and when I was at my labors there. They have a discipline instilled from infancy beyond anything we could hope to achieve. When they fight, they're like one body, pouring each self into the greater whole. The hardened spears have done something to even the balance, but they still have iron armor we cannot match unless someone knows how to make armor from tree trunks."

"But you're a sorcerer," Grannif said.

"And they have theirs, too, chief. I'm only just beginning to understand what that means. True, I am getting better each day, as Sravika can attest." He glanced her way again before continuing, "but that cannot compare to the hundreds or even thousands of years the Finaestari sorcerers have had. Our advantage is in secrecy. When they don't know where we will strike, they have to defend against everything. They pursue us, but we melt into the wilderness."

"One of our camps was recently destroyed," Grannif said.

Belarrin suppressed a flinch. "Yes, but one in how many years of resistance? Even ignoring their arms and armor, we aren't the Iron-Men and cannot become like them without years of practice free from raiding and deaths. We have courage and resolve that may well surpass theirs, but they have discipline such as we cannot hope to achieve. If we banded together, I'm as confident as you that we'd be successful in the first attack and maybe the next few. But in the end, unity only ensures our destruction."

Grannif frowned and scratched his jaw. "The same concerns we've all had, though I wonder that Belarrin exaggerates. What do you think?"

"I agree, Grannif," Kitiger replied. "Divided we are dying. Our only choice is to unite. Knowing the risks beforehand will allow us to minimize them. To my mind, we must decide how and when we are to join together and how best to make use of our combined strength."

They spoke further of plans and possibilities, but Belarrin had largely ceased to listen. The details no longer mattered to him, only that his warnings had been so quickly dismissed. He'd had his change of heart too late to make a difference. Was that always to be his fate?

He might even have agreed that there was a slim chance at triumph beyond all his doubts. But all that was meaningless with the stone. He could feel its weight around his neck, like a mountain pulling him into the earth. There was no way out. No way to be freed of it but by bringing destruction on these people. He couldn't flee and saw no choice more noble than to fight and die with them when that time came.

"Chief Jarkon," Kitiger's words broke through the cloud of Belarrin's thoughts. "You have been quiet for quite some time. What do you think?"

Jarkon leaned back, his large shoulders rolling. He glanced at Belarrin. "I came to this meeting convinced that unity was the answer, but there is truth in Belarrin's words. I'm not saying I agree with him, but nor can I agree fully with either of you. It's more than just a weighing of risks and choices. Could it be that we have become so embroiled in our war that we've come to neglect tomorrow in the face of today?"

Grannif's brow furrowed. "Our whole battle is for tomorrow. We've given up everything else to free our people."

"But is that the right choice? It isn't a matter of small bands or large, it's the futility in the course we've chosen. Belarrin's perceptions of the Iron-Men are as accurate as any I've heard and I'm certain he is right. If we join together, they'll track us down and destroy us. But remaining scattered is no better, as we have all come to know. Divided we die slowly, but no less certainly." Jarkon paused a moment, thinking, then said, "We have a chance to change everything. To change the whole war. We must let go of our old image for the Fallen Tree and claim a new one. The sacrifices would be different and no less great, but it's the only path I can see remaining to us. I suggest we join together just as we've discussed but not to raid. Instead, we leave."

"What madness is this?" Grannif cried.

Kitiger nodded. "Jarkon, there is no shame if your soul is weary from the fight. We know how valorously you've fought and would understand if you chose to set down your spear and seek a more peaceful life."

"I am not weary from the fight," Jarkon replied. "I'm telling you that the battle we've chosen is a futile one. We must choose a war we can win. We're dying, slowly but surely, and dead men cannot bring freedom. We need time and distance. We have former slaves who know smelting and, as I understand it, you were once a miner, Kitiger. We need to learn how to find ore, cut it from the rock, and forge weapons of iron. We need permanent towns and villages and time to prepare. Only when we can face the Iron-Men on their own terms will we have a chance."

Belarrin nodded, seeing the possibilities. Jarkon had spoken true, seeing beyond the immediate goals that held the Scions prisoners. And, even more than that, if the Scions did as he proposed, he could cast away his stone as they disappeared and be free of the Finaestari forever.

But Grannif shook his head. "I cannot do that. I cannot abandon all those people."

"Nor will I," Fedigni spoke for the first time. "My wife cannot have died in vain."

Kitiger frowned. "I cannot see your way, either Jarkon. You call for us to give up too much."

Belarrin's heart lurched between hope and despair as Jarkon said, "Those who we've lost have not died in vain. Every sacrifice paid is a worthy one, but we must ask ourselves if we are honestly making the difference we all yearn for. Are we freeing slaves to a better life? Instead of dying in bondage, they are slain as Scions."

"We all know the cost of our struggle and none of us shirk from the price," Kitiger said.

"I know, my friend, but is that enough? What does it say of us that only a pittance survive to see old age? I remember the stories I was told when I was still an Iron-Man. We were told that the Scions lived a meager existence, scratching out a life of want in dirty hovels in the wilderness whereas the slaves have shelter and food as they need."

Obaudes leapt to his feet, face flashing in anger. "Now he uses Iron-Man words against us? He betrays his true heart, that he seeks to destroy our cause!"

Jarkon looked up at him. "Even in lies there is a seed of truth and that kernel is what we must acknowledge if we're ever to become more than we are. But if you believe me the enemy, then strike me down. I will not resist."

For a moment, Belarrin thought Obaudes might, but Kitiger said, "Peace, Obaudes. If you knew Jarkon you wouldn't say such things. I won't have uncouth accusations, let alone the spilling of blood between friends. For we are all friends here."

Jarkon nodded immediately, Obaudes with greater hesitation.

"Perhaps we've been discussing too long," Grannif suggested. "It might be good for us to get some fresh air outside. When our hearts have cooled, we can continue. And is that roast venison I smell?"

"It is." Kitiger smiled. "Please follow me."

As Belarrin passed Obaudes on his way out of the shelter, the other man muttered, "Cowards, the both of you."

CHAPTER 33
Freedom

"I do not know what this day will hold or who, if any of us, will see its end. But that is of less import. It matters more to me who was present to see its beginning."

—Lord Arrik of Tuenosia

After the tension of the meeting, Belarrin just wanted to be alone. They wouldn't listen to Jarkon, at least not now. Only when a remnant survived the folly they proposed, but not even that could happen. His brothers were waiting patiently for his signal and would continue to bide their time. But if the Scions left the camp, the t'Okaedrin were sure to attack regardless of what Belarrin did. He wouldn't be able to hold them back.

Out of the corner of his eye, he saw Sravika waiting for him, but he turned away from her and the mouth-watering aroma of venison, heading into the forest. There the green of the wilderness surrounded him and the gloom of grey skies overhead matched his mood. More than any food, he needed to be alone. Only in solitude, as always, could he unleash his frustration.

Reaching the clearing where he'd practiced his magic, he sank to his knees in the center of it and bowed his head to his hands. "Highest Above, what am I to do now?"

Jarkon was right. They had to flee, but it didn't matter. Nothing mattered now because they wouldn't listen. T'Okaedrin were blinded from childhood by lies that sounded like truth while Scions were blinded by a fight they were too close to see.

He shook his head. All of those thoughts and arguments were meaningless. All that mattered was the stone around his neck. Plans and schemes, unity and disunity, they all ended with that stone. When Obaudes berated Jarkon, no one had rushed to defend him, a chieftain who'd spent decades as a Scion. If that was all his reputation warranted, how much reprieve might Belarrin receive if he confessed? An infiltrator mere days from seeking their destruction?

"I am a coward, just like Obaudes said." A coward because he couldn't bring himself to risk condemnation and death

He drew in deep breaths, letting his ears fill with the sounds of the forest. The creaking of tree limbs, the rustle of leaves. Cool wind touched his face rich with loamy scents. He could remember a time when he'd been troubled by the chaos of the wilderness, but that had passed. Now he found a simple peace in it he could find nowhere else.

The smell of venison came to his nose the same moment he heard boots scuffing behind him. He turned to see Sravika approaching with a bowl of stew in one hand and her spear cradled in the other.

She blanched as he looked at her. With so many emotions warring within him, he wasn't sure what expression she saw. But whatever it was, she smiled. "A peace offering."

The bitterest part Belarrin thought about refusing, but his grumbling stomach gave him away. He took the bowl. "Thank you."

Sravika sank down to her knees beside him. "I don't know what to say. I don't know what I can say. I could see in your eyes that Jarkon's words appealed to you. I confess, it has some appeal for me, too, but it's impossible. He doesn't understand the sacrifice he's asking of us. A few might listen, but only a few. And I'm sorry the others dismissed your words so quickly. If I was any part of hurting you, I'm sorry for that, too."

"You did what you had to do." She flinched and guilt washed over him. "You have nothing to apologize for. I owe you more than I can ever say."

"There are no debts between us, Belarrin."

It was Belarrin's turn to grimace as the word coward echoed through his mind. Too afraid to confess the truth and face death, did he have any courage at all? He was unworthy of anyone he had dared name friend. "There is a huge debt," he told her, "one I can never repay."

She touched his arm and he stared into his earnest eyes. "Belarrin, you must cast off your old life and old regrets. How I wish I could ease that burden for you."

"You don't understand."

"I don't have to."

"You do! If you knew!" Belarrin cried, pulling his hand way from her touch. Staring at her now, seeing Vitarria in her eyes, he knew he could hide no longer. No more fear, no more cowardice. It was better that she hate him, that he die. Then, at least, everyone else be saved. He sighed, then said, "Sravika, I am going to confess something and when you hear it, you'll hate me."

"I won't."

"Please, let me finish. You should hate me and you will. Hatred is the smallest measure of what I deserve. The only justification I can give, and it is no justification at all, is that I thought I was doing right. But I've seen that my path was wrong. You showed me that. You and Zoltha and everyone else. I will bow before any judgment you might give, even death. And I must confess everything to our people, too."

Sravika bowed her head. "Belarrin, I told you, you don't have to do this."

"I do, I must. Sravika, I'm not who you think I am. I didn't come here to..." He stopped as his eyes caught a glimmer of motion on the far side of the clearing. Belarrin turned to see a Finaestari woman in black flowing robes step out of the forest. Golden blond hair hung loose about her shoulders and a large two-handed blade was slung on her back. It was the Sword-Whisperer.

Belarrin blinked. A moment of terror, a moment of dread. Then instinct overcame thought. He leapt to his feet as golden lines blazed before his eyes. "Ae'irpiva aestari i'arpas!"

A hurricane wind surged from his outstretched hands.

"Setrinas asirda otyn!" the woman cried, flinging hands out to either side. A dark translucent sphere formed around her, breaking the gale like a horn of rock. The wind surged by on either side, tearing into the forest where uprooting brush and snapped tree limbs. After it passed, she dropped her hands and the sphere vanished.

"Peace!" the woman shouted as Sravika leapt up beside Belarrin, flinging her spear. It flew towards the center of her chest with deadly accuracy, but at the last moment, the Fin-aestari shifted her weight and slid aside. The spear passed by to bury its hardened tip into a tree.

"Peace!" The woman raised her hands up with palms open and toward them. "I come with a message for the man called Vistus."

Belarrin flinched, hearing the name he'd cast aside. "What do you want?"

The Sword-Whisperer lowered her hands slowly. "I am Ninanna, an ally of the Shadow-Servant, and I carry a warning."

"I want nothing to do with that murderer."

"Nor did I." Ninanna shook her head. "But His Highest Above had a different plan for me."

"But..."

"You are out of time, Vistus," she interrupted. "The t'Okaedrin are coming."

Ninanna reached into a satchel at her side, then raised her hand, palm up. Shards of black stone fell from her fingertips. "You weren't the only one."

"What?" A cold chill crept up Belarrin's spine.

"I only just learned."

"Who?"

"I don't know. These were in one of the Scion shelters, but I don't know who slept there."

"Wait!" Sravika cried. "Why is she calling you Vistus? Who is this?"

"I'm a friend you never knew you had." Ninanna's smile was grim. She looked back at Belarrin. "I know you hate the Shadow-Servant and with reason. He is as evil as he is good, but that doesn't matter now. The enemy is coming and I don't know how long you have. A few minutes, a few hours at most. Vistus, you know how the t'Okaedrin will destroy the camp. If I could stand with you, I would, but my presence would divide your people when they must unite. Hurry!" She bowed her head. "A new shoot rises."

Belarrin could only watch, stunned, as she turned on her heel and disappeared into the forest. His mind raced, but the hand pulling on his arm forced through his thoughts. "What did she mean? Who are you?"

"A coward. I waited too long. There should have been time!"

"Who is Vistus?" Sravika demanded, pulling him to face her.

His shoulders slumped. "It's what I was about to tell you. I was an Iron-Man named Vistus. The Finnies sent me to find and destroy you." He looked at her, not permitting himself the anguish of an excuse. "But I'm not one anymore. I don't want any of that. I want to be a Scion, to be free of who I was."

"An Iron-Man." Sravika's eyes widened. "I knew you were different. I knew that you had…" She cut off. "But I thought it was a human raid, not this. Highest Above, I never expected this!"

Belarrin watched Sravika silently, waiting for her to drive a knife through his ribs or at least to run away. But she did neither, only stared at him as tears bloomed in her eyes. "Please, Sravika, you must believe me. I should have told you long ago, but I'm a coward. I wanted a way out but couldn't see it and now it's too late. But please understand, that I'm not one of them anymore."

"I know," she said.

But he didn't hear her. She had to understand. He pulled the black stone necklace from beneath his shirt. "See, mine isn't broken. It's this stone that let the t'Okaedrin follow me. Breaking it is what tells them to attack. But I didn't understand I was wrong until it was too late. I was already here and I couldn't draw them away. They know where the camp is. They've known since we arrived. There was no choice, nothing to do. All I could do was not signal the attack until I found a way out. We had to run before I could break it so they'd never find us. I should have told you before. Please, Sravika, you must believe me."

"I believe you." Calm had fallen over her. But how? "Belarrin," she said, meeting his gaze, "just tell me how you killed Vitarria."

"Vitarria."

Belarrin stumbled back as the blood drained from his face. His knees collapsed and he fell to the earth. "How did you..." he managed to gasp before his throat closed tight.

She knelt down on both knees beside him, hands clasped in her lap, close enough to touch but he could feel the gulf widening between them.

"I... I wanted to tell you," Belarrin said. "But I was too weak, too afraid. I wanted to beg your forgiveness." He realized he was babbling, but couldn't stop. "She was in the first camp I infiltrated, the one you heard was destroyed. It was before I understood, when I was still one of them. She was my friend and I repaid that with murder. Highest Above, Sravika, I murdered them all!" Belarrin bowed his head. "Just kill me, I deserve to die."

He drew a deep breath, waiting, longing for the blow to fall. Waiting for the end. But it did not come. He looked up, meeting Sravika's eyes. She shook her head, blue eyes radiant in the flowing tears. How could she be so beautiful yet hate him so much? As if reading his thoughts, she said, "I don't hate you. That night when I saw the Tear of Isi glowing in your hand, I knew you were my sister's killer. I told you that I forgave you whatever you'd done. This is what I meant. Belarrin, I forgive you. I forgave you before we ever met."

"But how..." His voice cracked.

Sravika took his arm and, holding him at the wrist, gently yet firmly pulled him to his feet. He felt the walls between them collapse. "Another time. All that you have done is in the past. You're our salvation now and the Iron-Men are coming."

"Yes," Belarrin replied, his mind spinning. "Yes."

He forced all the questions, all the anguish from his mind and walked over to where Ninanna had stood. He'd been a coward and a fool, but if they acted quickly, they might still avoid disaster. The Scions could kill him later, but first he had to save them. Picking up the broken pieces of the necklace, he said, "My brothers will come in the hundreds. First they will encircle the camp, trapping everyone inside. Then they will attack, killing everyone except the chieftains. They want the locations of the other camps." Sravika gasped, but Belarrin's thoughts were clear now. "We must warn them. Can you go to Kitiger's shelter? They'll believe you more than me. I'll find others to rally the rest of the camp and meet you there." He took her gently by the wrist, holding her eyes with his. "What I said earlier is true. I know them. I was them. This isn't pride speaking. We must not fight them. If we fight, we die. Our only choice is to run and pray we can break through the perimeter before it's fully formed. As long as it isn't, we have a chance."

She nodded.

"Hurry!" Belarrin broke into a run. As he sprinted back to the camp, his mind churned. How could she have known what he had done? And knowing that, how could she forgive him?

He chased the thoughts away as he reached the camp. Those were questions for another time. Looking around, he was startled to see that nothing had changed. He'd imagined raging fires reaching up toward the gray clouds, the dead and dying scattered broken across the clearing. But all was quiet. The midday meal had past, and scattered Scions went about their daily tasks while children ran underfoot. Yrpel sat nearby fletching some arrows with bird feathers.

"Yrpel," Belarrin cried running up. The big man lifted his head. "Yrpel, do you trust me?"

"Of course, my friend."

"There's no time for me to explain. The Iron-Men are coming!"

Yrpel grinned and, grabbing his spear, leapt to his feet. "Then let us taste blood."

"No! They are too many. There will be hundreds of them, probably Finnies too. I don't know when they'll arrive, maybe moments, maybe hours, but our only chance is to run. Gather everyone you can and flee northward."

Yrpel snarled. "I am tired of running."

Belarrin rested his hand on Yrpel shoulder. "No, you must trust me, my friend. Run! There will be other chances, but for today, you must run!"

"I..." Yrpel's face flushed, but he nodded, his lips forming a thin line. "I will do as you ask."

Idysha stepped around one of the shelters carrying an armload of sticks to be crafted into arrow shafts. Belarrin looked at her. "Idysha, too. Please you must save who you can, but there's no time to delay. Flee!"

Confusion filled her eyes but she glanced at Yrpel who nodded grimly. That was enough for her. She dropped her load and drew her knife. "We will see it done."

"Good! Quickly and..." Belarrin hesitated. "And I'm sorry."

Before they could ask what he meant, he turned away and sprinted for Kitiger's tent. Behind him he heard the pair running to spread the warning. It would have to be enough. Pushing aside the entrance flap, he stepped into the shelter.

The Scions were all gathered around Sravika, Kitiger with arms crossed, angry. "I don't understand, Sravika, what do you mean?"

"Why are we wasting time arguing?" Sravika cried. "The Iron-Men are coming to destroy us right now!"

"We've heard nothing from the scouts. How can you be certain?"

"The scouts are dead already," Belarrin said, stepping forward. "I am certain because I once was t'Okaedrin. I was an Iron-Man and I know what they're doing."

All eyes turned on him, confusion shifting to anger. Kitiger, Fedigni, Laerdina, Obaudes, Argluf, Grannif, and even Jarkon. Belarrin returned all of their gazes, his own expression hard and certain.

"What?" Kitiger's eyes were wide, disbelieving.

"They sent me to be among you. To find your camp and as many others as I could. I was taught that you were the enemy, but living among you I learned I was the enemy."

"But that's impossible. You were a slave!"

"I joined a group of newly captured slaves and became one of them, all to find you." Confessing this time was easier, despite the pressure of the eyes upon him. Their weight was nothing before Sravika's. Belarrin lifted the black stone necklace from around his neck. "They gave me this stone, ensorcelled so they could follow wherever I went. They know where this camp is. They've known for weeks. When breaks they know to attack. Like this one." He opened his hand to reveal the broken stone. "There is a second Iron-Man here. He broke the stone."

"He blames others to confuse us," Fedigni said.

"Kill him!" Obaudes cried. Drawing a stone knife from his belt. Belarrin didn't flinch, he deserved no less. But Jarkon lunged forward, catching Obaudes by the wrist in an iron grip.

"There will be no murder here," he said.

"You're just like him." Obaudes spat. "Two traitors conspiring to butcher us."

"Be still!" Kitiger bellowed. It was the first time he'd ever raised his voice and everyone stopped stunned. "No killing, not until we know enough to judge. Argluf and Fedigni, please bind him. We must be sure."

"There's no time for this!" Belarrin said as the two took his arms and roughly pulled them behind his back. They tied his wrists together with rope. "Kill me now, I don't care. But run! Run now or everyone will die."

"He's a sorcerer," Grannif said, ignoring him. Grannif had picked up a spear and held it to Belarrin's throat. "Speak an incantation and I will drive this through your throat."

"Drive it through my throat then," Belarrin retorted, "then run!"

"Everyone stay calm," Kitiger said. "We must think."

"There's no time to think," Sravika pleaded.

"Sravika is right," Jarkon said, his hand still holding Obaudes' wrist. "The time for deliberation must wait, the moment has come to act."

Kitiger shook his head as if trying to wrest away the shock clouding his mind. "Sravika, how much time do we have?"

"It was a Finaestari woman who warned us. She said we have minutes, probably. Please, you must listen to Belarrin!"

Kitiger turned to Belarrin, pain and denial in his eyes. "I trusted you, and for this?" He shook his head. "And now you force us to trust you still. Speak."

Belarrin glanced over to Grannif and the spear hovering at his throat. "I was told when the stone is broken they would attack within two days. I don't know when that was done. Please, there is no time. I've done this before. They will kill all the scouts first and encircle the camp. The attack will begin once we're completely surrounded. They will come from all sides at once. There will be no escape. You must flee now before we're encircled!"

"You hold our warriors in little regard." Grannif snarled, his knuckles turning white from his grip upon the spear

"I am one of our warriors," Belarrin retorted. "But I'm not a fool. I know what the Iron-Men can do."

"Belarrin is right," Jarkon said, finally releasing Obaudes who stepped back, rubbing his wrists. "The Iron-Men will attack just as he says. Kitiger, you must rally your people and retreat. What does it cost if he lies? Nothing. But if he's right and we linger, we all die."

Kitiger nodded, his shoulders slumping. "Yes. Yes, you're right. Sravika and Laerdina, please spread the word."

The two women nodded and headed toward the entrance of the shelter, Sravika sparing Belarrin a glance filled with worry.

A scream echoed in the distance, followed by a second. "Iron-Men!" someone shouted.

All around him, faces turned white as Laerdina looked outside. "It's just as he said." She ran outside, Sravika on her heels.

Kitiger hesitated, glancing over to Belarrin, but Jarkon said, "I will watch him, go."

"You cannot fight them!" Belarrin shouted as the rest ran from the shelter. "Run!" He turned to Jarkon. "You understand. You must!"

"I do, but I cannot change them," Jarkon replied. "However, I can free you. Here, let me see your hands."

Belarrin turned around and raised his wrists. But instead of grasping the bonds, Jarkon lurched forward, the whole weight of his body crashing into Belarrin and driving him to the ground. Belarrin struggled against the man, expecting to be grappled at any moment, but Jarkon didn't move. Something wet splashed on Belarrin's cheek, dripping to the ground in front of him. Blood.

He looked up and met Jarkon's eyes. The chieftain gasped, bubbles of blood rising up in his throat. "The days of the Scions are over. You must make them see…"

Jarkon spasmed then fell still, the light fading from his eyes. Belarrin looked up as a spear tip hovered into view. "Such a sad fate, brother," Obaudes said. "Such weakness. The old traitor is dead, but you I'll keep for our masters. And you will know such pain."

"It was you," Belarrin whispered. Beyond the shelter, Scions screamed, fighting and dying.

"Yes, brother, and before you think to cast a spell, know that I will drive this blade through your eye without hesitation. It will be a loss for High Lord Tazil, but so be it." His lips twisted into a sneer. "So what was it that fouled your soul? The lies? The filth? That bleating goat Sravika?" He laughed. "They're all filth and fools. Worse even than the wildmen. But you're the bigger…"

The spear jerked, then clattered to the ground as Obaudes stumbled forward, collapsing to his knees. A faint gurgle escaped his lips as he crumpled to the ground.

Sravika ran to Belarrin and helped push away the body of Jarkon. "I had a feeling the traitor would try to kill you," she said, sliding her knife through his bonds.

Belarrin sat up. "You must run, Sravika. Please!"

"I know," she said.

"I'm sorry about all the lies, I'm sorry about everything, but you must go now. Please promise me you'll run and not look back. Anyone who lingers dies. I sent Yrpel and Idysha to gather as many as they could."

She rested her hand on his. "Come on. I know you're still learning, but with your sorcery you can still rescue us. I believe in you."

Looking into her eyes, Belarrin felt his heart tear within him. In a moment, he saw it all. He saw his fear, his cowardice, his shame. Every life that was lost today was because he had been too weak. He could help them, and would, but that wasn't enough. "I can't, Sravika. I have to free them."

"We'll free all the slaves together. Hurry!"

"Not the Kalilaer, Sravika, the Iron-Men. My brothers. I have to save them, too."

"Belarrin." Her voice was suddenly soft. The light in her eyes faded and he could see that she thought he was going to his death. Perhaps he was. It didn't matter. Then that slight lovely smile touched her lips, tinged in sadness, and she lifted the Tear of Isi from around her neck. He didn't flinch as she set it around his. "This is my promise to you, Belarrin. I will come back for you. I forgive you. Vitarria forgave you. I know this without you telling me. Return to me." She leaned forward and kissed his forehead. "But for now, save our people."

Sravika took up her spear and ran for the door. Belarrin watched her go in stunned silence. How could she…?

He jumped to his feet and hurried after her. Slowing at the entrance of the shelter, he looked outside onto madness.

The battle ravaging the camp was as bad as any of his nightmares. There were far too many Scions still present, fighting back to back near the campfire. T'Okaedrin ringed the glade on all sides, just as he'd warned, pressing forward in an ever tightening circle. Sravika ran straight toward the closest forest edge, right for a rank of advancing t'Okaedrin.

"She's mad," Belarrin hissed through clenched teeth. That or possessing far more faith than he could dream of. Urgency gave him focus and it took only an instant for the words to blaze across his eyes. "Donthae'a ykstaivusryhota kenatalet."

A great cedar, directly in Sravika's path, groaned and cracked. Its roots lost their purchase, rising up from the loamy soil as the massive tree toppled directly toward the t'Okaedrin. Discipline shattered and they scattered, a few too late as it struck the ground with a trembling crash. Sravika leapt agilely through the trembling branches. She looked back to flash him a grim smile, then disappeared into the forest.

Belarrin released a deep breath. If he'd lost her…

He crushed the thought, turning his attention back to the camp. Flames licked up in red tongues above most of the shelters. The Scions in the center tried to form a wall of spears against the closing t'Okaedrin, but they were too panicked to hold steady. He wanted to scream at them to run, to force their way through at one place and flee, but it was already too late for that. What was there left that he could do to save them? Nothing, except…

He looked up at the deepening gray sky, felt the cool wind choked with ash upon his face. The spell, he sensed, would take him to the edge of his ability. Perhaps if there had been more time to practice he would've been stronger. But it would have to be enough. At least Sravika was free.

She would survive and that was good. He closed his eyes, focusing on the one task before him and was startled how quickly the golden lines rose to his eyes. "Oesae yskaesot piteu'oesys. Ae'irpiva yskaesotsechwae Euvenypri'oesys. Itsoe'azhestva Asirda sypansypa!"

A moment, it felt like the world drew in a breath, drawing air from his lungs, from all the heavens. A moment of stillness, of silence without the screams of the dying, without the ring of swords, the crackling fires.

A gentle breeze brushed his cheek, tousled his hair, then sound returned in a torrent. Lightning flashed, touching the ground a dozen paces away. Thunder roared, its fury flinging Belarrin back against the outer wall of the shelter, driving him to his knees. A second strike as furious as the first. Then the heavens opened and wept. Rain fell in torrents, pelting like stones in an avalanche and over it all, the wind. It roared through the forest and across the glade, snapping trees, staggering Scion and t'Okaedrin alike, pushing to the knees those it didn't fling to the ground.

Another flash of lightning. A roar of thunder.

The skies darkened to night. Or perhaps it was shadows falling over Belarrin's eyes. He couldn't tell. His thoughts were too numb with shock and overwhelming exhaustion.

A voice shouted, "Run, Scions while we can!"

"Bless you, Mirnadd," Belarrin whispered.

Darkness claimed him.

CHAPTER 34
Price

"What is it that makes a home a home? Is it laughter? Is it tears? Does it grow from time or is it created in a moment? Is it a place of friendship? Or of comfort? Once you leave, can you ever return? What is it that makes a home a home? It is memory."

—Author Unknown

Lady Medreuneth sat at her window at the highest point of her tower, looking out toward the Timnar Mountains to the north. The nearest peak smoked in restless slumber, sending up a thin trail of smoke. The wilderness was under heavy cloud-laden skies, though Nahirazith and the coast were clear. It was on days like these that she was afforded the unique opportunity of seeing the mountains pierce the clouds like an arrow might puncture flesh with the tallest peaks standing tall in the afternoon sun. A day was coming soon when each of those peaks would be given a name.

The Cataclysm had shorn her people of the need to give title to every river, lake, hill, and mountain. From one year to the next, sometimes one day to the next, everything could change. But Isfalinis' troubled spirit was calming. Medreuneth had heard tell that the ice wall was retreating northward and had witnessed for herself the diminishment of earthquakes.

She took a sip from her goblet of wine, considering the mountains. Someone seeing her spend nearly all her waking hours at this window, in this repose, might have taken it for idleness. But she was not idle. The gift of the Aestari, both Syraestari and their wayward cousins, was time. Time to be, to think, to ponder and consider. Time to act only when the moment was right. That was something the Cataclysm, in its own impatience, had stolen away. Thus brashness bordering nearly upon human restlessness had been ingrained in many of the younger Syraestari.

But Medreuneth had long ago realized she could learn far more from watching than by doing. Or talking. Voices were always so much wind, a manifestation of the Breath of Isfalinis. Opposite her own inclinations, Medreuneth knew that was why she cared little for it. Unless, of course, she were the one speaking.

Her knowledge lay with the Flesh of Isfalinis and the rising mountains were the scabs and scars of that flesh. In understanding them, she could discern secrets that lay in the soul beneath. And that took time.

A tremor passed through her. Startled, Medreuneth instantly focused her thoughts. She closed her eyes, preparing to feel every earthen wave that rippled across the face of the world. But there were none.

Puzzled, she set down her goblet and rose to her feet. The trickle of smoke above the Timnar Mountains was unchanged. No, that was not the source. Curious. The only difference she could discern was that the clouds over the forest seemed darker than before. But clouds wouldn't cause a tremor. She concentrated on what she'd felt, reliving the moment. Not a tremor at all, not from Isfalinis. Something else. Something powerful. She could remember still, the last time such a sensation had washed over her. It had been on the day when the last of the Etyni and Cydion had been slain. But such power now was impossible.

Medreuneth chuckled to herself. Another lesson she'd learned was that nothing was impossible. It merely meant she didn't understand. And that meant that some events had no meaning for her.

She sat back down and, taking up her goblet again, resumed her study of the Timnar Mountains. One day she might come to know what had happened. Or perhaps not.

Belarrin opened his eyes to see Bridionis' grinning face staring down at him. "Welcome home, brother."

He groaned as he sat up and looked around. Bridionis, Hirnid, and his father were gathered around him in the center of Kitiger's shelter. He looked from face to face, trying to remember who he'd been. So much time had passed. So much had changed. His gaze shifted past them to Captain Eltirkar, standing a few steps away. Rage welled up in his heart. Here was one of the betrayers. One of those who had sent him to kill those who fought only to be free. To slay the new family he'd grown to love. He had killed Vitarria at Eltirkar's hand and so many others. Belarrin clenched his eyes shut, trying to quell the overwhelming sense of rage and grief. He took a deep breath and opened his eyes again, focusing on his brothers instead. Looking upon them, he saw only slaves. They were family, just as much as the Scions had become, bound in a servitude they couldn't even see. He swallowed, fighting down the grief. "Bridionis, father, Hirnid..."

"Rest easy, my son," Dalric said with a gentle smile, doubtless confusing the emotions that flitted across Belarrin's face. "It is good to see you. Are you hurt?"

"I think so," Belarrin said, rubbing the back of his head and thinking quickly. "I must have been struck. I cannot remember."

Bridionis patted him on the back. "You'll live."

Captain Eltirkar strode over. "What happened? Have you discovered any other camps? How do the Scions coordinate?"

Belarrin scrambled to his feet with his father and brothers and bowed low. After hating Finnies for so long, so openly, it was a struggle to regain control of himself. He channeled his anger into frustration. "I don't know, my Lord. The raid happened too soon."

"What happened to Liuticar?"

"Who is Liuticar, Lord?"

"The other t'Okaedrin," Eltirkar replied, pointing to the far side of the chamber.

Obaudes and Jarkon lay just as Belarrin had left them, both faces slack in death. Belarrin's eyes lingered over Jarkon, a slave who had broken free. And now he was dead. Belarrin forced his attention back to Eltirkar. "I didn't know him by that name."

"But what happened?"

"He went mad, my Lord. Both he and I were part of the chieftain's council and we were meeting when the attack came. He laughed, telling them their judgment had come. I don't know why he did that. It was reckless. This one," Belarrin said, pointing at Jarkon, "Killed Obaudes, er Liuticar before they all fled."

"Why didn't you stop him?" Eltirkar demanded.

Belarrin felt his face flush with anger and shame. "I avenged him, killing this Scion. But how was I to stop him? I didn't even know who he was until today. If I'd been told about a second infiltrator I might have restrained him or protected him before he brought his own death."

"That makes no sense." Eltirkar growled. "I want answers. Thirty t'Okaedrin died in this battle. It's an embarrassment. Never before have so many died in a single day!"

"I don't know what else to say." Belarrin felt his hands shaking. He couldn't stop them. He was a coward and a fool. If he couldn't hold his temper, he'd betray himself. He channeled his anger into false frustration. "I didn't break my stone. I was close to learning the truth! Just a few more days would've been enough. He signaled too soon. He must have lost his patience."

Eltirkar rubbed his jaw, grimacing, then said, "What were you close to discovering?"

"The location of two more camps," Belarrin replied. He saw no harm in telling the truth about that. "Two other chieftains arrived yesterday to meet with us."

"How did they communicate with the other camps?"

"They wouldn't tell me. Messengers, I think, but never ones who went on raids."

"So you know nothing."

"No, my Lord."

"Not good enough."

"It's not my fault, my Lord!" Belarrin cried. "I did everything that was asked of me. I lived for months in this filth only to have that fool Obaudes throw it all away!"

"Vistus, peace," Dalric said, resting his hand on Belarrin's shoulder.

Belarrin bowed his head, seeing the warning flash of anger in Eltirkar's eyes. He drew in a deep breath, stretching for a calm he didn't feel. Slipping into his old habits, his old debasements, churned his stomach. Would that he could burn Eltirkar to slag by pulling lightning from the sky. But then he'd have to kill his brothers, too. Maybe he should've run with Sravika. "Please forgive me, my Lord. I'm frustrated with myself and allowed it to show in my words."

"Indeed. Perhaps you were too long with these savages."

"Yes, my Lord."

"There still may be some hope," Eltirkar said. "We've take some prisoners. You will tell me if any are chieftains or their messengers."

"Yes, my Lord."

Belarrin and the other t'Okaedrin followed Eltirkar out the shelter. As he stepped through the door, Belarrin had to suppress a gasp. The glade that he'd come to call home was in ruin. Every shelter had been destroyed. Most were smoldering heaps. The stench of soot and blood hung heavy in the air and the dead lay scattered across the ground. There were several dozen fallen Scions that he could see and doubtless many more he could not. He stumbled as saw the body of Mirnadd, dead of a sword thrust through the chest. Poor Tayrja. Grannif's body lay a little further, barely recognizable for the deep slash in the throat that had nearly severed his head. Belarrin scanned for his friends, Yrpel and Idysha, Chostir, Henirgar, and… Zoltha.

No. The silent scream rose up in Belarrin's soul.

Zoltha was alive. Hands bound behind him, he knelt in the line of prisoners. His shirt was stained crimson by a deep bleeding gash in his side. It was all Belarrin could do not to cry out and run to his side. A strangled moan rose up in from his chest that he barely concealed by clearing his throat. And to intensify the tragedy, Chief Kitiger knelt next to him, a red wheal rising on his forehead where he must have been struck.

"Are any of these prisoners a chieftain?" Captain Eltirkar asked.

But Belarrin barely heard the question. What if, instead of trying to warn the chieftains, instead of sending everyone away, he'd unleashed his sorcery immediately? Would it have made any difference? Would Mirnadd have lived? Could he have saved Zoltha and so many others from this? This shame? He stumbled, falling to his knees.

"So many dead." Belarrin looked up to the captain. Yes, Eltirkar would burn for this. All the Finaestari would burn. Clenching his fists, he gathered his thoughts, focusing on the still-brooding heavens above.

"Vistus?"

Belarrin turned at Bridionis' touch upon his shoulder. His brother knelt beside him, concern heavy in his eyes. Belarrin met that gaze and his rage faded beneath overwhelming shame. He couldn't kill Eltirkar, not when he'd have to kill his brothers, too.

Highest Above, was there any choice that was right?

"So many dead," Belarrin whispered. Then he added, "So many brothers fallen."

Bridionis nodded, his eyes drawn.

"Where are the chieftains?' Captain Eltirkar asked again, more impatient this time.

Belarrin struggled to his feet and looked around the camp, forcing himself to face the price of his failures. He shook his head, praying none of the prisoners would be foolish enough to protest. "They aren't among the prisoners. Nor do I see any of the Scions who accompanied them from the other camps. There were only a couple. One of the chieftains I killed and that one there was Grannif." He gestured to the body. Then he pointed to Mirnadd. "And that was Kitiger, my chieftain."

"I believe it," Dalric said, looking down at Mirnadd's body. "That one killed three t'Okaedrin. I've never seen a spear pierce iron mail so easily."

"Cydion's Abyss, what a waste!" Eltirkar cursed. "Kill them all. Now!" He turned and stormed away.

Belarrin turned to Dalric, hating the words that came out of his mouth. "I will do it, father."

Dalric nodded. "It is your honor, my son."

It was his burden.

Belarrin took the blade his father handed him. He had failed his new family and the only thing he could offer now was a quick death from a friend. Better than from an enemy. It was his penance for failure. His steps were heavy as he walked over to Kitiger at the near end of the line.

"To think I called you friend," his old chieftain spat. "If you truly changed, then why didn't you tell us, why didn't you trust us?"

"I was afraid of what you'd do to me," Belarrin admitted. "I am a coward and deserve every curse you lay upon me."

"Worse than a coward. You're a traitor. Your weakness has doomed us all. I hope your soul burns in the Abyss."

"I deserve no less."

"Don't spare your self-pity on me!"

"Peace," Zoltha said. "We all knew the price of rebellion and it is time to pay our due. Face it with honor knowing that many still live because of Belarrin."

Kitiger's lips twisted into a grimace. "End it then, traitor, and know that I die cursing you."

Belarrin knew there was nothing he could say, there could be no absolution. There was only a sword thrust through the heart. Meeting Kitiger's eyes, he ended his life.

Stepping to Zoltha, Belarrin's heart quailed within him and his hand trembled so much he almost dropped the sword. Pain had tightened his friend's eyes and shortened his breathing, but he managed to gasp softly, "I always sensed there was something special about you."

"I am not who I once was."

"I know, my friend."

"How can you still call me friend?"

"Because you are. I see your heart. I understand now."

Staring into Zoltha's eyes, Belarrin's resolve melted. "I don't think I can do this."

"You must, Belarrin. I must die now if our people are ever to be free."

"But..."

"I once told you of the importance of hope. When I see you, I have hope. Your story isn't over, our story isn't over. I will die knowing that both my life and my death have had meaning. That is more than most men can say."

"I am sorry, Zoltha."

"No tears, my friend, for they will betray you. There is no more time, kill me now."

"Goodbye, my friend."

"Highest Above bless you, Belarrin."

Belarrin wanted to clench his eyes shut but forced them to stay open and locked on Zoltha's as he drove his sword through the man's heart. As the light in Zoltha's eyes faded, a part of Belarrin died, too.

Whatever price would be demanded of him in the days ahead, he vowed he would pay it.

Drawing in a shuddered breath, Belarrin stepped to the next prisoner in line. Unlike with the first band he'd destroyed, none but Kitiger cursed him. They each watched him silently, waiting for death. A few even nodded in acceptance as if they, like Zoltha, believed their deaths had meaning. Belarrin wished he could have such faith. He longed for curses instead, for condemnations rising from the throats of his enemies. Killing someone you named friend was far worse than killing an enemy. With each blow, his hatred grew. He hated himself but he hated the Finnies even more for what they'd done to both his families, Scion and t'Okaedrin. For what they had made him do.

When the task was done, he made sure his face was clear of the boiling rage and deep shame that roiled in his soul as he turned back to his waiting brothers. Arcomin had joined them, a wide grin on his face. That was more than Belarrin could bear. He walked up to his brother and struck him as hard as he could in the jaw.

Arcomin hadn't expected the attack and dropped to the ground dazed.

"I promised I'd kill you, brother," Belarrin spat as he shook out his hand from the force of the blow. "Be grateful I used my fist instead of my sword."

Arcomin rubbed his jaw and glared up at him as his eyes regained their focus. "I am your eldest."

"You are nothing!"

"Vistus!" Dalric grasped him firmly on the upper arm, clenching tightly to the edge of pain. "I don't know what has gotten into you, son. First you raise your voice to your Syra-estari Master and now you strike your eldest brother." His voice lowered, but hardened as he continued, "You are a hero to all the t'Okaedrin. I don't want to send a hero to the lashing post, but I will. Now apologize to your brother."

"Not after what he's done to me, father!" As anger flashed across Dalric's face, Belarrin took a deep breath. His father was right, if not for the same reasons. He had to get control of himself or he'd be able to do nothing. Zoltha and all the others would have died for nothing. "I'm sorry, father. After everything, today, these past months… I don't know how to explain. But I can't apologize to Arcomin. Not after what he's done to me."

"What was that?" Dalric said, his voice still hard.

"He took advantage of my position among the Kalilaer to torment me where I couldn't challenge him."

"Your brothers were commanded to make your life difficult. Your suffering compelled loyalty from the other Kalilaer."

"Not when I was on the Boards, father. There were no Kalilaer for a hundred paces and more, yet he struck me when I was helpless and it served no purpose but his own pleasure. He hates me, he has always hated me."

"Phaw!" Dalric cried. "I won't stand for this bickering. I'll send you both to the whipping post."

"Vistus is right, father," Hirnid said, stepping forward. "Arcomin took too much pleasure, not just in torturing Vistus, but the Kalilaer, too. I tried to convince him when we were alone, but that only pushed him more. It wouldn't surprise me if he was trying to break Vistus and force him to fail. But Vistus was stronger than that and he didn't."

Belarrin looked upon Hirnid as if seeing with new eyes. The other man had always been a friend, but he'd also been one of the meekest of his brothers. Valiant and obedient, always a follower. Standing up to an eldest in any circumstance took a kind of courage never expected from Hirnid.

Realizing that, Belarrin felt his soul tear within him. These men here were his brothers. They had no idea what the Finnies had done to them. He had to save them.

Arcomin rose to his feet, glaring between Belarrin and Hirnid, but he didn't speak as Dalric's face darkened to a deep red. "I hadn't expected such dishonor from my two greatest sons. It is a day of honor for our family, but one of tragedy as well. Thirty brothers died and I can only be grateful none were from our family. I have never before heard of such a thing. I won't taint this day by dwelling on the pettiness from either of you. Be warned, I still may send you to the whipping post and if either one of you touches the other, you'll both go to the Boards for a week like a common Kalilaer!"

Before he had become a Kalilaer and a Scion, Belarrin would've felt shame from his father's words, but now he felt only grief and anger as he watched his father storm away. When he was gone, Belarrin turned back toward the ruin of the Scion camp. He didn't look at Arcomin or care what his eldest did.

The other t'Okaedrin were already busy destroying what little remained of the Scion camp. The dead, as before, were piled in the central fire pit and burned. As he once had with Vitarria, Belarrin carried the body of Zoltha to the pyre. Zoltha was a small man, but Belarrin's feet dragged as though he were a heavy burden. Looking down upon the man's face, empty now in death, he longed to hear once more the gentle laugh and see the soft smile. Those were gone forever because Belarrin had failed to find his courage. He had coveted his own life over so many others nobler than himself.

He set Zoltha carefully onto the stacked wood. Carrying his friend wasn't even the beginning of penance, but Belarrin knew he could take one comfort. Yrpel had succeeded in escaping with over half of the Scions including all the children. No new boys or girls would be twisted into t'Okaedrin or Pi'aernoth. That fact enraged the other t'Okaedrin nearly as much as the death of the brothers and Belarrin understood why. He, too, had once thought they were saving the young from a life of apostasy. He shook his head. His brothers were the apostates, now.

When the camp was destroyed, they set out even though the day was mostly spent. No one wanted to spend a night on slaughtered ground, regardless of whether the dead were savages or not. Only a few t'Okaedrin families remained in the area, searching for Scion survivors. The main host camped a few miles away, setting out twice the usual number of guards against the possibility of attack. It was the first time in t'Okaedrin memory that they'd raided a Scion camp or wildman village and more than a handful had slipped through their trap.

There was rampant talk of the savage storm that had ripped through the camp. Most of the t'Okaedrin dead had been crushed by falling trees. A dozen or more theories were said, but not one guessed a sorcerer among the Scion. That was impossible. There were no human sorcerers. The older, wiser t'Okaedrin just shook their heads and said one word. Cataclysm.

As Belarrin shaved his beard away, he brooded on how nothing was the same as it had been before. His heart was different, as was his allegiance. Last time he had killed from a sense of justice, but this time the deaths were wrought by his failures, by his fears. But even as he wrestled with the grief ravaging his soul, he recognized another truth. There was some pleasure amidst the pain. Though he missed Sravika and the other Scions, he loved his brothers still and it was good to be among them again.

As he finished his shave, Belarrin ran his fingers across his smooth chin. He felt cold and exposed. His brothers laughed at his confused expression. As he joined in with a rueful grin, he remembered only a few weeks before when he'd been forced to laugh at Scion humor he didn't feel. His good humor vanished. Belarrin tried to evade the good-natured banter by fleeing to his bedroll as soon as night fell, but sleep evaded him. He tossed and turned restlessly, mourning for Zoltha and Mirnadd, worrying about Sravika and all those who had escaped.

He awoke the next morning tired and sullen. During the march, he constantly warred between the pleasures of being among his family again and the grief of all his failures. But his mood darkened the most whenever he contemplated that his brothers walked blindly in chains. Late in the day, they reached the t'Okaedrin camp where his brothers had hidden during his time among the Scions. The fort was surprisingly small for housing nearly five hundred t'Okaedrin and Pi'aernoth along with several dozen Finaestari. They had taken more than their usual care to blend the camp into the surrounding wilderness. No trees had been cut to clear the area for bow fire. The wooden walls themselves were masked by branches and brush.

"We weren't allowed to light fires between sundown and sunup," Bridionis told him. "And only scouts were allowed outside the walls. I must say that I'm glad the call came in to attack when it did. Tempers were getting frayed with all the waiting."

That night they feasted on venison. The Pi'aernoth archers had gone hunting in anticipation of a celebratory feast. The celebration didn't happen, but still they ate well. Few of the t'Okaedrin and Pi'aernoth seemed to mind. Grander schemes like the entrapment of the Scions were matters for their fathers and their masters. The duty of the t'Okaedrin and Pi'aernoth was to fight where they were sent. Surviving any battle was cause for rejoicing, especially when the cost had been so high. Belarrin noticed that few of the Finnies remained with the army. He hadn't seen Captain Eltirkar since the afternoon of the raid. Doubtless, they had already departed on horseback to Nahirazith with news of their failure.

He was gnawing on a haunch of venison, barely noticing the rich flavor when Elestis sat down beside him. She gave him a hug and said, "Welcome back, Vistus."

"Thank you," he replied, noticing the stiff formality of her embrace. He wasn't sure how he felt about that. Once it would have evoked dismay. "It's good to be home."

"What was it like spending so much time among those savages?"

Belarrin met her eyes. She was beautiful and even the smudges of dirt on her cheeks didn't detract from that. Her hair hung unbraided and wisped gently in the night breeze. But, he realized, she was no Sravika. Not in beauty, not in spirit. "I don't know. I became accustomed to it after a while. The clothing is coarser, but manageable. The food is mundane but there was enough. The shelters were crude but we weren't cold at night. Truth be told, it's strange coming back."

She nodded and hesitation entered her voice. "And you are well?"

There was more to that question than just what lay on the surface. He stared at her, looked deep into her eyes and saw her flinch. "You're marrying Arcomin, aren't you?"

Her mouth dropped open in surprise, but she quickly closed it again and pressed her lips together, frowning as her expression transformed into a glare. "You haven't been around, Vistus. I can see it in your eyes, too. You're going to do it all over again. Sneaking into one Scion camp after another, again and again until they catch you and kill you."

"I understand."

"I'm not going to marry a husband I'll never see. I'm a good Pi'aernoth, I deserve better than that. My mother has spoken to your father and it's all arranged. Arcomin and I are to be married after we arrive home."

"I understand," Belarrin repeated, gently touching her hand.

Elestis' eyes narrowed. "You aren't angry. Why aren't you angry?"

Belarrin sighed. "I'm not the man I once was. You're right. My time with the Kalilaer and Scions changed me. I can't be the man you need me to be."

She glared at him. "You could at least be a little mad."

Belarrin laughed. "Maybe a little. So much has changed, Elestis. If only you could understand what I understand." If only he dared tell her. "But be careful with Arcomin. Be sure he is the one for you."

"There's the old jealousy." A smile grew on her face.

"Elestis, he isn't a good man."

It was her turn to laugh. "He is to me. I know you two have your problems, but he's always treated me right." Belarrin opened his mouth to speak, but she cut him off. "And don't worry. If he tries anything, I've got a knife handy."

Belarrin grinned despite himself. "Then I guess all I can say is that I wish you happiness."

"Thank you, Vistus." Elestis rose to her feet and hugged him again. This time the embrace was warmer.

Belarrin watched her walk away from the fire and disappear into the night. "Cydion's Abyss," he cursed under his breath. He really had changed, more than just in his allegiances. He wanted to be angry, just as Elestis had wanted, but he wasn't. In that step from t'Okaedrin to Scion, he had let so much go. He'd found so much new to cling to. He still loved Elestis and always would. But it had become love as for a sister, not a woman he wanted for a wife. It was the same way he felt for Bridionis, his father, and all those still in bondage.

During the journey southward, others came to talk to him as well. Mostly those of his own family, but other t'Okaedrin and more than a few Pi'aernoth. The brothers, one and all, were curious, and none blamed him for his failure. Belarrin's lie had permeated the camp and guilt lay firmly with the one he'd known as Obaudes. His Pi'aernoth visitors were more interested in him, now that word had passed that Elestis was with Arcomin, but Belarrin paid them no mind. There was another woman who had stolen his heart.

He sensed only darkness on his path ahead, but Sravika's final words to him rang in his ears. She said she'd come back for him and he believed it. But he had also seen his death in her eyes. Perhaps that was for the best, anyway. It was the least he deserved. He had let fear for his own life keep him from doing what was right. That, he vowed, would never happen again. He would do everything he could to save his brothers. Being with Bridionis and Hirnid again only affirmed that need, yet he was uncertain how best to proceed. He wouldn't delay too long this time, though.

When they reached Nahirazith, Belarrin stopped on the edge of the forest and blinked up at the open sky and radiant sun. The day was cool, the wind biting for early autumn, and far in the distance he could see hear rumbling surf. He had loved that sound, but now his eyes were drawn to the Kalilaer camp where hundreds of slaves toiled. Doubtless Regund and Fritten were still there. He understood Sravika's passion, her unwillingness to leave so many in bondage.

"Glad not to be going there this time?" Bridionis said, laughing as he followed Belarrin's gaze.

"Yes." That answer, at least, was honest. But the t'Okaedrin barracks were little better. As the marching column turned toward home, Belarrin's eyes lifted to Nahirazith on the hill above. Suppressing a flash of anger, he saw that dozens of banners he didn't recognize fluttered above its high walls. The largest was a crimson one atop High Lord Ushtyl's palace. "Why the banners?"

"Rumor is the empress and all of the high lords are in the city, waiting to hear word of our triumph."

"I suppose they'll be disappointed."

Bridionis slapped him hard on the back. "Perhaps, but not with you. You did everything you were supposed to. So did we. You should be proud of what you've done."

"I am," Belarrin replied, still staring at the flags. "Of some of it."

CHAPTER 35
Blood

"I walked that day among the fallen. Some had faces locked in eternal terror, others contorted in agony, while a few might merely have been sleeping. And I laughed as tears of joy streamed down my face. I did not laugh for them, but for myself. The anger, the pain, the shivering night sweat would haunt me later. But for that day, in that moment, only one thing mattered. I had passed through the inferno of battle and had lived."

—Kharlas of Delnios on the Field of Kienan

Sravika stared out from the interwoven branches of the thicket. She had heard no sounds since she'd taken refuge there late the day before. A few Iron-Men had passed just after her escape, but through the night all had remained quiet. Despite all that time, she was still in shock. Too much had happened, too much revealed, too much pain. And it all centered around Belarrin.

He'd killed her sister, just as she'd known, and he had saved her life just as she'd known. But an Iron-Man? That she had never guessed, had never dreamed. And it meant that Vitarria had been alive up until only a few months ago. They had been so close but never knew it.

Forgiving Belarrin had been hard, yet much easier than she'd dreamed. Vitarria would have been proud. He was a good man, the best of men, but darkness had always lain between them. Yet in the very moment it had begun to lift, he'd been torn away in a day of blood and slaughter.

"Oh Mirnadd." Sravika buried her face in her hands. She had seen him, Tayrja, and so many others still in the camp. Perhaps Belarrin had helped them escape, but she couldn't see how. It wasn't supposed to be like this. They should've been safe in the forest. But nowhere was safe anymore. She tried to remember who else she'd seen. Zoltha, alas, and Kitiger and so many others. In the madness, it might have been all of them. She might be alone.

But even if she was, she had sworn to Belarrin that she'd return to him and she would, even if it killed her.

Sravika pushed herself flat against the ground and, spear in hand, carefully crawled out of the thicket. On the far side, she rose to her feet and listened again. The forest remained silent. With a last look southward to where their camp had been, she turned the opposite way. If there were survivors, they'd head north.

She walked without haste, wary and ready. The forest was her ally, but that didn't mean an Iron-Man ambush was impossible. The day before had proven that well enough. She came across a small stream and washed her face. Cleaning the dirt and spattered blood from her cheeks went a far way towards clearing the clouds clinging to her mind. Morning passed into afternoon and still without a sign. Her stomach gnawed and she knew she'd have to stop to hunt if she didn't find someone soon. Pausing to stretch her weary muscles, she peered into the forest around her. Every direction was the same. Maybe she would never find them. Maybe there were no other survivors and she was alone again, just like when she'd lost Vitarria.

A thrush twittered in the distance and she hesitated, listening. It sang again and a smile broke out on her lips. She could recognize Henirgar's signal anywhere. Still, she crept ahead slowly. He would be as wary as she was. But the foliage suddenly flung back and Henirgar leapt toward her, his arms open wide.

"Sravika!" he cried, "Highest Above be praised."

"Henirgar," Sravika barely managed to gasp as he engulfed her in an embrace. She realized that tears were falling down her face. "How many?"

"Nearly forty now," he replied. Releasing her, he stepped back. "As soon as we heard Yrpel and Idysha's warning we grabbed all we could and fled."

"Thank His Highest Above," Sravika whispered. "I managed to slip out with Belarrin's help after the attack."

Henirgar hesitated a moment, then said, "Is it true that Belarrin is an Iron-Man?"

Sravika frowned, unsure how to explain what she knew in her heart. "Yes and no."

"What does that mean?"

"He was, but not anymore."

"Can you be sure?"

"I've never been more certain of anything. Everyone that survived yesterday is alive because of him."

"Still. It's hard for me to accept."

"Me, too. But at last I think I begin to understand."

"If you say he became who he claimed to be, then that's good enough for me." Henirgar shrugged as if pushing a weight off his shoulders. "He was my friend, too. Come and join the others. They'll be glad to see you."

"Is Tayrja or Mirnadd with you?" she asked as Henirgar guided her through the forest ahead.

"No."

Sravika's face fell. "I saw them trapped by Iron-Men, but still hoped."

"Chief Kitiger hasn't made it either. Nor Chief Jarkon or Chief Grannif."

"Jarkon was killed by Obaudes." At Henirgar's look, she continued, "Obaudes was an Iron-Man, too."

Henirgar shook his head. "Two of them and we had no idea. What chance do we have if they can become one of us so easily?"

Sravika stopped, her mind suddenly racing.

"What is it?" Henirgar asked. "Is something wrong?"

She smiled sadly. "No, I just understand what Belarrin and Jarkon were trying to tell us. They were right. We cannot be what we were."

"I don't know what we are now anyway," Henirgar replied. "But we're still a family, at least. Come on."

She followed him into a shallow depression, ringed on all sides by dense trees. The remnants of their band sheltered near the bottom. Not far away, Yrpel sat on the ground, his head in his hands. Idysha knelt beside him. "We saved everyone we could."

"It wasn't enough. Not enough!" The big man hunched further in on himself. "I couldn't find Zoltha. I promised Belarrin I'd save everyone I could, but I couldn't find Zoltha. I didn't see Mirnadd or Tayrja either! I failed him, I failed them!" Sravika had never seen him in such a state. Always furious, aggressive and relentless, but never broken.

"No one blames you. We know you did all you could," Idysha said. She looked up and, seeing Sravika, a bright light shone through the sadness in her eyes. "Sravika!"

She jumped to her feet to throw her arms around Sravika, but Yrpel barely stirred. He looked up at her with bloodshot eyes. Tears smudged the dirt on his face, forming runnels of mud. "I'm sorry, Sravika, I've failed again. First my village and now here. I'm not worthy to be called a warrior."

"No, you didn't fail."

Henirgar touched Sravika's arm, pulling her attention. "I'm going out again to look for others. Call me if I'm needed."

Sravika nodded, then turned her focus back to Yrpel. She knelt down beside him. "Idysha is right. It's a miracle you saved as many as you did. We were completely surrounded."

"But so many died."

"Enough, Yrpel!" Idysha knelt across from him and lifted his face in her hands to meet her eyes. "This isn't the Iengian warrior I know. You've seen death before, plenty of it. Everyone who died knew the risks of becoming a Scion. They made that choice. Grieve for them, vow your vengeance, but no more of this weeping. I won't see you broken by this!"

Yrpel rubbed his hand against his cheek, clearing away the muddy tears and looked up at her. "You're right, of course. I shall try."

"You will do more than try!" Idysha replied, softening the statement with a grin.

"You did well," Sravika said, patting him on the back and rising to her feet. Turning, she saw Fedigni and Laerdina walking her way. They were followed by one of the men who'd come with Chief Jarkon. Dirbructi, she thought his name was. "Sravika!" Laerdina cried, running forward. They embraced, then Sravika turned to Fedigni. His face was like stone, but his eyes burned deeply with anger and sorrow.

For all that, he hugged her warmly. "I'm glad you escaped," he said. "Would that I had not. Not to see this."

Stepping back, Sravika looked him over, concerned, but he only shrugged and turned away. Laerdina was watching him, too, her face wrinkling with worry-lines. She turned to Sravika. "Did you see anyone else?"

"No," Sravika replied. "Until a few minutes ago, I was afraid no one lived but me."

Laerdina shook her head. "I know what you mean. I'm surprised Fedigni and myself even got out alive. How did you escape?"

Sravika told them of her flight. When she recounted that Belarrin had opened the path for her by pulling down a tree, Fedigni cursed under his breath, "Iron-Men among us. To the Abyss with them!"

"I believe we're all that remains of our council," Laerdina said with a sidelong glance at Fedigni. "We will need to appoint a new chieftain."

Sravika nodded. "And decide what to do now."

"So long as we kill Finnies, I don't care who leads us," Fedigni growled.

"First, we need to give ourselves time recover from this ordeal," Sravika suggested. She could only hope that Fedigni's rage cooled. First his wife and now the camp itself. But for that matter, it was a wonder any of them were holding themselves together. For herself, Sravika knew she was afraid of quiet. As long as she could keep busy, she wouldn't have to think of all the dead.

"A little," Laerdina said, "but not too long."

"We need nothing," Fedigni said. "I'm ready to begin killing now."

"Not while vengeance and grief clouds our thoughts," Laerdina replied.

"Unless it makes our thoughts clearer, our courage stronger," Fedigni said.

The snapping of branches turned Sravika's head. Henirgar stumbled from the underbrush, a woman in his arms. She was so covered in blood it took Sravika a moment to recognize Tayrja. Sravika and the others ran to her side and helped Henirgar ease her to the ground, leaning up against a tree trunk.

"What happened? Are there Iron-Men near?" Sravika asked as Laerdina lifted up the edge of Tayrja's shirt to reveal a long gash down her left side.

"No. Just..." Tayrja broke off with a cough. "Just one Iron-Woman. Dead." Idysha gave her a flask of water and she drank eagerly. "Surprised each other. I was quicker."

"The wound doesn't look deep," Laerdina said, "but she's lost a lot of blood. I'd better sew it up quickly."

Sravika nodded, but Tayrja reached up to clutch her wrist. "Others too. A dozen, all hurt. Hiding. Find them."

"Where?" Sravika asked.

"The knotted oak."

Sravika knew the place. It was no more than a mile from the where the camp had been. It was a wonder they'd managed to find a place to hide that close. "Is Mirnadd with them?"

"No." Tears fell down Tayrja's cheek and her voice cracked. "Chostir. Argluf and... and others."

Sravika rested her hand on Tayrja's brow. "Rest now. We'll find them and bring them in." She looked up at Henirgar and he nodded.

From the opposite side of Tayrja, Yrpel spoke. "I'm going too."

"And I," said Idysha.

Ninanna knelt down and touched the red stain upon the leaf. It was blood. Looking ahead, she saw a snapped twig and further, a scuffing in the soil. If this was a Scion, the rebel was far more careless than normal. Wounds could do that. He or she might be thinking of nothing more than panicked flight, leading her down a trail to nowhere. Ninanna crushed the thought. She had to be calm.

She wiped the leaf dry then broke the twig again so the damage was hidden beneath an overhanging leaf. Next, she smoothed the disturbed earth, scattering leaves to better hide the path. Then she continued onward, pausing often to mask the trail, to listen, and watch. She forced patience where she felt none. A thicker pool of blood and an unnatural shifting of leaves marked where the human had paused to rest. Those were harder to conceal, but it was worth the effort. She had to be certain no one else could follow.

Then she found what she had longed to see. A second pair of tracks. They joined the wounded one and it was clear from the droplets of blood there had been a pause. Only one set of footprints departed, leaving heavier impressions in the soil.

She followed quicker now, but still pausing to hide all signs. Her ears strained for any disturbance in the forest around her until finally, she heard it. Voices. A smile rose to her lips. They were distant enough to be murmurs drifting through the wilderness, barely discernable over the whisper of the wind through the leaves. A shadow flickered between the trees ahead and Ninanna dropped to her stomach, watching carefully as a Scion walked by holding a spear. The warrior was alert, carefully scanning the woodlands, but he didn't see her. He might have, had she been slower.

Ninanna waited for him to pass out of sight, then carefully unslung her sword and hid it in the underbrush. Lowering again to a crouch, she crept toward the voices. As she drew closer, she dropped to her knees and crawled until she reached the edge of a shallow depression heavily concealed by closely grown trees and thickets. It was an admirable hiding place. If she hadn't found the trail of blood, she would never have passed close enough to even hear the voices that drew her in.

Within the small glade, she saw huddled clusters of humans. The nearest groups knelt around a wounded woman who was biting down on a stick as another Scion sewed up a wound in her side using a needle of bone. Ninanna let out a slow breath of relief. The human still lived.

But as she watched, the woman's eyes rolled up, her head lolled and the stick fell from her mouth. "Blood on the Bridge!" the Scion with the needle cried. "She's lost too much blood."

"Finish the task, Laerdina," a man told her.

"She's dying, Fedigni!"

"Not yet," the man retorted. "Don't give up on her."

"I'm not!"

Ninanna cursed silently. She didn't really have a plan, but what she was about to do hardly felt like the wisest course. Yet she had to. Ninanna rose to her feet and stepped into the glade. No one noticed her, their eyes locked on the dying woman. Ninanna walked forward until she stood behind the kneeling group. Their eyes lifted as her shadow fell across them. Before they could respond, Ninanna stretched her hand toward the wounded woman. "Sinahastir itavyly yskaesira."

The man, Fedigni, recovered from his surprise first. He leapt to his feet, spear in hand and thrust it at Ninanna. She shifted back a step, twisting from the attack, and swung out with her hand. Grabbing the spear a forearm's length from the point, she continued her turn and wrenched the weapon from the surprised man's grasp. She flung her hand back, casting the spear away behind her. "Peace."

But they didn't listen. Two more men rushed towards her with spears outstretched. Ninanna dropped into a roll, both points passing less than a hand's breadth from her face. She jumped back to her feet, now behind the two assailants and reaching out, pushed them both away. "Peace!" she cried again. "I've come to talk and carry no weapon."

The Scions gave her no mind and gathered around her in a circle, more and more joining until twenty faced her with spears held ready. Ninanna cursed. "I don't want to hurt you." Raising her hands, palm outwards, she turned in a full circle, watching carefully. "I have come alone. I want to talk to the one named Sravika."

From behind the circle of warriors, a woman groaned, then Laerdina cried out, "Wait! Tayrja is awake."

The encircling Scions paused and Ninanna breathed a sigh of relief. She lowered her hands and waited. A moment later, Laerdina stepped through the circle and walked up to Ninanna. "What did you do?"

"I gave her strength enough to endure your mending," Ninanna replied.

"Why shouldn't we kill you?"

Ninanna looked down on the shorter woman, wishing for once that she wasn't so tall. A little smaller and she might not be so imposing. Then again, perhaps she could use that. "You couldn't. And I have no desire to harm any of you. But we must talk, for the good of your people and mine. I don't see Sravika. Is she not with you?"

Fedigni stepped from the circle. He'd picked up his spear again and held it clutched tightly in his hands. "How do you know Sravika?"

"I have met her once before."

"Lies!"

"I warned her and Belarrin of the attack upon your camp."

"Sravika is no friend of the Finnies," Fedigni snapped. "Who are you?"

"I am named Ninanna, once a Sword-Whisperer."

A gasp of horror passed through the crowd and instantly Ninanna regretted her words. They knew of Sword-Whisperers but didn't understand.

"Monster!" Fedigni cried and the circle of Scions charged forward.

"Setrinas tefiral!" Ninanna shouted. A sphere of shadow burst around her, pushing outward like a wall. It struck the circle of Scions, pitching some backward through the air and sending the rest sprawling. She resumed her place with hands folded in front of her and repeated, “Peace! If I intended you harm, how many would be dead already?”

Laerdina flung out her hands. “She’s right.”

“You don’t command here, Laerdina,” Fedigni snapped.

“And neither do you,” she retorted then turned back to Ninanna. “Belarrin said the Iron-Men found our camp because of a black stone he had.”

Ninanna nodded. “I came alone and carry no stone. All I have is the clothes I wear. I will allow Laerdina to inspect me.”

“What if she dropped it in the forest nearby?” Fedigni demanded as Laerdina stepped forward to look her over.

“Then you had best run,” Ninanna said evenly, “because I cannot remove all the trees to satisfy you.”

“The Finnie has no stone and no weapon,” Laerdina said, stepping back. “But you demand much trust from us, Ninanna the once-Sword-Whisperer. You are one, but we are many. If you deceive us, the greatest cost to you is a single life, but the cost to us is everything. Your Iron-Men have already slaughtered half our people. If you want us to trust you, I demand one more act.”

“Speak,” Ninanna replied.

“You have proven your prowess, now prove your trust to us. Allow us to bind your hands.”

In reply, Ninanna lifted her arms with wrists together.

“Some twine,” Laerdina called behind her. Another of the Scions ran to fetch some. When he returned, Laerdina took it and bound her hands.

Fedigni stepped forward and smiled. "Now that she cannot resist, gag her so she cannot use sorcery."

Ninanna drew herself up and glared down at the human. "You've already tried to kill me twice. I forgive it because I know you're in pain. But that doesn't mean I will leave myself defenseless."

"You cannot stop us now."

She quirked her eyebrow. "If you're wrong, the price may be your life. I've caused no harm because I intend none, but breech this trust and I won't be so restrained."

Fedigni growled and took a step forward, but Laerdina grabbed his shoulder. "This is enough, Fedigni. She did as we asked and now we will wait."

"Fine." He spat. "But we're searching the forest, too."

Sravika crept carefully between the trees, ears straining to hear, eyes watching for any movement. After three days of furtive travel, expecting ambush at any moment, she was exhausted. A full day and night's sleep wasn't too little to ask. Weary as she was, even her forestcraft was suffering. Every tree began to look like the one before and she could no longer be certain they were headed in the right direction. If they were, the hiding place would be nearby. If not, she didn't know what she'd do. Unfortunately, Yrpel and Idysha weren't much help. They were too new to this part of the forest while those they'd rescued were too hurt.

Just as Tayrja had said, they'd found a dozen Scions, including Argluf and Chostir. All of them had been wounded in their escape and it was a small miracle they'd managed to find a decent hiding place so close to the old camp. Sravika, Idysha, and Yrpel had done their best to bind their wounds, but three had been beyond help and died. The return journey had been slow, both for worry of attack and because of the weakness of their companions. And that meant no rest for her, Yrpel, or Idysha.

The brush rustled ahead and Sravika froze. Her eyes scanned the wilderness, but saw nothing. A squirrel, perhaps. But maybe not. She tightened her grip on her spear, then gave a thrush call.

A moment later, a thrush responded. Sravika's shoulders slumped as relief flooded over her. She straightened as Henirgar emerged from the forest ahead. He flung his arms around her. "Sravika, welcome home."

It was all she could do not to collapse into that firm embrace and fall asleep. But she straightened and gave a second, louder bird call to signal the group following behind her. "Am I glad to see you," she told Henirgar as they waited for the others.

"Things have changed since you left."

Sravika's brows narrowed at his tone. "What?"

"Better if you come see."

When the rest of Sravika's party arrived, they passed through the last stretch of forest together. Stepping out of the trees, Sravika's heart lurched in her chest. At the center of the glade, a Finaestari woman sat, cross-legged with arms bound. She appeared to be sleeping, with head drooped. Around her four Scions stood guard with spears at the ready.

But before she could speak, she and the others were engulfed by happy Scions gathering around them. To her left, Argluf was shaking Fedigni's hand. To her right, Chostir had flung her arms around Henirgar in an enormous hug. Laerdina brought in a swarm of men and women to tend to the wounded.

"What happened?" Fedigni asked them.

"Didn't Tayrja tell you?" Sravika asked.

"She's been sleeping heavily these past few days. She nearly died of her wounds and is still very weak."

"We all should have died," Argluf said. "The Iron-Men had us completely surrounded, but then the heavens broke around us. You must have felt it? It was as if His Highest Above had lowered his hand and brushed our enemies away. It was still a hard fight. Lightning struck all around, rain and wind blinded us. But it did the same to the Iron-Men. We still lost far too many, but the storm caused enough chaos for us to slip through."

"You were lucky indeed," Henirgar said.

"It wasn't luck," Sravika replied. "It was Belarrin."

Fedigni spat. "I hope that Iron-Man traitor died in the battle. We should've killed him when we had the chance."

"You're a fool, Fedigni!" Sravika snapped.

"And you're smitten blind! Belarrin came to destroy us."

"Until he saved us." Sravika felt heat rise in her face. "Are you going to be furious for what he was, or grateful for what he became? You can't be both. We are Scions of the Fallen

Tree, not the Fallen Tree itself. The tree is dead and we've risen from it."

"I hope you're right." Argluf said, but Fedigni only turned away.

"Our life is the future," Sravika told him, "not the past. By rejecting what he was, if anything, Belarrin has shown us what it means to be a Scion."

"You're as bad as that Finnie," Fedigni muttered.

Sravika turned to look toward the center of the glade. The woman had risen to her feet and was watching her patiently. Her four guards still circled her, their spears hovering inches from her skin, but she appeared not to notice. Even under heavy guard and with wrists bound, there was a magnificence to her, a grandeur Sravika couldn't even hope to achieve. It was in her posture, in the smoothness of her face, in the depths of her eyes. Meeting those, Sravika realized she had seen the Finaestari once before. "Why is she here?"

"Because Laerdina is a fool," Fedigni said. "She should be dead."

Henirgar said, "She is unarmed and, as best we can tell, came alone. She insisted on speaking to you."

"Me?" Sravika crossed the glade to stand before the Finaestari. She forced herself to keep her hands loose on the spear, though she wanted to clench it until her knuckles burned. "Why are you here?" she asked the woman.

"I'm here because you need me, just as I need you."

"We don't need you and I don't care what you need."

The woman dipped her head. It was a very human movement. Sravika didn't know what it meant for a Finaestari, but from a human it would have signaled that she acknowledged the statement, disagreed, but wouldn't argue it. "Who are you? Why did you ask for me?"

"My name is Ninanna," the woman replied. "I asked for you because I know you are important to Belarrin."

That name drew a host of murmurs from the other Scions who'd gathered around to listen. Sravika felt her jaw tighten. "Why do you know Belarrin?"

Ninanna's lips twisted in distaste. "I commanded the raids where he was first slipped in among the prisoners."

That brought angry mutters from the Scions and Yrpel yelled, "Then you killed my people!"

Ninanna flinched though Sravika couldn't tell if it was from the ferocity of the denunciation or from the truth of it. "That isn't a wise claim to make in this company," Sravika told the Finaestari. "If you led the raid and helped Iron-Men infiltrate us, then you're our enemy. Why do you claim to be an ally, now?"

Ninanna grimaced. "The world I live in isn't always a pleasant one."

"And ours is?"

"You misunderstand me. I only meant that sometimes a person has fewer choices than it might appear. I commanded the raid with great reluctance. I didn't know of Belarrin or the other infiltrator until long after the deed was done."

"You were commander. How could you not know?"

"Syraestarin politics are… complicated. I wasn't well regarded by my people then. I am in even less favor now. I don't expect you to believe this statement, but I am named a 'human-lover' by my own kind and am mistrusted because of it."

"And are you? A lover of humanity?"

"Yes."

"That is an easy claim to make," Sravika said. "How do you intend to prove it?"

"The only proof I can offer is that I am here. Alone."

Fedigni stepped up beside Sravika. "I'm tired of this! This troglyd spawn has been saying the same clever words ever since she arrived, tempting the weaker and more good-hearted of us to false delusions. The answer is simple. She is a Finnie. She must die."

Ninanna turned to face the man. "Tell me, Fedigni, have none of your race ever subjugated another into slavery? Have any of your race ever committed murder?"

Fedigni's eyes flashed. "I have not."

"Neither have I," Ninanna replied. "Kill me for who I am or for what I've done, but not for the crimes of others of the race to which I was born. If you kill me for the blood in my veins, then you're no better than the worst of my kind."

"You play well with words, Finnie, but I won't trust you."

"I do not play, Fedigni, and I know you do not trust. You're wise not to. In your place, I would not. All I desire is that we may talk without killing each other, but you refuse to consider anything beyond the simple world your eyes show you. It is the same trap that enslaves the t'Okaedrin. You refuse to see what lies beneath."

"I see the blood of my people on your hands!"

The Finaestari rolled her shoulders as if physically warding off anger and frustration. She turned to Sravika. "I am done with this sparring. You will decide now. Three choices lie before you. Hear what I've come to say, send me away, or kill me, if you think you can."

"You will not order us, butcher," Fedigni retorted.

"Then name a fourth choice and take it," Ninanna replied. "But I already know which you would choose, Fedigni, and if it is the greater answer, then I shall face it as I may."

Sravika rested her hand on his shoulder. "The Finaestari is right. We should hear what she has to say before we decide anything else."

Fedigni pulled back from her touch. "You aren't chieftain here."

"Nor are you, Fedigni."

"No one is," he retorted. "Because she murdered him!"

Determination flashed across Fedigni's face, a moment before he moved. Sravika raised her hand to stop him, but he was too fast. He leapt forward with spear outstretched, driving straight toward Ninanna's midriff.

The Finaestari shifted. It was like watching the wind given shape as Ninanna twisted her body around the lunge. Her bound hands lifted as the spear point slid past her face, grasping the haft between them. She pushed up, catching the spear in her binding ropes, deflecting the strike. As she straightened, her foot last out, catching Fedigni in the stomach. He dropped, stunned, and she pulled the spear from his grasp.

"Syrfinet ivakemai ichisi," Ninanna said and the rope binding her wrists tore into individual fibers and fell away. Then she turned and flung the spear into the wilderness behind her. Sravika could only watch in awe. Ninanna had been right. If she wanted them dead, they would be. All of them.

Ninanna's face reddened in fury. "I had hoped to find wisdom here, better than that of my own kind. I had hoped to find allies, perhaps even friends, but I see only wounded souls, so damaged that you know only hate. I truly hope that you survive, but if hate is all that remains, you will destroy yourselves as surely as my own people would." She turned on her heel. "His Highest Above's blessings upon you."

Stunned, the surrounding Scions stepped back and allowed her to pass through. As she watched, Sravika felt a part of herself die, though she couldn't say why. Perhaps it was a final link to Belarrin tearing away.

CHAPTER 36
Oath

"As I witnessed the horrific loss of the Cataclysm, I deluded myself with the hope that it would be like a smelter's fire, searing away all impurities until only the good remained. I was a fool, for we remained unchanged, unrepentant, and no wiser for the trial. I realized then, as I should have long before, that there could be no paradise this side of death."

—Unknown Aestarin

"Wait," Sravika heard herself say. "Please."

The glade was silent, all eyes upon the retreating back of the Finaestari Sword-Whisperer. Ninanna paused beside a cedar at the forest edge and reached out to touch its rough bark. Her shoulders heaved in a deep sigh as she spoke without looking back, "Why should I continue to waste my time here? I've come only to speak words, yet have been attacked not once, but three times without retaliation. What else need be said?"

"Three times?" Sravika glared at Fedigni.

He staggered back to his feet, still clutching his stomach, and matched Sravika stare for stare. "Who are you to judge me? She's a Finnie so there can be only one answer."

"Is that all you see?" Sravika asked, realizing she was mirroring Ninanna's words.

"We're both members of the council, your voice is not greater than mine. You are no chieftain."

Sravika frowned, unsure of what to say. Fedigni was in pain, she knew that. But it was not his alone. The losses of the days before lay like an open wound across them all. Laerdina spoke quietly into the silence, "She should be."

"And throw our lot in with this monster?" Fedigni cried.

Laerdina turned to Argluf who stood nearby. "Who do you believe should be chieftain?"

"Why does my word matter?"

"You are the only other surviving member of the council. We make our choice and bring it to the people for consent."

Argluf looked at Ninanna, still standing at the edge of the glade with her back turned. "I don't know how you can ask me. I've only been here a short time."

"You've fought beside us, you've bled with us, you've lost with us," Laerdina replied. "What more must you do?"

Argluf swallowed. "I hate the Finnies for what they've done to me, to my people. Ten years of my life were consumed in toil in their camps. Before that, they killed my wife and stole my children away to be raised into Iron-Men. For ten years I've wept and dreamt of vengeance." Fedigni nodded as Argluf spoke. "But I am tired. I'm weary to the heart in a way that no amount of bloodshed can sate. We ignored Chief Jarkon when he agreed with Belarrin that we should flee. We ignored him and condemned Belarrin instead. I choose Sravika. I've never heard her say a rash word, nor have I ever seen her show anything but compassion and determination for myself and our people."

"But you already know what she'll do!" Fedigni cried. "By choosing Sravika, we choose to bind our lives to this spawn of Cydion!"

"Maybe," Argluf answered, "but we should listen to her first, just as we should have listened to Belarrin's warning. I won't make that mistake again."

Laerdina turned to Dirbructi. "You aren't a member of our council or our clan, but you have fought with us side by side. Have you any thoughts on the matter?"

"As much as the thought of an Iron-Man among us turns my stomach," Dirbructi said, "I cannot but admit that Belarrin and Sravika are the ones who saved us. I have no ill word to speak of her."

Sravika was surprised that Fedigni held his tongue, though his face purpled. Yet she was not angry. Her heart knew only pity. Fedigni had once been a gentle man, kind, and careful. But this war was corrupting them all with its pain and its loss.

Laerdina turned to the assembled Scions. "The Council has chosen Sravika as our chieftain. In quieter days we might have had time to consider longer and deliberate, but these are desperate times and we must decide now. You know that

Sravika would have us listen to the Finnie and if we accept her, we agree with that choice. What say you?"

A cry of joy rose up in the glade. "Sravika!"

Sravika felt her cheeks redden at the accolades as Laerdina turned to her. "The people have decided. Do as you've chosen, chieftain."

Sravika nodded. There would be time later to begin the healing with words of courage and kindness. But for now, the greater question lay before them. Deciding to take a symbolic gesture, she took several steps forward, moving away from the apparent safety of the gathered Scions toward Ninanna. "Please return, Ninanna. Speak and we will listen."

"Fah!" Fedigni muttered under his breath, but otherwise held his peace.

The Finaestari turned slowly and Sravika saw the sheen of tears on her face. The other Scions were far enough away she doubted they could see, but Sravika felt her own anger and pain diminish at the sight of them. Ninanna returned to stand face to face with Sravika. The Finaestari was a full head taller, but she lowered her chin to meet Sravika's eyes. "Thank you," she said with hushed voice. She scanned the gathered Scions before. "Before I begin, I believe I should apologize."

"For what?" Sravika asked.

"I have failed your race. I spoke truthfully before when I said that I've never done humanity wrong, but that isn't enough. For far too long, I chose the slow path, seeking to change my people from within and all the while your people suffered and died. I am Syraestari, what you call Finaestari, but unlike most of my kind, I am still in many ways Tirnaestari."

"I don't know what that means," Sravika said.

Ninanna smiled. It was a gentle expression tinged in sadness. "Just words. Titles we give to hate our enemies and love ourselves. My people have been divided for two thousand years. We were broken by our Oath. One which my people no longer follow but I have never surrendered."

"I don't understand. What oath?"

Behind her, she heard Chostir whisper, "The legends are true."

Ninanna's eyebrows rose. "I forget sometimes how much knowledge has been lost. This Cataclysm has inflicted a thousand kinds of evil, not least upon our memories." She drew in a breath. "In ancient days, when death entered the world, it didn't touch my people as it did yours, the Bergrist, or the Ie'dhae. To stop the annihilation of your races, His Highest Above granted the gift of birth through his Etyni. But the Etyni were worried about the strength of the Aestari. Since we do not age, it was felt that we would become masters over the world, subjugating all others. Thus birth was denied us even though we longed for children of our own.

"In the end, the Etyni relented, but only in exchange for an Oath which demanded that we seek as much good for the other races as our own. But with time, the Oath became a cancer that gnawed at my peoples' hearts. There were some who felt it was an enslaving chain holding us in eternal servitude. My people split in a bloody Schism with those who kept the Oath naming themselves Hiraestari – which means higher – for we believed we held the greater purpose. But our enemies called us Tirnaestari, or bound, for we remained enslaved to the Oath. Those who turned from the Oath took on themselves the name Syraestari, or true, for they felt that they became the true version of what our people were meant to be. We who kept the Oath named them Finaestari, or dark, for the shadows that lay upon their souls."

Sravika wondered who the Bergrist and Ie'dhae were, but that wasn't the important question of this moment. "But you claim to uphold the Oath, yet you are from the Finnies. I mean, Finaestari."

Ninanna nodded. "I am of both yet of neither. I am true and bound, high and dark. The story of how I came to be who I am is long and complex. Suffice it to say, I was cast out from the Hiraestari. Despite holding the Oath, I was accepted among the Syraestari, albeit grudgingly. But now that, too, is ended."

"But these are just words," Argluf said. "I've heard oaths given a hundred times and ninety-nine were broken."

"Not this Oath," Ninanna replied. "It came from the Etyni and pierced our souls. It was not something easily broken and that breaking carried a price. As a final proof of my devotion to it, I shall recite it again that you might hear and see that its power remains undiminished." She knelt down on both knees and with head bowed, clasped her hands in front of her. A hush fell over the glade and Sravika got the sensation that even the world itself bent forward to listen. "I swear beneath the eyes of His Highest Above and all of his Etyni that I shall uphold this Oath. That through the benevolent foresight of Ainii, our Shaper, I am freed of the curse of age and infirmity and of the death that follows from it. That by the granting of the gift of birth, we of the Aestari race might grow and multiply. That I shall not use this Gift to subjugate the Bergrist, the Human, or the Ie'dhae. That I will bend the knowledge and wisdom we gain through our prolonged lives as much to the betterment of these other races as to ourselves. This I so swear, to neither rule nor be ruled, but to aid in eternal friendship, never forgetting the blessings that have fallen upon me nor the source of this benevolence."

As Ninanna spoke, Sravika sensed a warmth rising up from deep within the Finaestari. It grew in strength as she continued, transforming into a golden glow that surrounded her. It reminded her of the sorcery of Belarrin, filled with power and wonder beyond the strength of mere words. But there was something deeper, beyond mere sorcery, delving to the very foundation of creation. When Ninanna finished, she fell silent, breathless. After a long moment, she rose slowly to her feet as one shrugging off a great weight and blinked, her eyes regaining focus on Sravika. "Now, with your agreement, we can speak of present things."

"Yes," Sravika replied. She had to mentally shake herself. There was power here, but that didn't mean she could relax. Whatever Ninanna's intentions were, she was still an outsider, a Finnie.

"It is important that you understand that not all Finaestari revile humanity," Ninanna said. "I must confess that few have kind feelings for your race, but most are indifferent rather than hateful. Even among those who are indifferent, there are some who believe that slavery is not the right course. It has long been my hope that my people all come to this conclusion. They wouldn't do so for your sakes, but their own. Our original intention was to find a land of our own, free of any other races, where we might be our own people, but the Cataclysm forced us in our desperation to try and carve a land that wasn't secure. Unfortunately, that turned us to slavery. The Cataclysm is ending. The fires cool and the ice recedes and we should be departing, but many of my people no longer wish to. They have become fond of the power and opulence their slave-world permits." Ninanna looked out at the surrounding Scions. "You may not know it, but your raids have terrified my people. No one dares live beyond the walls of our nine cities. The unpredictability of your attacks mean that we can only defend ourselves from positions of great strength. We simply lack the numbers to do more." She let out a slow sigh. "But despite all this, I fear your cause is doomed in the end."

"What madness is this, then?" Fedigni cried and was echoed by dozens of others. "I warned you not to listen to her!"

Sravika's ears burned, too, but she said, "Let Ninanna finish."

"I don't mean to enrage you," the Finaestari said, "but plead that you will see your own desperate fate. You know the cost that accompanies your raids and I won't insult you by addressing it. But do you realize what this existence is doing to you as a people?"

"What are you saying?" Sravika asked, but even as she did, she suspected she knew the truth.

"This struggle has so consumed you that you see nothing else," Ninanna replied. "It is destroying you from within as surely as my people are destroying you from without. You aren't growing in numbers or in knowledge. This Scion war has waged for over a hundred years, but your strength is unchanging. Yes, the realm of my people remains frail and yes, our expansion is stilted, but it is not stopped. For generations you have fought the Iron-Men, yet you are no closer to recovering the secret of iron for yourselves. You scavenge what you can, and use it, but that's all. That is why you are failing. You need villages, towns, people to work the fields, people to learn the forging of metals, people to write and record. This cannot be achieved as long as you scatter to survive."

You're suggesting we unify," Sravika said. She glanced over at Laerdina and Fedigni. "Jarkon said much the same thing in the council meeting before the raid. I didn't like what he said then, but given what we've just been through, I'm beginning to see the wisdom of it."

"But Jarkon wanted to run away," Fedigni protested. "Have you forgotten everyone who died? Think of Chief Kitiger and Mirnadd and Zoltha. Think about my wife! Did they die for us to bow before this monster and flee just because she asks us to?"

From near the back of the Scions, Yrpel spoke, "You didn't know Zoltha. Vengeance may be the life I know, but it was not his way."

"Or Mirnadd's," Tayrja said. Still weak from her injuries, she leaned on Henirgar for support. "I saw the light leave his eyes," her voice choked off. "He didn't save me for vengeance, but because he loved me. He wanted me to live on even if it was without him."

"But we're saving more slaves than ever before," Fedigni said.

"And the cost has been greater, too," Sravika said. "One Scion band was totally destroyed and ours is in tatters."

"We always knew this war had its risks. You knew that, too, or have you forgotten? Just days ago you played with my anger, Sravika, pushing me to set aside caution for the sake of this war."

Sravika bowed her head. "I know, Fedigni."

He flung his hand out, pointing an accusation at Ninanna. "And now you want me to trust her? A Finnie? I would rather trust in ourselves. I would rather trust His Highest Above. He sent the Shadow of Zaris who has pointed us unerringly where to strike."

Ninanna's sigh interrupted Sravika's response. "The creature you know as the Shadow of Zaris is no such thing," she said. "He is another Finaestari."

"Lies!"

"My people know him as the Shadow-Servant. He is a spy and assassin. He doesn't love humanity, nor does he feel any compassion for your plight. He wants our people to leave this place and sees the Scions as tools to help him achieve that."

"How is that any different than you?" Sravika asked.

"From your view, I doubt you can see a difference. We both want our people to abandon this dominion we've created, but I also wish for humanity to thrive."

"You can't prove any of this," Fedigni said.

"You're right," Ninanna replied.

"So we're just supposed to take your word for it?"

"That is for you to decide. With time, you may be able to verify some of what I say, but time is what you have least. But if it helps you understand, it was this Shadow-Servant who told Belarrin he is Siharrin. A sorcerer. He also told Belarrin that his life as a t'Okaedrin was a lie. In order to convince him that his heart had changed, he attacked you, Sravika. By forcing Belarrin to face losing that which he valued most, he made Belarrin see who he really was."

"What!" Yrpel cried. "It wasn't me?" The big man stumbled and might have fallen had Idysha not caught him. But Sravika could only nod, feeling suddenly warm. Belarrin had changed for her? Yet everything Ninanna said fit together better than anything she'd known before.

Ninanna turned to face her. "I must beg forgiveness for his actions, Sravika. As I said, he sees humans as a tools to manipulate. When Belarrin learned of it, he banished the Shadow-Servant."

"But when you warned us of the raid, you said you were working with him," Sravika replied.

Ninanna nodded. "I am. He is aware of my beliefs and now that we're working together, I believe that will restrain him. He is dangerous, but so am I."

Sravika looked at Fedigni, but his lips were compressed to a fine line. From his eyes, she could see that he, like herself, saw the truth in the Ninanna's words. "What you said before, it sounded a lot like what Chief Jarkon wanted us to do." She turned to address the gathered Scions who hadn't been in the council meeting. "Jarkon wanted us to join together, not to fight, but to flee. He saw that we will never be strong enough to defeat the Finnies as we are now. But we are strong enough to find a place of safety for ourselves and establish a true kingdom of our own. We will learn how to mine, smelt, and forge iron. We will learn how to fight as the Iron-Men fight and we will grow strong. Then, once we're strong enough to stand against them, we will return to the battle to free our people."

Murmurs passed through the crowd, mostly grumbles, and Sravika didn't blame them. Jarkon had explained it so much better and, at the time, she'd disagreed with him. She still wasn't sure in her own mind. She turned to Ninanna. "It is hard for us, myself included, to give up this fight. It feels cowardly."

"That's because it is," Fedigni snapped.

"Sometimes wisdom can look like cowardice, but sometimes patience is the only path to survival," Ninanna replied. She smiled gently. "Your friend Jarkon was right, I believe, but there is more to what I propose. And this may make the decision more palatable. You must flee to marshal your strength if you are to survive, but before you do, I see an opportunity to bloody the noses of my people as never before. Strike them hard enough and they may choose to flee to a distant refuge as I hope. Yet even if that fails, you may be able to liberate the slaves of an entire city and so damage the faith of my people in themselves that they'll be forced to treat humanity with greater respect."

"What is this opportunity?"

"Unite as many bands as you can, just as you proposed," Ninanna replied. "From what I understand, you have members of two other bands here with you now. The Shadow-Servant, acting as the Shadow of Zaris, has found five more of your bands and told me their locations. The t'Okaedrin would never expect a coordinated attack from eight groups of Scions at once. Furthermore, you have allies on the inside. Myself, the Shadow-Servant, and Belarrin."

"Why not continue the fight, then?" Fedigni asked. "None of that will change after a single battle."

"Belarrin will be exposed once he acts and you must understand that sorcerers, for all their power, are also vulnerable. A single Siharrin among a host of humans will draw the attention of every Syraestari sorcerer like vultures to a dying animal. But more than that, my people will change, too. Eight bands and hundreds of freed slaves won't be able to hide in the wilderness. My people have grown lazy in this raiding war, but a pitched battle like this will rouse them. Not only will they amass their host of t'Okaedrin, but they may well send their own warriors into battle. These are men and women with hundreds of years of experience, many in both swordplay and sorcery. If you linger, it will become a war of annihilation, one you cannot hope to win."

Sravika found herself nodding. "Yes, such a raid would give us both the pleasure of justice and vengeance for what the Iron-Men did to us. And with a thousand freed Kalilaer, it would be the greatest victory the Scions had ever experienced."

"And they would make a powerful army to continue the fight," Fedigni said, crossing his arms.

Laerdina touched his shoulder gently. "My friend, you know that's impossible. We can't hope to hide a thousand Kalilaer from vengeful Finnies and most would take months or years before they're ready to fight alongside us."

"But..." Fedigni could only shake his head. It took a long moment to say more. "It is a hard hard thing. I love the idea of freeing an entire city, but knowing we have to run afterward?" He sighed. "Yet I know you're right and saying otherwise would only be folly. That doesn't mean we should blindly follow Ninanna, though. She may be what she claims, but she may be an enemy in the guise of a friend."

Sravika turned to the rest of the Scions. "Does anyone else have a question or a doubt? Or do we all agree?" Yrpel raised a hesitant cheer, but otherwise, they were silent. Everywhere she looked, though, Sravika saw heads reluctantly nodding. She turned to Ninanna. "It would seem you've convinced us. I can only pray that you're leading us true."

"In the days to come, I hope to earn that trust."

Now that they had made the decision, Sravika felt her confidence growing. Perhaps Ninanna was right, and Jarkon and Belarrin. Had she allowed herself to be so preoccupied by what lay beyond the end of her spear that she could see nothing else?

She looked to her councilors. "It is good to have a purpose again and there is much to be done."

"Medienasovel trest'Onath sarnifoeka amdelis."

Reigliff sensed more than saw the shadowed sleep spell fall over the courier. Once it was fully in place, he slipped the door fully open and stepped inside. Shutting the door behind him, he lit the candle he'd brought and set it on the nearby table. He wouldn't risk someone being overly alert and noticing that the room's own candle had burned down inexplicably.

He surveyed the room. It contained a bed, a storage chest, and small table along with a single chair. This room in Fuldynathir, home to High Lord Ovirkar, might have been a testament to his lack of creativity had not all the other guest chambers in all of the other cities been just as drab. Did that blandness speak to a common attitude of Syraestari high lords toward their guests?

Reigliff walked up beside the courier and checked to make sure that his breathing was normal for one in a deep sleep. It had taken him nearly a week to track the courier down. Onath, the empress' personal messenger, was always on the move. Which, of course, meant he was cursed to stay in many of these lifeless rooms. Yet Onath was known for his dogged loyalty and diligence. A requirement for carrying royal correspondence with the utmost of circumspection.

The storage chest was locked, but it took Reigliff only a moment to pick it. In this case, he was willing to risk a few minor scratches on the already battered lock, rather than spend the time of study required to discern the best magical phrase to open the lock without damaging it.

Inside the chest lay the courier's satchel containing a dozen letters. Sitting at the table, Reigliff quickly scanned through them. They each were carefully folded and closed with the empress' personal seal. Every one of them, he knew, was a private message. For more general business, Kayrstana would have used more normal means. He flipped through them closely, scanning each. Most were addressed to a high lord, though one was to the sorceress Medreuneth, and another to a significant merchant in Sarhystoeka. One, though, was unmarked.

Curious. That meant only Onath could know its recipient should idle eyes fall upon the letters. Reigliff rubbed his chin, pondering. It could be nothing, or everything. He took out his knife and warmed it against the candle flame. When the blade was well heated, he lowered the letter to the table and slid it against the wax.

A faint curl of smoke rose from the seal and Reigliff drew back, cursing under his breath. If he hadn't been concentrating, if he hadn't known the spell, everything would have been ruined. He paused, lifting the letter again and inspecting the seal closely. Yes, it was definitely ensorcelled. If tampered with, it would burst into flame. But there were ways around such things. In this case, the Flesh of Isfalinis could work as a fine counterpoint to smother the violence at Isfalinis' Heart.

Reigliff warmed his knife blade again, but this time as he pressed it against the wax, he whispered, "Masaer foesadoti'oe ipainyn." The wax discolored, faintly, as it tried to incinerate the letter, but his spell prevented flame. When he was done, he eased the letter open. The wax held its shape and only one watching closely would notice the change in color after he resealed it.

He sat back in the chair and read. "Cydion's Abyss!"

It was from Kayrstana to Ushtyl. "Her love." That meant the two most dogged rivals were actually in collusion. Reigliff quietly scanned through the letter but the contents themselves were of little importance. Just idle words passing from one love to another. But the fact of that love changed all of Reigliff's assumptions about the high lords' conspiracy. No, not a conspiracy at all, but a trap. One with many victims. It was clever. Brilliant, even. But very dangerous, too. It had already claimed Ninanna and could well claim the empress herself if she weren't careful.

Reigliff eyed Onath, who still slept soundly, then turned his focus back to the letter. Knowing the incantation that had set the trap, it was easy enough to seal the letter again and put it back into place. Then he returned the satchel with its collection of letters back to the storage chest and locked it. When Onath awoke the next morning, he might be surprised at how deeply he slept, but there would be nothing to draw suspicion that anything had happened.

Blowing out his candle, Reigliff gave it a moment for the wax to cool before returning it to his satchel. Then he opened the door a crack and looked out into the hallway. All was silent. He slipped into the hall, out of the palace, and into the night.

CHAPTER 37
Discord

"There is nothing in this life so addictive as power. It is a fount that, rather than quenching, evokes even greater thirst. It is the rare man indeed who, once having drunk deeply of that spring, can cast it all away, even for the sake of love, duty, or honor."

—Queen Cathryn of Tuenosia

"My name is Talikae." The Stone Sister smiled at Belarrin. "In the room beyond, a bath has been drawn. When you're done, return here and I will see that your hair is groomed and that you're properly shaved."

"I can shave myself," Belarrin replied.

"No doubt," Talikae replied. "But I will be the one punished if you aren't to Her Imperial Majesty's standards."

Talikae's light-hearted tone regarding the harsh punishment that might await her startled Belarrin. But then, he might have said something similar when he still believed the Syraestari to be one step short of perfection. Now, though, it startled him to contemplate how easily the lash had become such a basic part of life for his brothers and sisters.

"Very well," he said and stepped into the bathing room. Talikae closed the door, sealing him in his solitude.

Steaming water had been poured into a large wooden basin. It smelled faintly of wildflowers. He carefully eased himself into the hot water and felt tightness leech from his bones. If only it could release the deeper tension constricting his soul. Everything he'd witnessed since his arrival home reminded him of how different he was from who he had been. Every act that had once given him pride now turned his stomach. And he was reminded again and again of the slavery he and his family suffered blindly. He was uncertain how much longer he could uphold the lie. But as long as he was here among his brothers, he wanted to believe that there was some good he could do, both for his old family and his new one.

Belarrin shook his head, whispering to himself, "I can't remember the last time my life wasn't a lie."

In a nearby room, his father was undergoing the same preparations. They'd been summoned to Nahirazith earlier that morning. The empress was in the city with all of her high lords and wanted to personally meet the infiltrator. It was an honor never before afforded to a human and his father was bursting with pride. But Belarrin was terrified and furious. He was about to step before the throne of the most powerful ruler in the world. A ruler who had subjugated his people into slavery.

When he'd finished washing, Belarrin stepped from the tub and dried off. On the nearby table, he saw that Talikae had laid a new set of clothing for him. It was a stylized variation of the normal t'Okaedrin garb, a linen burgundy tunic with brighter red trim at the cuffs and collar. The cloak was crimson and the breeches black. He pulled on the clothes and found them to be far more comfortable than what he usually wore. They fit perfectly, even the leather boots that were buffed to a gleam. At his father's direction, he'd also brought the ring Lord Tazil awarded him after his first infiltration. He shivered as he slid it onto his finger. It was his reward for murdering Vitarria. And now he was to be acclaimed for a host of new murders.

Stepping back through the door, Belarrin saw Talikae waiting for him. She gestured him toward a stool beside which she had set a comb, a blade, and a basin of warm water. She started with his hair, running the comb through, and pulling out all the knots. She was firm but not harsh, no matter how many times it snagged.

"You're the one who lived among the Scions, aren't you?" she asked after a while.

"Yes."

"What is the forest like?"

"The forest?" Belarrin said, surprised at the question. He'd been approached by many t'Okaedrin and Pi'aernoth since his return and all the questions had been the same. How had he been able to endure living among savages? How did they survive with only wood and bone for tools? What was it like, sheltering in homes of mud and twigs?

"I've only seen it from a distance." Talikae hesitated a moment, then added, "I was afraid of it once, but I'm curious now. Is it frightening living inside?"

"No," Belarrin replied. "It's more alive than life here on the plains, and very green and very crowded." He continued describing the forest as she worked and Talikae hung on every word. She asked him about the trees, the wildlife, its smells and its sounds, but she said nothing of the Scions or the war. It was, he realized, the most pleasant conversation he'd had since returning to the t'Okaedrin. When she was done, his hair had been trimmed and combed, his chin shaved closer than he'd ever managed himself.

The door opened and Dalric walked in with an older Pi'aernoth. His father was also newly groomed and wearing fine new clothing. He grinned at Belarrin as he sat down on a nearby stool. Belarrin matched his smile even as a new thought emerged into his mind. Dalric wasn't his father. For the first time in his life, he wondered who his real parents had been. Had they been slain when he was taken or were they slaves toiling for their masters, still grieving the son they'd lost long ago? Yet he loved Dalric. He was a slave, too.

"Now," the older woman said, "I will instruct you on the etiquette of the court. Attend closely or we all may lose our heads."

When the doors swung wide, Belarrin's mind roiled with all the information that Talikae's mother had given him. He and Dalric walked in front and the two women followed as attendants.

Rather than holding court within High Lord Ushtyl's palace, the empress had convened in the large courtyard outside, where all the people of Nahirazith could attend. Beneath the palace itself at the head of the circular plaza, the eight high lords and ladies sat with the Empress Kayrstana at their center.

Belarrin blinked in the bright sunlight. It gleamed off the high roofs of the surrounding buildings, the sorcerer's tower, and temple where the alabaster statues of the lost Etyni seemed to come to life. A chill autumn wind whipped through the wide streets, rustling the dozens of banners and pennants. Syraestari ringed the plaza, perhaps the entire population of the city bolstered by even more from across the realm. They all wore their finest clothes, robes, gowns, and tunics, in reds, blues, and purples colored from the richest dyes and trimmed in silver and gold. Even the meanest Syraestari had rings on their fingers, the woman wearing precious stones in their ears and on bracelets at the wrist that sparkled in the sun. Their eyes, one and all, were painted, some simply around the lids but most in elegant representations of bird wings, talons, wind, or rain. Interspersed among them were Pi'aernoth attendants, easily marked by their simpler garb, though it still was far finer than anything a Kalilaer might wear. A handful of t'Okaedrin were present, too, from Belarrin's own family. They had been given new crimson cloaks for the occasion and stood in two ranks on the far side of the plaza, still and formal in their pride.

As he walked toward the center of the courtyard, Belarrin felt all eyes shift towards him. It was a pressure unlike anything he'd sensed before, pushing against his mind. He made himself ignore the stares of slavers and slaves to focus only on the empress herself. Her Imperial Majesty, the Empress Kayrstana, was a striking woman, noticeably tall despite being seated. Her curled black hair had been lifted into a tower cascading around her golden crown. Her eyes, a gleaming blue, stared at him from the depths of dark eye makeup fashioned to flare up towards her brows and down her cheek like elegant feathers.

He and Dalric stopped a dozen paces before the empress and bowed, dropping first to their knees then prostrating themselves flat upon the ground. Behind him, Talikae and her mother did the same. Face pressed against the smooth stones of the courtyard, anger flared in Belarrin's heart. He was not a beast. No, he was the equal of any who stood or sat before him.

"You may rise," the Empress said. Her voice was melodic and gentle, yet full of authority.

Belarrin and his father rose to their knees. That was as much as a human could ever rise before the empress.

"So, this is the t'Okaedrin who brought two Scion camps to their knees? You have impressed us with your skill and devotion. You are the example to which all of humankind should aspire."

Belarrin said nothing. Talikae had instructed him to be silent unless he was asked a direct question.

"Even Syraestari should aspire to your devotion," she said and rose to her feet. Murmurs trickled through the crowd. According to Talikae, the empress almost never rose from her throne during an audience. Certainly not one with humans. A tendril of fear trickled through Belarrin. Had she seen something that betrayed him? But if she had, her first act would have been a call for the headsman. Instead the empress walked towards him, stopping when she was only three paces away. Belarrin didn't look up, but he could see the soft red slippers upon her feet, peeking out from the bottom of her flowing gown.

When the empress spoke next, her voice was soft, as if meant just for the two of them, but in the silence, he had no doubt it carried across the courtyard. "What is your greatest duty, Okaidir?"

Belarrin answered loudly, for he sensed that was what was demanded of him. "There is no greater duty than to kill in the name of the Empress!"

"And what is your greatest honor, Okaidir?"

"There is no greater honor than to die in the name of the Empress!" Though he spoke the words without inflection, his stomach turned. He should kill her now. She deserved no less and none would be able to stop him. But then another would replace her and slavery would continue as it always had. Her death wasn't enough.

"Yes," the empress replied softly. Turning to face her throne and the attending high lords, she repeated more loudly. "Yes! From the lips of a human, wisdom. From his heart, courage. From his soul, duty. Would that all my subjects aspired to such greatness!" She walked back to her chair and sat down as a hush fell over the waiting crowd. No one spoke in the long silence that stretched until Belarrin began to wonder if he'd been dismissed.

But then, the empress spoke again. "This Okaidir infiltrated a camp of the Scions of the Fallen Tree. Hundreds of his brothers and sisters awaited his summons in the heart of the wilderness to destroy the enemy and recover him. But in the final moments, there was failure. Why?" The empress turned to face the high lords still seated on their thrones. "Why is it that thirty of our t'Okaedrin were lost and at least half the enemy camp escaped our trap? It was not our human servants that failed us. It is not the fault of this man. No, the blame lies here. Too long have our people been divided by the ravages of the Cataclysm. We scattered of necessity while we wandered, eking out a living little better than wildling humans, but no more. We have established a realm. A home. We are here together in one place as one people yet we remain scattered in spirit. It is our bickering, our waywardness, our insolence that poisons our hearts.

"No more! No more will I brook defiance from my own people. I am not blind. I know in whose hearts rebellion lies. I know who would sacrifice the good of our people for the aggrandizement of self. This is my final warning. Cast all such things aside and submit to the future of the Syraestari, a future of glory, prosperity, and security as we haven't known for a thousand years. We are freed of all shackles.

The throes of the Cataclysm are ending. A new age is upon us!"

A cheer rose up from the assembled Syraestari, ragged from some quarters and exuberant from others. When he turned his head just slightly, Belarrin could see the high lords out of the corner of his eye. Cold fury was written on nearly all their faces. The empress' speech wasn't for him, he realized, but for them. He was merely a symbol to bring unity. It was strange to realize that the Syraestari might be so divided. He knew they had disagreements as the Shadow-Servant had alluded to, but nothing as venomous as this. If the empress succeeded in achieving unity, would that be better for the Scions or worse? He couldn't be sure, but feared the latter.

As the cheers faded, the empress turned back to Belarrin. "But you, t'Okaedrin. Father and son and all your brethren. You have shown us duty and honor. You have our thanks and are dismissed from our presence with our blessing."

Belarrin and his father rose to their feet and followed the two Pi'aernoth through the circle of attending Syraestari. This time, little all attention was on them. The Syraestari whispered among themselves with an air of excitement and, perhaps, apprehension.

When they reached the human quarters beneath the palace, Dalric clapped Belarrin on the back. There were tears of pride in his eyes. "You did well, my son. Such honor! I never dreamed that one of the brethren, let alone my own son, might see such a day when the empress, His Highest

Above shine upon her forever, blessed us so. We shall return and share this joy with our family."

"Yes, father," Belarrin said, turning to follow Dalric. But as he did, he caught sight of a perplexed expression on Talikae's face. "What is it?"

"I..." she began to say, then flushed and glanced hurriedly at her mother. "It is nothing. Blessings upon you Vistus."

"And you," Belarrin replied before hurrying after his father. But he understood now. Just like himself, she had seen and recognized the imperfection. Was it possible that there could be others among the t'Okaedrin and Pi'aernoth who weren't blinded by the majesty of their masters?

"Are we going to slink back to our cities and do nothing, then?" High Lord Tazil asked, running his eyes across the other high lords.

Ushtyl had gathered them once more in the Room of the Arching Cedars in the lower parts of his palace. The general darkness of the room and the chairs, gathered in a circle, gave the gathering the conspiratorial air he desired. There was also the advantage of hosting them here while the empress slept in her quarters up above. Ushtyl waited for Tazil's eyes to meet his, then gave a slight nod of encouragement. They all felt the pressure of the imperial decrees now, and needed to be pushed. But he knew he couldn't push them too hard. Just enough to break them.

"Of course not," Sizras replied. "I merely suggest we proceed carefully. The empress has displayed all her intentions for the world to see and we must be careful how we respond."

"Caution has served us poorly enough so far," Arkesh growled.

"I disagree," Ushtyl said, seeing an opportunity. "Yes, we're feeling the retaliation of the empress, but we have to ask ourselves why. She hasn't been this aggressive before. Her own fear is making her bold. The stroke against Ninanna touched close to her heart so she's lashing out. If we respond wisely, we will triumph. We must be careful, certainly." He turned to look at Sizras. "But we cannot long delay, either, or our opportunity will be lost."

"No secrets, though," Tazil said. This time there was a hardness to his gaze as he looked at Ushtyl. "Whatever we do, we do together and openly."

Ushtyl forced himself to hesitate. He didn't want to appear too eager. He was the target of Tazil's comments, though the others might not know that. Ushtyl, on his own initiative, had sent in the second t'Okaedrin infiltrator. It was a pity that the fool had panicked and ruined everything. Tazil's ire from that discovery had weakened their alliance. Compressing his lips to a thin line to suggest he was annoyed, Ushtyl nodded slowly. "Then what options do we have?"

"Only two," Sizras answered. "We bend our knees or we stand in defiance."

"I will not surrender my rule," Arkesh said. Nodding heads around the circle said the rest were with him.

"It must be at a time of our choosing and our defiance must be open and honorable. Anything less and the people won't follow us," Sizras said. "At the moment, all we have are words from the empress. When she next oversteps herself we must act."

"I say we don't wait," Tazil said. "That's all we've ever done. We need to start the confrontation this time. But it must be subtle. We must goad her to try to claim something that has been our responsibility."

"Such as what?" Ushtyl asked. He liked where the conversation was heading. The tension was increasing to a breaking point and the sooner the high lords were broken, the better.

The other high lords all watched Tazil as he considered. Such ideas had always been his strength. He paused, considering, then said, "Perhaps we should return to where this began. With the wildmen. We've driven the greater part of them away from Raefi'ernyn and Nahirazith, but there are many tribes further west threatening the lands of Sizras and Zaerina, not to mention Tyrnis and Jesaelyn. This time, not two cities but six join together to form an army under our own guidance. We can expect the empress to challenge us, just as she did for myself and Ushtyl. But this time, we stand firm as we should have then."

Sizras nodded. "Yes, if she does nothing than her triumph from the first raid loses all meaning. But she cannot make six of us bow. Not when the security of our borders has always been entrusted to us."

"That Tyrnis and Jesaelyn's cities will benefit as well is to our benefit," Zaerina spoke for the first time. "They may disagree with our actions, but they cannot deny the greater security the campaign will bring."

"I like this plan of yours, Tazil," Arkesh said and Ushtyl leaned back, smiling. At last Arkesh was willing to work side by side with Sizras and Zaerina. The conversation was going perfectly. There was little he needed to add now. Let the others carry it forward to the final confrontation.

"But rebellion?" Ovirkar said. "Do you think it will come to that? I hate to take that desperate step."

"As do I," Tazil said. "It turns my stomach, but if we remain strong and determined, we may yet avoid it." He turned to Sizras. "I know you're at least as troubled by rebellion as I am, but you will stay with us if it comes to open war?"

Sizras grimaced. "When I joined this alliance I said I would not, but circumstances are changing and my heart misgives me. With her brazen militant words, the empress has given us little choice. Who among our people could not recognize the cold denunciation she laid directly at our feet. In the hearing of humans, no less!"

"The words of a coward," Arkesh spat.

"Not a coward," Sizras replied, "but a very determined woman. It is possible that, were I in her place, I might have done no less. But I am not. She means to rule us with a scepter of iron and we mean to keep our rights. It's as simple as that. If it does come to rebellion, and I pray to His Highest Above that it won't, it must be quick and decisively executed. We must shed as little blood as possible lest we truly become villains in our peoples' eyes – and our own."

"Enough to bring her down and quell any loyal resistance," Tazil said.

"Yes and then peace and amnesty. We must be whole again as quickly as possible."

"The t'Okaedrin must not become involved, not on either side," Tazil said. "Can you imagine if they were sent to kill Syraestari? Their loyalty would be shattered and we might never be able to trust them again. In sending them off on this raid against wildmen, I think we can avoid that, at least."

"Then I think we are agreed," Sizras said, looking around the room. Ushtyl was pleased to see every head nod in consent. "We begin our planning for a new raid and stand together when the empress challenges us."

"Yes and speak of it only to our most trusted housecarls," Ovirkar said. "If word gets out before we act, we'll all kneel before the executioner's block for certain."

"All the more reason to be careful," Ushtyl told them. "Wayward lips and blood will flow, ours and our peoples."

"There is another choice we haven't considered," Zaerina said. When all eyes turned on her, she continued, though her voice was reluctant. "If the empress were to die suddenly, there would be no need for war."

Stunned silence met her announcement, except Sizras who jumped to his feet. "Lady Zaerina, I protest."

"I don't like it either," she said, "but does one life outweigh the scores that might die otherwise?"

"No," Sizras repeated. "I said no subterfuge and I meant it. I've been plagued by nightmares for even relenting to the framing of Ninanna. I won't abide the murdering of our liege."

"Nor I," Tazil echoed and Ovirkar voiced his agreement a moment later. "One such killing would open the door for more and where would that end?"

Looking at each face, Ushtyl saw that only Arkesh was considering Zaerina's words. And then, an idea sprang to life in his mind. A path for all his own ambitions to come to fruition. It would be more magnificent even than manipulating these high lords to be broken by the empress. It could place him upon the throne itself. He rose to stand with Sizras. "I also cannot countenance murder. We will find another way." He looked to Sizras. "An open, honest way. Rebellion if we must and an appeal to the people."

"As you wish," Zaerina said. "I didn't like the idea any more than you, but neither do I like my people dying for the ills of another."

"Then we're all agreed," Sizras said. "And if we do rebel, there will be no murder. Not even execution. I won't see Kayrstana's life forfeited in this. Abdication will be necessary and, perhaps, banishment."

"It seems an unnecessary risk to tie our hands this way," Arkesh replied, "but if you will not bend then I agree."

"As do I," echoed Tazil.

The words were repeated around the circle until it came to Ushtyl. "I also agree," he said. But the fools had opened themselves to vulnerabilities they couldn't even imagine.

The moment of his ultimate triumph approached far faster than he'd anticipated.

Belarrin stood on the high bluff overlooking the sea. It was wondrous, feeling the wind rush through his hair, listening to the roaring surf below. He'd always loved the wind and even the rain. Now with his affinity to the Breath of Isfalinis, he knew why.

Nahirazith loomed in the distance to his left and the Kalilaer camps were far enough behind him that the toiling slaves were mere specks in the distance. He'd been home only a handful of days and already he had to get away. Every word falling from t'Okaedrin lips that did not sadden him brought rage instead. Every slight he saw from the Finnies drove him to a fury. If he didn't find his self-control, he would say something that would get him killed. It wasn't that he feared death. He knew he deserved it. Kitiger's dying curse echoed in his mind, and even more than that, the brand of coward. Every time he closed his eyes, he saw Zoltha's earnest face looking up at his, or Mirnadd's, or Vitarria's. But whenever Belarrin did die, it had to be for a reason. He had to repay at least some of the cost he'd exacted in his life.

Realizing he was rubbing his clean-shaven chin, Belarrin forced his hand away. He still wasn't accustomed to it. But it was good to have the familiar weight of his sword at his side, though strange and troubling, too. It sometimes felt like a lodestone, pulling him back to his previous life.

He had to tell Bridionis the truth. Ever since his audience with the empress, he'd known he must. Bridionis, his best friend, would be the first. But he was not sure how. How did one go about telling a friend that the only world he knew was a lie? But Belarrin felt like he was running out of time. His family had all been present when the empress denounced her high lords and Belarrin had to act while that memory remained fresh. He could only hope that witnessing those flaws planted the seed for what he had to do. It was hard to admit, but he knew he was afraid.

"It is good that you are alone," a voice said behind him.

Belarrin spun around and drew his sword. His eyes fell upon the black-robed form of the Shadow-Servant, seated on a rock several paces away. "I told you I will not be your tool and that hasn't changed." Belarrin spat.

"Lie to yourself all you wish, but you're doing exactly what I want."

Belarrin felt his face flush red. "I have no interest in exchanging words with you. Have you come to kill me?"

"No."

"Good." Belarrin slammed his sword back into its sheath and strode off toward Nahirazith.

"Then you have no interest in hearing the fate of your friends?"

Belarrin stopped and reluctantly turned.

"Sravika, Yrpel, Idysha, Chostir, and Henirgar escaped. I assume you know about Mirnadd."

"Yes," Belarrin said, dropping his head. The news was a weight off his heart, but that didn't make this creature his friend. "You spied on us even after I refused you?"

"You are not my only pupil."

"I'm not your pupil!"

The Shadow-Servant shrugged. "Regardless, I did not remain. I follow many things, do many things. It was Lady Ninanna who watched you and, as you know, warned you."

"You're working with her now?'

"It might be better to say we have decided to tolerate each other." Belarrin's laugh at that was bitter, but the Shadow-Servant didn't seem to notice. "Lady Ninanna actually cares about humanity, while your kind is of marginal concern to me."

"Honest words for once."

"I have always been honest," the creature replied calmly. "Whether you were willing to listen was the question."

"Honest as you were with the attack on Sravika."

"I said honest, not open. But is this really the best use of our time? To bicker over old wounds that will not be healed?"

"Agreed. I'm done, Shadow-Servant."

Belarrin turned away, but the creature's words stopped him again. "Ninanna is with Sravika and your friends as we speak."

"What do you mean she's with them?"

"Living with them, talking with them, advising them. Something I would never do."

"And this is supposed to make me trust you?" Belarrin faced the Shadow-Servant again.

"Never me. But perhaps her."

"Since you recommend it, I cannot trust her."

"Do you trust Sravika?"

"Yes."

"Sravika is chieftain, now. She's the one who decided to let Ninanna remain."

"You're taunting me with knowledge again, Shadow-Servant. Say what you want and leave me be."

The creature's head tilted to one side. "Is it beyond consideration that I merely wished to see you again?"

Belarrin laughed, but didn't reply.

"Perhaps you're right. Then I come with a warning for you to be ready. Your Scions will have need of you in the days ahead. They are uniting many bands into a great army for a raid on this city."

"But they can't! They'll be destroyed. Even if they succeed, they'll never be able to hide again."

"Hiding is not their intention. After the raid, they are going to flee."

"Flee." Belarrin let out a slow breath. It was what Chief Jarkon had pled for. He wondered how they had come to that hard conclusion. He realized his heart had begun to race. This was all he could have asked for. An end to the hopeless war, an escape from the chains of the t'Okaedrin. But even as the excitement took him, he hesitated.

"Something has occurred to you," the Shadow-Servant said.

Belarrin glared at him. "You have not earned my trust."

"Hold your own council if you choose." The Shadow-Servant rose to his feet. The motion was almost like that of a snake uncoiling. "But your face shows much. You intend to confess to your family."

Belarrin felt his face flush with anger. How could this monster read him so easily? "What if I am?" he snapped.

"If you do, your family will destroy you. Even Bridionis."

"He is my brother. He needs to know."

"He is t'Okaedrin."

"So am I!" Belarrin retorted. "I saw the truth and he deserves the same chance. All my brothers do."

"You saw the truth by living among the Kalilaer and the Scions. How many of the t'Okaedrin have experienced what you have? How many have seen this life from different eyes? And even if they did, do you think they would see clearly? The other infiltrator did not. If you tell your brother, he will kill you or you will have to kill him."

"I won't kill him."

"Then you will die."

"He will not kill me."

"When the Scions strike Nahirazith, they will need you. They will need your place of secrecy among the t'Okaedrin. They will need your sorcery. If you cast your life away, how many Scions will die for your choice?"

"You don't care about the Scions."

"But you do."

Belarrin took a step forward. "It was you and your people that stole life and soul from my brothers. If you lack the courage to fix the injustice, then I will do it and the only way you can stop me is by killing me."

"It will be your dearest brother who drives the knife into your heart."

"And I will let him." Belarrin turned on his heel and strode away. Nothing the Shadow-Servant could say would stop him this time. No one would. This was the price for his life he had been looking for. Judgment for himself. Justice for his brothers. Sravika would have to understand. If he failed, he would have to trust to the Scions courage to see them through.

Despite his resolve, it still took Belarrin a few days to find Bridionis in a place where they could speak. But finally, they sat together in the meal hall alone after a late watch guarding the camp.

Belarrin looked across at his brother. "There is something I have to tell you."

"Of course, my friend," Bridionis grinned.

Belarrin hesitated, then forced himself to continue. There would be no better time. "First you must promise to listen to everything I have to say before you respond."

"What is it?" Bridionis eyed him askance, then his eyebrows twitched. "Did you put ants under Arcomin's bed sheets like we did as children? You should have told me and I'd have helped."

Belarrin laughed. His brother always had a knack for putting him at ease. "No, my rivalry with Arcomin is over. But I'm being serious."

Bridionis looked him in the eyes and his smile faded. "I don't believe I've ever seen you so grim, Vistus. Yes, yes, of course I will listen."

Belarrin nodded and drew in a deep breath. Now that he was about to begin, doubt assailed him, but he pushed on. "I've learned many things over the past few months."

Bridionis' eyes narrowed. "When you were with the rebels? Highest Above, Vistus, don't tell me you listened to their lies."

"Let me finish. You promised."

"Yes, you're right," Bridionis replied. "Continue."

"I've learned many things over the past few months. About myself, about our people, the Syraestari, and the world. Bridionis, I'm a sorcerer."

His brother laughed. "Vistus, you're having sport with me. I thought you were being serious."

"I am serious."

Bridionis leaned forward. "Vistus, there are no human sorcerers. The only ones were apostates in service to Cydion during the Great War. It is a power belonging only to the wisdom of the Syraestari. They train for centuries from what I've heard."

Belarrin had anticipated this. He reached into his pocket and pulled out a small leaf. Holding it up, he concentrated until the familiar golden lines flashed before his eyes. "Eusy'arjev tae'oekym rykatriv naeroda'oesys!"

As it burst into flames, he dropped it. The leaf disintegrated into flakes of ash as it fell. Bridionis cried out and leapt back, stumbling over the bench as he moved. "Highest Above, Vistus! What have you done? How did you…"

"I am a Siharrin, Bridionis. It's a rare gift. The words come to me and I speak them." Belarrin gestured to the seat. "Please."

Bridionis eyed him in awe and a little fear, but edged back to the bench. When he was seated, Belarrin said, "I realize now that I've always had this gift. I think I used it to push the rafters back when the barracks collapsed on me as a child. I know I used it to move the cart that fell on you. My greatest strength is with wind, but I can create fire and heal, too."

"But Vistus, I don't understand."

"It's impossible, right? There are no human sorcerers."

Bridionis nodded.

"We are flawed and imperfect. Lacking wisdom, if left to ourselves we will invariably turn to evil. Only under the guidance of the Syraestari can we thrive, right?"

Bridionis nodded again.

"You were at the audience where the empress spoke to me. Tell me, Bridionis, did you see wisdom and purity?"

"I don't understand."

"The Syraestari are no wiser than we are. You heard the empress' words. She was talking to the high lords. She rebuked High Lord Ushtyl and High Lord Tazil, both of whom we have served, accusing them of greed and rebellion. Those aren't the words of a wise and unified people."

"Vistus..."

"We've been lied to, Bridionis, all of our lives. There have been good human sorcerers as well as evil. There have been good and bad human kingdoms. We are not a lesser people than the Syraestari. We are not fated merely to be their slaves, dying for them, killing our own kind."

"You've become one of them," Bridionis hissed. Fear edged his voice as his face turned white as a snowbank. "They corrupted you."

Bridionis drew back and Belarrin reached for his hand to steady him. But his brother pulled it away and scrambled to his feet, eyes staring at him as if facing a poisonous snake.

"Bridionis, you promised you'd let me explain."

"I promised my brother, not an apostate! I don't know what you are!" Bridionis cried, backing away and drawing the sword at his side.

Belarrin rose slowly to his feet, a thousand curses flying into his mind, none of them strong enough. Staring at his brother's blade, he wondered if Bridionis would kill him. "Please, listen to me. I can explain."

"I won't hear your words!" His brother backed into the hallway and frantically looked either direction as he cried out, "Apostate! Vistus is an apostate and a rebel. He has betrayed us to the Scions!"

Belarrin cursed again and dashed for the door. His brother flinched back as he pushed past, but the hallway was already filling with other t'Okaedrin. Belarrin charged for the outer door, barreling past one, two, then three of his brothers, each more surprised than aggressive. Then someone leapt onto his back. Belarrin struggled against the sudden weight as another brother lunged from the side, knocking his feet out from under him. Belarrin twisted in the air, then landed hard. His head struck the floor and the world went dark.

CHAPTER 38
Emptiness

"Each step I have taken, each one so carefully considered, so apparently reasonable, the best choice at its time. But now at the end of my life as I look back, I can see how each innocent choice was but one more step on the path to ruin. How therefore, I ask, could I have done anything else?"

—King Ardrathon of Ithia

"Are the other t'Okaedrin still to be trusted?" Ushtyl asked, eyeing the unconscious form of Vistus sprawled atop the Boards. They had brought him down to the deepest cells of his palace rather than the Boards out by the Kalilaer camp. This kind of betrayal was not for public spectacle.

"I believe so, my Lord," Captain Eltirkar replied, his face glimmering in the faint golden torchlight of the dark room. "It was his closest brothers who captured him as soon as they realized what he'd become."

"Good. But I want his family watched closely over the next few months." Ushtyl turned to Medreuneth. "Do you have any advice, Lady?"

The sorceress held one of the spears they'd recovered from the raid and she turned the haft idly in her hands as she stared at Vistus. "Forge stronger armor."

"What?"

Medreuneth looked at him. "The spears. I have no affinity with the Spark of the Heavens, but I am sure it has been enchanted somehow. This spear is harder than steel and not brittle. Therefore you might want stronger armor if you plan to fight Scions armed with these."

"Then he is Siharrin as he claimed to his brothers?" Ushtyl asked.

"The one who denounced him claimed he set a leaf on fire with his voice. I can't imagine there is anyone of skill to teach him as you and I were taught. I am reminded of the day of the attack on the Scion camp. Even from here I sensed something strange on the wind. I dismissed the possibility of sorcery, then, but it would seem I was wrong. And, of course, there is this." Her eyes dropped again to the spear and the corner of her lip turned up in a half smile. "Very clever. Brilliant, really. I've never heard of such a thing, even in the age before the Cataclysm. Maybe if you had picked someone more stupid to infiltrate the Scions..." she cut off, but not at Ushtyl's deepening frown. Her gaze was still fixed on the spear. "...no, that wouldn't have worked either. You cannot have a fool carry out such a task. It would be beyond their capabilities."

"Lady Medreuneth," Ushtyl said firmly.

She looked at him. "It seems you have created yourself a conundrum, High Lord. If you pick a fool, they will get caught. If you pick someone clever, they will see through the lies we've created for them. Interesting, very interesting indeed."

"Yes, Lady Medreuneth. Thank you." Past experience had taught Ushtyl that it was pointless to argue with her. She was unlikely to even notice. "Do you have any advice on how to handle the prisoner?"

"It is said that most Siharrin eventually go mad." She tapped her chin with her forefinger thoughtfully. "Curious. I wonder why that would happen? The very definition of Siharrin is one who can navigate the Paths of Power safely. Anyone else who dares risks death, madness, or the scarred mind of a simpleton. I, of course, have managed it safely a few times when necessity demanded it. But he can walk those paths naturally. Why then, would so many Siharrin choose to embrace madness? Embrace." She frowned as she repeated the word, staring off into the darkness. "A curious choice of phrase. I wonder, did I stumble across it with reason?"

"Lady Medreuneth!"

She blinked and turned to meet his gaze again. "I expect you will have to kill him." She shook her head. "Unfortunate. I would have enjoyed learning more of him. I have known of Siharrin, but to actually understand how one's mind works. An unfortunate loss, but unavoidable."

"I want him questioned," Ushtyl said. "Could you stop him if he tries any sorcery?"

"A curious question. One I'd like to know the answer to," Medreuneth said. "But the only way to discover is to try. It might even be worth dying to learn."

"I have no intention of dying," Ushtyl growled.

Medreuneth shrugged. "Then I can be of little use. The best you can do is press a knife to his throat. If you hear any words you don't understand, then kill him. Of course, he'll know that, too, and may choose death over pain. So you can't press him too hard."

Ushtyl nodded. Finally, he was getting somewhere. All Medreuneth's blather had been worth it. "Too little and he won't answer. Too much and he'll force us to kill him. This will require finesse. Lady Medreuneth, you are welcome to stay, should you choose."

She glanced over at Vistus. "I suppose you shall question him on such mundane things as Scions and Kalilaer, even though the finer points of sorcery may be far more telling."

"Regrettably, I doubt we'll have time to discuss sorcery, especially with him so dangerous."

"Ah well, it is as I fear." Medreuneth offered a slight bow. "Then I shall take my leave. Please inform me, High Lord, should anything interesting be said."

After she left the room, Captain Eltirkar muttered under his breath. "Crazy woman."

"Focused, not crazy. And worth tolerating," Ushtyl told him. "Bring in housecarls to ungag and revive the prisoner."

Belarrin lurched awake as a bucket of cold water was poured over his head. He jerked forward in surprise then opened his mouth to scream as lances of pain coursed up and down his arms. But a gag was crammed in his mouth that only sank deeper, choking off his cry. He fell back, striking his head against a hard wood surface.

Tears of pain stung his eyes as he looked around. He was in a small dimly lit room with Ushtyl, Eltirkar, and two housecarls standing opposite him. Ropes bound wrists and ankles, stretching his limbs out away from his body.

Highest Above, not the Boards!

A whimper stole from his throat before he could stop it. Belarrin clenched his eyes shut, trying to slow the panic welling within him. But old nightmares flooded over his mind. Memories of his last time on the Boards, memories of being buried in the darkness.

It was all he could do not to writhe and spasm in his relentless bonds, to scream into his gag. He breathed deeply through his nose, trying to slow his racing heart, to calm his panicked mind. Finally, when he felt he had regained a semblance of control, he opened his eyes.

Eltirkar had stepped forward to loom over him. "Tell us everything you know, traitor, and your pain can end. I don't know if you're Siharrin or not, but say a single word I don't understand and your throat will be opened." He nodded to one of the housecarls who pressed a knife up against Belarrin's neck then tore the gag from his mouth.

Belarrin ignored the blade point. The pain of it pricking his flesh was as nothing compared to the burning fire from his stretched limbs. "Traitor to what? You? A slave cannot be a traitor."

Eltirkar struck him hard in the face, driving Belarrin's head back against the Boards. Darkness edged Belarrin's vision as Eltirkar said, "Where are the other Scion camps?"

Belarrin spat at him.

Drawing a cloth from his pocket, Eltirkar dabbed at his face. Then, he grabbed the rope tied to Belarrin's right arm and pulled. The fiery pain roared into an inferno. Belarrin screamed, his world shrinking to a crucible of agony where thought and meaning died.

After an eternity of moments, Eltirkar released the rope leaving Belarrin heaving to draw breath to his tortured lungs.

In an even voice, Eltirkar asked again, "Where are the camps?"

"Kill me, spawn of Cydion, or I'll kill you," Belarrin retorted, gasping for breath. "I swear it. I'll slaughter you all!"

Eltirkar shrugged. "You can force us to kill you if you're ready to cast it all away now, but I don't think you've given up yet. You still want to live. Or do you simply desire a death less pathetic?" His lips turned upward into an amused smile. "Where are the camps?"

The ropes tightened and Belarrin screamed, rage and agony burning together within him.

"It's wonderful," Ninanna said, looking down at the parchment. Sravika grinned, pride swelling in her heart. "You're very own alphabet from nothing? This is what most impresses me about your race. With short lives, you can lose so much, but you aren't just trying to bring back the past. You look beyond your misfortune."

"I cannot take all the credit," Sravika said. "The idea came from a friend of mine."

"Belarrin?"

"No." Sravika fought down a wave of sorrow. "Zoltha did not survive the raid."

"I wish that I could have done more."

Sravika shook her head, surprised that she was comforting a Finaestari. "Without your warning, none of us would have lived."

Ninanna nodded, returning her gaze to Sravika's writing. "And these words, they are the spells Belarrin cast?"

"Yes, but I've never been able to mimic what he's done."

"It isn't as easy as that." Ninanna smiled. "You must understand the words, their every nuance and then focus all your thought upon them."

"But anyone can cast a spell?"

"Nearly," Ninanna replied. "There are a few who cannot touch sorcery, but this means they also cannot be touched by it. The more powerful one is, the more vulnerable one is. And Siharrin are always very powerful. Belarrin may well be the strongest sorcerer in centuries."

"But the Finaestari haven't forgotten the words, right? And you were a Sword-Whisperer. Doesn't that mean you use magic in battle?"

"Yes, but my skill comes from long practice. Sword-Whisperers chant their magic as an aid to memory and focus."

"Can you teach me?"

"Learning sorcery is a long and difficult process. It requires many hours of study and focus for which we do not have time. But perhaps we can try a little. Ninanna uncoiled her legs and rose to her feet.

Sravika eagerly stood as well.

"I will teach you the words I used to give Tayrja the strength she needed to survive her wounds. It comes in three parts. First, the Residue of Creation must be called. It is the essence, the power from His Highest Above that he granted to the Etyni when the world was first shaped. Only a remnant remains now, an echo of what once was. But it is enough for what we do. In this case, the first word is 'Sinahastir'. It is one of the Sparks of the Heavens, the greatest gift of His Highest Above, the fire of life. It speaks to life's resilience, its potency and will to endure. The second word, 'Yskaesira,' is a command to strengthen. For in speaking these words, we seek to give resilience to that which already exists. 'Yskaesira' does not actually heal, but it hardens the body to preserve life, giving the time it needs to heal naturally. For the final word, I said 'Itavyly,' woman, because I did not know Tayrja's name. The more precise you can be, the greater the power you can summon." Ninanna closed her eyes and drew in a deep breath, then opened them again. "Sinahastir yskaesira Sravika!"

A flush of warmth passed over Sravika. The air suddenly tasted crisper, the leaves were sharper. Her heart raced and she felt as though she could run for a day. She wanted to leap up and dance, crying aloud with joy. Sravika laughed. "That's incredible!"

"Now you try."

It didn't come to her as easily as she had hoped. A dozen times, she said the words with Ninanna correcting her each time. Each sound had to be perfect, the infliction, the pitch. But even when Ninanna approved, nothing happened. Sravika tried again and again. She shook her head in frustration. "Belarrin told me something about affinities. Could it be that I don't have the right one for this?"

Ninanna laughed. It was a gentle sound like water rippling in a creek bed, without a hint of malice. "Humans are always so hasty. It is too soon to leap to that conclusion. Sorcery takes practice and time. You must allow yourself to be patient or you will never succeed. Now try again and pour all of your focus into each word. Think on the meanings and on what it is you desire."

Sravika did as Ninanna said. Closing her eyes, she thought of health, of vibrancy. The strength of the sun and the wind, the feeling of blood racing through her veins, of life and hope and the will to persevere.

"Sinahastir yskaesira Sravika." Nothing happened.

"Good," Ninanna said quietly. "Again."

Sravika thought of her friends, all she had lost. They had fought to the last. She thought of Darr running wounded through the woods so that they could lead Belarrin and the others from the slave camps. She thought of Mirnadd and Chief Kitiger, fighting on against the encircling Iron-Men, knowing they would die but fighting anyway. She thought of her own wounding when Belarrin had pulled her back from death. She had not wanted to die, she had clung to life, to breath to her racing heart."

"Sinahastir yskaesira Sravika."

Even before she finished speaking, there was the sensation of something washing over her. A freshness like the dew on a new spring morning. Just a fleeting sense, then wind rushed in her ears, her heart leaping to exuberant life in her chest. Her muscles tautened with the thrill of strength after a long exercise, yet still the freshness of first waking with a buoyancy that said she could run all day and not grow tired. She realized she was breathing hard. "Highest Above, is that how it always feels?"

"Not always." Ninanna replied. "There is something in the Spark of the Heavens, as though it carries its own joy. There are eight facets of magic and each carries its own taste. They work with and against each other. Think of them as eight spokes of a great wheel, half raised to the heavens, half descending to the world at our feet. They are the Blood, the Flesh, the Breath, and the Heart of Isfalinis and the Beacon, the Void, the Veil, and the Spark of the Heavens. The Void is twisted, a weapon of Cydion, and is filled with corruption.

Only those who are willing to destroy their own souls can use it."

"Belarrin said his strength was with wind."

"The wind is but one part of the Breath of Isfalinis, but it is so much more. I have the greatest affinity to the Blood of Isfalinis."

"Blood?" Sravika asked, wrinkling her nose.

"Not our blood, the blood of the world," Ninanna said. "Rivers and oceans and all that draws from that. Water is clever, it is agile, it is relentless and strong. The Spark of the Heavens, that which you just used, lies close to both the Blood and the Breath."

"What determines a person's affinity?"

"Random chance?" Ninanna shook her head. "His Highest Above only knows. The great Syraestari sorceress Medreuneth is strongest in the Flesh of Isfalinis, the personification of rock and earth, of fortitude and will. The Shadow-Servant's strength lies with the Veil of the Heavens where shadow, deceit, and subterfuge lie."

Sravika suppressed a chill. She wasn't sure what she felt about such a creature aiding Ninanna.

Seeing the expression on her face, Ninanna said, "You are wise not to trust him. I don't trust him either."

"Then why do you ally with him?"

"Because I need him, just as you do." Ninanna let out a deep sigh as if considering her words. "He is not evil. That is too simple a word for so many things. But neither is he good. His only purpose is the betterment of my people and he does not balk at the cost that might mean for anyone, even individuals of our own kind. For now, he hates slavery, and that makes him an ally. But should the tides shift, as they no doubt will one day, he might become an implacable enemy." She shook her head and laughed. It had a bitter sound to it. "Always he has his one singular purpose. If it did not come at such great cost, I would admire it."

Sravika looked up as Henirgar, Idysha, and Yrpel approached. "The first clan has arrived. It is Grannif's people," Henirgar said. "Runners report that three more should be here before midday tomorrow."

Sravika nodded. Every band they spoke to had been reluctant at first, but the arguments were irrefutable. After a period of grumbling, each had agreed. Like herself, that agreement had moved quickly to eagerness, both for the battle to free so many Kalilaer and the hope that such a rescue promised. Sravika began to wonder if they truly had lost sight of hope before this.

"I should leave tomorrow, then," Ninanna said. "There is still a lot to do within the empire to prepare for your attack."

"Many remain concerned that you are leaving us," Sravika said. "Not everyone trusts you."

"That's what I'm for," Idysha said, grinning impishly. "Just tell the doubters I'll have my eye on her."

Yrpel crossed his arms and glanced out of the corners of his eyes at Idysha. "I still think I should be joining you. It isn't safe for any human to be in Finnie lands."

"One is dangerous, but necessary," Ninanna told him, "but two would be far harder to hide. Have no fear, though, I will watch over Idysha and see that she returns safely."

Idysha laughed. "And I will make sure Ninanna returns safely!"

Ninanna smiled but, as she faced Sravika, her expression became serious. "I want to thank you for the trust you have placed in me. I know it isn't an easy thing and I swear to you that I will not cast it aside."

"Thank you, Ninanna."

"And when I've reached Nahirazith, I will check on Belarrin as soon as I am able."

Sravika let out a deep breath. Belarrin. She hoped he was doing well.

Belarrin lay back against the Boards, mind and body swimming in a fog of pain and delirium. He had long since lost track of time. There was only night in the bowels of his cell. He dwelled in an Abyss of darkness, broken intermittently by questions and torture that made the agony of his eternities of empty solitude seem like periods of rest by comparison.

He didn't know why he carried on. His only allies, the Scions, were a people whose trust he had abused, whose kindred he had murdered. They would not and should not care if he were tortured. And even if they did care, they couldn't reach him here with their wooden spears and leather armor. Not against all the mighty defenses of Syraestari warriors born of another age. But he couldn't surrender. Through the pain, the darkness, the stupor that gripped his mind, he couldn't relinquish the belief that there had to be more. That his death, when it came, would be something greater than the pathetic opening of his throat by Eltirkar's knife. And then there were the debts he owed, the penance he could not assuage by some quick coward's escape.

He tried to cling to his debts, to his shame. But he found that the longer he lay in the darkness alone, the more his memories vanished into shadow. Strangely, it was in the moments of fiercest torture where he remembered most. When he knew who and what he was. When he clung most strongly to what he increasingly doubted would ever be. But when even his torturers abandoned him to writhe in duller torment, his limbs splayed wide, it was difficult to remember.

As his mind swam through the shadow of these thoughts, the small corner of it that remained alert realized he was no longer alone. He opened his eyes and squinted in the blinding light of the single wall sconce opposite him. Perched on a stool beside the Boards sat High Lord Tazil.

Looking up into the Syraestari's brown eyes, Belarrin remembered the first time they had met face to face. It seemed a lifetime ago when the Syraestari had held a place of sanctity just beneath the Etyni. When there was no greater honor than to bow and obey. Tazil was different, too, from the Syraestari he recalled from that day. This man before him stood with stooped shoulders. Syraestari faces did not wrinkle under the weight of the elements or with the passage of years, yet there was a sense of age and burden upon his features beyond the heavier shadows cast by the torch.

"I am not here to torture you," Tazil said, "but I do have questions. I realize you cannot answer other than to nod or shake your head and even in that, I will not force you." He paused, perhaps expecting some movement from Belarrin, but Belarrin gave none. He saw little point.

"I don't understand why you've turned your back on us," said Tazil after a long moment. "What we did, what I did, was never for the best of humanity. When we created the Kalilaer, t'Okaedrin, and Pi'aernoth it was to protect ourselves from the devastation we suffered during the Cataclysm. Your kind breed and grow, even in iniquity, and our only chance of survival seemed to be fixed on using humans against humans." He shook his head. "I am no Ninanna, but neither do I despise humanity like some of my people. As we forged the t'Okaedrin, I saw a brotherhood of humans different than what had come before. Different even than the bickering fools my parents told me of from the Lost Age. You were proud, dutiful, focused, and honorable. You were a force to be reckoned with. I was pleased with what you and your brothers had become." Tazil leaned forward. "Was I wrong? Do you truly prefer the squalor of life among the Scions to all we've given you?"

Belarrin considered ignoring the Syraestari, but there was something in his demeanor. It was almost a desperation to understand. And unlike with his torturers, Belarrin saw no value in denial, not even pleasure. He nodded his head.

"You prefer the wilderness?" Tazil asked again and Belarrin nodded.

"Then you hate the t'Okaedrin?" When Belarrin shook his head, Tazil said, "But you hate what they are."

Yes.

"Even if it is a good lie that leads you to a better life?"

Rather than answer, Belarrin only glared at him.

It was Tazil's turn to nod. "I see." He stared down at Belarrin for a very long time as if trying to read his thoughts. Then he rose to his feet and drew his knife. "I would hear your words, Vistus. I dislike what Ushtyl is doing to you. An honest execution would be better, but I won't countermand him. Please don't make me kill you."

After Tazil removed the gag, he lifted a flask to Belarrin's lips while his other hand held the knife to Belarrin's throat. Belarrin drank deeply, thankfully. Then he looked up at Tazil. "I was not the first. I will not be the last."

Tazil did not answer, only staring down upon him, eyes focused in deep thought. Then he returned the gag to Belarrin's mouth. "Thank you, Vistus. I cannot say I hope your fate is a good one, but I hope it is better than this."

Then he snuffed the torch and departed.

Belarrin stared up into the void of darkness overhead. Was that enough? Had his life served sufficient purpose, giving doubt to one of his masters? No. It wasn't enough. Not enough at all.

As the empty loneliness of his splayed torments stretched on, memory of the conversation faded. It became but one more dream blending with those of life before the Boards. One more haunting idea. As he writhed in pain, unable to find sleep or rest, he wondered if the visit from Tazil had even happened. Was it only a dream, a delusion?

He tried to call up good thoughts, of sun, rain, and wind. Of laughter and joy. Of his brothers old and new, t'Okaedrin and Scion. Of Sravika. But each of them slipped further and further out of reach until even the memory of them became pain. Until features failed him. There was only the torment in arms and legs unable to relax beneath the tight bonds of his ropes. There was only the thunder of agony in his head, behind his eyes. The parched sandy grit of his throat. And the total darkness. Always darkness except for the hours of questioning.

Yet within that darkness there were times when he thought he saw things. Delusions, after images perhaps. They reminded him of what he saw when he sought the right words to speak sorcery. Flecks of light moving across a canopy of darkness. But now, he also caught fleeting glimpses of a distant crimson ribbon of cloud, vaporous and half seen. He'd noticed it once before when he'd overstretched himself hardening the spears a lifetime ago. It was stronger now, strangely tantalizing yet terrifying, too. He fled from it, seeking the darkness alone, just the darkness. And he was all alone.

When the door to his cell finally opened again to reveal the arrival of Eltirkar, his tormentor, Belarrin chuckled in gleeful anticipation. It was half whimper. He was no longer alone. Pain would come that made all the dark eternity like bliss. But he was no longer alone. And there was light.

A housecarl stepped up beside the Boards and, holding a knife to Belarrin's throat, removed the gag from his mouth.

"Where are the Scion camps?" Eltirkar asked.

Belarrin only laughed. It rang mad in his ears. Was it good that he realized that?

The housecarl pulled on the rope binding his right arm and Belarrin screamed in agony.

"Who helped you?" Eltirkar asked. "You could not have acted by yourself."

"Ushtyl." Belarrin laughed. "The Empress. His Highest Above!" He could no longer remember why he endured. Why didn't he just speak sorcery and end it all? A faint whisper arose in the back of his mind. Because he had failed Vitarria and Zoltha. Because he had been a coward unwilling to face his own death and thereby bringing a slaughter. Because his death had to have meaning and that meaning was the death of the Finaestari. They would pay for the evil they wrought.

As the bonds tightened, Belarrin screamed again, body and mind flooding with pain. He clenched his eyes shut until the stars shifted across his vision again and the ribbon of red drifted closer. Madness. He realized that was what it was. An oblivion stronger than he was, offering an escape from his pain. From himself.

But no, he didn't deserve oblivion. He deserved the pain. It was a searing agony that filled him, became him, until there was nothing else.

"I don't know what I'm doing anymore," High Lord Tazil said.

He and his wife sat in their familiar places on the couch in the main room of their quarters, feeling the warmth of the fire. It was good to be home again and in this comfortable place, if only for one night. In the rush of activity over the past few months, he'd missed these quiet evenings with his wife. That their son was home, too, made it all the more wonderful, though Nethzir had already retired for the night.

Aerharyndra smiled back at him. "You are as you always have been, my husband. Perhaps you saw less clearly then than you do now, rather than the other way around."

Tazil chuckled. She always knew how to make him laugh and, at the same time, challenge his thoughts. He picked up his goblet of wine from the low table in front of them and took a sip before saying, "But could I have been so wrong? Was it a flawed choice we made to create these t'Okaedrin? To create even the Kalilaer?"

"Is that the question you should be asking?"

"What am I not seeing?"

"That the man who decided our survival depended upon bending humans to servitude is the same man who sees this construct cannot sustain itself."

"You're saying I was right then and I'm right now."

"We made the best possible choice we could. Might there have been better?" She shrugged. "Perhaps. But it was one we made and one that has seen us endure. Yet now we see the cost of that choice. Their loyalty is frayed and their contentment is doubtful. I have heard others say that the use of them is taking a toll on us as well. In our reliance, we are becoming weaker."

"Others like Ninanna," Tazil said.

"It sounds as though you and she agree more than you might have thought."

Tazil barked a laugh and Aerharyndra smiled at him. He rose to his feet and walked over to the balcony door. As he pushed it open a gust of cool night air met him. He looked down on his city below. The streets of Raefi'ernyn glimmered in lamplight, while softer golden rays shone through the windows of its many houses. But beyond the walls, there was only darkness. On the plain, the Kalilaer had all been locked in their barracks for the night. To the south, the sea wracked the coast with its endless energy while to the north, the invisible forest loomed impenetrable and silent beneath the moonless sky. "I have come to love this place we've built. From the ruin of everything, we lifted it stone by stone."

"With Kalilaer help," Aerharyndra said, joining him. She had wrapped a shawl around her shoulders against the chill.

Tazil nodded. "But perhaps it is wrong. Perhaps this love is a lie, a trap that ensnares us. If Vistus is but the first of many, and he claimed there were others before him, how can we hold back the tide? In the end, whether it be a century or a thousand years, can there be any other fate but our own trusted warriors rising against us?"

"Few realms endure a thousand years, even Aestarin ones."

"But is that enough? To leave the solution to future centuries when we're more trapped here than ever before. Perhaps refuge is the better answer."

"Perhaps it is." Aerharyndra slipped her hand through his arm. "But ruin will not come tonight. And certainly the answer won't come from an open door that banishes all the warmth of our chamber."

"Of course not." Tazil smiled as he closed the door again. Returning to the couch, he took another drink from his wine goblet. "I regret that we haven't had many evenings like this of late."

"We will again. You must leave tomorrow morning?"

"Yes." Tazil frowned. "The empress is enjoying having all of us under her thumb, I think."

"I am glad our son is going with you. He's the only one you can trust. Do not lean too much on the empress or on your friends."

"Ushtyl I trust, even though he keeps his own secrets," Tazil replied.

"As you say," Aerharyndra replied, though her tone held doubt. "Just be careful."

CHAPTER 39
Sacrifices

"What is the value of a life? Of lives? There are some who say that no end is worth the price of a single life. There are others who pour out lives like rain from the heavens for some perceived good. Both are right and both are wrong. Those who forget this truth fall prey to the tyranny of the one or to the tyranny of the many."

—Jhoacen, the Philosopher-King of Rynaeca

The friend you think you have is no friend.

The Empress Kayrstana stood in the middle of her quarters and stared at the corner of the room where the Shadow-Servant had vanished. His final words of warning were fixed in her mind. As ever, he had arrived and departed behind a veil of darkness. But for all of his enigmatic behavior, she didn't dismiss what he'd said, remembering her father's warning as a child. The Shadow-Servant was a creature solely devoted to the Syraestari people. He should be heeded with caution, but he would never be tamed. So her own experience with him had proven.

She turned back to the warm fire blazing in the hearth. Autumn was pressing onward toward winter and early mornings had a clinging chill. Through the windows beyond, she saw the first reds of dawn as the sun's newborn rays breeched the outer walls of Nahirazith.

Who was the friend that the Shadow-Servant believed was false?

Surely it wasn't High Lord Tyrnis. He was like an uncle to her. It couldn't be High Lady Jesaelyn, either. She was far less ambitious than her peers. Of all the high lords, those two were the only ones whose loyalty she could trust, except for her beloved Ushtyl of course. The other five high lords had never been her friend. Ninanna? The empress shook her head and sat down on the couch opposite the hearth. Ninanna had been a friend, but was hardly one now and regretting that rift resolved nothing. Could the Shadow-Servant have been talking about himself? But, of course, he had no friends. If only he'd spoken plainly for once! But such a desire was just as useful as wishing for wings. Or for her father back alive.

She shook her head. The time for guessing was over and she would do just as the Shadow-Servant had recommended. Time would reveal its answers. Kayrstana reached over to the nearby end table and rang the bell resting on it. Not for the first time, she wished she had brought her own Pi'aernoth attendants with her. They knew her tastes and her mood. But then again, perhaps it was better that she didn't know the one who would come.

"Enough is enough, Talikae," Draatha said. The glare she cast from the opposite side of the washing basin took the sting out of her words. "You will be the death of mother and bring her wrath on the rest of us."

"You know I don't mean anything," Talikae said. "I have dreams, vivid dreams. All I want to do is walk once beneath the trees and see." Whenever she closed her eyes, she saw the images Vistus had painted with his words. That he was now denounced as apostate didn't make the forest any less real.

"Pi'aernotha Kaupet don't go running through the forest." Draatha laughed. "What do you think you are, an Osnoeda?"

"I know who I am," Talikae grumbled. She knew it was a foolish obsession. What was the forest but a mass of trees? Yet it had seized her mind, a promise of a broader world beyond the simple one she lived in now. If only she could walk beneath its boughs just for a few minutes. To hear the wind in the branches, feel the cool upon her face, see the lattice of sunlight through the leaves and be surrounded by all that life.

"You used to be the best of us and I don't know what happened. I don't know how many more chances mother will give you before you're sent to muck out the stables for the rest of your life."

Lady Ninanna happened. And then Vistus. He had seemed like such a nice man.

The washroom door flew open and they both leapt to their feet to face their mother standing on the threshold. Hands on her hips, she looked them over, eyes stern. "Draatha, the empress has summoned you. Go now and see what she needs. I expect you to do all she demands with grace and aplomb."

"Yes, mother." Draatha dried her hands on a towel, then with a warning glance to Talikae, departed. Talikae took the full meaning. If you had behaved, it would have been you serving the empress. Behave now and maybe you will one day.

"Talikae, the housecarls in the lowest level need their breakfast. Go to the kitchens and carry it down to them."

Talikae swallowed. She knew what the lowest level meant. That was where the cells were. They stank of filth and blood. That was where Vistus was being held prisoner on the Boards. She had heard his screams through the cell door. But with Draatha's warning in her mind, she dipped her head deferentially. "Yes, mother."

"When you're done come back here and resume your washing."

"Yes, mother."

The morning was bright under a cloudless sky. A beautiful day and full of promise. High Lord Ushtyl waited with the other high lords and ladies on the outer steps of his palace. Behind him, the central fountain gurgled merrily, the droplets shining like diamonds as they caught the brilliance of the sun. His people, along with the occasional Pi'aernotha Kaupet, passed busily along the edges of the plaza about whatever tasks or leisure the day had for them. More than a few Syraestari lingered, though, doubtless on the hope of catching sight of the empress as she went on her daily walk through the streets. A new sort of normalcy had descended on the city with Kayrstana's lingering presence. To Ushtyl's pleasure, his compatriots took issue with such routines, because it bound them to be present more than not. They took it as but one more silent assertion of the empress' authority over Ushtyl and, by extension, themselves. It was one they could hardly resist, though, as it had always been the right of the empress to impose upon the hospitality of her high lords. While they planned their new raid, they bided their time in silent fuming. Ushtyl feigned his own dissatisfaction, though he remained secretly pleased. Kayrstana's close proximity in his city served only to further his plans, especially on this particular day.

The other high lords in attendance waited at the base of the steps, doubtless enjoying the warm sun that was so pleasant with the deepening of autumn. Ushtyl amused himself by reading each of their stances and attitudes. It also served, he admitted silently, to distract himself from the fluttering of his own nerves over what the next few hours might yield. Tyrnis and Jesaelyn stood together, their distance from the others and proximity to the central steps an unspoken proclamation of their unquestioning loyalty to the empress. Sizras and Zaerina also waited side by side. Though they were in defiance of the empress like Ushtyl and the others, their insistence on refuge over dominion set them apart. Then there were Arkesh and Ovirkar, standing nearest to Ushtyl. They were at the core of the conspiracy, the former so transparent even when he thought he was secretive, the latter ever the follower even against his own better judgment. It was curious that Tazil, so often the mediator, didn't wait with them or with Sizras. He stood by himself on the far side of the steps, a brooding frown etched upon his features.

Ushtyl didn't think Tazil was still angry about the failure of the second infiltrator. Not after Vistus, too, had proven false. It was something else. On any other day, Ushtyl would have approached to see what was wrong, but not today. The pretense of caring hardly mattered anymore anyway.

The doors to his palace creaked as they swung wide to reveal the Empress Kayrstana on the threshold. There was something irksome about waiting attendance on another in his own home, even if it was Kayrstana and even if he knew it was necessary for the outcome he desired. Kayrstana smiled down upon her high lords and ladies as ten of her t'Okaedrin bodyguards hurried past her to line the steps on either side. It was a curious smile, one Ushtyl was unfamiliar with, and he thought he knew them all. A stab of fear leapt to his heart, but he dismissed the thought. There was no way anything could go wrong. He forced his focus to the bodyguards. He was continually amazed at how easy it was to sculpt human behavior to such duties. True, there were the occasional failures, with Vistus as proof. But in general, a well-trained human made the perfect servant and protector, devoted and diligent. The empress had begun to call these humans her Kal t'Okaedrin, Royal Brothers, in recognition of their elevated duties. Ushtyl nodded to himself. The name had a pleasing ring to it, one he was sure to retain.

Once the Kal t'Okaedrin were in place and all attention across the plaza was fixed on her, the empress passed through the palace gates and walked down the steps with Captain Sarroth trailing to her right. She wore a fine gown of flowing purple edged in lavender and gold. Her crown, as ever, was set deep in the mountain of dark curls that cascaded around her face. There was a peculiar stiffness to her step, yet she remained every bit the regal monarch surveying her domain.

As Kayrstana passed the midpoint of her descent, a blur of motion streaked across Ushtyl's vision. The empress jerked backward, face turning white as a crimson stain expanded outward from an arrow buried in her chest. Then she stumbled and collapsed to the palace steps.

An eternity of stunned silence passed, broken only by the timeless gurgle of the fountain and the soft breeze rippling through the flags overhead. Ushtyl forced his gaze to look up toward the rooftops. "Assassin!" he cried, pointing at the dark-cloaked figure standing atop the temple roof, bow in hand.

Ushtyl's words broke the spell of frozen shock. Heads turned to mark the figure, then a half dozen housecarls dashed across the courtyard toward the temple with High Lord Arkesh following. Screams of shock and fear arose from every corner of the plaza. Many of the Syraestari fled in panic and just as many remaining transfixed. All the high lords save Arkesh ran to the empress' side as the Kal t'Okaedrin closed around them in a protective ring, their faces white and brows grim with studied determination.

Captain Sarroth knelt at Kayrstana's side but stepped back at a curt gesture from High Lady Jesaelyn. Ushtyl stooped beside her as she rested her right hand on the empress' brow and her left on the flesh around the arrow. The purple gown was stained in blood, but the high lady didn't seem to notice. She muttered under her breath, then closed her eyes. "Sinahastir koenasi ondae." A wince, a frown, and Jesaelyn shifted so both hands covered the wound. "Ansaere saeklae'eus yskaesira." She shook her head, checking Kayrstana's forehead again before exhaling a long slow sigh as she looked up at Ushtyl. "She's gone."

"Gone?" Tazil hissed. Eyes wide, he bowed down to the steps opposite Jesaelyn and Ushtyl. "No, no, no, not like this." It sounded like a prayer on his lips.

Ushtyl met his gaze, curious at the response, then, schooling his own features, looked to the others. They all crowded around, eyes wide with shock, alarm, and in some a little fear. All except Tyrnis. That was strangest of all. He was practically an uncle to the empress, yet Tyrnis stood a little back from the others, arms crossed and brow furrowed, his attention as much on the temple where the assassin's arrow had come from as the body of his liege.

"What do we do?" Zaerina asked.

"Bring her inside," Ushtyl said gently. "We cannot let the people know she died here upon the steps."

"Ushtyl's right," Tazil said. Jesaelyn nodded reluctantly and rose to her feet to give Ushtyl and Tazil room to carry her. They cradled Kayrstana's body between them as they climbed the steps. Captain Sarroth led the way, opening the outer doors for them to pass through. In their wake came the high lords while the Kal t'Okaedrin held their same determined circle as if she were alive. Maybe the fool humans still thought she could be saved.

Inside the palace, Ushtyl guided them to a private sitting room off the main gallery, where a fire still burned in the hearth. They carefully set Kayrstana's body reclining upon a couch, then stepped back.

Ushtyl looked around the room, gauging his peers. Most were still in stunned shock, but he could see calculation beginning on the features of Sizras. Tazil was considering, too. Only Tyrnis, standing near the outer door, was unreadable, his face a mask. A thousand thoughts flitted across Ovirkar's startled visage while Zaerina collapsed as if exhausted on a chair opposite the empress. Jesaelyn knelt on the floor beside Kayrstana's head, her hand brushing back a lock of hair that had fallen over the empress' face. Captain Sarroth stood above the pair of them with arms crossed, a sentinel over his fallen liege.

No sooner had they claimed their places then a side door opened and a handful Pi'aernoth hurried in with trays holding goblets of wine and a plate of fine cheeses. Ushtyl almost smirked. Death or life, they carried out their service. But when no one responded to them, they set the food and drink on the central table and withdrew like ghosts to the outer edge of the room, joining the Kal t'Okaedrin who'd taken station there.

"What now?" Zaerina said, rubbing her brow as she broke the long silence. "What do we do now?"

Ushtyl glanced to Sizras, whose eyes were still locked on the empress. Sizras and Tyrnis would be his most implacable foes in the minutes ahead. For the moment, he had to move cautiously, but he had to be careful that everyone felt his concern and grief, too. "Whatever we do, we must act quickly before rumors spread too deep."

"But who did this?" Zaerina asked. "How did this happen?"

Ushtyl looked at her, voice cold. "I recall you voicing this very act."

Zaerina's face turned white as a snowbank.

"What's this?" Jesaelyn said, tearing her gaze from the empress' face. Sorrow was replaced by fury. "What did you do?"

"Nothing. I've done nothing," Zaerina protested.

Jesaelyn rose to her feet and straightened her dress as she looked around the room, oblivious to the streaks of blood her hands left behind on the fine fabric. "Was this your conspiracy? Were you all part of this? I'm not blind to your scheming." Her eyes locked on Ovirkar, the weakest of them.

He flinched under her gaze, but said, "Never. I would never kill my liege."

"Nor I," Tazil said when her gaze shifted to him.

"I cannot believe any of us did," Ushtyl said, stepping forward. "Nor are blind accusations helpful. With luck, my housecarls will arrest the assassin and we can get to the bottom of that plot, but in the meantime, we must move forward. The people are in shock and these tremors will echo through the realm."

"High Lord Ushtyl is right," Sizras said. "This horrendous murder forces us to face one unpleasant truth. We have become weak. Our dependence upon humans has left us vulnerable. Not merely a weakness of our fortitude, but a corruption in our souls, as this murder clearly proves." He gestured at the still form of Kayrstana. "The time has come to abandon this ephemeral dominion of idleness and return to the people we always intended to be."

Ushtyl hid a smile of triumph. Sizras had acted too quickly and left himself vulnerable. "How can you turn this tragedy into a ploy to achieve your own ends?" he demanded. "The empire is troubled and driving that choice now would only divide it further."

Sizras turned on him. "I know well your heart, Ushtyl. Don't turn your own twisted mind upon me. You've become bloated on the false power of this land and would feed further until you burst. I won't let this tragedy become yet another excuse for dithering and delay while our society continues to rot."

Ushtyl kept his expression smooth even as his heart roiled within him. He had been wise to be watchful of Sizras, but the other man lacked one advantage. The only one that would matter in the end. The empress had died here and all the high lords were here, in his city. He would do what had to be done. By force, if necessary. Sizras would likely have to die and Tyrnis, too. But if he remained unruffled he could bring the others around. Ushtyl extended his hands out from his sides, palms forward in a gesture of calm. "Sizras, your words wound me after how closely we've worked in the past. I know we haven't always seen eye to eye, but surely we can step back from such hard words in a time of crisis like this."

Tazil stepped up to Sizras and rested his hand on his shoulder. "Ushtyl is right in this, my friend. Not today, not with the shock still so strong. I, too, am troubled by what is becoming of our people, but we must be calm and ordered before we come to any conclusion."

Ushtyl felt a glow of triumph as Ovirkar stepped to the other side of Sizras. "Yes, we can discuss this, but later. Once we know who was behind the death of the empress."

The room's outer door swung open to reveal High Lord Arkesh on the threshold, a smile of triumph on his face. "Lords and ladies," he said. "I can answer that question."

Arkesh sprinted across the plaza following the handful of housecarls toward the temple.

The empress was dead.

If he hadn't seen it with his own eyes, he might not have believed. But that shot, impressive for the distance, had been a killing blow. And he would be the one to apprehend the assassin. Let the others remain behind and bicker over scraps. When it was all over, the people would remember the one who acted. The blemish of Ninanna stealing his sword would be washed away.

"Watch the sides and back!" he bellowed to the housecarls in front of him as they reached the temple. They obeyed instantly, several breaking off to the left and right. The first two, however, ran straight through the doors with Arkesh fast on their heels.

At this time of the morning, the central chamber of the temple was empty. Rows of polished cedar pews ran down either side of the room, split in the center by a purple carpeted aisle. Five alabaster statues looked down from the left and right walls while a great white disc representing His Highest Above hung directly above the chancel ahead. Its silver trim gleamed faintly in the dim light.

Arkesh drew his sword and followed the housecarls to the right side of the chancel and up the stairs. They wound in a tight circle ever higher but none of them slowed their pace. Perhaps it was best that he wasn't in the lead, Arkesh realized, breathing heavily from the exertion. At their pace there was no way to see more than a pace or two ahead. If the assassin were descending or lying in wait, the first of them would be dead before they knew it. Let one or two of them die, but Arkesh would see the deed done. He was a hero, not a fool.

But there was no ambush. He rushed after the others through the final arch and out onto the rooftop, blinking in the sunlight as it gleamed off the white stonework. Then he stopped and lowered his blade, the two housecarls doing likewise. They were too late for glory.

Near the center of the roof, Captain Eltirkar stood with bloodstained blade over the black-robed body of the assassin. Eltirkar looked over at him, drawing a deep heaving breath. "No chance. He rushed at me and the only choice was kill or die."

"No one will blame you, Captain," Arkesh said. Thrusting his sword back into its sheath, he strode up beside Eltirkar and knelt down over the body. The assassin had fallen face first, his own blade a pace from his outstretched hand. With a grunt, Arkesh rolled the body onto its back and tore back the hood.

"Black Abyss of Cydion!" he cursed, staring down into the vacant eyes of Captain Nethzir. "But if he's the assassin, then... then..."

"...his father Tazil must have ordered it," Eltirkar finished what he could not bring himself to say.

Arkesh shook his head, not wanting to believe. What madness must have possessed Tazil to do this? True, Arkesh had considered assassination when Zaerina first mentioned it, but later in his own mind he'd dismissed the folly. It could only bring recrimination and chaos. If one killed an empress, how much easier would it be to kill a high lord?

Arkesh grunted to hide the exhalation of shock that forced its way up his throat. He stood and looked at Eltirkar then the waiting housecarls. "Come, we'd best bring his body back to the others. They will need to know."

Eltirkar nodded to the housecarls who immediately ran forward and lifted Nethzir between them. As Arkesh followed them back down the winding steps, it occurred to him that despite the tragedy, despite the inevitable doom of Tazil, a man he once had considered a reasonable ally, he still would come out of this ordeal in a good position. He might not have slain Nethzir, but he was there to take command of the body and bring it to the others. He would oversee the arrest. That would be remembered far better than the unseen duel between Eltirkar and Nethzir. Arkesh would be the hero, as it should be.

CHAPTER 40
Life

"Are you afraid to live or afraid to die? Does it matter? We usually get that which we dread most."

—King Ardrathon of Ithia

From the adjoining room, Kayrstana could hear them squabbling over the still-warm corpse they believed was hers. She heard Arkesh arrive and announce the assassin. The other high lords and ladies had instantly pounced upon Tazil, trussing him up despite all protests between his sobs of unremitting grief. And what cause had they to consider anything else? Nethzir had been caught in the very act of leaving the rooftop.

But that revelation had barely slowed them from turning on each other, Sizras and Ushtyl especially, the former attempting to tear down the empire while the latter tried to devour the whole thing. He probably would, too, if nothing else changed.

Betrayal heaped upon betrayal. Not just from the high lords. She'd come to expect that. But from Ushtyl? From her beloved! She had never considered the impossible because it was impossible. If she hadn't witnessed the murder with her own eyes, hidden beneath veils of sorcery on the temple roof, she never would have believed it.

She wanted to scream, to weep, to throw herself upon her bed in a heap of uncontrolled sobbing, but she couldn't. She was not some simpering girl. She was the empress, the ruler of the realm. Long ago, Ninanna had told her that the crown carried a burden all its own. Kayrstana choked back a sob. She had betrayed Ninanna because she believed in Ushtyl and his plan, but now he had betrayed her. It all had been for nothing.

Unable to restrain herself any longer, Kayrstana flung the door open and stepped through. Cold satisfaction seeped through her fury as all eyes turned on her in expressions of amazement and horror. Only Tyrnis was unmoved, but that was no surprise. She had been impressed by his restraint.

"Is this the best that the greatest lords and ladies of the realm can offer my people?" she demanded as the other ten members of her Kal t'Okaedrin entered behind her followed by another twenty t'Okaedrin. "Bickering children squabbling over their parents' scraps, over treasures not theirs?"

"Your Majesty!" Ushtyl gasped, taking a step forward, but Kayrstana stilled him with a raised hand. Her eyes met Tyrnis, still standing stoically beside the door, then Jesaelyn, rising in stunned amazement from kneeling beside the body, tears gleaming on her cheeks. "Only two here are worthy of the name high lord and high lady. Only two know true honor and nobility."

"Your Majesty," Ushtyl protested, "forgive us, for we are stunned that you live. All you might have heard was but concern for the realm, for the care of your people. I'm certain I speak for the joy in all of us that this tragedy has been avoided."

"Has anything but poison ever passed between your lips, Ushtyl?" Kayrstana snarled.

He recoiled at her reply, but before he or anyone else could speak, she flung out her hand. "Captain Sarroth arrest them, all but Tyrnis and Jesaelyn. Arrest Eltirkar, too. If any resist, kill them."

Ovirkar and Arkesh's eyes flickered around the room as if measuring their chances against Tyrnis, Sarroth, and a room full of t'Okaedrin, but they held their place. There was no sign of resistance from the others, not even Ushtyl. The snake probably thought he could charm his way out of his bonds once she calmed. But she knew him now. As his hands were bound, his eyes remained fixed on Kayrstana, brimming with hurt. That, more than anything, churned her stomach.

"Might I ask the reason for this arrest, Your Majesty?" Sizras said.

"Yes, Your Majesty," Arkesh added. "You live and the disaster is over."

"Is it?" Tazil asked, his voice heavy with bitterness. "My son is dead. Why is my son dead?"

Kayrstana turned to Ushtyl. "Perhaps you can answer that, my love." That last with a note of acid.

A glimmer of shock flickered across Ushtyl's face, just as quickly to be replaced by steady reserve. "I don't know what you mean, Your Majesty."

"Yes, I suppose you would choose the path of the coward," she replied coldly, then her anger rose up in her throat. "Do you think me blind? Am I a fool captivated by your fancies while all along you sought only to replace me! Not consort, but emperor!"

"What does she mean?" Sizras asked Ushtyl, his voice hard. "What have you done?"

"Murder," Kayrstana replied. "He feigned friendship. He promised unity by breaking the rest of you malcontents by your scheming. There was more he thought to hide from me, but I was there watching, hidden on the rooftop. I saw the actual assassin. He came to the rooftop carrying an unconscious Nethzir on his shoulder, both in black robes. After the killing arrow was shot, it was a simple task to toss his own robes aside and then kill Nethzir. Then he would appear to be the savior when the guards arrived, sent by his master."

"Eltirkar!" Arkesh breathed.

"Then Ushtyl gave the command," Sizras said.

"Yes," Kayrstana replied, eyes still locked on Ushtyl. He met her gaze evenly without a glimmer of fear or regret. "What was it you wrote for Ninanna's trial? 'Crimes against a high lord are but one step beneath crimes against the imperial throne itself and there can be no mercy.' From your own mouth you condemn yourself."

"Your Majesty," Jesaelyn spoke, still lingering beside the body of the couch. Her voice was still choked with grief and shock. Forgive me, but I felt your life flee beneath my hands. I thought I'd lost you. Who, then, is this?"

"A Pi'aernoth," Tyrnis answered.

Kayrstana nodded. Her old friend, unable to touch magic and untouched by it, had been the only one to see through the guise. And that he had said nothing until now testified to the measure of his loyalty. Kayrstana walked up to stand beside Jesaelyn and touched her gently on the wrist. "I know what you did for me, how you suffered. And I will never forget." Kayrstana stooped to touch the dead woman lightly on the forehead. "Tras natalis oezheut." The body shimmered a moment as the Veil of the Heavens dropped away to reveal the form of a human woman, dark haired like herself and young with smooth skin pale in death.

"Draatha, no!" One of the Pi'aernoth standing attendance near the hearth screamed in sudden horror. She ran forward to throw herself weeping upon the body.

Kayrstana closed her eyes. Again, it seemed that a human understood grief and loss far more than all her high lords except Jesaelyn. If they had responded in a similar manner instead of instantly squabbling over the scraps of empire, she might have been inclined to mercy. She opened her eyes again to see an older Pi'aernoth, doubtless their mother, hurry abashedly to the center of the room. "Hush, Talikae," the mother said with a hiss. At a snap of her fingers, several more Pi'aernoth rushed forward to help pull their distraught sister from the room. The mother followed, bowing deeply as she backed away.

"Your Majesty," Sizras said. "I commend you for overcoming Ushtyl's plot against your life. I had no part in any such treacherous scheme. Why, then, am I still bound?"

"Do you think your own sins are unknown?"

"I have committed no crime."

"No crime but rebellion. Yes, I know of all your plans, your schemes to overthrow me, to cast me aside. To banish me!"

"Ah, yes. That would be the plot you and Ushtyl so carefully orchestrated to ensare us? Who is witness to the scheme? Him?" Sizras said, glancing at Ushtyl. "He whose every word you have proclaimed to be poison?"

"Not his testimony, but mine," a new voice spoke from the corner of the room.

Kayrstana turned, as shocked as the others, to see the Shadow-Servant standing there. He stood stoically, with hands crossed in front of him, black robes flowing from his shoulders and white mask gleaming within the shadows of his hood. Tyrnis and Sarroth drew their swords in alarm.

"Hold!" Kayrstana ordered. They relaxed at her command, but didn't sheath their blades.

The Shadow-Servant glanced at them, idle amusement in his eyes before looking at Sizras. "I was there in the bowels of this palace when you conspired. I heard every word spoken when each one of you consented to open rebellion. Of forcing the empress to abdicate and then casting her out. Each of you consented in turn."

Sizras rolled his shoulders back, open defiance in his gaze. "And who then, creature, are you that knows so much?"

"I am the Shadow-Servant."

"All the Shadow-Servants are dead. I witnessed their fall a thousand years ago."

Rather than reply, the Shadow-Servant reached out with one gloved hand and flung the hilt of a blade onto the central table of the room. It clattered against the hard wood as it landed, sending a hush of awe through the room. Tyrnis stepped forward and picked up the hilt and spoke in a voice full of wonder. "This is the blade that was thrust into Cydion's back."

He turned back toward the Shadow-Servant and Kayrstana's gaze followed his. But the corner of the room where the Shadow-Servant had stood was empty.

"Enough!" Kayrstana said, clapping her hands. "Guilt has been established. Murderers and rebels will alike die for what they've done. Captain Sarroth, please escort these prisoners out to the plaza. I must announce that they have failed and I yet live. High Lord Tyrnis, High Lady Jesaelyn, please attend me as well."

This time, it was Ushtyl who scanned the room with measured eyes. But he had allowed his hands to be bound and his sword taken. Though he'd once been a Sword-Whisperer, he was no Ninanna. Kayrstana smiled with savage pride. Through sorcery, Ushtyl might have attempted escape as her former guardian had, but she could see him discard the idea as he turned toward the door at the prodding of two t'Okaedrin.

Sizras followed with head held high in unbroken pride. Always an implacable foe, Sizras at least had honor. He was followed by Arkesh, Ovirkar, and Zaerina, each with shoulders bent in numb disbelief. Tazil came last of all, a hunched and broken man, the paint around his eyes smeared by tears for his fallen son.

The plaza was already nearly full with idle populace. They talked loudly to each other in heated discussion, doubtless drawn as word of the morning's crime spread through the city. Sarroth had a trumpeter sound his horn, drawing any others who yet remained away. As the prisoners descended the steps with hands bound and, last of all, Kayrstana herself appeared again alive and hale, the populace fell silent in stunned and satisfying awe. Then applause began, intermittent at first but growing gradually to a loud cheer like the slow onset of a spring rain.

Kayrstana strode forward until she stood above the top step and there she waited in patient silence for the crowd to grow until it comprised the whole population of the city. They waited with nervous patience, the quiet broken only by fervent whispers.

"People of Nahirazith!" Kayrstana cried. "My beloved people. The schemes of assassins and rebels have failed. I stand before you healthy and whole – yet also with a heavy heart. Many of you today witnessed the attempt that was made against my life. The assassin was none other than Captain Eltirkar, acting on the commands of High Lord Ushtyl."

Murmurs of anger and shock rippled through the crowd. Kayrstana nodded to herself, satisfied that Ushtyl's own people were appalled at the deed.

"For their crimes, Ushtyl and Eltirkar shall both die, but they shall not die alone. Though I believe the protestations of Sizras, Arkesh, Tazil, Zaerina, and Ovirkar, that they were unaware of the plot for regicide, they are guilty of planning sedition and rebellion against me and the empire. Their punishment shall likewise, therefore, be death.

"But not all is dark upon this day for High Lord Tyrnis and High Lady Jesaelyn have once again proven their loyalty and duty to you, to myself, and to this realm. Likewise, I honor Captain Nethzir of Raefi'ernyn, who was himself murdered by Eltirkar. That he died of pure heart, devoted to all our people, I do not doubt. His sacrifice shall not be forgotten."

Kayrstana paused to allow the people time to understand all that she'd said, but she did not move. Though hushed words were passed among the crowd, her continuing presence was a weight upon them and after a long moment, she felt all eyes return to her.

"Finally," she said. "Today is a day of declaration. For a thousand years, you my people, have lived in doubt and worry. In the ravages of the Cataclysm we were driven onward in desperate migration, searching for food and safety. A century ago, we decided to linger here, to build a defensible place until we could find a refuge free of the predations of human barbarism. There has been much debate in recent years about when that migration should begin, with many beginning to question whether we should leave at all. This place that was to be a temporary shelter has become a home. And thus, today, I proclaim it! This place is our home. Here, upon the foundation of these nine cities we shall rebuild all that was lost. There will be no more fevered flight, no more looking over our shoulders worrying about the morrow. This land, here, is our dominion, not just for today and tomorrow, but forever!"

Shouts of joy filled the plaza as her people flung their hands in the air or turned to embrace those standing beside them. The sounds rolled like the tide over her, filling her with pride. Kayrstana smiled beneath the torrent of accolades, pleased at their affirmation. But in truth, the reasons she had named were not her reasons. It had been during the long wandering that the once-loyal high lords had become wayward. Having finally regained unquestioned authority over the entire realm, she wasn't about to risk that again by another migration to a place of refuge, no matter how pleasing that land might be.

She waited until the rejoicing had calmed, then said, "Until this day I have accepted the voices of debate. I have listened to all, weighing each word for I was not yet settled in my own mind. All those who argued for leaving these lands for a new place of refuge bear no guilt or shame for their words. But today, I have spoken. The decision has been made and there will be no further debate or dissention on the matter. Word shall be sent out to all the cities declaring the rise of our homeland. Rejoice, my people, for our Empire is at hand!"

Kayrstana drank in the loud cheers a moment longer, then turned on her heel and strode back into the palace.

Darkness lay heavy on the corridor, heavier still than the night above, despite the handful of flickering torches. The darkness here was drawn as much from an absence of hope as an absence of light. It was a place where joyous laughter had never been heard and screams sank deep into the cold stone walls. In his present mood, it reminded Reigliff of another prison long ago, and another bleak choice.

From the deepest shadows, he contemplated the guards outside the door at the far end of the hallway. Both were Syraestari housecarls, lounging in idle boredom. It would be quickest and easiest to simply kill them. Doubtless Ninanna and so many others would think that his first choice. But deaths lead only to questions.

"Tras prethnytaso ipainyn," he hissed.

The torches fluttered a moment in what, for a living thing, might have been panic, as the surrounding shadows enveloped them, snuffing out their life.

"Blood on the Bridge!" one of the guards cursed.

"I hate this Abyssally cold hallway," the other echoed. "Wait here while I find another torch."

Reigliff slipped down the black hallway, passing the first guard midway down then sliding past the second, who was still mumbling to himself. The cell door opened silently and Reigliff passed through. There was no light within either, but he didn't need it. He knew all of the rooms in Ushtyl's palace. He leapt upwards, seizing a rafter and pulled himself to the peak.

"Itazh asirda miresh."

Nothing changed, but he didn't expect it to. Not until the guards entered. The door swung open again a minute later and the pair peered in, each one holding a torch. But as with all creatures, both human and Syraestari, they failed to truly see with their eyes. They didn't notice that the shadows at the top of the ceiling were thicker than normal.

"Nothing," a guard said.

"Close the door then. I hate the smell of blood."

"Ha!" the first laughed. "It's the stench of humans that turn my stomach."

The door shut behind them again, pulling the room back into darkness.

Still Reigliff waited. Patience was always the key. He sat in the stillness, listening, hearing only his own soft breath and the ragged breath of the prisoner below. When he was satisfied that the guards would not return, he hissed, "Itazh li'as anjoeda. Itazh oetsyr kilys." The thin barrier of shadow coalescing around the chamber would have been barely discernable in torchlight, but it was enough to seal off all sound. Dropping to the floor, he withdrew a small tallow candle from his robes. "Eusy'arjev heti loesyns."

His affinity with the Heart of Isfalinis was feeble, but he could at least conjure a small spark to light the candle. As it flared to sudden life, he grimaced behind his mask. The room was small and cold with harsh rough cut stone walls that held in the pervasive stench of blood and filth. Splayed across the Boards at the chamber's center, lay Belarrin. Where the ropes bound him at wrist and ankle, his flesh was red and raw. His nose was blackened with blood that had splattered red across his cheeks and matted his hair.

Belarrin trembled at the effort of raising his head to match Reigliff's gaze. His eyes were fevered and bloodshot. Beneath the torment in them there burned a stark fury of startling strength. Not many could hold such rage in the face of torture, where pain and fear consumed all other thought.

Reigliff set down the candle on the edge of the Boards and let out a slow sigh. "I warned you that it would come to this. Your brothers are bound in a cycle of lies that cannot be easily broken. I consider it a small miracle that even you, with everything you witnessed, broke free."

Belarrin's head sank back to rest again upon the Boards, the effort of lifting it apparently too great.

"What I say next," Reigliff said, "is not to give you hope. There is no hope. It is, instead, to prepare you for what must come. Your allies among the Scions are planning for a great attack, an attack I helped to build. But I can no longer allow it. The empress, has declared the foundation of our dominion, here. I will not gainsay her and therefore must support her, though I still might wish otherwise. I can no longer aid you, nor even allow you and the Scions to tear down these cities we have built."

Belarrin spasmed on the Boards. It was a heart-wrenching movement, and Reigliff was startled to realize it pierced him deeply. Perhaps he'd been wrong and Belarrin was no longer capable of clear thought. He couldn't be certain if the spasm was in response to his words or the long pain of the Boards. Belarrin's eyes were opened wide, staring into the darkness of the upper rafters as if seeing the Abyss itself. A single tear trickled down his left cheek and fell to mingle with the dried blood of the Boards.

"I regret it has come to this, but too much remains at stake for me to live in a world of remorse," Reigliff said. He wondered what Ninanna would say. She wouldn't understand. Would she see it as yet another betrayal? Unfortunately, she probably would. "I won't destroy the Scions, if I can see that done. My people need them gone, not dead. I will help them flee if I can, but I will promise nothing more than to try."

It was curious that he felt the need to explain himself. Why? He never had before except once. Was this some strange influence from Ninanna? He certainly didn't feel any better for it. Words were never as clean as a blade, never as simple.

Reigliff took a step forward, standing near Belarrin's head. The prisoner shifted his gaze to meet his eyes. The fury was gone, now, leaving only emptiness. It was like staring into the eyes of one already dead. "The best I can do for you, the only thing I can offer, is to grant an escape from this life of pain."

It was not the first time he had killed from mercy, but he hoped it would be the last. He could still remember as if it were the same night, another dark cell long ago where he'd taken another life. Where he had saved a soul from torments worse than death. Belarrin didn't move. His vacant eyes didn't even flicker. Reigliff matched him gaze for gaze. He deserved at least that.

Reigliff reached forward with his left hand to pull back Belarrin's shirt to ensure a clean thrust to the heart. Not that he was clumsy, but such a death had to be clean. Something flickered at the edge of his vision. Breaking his gaze with Belarrin, Reigliff looked at the human's chest. Revealed from beneath the tattered cloth of his shirt lay a gemstone on a leather cord. It was a pale blue, nearly white. But as Reigliff reached towards it as one entranced, the stone blazed into a brilliant crimson. Its searing light, a thousand times brighter than the flickering candle, burned his eyes.

"Blood on the Bridge!" Reigliff lurched back. Then realization took him and he stumbled, collapsing over his own feet and falling to the floor. Pain washed over him and loss and despair in equal measure, but worst of all hope. Without hope, the pain would have been empty. Curses tumbled from his lips, his mind too staggered for coherent thought. "Blood on the Bridge. Henji's Blessed Blood on the Bridge!"

He realized he was weeping. Tears poured down his cheeks, burning against the raw flesh of his face like fire. In agony, he tore off the mask, but that pain was as nothing to the torment welling in his soul. Trembling, he pushed himself to his knees and crawled over to the Boards, raising himself to stare in horror at the stone blazing upon Belarrin's chest.

Isi.

The other death from mercy. A woman, an Etyni, enchained, unsaveable, and so he'd done the only thing he could. Pure tears of blood had fallen upon the world, a dozen of them. Tears pouring from his dagger that burned his soul like fire. He remembered her sad smile, her kind words without judgment. It was the single greatest regret of his life, the one black blot he could never remove. The one deed for which he could still see no other choice. "You must forgive yourself", she had said, but it was the one crime he could never forgive. And now her tears had found him again. Here in a place just like he'd left her.

With shaking hand, he reached out to touch the crimson gem. It held him spellbound as words fell from his lips. "Tears from iron, blood from stone. The heavens tremble, the earth doth groan." He shuddered at the power of those ancient words. Drawing in a rasping breath, he remembered what else had been prophesied. "Harbinger raise thy final hand, stayed at last by crimson brand." He looked at Belarrin. The human's head had turned enough for their eyes to meet again. The emptiness was gone from Belarrin's face, but Reigliff couldn't be certain what lay behind those bloodshot eyes.

"Do you understand?" Reigliff rasped, pushing himself unsteadily to his feet. "I do not. I cannot see it." Belarrin did not stir. He did not even appear to notice Reigliff's ravaged face. The Shadow-Servant stooped to recover his mask, but only held it in his hand as his mind raced. He had to push away from that overwhelming pain and think of today, of the man lying bound before him. "It isn't over, but neither can I see the end. Vaenna knew. Her prophecy foresaw this even from the moment of Isi's death. Everything has been in motion since that day and the story isn't done."

Reigliff closed his eyes, bringing calm and control back to his mind. How long had it been since he'd so lost himself? Two thousand years. Heart still raw, he slid his mask back into place, then leaned forward until he was looking down on Belarrin once more.

"For years I have yearned, anticipating this prophecy, thinking I understood its truth. But I know nothing. We walk the lines of prophecy now, as blind as if its words were unknown. All that has been set in motion is larger than you and I. So I will do nothing. I will not kill you nor hinder the Scion raid. But I cannot free you either, for I don't know what that would mean and I am afraid. I am paralyzed by the stone upon your chest and all I dare do is strengthen you for the ordeal ahead. Then I must ride upon the shadows to see what unfolds."

Reigliff pulled Belarrin's shirt back in place to hide the stone again, then rested his hand on the human's forehead, unmindful of the dried blood. "Sinahastir Belarrin yskaesira. Sinahastir Belarrin sarnif'koepiri yskaesira."

CHAPTER 41
Mercies

"Like a rooster crowing at the moon or a pig holding court over half-eaten cobs of corn, so is the man who thinks he can see all ends."

—Lord Nitalis

Sravika looked southward, squinting in the afternoon sunlight that filtered through the canopy of leaves. They were still days from Nahirazith, but she couldn't help peering forward as if the city were visible in the distance. Fourteen Scion bands marched with her. She could hardly believe they'd managed to muster over a thousand warriors in a few short weeks. The meetings with the other chieftains had been strained and wearying, but in the end, each had seen what she saw. That they must save what they can, then save themselves.

The bands were scattered across the wilderness, now. It was strange to march in such a manner which made it impossible to hide their passage. No, this time they made no effort to conceal their path. Any t'Okaedrin who might stumble across their trail would find such a chaos of snapped twigs and footprints that it would have been without meaning. Not that there was much chance of one being out here before it was time to retreat again. At that point, the chaos layered upon chaos would do even more to confuse their vengeful pursuers.

She lifted her water canteen to her lips and took a slow drink. As she lowered it, she saw Henirgar approaching. With her elevation to chieftain, he'd taken her former place on the council. He took the canteen she offered him and drank, too.

"He will be waiting for us, Sravika. Idysha and Ninanna will make sure he is ready."

She turned to look south again. "I know." There were some who still doubted Belarrin, but she didn't. He'd changed sides once easily, they argued, so what if he had changed back again? No one who witnessed his anguish and his anger would ever believe such a thing. She understood him now, at least in so far as any woman could understand any man. Ninanna had explained the pieces of his past that had been beyond Sravika's knowledge. She'd known that the Finnies ensnared the minds of the t'Okaedrin when they were young, but it was one thing to be aware of it and something wholly different to understand how it had been done. She pitied them now, even more than the Kalilaer.

"I know, Henirgar," she repeated, tucking her canteen back into her belt. They walked forward together as other Scions flitted between the trees around them.

We are coming, Belarrin.

"You do not have to be here for this, Your Majesty," Marshal Sarroth said.

Sarroth bore the new rank well. He was no longer merely captain of her housecarls, but also commander of all warriors of her legion. So far they'd only had time to reorganize the once-housecarls of Nahirazith, but with time, Sarroth would oversee all the warriors of the dispossessed high lords.

"I do, Marshal," Kayrstana told him. She looked also to the two other legionnaires accompanying them. It was a message she wanted spread throughout the realm. "The t'Okaedrin are sworn to me and that makes Vistus my responsibility. I will do what must be done."

"Yes, Your Majesty," Sarroth replied. He glanced down the dark hallway toward the door at the far end. A Pi'aernotha Kaupet had just emerged from the cell. She carried a basket of filthy cloths with a scrub brush perched on top. The human woman hurried down the hallway toward them, dropping to a quick bow without losing stride. Kayrstana recognized her as the woman who had wept for the Pi'aernoth that died in her place. Doubtless, her mother had sent her here as a punishment, though Kayrstana thought no less of her. The t'Okaedrin and Pi'aernoth had been raised as brothers and sisters. It was natural to expect grief at the death of a sibling, even if it had been a worthy sacrifice. "The room has been cleaned as much as possible, Your Majesty," Sarroth continued, "but the stench is still quite strong."

"I am prepared, Captain. Lead on."

Sarroth dipped his head in a shallow bow, then guided the way down the hall. Two legionnaires stood guard at the door and bowed as they arrived. Then one opened the door. As she stepped across the threshold, Kayrstana had to stifle the urge to gag. Sarroth had not exaggerated. The scent of blood and waste was heavy in the room. It had soaked into the Boards themselves, an uncleansable testament to the torments that had been unleashed upon it.

The prisoner lay sprawled across the implement of torture. Though she had seen the Boards before, she'd never troubled herself to draw near to one. Vistus' hands and legs were stretched nearly taut, wrists and ankles enflamed where flesh had been rubbed away by the coarse fibers of the ropes. He had been cleaned of whatever blood and filth had been caked on his skin, leaving only the scars and welts of open and half-healed wounds. His hair was damp, but still bedraggled from filth and sweat that couldn't be easily washed away. And though much had been cleaned, his clothes had not been touched. They were matted and crumpled, reduced almost to rags. Vistus' head rested against the Boards, his gaze fixed on the dark rafters above. He did not stir as she entered. It was as if she didn't exist.

"How long has he been here?" she asked.

"Three weeks," Sarroth replied.

Kayrstana marveled that he still lived. Perhaps her people's problems with humans stemmed in part from a refusal to acknowledge that race's resilience. As if anticipating her question, Sarroth said, "He is given a little water every day and some broth to keep him alive, but only enough."

"He is aware of us?"

"He always has been until now, Your Majesty."

Kayrstana nodded. "Then you may begin."

"Yes, Your Majesty."

Kayrstana withdrew to the back wall of the small cell as Sarroth and one of the legionnaires stepped up to the Boards. The legionnaire undid the gag in Vistus' mouth and pressed a knife to his throat. Then Sarroth said, "Are you prepared to escape your torments, Vistus? You know what we wish to know."

Vistus' eyes came slowly into focus. His head lifted to look at Sarroth, then he glanced past him to Kayrstana. As their eyes met, Kayrstana wanted to tremble at the fever and fury within his. Vistus laid his head back. "I am Belarrin. Vistus is dead."

"Your name is nothing," Sarroth replied. "You live only to answer me. Speak and I will free you."

A crazed smile touched Vistus' lips. "I live because I choose to live. Or would you care to prove me wrong? Where are Eltirkar and Ushtyl? Don't tell me the reek of my Boards was too much for them to endure." A laugh rose up from his throat. Kayrstana might have thought it tinged with madness but for the look they'd shared when their eyes met. No, he was startlingly frighteningly aware.

Sarroth laughed, too. "I have some news that might loosen that tongue. Your brothers have just returned from the wilderness where they tracked down the last of your sorry Scion band. Each one of them has been executed. Speak now and I will let you join them in merciful death."

"I care nothing for your lies, Finnie. I am not a fool."

"And yet here you are, dying slowly upon the Boards."

"If they were dead, you would have brought me a corpse." Vistus closed his eyes. "Leave me be or kill me."

"No, we are not yet done," Sarroth glanced back to Kayrstana and she nodded. It was regrettable, but had to be done. Sarroth turned to the second legionnaire standing near the door. "Bring him."

The legionnaire bowed, then exited the cell. As he did, Vistus lay still as if no one were present. A moment later, the legionnaire reentered the room, escorting a t'Okaedrin. The human warrior glanced at Vistus and a grimace flashed across his face. Kayrstana was not familiar enough with human expressions to know whether it was from alarm at Vistus' state or disgust at Vistus' treason. The t'Okaedrin looked to Sarroth, waiting dutifully to be commanded.

"Your brother, Vistus," Sarroth said. "And I am told he was your closest friend."

At those words, Vistus opened his eyes again and looked to the t'Okaedrin. "Bridionis, I'm sorry they made you see me like this. I understand why you did what you did, and I forgive you. We all bear heavy chains."

Bridionis opened his mouth to speak, but it appeared that words failed him, for he clamped it shut again.

"You still care about your brother, then," Sarroth said. "I knew you would. Tell me what I want to know and he shall be spared."

Vistus laughed. "No he won't. You cannot risk it now. By the very words you speak, you prove the truth of who you are. You prove that all I said was true. Whether I speak now or not, he is dead."

"You have other brothers, too. Speak or I shall bring them here to die, one by one."

"Bring them, then!" Vistus roared, his body shaking violently in his bonds. "Do you think the lives they live are better than death? They are slaves, bound mind, body, and soul, worshipping their tormentors, bearing guilt for their masters' sins. Kill them all and set them free. Yes," he continued, meeting Bridionis' eyes. "My brother sees who you are now. He is the first you've freed. You cannot continue down this path and expect servitude from my kindred. Bring them all before me and free them one by one from this life of chains."

Sarroth's face darkened with anger, but it was Bridionis who spoke, his voice a whisper. "Yes, brother, I see now. Forgive me for not trusting you."

"The fault is not yours, but theirs, my brother."

Bridionis opened his mouth to speak again, but before he could, Sarroth drew a knife from his belt and plunged it into Bridionis' heart. His brother blinked once, then his mouth went slack and he crumpled to the floor.

"Bring another one!" Vistus spat. "Free them all!"

"So be it!"

"Marshal Sarroth," Kayrstana said. Sarroth turned to her, face crimson with anger and for a moment she thought he might yell even at her. But he regained his composure and dipped his head.

"Yes, Your Majesty?"

"I have seen enough. Gag him and join me outside."

"Yes, Your Majesty."

Kayrstana stepped gingerly over the body of Bridionis and left the cell, Vistus' mad laughter following her. Only it wasn't mad, it was frighteningly cogent, just as his words had been. A minute later, Sarroth and the two legionnaires joined her. "I beg your forgiveness, Your Majesty," Sarroth said, bowing his head lower this time. "I allowed him to anger me and overstepped myself."

"It is forgiven. Waste no more time in questioning him. He will never reveal the secrets we want." Ushtyl and Eltirkar should have seen that at the beginning, she realized. This prolonged torture was a revolting affair. She might order all the Boards destroyed after this. Kayrstana glanced back at the door and replayed the conversation in her mind. This was her own fault. She and her people had betrayed their t'Okaedrin. The brothers were forged to be dutiful servants and she had failed them. She had forsaken the trust Bridionis had rendered so faithfully, but also, perhaps, Vistus' own. But that was a question for another day. Sometimes the master craftsman had to cast away the clay she'd shaped with so much care. "I want him kept alive for the time being. In his death there is one more purpose he will yet serve."

Imeskir flowed through the tall grasses, shifting his stance as he whirled his greatsword over his head. He sliced and parried, cut and blocked, moving the weapon through the drills, honing his mind past thought toward instinct. None of the motions were fully practical, but they gave him a bond with his weapon, a sense of where it was, a sense of it as a part of him. There was a simplicity in the blade that he loved. It was deadly, and by it he would likely one day die, but that was the price all faced when they took up the sword. It was a far cleaner fate than many he had witnessed.

Around him, the other twenty Sword-Whisperers moved in similar drills. In time, when they were warm and the heat flowed through them, they would join together and train as one. They would chant the war spells for the next battle, the next war. Wherever the empress might send them. Perhaps that would be nowhere. The Sword-Whisperers were out of favor of late. The empress had left them behind when she and so many others traveled to Nahirazith. Rumors cast the blame on the shoulders of Ninanna, no matter how gallant the tales of her escape had been. She'd fought past a dozen guards without inflicting more harm than a scratch, but even that couldn't save her reputation. Yet Imeskir wondered if the greater blame lay with himself. How, in that moment of Ninanna's flight, he had only watched.

Imeskir faltered a step, his concentration overcome by the emotions flowing through his mind. He lowered his sword and looked out over the wide bluff, past the rocky overlook and to the endless blue sea beyond. He closed his eyes, feeling the wind flow over him, listening to the whisk of his companions' blades slicing the air.

He let out a deep sigh and opened his eyes. There could be no peace in his mind at this moment, it was a storm to be weathered. He turned away from the sea, back toward the wide fields with Thusaeyanin rising like a gilded crown in the distance. Two figures approached, but not from the city. As they drew nearer, he saw that they were both women. One was Syraestari, tall, fair-haired, and garbed in a black robe, while the other was a crimson-haired human in Kalilaer dress. He let out a soft gasp, recognizing the first. "Ninanna."

The other Sword-Whisperers stopped their drills and turned silently to watch. Imeskir sensed an uneasiness in the air. All of them knew and admired Ninanna, but she was a fugitive now, severed from the Syraestari. None had been present to witness what he saw at her trial and, heavy in his own mind, Imeskir had shared nothing.

The two women stopped a dozen paces away and Imeskir was started to see the human run her eyes curiously across the faces of the twenty warriors without the docility or fear he had come to expect from the Kalilaer.

Imeskir slid his sword into its sheath, then advanced to stand before Ninanna. Her face was harder than he had ever seen it, her eyes an age older. But as she met his gaze, a tender smile spread across her lips. "Imeskir, do you trust me?"

All of the warring emotions that had been unleashed during her trial rose up from his heart. It wasn't her words that captivated him, but her escape. It was astounding that he had failed to understand who she was after the thousands of times they'd drilled together. But perhaps such wonder could only be witnessed in true battle. He had seen such majesty only one time before. On that day when his life changed.

He dropped to his knees before her. "I would follow the Savior of Dahiraetin into the heart of the Abyss."

A gasp rippled through his companions as they understood the implication of his words. They all had heard his story countless times and many had fought in the battle. Each of them knew exactly what that meant to Imeskir, to the Syraestari people, to themselves. There had been no greater Syraestari hero since the end of the Great War.

Ninanna bent down and, taking his hand, raised him back to his feet. Then she embraced him. "I have missed you." Stepping back, she turned to the human woman. "This is Idysha. She is a Scion and a friend. There is much work that we must do and we need your help."

"A Scion?" Imeskir blinked. But it didn't matter. If Ninanna wished it, he would see it done. "I am yours. We are yours."

Behind him, the other Sword-Whisperers echoed, "For the Savior of Dahiraetin, we are yours."

"Thank you, my friend. I'm glad you know, now, yet sad also. I've never been and can never be the hero you remember from that day. You owe me nothing. We're kindred in blood, you and I, and that is enough."

Imeskir wanted to protest, wanted to proclaim all that that day had meant for him, yet he knew Ninanna well enough to realize he should not. She already knew everything he wanted to say. He would speak by his deeds as she had spoken by hers. He would follow wherever she led him without question or doubt.

"Before I tell you of the storm that is coming, Imeskir, I need to know what news there is in the empire. I've been gone many weeks."

"There's been more news in the past few days than in a hundred years." Imeskir barked a laugh then told her about the assassination attempt on the empress and the judgment against the high lords.

Ninanna frowned as he spoke but, when he was done, asked, "There was a raid on a Scion camp several weeks ago. I'm curious if you know anything about the Okaedir who infiltrated the camp. His name was Vistus."

Imeskir shook his head. "The human sorcerer? That's a second story, nearly as startling the first. He tried to corrupt one of his brothers and was arrested."

Ninanna's eyes widened in alarm. "Where is he? Does he still live?"

"I believe so. Last I heard, he was being questioned in the cells beneath Nahirazith."

"On the Boards?"

"I expect so."

The human woman drew in a sharp breath. "We must rescue him, Ninanna."

"We will, Idysha, I promise."

"I've heard that the high lords are to be executed in Nahirazith in a few days," Imeskir said, "and the rumors say Vistus is condemned to die with them. It is a final mark of their treason that the high lords be killed alongside a human. Lady Ninanna, I will do whatever you ask of me. I owe you that, but please look to the welfare of our people. I know these humans have their grievances, but your people are vulnerable, too."

"I know, Imeskir. There are oaths binding me to both peoples and I will do all I can to aid each. I'm afraid, though, that we've gone too far down this path. The shedding of blood has become inevitable."

"I pray it will not be much."

"As do I." Ninanna ran her eyes across the ranks of waiting Sword-Whisperers, then met Imeskir's gaze again. "Idysha and I must hurry now, like the wind, but I ask that you follow us to Nahirazith. We will be needed there before the end."

"We are yours to command."

Ninanna slid past the cell door into the deeper darkness beyond and closed it softly behind her. Reaching overhead, she felt a heavy wooden crossbeam and, grasping it in both hands, vaulted herself onto it. As she did, she wondered if the Shadow-Servant might have entered the room the same way. It was convenient to have the cell placed at the end of a drafty corridor where an errant gust of wind might just snuff the torch.

A few minutes later, the door opened again and two guards, holding torches, looked in. "I hate this watch. I'll be glad when they finally kill him," the first said. "It's getting so I can't wash away the foul stench of this place. And then there's that Cydion-accursed breeze always killing the torches."

"Unless it was the Shadow-Servant sneaking about down here. Maybe come to murder us."

"Quiet, fool!" The first guard said, slapping the back of the second's helm. They both glanced around one final time, eyes wider than before, then slammed the door shut again.

Ninanna waited several minutes until she was content that she wouldn't be disturbed. Lowering herself down to the floor, she spoke the Words of Power to light the candle she'd brought with her.

"Highest Above," she cursed under her breath as she saw the prison cell for the first time. It was worse than she'd expected, worse even than the foul stench assailing her nose suggested. Was this to be the legacy of the Syraestari? Looking down on Belarrin's ravaged body, she knew she owed humanity a great deal. She owed Belarrin even more.

He opened his eyes and stared at her when she rested her hand on his forehead. His skin was hot to the touch. "I'm sorry, Belarrin. I came as soon as I learned what happened to you." To her surprise, there was no anger in his expression. No hope, no fear, only pain. She sighed and took a seat on the edge of the Boards beside him. "We both have reached a place of decisions. I will tell you all I know and then give you your choices. If you want to be freed, I will see it done tonight and will heal you as best I can. You will understand in a moment why I delay."

Belarrin nodded and Ninanna hid a sigh of relief. "The Scions are coming to free the slaves of Nahirazith. Sravika leads your old band and has gathered together many more, over a thousand Scions in all. They will attack when the Syraestari are preoccupied with your execution tomorrow. Six high lords have been found guilty of conspiracy and are condemned to die alongside you. I expect that will bring all of the Syraestari into the city, leaving the Kalilaer settlement attended only by t'Okaedrin, who will be outnumbered." She paused a moment, then continued, "But I'm worried, Belarrin. Once they realize there is a raid of this magnitude, my people will intervene. There are many skilled warriors and more than a handful of sorcerers. Though only Lady Medreuneth has any great strength, the sheer numbers of them could be overwhelming. The Sword-Whisperers will do what we can to keep the Syraestari contained in the city, but I don't think the twenty of us will be enough. We need your help."

Belarrin mumbled something into his gag and Ninanna leaned forward to loosen it from his mouth. Then she pulled out a water flask and gently poured it so he could drink. After he had, he said, "I am not afraid of dying."

"I don't want you to die, Belarrin. For all of my failings, I owe you at least that. I will free you when the battle begins."

"You are afraid of me," Belarrin said.

Ninanna flinched. Then she folded her hands in her lap. "Yes, but not for myself. For my people."

"Slavers and murderers."

"I cannot deny nor defend what my people have done to you and your brothers. I will only say that out of fear and desperation we allowed ourselves to make an evil choice. But my people are no more evil than any other. I plead for their mercy. I know that there will be death tomorrow. That cannot be avoided now. I know that in unleashing you, I will give you full reign of your vengeance, but I hope, I pray, that you can find compassion."

Belarrin laughed. It was a biting sound, bitter and filled with pain. "I don't know what mercy looks like."

Ninanna's answer was soft. "I understand."

He coughed. It was a wracking movement that made his whole body shudder. He clenched his eyes shut until the spasms had ended. Opening them again, he said, "You are asking that I remain on the Boards one more day. That I walk out to face my execution."

"Yes."

"That's why you haven't healed me. Because if I was found without blemish, they would know something was wrong."

"I know it is a monstrous request after you've endured so much. I can only beg your forgiveness and promise that I will do all I can to free you and see you reunited with Sravika."

"No," he rasped. "Sravika doesn't need the likes of me. I murdered her sister. I brought death upon her people."

Her sister! Ninanna stifled a gasp, but Belarrin saw it and smiled bitterly.

"Yes, she knows. She knew before I even told her," he said. "I will remain here as you ask. I will march to my execution. It is far less than I deserve."

"Belarrin you do not..."

One look from him silenced her. The pain she saw now was not from the Boards ravaging his body, but from the depths of his soul. "So much blood has spilled and only blood can wash it away." He closed his eyes for a long moment as if drawing from some deep inner strength or perhaps deeper pain. "But mercy? I don't know if I can find what none of us deserve."

"I can only ask that you try."

He looked up at the ceiling overhead. "If there is nothing else, you had best leave me to my darkness in case the guards come."

"Is there anything you want me to tell Sravika?"

He shook his head. "No. It would be better that she forgot me."

Ninanna rose to her feet. "I will heal you more fully tomorrow, but for now I can at least give you strength to help you endure."

"The Shadow-Servant already did as much when he came here."

"The Shadow-Servant was here?"

"Yes, he came to kill me. I wish he had."

"Why didn't he?"

"Because he is mad, just like me. He carries a pain as deep as my own and a guilt that is far deeper." Belarrin frowned as though he'd said more than he wished. "I am ready."

He did not move as Ninanna replaced the gag in his mouth, nor when she cast the spell of strength over him. But his eyes held hers until she blew out the candle. She could see now that he had no intention of surviving the morrow. He wanted to die for the guilt he felt. Perhaps he even welcomed the pain. There was only one way to save him, and to save as many of her own people as she could. She needed Sravika.

CHAPTER 42

Evening

"It is the curse of empires to be forever hungry, reaching often beyond their means. In each clutching grasp new enemies are made, as often from within as from without."

—Tae'irfynon of Kayrkoreth

The Empress Kayrstana leaned back in her chair and, cradling a wine goblet in her hands, closed her eyes. In the tumult of the past few days, she'd been so busy that there had been little time for clear thought. Her expectations, her dreams, even her simplest thoughts had been ravaged, both by the treason of the high lords and the devastating betrayal of her once-beloved Ushtyl. She longed for but a few hours to collect herself more fully, to consider everything.

"Your Majesty?" High Lord Tyrnis said.

But not yet. Not until Ushtyl was dead. Highest Above, she missed Ninanna, a voice she could trust without looking for hidden ambitions, a person on whom she knew she could unleash all of her burdens. But she had been a fool. She had allowed herself to be guided against her better judgment and had driven her closest friend away. All for a man who'd sought only to use her. To kill her. Kayrstana opened her eyes. "Yes, High Lord."

They sat with High Lady Jesaelyn in the receiving room of the palace in Nahirazith. It was here that Arkesh had feigned the attack that brought Ninanna down. During the daylight hours, the room was filled with light from the large windows and bright walls, but Kayrstana preferred it at night. With only a pair of lamps lit on either side of the room, she could look up through the windows and see stars twinkling faintly above. A reminder of peace that she did not feel.

"I am concerned about your intentions for tomorrow, Your Majesty," Tyrnis said. "Word has gone out to all the cities by now, and I'm hearing mixed reports. Some are jubilant, but many are not. There is grumbling, especially from the cities of the arrested high lords."

"Former high lords."

"Yes, Your Majesty. I have heard of nothing beyond talk, but that may change at any moment. I fear it may already have changed."

"The executions tomorrow will end that," Kayrstana replied. "With the traitors dead, there will be no one for the dissenters to rally behind. The empire will be secure and we shall move forward as one people. In fact, I have been thinking. An execution in the square isn't enough. I want their treason displayed to the world. Let them die the base deaths they deserve among the Kalilaer on the plains below."

"Your Majesty," Lady Jesaelyn said, leaning forward. Her eyes were downcast deferentially, but her voice was earnest. "I ask you for clemency."

"For murderers?"

"Not for Ushtyl or Eltirkar, but for the others. I understand your anger and support whatever you decide. But the others, they were not involved in Ushtyl's plans. He manipulated them." As much as Ushtyl manipulated you. Kayrstana heard the unspoken suggestion and her face flushed.

Perhaps sensing she'd pushed too far, Jesaelyn ducked her head and fell silent, but Tyrnis spoke for her. "Your Majesty, I have heard confessions from their own lips, both when they thought you were dead and also when I questioned them after. I don't know that they committed any greater grievance than a shared frustration at some of your demands. Their anger might have led them to conspire in the future, but not yet."

"They were closer to open rebellion than they'll admit. There was already an agreement to overthrow my regime and banish me."

"I do not deny it, but I think they're ashamed at how Ushtyl used them."

"And so I should risk them rebelling against me again? Killing me again?" She closed her eyes and raised her hand. "Please, leave me. I am very fatigued."

"Yes, Your Majesty," they both said, rising to their feet.

"High Lord Tyrnis, please issue commands to the workers. The judgments will be carried out on the plains below, not in the city. I know it will require some changes, but see it done."

"As you command," Tyrnis said. They bowed quietly and withdrew, leaving her alone in the dark room.

Kayrstana stood as well, walking around her chair to stand by the windows. Looking up at the night sky, she whispered, "Blood on the Bridge, Ninanna. What have I done? I could use your advice now." With Ninanna she might have shared what she intended on the morrow, but no other. It had to appear a spontaneous choice.

"Kayrstana."

The empress' eyes widened in alarm as she recognized the voice behind her. Summoned as if wished for. But this was not a dream and no amount of wishes could undo what had been done. She was the empress and she had spoken. She had to abide by the words that had been said and the decisions she had made. Kayrstana made sure her face was smooth before she turned around. "Ninanna, should I summon the guards?"

Her old guardian stood in front of the closed door, her hands clasped behind her back. "If that is all you wish of me, then I shall leave."

Kayrstana shook her head, then returned to her chair and sat down. Being seated always lent an air of authority. "I would not have executed you. Condemned, yes, because I had to. But I would have ensured your escape."

"If that is an apology, it is insufficient. If it is not, your words are meaningless. My life does not matter."

"It is the best I can do."

"Then do nothing. But I didn't come here for your apology."

"What do you wish, then? A pardon? With the execution of your accusers, I was planning on it."

"You are on the threshold, Empress," Ninanna said. "I'm sure you believe yourself to be on the verge of a glorious triumph and perhaps that will be true. But you are likewise on the edge of destruction."

"All threats to my reign have been removed. Unless you count yourself my enemy, now."

"I have never been your enemy, not even after your betrayal" Ninanna replied. It was startling how steady her voice was, even after all she'd been through. There was no pleading in her tone, nor any air of menace. She stood just as she always had, rigidly formal yet loose as well. "You are your own worst enemy. That is the truth of all of our people. It always has been."

"With the high lords broken, the people follow only me."

"The high lords are nothing. It is humanity that should fill you with terror. You have created a dominion you cannot possibly hope to control. You are sailing upon rough seas and are but skirting the edge of the coming storm. In time, the tempest shall grow until its full fury leaves you with little choice but to hang on and wait for your vessel to be torn asunder and the deeps to swallow you."

"We have broken the humans to our will."

Even Ninanna's barked laugh was controlled. "This is no idle discussion as in the days before. This is a warning. Humanity cannot and will not be controlled. When we first began to capture humans, the plan was to leave when the time was right. We intended to hand over the leadership of this empire to the t'Okaedrin and go our own way. That time has arrived and opportunity is short. Free the Kalilaer, give the t'Okaedrin the ownership they have earned, and leave before this beast you've birthed devours you."

Kayrstana rose to her feet, anger flushing her face. "I always tolerated your love of humanity, but this passes beyond that. You would betray your own people."

"I speak of our salvation. The storm is here, Kayrstana. Please, for our own good."

"Enough! If this is all you came to say, Ninanna, then you have said your piece."

Ninanna sighed. "So I have. This is my final plea before I go my own way. It is possible we will never speak again."

Kayrstana sank back into her chair, regret returning to her again. But all the words that could be said had been. There was nothing else to be done. "Then live well, Ninanna."

"And you, Kayrstana."

Kayrstana blinked at the words. There was far more warmth in them than her betrayal of Ninanna deserved. Almost Kayrstana lifted her hand, but already Ninanna had turned away and passed through the open door.

Darkness surrounded him. Had there ever been anything but darkness? Had he lived prior to the endless night? There were dreams, yes, but had any of it been real? These dreams of sun and wind and rain, of warmth without pain, of smiling faces, of laughter. The words felt familiar and, if he could concentrate, he could almost see them. But feel them? No, he couldn't remember that. He couldn't be sure they ever had been. Nor could he be sure of who he was, or even if he was. Vistus, he had once been called, and Belarrin. Was he both, one, neither? Names, what did they mean?

And names of visitors, too, entering into his darkness with a momentary flash of light. Yes, there must have been light once. He was sure he knew that. Tazil, and the Shadow-Servant, and Ninanna, they had been called. The first came in doubt, the second to kill, the third near pleading. Others had come, too, with pain. Eltirkar and Ushtyl and the empress. That was clearer, more real. He could remember those moments when the ever-present pain was sharper. Pain and darkness were all he knew, all he could be certain of... except for one thing. He deserved it. He deserved the darkness. He deserved the pain.

Every time he looked into the darkness, every time he closed his eyes, every time he dreamed, their names came as a litany to his lips. Vitarria and Zoltha, Bridionis, Parvik, Inban, Kitiger and so many more. So many he had murdered and so many others he had failed. Mirnadd, Wiersa, Jarkon. So many. Did he still have the strength to do all he must? Could he think past the pain? Even with the healing given him he could feel his life, his mind, failing. He drifted ever more among that sea of stars with the crimson ribbon of madness beckoning him to its warm embrace. There was strength there, but also the death of self. And, though he deserved to die, he would save his friends first.

"What? No!" Sravika said, her mind whirling.

"He needs you, Sravika," Ninanna replied.

Sravika leaned forward and rubbed her forehead. It had begun throbbing earlier in the day. So much was at stake, of herself, of him, of everyone. The darkness around them was startlingly silent. Several hundred Scions within a few miles and barely a sound broke the night. There were no fires, no warm cheer or laughter. Just waiting and wondering if the dawn would herald a glorious triumph or a slaughter. "I cannot. These people need me too. I pulled them together. I promised them and they're depending on me to lead them."

"He's been down there for weeks. He's overwhelmed by anger, pain, regret and something more. I don't know. I just know he needs you."

"Then why didn't you bring him out?" Sravika snapped.

If Ninanna felt the bite of her words, she didn't show it. Her reply was gentle. "Because you need him there. He is the key. When the battle begins, you need all the surprise you can manage. Between him and my Sword-Whisperers, we can hold the Syraestari in the city."

Sravika flung up her hands. "How can I weigh a thousand lives against one, even if I… even if it is him?" She shook her head. "I cannot. Not even for him. He was a warrior. He is a warrior and he knows what it means to lead."

"As do I. But this isn't the same thing."

"It is the same. You left him there and I will have to rely upon you to bring him out." Sravika drew in a ragged breath. "Please bring him out."

"I will do everything I can." Ninanna rose to her feet. "Highest Above be with you tomorrow."

"And with you."

Sravika waited until Ninanna had vanished into the darkness before she allowed the tears to fall. As the wind rustled through the trees, they burned cold against her cheeks. She wanted to do all Ninanna had said. She wanted to run to him, embrace him and hold him and tell him all she felt in her heart. But she couldn't. Not tomorrow. Not when so many other lives hung in the balance. "Belarrin. Blood on the Bridge, what did they do to you?"

Looking up at the starlit sky, Ninanna wondered what other eyes must be turned heavenward on this night of 'Before'. Did they know what lay before them? Did she? Her night had been filled with visitations in the city and in the wilderness. But now, all she could think to do was done. With the morrow, how many would die, how many would walk free? How many chains would break and how many would clasp?

She leaned back against a tree with her greatsword cradled in her lap and looked southward to the dark silhouette that was Nahirazith. What would this field and those heights look like with the dawn? And with the dusk that followed?

Clouds rolled across the heavens. They were invisible in and of themselves, known only by the stars that one by one were consumed until only darkness remained. Closing her eyes, Ninanna drank in the cool wind that brushed her cheeks. Autumn waned and winter approached, a time of stagnation and death. Or perhaps, of life. Branches rustled faintly against each other in a haunting melody. Most were skeleton-like, their leaves a colorful carpet on the ground below. But among them, there was one sound that did not fit. Yet only barely. It was instinct honed over the centuries that told her different.

"Are we still allies?" she asked the darkness.

"I would like us to be," the Shadow-Servant answered.

"Then tell me again what it is you want. What change drove you to kill Belarrin and then changed again to let him live?"

"What I want is what I've always wanted."

"Then what is best for the Syraestari has changed."

"Yes."

"Why?"

She opened her eyes as Reigliff stepped from the darkness of the forest behind her and sat down in the grasses a pace away, his legs crossed. "Because the empress has spoken," he answered. "When she declared the new dominion I was left with two choices. Become a rebel like those that tried to murder her or remain an ally upon whom she could rely. It was under Ushtyl's influence that she made so many poor choices, including your condemnation. She has realized that now and the folly of yesterday has given her new wisdom. I believe she regrets what she did to you."

"Only after her own betrayal was revealed. Too late." Ninanna grimaced. "And even if she regrets, she is not truly penitent."

"That is for you to judge, not I. But regardless of how she's wronged you, the Syraestari need the empress, strong and certain, and therefore the empress needs me as an ally. My dream for refuge has died."

"As simple as that?"

"Simple?" Reigliff shrugged. "If that is the name you choose."

"Then what of the humans?"

"They are, as they always were, an impediment."

"But you spared Belarrin. If you want a stable empire, then he and the Scions are all a threat to be destroyed or driven off. Syraestari will die tomorrow, no matter what we do. Highest Above, it terrifies me. What if I chose wrong? Deaths could number in the thousands, both Syraestari and human."

"I am less concerned with tomorrow than what will happen after. What will we become? What will the Scions become?"

"This is why I still doubt my trust in you," Ninanna replied, amazed that despite all that, she could speak openly to him from the heart. "Yes, the days that follow matter, but you don't see individuals. You see only peoples, societies, plots, and inclinations. But all of that comes from the many persons that are a part of them. A thousand individuals, each deciding what they think is best. Tomorrow matters, because each of those people will be deciding. You, me, Belarrin, the empress, and dozens of others, perhaps even someone unexpected whose hand will change everything. The arrow unseen, the word unexpected, a shift in the wind."

"I see them all, Ninanna," Reigliff said softly, "but not in the same way you do."

"Then why don't you fear tomorrow? You spared Belarrin, so I want to believe that we remain allies. Tell me how I can know."

"Because I have seen tomorrow. Vaenna's words are about to be given life and breath."

"The prophecy?" Ninanna asked, but her usual sneer died on her lips. There was something earnest in his voice that made her doubt. "Explain it to me."

Reigliff hesitated, then shook his head. "I cannot. There are secrets within it I cannot reveal, dark wounds that have bled for centuries."

"You become poetic when you try to evade. If you won't tell me of the past, fine. But explain tomorrow."

"It is best that I refuse. A prophecy understood can be worked against, whether we mean it or not. What did I see that made me spare Belarrin? I learned that even a master of shadows must sometimes bow to what must to be. In a way, you were right to doubt the prophecy. Tomorrow you need to be Ninanna unfettered by supposed interpretations."

"But you know it. How has that changed you?"

"I know what must be, but I do not know what will be." Almost she thought he grinned at her behind his mask. "I know that's a riddle. For me, too. I don't know what I'll do. Perhaps nothing at all."

He leaned forward, the movement so sudden, Ninanna instinctively drew back. "Join with me, Ninanna. I have declared myself, now. Our people know that a Shadow-Servant lives and walks among them. Too long, I have been alone and in secret. Join me and become the second of a new breed of Shadow-Servants. I know you care about our people, just as I do."

Ninanna grimaced. "I would prefer the opposite."

"The opposite?"

"Cast off that name. Let the Shadow-Servants die the final death they deserve. You and your kindred have done at least as much evil as good. Claim a better, greater name free of that tainted lineage."

Reigliff sat back, hands resting on his knees. "There is good and evil in all of us. We make the best choices we know and live or die with them. A Shadow-Servant is what I am and what I will remain."

"Then we are what we are. But whether that means ally or enemy depends on tomorrow." She leaned forward and met his eyes, as much to soften the hardness of her words as emphasize how important they were. "You know what I believe. You came to me when my heart was in ruin and for that I have trusted you and will trust you until I can no longer. But if that trust is destroyed, if we must become enemies, I will not shrink from it."

"I know. And that's why I admire you. I will only say that I do not wish harm upon Belarrin. Nor do I wish ill upon the Scions you've come to love. If the Empire is rid of rebels, so much the better. If tomorrow can end with that still true, than I wish it, too. But be warned that my purpose remains unchanged. I will do whatever I must to see our peoples' future secure."

"Then we will see."

"Yes, my friend, we will see."

"For now, I will pray. Nothing else remains to be done."

"Then pray for all of us."

CHAPTER 43
Condemned

"Justice? I have not seen it upon this earth, for who is perfect that he might judge me? Who knows my heart? Who sees the wars that have waged in my soul? Who sees the suffering, the torment, the toll each choice has taken within? Condemn me, then, but do not pretend to know me. Do not pretend to understand me! Condemn me, but know that your heart is as black as my own."

—Tars, the Butcher of Dinmala

Elestis peered through the foliage and smiled to herself. What had started as a bleak gray dawn had suddenly become a morning of promise. Fifty paces away, a Scion woman crept through the forest. Elestis had never seen one roaming so close to the edge of the wilderness. Very rarely, a Kalilaer might be lucky enough to escape this far, but no Scion would wander here by chance.

Elestis' fingers drummed across her bowstring as she waited for the perfect moment to strike. A dozen paces away, two of her sisters readied as well. Her shot would be a long one, and difficult because of all the forest boughs. Yet she was afraid to draw any nearer. The Scion moved slowly, carefully, scanning the woods all around her and, if Elestis dared to move, the woman would almost certainly see her. The Scion was short and thin with light brown unkempt hair that touched her shoulders. Not surprisingly, she twitched nervously with each step, head swiveling at the creak of every branch, hands trembling as she gripped her spear too tightly. She was like a deer that senses hunters nearby. Perhaps this one was lost. Elestis' smile widened. Better to capture her alive then. She would take the woman to Arcomin and he would make her talk. If they located a Scion band preparing to raid nearby, there would be great honor for the both of them.

The Pi'aernoth and t'Okaedrin needed that to overcome the shame of Vistus' fall. She squeezed her eyes shut, fighting back a wave of sorrow. Why did he have to walk among the rebels? She had loved him, once. A part of her still loved the man he'd been before it all.

The Scion woman angled a little closer, passing along the base of a small cliff that finally forced her to walk at the edge of a glade. As she stepped fully into the open between two trees, Elestis drew a breath and raised her bow, touching fletchings to cheek. She exhaled then loosed.

The bowstring sang as the arrow leapt forward. The Scion turned, sensing motion, but it was too late, and the arrow took her in the right calf. She screamed as she fell to the ground, spear flying from her hands.

Elestis leapt from her hiding place with short sword drawn, followed closely by her sisters. Seeing them, the Scion woman cried out. She tried to stand but her wounded leg buckled. Falling back to the carpet of autumn leaves, she scrambled for her spear. But Elestis was quicker. Gouging her boot into the woman's right arm pit, Elestis forced the Scion's hand from the spear. The woman wriggled beneath the weight, trying to twist away, but Elestis drove her other knee into the woman's back. Her sisters arrived, one kicking away the spear while the other grappled with the woman's hands, but still the Scion fought. Clawing savagely, she was more wildcat now than deer. A hand broke free to scratch runnels in Elestis' cheek. Cursing, Elestis drove her knees deeper as her sister took the woman's hands again, wrenching them painfully back until the Scion shrieked in pain. Before she could recover, her hands were bound tight, and then her legs. But still the Scion fought, kicking out, lunging to bite with her teeth.

Elestis plunged her sword into the ground next to the woman's neck and hissed. "Keep fighting and I won't kill you. I'll take out your eyes. First one, then the other." She meant it, too, though she would hate it at the same time. Thankfully, the Scion whimpered, then finally fell still.

"Good. Now we go quietly," Elestis said, dragging the woman to her feet. She turned to her sisters and grinned. "There will be great honor for the Pi'aernoth today."

"Do you remember me?" the Pi'aernotha Kaupet said. Belarrin looked up at her from the Boards. The guards had released his hands and feet several hours before, then they'd lashed his ankles together and his wrists behind his back. His gag remained. Bringing in his arms and legs had raised a fire in his tortured limbs as agonizing as any moment stretched out on the Boards. He had lain there ever since, whimpering as awareness came and went. The Pi'aernoth spoke again, "Talikae, the one you told about the forest."

Belarrin squinted. The name was familiar, like from before a dream. Then he remembered. It was the woman who'd prepared him to meet the empress.

"I've been sent to bring you outside. You are to be executed," she told him.

Belarrin nodded. His mind was clearer now.

"It is time to rise." There was surprising gentleness in her voice. He tried to push himself upright, but his whole body trembled at the effort. She took his shoulders gently and pulled him to a sitting position. "You do not need to stand alone."

Talikae slipped her hand under his arm and across his back as he tottered to his feet. Pain arched up his legs and he buckled, but a second Pi'aernoth rushed to his other side and, between them, they held him up. He didn't look to see the other woman. It was too much effort even to lift his head and there was no point.

"We have you and won't let you fall."

Belarrin laughed into his gag. She was worried about his knees scrapping the ground as she marched him to the headsman's axe. But his death awaited and he would not flinch from it. Ninanna had promised to free him, to see his escape, but that was not his plan. He didn't care about his own life. No, he had done too much evil and deserved to die. He had killed friends and family. The blood of Zoltha, of Vitarria, of Bridionis and so many others lay upon his head. He would face death with courage. But if Ninanna did free him, he would do as she asked. He would kill Syraestari and see to it that Sravika lived. It was a far cry from redemption, but it was the best he could do.

Step by aching step, he and his Pi'aernoth minders climbed up from the bowels of the palace. He sensed house-carl guards following them, but he had as little interest in them as he did in Talikae's companion. He stumbled countless times and, more than once, was not sure he had the strength for the journey, but the two Pi'aernoth caught him each time, holding him up, until finally he reached the palace threshold.

As wind caressed his face for the first time in an eternity, a whimper of joy and pain escaped his lips. He lifted his eyes to squint at the brilliant cloud-borne heavens. In the far distance, he even thought he could hear the rush of the surf, flowing in and out like slow drawn breaths.

The Pi'aernoth guided him out through the stable gates and then around the side of the palace to the main plaza. His feet stumbled on the grooved cobbles, but again they kept him from falling. He wondered at the gentleness of their grasp. After the harsh treatment of his tormentors, he could sense the greater care they showed even in the way they held his upper arms. He knew how much weight they were carrying and how hard it must be on their arms crossed behind his back. They should have just let him fall. Another bruise on the body of a walking corpse made no difference.

The streets of the city were surprisingly empty of all but Pi'aernoth about their duties. He didn't see a single Syraestari except for his guards and a handful up on the walls. But then, he didn't care about that either. They walked together, at his slow shambling pace, past the plaza and down Nahirazith's central street.

Belarrin stumbled as he realized what that meant. Ninanna had said he and the high lords were to die in the plaza, but that was already behind them. Where, then was he to face his end? Had Ninanna's plan come apart already?

They passed through the city's outer gates, where the sea stretched out before him in magnificent glimmering blue. Even beneath a clouded sky it was too bright for his light-deprived eyes. He walked the path he had walked before, down the city bluff and out onto the plain. Ahead of him waited a familiar sight, the Kalilaer camp and the field edged by Boards. But the field was different now. Eight posts had been erected near the center and a high viewing platform stood opposite them. Encircling the field waited the populous of Nahirazith. A throng, gathered to see him die. More likely, they were interested in the high lords the empress had condemned, but he decided to take the pleasure himself.

A few murmured in idle curiosity as he walked through, though most ignored him as Talikae guided him to the nearest of the posts. Under the watchful eye of his Syraestari guards, Talikae and the other Pi'aernoth carefully untied his hands, then bound them again behind the post. Standing after being stretched so long was agony, but by leaning against the post, Belarrin was able to hold himself upright. Barely. When they were done, the other Pi'aernoth withdrew, but Talikae lingered a moment.

"I am honored to have known you," she said in a soft voice. Honored? Was she mad? "There are two people I have come to respect more than any other and they both have fallen. My mother thought making me tend you was a punishment, but it was not."

He looked up and met her eyes, intense and earnest. Then she turned away.

"I don't know anything. I was lost!" the woman cried. She had given her name as Chostir. Hirnid recognized her from the smelting camp that Vistus had been assigned to, but he doubted Arcomin would. Such things were beneath his notice. Chostir was lashed to one of the whipping posts used to punish willful young t'Okaedrin. Hirnid had been an obedient child and only faced that lash once. But Chostir was bound with her back to it, facing outward. Already her nose was broken and one eye had swollen nearly shut. Her shoulder had come out of joint and her calf oozed blood from where Elestis had shot her with the arrow. "Water, please!"

"You get water when you say something useful," Arcomin snapped, then struck her again.

Hirnid's stomach clenched and he turned away from the circle of brothers. Scions were supposed to be hunted down and executed, not treated this. They were apostates, not beasts.

"What's wrong, Hirnid?" Arcomin called to him. "Going soft on rebels like your friend Vistus?"

"No." Hirnid forced himself to face his brother and the beaten woman. If Bridionis were here, he'd have said something. He would have stopped Arcomin, but Bridionis was gone. Rumor said he'd been assigned to the Kal t'Okaedrin, but no one really knew. No one but Bridionis and Vistus had ever been strong enough to stand up to Arcomin. Especially now that he was eldest.

Arcomin flashed a frown his way, suggesting once again that he was more in control than his behavior often suggested. Turning back to the woman, he raised his hand to strike her again.

"Please, no more!" Chostir cried out, flinching from the hovering fist.

"Then answer! Where are they?"

She sagged in her bonds and her voice became small. "About five miles into the woods northwest of here."

"Not good enough. The forest is huge."

"Please," Chostir whimpered. Tears fell from her eyes. "Highest Above forgive me."

"He'll forgive you when you speak."

"Near the hillock. The one with the river that wraps around the base on the southern side."

Arcomin glanced over at Elestis who stood among the gathered brothers. "You know it?"

She nodded.

Arcomin turned to face his family. "Brothers, get ready to march. I'm going to bring this news to father and then you can be sure the orders will come. The ground will drink Scion blood this day!" Arcomin smiled. "Go now! All except Hirnid."

As his family scattered to gather their full gear, Arcomin walked up to Hirnid and stabbed his chest with his forefinger. "No glory for you, today. You've grown too weak in the face of duty. That's what took Vistus and, if you're not careful, it will take you to. Remain here and watch over the Scion since you care so much about her." He shook his head. "So weak in the stomach, I'm not sure you deserve the name brother."

"Yes, Eldest," Hirnid answered as Arcomin left. Perhaps he was weak. He didn't know. Arcomin only mocked him to bolster his fervor and, at one time, that would have worked. He couldn't say what had changed. Except Vistus' fall. With a sigh, he walked over to Chostir and, unstoppering his canteen, let her drink.

"Thank you," she said, when she was done drinking.

"Don't thank me for keeping you alive," Hirnid replied.

"Belarrin is your brother, isn't he? I remember you from the slave camp."

"Vistus. He only went by Belarrin when he infiltrated your people."

"Vistus is dead. He is Belarrin, now."

"Yes, I suppose that's true," Hirnid replied. And soon, Belarrin would be dead, too. He looked up to the walls of Nahirazith where Belarrin was imprisoned, thinking of the days when he'd given Vistus water on the Boards.

"We had cities like that once," Chostir said. Her voice was hoarse, but she continued anyway. "Before the Cataclysm there were magnificent cities with tall buildings and fountains. One even had a waterfall that flowed straight through it."

Hirnid shook his head. "How can you talk of fantasies and dreams at a time like this?"

"What else should I think about? That I can hardly see and barely stand? That your brothers are going out to slaughter my people?"

"I don't know," Hirnid muttered. He knelt down to wrap a cloth around her bleeding leg. He wished she would stop talking. The more she talked, the more he hated himself.

When the task was done, he rose and stood side by side with his prisoner, watching his brothers gather. They moved with quick efficiency, nearly the entire brotherhood of Nahirazith. Over half a thousand strong, they grouped by families of about twenty apiece, forming squares four across and up to five deep. Eldests stood at the front, signaling their fathers when all was ready. Helms and banded shields gleamed dully in the light of the overcast sky. There was always a startling quietness to such gathering with commanders calling their orders like birds of prey piercing the heavens and the brothers themselves obeying with quiet certainty, their only voice the gentle chink of metal on metal. Against such a force, the Scions would stand no chance. It would be a day of glory with little loss.

Why, then, did he feel no regret at being left behind?

Sravika crawled on her hands and knees through the outer verge of the forest. Head peaking just above the tall grasses that grew beneath the shade of the trees, she looked out on the slave settlement beneath Nahirazith and her eyes widened.

"See what I mean?" Henirgar said. "It wasn't supposed to be like this."

Heart rising up in her throat, Sravika doubted she could speak, at least not quietly. She could only nod as she stared out at the gathered throng of Syraestari on the edge of the encampment. There had to be over a thousand of them and more were walking down from the city to join them. Though none of those in sight were armed or armored, with lifetimes measured in millennia, she didn't doubt that hundreds of them could make for terrifying foes.

"Why are they here?" Henirgar asked. "The execution was supposed to be up in the city."

That meant Belarrin was only a few hundred paces away, waiting to die. Sravika exhaled a slow breath through pursed lips. "I don't know."

"What do we do, now?"

"The only thing we can."

The Empress Kayrstana stood in the atrium of the Nahirazith palace and looked through the open doors to the plaza outside. After today, her work here would be nearly done and she could return to her own city of Thusaeyanin.

She was happy with her choice of the night before to move the execution beyond the walls. There was a satisfaction in the humiliation her enemies would suffer to die among the humans, especially Ushtyl. The craftsmen had worked through the night ensuring all was in readiness.

Looking out one of the high palace windows, she had watched her people walk down to the plain below to witness the day's events. There were many more than just those of Nahirazith present, several hundred from the other cities of the realm had made the journey over the past few days to witness the spectacle. To her pleasure, none had protested her judgment.

When the prisoners were marched onto the plain, she'd watched that, too. First Vistus, a husk of the man he once had been, stumbled his way across the plaza. Once he was secured below, the high lords followed. Sizras and Ushtyl, her greatest threats, strode out with heads unbowed, but the others were stooped and broken, Tazil by more than just his fate. It was unfortunate his son had been murdered. Under any other circumstance, she would have been first to offer him commiseration.

As the last of the prisoners passed from sight, Kayrstana turned to High Lady Jesaelyn and Marshal Sarroth who waited in attendance. "Where is High Lord Tyrnis? He should be here by now."

"I don't know, Your Majesty," Jesaelyn said. "I haven't seen him this morning."

"Nor I, Your Majesty," Sarroth said.

Kayrstana frowned. She needed his presence as much as she needed Jesaelyn's to solidify the prestige of her throne. But at the same time, she couldn't delay the executions either. The prisoners and the populous might interpret that as doubt. She turned to her Pi'aernoth attendant waiting nearby. "Find High Lord Tyrnis and tell him his empress needs him immediately."

"Yes, Your Majesty." The Pi'aernoth dropped into a deep bow before hurrying for the interior door.

Time passed and it was all Kayrstana could do not to tap her foot with impatience. When she was just about to send out another attendant, the Pi'aernoth returned. Dropping to both knees and bowing her head to the floor, the woman said, "I'm sorry, Your Majesty, but we couldn't find High Lord Tyrnis. He is not in the palace, nor on the battlements, and he wasn't seen in the city either."

"Blood on the Bridge," Kayrstana cursed. She glanced to Jesaelyn and Sarroth. "I cannot wait any longer. I want the search for Lord Tyrnis continued and orders left at the palace for him to ride with all haste to the execution field once he returns."

"I will give your orders to the Captain of the Guard as we depart, Your Majesty," Sarroth answered.

Kayrstana extended her arms to allow the Pi'aernoth in attendance to straighten her gown. When all was in readiness, she took a slow breath and walked with a regal steadiness she did not feel out of the palace and down the steps. Sarroth and Jesaelyn followed and a perimeter of Kal t'Okaedrin marched around them, eyes darting everywhere for potential assassins.

Groomsmen had their horses waiting at the base of the steps. Lady Medreuneth was already mounted. A subtle frown touched her face as, eyes downcast, the sorceress muttered quietly to herself. As Kayrstana arrived, Medreuneth gave her a dignified bow, then promptly resumed her distracted thinking.

Two Kal t'Okaedrin held the reins of Kayrstana's horse as she mounted. Then they mounted as well, all twenty of them. Once all was in readiness, Kayrstana nodded to Marshal Sarroth, and he gave the command for the imperial entourage to march. They rode at a dignified walk down the wide main thoroughfare of the city, their only audience a host of Pi'aernotha Kaupet about their daily duties. The Sisters of Stone bowed as she rode by, then resumed their tasks.

As they passed through the outer gates, the two Syraestari legionnaires standing watch sounded their trumpets to herald her approach. The melody rolled majestically across the plain. Kayrstana looked up to them and smiled. A little over half of the legionnaires in Nahirazith had once been housecarls in service to Ushtyl. They'd sworn their oaths to her, now, and their diligence had been unrelenting in the past days. It was further evidence that her people blessed her choices and acknowledged the wisdom of her rule.

Looking across the plain as she followed the path down from the city, Kayrstana saw the host of Syraestari gathered at the execution field. It was good to see so many of her people gathered in one place to attend her. Everywhere she looked since the vile assassination she saw signs of unity and loyalty.

But her eyes didn't stay on the execution field long, caught by a swarm of activity among the t'Okaedrin barracks to her right. There were hundreds gathered there, too, but these formed into orderly squares of warriors. Many had already begun marching, passing the gathering of Syraestari, and heading into the forest to the northwest. "What are the t'Okaedrin doing, Marshal Sarroth?"

"A Scion straggler was captured this morning, Your Majesty. Under questioning, she confessed there was a raiding party gathered nearby."

Might this have been Ninanna's warning from the night before? No, she couldn't have been so enamored of humans to think that a single Scion raid threatened to topple everything. "Yet another good omen for the establishment of this empire."

"Yes, Your Majesty."

CHAPTER 44
Judgment

"It is a simple thing to raise your sword and strike down the enemy. Knowing when not to is the greater challenge."

—Deylos Velparysis

Kayrstana's subjects encircling the execution field dropped to one knee as she rode by. All except the inner ring of three hundred legionnaires who held their place with left hand on hilt and right hand touched to chest. She looked for High Lord Tyrnis among them, but he wasn't there. A herald stationed at the base of the imperial platform bellowed, "Behold! Her Imperial Majesty, the Empress Kayrstana, Guardian of the Nine Cities, Keeper of the Staff of Kayrkir, High Lady of all the Syraestari!"

She guided her horse to the platform, where half of her Kal t'Okaedrin quickly dismounted. Eight ran to take up station on the platform while two held her horse's harness for her to dismount. When she was on the ground, Jesaelyn,

Sarroth, and Medreuneth followed, then the second half of the Kal t'Okaedrin dismounted, too. Kayrstana climbed the steps at the back of the platform, then took her seat on its single chair. It was hand carved and, though a simple work for a master craftsman, still held the majesty of a throne in its curved lines and high back. Settling onto its soft cushion, Kayrstana looked out on the field.

Before her stood the eight condemned, each tied to a stake. Ushtyl, Sizras, and Eltirkar met her gaze with hard eyes, but Arkesh, Tazil, Ovirkar, and Zaerina's heads were bowed. The human, Vistus, swooned in his bonds, seemingly unaware of what was happening. Around the field, her Syraestari had formed into a great circle. Kayrstana looked past them to the forest sweeping north and west, her eyes following the t'Okaedrin on their march into its western fringe. Behind her, the ocean surf rumbled its steady rhythm.

"Rise," Kayrstana commanded her people.

They obeyed, standing and watching in expectant silence. "Thank you, my people, for attending me this day. It is a hard day, and yet a necessary one, as is any day when judgment is passed upon those we once considered friends and kindred. I thank you for the fortitude with which you have weathered these uncertain times. Your courage and tenacity, as ever, are a tribute to our people and give you cause to feel great pride in who we have become." She turned to Sarroth who stood at her right. "Marshal, please read the charges."

Sarroth dipped his head then his eyes lifted, looking past Kayrstana toward the horizon. "Your Majesty."

Kayrstana turned to the southwest and saw three riders crest the small hill on the far side of the Kalilaer settlement. The first had the characteristic easy horsemanship of High Lord Tyrnis. At last. But why today of all days did he decide to go for a ride? As she watched, Tyrnis gestured with his hand and one of the men with him turned toward Nahirazith while he and the other rode toward the execution field. There was something urgent rather than relaxed in their gait. She would learn soon enough. Kayrstana turned back to Sarroth. "The charges, please."

"Yes, Your Majesty." Sarroth stepped to the forward edge of the platform. The people below waited attentively. Gathered as they were in the lower ground, they wouldn't have seen what Kayrstana had. Sarroth drew a scroll from a pouch at his waist and unrolled it. Then in a loud and commanding voice, he read. "Behold the charges and the judgments passed upon these traitors of the empire. It is found that the former t'Okaedrin Vistus is guilty of betraying his oaths to the imperial throne, that he aided Scion rebels and attempted to subvert his loyal brothers with treasonous words. It is found that the former high lords Tazil, Ovirkar, Arkesh, Sizras, and Zaerina are guilty of conspiring against the throne, of willfully disobeying imperial decrees, and of preparing for armed rebellion in direct defiance of their oaths of fealty. Finally, it is found that Ushtyl, once High Lord of Nahirazith, and Eltirkar, his former captain, are guilty of the aforesaid charges and are further guilty of the murder of Captain Nethzir. Further and most heinous, they are charged with the attempted regicide of their empress against all laws of

His Highest Above, the blessed Etyni, and the Aestari. It is a violation of their fealty and trust and there is no greater crime this side of the Abyss." Sarroth rolled up the scroll. "For these crimes, each of the condemned shall be beheaded. Headsman, prepare the axe."

A hush fell as the executioner appeared from around the side of the platform. He was a large Syraestari in plain tunic and breeches with a heavy hood upon his head. On his shoulder he bore a large two-headed axe, the haft of which was longer than he was tall. He strode in a slow pace to the block on the side of the field to the empress' right.

At the nod of Sarroth's head, two legionnaires stepped up to Arkesh, the first prisoner in line. But as they reached for his bonds, Kayrstana rose to her feet.

"Hold!" she cried, letting her voice echo out across the silent field. Stillness washed over the assembly, broken only by the soft rumble of the surf at her back, then scattered murmurs rose among the gathered people that only stopped as she spoke again. "I have decided this day to demonstrate mercy, though none has been accorded us by these fallen lords. My dream is for a united and whole empire, freed of disunity and strife. For this reason, I am prepared to show mercy to those lords and lady guilty of the lesser crime of conspiracy. I am willing to believe that they acted, however misguidedly, in what they thought was the best for our people. Ushtyl, Eltirkar, and the human Vistus must die for the greater depth of their crimes, but the others I will pardon and even restore to their former places."

A rush of whispers rippled through the crowd. Kayrstana allowed her gaze to flicker among the people and she saw excitement. Yes, this was the better choice. By showing mercy, she became not only the victim of a treacherous conspiracy, but the benevolent ruler who rose above petty ambitions. "I demand only two acts in return. First, they must swear the deepest and most binding of ancient oaths of eternal loyalty to my person. I am unwilling to again subject my people to the uncertainty we have witnessed these past days. Second, they must likewise direct their housecarls to submit to my authority, rather than their own, as members of the imperial legion." She looked down upon the condemned. "Arkesh, will you accept my mercy?"

Without hesitation, Arkesh bowed his head. He spoke loudly, with a voice choked by relief. "I submit to all you demand, Your Majesty. I swear upon my life and my honor, that I will serve you fully as you demand, a faithful servant of Your Majesty."

His response was no surprise. Kayrstana had chosen him as the first to die for a reason. "Then so you shall be restored," she said. The oath would be formalized later, but his vow would serve until then. She turned next to Ovirkar. "Will you likewise accept my mercy?"

"I will, Your Majesty," Ovirkar said. His face had been ashen all morning, but as he spoke, she saw the first glimmer of color return to it. "I also swear, Your Majesty, that I will serve at your mercy as a humble and obedient servant."

Kayrstana paused as hoof beats pounded a heavy tattoo upon the earth. Tyrnis and his companion rounded the nearest Kalilaer encampment, driving their horses at a gallop. The hide of both beasts frothed from the exertion. Kayrstana cursed silently as they arrived. Late to the judgment and now making so much noise it detracted from the ceremony. Tyrnis reined his horse to a halt at the rear of the platform and practically leapt from the saddle. Handing the reins to a nearby Kal t'Okaedrin he hurried up the steps and bowed low before the empress.

"It is good of you to join us, High Lord," Kayrstana told him coldly in a voice pitched to carry no further than the platform. "You knew I had need of you this morning."

"I know, Your Majesty, and I beg your forgiveness. It was not without reason that I departed soon after we talked last night." At a sign from her, he continued, "As you know, I placed scouts to watch over the cities that once belonged to the condemned high lords. Yet it seems that despite their watchfulness, an enemy army has gathered in Raefi'ernyn under the command of Tazil's wife. They must have done it in ones and twos to avoid notice and now they are marching on Nahirazith with a force of some eight hundred housecarls."

"But no t'Okaedrin?"

"No, Your Majesty. But the army is fully mounted and coming at speed. They will be here in little more than an hour. I urge you to delay these proceedings. Call out the t'Okaedrin. Between them and the legion, we will be strong enough to hold the walls of Nahirazith." He shook his head. "I regret to report that the empire is torn by civil war."

"Not yet," Kayrstana replied, firmly. "Already, Arkesh and Ovirkar have thrown themselves at my mercy. By the time Aerharyndra arrives, the high lords will be firmly in my hand."

"Even Sizras, Your Majesty?"

"If he doesn't bow, he will be executed. I hardly expect my Syraestari to die for a martyr. Aerharyndra's army will disburse to their homes having witnessed both my mercy and my authority."

"At least gather the t'Okaedrin, Your Majesty. Have them set a perimeter about the encampment and prepare the city for siege. If there are any surprises, then, we will be prepared."

"The t'Okaedrin are in the forest," Sarroth said.

"All of them?" Tyrnis asked the marshal.

"Nearly. They're in pursuit of a Scion raiding party located nearby."

"Coincidence?" Tyrnis frowned, then shook his head. "Of course, it must be. Your Majesty, this makes the situation even more urgent. The legion here is only three hundred strong and many were recently in Ushtyl's service. Recall the t'Okaedrin and I'll send out riders to Thusaeyanin, Kinansath, and Kikara for reinforcements."

Kayrstana narrowed her eyes, considering. "I will not cast aside a chance to strike a blow against the Scions because I allowed myself to panic. Marshal Sarroth, recall half the t'Okaedrin. The remainder should still be strong enough to handle any Scion threat. In the meantime, I have judgments to carry out. Tyrnis, please stand beside me."

"As you command, Your Majesty." If he disagreed, there was no sign of it in his voice.

Kayrstana looked down on the execution field as Sarroth hurried down to the base of the platform to send messengers. Her people had begun talking avidly amongst themselves during the lull. Though they were all too far for her to hear their words, the tempo of their collective voices spoke of curiosity edged by fear. It was time to bring their attention back. Kayrstana looked down upon the high lady bound below. "Zaerina, will you likewise accept the mercy I offer today and return to my side?"

Belarrin chaffed in his bonds. The post was better than the Boards. Anything was better than that. And to see light again. It made his eyes burn after so much darkness. But light did exist. It hadn't been some tormented dream. And the wind, cool and fresh upon his face was like the breath of His Highest Above. He could close his eyes and lose himself in the wonder of it. If only those fool Syraestari would be silent.

A crowd of hypocrites, watching, judging, or in bonds like himself. They were all the same, standing tall and arrogant as they bickered over empty things. Their pride was a mockery of what they had done and even now did not see. Each of them, high and low, was a slaver, a murderer of humans. Soulless monsters who had twisted his own heart and those of his brothers, turning the t'Okaedrin into murderers like themselves.

What mercy did Ninanna beg for these beasts? What grand people did she hope to preserve? Just a band of marauding brigands who apparently couldn't agree on anything but the killing of humans.

Belarrin wished they would just execute him and be done with it.

"I bow before your mercy and beg your forgiveness, Your Majesty," Zaerina said, "and I swear my life to your service as an obedient servant."

Kayrstana smiled. The easiest three, the ones she had been most certain of, had broken. But now, the greater challenges. Kayrstana turned to Sizras. "Will you also accept my mercy and bow before the throne?"

Sizras lifted his head to meet her eyes and she saw the denial in them even before he spoke. "This was always your plan, wasn't Empress? To break us one way or the other, by driving us out to open rebellion or down to be slaves at your feet. You may condemn me as it suits you, as you have planned it. But I am guilty of no crime and therefore have nothing to repent. It is the right and obligation of every subject to challenge the injustice of their ruler. You have the power to execute an innocent man as your whim takes you, but I shall die today with honor. My murdered blood will forever stain your hands, tainting everything you do forever."

"You may spurn me as you wish," Kayrstana said coldly, "and attempt to cloud your treason with honeyed words. Were our places changed, I already know what you intended, banishment or death, yet you mock my offering of life and restoration. So be it." She turned to Tazil. "Do you, Tazil, accept my mercy or will you also spurn this offering of peace and life?"

When Tazil met her gaze, she saw that his eyes were bloodshot and haunted. She'd left him for last, counting him a broken man and therefore unpredictable. Even now, she couldn't hazard what he would say. The only blessing was that he didn't know his wife was coming with an army.

When Tazil spoke, it was from a voice rasping with inner pain. "I do not know what we are anymore," he said. "This realm I helped create splinters all around me, this world of devastation I dreamed of restoring to lost glory has showed me there is no glory left in it. And it has taken my son. What can I do now that would bring him back to me? Nothing." He shook his fevered head. "If life offers more of the same false hopes, than I choose death and to rejoin the son I lost."

Kayrstana's heart broke, listening to the wailing cry of his soul. Speaking softly, gently, she asked, "I will still offer you mercy if you swear never to raise your hand against me in word or deed. You do not need to return to your place as a high lord. You do not have to stay in this realm."

"Alive I remain empty. No, death is the only path left to me."

Kayrstana nodded slowly. "As you desire, I will not deny it." But when the other condemned traitors were dead, she resolved to pardon him anyway. She had seen the wasting illness that came with the breaking of the Syraestari soul. Tazil was doomed to die either by her command or by his own self-recrimination. The least she could do for him was forgive him and ease his passage. His wife would surely relent in her efforts at civil war, then.

Breaking her gaze from Tazil, she turned to Ushtyl. The man she had once loved would be shown no mercy. Her features hardened as she looked down upon him. "Mercy has been offered," she announced, "to those still worthy of it. But there are those who are beyond forgiveness. Let their souls be consigned to the Abyss. Ushtyl first! Guards, bring the traitor to the execution block."

"Why aren't they in the city?" Laerdina asked, gesturing out toward the slave settlement beyond the trees.

"No plan ever goes perfectly," Sravika replied grimly. They had watched from their hiding places as the Iron-Men marched past, between their position and the slave settlement, entering the forest to their right. Turning back to her left, Sravika stared at the gathering of Finaestari. "We knew there would be serious risks."

"Serious? Risks?" Fedigni exclaimed. "I want to die killing Syraestari, but today will be a slaughter. Ninanna must have betrayed us."

"We can't know that," Sravika replied. "I certainly don't believe it."

"Nevertheless, we need to delay," Laerdina said.

"We can't delay this any more than we can stop it," Sravika replied. "We've already sent dozens of our people into the camps where they will be discovered by nightfall at the latest. The t'Okaedrin are away and we won't be able to get them out of the city again. And Belarrin will be dead in minutes, leaving us with no sorcery at all." She tried not to think of the personal cost to herself if he died. "Besides, it's impossible. We have an army a thousand strong scattered along the edge of this forest. There is no way we can call them all back and remain hidden at the same time."

They stared back at her. Finally, Laerdina said, "We're all dead, then."

"I can think of no better day to die." Sravika rose to her feet and took up her spear. It was one of the thirty sorcery-hardened ones they still had. Without looking to see if any followed, she walked out of the forest.

Kayrstana watched with grim satisfaction as two legionnaires untied Ushtyl from his post and pulled him toward the execution block. He walked without resistance, his eyes locked on Kayrstana's. She felt them burrow into her mind, pushing at all her certainty. Once, she had stared into those eyes and felt her heart melt, but what had once been love had been seared away by pain and betrayal. She forced the shadow of a triumphant smile to her lips, even though she did not feel it. A few moments more and she would be freed of him and his accursed eyes forever.

"Your Majesty," Tyrnis said softly beside her, an edge of warning in his voice.

Breaking her gaze with Ushtyl, Kayrstana's eyes were immediately caught again by movement in the wood line a mile to the northeast. A woman ran from the forest holding a spear and wearing crude leather armor. A Scion. Moments later, more emerged behind her, at least fifty in number. But the t'Okaedrin had been told the Scions were further to the west! Even as the thought passed through Kayrstana's mind, the whole of the forest edge for hundreds of paces to either side of the Scion band rippled with movement as hundreds, no, a thousand more emerged onto the plain and began to advance at a slow loping run. A ripple of alarm passed through the assembled Syraestari as those along the northern edge realized what was happening.

"Legionnaires!" Tyrnis bellowed. "Form ranks on the north side of the field. Prepare to engage raiders!"

Kayrstana clenched her hands into fists. How was this possible? Scions never attacked in numbers anywhere near a hundred, let alone a thousand. Her eyes shifted to Vistus, but he stood unmoving against his post. With head bowed, he was seemingly unaware of what was happening. "They've come for him."

"I don't think so," Tyrnis replied. "They're heading for the Kalilaer settlement. Your Majesty, we must attack the enemy before they free all the laborers. We'll be outnumbered, but with our skill and weaponry, your legion will far outmatch them."

Perhaps he was right, though the closest part of the camp was a bare hundred paces away. "Do it. Keep just enough legionnaires here to guard the prisoners. I will depend upon Lady Medreuneth and my Kal t'Okaedrin for my protection."

Tyrnis turned to Sarroth who had just returned to the platform. "You remain here and guard the empress with your life. I will lead the attack."

"By your command," the marshal replied after a confirming nod from Kayrstana.

Tyrnis raced down the platform steps, shouting, "Legionnaires, two ranks remain with the prisoners, all others form behind me and prepare to attack!"

But as soon as he'd spoken, Kayrstana's eyes were drawn to movement within the Kalilaer settlement itself. A woman had emerged from the nearest buildings. With loose golden hair dancing in the wind, Ninanna stood alone and weaponless as she faced the three hundred legionnaires forming in front of her. When she spoke, her voice was lifted on the winds by sorcery. It was with a tone of authority that Kayrstana, after hundreds of years of wearing the crown, could only aspire to.

"Stand aside, Syraestari, these humans are not for you."

CHAPTER 45

Now

"I enter every battlefield as a dead man. One day I will cease to be surprised."

—Marshal Zarthin of Thres

Heart in her mouth and spear clutched in hand, Sravika ran across the open plain, the tall grasses rippling like waves about her knees. She had never before felt so vulnerable. This was not how Scions did things. Subterfuge and darkness with the enemies unaware, that was their way, not boldly marching beneath open heavens, no matter how cloud-laden. Never with a host of Syraestari gathered nearby. That had not been the plan. But before her lay everything she had wanted, what she had dreamed of.

She had to be certain of triumph for the army following her regardless of what enemy stood before them. The slightest faltering and it could all unravel. Fedigni ran a pace to her left and Laerdina to her right. Henirgar, Tayrja, and Argluf all came after, friends old and friends new. Other bands fanned out to the left and the right, sweeping forward to the camp where slaves had dropped the implements of their toil and looked on in amazed awe. She could feel the ghosts of so many others following behind. Of Vitarria, Darr, Mirnadd and all the sacrifices that had brought her here.

Highest Above, she prayed. Let them know their deaths mattered.

She looked to her left, to the execution field, and knew that Belarrin stood in the midst of the Syraestari. Her heart lurched, but she clenched her teeth and ran on. She longed to run straight for him, no matter the enemy between, but a thousand Scions and as many slaves were depending on her.

Yet fear edged into her mind. There were so many Syraestari. Several hundred warriors were already massing to counterattack and against them stood one solitary figure in robes of black. They were too many, no matter Ninanna's valor. This was no quick and clean raid, but one that would be stained in blood. One that might see the ultimate destruction of the Scion cause.

"Highest Above," she whispered, "let it all be worth the price."

"Hold your place and no one will die today," Ninanna commanded the legion facing her. The cool autumn wind brushed her face. It had been a long time since she had felt so alive. No matter how the day might unfold, it was good to finally be doing something she knew in her soul was fully just. The legion ranks forming in front of her eyed her cautiously. They had all heard of the battle after her trial by now, but they were three hundred and she was one.

"It was my intention to pardon you, Ninanna, of the charges laid against you," the empress said, her voice likewise raised by sorcery. "But this I cannot do if you defy me and our people."

"It is the place of the wronged to pardon, not the transgressor." Ninanna sensed the Scions drawing nearer. Some had begun to fan out behind her, forming an unsteady line of spears, a cordon from the settlement to the forest, while the rest ran still toward the slave encampments. "I have come for the good of two peoples. Turn from the path of slavery that binds us as surely as it does the Kalilaer. I do not wish to kill, but this battle is not about me and I cannot stay my hand."

"Enough!" Kayrstana's voice boomed across the plain. "Stand aside, Ninanna, or meet the fate of a rebel. For all your prowess, you alone cannot stop the legion from reclaiming what is ours."

"I am not alone."

Ripples of uncertainty passed through the legion ranks as twenty Sword-Whisperers emerged from the buildings behind Ninanna, half to stand at her left and half at her right.

"Sword-Whisperers!" the empress cried. "Do you follow this outcast? Withdraw now, and be forgiven or be branded forever traitors to the realm!"

Imeskir, standing at Ninanna's right hand, stepped forward. When he spoke, it was not with a voice magnified by sorcery, yet his bold shout rang loud enough over the execution field. "The Sword-Whisperers follow the savior of the Syraestari people. We follow Lady Ninanna, the Hero of Dahiraetin!"

The empress recoiled as if struck, then her face darkened to red as gasps rippled through the attending crowd. "Legion, attack!"

The line of warriors roared in response to her command. A horn sounded and the legion surged forward. Beside her, Imeskir handed Ninanna her sword. "We cannot pretend to understand all that is happening," he said quietly, "but we are with you."

"We must kill, for I see no other way," Ninanna told them. "Strength and unity."

The other Sword-Whisperers raised their blades and began to chant as she had commanded. The words were ancient, from the dawning of the world, and they rippled up and down their line with a heat reminiscent of billowing fire that settled on her skin and burrowed into her flesh. She felt her mind sharpen, her muscles knit more tightly, and with it came a sense of oneness. A feeling of concert with the men and women standing to her right and to her left, an understanding of their focus, their concentration, a preternatural sense of what they each would do. Sensation flowed across her like a wind, trembling in the hairs of her arms, enlivening the surrounding scents of sweat and dust, the taste of the cool autumn wind upon her lips. "Charge!"

The tiny Sword-Whisperer line lunged forward to meet the Legion wave with a clash of hardened steel.

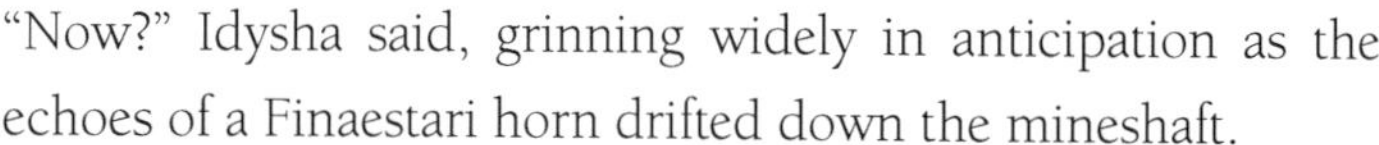

"Now?" Idysha said, grinning widely in anticipation as the echoes of a Finaestari horn drifted down the mineshaft.

Beside her, Yrpel looked upward to the circle of daylight overhead, then back down to the score of shadowy figures looming in the darkness around them. "A little longer. We cannot emerge too soon."

She could feel his restless energy as he drummed his fingers on the rope in his hands. She could feel it inside herself, too, the white knuckled grip on her own rope, the racing of her heart in fear and anticipation. Around them, the miners leaned closer in thirsting hope. Many had been down in this pit for a dozen years and more, with nothing but a circle of light to remind them of the world above. No longer.

"Now," Yrpel said. He took a step forward and, dropping the end of the rope, began to twirl it. The iron grapple on the end, a gift from Ninanna, sang as it whirled. Idysha stepped a few paces apart from him and began to swing her own rope. They launched them at the same moment, up and over the lip of the mineshaft.

She tested her weight against the rope, then flung herself upward, and hand over hand, began to climb, following Yrpel on his. "Come, my friends!" he cried. Behind them, the miners roared, then one by one, began to ascend.

Her lungs were heaving by the time she pulled herself out of the mine. She stumbled to her feet beside Yrpel and stopped, heart rising up in her throat. Instead of a camp emptied of enemies, there were hundreds of Syraestari charging their direction.

The first miner climbed out of the hole and joined them. "Never let it be said we were afraid to fight," he said.

Yrpel glanced at Idysha and nodded. She clenched her spear tightly as he shouted, "Defend the mineshaft until all are free. The enemy is coming!"

Hirnid watched the Scions flowing across the plain, transfixed. It was madness for them to attack in the daylight with the Syraestari legion so near. But they didn't flee in terror as he expected them to. No, they charged onward to certain death.

Near the execution field, the battle joined first with the clashing charges of the Syraestari Legion and Ninanna's Sword-Whisperers. But the Whisperers were too few to hold back the entire legion. More than a hundred ran past them, to the right and the left, and clashed against the Scion cordon. The rebels met them and, to Hirnid's surprise, held. They gave ground only grudgingly, though many fell. More of their number pressed onward into the Kalilaer camp heedless of the danger all around them. It wasn't madness, he realized, but courage.

And they had come from the stretch of woods to the northeast, not from northwest as Chostir had claimed.

He turned to her. She was limp in her bonds, more broken ragdoll now than human. "You lied."

She lifted her head to look at him. Even that motion caused a flicker of pain to flash across her face, but she grinned widely through broken lips. "Yes."

"Then you did this on purpose. You let yourself be tortured?"

"If Belarrin can survive weeks on the Boards, I knew I could endure one morning here. Are you going to beat me now that you know the truth?"

"No, I..." Hirnid turned away, overwhelmed. It was devotion a t'Okaedrin could only aspire to. What delusion must have possessed her to throw everything she had away?

She spoke behind him. "You Iron-Men know how to die, but we know how to live."

"Live like this?" He faced her again, gesturing at her broken body.

"Not my life." Chostir's smile was just as strong and defiant as before. "Theirs."

He looked back to the Scions, some thousand strong. Weighing those numbers against the cost of a single life to pull the t'Okaedrin away, any wise commander would have called that life a worthy sacrifice. But how could the one whose life was thrown away make that same claim? The courage and faith humbled him. Maybe it wasn't a delusion after all. It was a dream, a mad dream just like the one that had claimed Vistus. If only he were strong enough to dream such dreams. Hirnid knew he wasn't strong enough himself, but he could follow those who were.

"No," he whispered, shaking his head. "Your life, too." Then, before his resolve left him, he stepped up to her. Holding her gently with his left arm, Hirnid sliced through her bonds.

She sank into his arms. "I have no strength to stand."

"Then I shall carry you."

Hirnid lifted her into his arms and ran toward the battle.

Ninanna shifted back and lifted her blade to deflect a quick thrust from the legionnaire opposite her. He was far less experienced than her, though still very quick. Unfortunately for him, with so much at stake, she had no time for the mercy of a crippling blow. She pivoted and brought her sword down in a heavy slashing cut, using the full weight of her heavier weapon to bore through his defenses. His sword buckled in his hands, wrists bending back beneath the pressure, then her blade met his collarbone, snapping through the scale mail to tear flesh.

"Forward, Sword-Whisperers," she cried. They had to reach Belarrin. Everything depended upon that. But as she took a step forward, two new legionnaires advanced to fill the place of the one she'd slain.

The plan had been simple. In the city where the execution should have occurred, twenty Sword-Whisperers could have held the gate closed for hours leaving no one to stand in the path of the Scion rescue. But not out here. There was no way to stop the legion from sweeping around either side to prey upon the vulnerable humans. There was little enough she and the other Sword-Whisperers could do to protect their own flanks. Already their line had bowed into an arrowhead with herself at the point.

She gritted her teeth, then rejoined the chant of her companions, feeling anger, pain and worry drain from her mind. She fueled her resolve, focusing on her words as she felt the sorcery suffuse her body. It was a battle against time, now. A battle whose end she could not foresee. One whose end she dreaded to know. It was another Dahiraetin, except this time was worse. This time the enemies she killed were friends instead of monsters.

Words and thoughts drifted through Belarrin's mind, but none of them mattered. He was exhausted, in soul and in body. He had fought for so long, straining to believe that there was something more, something better. That he was a part of it. But he was not. Only a helpless witness of slaughter.

By turning his head as far as he could to the right, he could see the lines of legionnaires and Sword-Whisperers locked in savage combat. But not even the Sword-Whisperers mattered. They were too few.

That there were fewer Syraestari than Scions, mattered little. Not with the centuries of experience the Syraestari possessed. Not when the Scions held weapons of stone and wood. Had this been the grand plan of Ninanna's? It was not enough. A remnant of the Kalilaer and Scions might escape, but most would die. And no one was near to reach him and free him. Ninanna herself was the closest, but still over a hundred paces away, with an army between them.

Perhaps that was for the best. He had been a harbinger of death, killing all the good and just who crossed his path. It would have been better had he died long ago as a child in that earthquake or in any of the dozen battles since. He should have died so that all those he'd slain could live to see this day.

But for his own life, it did not matter. Like smoke above a candle flame, empty and meaningless, billowing to nothing. The nothing he should have embraced long ago. He prayed that the Scions would free as many of the Kalilaer as they could, but even more, he gave thanks that no one else would die because of him. For that alone, he might claim joy in these, his last moments.

Ushtyl stood forgotten near the base of the imperial platform, the headsman's block at his feet. The empress' attention had turned toward the battle between her legion and the Sword-Whisperers. He looked to the headsman standing before him, then glanced to his jailors, one at his left and the other at his right. Both had been his housecarls before his arrest.

"It is weakness that brought our people to this place of chaos."

"Hold your tongue, traitor," the headsman growled.

Ushtyl ignored him. "This is but the first sign, the beginning of a civil war that will ravage our people. It will be another schism. Who do you wish to follow in a time such as this, the weak hand or the strong one?"

"I said be silent." The headsman grasped the haft of his long axe and stepped forward. But even as he did, Ushtyl's two jailors moved and in a swift motion, sank their daggers into the headsman's chest. As he crumpled, the jailors turned to him. "We have chosen."

While one cut through his bonds, Ushtyl turned to the other. "I will need your sword."

"Yes, my liege," the man replied, handing him his blade.

Ushtyl lifted the sword high in the air as joy and strength flooded over him. It had taken all his willpower to hold his dignity in that moment when the empress had walked alive and whole through the door of his palace to arrest him. From that hour, he had thought his fate sealed, to be faced only with unbowed knee. But then, this moment of opportunity. Of glory!

"Vehondai detroe'ydalot osmyt!" He could feel the power of the wind rise up in his throat as he spoke, carrying his voice loudly over the field. "My people!" He bellowed, the wind magnifying his voice. "The time has come to cast aside weakness, to topple an enfeebled throne. Join me and we shall forge an empire worthy of our names!"

Stunned silence met his words. He sensed them rippling through the rear ranks of the legion, among those who weren't embroiled in the fighting. Then the air was punctuated by cries of jubilation. The legion churned as warrior faced warrior, each gauging the resolve of those around them.

"Treason!" Kayrstana cried from her place on the podium, but no magic had lifted her voice leaving it enfeebled next to Ushtyl's own glorious proclamation. "All loyal warriors of the empire to me."

The legion battle lines churned like water boiling in an iron pot as warrior turned on warrior in a chaos of blood. Of freedom. Ushtyl turned to his former jailors, forcing calm command into his voice. "My friends, free Eltirkar and then kill that human sorcerer, Vistus. I want Sizras and Tazil executed next, then rejoin me. I will take care of the empress."

"My Lord," the two warriors bowed, then ran to do as he'd commanded.

Ushtyl strode forward toward the platform. There was no hurry, now, and dignified poise would matter more for how this day was remembered than anything else. Four Kal t'Okaedrin defended the base of the platform with blades raised and ready.

"Stand aside or die," Ushtyl snarled.

"There is no greater honor," they replied and attacked.

Belarrin watched unmoved as Syraestari turned on Syraestari. It didn't matter to him who reigned, Kayrstana or Ushtyl. Both had tortured him, both would see him dead. Yet the old part of Belarrin's soul felt pride as he watched the Kal t'Okaedrin gallantly stand in Ushtyl's path. It was a battle against an ancient warrior they couldn't hope to win. But the newer part of

Belarrin's soul felt sorrow as he also saw slaves dying blindly for their mistress.

As Ushtyl battled and warrior turned on warrior in the frenzy of civil war, the unmartial Syraestari fled for the refuge of the city. They had lingered when the Scions appeared and when Ninanna defied the empress, doubtless both curious and still feeling safe. But now, that security was gone.

Nearer to hand, Ushtyl's two jailors ran to where Eltirkar stood bound and set him free. He clapped them both on the back then accepted the sword one gave him. Eltirkar's eyes ran across the other high lords who all still waited, bound and helpless. Then he turned to look at Belarrin and smiled. There was death in those eyes.

Belarrin matched his gaze, empty of feeling. His life had been like waves upon the ocean with crests of joy followed by troughs of despair again and again. During his weeks of torture, he had accepted that his life would end in darkness. With all the blood on his hands, he deserved no better. Every ruin had been of his own making and now even his death would be without the meaning he'd sought. But he was too weary to care. Ninanna still had a battlefield to cross to free him. Perhaps in the city it would have been different. But at least out here he had seen the open sky once more and felt the wind upon his face. That would have to be enough. He would die content.

A woman stepped up from behind him and turned to face him. It was the Pi'aernoth, Talikae. She glanced over her shoulder at the approaching Syraestari, then said, "I would like to hear the wind in the boughs." Belarrin blinked, uncomprehending as Talikae reached up and eased the gag from his mouth. "I want to feel the loamy soil beneath my feet. To understand what life is. To laugh..."

She spasmed, eyes widening in sudden shock, then her face slacked and Belarrin could only watch transfixed as the light faded from her eyes. She sagged forward, falling against his chest, then crumpling to the ground.

Vitarria. It was Vitarria all over again! Belarrin looked up to see Eltirkar, sword extended, mouth wide in a smile of triumph.

Fire and rage poured through Belarrin's veins, a burning sun erupting within his chest. There was no effort, no thought, as he pulled the lines of gold across his eyes. "Itsoe'azhestva ryhota Eltirkar!" He screamed his anguish.

A moment was all Eltirkar had to realize what had happened. His smile had barely begun to fade when blinding light flooded over Belarrin's vision. A flash of pure white.

Light faded to reveal a charcoaled husk of flesh standing before him, skin, hair, and clothing all burned away. Only his blade remained, seared to an untarnished gleam. It clattered to the ground as the body collapsed into a cloud of powdered ash. The two rebel housecarls behind Eltirkar froze in stunned awe.

Belarrin snarled. "Ae'irpiva asir'vimoes tefiral'unavai!"

Wind roared in his ears, a tumultuous fury that blasted outward from the ground at his feet. It crossed the field, a wave of air that struck the pair of hapless warriors and pitched them head over heels as if they were leaves caught in a storm. The wind continued outward, buffeting the other bound prisoners and heaving them heavily against their bonds. Still it flowed, lifting dirt into a hail of pebbles that battered the backs of the warring legionnaires, buffeting their ranks into disarray. Then the wind faded, calming to a whisper before vanishing entirely.

Breath heaving, Belarrin looked across the field, from the prisoners still bound as he was, to legion fighting itself as much as the Sword-Whisperers, and beyond them, to where the embattled Scions tried to hold a line of spears against the heavy press of Syraestari warriors.

He looked up to the imperial platform. Kayrstana clung to her throne watching in fear as Ushtyl carved his way through her guardians. Sarroth and the sorceress Medreuneth stood beside her. Here, then, were the orchestrators of all his pain. The ones who had enslaved his brothers, his people, his mind. He flung his head back and drew on his pain as a parched man would drown himself in water. Golden lines rose before him.

"Itsoe'azhestva ryhota sypansypa!" he cried, drawing a flash of lightning down from the heavens to strike the empress on her throne. But even as the bolt of white fury seared down from above, a cloud of dust rose up around the platform and solidified into a hardened sphere of earth. The lightning touched it and died. Vanishing in a heartbeat, the bolt left behind only the harsh sense of unleashed power flickering against his skin.

The cloud of dust fell away to reveal Medreuneth facing him, eyes tight with determination. She lifted her hands and, at the base of the platform, the ground swelled like an ocean wave. With a groan like an earthquake, it rippled forward, directly toward him. Still bound hand and foot, Belarrin couldn't move as the ruin of stone and earth bore down upon him. His exhausted mind could think of no way to stop an earthen wave and all he could do was clench his eyes as it struck.

The wave pitched him into the air, stones flying past cut into the skin of his hands and cheeks. But even as he fell, he drew golden fire across his eyes. "Ae'irpiva asir kilys!"

A gust of wind welled up beneath him, catching him in its vaporous grasp and lowered him gently to the earth. As he descended, he shouted again, "Eusy'arjev ivakemai'o naeroda," and winced as the ropes binding him to the post caught fire and burned away.

He landed on the ground and stumbled to his knees as his battered legs gave out beneath him. He flung a hand toward Medreuneth, roaring, "Ki'anpahityn oedva'ryhota ult!"

Wind whistled past him, the fury of a gale. Plucking rocks and pebbles from the ground, the tempest flung them toward Medreuneth and Kayrstana with the force of a thousand slinger's stones.

Medreuneth raised her hands and a cloud of dirt lifted skyward, solidifying into a wall of earth. The flung stones rattled against it like heavy hail, then fell to the ground, spent. As soon as the gale had passed, the wall of dirt collapsed to reveal Medreuneth gesturing toward him. The words she shouted were lost to a sudden roaring of the earth. With a crash to rival the thunder, the ground cracked open beneath Belarrin's knees. He flung his hands out futilely as the abyss widened in a stream of dust and pebbles. "Ae'irpiva asir ekynd!"

An upwelling of wind caught him again, flinging him out of the rent to roll across the ground safely to the side. Breath heaving, he pushed himself up on hands and knees to looked at the platform. What wind could overcome a wall of earth? He couldn't think. Was this all that was left for him? A pitiful duel with a sorceress he couldn't defeat while his little remaining strength flitted away and his people died in a battle they couldn't hope to win?

He drank in his fear and frustration, unable to think of anything but to draw upon his rage. He pulled down a second lightning bolt from the sky and then a third before Medreuneth could counterattack. A fourth, a fifth, a six, on and on until the afterimages of white blinded his eyes. But it was not enough. Nothing was enough!

Beneath the relentless barrage of lightning, Kayrstana had fallen to the wooden floor of the platform, cowering with hands over her ears against the relentless roar of thunder. How Medreuneth could stand above her against that unceasing barrage, she did not understand. Sweat poured down the sorceress' face and she bit her lip in furious concentration.

The lightning pouring over them had done nothing to slow Ushtyl either. Kayrstana looked over with growing dread as he cut down the last of the Kal t'Okaedrin. Marshal Sarroth stepped forward to block his path. The marshal was a good man and a strong warrior, but Ushtyl had been a Sword-Whisperer. There could be only one outcome. She would be spared death at Vistus' hands only to die on Ushtyl's blade.

"Do something!" Kayrstana yelled to Medreuneth, even though she knew it was impossible.

"Must everyone die before you fall, Kayrstana?" Ushtyl shouted over the storm as he lunged for Sarroth. The marshal parried the blow but barely, and the point of the blade tore a shallow gash in his upper arm. "Too many good men have died to preserve your weak rule. A rule too feeble to hold this empire together. Too feeble to scour the land of humans. You can die certain that I will not balk, fainthearted, where you have failed."

"Medreuneth!" Kayrstana screamed as another cut opened the fleshy part of Sarroth's thigh. The marshal stumbled, barely deflecting a killing stroke for his heart.

"I cannot," Medreuneth gasped. The sorceress clenched her eyes shut and her hands trembled over her head. A bead of blood trickled from her nose. Maybe they would die to Vistus after all.

Kayrstana looked up at the swirling sphere of dust that encased all of them, heart fluttering and mind in panic. There was but one chance, one final chance. "Jump, Sarroth," she screamed as she lunged toward Medreuneth. She caught the startled sorceress about the waist, clutching her and dragging the two of them off the platform.

They struck the ground below hard enough to drive the Kayrstana's breath away. Lungs heaving, she struggled to her knees as, looking up, she saw Medreuneth's sphere of earth fall away. Lightning seared across her eyes.

Again and again Belarrin brought lightning down from the heavens until there was only his voice, the fire, and the roar of searing light. But it meant nothing, it was nothing. A war of futility without end and without escape.

But then, the sphere of earth surrounding the platform vanished. Belarrin blinked in stunned awe, startled in mid-incantation as two people tumbled from the platform to land hard against the ground beneath. Then Sarroth staggered back from an attack by Ushtyl and, losing his footing, fell off the other side. Ushtyl took a step forward, his eyes lifting to meet Belarrin's across the distance.

Belarrin smiled and lifted his right hand to the heavens. "Itsoe'azhestva ryhota Ushtyl!"

Nothing impeded the bolt of lightning as it plunged down from on high, drawn to Ushtyl's outstretched blade like a moth to the flame. A moment earth and heaven were connected by a line of purest white, then the platform exploded in a wave of heat.

Belarrin raised his hand as the fierce gust washed over him. He realized he was laughing in desperate mirth. Then his eyes dropped to the base of the ruined toward to see two women huddled there, Medreuneth and Kayrstana. "Burn!" he roared, pulling down another line of fire from the sky. But before the lightning could strike, a shell of earth rose again to enclose them.

Belarrin stumbled and fell to his knees. One of his great tormentors was dead, but he would never touch the other. It was impossible. His laughter died as despair filled him, leeching what little strength remained away. He looked over his shoulder to where the battle still raged. The Sword-Whisperers were fully engulfed, now, and the Scions reeled back against the legion assault. Their line of spears faltered on the verge of crumbling. Once that broke it was all over.

And then his gaze lifted to the forest on the far side of the Scion and Syraestari battle as rank upon rank of t'Okaedrin emerged from the wilderness, cutting off the line of escape. A whimper stole through Belarrin's ravaged lips. There was too much. Too much ruin, too many enemies and he had burned away what little strength he had in a futile duel. He closed his eyes against a wave of dizziness and saw the face of Talikae rise up before him, bleeding. He shook his head to banish the vision, but her face was only replaced by Zoltha, then Vitarria, then Bridionis all bathed in blood.

There was nothing left for him.

His body was too ravaged by weeks of torture, his mind scarred just as badly. His strength was gone and his focus faltered. But the Scions needed him. Sravika needed him. He tried to concentrate, only to have his thoughts slide away. Not even anger could hold them against the all-consuming exhaustion.

He slumped down to his elbows, rocking forward till his forehead touched the earth. With eyes closed, he could feel the wind rippling through the rags that were his clothing. He could hear the echoing clash of blades, the screams of the wounded and the dying. Familiar stars floated past his eyes, but he had no strength to reach them, to search for the words that could save his people.

To think that Ninanna, that Sravika, had put so much faith in him. They had trusted a fool who had never been able to save anyone he loved.

Belarrin opened his eyes to see that the Tear of Isi had fallen lose from his garments, dangling to touch the brown earth in front of him. How was it that, through all his torture, the stone had never been taken from him? Didn't they know what it meant? A smile from a stranger who pulled him from the darkness. A smile broken by blood. Vitarria.

The stone is where it had all begun.

He pushed himself up from the ground and rocked back onto his heels. Grasping the Tear in his right hand, he looked down upon its perfect clear facets. Tears from iron, the Shadow-Servant had once said. Sravika, too, he realized. How could they know the same words? Blood from stone. Yes, blood had flowed from his hands, crimson and burning. He closed his eyes. He had to try.

The pinpoints of light rose up in his mind, faint and elusive. But among them loomed that which he had known he would see. A distant ribbon of crimson cloud. It was the madness that had sung to him in the darkness of his cell, promising a release from pain and strength unmatched. He cared nothing about the pain now, but strength was what he needed. Strength to make the heavens tremble, no matter how it burned his soul.

"Highest Above, let it be enough," he whispered as he leapt forward with his mind. It was as if the veil of red had only waited for that call. It poured around him like a living thing, enveloping, burning his mind. No pain? That was a lie. But strength, such strength.

Belarrin screamed as power washed over him.

CHAPTER 46
Tempest

"She strode there, over the great divide against the onrushing darkness, surrounded, but never consumed. Two blades as twin stars, piercing the Abyss. But it was not the day for the Abyss to fall, and so she fell instead, sundering the darkness with her final breath."

—Excerpt from "Henji's Blood on the Bridge," Author Unknown

"Courage Scions, we are their equals!" Sravika called out over the fray of battle, then ducked low at the sword swipe from a Finaestari legionnaire that nearly took her head. But they were not equals, not even those few with Belarrin's hardened spears. "Hold the line!"

The Scions stood shoulder to shoulder, presenting a wall of bristling spears, but there was little enough the stone-tipped points could pierce. Beneath the arm where it met the shoulder, the face and upper neck. Otherwise, they may as well have been stabbing rocks.

Over the immediate cacophony of battle, thunder roared in ceaseless barrage. Ninanna had done as promised and Belarrin was free, but Sravika couldn't see where the lightning struck. Only that it hit again and again, the same place far away.

The Scion to her left fell with a gurgling cry as a blade tore out his throat and the line of Scions faltered. This is what Belarrin had meant by unready, she understood that now. But there was no choice, no other chance. "Stand and fight!" she shouted. "Show them we are not cattle to be herded."

A cheer met her cry, though it was more ragged than she'd hoped. Sravika thrust with her spear, not toward the expectant Finaestari facing her, but toward the one a pace to the right. The superior length of the spear was her advantage, and he must not have expected the hardened tip. She felt the satisfying tug as it pierced the scale mail of his right side, and drove deep into flesh. "They can die!"

As she withdrew her spear, the Finaestari to her front lunged again. Sravika leapt back, her foot catching on the dead Scion behind her, and fell. But even as the Finaestari followed forward with his attack, a slave leapt over Sravika and threw himself at the started legionnaire. A resounding roar, visceral and raw, echoed behind her. Sravika scrambled back to give her savior room to fight and looked back to see dozens of slaves armed with spears charging forward to bolster gaps in the line. Their faces and hands were stained black with dirt and filth. With them ran Yrpel and Idysha.

Sravika spared a quick glance to the left and the right as her friends joined her. Slaves were streaming from the settlement by the hundreds, some joining the fight as the miners had, others running along the back of the line toward the forest beyond.

But then, the ones nearest the forest edge screamed and stopped their panicked flight to recoil away from the trees.

"What…" Sravika began to say as she stepped forward to see. Then her heart froze in her chest. Out of the line of trees behind them, hundreds of Iron-Men had appeared. "Cydion's Abyss," she cursed, "we're about to be cut off."

"We have to hold," Yrpel said, his face twisted into a snarling grin. "We have to give Belarrin time."

Idysha nodded and turned to Sravika, "You hold the legion back, we'll face the Iron-Men."

Yrpel bellowed. "Miners with me! To your backs, the Iron-Men are coming."

Chaos gripped the field of battle with the Scions assailed by Finaestari on one side and Iron-Men on the other. But Yrpel didn't care. Battle was chaos and this time, he was ready for it. This time the world would see what it meant to be Iengian. "To me! To me," he bellowed running forward with a hundred or more Kalilaer at his back and Idysha beside him. That was a woman who knew how to fight, how to live. They would live and die together.

The heavens roared behind him in tattoo to his steps as he ran across the open field, grass waving at his knees. The Iron-Men stood waiting for him in ordered ranks with swords drawn and shields out. As the two lines closed, the t'Okaedrin began to walk, and then to run until both sides charged across the distance. Fifty paces, forty, then thirty. Then there, across from him, his eyes looked into the face of a man he knew. A man he had cursed a hundred times and would never forget. Arcomin. Yrpel laughed in bestial fury. Today was the day of his revenge. "Dog!" he roared. "Who is the coward today? Fight me and die!"

What little caution Yrpel had vanished as the two lines closed. At ten paces he took a double-step forward and threw his spear with all of his might. Arcomin raised his shield, but it was not enough. The ensorcelled point of Yrpel's spear met the shield and pierced it with a loud crack, driving through to penetrate mail and flesh.

"Or just die!" Yrpel cried, leaping forward to withdraw his spear from Arcomin's chest and thrust it at the Iron-Man who followed behind.

The stunning brevity of Yrpel's attack was the only thing that saved him. Rather than thrust with his sword, the Iron-Man raised his shield and Yrpel crashed full-force against it, sending the pair cartwheeling back. Yrpel tucked in his shoulder and rolled with the fall. Leaping back to his feet, he realized he stood behind the last rank of the enemy line all alone.

Five Iron-Men turned towards him, each brandishing sword and shield. Yrpel faced them, lungs heaving. He had no fear of death, now. Since his days at the smelter he'd seen true courage over and over again. Still, it would have been nice to die beside Idysha.

"Five against one," he snarled, readying his spear. "Sounds about right."

Then the heavens roared.

Pain. Pain unimaginable burning through his mind, flowing through his veins like fire. The thousand pinpoints of light seared like suns in Belarrin's eyes and he felt words unveil before him. But first, he screamed. There were no words, just pain, shrieking across the heavens. He felt his voice wash across the gathered warriors, Finaestari, Scion, Kalilaer, and t'Okaedrin. It was as if he was beyond them, above them, seeing every heartbeat, feeling ever sword thrust.

"Itsoe'azhestva asirda sypansypa!" The heavens opened and lightning fell. Not just one bolt but dozens. They lashed out from darkened skies to touch drawn steel, exploding in bursts of light. The earth shook with the pain of it, dirt, stones, and flesh flying.

"Burn!" He summoned the lightning again, then a third time. "It's not enough," he screamed. It could never be enough. There were hundreds of Finaestari, a thousand t'Okaedrin, all within his grasp. All beneath his rage. They all had to share the tempest of his wrath, his agony. With the Tear of Isi clutched in his hand, he thrust his fist skyward.

"Eswynoth asir'da eh'daekir'oesys hae'avyt!"

Energy crackled around him, coruscating ribbons of blue-white light lancing outward. It was as if the gemstone felt his pain, his betrayal, his guilt and anguish. It fueled him as much as he fueled it, drawing on his rage until it glowed through his clenched fingers like newly fallen blood.

Overhead, the grey clouds darkened to black. Shuddering, they began to roil like a tumultuous sea. And the wind grew, swirling around him, faster and faster. It expanded outward, stretching to encompass the judgment field, and still it grew in size and fury. He screamed as he poured his entire being into the tempest, surrendering everything else.

Ninanna staggered against the growing wind. Her battle had lost all focus, all meaning, since Belarrin broke free. But at least he was free. She could only pray that his release was cause for hope as lightning seared the heavens and the clouds roiled. It was a storm more relentless, more powerful than anything she could have imagined.

"Wall of Shadow!" she screamed over the tempest.

The Sword-Whisperers obeyed with the immediacy she'd come to expect from her brothers and sisters. In mid-sentence one chant ended and another began. The words billowed out from them in a veiled sheen of translucent grey. The protective shell encompassed their closest enemies, too, but that didn't matter. Where wind and shadow met, the tempest rippled around or over.

But that was only half the battle, the struggle of survival. Too few of the legion were held in check by their assault. She had to do more. "Sword-Whisperers advance!" she bellowed, stepping forward. Her blade whirled with deadly efficiency, breaking scales, drawing blood. Their enemies fell back before them, but the legion, too, had courage and did not flee. Alas for fool courage.

Step by bloody step, Ninanna advanced toward the wavering line of Scions. Her part had become but a flickering candle against the inferno of Belarrin's rage, but she would do all she could.

The eye of the storm was no place of peace. With hand uplifted, Belarrin felt as though his flesh were burning away. The Tear of Isi blazed brightly in his clutched fist, brilliant as the noonday sun, but crimson as the dawn. Yet for all that, it was the only part of him that felt cold as heat seared through his body. That one stone, a gift taken in death and given again, it had become all his focus. It was as if by clinging to it, he clung to the few strands of life that still remained.

He pulled lightning from the storm, to burn enemies across the battlefield. But as much of that heavenly fire fell of its own accord as from him, striking where it chose without guidance.

"Eswynoth hae'avyt'seunae'os. Seunae'os!" He screamed. The tempest wasn't enough. Not yet, it had to grow and grow until no evil could stand. Pain surrounded him, increasing even as the maelstrom expanded, piercing mind and heart, a coursing fire flowing through his body like the blood in his veins. But it wasn't enough. Not just to destroy the enemies beyond, but to destroy the enemy within. The one who had slaughtered Vitarria, who had struck down Zoltha and condemned Bridionis. Every life taken had to be repaid.

Wind whipped around him, faster and faster, until he could see nothing beyond the twisting column that stretched straight up from his hand to the clouds above where the skies churned like a massive whirlpool. Earth and stone swirled around him, swords, and shields, broken flesh all lifted into the air.

"This, this shall be my justice!" He bellowed, his voice drowning in the storm he'd created. But there would be no true justice until his own soul burned away.

"No more!" Sravika had to scream to be heard above the wind. "Back no farther. The line holds here!"

The day had darkened to twilight, grim and bleak beneath the tortured sky. A tempest blotted the light of the sun. But there was light, burgeoning to the tempo of the thunder, lancing in arcs down from the sky. And where each bolt struck, someone died. There was another light, glowing through the storm ahead of her, gleaming small yet blinding like a crimson sun that cast all the ranks of the legion facing her as dark silhouettes.

"If your heart falters, you kill your brother, your sister. No farther!" she cried, setting her feet and thrusting again with her spear to keep the Finaestari at bay. The enemy had gained a healthy respect for the stronger spears, but it hadn't stopped them. Their pressure was relentless and Sravika could feel the spirits of her own people wavering. There was only heat and cold, with no place for fear or for courage. Those were thoughts that required time, required perspective. All that was left was instinct, and the resolve that kept her in her place on the line. Buying time with sweat and blood for as many slaves as possible to run through the tightening cordoned pressed on one side by the legion, the other by the Iron-Men.

Her own soul trembled at every scream that echoed out of the heart of the storm. Most of those around her wouldn't understand it. They wouldn't know what those screams meant. Belarrin. Such pain. Impossible pain. The storm he had conjured in the forest was as nothing before this tempest. She didn't know how he could summon it and live.

And with each of Belarrin's scream, the storm grew. Stronger and stronger until fighting came only second to simply standing, to seeing amid a staggering wind that blinded the eyes as much as it battered the body.

Is this what Ninanna had foreseen? Sorcery blended with madness and pain. Sravika could feel the frenzy in it, even had she not heard his screams of maddened agony rolling upon the storm.

Lightning struck in front of her. The heavens roared, a blast of sound and wind more deafening then all that had come before. Sravika tottered back, reeling, and had to use her spear more as a crutch than a weapon to keep from falling. All around her men and Finaestari lost their footing. Some fell. One or two were plucked by the storm and whisked away screaming.

A second flash behind her and, at the same moment, its roar. The power of it buffeting her forward in a staggered lurching run. She stumbled and fell to her knees.

That one had fallen among the fleeing Kalilaer. "Highest Above, he's lost control of it," she whispered, her words immediately taken by the wind.

There was no more battle now, no fighting at all. Just clinging, surviving amid the raging tempest, the relentless storm of wind and fire.

"Belarrin!" Sravika screamed as tears fell from her eyes and were immediately plucked away by the wind.

She tried to stand, but it was beyond her. No strength, not against the maelstrom. So she crawled on hands and knees, through the writhing, cowering bodies of the Finaestari legion, those who still lived curling on themselves with no hope left but to survive.

But she couldn't only survive. Belarrin needed her if any were to live through this. If he were to survive. She looked to the glowing nimbus at the heart of the storm and crawled. Her spear was lost and forgotten as hands and knees scratched across the earth, each effort a trial of will and strength against a fury that threatened to lift her and carry her to oblivion.

Tyrnis advanced across the field, leaning into the wind with sword drawn. Even for him, moving was a struggle. For the first centuries of his life, he'd considered his inability to touch sorcery a curse among a people so gifted with magical knowledge. That immunity had cost him his eye at Dahiraetin when another man might have had his sight healed. But that immunity was a gift as well, once he took the time to look for it.

Amid this storm of sorcerous madness, the conjured wind and lightning were as nothing, dying at his touch. But even summoned storms birthed true wind and that is where the struggle came.

With the treason of Ushtyl and the unleashing of the human sorcerer, Tyrnis had found himself surrounded by the heat of battle against the Scions. Even now, he could only pray that the empress still lived. And he cursed that Vistus still did.

The human's place was marked upon the ravaged field by the penumbra of crimson light piercing through darkness of the tempest, wavering like moonlight through a thin cloud. And that was good. For the ground he walked was not the ground he had known an hour past. It had been scoured by the raging wind until every direction looked like the other.

No one else stood upon the field of battle that he could see and few moved. To his right, the prisoner stakes remained and he couldn't tell if the high lords bound to them were dead or alive. To his left, a human woman crawled in the same direction he walked, but he paid her no mind. It was the source he had to staunch and each firm step brought him closer.

He could see Vistus, a vague wind-wracked figure at the eye of the storm, standing with one hand upraised, a hand that burned brighter than the setting sun. Only ten paces, now, and the storm would cease.

A shadow rose up from the ground. A figure in a writhing black robes. It was ringed by a sphere of translucent shadow that flickered in and out of existence beneath the relentless buffeting of the storm. The figure's cloak danced in the wind, splaying out behind him like a great black flag. The storm tore back the hood to reveal the white-masked face of the Shadow-Servant.

"What are you doing?" Tyrnis screamed to be heard above the storm. "Stand aside and I shall end this."

"It cannot end, not yet." The Shadow-Servant gestured to its right and Tyrnis glanced over to see the human woman he'd noticed before. She was crawling across the same ground he'd walked, slower, far slower, but relentless.

Who was she? Some Scion? What did she matter? The storm, the source of death lay ahead. Tyrnis brandished his blade. "Who do you think you are?"

"The silent sentinel, watching over the souls of our people. The harbinger. The Shadow-Servant!" A roar of thunder behind Tyrnis punctuated the words.

"You are a traitor!"

"How many times has that word been cast about? Has it lost all meaning?"

"Not to me! Our people are bleeding!"

"Every race could do with a bit of spilled blood!" the Shadow-Servant cried. "This is the scourge, the price for our complacency, the retribution for our failures. There is no growth without consequence, no learning without pain. Let this agony drive us from our folly, break our flawed empire, and renew who we once were."

"Is that all that concerns you?" Tyrnis roared.

"There is no other way. None but humanity unleashing its fury in a rage far greater than this. Not just a century of nurtured hate, but millennia, by a people stronger and more furious while we descend into idle weakness. A hundred deaths now will be as nothing before the thousands we will reap if we stay this course."

"I will not accept that. I won't kill my own people no matter how noble the cause. Now stand aside!"

The Shadow-Servant did not move.

Tyrnis growled. "Your sorcery won't touch me, assassin. Do you think you can stand face to face against a warrior untouched by your tricks?"

The Shadow-Servant might have shrugged beneath the billowing cloak. "I do not wish to find out, but it seems you leave me no choice."

Tyrnis leapt forward, thrusting with his blade, but the Shadow-Servant wasn't there. The creature spun away, letting the wind carry him two paces to its right. From the folds of its cloak, a blade lashed out, long yet startlingly thin. Tyrnis parried the strike easily and countered with his heavier weapon, breaking through the Shadow-Servant's defenses. But the creature danced back again, letting the two weapons slide past harmlessly. Tyrnis gave no respite, stepping forward he swept up in a slicing attack for the Shadow-Servant's throat. Again it parried and countered, but its own strikes were feeble. Tyrnis advanced again, growling. The vile butcher meant to waste his time in meaningless battle and all the while the storm raged and their people died.

There was no time. None for this. Not anymore. Tyrnis attacked again and again, shifting his stance so the Shadow-Servant had to turn into the wind. There would be no more sliding easily away. The Shadow-Servant must not have realized what he was doing because it didn't fight for the position. Tyrnis grimaced, his heart hard. The Shadow-Servant had saved the empress' life when no one else could and he owed it that. But not for this. Tyrnis lunged forward in a hard cut, straight for the heart. As expected the Shadow-Servant blocked it, but before the creature could recover, Tyrnis pivoted and brought his blade against its weaker side with a sweeping slice for its head. But even as his blade closed, the Shadow-Servant leapt toward him, casting its own sword away. Tyrnis had no time to set himself as the creature struck, bearing him to the ground.

Sharp pain lanced through Tyrnis' abdomen with the bite of cold steel plunging deep. With a deep sigh, he looked up into the Shadow-Servant's eyes, hovering before his own. He felt the creature's hand take his own and guide it down to the hilt of the knife in his stomach, already slick with blood.

"Not a killing blow," the Shadow-Servant said, "but a crippling one. You won't want to remove the blade until the storm abates. Out too soon and you'll bleed to death. Wait as I asked, holding it steady, and you'll live to curse me."

Tyrnis clenched his eyes against the pain building within him. When he opened them again, the Shadow-Servant was gone.

Storm. Wind. Rage. Fire.

Once there had been a man named Vistus. A man who had believed he was a sword of justice, a defender of wisdom and civilization against the darkness of ignorance and corruption. But he had been a murderer, destroying what he should have defended. Killing innocence, killing purity, a pawn for evil.

Once there had been a man named Belarrin. A man who believed he could step beyond his own failings. A man who believed he could save old family and new alike. But he had been a fool and in his fear had wrought the deaths of those he'd sought to save, new and old.

Now there was only the storm. Only the wind, with rage burning in insatiable fire. The man once known as Vistus, once known as Belarrin, screamed at the ravaged heavens with hands upraised, knowing that the fury of the skies could never come close to absorbing all of his pain, all of his anger, all of his self-loathing. But he would try. He poured all of his being into his sorcery unheedful of his eyes, blinded by the relentless red-gold glow that filled his vision, deaf to the thunder that pounded in his head louder even than the hurricane gale.

It was not enough. It could never be enough. Not even if every Finaestari since the dawn of time were burned into a blackened cinder. It was not enough to cleanse it all.

Beneath the relentless torrent, beneath pain so intense it seared away all thought and memory, every feeling was overwhelmed. Hands and feet, flesh and bone, eyes, ears, and heart all faded until even the relentless agony vanished. There remained only fire and storm and oblivion. Nothing more. Nothing else mattered but the wind. The storm was all.

CHAPTER 47
Calm

"There is a place between calm and rage, between hope and fear, between vengeance and forgiveness, between life and death. It is a place I have ventured but once and I dread being pulled there again. It was a moment more pure than any other. It was a moment of agony as my soul was flayed bare. Nothing I have experienced since has been more wondrous or more calamitous."

—Lady Syrdrana of Aveonfaili on the Field of Kensethir

Heart in mouth, Aerharyndra spurred her horse forward. The poor beast was exhausted, but she could not relent. The gloomy morning sky had turned into a maelstrom more turbid than anything she'd seen throughout the Cataclysm. And all of it loomed above where her husband, Tazil, stood imprisoned.

"Highest Above, not him too," she whispered for the thousandth time. "Not Tazil too." Son dead and husband's life on a tether. Not him.

Her army followed, though not as fiercely, strung out on winded horses. Nearly a quarter were her own loyal house-carls, while the rest came from the other condemned high lords' cities. Their reliability was doubtful, but they followed because she led them to their masters.

The storm had begun to abate. Lightning flashes danced more across the heavens than touched the earth. The clouds seethed still, but without the relentless energy of before. It was all proof that a hand had touched them and she could think of only one source. The human sorcerer. No one else could have such strength. And he would have no reason to spare her husband. "Highest Above," she resumed her litany as she began to climb the final rise.

But as she reached the crest, there was no storm. No wind. Only silence beneath a gloomy gray sky.

She reined in her horse, stunned, barely aware of her companions coming up alongside to join her in disbelief.

Silence.

Then a murmur against the void. A faint hiss, soft, of sand dancing upon a breeze. A rush, distant. A ripple, rolling and gentle. A wave washing upon some far shore. Then warmth, falling upon flesh softly as the dawn after a long chill night. Cool, but with the promise of heat to come.

He opened his eyes, then, and realized he knelt upon the ground with head bowed. Scoured earth, brown and hard, lay before him. He blinked, feeling as if there should be more. Afterimages, lingering… something. But there was only silence, blessed silence. He drew in a deep breath, bracing for pain, but there was none. Only a sense of weariness like at the end of a long day's toil, ushering in a night of restful sleep. His mouth was dry like sand in the desert.

It was an effort to stand, but he felt a sudden irresistible urge driving him upward. He stumbled at the effort, limbs weak and clumsy, balance awkward. His head turned, looking around, knowing what he saw, yet mind thick and uncomprehending. The world was ravaged. There had been buildings, once, he knew. There had been people, a thousand and more, surrounding, fighting, dying. But now the land lay lifeless. Heaps of detritus scattered across the plain, some wood, some stone, some flesh. Seven posts, driven into the earth, remained. Limp forms hung from five in stupor or death. There had been an eighth post, once, but it was gone. Here and there, he saw movement. But whether it was faint flutterings of ragged cloth in the wind or inklings of life, he could not say. He knew it had to be important, yet such comprehension lay beyond him.

His eyes lifting to the rolling hills beyond the plain. A line of figures on horseback. Were they friends? Why were they watching? But no friends of his had horses. At least he didn't think so. He took a staggered step forward and nearly fell. Off balance, he stumbled down to one knee. Standing carefully again, he realized the movement had turned him. A high bluff lay before him now and on it perched a city. The walls stood unmoved by the noise that had come before the silence. Above the stone parapets rose spires, glistening and flawless. It was a place he had known, though he could not recall the name. But looking upon it now, he knew it was the home of his enemies. He frowned. That meant there was more still to be done.

Feeling a flush of anger, he clenched his fists and felt something hard in the palm of his right hand. Opening it was an effort, like prying a reed into a basket that hadn't soaked long enough. He felt the skin of his palm tear as his fingers stretched wide, raising a trickle of blood dribbling down his wrist past the stone he held. It was clear and faceted and beautiful.

No. He shook his head. He was angry and couldn't be distracted. There was still more to do. He lifted his eyes to the city on the hill.

"Belarrin."

A voice spoke behind him, saying a name he had once known. The name, he realized, was his own. It was one of the names he'd possessed. The better one. He knew the voice, too, and turned, though the movement caused him to stumble and nearly fall again.

A women knelt on the ground a few paces away. Her clothes were tattered and ragged, her cheeks streaked with filth dampened by tears. Bedraggled golden hair fell in unkempt locks around her oval face.

"My work is not done," he told her.

"It is done," she replied, pushing herself back so she knelt before him. By her stiff movements, she seemed as exhausted as he felt.

"No." He shook his head, feeling the anger that lurked with in him. He didn't know why he was angry, only that it was with reason. "They cannot be allowed to live. Not one of them. Not for what they have done." He couldn't remember who they were or what they'd done, but he knew he was right. That was all that mattered.

Something landed on his cheek and he lifted his hand to touch it, puzzled. His fingers came away damp. He looked skyward as more water landed on his face and hands. Rain, falling from above. The clouds were gray and calm, though he knew it hadn't always been so. There was something cleansing in the water, clean and pure. That reminded him of something, something he couldn't quite bring to mind.

The woman tried to stand, but stumbled. He walked to her, his own legs still unsteady and lowered his hand. She took it but, instead drawing her up, she pulled him down to his knees facing her. Meeting her blue eyes, rimmed in sadness, he knew he should know her. He stared into those beautiful eyes, struggling to call her name to mind. The effort brought forward flashes of pain, but at last he had it. He smiled. "Vitarria."

The faintest of flinches flitted across her face, but her lips firmed as she replied, "Sravika."

Memory flooded over him.

He reeled back and tried to stand, to flee, but his feet gave out and he fell again as his soul unleashed a silent wail. All that he had lost, all that had been burned away returned, the pain and rage of it pouring over his mind. Faces flooded across his vision. All those he'd slain, all those upon whom he'd brought death. And the dark pain that had been his crucible, his tomb. He scrambled backward on hands and heels, fleeing the pain, the shame.

A glimmer of light on the ground to his right stopped him. He looked down and realized he'd dropped the stone in his haste. The Tear of Isi, he remembered as he picked it up. It was pure and radiant with no hint of the crimson flame that had once burned within.

"Belarrin," Sravika said again. She crawled to him and knelt at his side. Mind still reeling at the return of all the regrets he'd lost, Belarrin didn't resist as she took his hands in hers, cupping them around the cold stone.

"Hate me, Sravika. I murdered your sister."

"No." She shook her head. "Not anymore."

"But you must. I am a monster. I am the enemy."

"You were never the enemy. You were the price," she replied.

"What does that mean?" he managed to ask though his voice stammered. Looking into her face, he longed to find hope again yet he dreaded that, too. He didn't deserve hope. He blinked, trying to look away from her gentle gaze, but couldn't. Tears fell from his eyes, mingling with the falling rain.

Sravika reached up to touch them. "Tears from iron, blood from stone, the heavens tremble, the earth doth groan. His hand in crimson fury shine, taketh my life but saveth thine." Belarrin could only tremble in response, knowing, yet fearing to know. "My sister wasn't just a priestess, she was a prophetess with the Eyes of Vaenna. She spoke those words when we were still children," Sravika said. "I hated you for years because of them, but Vitarria told me not to. She knew I couldn't and she was right. I don't."

"You should. For everything I've done."

"I knew who you were from the moment this stone turned red in your hands all those months ago. Did I flee from you knowing that?" She shook her head. "No, I see what Vitarria saw. A man always trying to do right."

"But I always failed. I always did the opposite." He pulled away from her and scrambled to his feet. Untarnished Nahirazith beckoned to him in the distance and, as he looked around, he saw the field stirring. The plain was not dead as he had thought, but returning to life, Scion, Kalilaer, t'Okaedrin… Finaestari. Hundreds, however, did not move. Blackened husks where lightning had burned Finaestari to cinders, blood-stained bodies of Scion and slave, slashed beneath the blades of their oppressors. But the battlefield was still alive with hundreds more, perhaps even half those who had once stood upon it, rising in stunned awe.

A growl rose up from deep within Belarrin's soul. "And the task isn't complete. I've been shaped into a monster and won't allow anyone else to be pulled down my path." He turned to where the imperial platform had once stood and saw the empress kneeling on the ground nearby. Beside her lay Medreuneth, dead or in unconscious stupor. The empress watched him with haunted eyes. Her crown had been torn away, her dress shredded to rags, her face covered in filth. Just another woman, just another life of no greater value than any other. Less. He flung out his hand, pointing to her and she flinched back. Was there innocence in fear? No, but there was honesty. The yearning for life. He wanted to be able to fear again. "Today, it all comes to an end."

Sravika stepped in front of him and took his hand again. "No, Belarrin, don't you see? You are not a monster and never were. You haven't failed. Every choice you took was because you thought it right and just. You were wrong, but didn't know it. Release that now, forgive yourself, forgive them."

"Forgive them?" Belarrin's question came out a rasp.

"Forgive them," she answered. "Their army is broken. Our people are free. You have done what you came to do. I know there is more to you than your anger and your shame. I saw that once and it hasn't changed. Only you remain in chains, stronger than those when you were Iron-Man or slave. They are the chains of your hate. If you ever want to be free of them, free of everything, you must forgive the Finaestari. Until you do, they will bind you as strongly as they ever did."

"I deserve nothing less than chains!"

She stepped closer to him, the rain washing through her dust-filled hair, sending runnels down her cheeks. "What was it Vitarria said before she died, the last thing she said before you killed her?"

"I..." Belarrin flushed and turned away. "How can you know what she said?"

"Because she was my sister. What did she say? What did she want you to become? Was it this?"

"She... she forgave me." He drew in a long hissing breath.

"Your war isn't against the Finaestari, Belarrin. It has always been against yourself and only you can end it. The Scions need you. The Kalilaer need you." She hesitated, then added more softly, "I need you."

Belarrin closed his eyes. He could feel the rage and pain that lurked within him. The shame that whispered to him that he was unworthy of anything more. That the Finaestari deserved to be destroyed and so did he. But Sravika's voice, so calm, so kind. The one who should hate him most didn't and neither had the one he had stolen from her.

Wind rushed past his face, modest now, but with the promise of a hidden fury. He had only to call upon it once more to finish what he'd started. Or he could release it into a gentle breeze. He felt the stone of Isi, cool in his hand. It had two faces, too, crimson for the path of vengeance, judgment, and death, or clear and pale for the path of hope, forgiveness, and life. For the first time in a long time, he admitted what he wanted to do. But could he?

The words of Zoltha drifted into his mind from a time before his heart had changed. If consequences didn't exist, then our lives would be without meaning. For us to be able to choose, we must be allowed to create a Cataclysm.

"Or not create one," he whispered, opening his eyes. Sravika met his eyes, confused and concerned until he smiled. It felt strange upon his face. When was the last time he'd smiled? "I forgive them," he said. She smiled back at him. He had never seen her more beautiful.

Belarrin turned to look across the field. He saw the new army of horsemen on the far hills, he saw figures lining the walls of Nahirazith. On the plain itself, he saw Finaestari, Scions, Kalilaer, and t'Okaedrin, all staring at him in silent wonder and fear.

It was a small thing to draw the sorcery to his lips that magnified his voice to boom across the field. "I forgive you." His words rose high upon the wind. Then, "We are leaving. You will not follow."

His first step was so easy and yet, as he took it, he realized how momentous it was. He was walking away. They all were walking away. Forever. It was the vision he'd first dared to seize when Zoltha pulled him from the delusion of servitude. It had been a dream he could never quite see, yet it lay before him.

But even as he began, an unmoving body pulled his attention from his path. He knelt down and brushed back the locks of hair to reveal the dead woman's face. "Talikae," he whispered and looked to Sravika. "Without her..." He shook his head, unable to finish the thought. "All she wanted was to the see the forest."

"Let her rest there, then."

Belarrin nodded. He stooped to lift her into his arms, but in his exhaustion, it was an effort to rise. With Sravika's help, he did. Still the world watched them apprehensively. What would the Finaestari do if they knew how spent his strength was? Belarrin doubted he'd ever again be able to summon a fragment of what he'd wrought in his fury. But that no longer mattered.

A few of the Scions and Kalilaer had begun to shift, trickling toward the forest at a slow walk, as if afraid anything more might break the spell and bring destruction back upon them. But most lingered, transfixed. The hundred or so surviving warriors of the Syraestari legion stood between Belarrin and his people, but they drew back stiffly, clearing a path as he neared. They watched with careful eyes that couldn't hide stunned awe and fear. In their midst stood a handful of warriors clothed in black. He knew only the woman who led them, but had witnessed all they'd done, however futile.

He stopped in front of them, Sravika by his side. "You and your people are welcome among us, Ninanna. As friends."

Ninanna glanced to the man beside her and a wordless message passed in that gaze. Looking at Belarrin again, she said, "I will follow, but myself alone. Imeskir and my companions have a different path."

"As you wish."

"You are weary," Ninanna said looking down at Talikae. "Let me ease your burden."

"She is not a burden."

"Talikae matters to me, too."

Belarrin nodded and let the Sword-Whisperer take her. Then, he turned again to the forest, feeling the breeze flush across his face and the soft rain it carried. Weeping, yes. It was appropriate that the world weep for joy and for sadness. At his side, Sravika slipped her hand into his and he clung tightly to it as if it were only line leading out of the dream that surrounded him. And still the Finaestari watched, unmoving, as he passed through.

The Scions waited beyond. Those he had called friends, those he had betrayed. He deserved only their curses, but was met with smiles. From Yrpel and Idysha, from Henirgar and Tayrja. But looking upon them, he realized one precious face was missing. If even one more friend from his ordeal in the smelting camps were dead, he couldn't say what he might do. He could feel the rage, still, threatening to overwhelm him. "Where is Chostir?" he asked, voice rasping at the edge of grief.

"She is here, brother," a voice said behind him.

Belarrin turned. "Hirnid."

The t'Okaedrin held Chostir's battered body in his arms, but she looked up at him and smiled through tattered lips. "They never broke us."

Belarrin pulled his hand free of Sravika's and set it on Chostir's head. Healing was almost too much for him and he staggered even as the golden lines flashed before his eyes. "Sinahaster anditrasaChoestir atiro."

Beneath his touch, he felt her flesh and muscles tremble as they knit back together. His knees sagged as a wave of exhaustion struck him and he would have fallen but Sravika steadied him with an arm around his shoulder. Belarrin blinked the stars clear from his vision and, as they faded, he saw Hirnid looking at him in amazement.

"Everything is true," Hirnid said.

"Not everything," Belarrin told him. "But most. It is good to see you, my brother."

"You showed me." He looked down to Chostir who he carefully lowered until she stood beside him. "She showed me. That there is something better."

"Something better," Belarrin murmured. He turned to see the host of Scions and Kalilaer who had gathered around them. Smiling faces. Faces filled with expectation and hope. "We have no families," he called to them. "That was taken from us, but no more. Every one of you is my brother and my sister. We are all kindred freed from long chains. The war we've fought, whether it was with bowed backs or heads raised, in dirt or in blood. That war is over and now we depart."

There was no jubilant cry to his announcement and that felt right. Instead, as Belarrin turned toward the forest, they formed around him and followed in silent hope. His friends. His family. He didn't look back again to the Finaestari or to the t'Okaedrin who had once been his brothers. He didn't need to. They would not strike now. They would not hazard a second storm.

As the shade of the trees fell over him, Belarrin let out a deep sigh, feeling as if the shackles upon his soul had truly fallen away. He was home. Sravika's hand met his again, intertwining fingers. His heart leapt at the warmth of her touch as they marched northward to their new world.

EPILOGUE

Fog lay heavy upon the forest, but where the trees fell back, the fog died beneath the warm rays of the late morning sun. Reigliff crouched on one of the outer tree limbs at the edge of the white mantle and looked outward upon the settlement. But a handful of years and already it had burst into a thriving village. He knew it was but one of dozens. He could see the blending of worlds in the architecture of each building, of Scion, t'Okaedrin, Kalilaer, and even Wildman. Walls of rough or smooth stone, blocked or shaped wood, some tall and storied, others squat with arching rooftops of wood or thatch. There was joy in the measured disorder. Smoke curled up from a smithy accompanied by a ring of its hammers. That was a mark of pride for the humans who dwelt there. Earthen works had been raised around the village, only waist tall at the moment, but growing and marked by strongpoints of stone.

The central Great Hall would not have been called great by the peoples that had walked these lands before the Cataclysm, but he could see self-confidence in its sturdy beams and carved eaves. That pride was proclaimed by a gently billowing green banner emblazoned with a disc, half red and half white. Already he had heard some calling it the emblem of the Kingdom of Belarria, doubtless to the consternation of its reluctant ruler.

Three children ran playing in the dusty streets, two boys and a younger girl, each with golden hair and laughing eyes. They bore names heavy with memory, names that one day they would understand. Zoltha and Bridionis and Vitarria. With a cry of delight, they ran to the door of the Great Hall as their parents emerged. The queen knelt down to embrace her sons while the king scooped Vitarria into his arms and held her close. But Reigliff's gaze was pulled from them to the tall serene woman who followed. Though her greatsword remained on her back, Ninanna had doffed the black robes of a Sword-Whisperer in exchange for grey ones.

Ever the warrior and guardian, her eyes scanned the village and the forest, stopping as they met Reigliff's across the distance. Only she would have noticed him there amid the tendrils of fog. Ninanna stepped away from the monarchs as two other women approached the queen. The first, red-haired Idysha, held the hand of a small boy, already with shoulders broadening to match his father's. The second, Chostir, held a baby cradled in her arms. The future of humanity was secure.

"Yes," Reigliff murmured to himself as Ninanna approached. "It would be wise, Empress Kayrstana, to heed the wounds that have been opened, for they do not all heal with time."

The once-Sword-Whisperer walked with an easy gait. She was far more relaxed than he'd ever seen her. Some wounds, at least had closed, though the scars wouldn't vanish easily. Reigliff slid from his perch and awaited her at the edge of the forest.

Ninanna stopped a half-dozen paces away, arms hanging loosely at her side, blond hair fluttering softly in the breeze. Her eyes were sharp and clear, but he sensed wariness at the edge of them. "Is all well?" she asked.

Reigliff had long considered his answer to such a question. Should he tell her of the departure of Sizras and Tazil to the refuge they'd long sought? Should he report that Imeskir had led the remnant of the Sword-Whisperers after them? Did it matter that the empress had restored the other high lords or that she'd found a husband in Sarroth, the only Syraestari to stand between her and the treacherous Ushtyl? Certainly Ninanna would care that the Boards had been abolished and that the burdens of the remaining Kalilaer had been lightened. That a child becoming t'Okaedrin was now a source of pride for the parents instead of tragedy. But looking in her eyes, he saw that she was haunted still, haunted and trapped between two worlds. There would be time enough later for pain and worry. Today was a day of healing. He glanced past her, taking in her new family, her new hope, before meeting her eyes again.

He smiled from beneath his pale mask. "All is well."

GLOSSARY

Aerharyndra (AYR-harr-in-drah) – The wife of High Lord Tazil

Aestari (AY-star-ee) – One of the four races. Aestari are fair skinned, tall, with sharp noses, angular features, and pointed ears. Though unaging, they can be slain or die of despair.

Ainii (EYE-nee) – A Cyrleni, shaper of the Aestari.

Arcomin (AR-koe-min) – Vistus' brother, a t'Okaedrin

Argluf (AR-gluf) – A Kalilaer

Arkesh (AR-kesh) – High Lord of Yeltikar

Auphni (OWF-nee) – Vistus' mother, a Pi'aernotha Osnoeda

Belarrin (BELL-ar-in) – Vistus' name as a Kalilaer

Bridionis (BRID-ee-oh-niss) – Vistus' brother, a t'Okaedrin

Cataclysm, The – The ruination of Isfalinis caused by the violent deaths of Cydion and the Etyni during the Great War. The Cataclysm wrought a string of natural disasters including earthquakes, floods, and volcanic eruptions that culminated in an age of ice. It reshaped the world and caused the deaths of all but a remnant of the peoples of the world. Its exact length is uncertain but is believed to have lasted at least a thousand years, possibly twice that.

Chostir (CHOE-steer) – A Kalilaer

Cydion (SIGH-dee-on) – Lord of Life and Death. The Great Betrayer. The Lord of the Abyss. Cydion created the fires at the heart of Isfalinis in the dawn of creation before he betrayed His Highest Above and sought to rule the world. He played a major role in the Schism of the Aestari and most other upheavals of the Lost Age. At the end of the Great War, he was slain by the Etyni Itesa on the Hill of Kensethir.

Cyrleni (KIYR-lin-ee) – The secondborn of His Highest Above. Their exact number is uncertain, but the Cyrleni are known to number many more than the Etyni. Famous among the Cyrleni are Vaenna the Prophetess, Ainii the Shaper of the Aestari, and Ilsul the Shaper of Humans.

Dahiraetin (DUH-heer-ay-tin) – A battle approximately a century before the founding of the Kayrstaran Empire between the Syraestari and numerous tribes of humans who were pursued by ash monsters called troglyds. In the aftermath of the battle, the Syraestari resolved to end their long migration and reestablish an empire.

Dalric (DAHL-rik) – Vistus' father, a t'Okaedrin

Dirbructi (DEER-bruk-tee) – A Scion of the Fallen Tree

Draatha (DRAH-thuh) – Pi'aernotha Kaupet

Edrethyn – A word with no perfect translation. A guardian and protector of the body, the mind, the heart, and the soul.

Eicai (EE-kai) – An Etyni, shaper of the wind. Brother of Naedda.

Eldest – The combat leader of a family of t'Okaedrin or Pi'aernoth. The Eldest is not necessarily the oldest of a family but holds a place of preeminence among his or her peers.

Elestis (EE-less-tiss) – A Pi'aernotha Osnoeda

Eltirkar (EL-teer-kar) – Captain of Lord Ushtyl's housecarls

Etyni (EH-tin-ee) – The firstborn of His Highest Above. The Etyni were ten beings of immense power. Along with the Cyrleni, they were entrusted with the creation of the world. They originally numbered eleven until Cydion rose up in rebellion. In the Great War, all of the Etyni were slain defeating Cydion. Their names are Fenr, Itesa, Henji, Lelpfios, Eicai, Naedda, Niella, Oltos, Isi, and Zaris.

Fedigni (FED-ig-nee) – A Scion of the Fallen Tree

Fenr (FEN-nur) – An Etyni, shaper of the mountains. Brother of Itesa.

Finaestari (FIN-ay-star-ee) – The name given the Syraestari by their enemies. Literally "Dark Aestari", they are condemned for betraying their Oath. For further details, see Syraestari.

Finnie (FIN-nee) – A slur for Finaestari.

Fritten (FRIH-tin) – A Kalilaer

Grannif (GRAN-if) – A chieftain among the Scions of the Fallen Tree

Great War, The – A war at the end of the Lost Age when Cydion, Lord of Life and Death, sought to conquer all of Isfalinis. He was slain by the last of the Etyni on the Hill of Kensethir. The unleashing of power from the deaths of Cydion and the Etyni brought on the Cataclysm.

Henirgar (HEN-eer-garr) – A Scion of the Fallen Tree

Henji (HEN-jee) – An Etyni, carver of rivers. Sister of Lelpfios. She died on the Bridge of Vasyr during the Great War.

High Lord – The highest nobility of the Kayrstaran Empire below the empress herself. There are nine high lords and ladies each of whom reigns over one of the nine cities of the realm. The empress is also a high lady of the capital city, Thusaeyanin.

Hiraestari (Heer-ay-star-ee) – One of the two branches of the Aestari. They are called Tirnaestari by their foes. Literally "High Aestari," the Hiraestari remained true to their Oath to His Highest Above and the Etyni during the Schism in the Lost Age. The Hiraestari are proud to stay true to their word while they see the Syraestari who betrayed it as having darkened their souls.

Hirnid (HEER-nid) – Vistus' brother, a t'Okaedrin

His Highest Above – The Creator. He formed Isfalinis from the Void and created the Etyni, Cyrleni, and the souls of the Four Races.

Housecarl – Syraestari warriors sworn to one of the eleven high lords.

Idysha (IH-dee-shah) – A Kalilaer

Imeskir (IM-esk-eer) – A Sword-Whisperer

Inban (IN-ban) – A chieftain among the Scions of the Fallen Tree

Isfalinis (IZ-fall-ee-neese) – The world. It was brought into being by His Highest Above and shaped by the Etyni and Cyrleni.

Isi (EE-see) – An Etyni, creator of sound, voice, and song.

Itesa (EE-tess-ah) – An Etyni, delver of valleys. Sister of Fenr. Mortally wounded, she struck down Cydion on the Hill of Kensethir at the end of the Great War.

Jarkon (JAHR-kon) – A chieftain among the Scions of the Fallen Tree

Jesaelyn (JES-ay-lin) – High Lady of Kikara

Kalilaer (KAH-lee-layr – Laborer. The human workers, both male and female, of the Kayrstaran Empire.

Kayrstana (KAYR-stan-ah) – Empress and High Lady of Thusaeyanin

Kayrstaran Empire – The realm of the Syraestari ruled by the Empress Kayrstana. It is comprised of nine cities, each ruled by a high lord or lady.

Kitiger (KIT-ih-gur) – A chieftain among the Scions of the Fallen Tree

Laerdina (LAYR-dee-nah) – A Scion of the Fallen Tree

Lelpfios (LEHL-pfee-ohs) – An Etyni, master of oceans and seas. Brother of Henji.

Liuticar (LOO-tih-kar) – Vistus' brother, a t'Okaedrin

Lost Age, The – The period from the Creation of the Isfalinis to the onset of the Cataclysm at the end of the Great War. Most records of this era were lost, especially among human peoples.

Medreuneth (med-ROO-neth) – A Sorceress of the Breath of Isfalinis

Mirnadd (MEER-nad) – A Scion of the Fallen Tree

Naedda (NAY-dah) – An Etyni, bringer of rain and the clouds. Sister of Eicai.

Nalsuntha (NAHL-sunth-ah) – Vistus' Eldest, a t'Okaedrin

Nethzir (NETH-zeer) – Captain of Lord Tazil's housecarls

Niella (NEE-lah) – An Etyni, forger of the Sun.

Ninanna (NIH-nah-nuh) – Kayrstana's Edrethyn, a Sword-Whisperer

Oath, The – An oath given by the Aestari in the Lost Age to His Highest Above and the Etyni that they would seek the betterment of the other races as much as their own. Some Aestari began to regret this swearing, feeling it a form of bondage. This debate flared into the Schism of the Aestari people between the rebel Syraestari and the loyal Hiraestari.

Obaudes (OH-bow-dees) – A Kalilaer

Okaidir (OH-kai-deer) – Brother. See t'Okaedrin.

Oltos (OEL-tohs) – An Etyni, the Lord of Balance.

Onath (OH-nath) – A courier

Ovirkar (OH-veer-kar) – High Lord of Fuldynathir

Parvik (PAR-vik) – A Scion of the Fallen Tree

Pi'aernoth (PEE-ayr-noth) – Sisters. Warriors and high level human servant women of the Kayrstaran Empire. A general term that includes both the Pi'aernotha Kaupet (Sisters of Iron) and Pi'aernotha Kaupet (Sisters of Stone). Pi'aernoth are formed into families like t'Okaedrin.

Pi'aernotha Kaupet (PEE-ayr-noth-ah Kow-pet) – Sisters of Stone. Female human servants who see to the daily needs of the Syraestari in the Kayrstaran Empire. They are the only humans who reside within the walls of the imperial cities.

Pi'aernotha Osnoeda (PEE-ayr-noth-ah OZ-noh-dah) – Sisters of Iron. Female human warriors of the Kayrstaran Empire. They serve predominantly as scouts and archers.

Regund (RAG-und) – A Kalilaer

Sarroth (SARR-oth) – Captain of Empress Kayrstana's housecarls

Schism, The – A bloody war in the Lost Age that ravaged the Aestari people. Caused by a disagreement over the Oath, the Syraestari rebelled against it while the Hiraestari remained loyal and held their word. The war split family and friends and the two factions remain blood enemies.

Scions of the Fallen Tree – Human rebels against the Kayrstaran Empire. Some joined the Scions from wildmen tribes but most are escaped Kalilaer.

Sizras (SIHZ-rass) – High Lord of Sarhystoeka

Sravika (SRUH-vee-kah – a Scion of the Fallen Tree

Syraestari (SIHR-ay-star-ee) – One of the two branches of the Aestari. They are called Finaestari or Finnie, by their foes. Literally "True Aestari," the Syraestari broke the Oath they swore to His Highest Above and the Etyni during the Schism in the Lost Age. The Syraestari believe that they live as their race was intended to be. Thus, they call themselves true, while they see the Hiraestari, who follow the Oath, as still bound in slavery to it.

t'Okaedrin (TOE-kay-drin) – The Brothers. The male human warriors of the Kayrstaran Empire. They serve predominantly as formed foot soldiers armed with swords and shields though some are mounted warriors. T'Okaedrin are formed into families, usually of approximately twenty warriors. They are raised and mentored by their Father (a t'Okaedrin) and Mother (a Pi'aernoth). In battle, they are led by their Eldest, the senior brother of the family.

Talikae (tah-LEE-kay) – A Pi'aernotha Kaupet

Tayrja (TAYR-jah) – A Scion of the Fallen Tree

Tazil (TAH-zill) – High Lord of Raefi'ernyn

The Shadow-Servant – An assassin

Timnar Mountains (TIM-nahr) – A mountain range north of the Kayrstaran Empire.

Tirnaestari (Tihr-ay-star-ee) – The name given the Hiraestari by their enemies. Literally "Bound Aestari", they are so named because they remain enchained to their ancient Oath. For further details, see Hiraestari.

Tyrnis (TEER-niss) – High Lord of Kinansath

Ushtyl (USH-till) – High Lord of Nahirazith

Vaenna (VAY-nah) – A Cyrleni, creator of the Moon. A prophetess who foresaw the Schism, the Great War, and the Cataclysm.

Vistus (VIH-stuss) – A t'Okaedrin

Vitarria (vih-TAR-ee-ah) – A Scion of the Fallen Tree

Wiersa (WEE-ayr-sah) – A wildman

Wildmen – Human tribes inhabiting the wilderness north of the Kayrstaran Empire. Wildmen tribes live a semi-nomadic life subsisting on hunting, gathering, and a small amount of farming. They have no knowledge of metallurgy and use weapons and tools of stone, wood, or bone. Known tribes include the Lothyn, Iengian, Tatyrni, Zengris, and Isyren.

Yrpel (ER-pil) – A wildman

Zaerina (ZAYR-ee-nah) – High Lady of Terni'andarn

Zaris (ZAER-iss) – Leader of the Etyni, the bringer of time.

Zoltha (ZOEL-thah) – A Kalilaer

Made in the USA
Middletown, DE
12 January 2019